Praise for KRONOS

" . . . a master class in the suspension of disbel. . . .
niscent of the work of Michael Crichton (Jurassic Park, Congo) in that
it weaves together an exciting and gripping yarn which, despite depict-
ing fantastical subject matter, doesn't insult the reader's intelligence by
appealing to the lowest common denominator."

– Krank.ie

"Batten down the hatches and brace yourself . . . Hawthorne delivers
suspense at a breakneck pace in his terrifying debut."

– Ryan Lockwood, Author of *Below*

"A word to the wise: if you bite your nails, you'd better wear oven mitts
when reading Kronos Rising. It will drag you down to the depths of fear
and take you back for a breath of air as fast as you can turn the pages.
Readers beware: a new master of marine terror is in your bookstore,
and his name is Max Hawthorne!"

– Stan Pottinger, NY Times Bestselling author of *THE BOSS*

"This is the most realistic story I've encountered that brings prehistoric
creatures into the present. The story is punctuated with extraordinary
detail and facts, bringing both the technology and the creature a level
of realism not often reached . . . Hawthorne's mix of science fiction,
adventure, and character development puts his books squarely on the
shelf next to Michael Crichton's."

– Jess Terrell, *For the Love of*
All Things Edgar Rice Burroughs

" . . . a great addition to this genre, worthy of sitting on the shelf next to
Peter Benchley's *JAWS*."

– Publisher's Weekly/City Life

" . . . a fabulous debut by Max Hawthorne. Simply put, it's got teeth. Big
ones!"

– Chris Parker, screenwriter (*Vampire in Brooklyn,*
Battle of the Year, Heaven is for Real)

Kronos Rising:

KRAKEN

(Volume 1)

A Novel

Max Hawthorne

Copyright © 2015 by Max Hawthorne

ISBN-13: 978–0692658147
ISBN-10: 0692658149

Published in the United States by: *Far From the Tree Press, LLC.*

Visit *Far From the Tree Press, LLC* online at: www.farfromthetreepress.com

Manufactured in the United States of America

First Edition

For my dad Joe, who bought me my first Aurora "Prehistoric Scenes" Allosaurus model when I was five. Here's to nine kids in one car, Rockaway Beach bungalows, museums, mammoth bones, and Megalodon teeth. Not to mention all the fishing trips, Star Trek reruns, and Ray Harryhausen movies we could muster.

This one's for you, Bluegill King.

"How many things are now called the worst evil, which are only twelve feet wide and three months long? But some day, greater dragons will come into the world."
--Friedrich Nietzsche
Thus spoke Zarathustra

ACKNOWLEDGMENTS

It is with great humility and pride that I acknowledge the following individuals for their support and/or contributions.

First and foremost, I wish to express my heartfelt gratitude to my intrepid publishers at *Far From the Tree Press*. Thank you for believing in my vision and for allowing me to let my imagination run wild.

I'd also like to extend my thanks to my ever-growing list of publicity and marketing contacts. Without your professionalism, consideration, and tireless toiling, many would never know the Kronos Rising series exists.

A *huge* thank you to paleo-artist supreme Davide Bonadonna, whose amazing skill and ability to work with me over weeks and weeks, conceptualizing and finalizing my vision, were responsible for the magnificent "Pliosaur VS Megalodon" painting "Old Scores" that now graces the cover of this book. Davide, you are, indeed, "the man"!

A special shout-out to my friend and mentor, screenwriter extraordinaire Chris Parker. Thank you very much for your patience and guidance in the beginning and your recent (and ongoing) efforts to make me a passable screenwriter. Rock on, my brother.

I'd be remiss if I didn't mention the individuals who were kind enough to read and contribute to *KRONOS RISING: KRAKEN* during its conception and editing stages. This includes my intrepid brother Stephen, AKA "Jaws", my go-to graphics girl, the talented A. Celine McKenzie, and my Grammar Nazi-slaying friend, Willis Beyer. Without their combined efforts, this book would not be what it is today. Thank you for contributing some much-needed feedback, and for giving my manuscript that last bit of spit-and-polish every novel needs.

Last, but certainly not least, to my incredibly supportive family: my everlasting devotion. And to my readers, including the always enthusiastic *"LEGIONS OF KRONOS,"* thank you for your ongoing support. I'm honored that you continue to allow me and my monsters into your hearths and hearts. You have my ongoing promise to always do my best to keep you entertained.

Or if that fails, to at least shock the hell out of you.

Max Hawthorne

ONE

The old gods hungered.

Fifty miles off the coast of Florida, the male *Physeter macro-cephalus* the world called *Avalanche* descended through the frigid waters of the Blake Plateau. With deceptively gentle strokes, the bull sperm whale's twenty-foot flukes powered him along, propelling his giant body ever deeper into the void. The sunlit phototropic zone was already far behind him and the bull emitted a noisy series of broadband clicks as he traveled. The thousand-yard cone of sonar reverberated back, giving the great beast a detailed picture of the eerie seascape surrounding him. At the 1,500-foot mark, Avalanche slowed. The entrance to the vast submarine canyon known as Ophion's Deep lay directly ahead. Extending from its unplumbed depths, a network of mile-long crevasses spread like hungry tentacles, splaying forth from the Ninth Circle of Hell.

Hovering head-down over the nearest chasm, Avalanche scanned it with his sonar before resuming his dive. The ice-cold seawater he drew in served to cool the spermaceti wax stored within his enormous head, adjusting his buoyancy and allowing him to descend without effort.

As he scattered a frightened school of fish at 3,000 feet, the bull sperm felt the familiar sensation of his flexible rib cage beginning to compress inward. His lungs were collapsing to reduce the inevitable nitrogen intake caused by the crushing water pressure. His heartbeat and metabolism slowed to conserve oxygen as he glided ghostlike downward, a pallid titan of the deep.

At a solid seventy feet in length and weighing over ninety tons, Avalanche was practically the mirror image of his sire, the powerful alpha male sperm whale that perished in this same region thirty years prior. There was one significant difference between the two, however; Avalanche carried a rare leucistic gene. Whereas every other sperm whale in the world was a dark grayish hue, he was white. From the tip of his battle-scarred snout to the edges of his notched flukes, he was the color of snow. The humans, obsessed with the irascible beast, had hounded him since his birth, some sixty years past. As an adolescent, whenever he'd approached the coastline, they'd pursued him relentlessly with their noisy boats, trying to get close and annoying him to no end.

The big bull eventually learned to tolerate such humans, however. It wasn't the gawking groups with their tiny flashes of light that he was wary of. It was the murderers – the assassins. They were the cowards that scurried atop their noisy metal ships, belching black poison into clear blue skies as they slaughtered his kind. Their explosive-tipped weapons had claimed nearly a million sperm whale lives over the decades, with the traumatized survivors carrying the collective memories of the slain.

But Avalanche knew well the chilled waters where the remaining human hunters lurked and he avoided them. The whaling ships and the heartless men that manned them were no longer a source of concern for him. Nowadays, the humans had their own problems.

A sudden shift in pressure drew Avalanche back from his ponderings. In the dark, a second bull sperm whale took up position off his left flank. The big whale shifted in the water, emitting a quick coda in response to the newcomer's greeting as the pair continued on in unison. Although the pitch-black depths concealed even Avalanche's milky-white skin, courtesy of their advanced sonar sight, the two bulls could view one another as plain as day.

As huge as Avalanche was, the newcomer was bigger.

In fact, he was a giant.

Measuring eighty-four feet in length, and weighing 152 tons, "*Tsunami*", as the humans dubbed him, was the size of the sperm whale that sank the 19th century whaling vessel *Essex*. The granite-hued behemoth was a genetic throwback. In addition to his remarkable size, there was another abnormality cetaceanists found intriguing about Tsunami – his jaws. Unlike most sperm whales, which had heavy, prey-penetrating teeth in the lower jaw alone, Tsunami's dentition showed indications of an opposing set beginning to appear in his maxilla as well.

As the two bulls continued their descent, they made it a point to actively scan the waters around them. The days when the great cachalots were the ocean's apex predators were gone. They had other carnivores to contend with now.

Worse, they knew what it meant to be prey.

The first time Avalanche encountered a "whale-eater," it was unlike anything he'd ever seen: a monstrous, short-tailed crocodile, with four powerful flippers and a mouth filled with sharp-ridged teeth. It was as big as he was, and incredibly fast. In the resultant battle, the old whale barely escaped with his life.

Soon, whale-eaters were everywhere: unstoppable predators with insatiable appetites that favored whale flesh above all others. Every cetacean in the sea became vulnerable to attack, from the smallest of dolphins to the largest of blue whales. The defensive Marguerite formation that the cow sperms used against their traditional enemies, the Orcas, was useless against the giant reptiles. A whale-eater would circle a sperm whale pod like a hungry shark, then dash in at a frightful speed, disemboweling a cow or calf, and then returning to gorge while the survivors fled.

In the end, the traumatized whales did what instinct told them; they changed pod formations and altered their migratory routes, spending their summers in frigid climes in an attempt to discourage their cold-blooded pursuers. For the most part, the tactic worked. The whale-eaters seemed disinclined to follow them and food was abundant. Of course, coldwater regions had threats of their own – human and other – and pregnant cows still had to travel back to temperate waters to birth their calves. Even with young bulls accompanying them as sentries, many were lost.

As Tsunami drifted a few yards closer, Avalanche focused his sonar on the younger animal. He studied the ragged punctures that ran like rows of bloody harpoon wounds across the top of the huge male's head and through one flipper. They matched the bite marks he had around his torn-up jaw and eye. The festering wounds were deep and painful, and bore testimony to the pair's recent life-or-death struggle with a gigantic whale-eater.

The two bulls had discovered that, by working as a team, they could fight back. Moreover, during their last encounter, they had the good fortune to detect a weakness in their predator's arsenal, one that could be exploited.

Out of nowhere, the monster had appeared. Like a white shark tracking an elephant seal, it began stalking them during a deep-water dive, locking onto them with its own sound-sight. There was no mistaking its ratcheting calls, even from a mile away. As it closed the distance, the two bulls dove deep. Then, at the last moment, they split up and went on the offensive. Toothy jaws spread wide and firing the tightly-focused sonar bursts they used to stun squid, they flew at it like giant pincers. The blasts from their sonar beams had no chance of incapacitating the massive reptile, but when it stopped emitting its telltale sonar clicks and began whipping its wedge-shaped head about, they realized they had somehow scrambled its sound-sight.

The whale-eater was temporarily blind. At that point, the sperms knew they had the advantage.

Tsunami rushed forward with youthful recklessness. Hammering into their sightless pursuer, he locked his jaws around the predator's thick neck and held on with all his strength. With flight no longer an option, the die was cast; this would be a battle to the death.

As the two titans struggled back and forth in the darkness, Avalanche joined in. Swimming in figure-eights, he rammed their opponent repeatedly. The enraged whale-eater, frustrated at finding itself hamstrung, fought back like a demon, writhing and snapping at anything it could sink its teeth into. Eventually, however, the tremendous bludgeoning forced out its air supply and weakened it, until finally, with a Herculean effort, Tsunami was able to torque his body into a gigantean death roll and break its neck.

Desperate for air and trailing blood, the victorious bulls made for the surface. Behind them, the body of their would-be killer sank soundlessly into the depths, a nightmarish demon returning to the abyss from whence it came.

Avalanche's scarred brow wrinkled up at the memory. A spasm of pain shot through him and he shifted his injured jaw from side to side, trying to dissipate some of the ache. An enthusiastic series of clicks from Tsunami told him they were approaching their favorite hunting grounds.

At six thousand feet, the rocky slopes of Ophion's Deep temporarily leveled off. The bulls switched to the high-frequency emissions they used to home in on prey and began to hunt in earnest. Beyond pale crabs and a few tiny squid, however, they found nothing.

Tsunami swept his cottage-sized head from side to side. Impatient and heeding the growls of his prodigious stomach, he moved on. A thousand yards ahead, past the rocky outcroppings and underwater ravines that housed their usual quarry, the canyon made another precipitous drop. This one continued all the way to the bottom; a 4,000-foot fall into oblivion.

As Tsunami accelerated toward the drop-off, a curt sonar blast from Avalanche stopped him in his tracks. Confused, the giant bull swung back, his head cocked to one side as he absorbed a harsh series of clicks – the sperm whale's version of a scolding. The message was clear: There were some places even the monarchs of the sea did not venture.

As they resumed their search, an excited squeal from Tsunami heralded the presence of prey. Pulling up alongside him, Avalanche studied the prospective meal. Their target was a hundred yards ahead – a large school of *Saepia inferni*. Known as the "Cuttlefish from hell," the pack-hunting cephalopods were a recent development, and appeared around the same time as the whale-eaters. Reaching thirty feet in length, with tentacles bristling with razor-tipped suckers, the thick-bodied squid were voracious predators that would pounce on anything from full grown sharks to smaller specimens of their own kind. To the two giants closing in on them, however, the mollusks were an irresistible buffet.

As the hungry whales loomed in the distance, the alarmed squid grew animated. They began to clump together, their bodies and tentacles intertwining until they formed a single, gelatinous mass, every bit as large as either whale. The conjoined colony of squid began to shimmer, emitting angry bands of red and green bioluminescence, with bright white sparks toward the front: a glittering, oval-shaped pattern – like a huge mouth. The entire mass moved deliberately toward the whales.

Avalanche uttered a snort of amusement. It was an impressive bluff. And a wasted effort. Funneling their sonar emissions into tight beams, the two bull sperms blasted away like giant shotguns at their significantly smaller adversaries. From fifty yards out, they could see their pulses taking effect. The glimmering waves of bioluminescence sputtered and stopped, and the dazed mass of squid began to drift to one side.

A second later, Avalanche and Tsunami smashed into them like colossal battering rams. Their combined 240+ tons annihilated the squids' defenses, scattering them like leaves as the whales plowed straight on through, their powerful jaws snapping.

Avalanche swung back in a tight arc, gulping down a frantically struggling squid as he prepared to re-attack. Tsunami was already in the thick of it, his huge jaws, lined with fourteen-inch teeth, greedily snapping up one dazed cuttlefish after another, pulverizing the bony gladius that gave their bodies rigidity and choking them down. For the harried sperm whales, the presence of the new squid represented hope. Food in such abundance was not always to be had. They might die tomorrow, but today they would feast.

As Tsunami cornered a trio of disoriented squid, a trickling of sand cascading down from an outcropping directly above him drew Avalanche's attention. He scanned the huge mass of stone with his sonar, increasing the frequency as he sought the source of the disturbance. Something about the rock's density was off . . .

Avalanche snorted in alarm as the entire mountaintop above Tsunami suddenly came to life. Spouting bubbles, the white whale uttered a shrill warning cry that echoed like a steam whistle throughout the submarine canyon.

His gluttonous impulses interrupted by the older whale's call, Tsunami looked up in confusion. His oval-shaped eyes peeled wide as the ledge above him began to shake, shedding voluminous clouds of sand. Its surface texture changed, becoming wrinkled and misshapen, and it started to grow. Dark and monstrous it rose, until its craggy dome stood nearly as high as Avalanche was long. Protruding from its base was a writhing nest of sea serpents, lined with hungry mouths, and as black as pitch. Then, as a pair of malevolent eyes opened and focused on the immobile whale below, Avalanche trembled.

It was some sort of octopus, but impossibly huge; it dwarfed even Tsunami. The old bull felt cold fear settle in all four of his stomachs. Despite the fact he had never laid eyes on a creature like this before, he instinctively knew what had found them.

It was The Great Enemy.

To the frightened sperm whales, the cephalopod was a nightmarish apparition. It was a whispered warning, one that was passed down from generation to generation and carried in their most primitive instincts. This was the hunter of hunters, the lurker in the darkness, and the reason why the great cachalots avoided the extreme depths. Whales that went too deep often didn't come back. And now, the thing that lay in wait had come to them.

They were going to die an agonizing death.

Tsunami sat frozen in fear as the gigantean octopus rushed forward. Despite its size it was lethal quicksilver, yet to his adrenalized eyes it moved in slow motion. It loomed over him, its swirling yellow orbs boring into his, holding him in its power, gleaming with ravenous intent. Tsunami could do nothing. He saw the arms, lined with suckers as big as trash can lids, reaching out from every possible direction to seize him in their lethal embrace. The giant bull felt pure terror run through him in waves.

WHUMP!

With a sound like thunder, Avalanche plowed into The Great Enemy. His toothed jaws slashed at the nearest tentacle as he threw a sonic shriek at Tsunami, breaking the younger whale free from the cephalopod's hypnotic spell. The impact of the white whale's 90-ton body knocked the octopus off balance, and he saw Tsunami shudder and regain the ability to move. Flukes thrashing, the younger whale started to ascend.

They had to make for the surface. It was their only chance.

Seventy-five yards up and accelerating, Avalanche felt an iron-like grip on his peduncle, coupled with an agonizing burning sensation. A second later, he was yanked violently back down and enveloped. A rockslide of writhing tentacles as thick as bridge cables swarmed him like a pack of anacondas, smothering him, pinning his flukes and fins. Searing waves of pain wracked his body and he twisted and turned, desperate to break free. A cold fury took over, and he clamped down on the nearest arm. Crunching through layers of rubbery tissue, Avalanche shook his head from side to side, until blue blood filled his mouth and the tentacle hung by scraps of skin.

It was to no avail. Even amputated, the writhing tendril reattached itself to him, its suckers eating into his skin as it wrapped around his face and head, pinning his mouth closed.

Through a tiny opening in the wall of tentacles, Avalanche saw an infuriated Tsunami returning like the tidal wave he'd been named for, his teeth bared and eager to fight. The older whale could feel the big bull's high-speed sonar pulses pummeling their enormous adversary, but to no effect. The octopus's craggy exterior was too tough; it shrugged off the sonic blows like they were bits of seaweed.

As the cephalopod extended several of its arms to claim its second victim, Avalanche thrashed his huge body from side to side. His flukes flapped wildly as he fought to muscle his way free. He failed, but his powerful struggles forced their enemy to refocus on him. Realizing that the younger whale was not going to give up, Avalanche emitted a desperate series of clicks, ordering Tsunami to flee. His codas turned to squeals of pain as an enormous beak tore savagely into his side, slicing through blubber and muscle, and cracking apart the ribs underneath.

Avalanche felt himself being shaken and he tasted rust. He experienced a sudden embrace of warmth and realized it was his blood, clouding the chilled waters around him like a blanket. He managed one last warning to Tsunami and was relieved to see the younger bull finally accept the futility of the situation and veer off. There was a sudden spasm of pain as he felt his lungs being punctured and seawater flooded his chest cavity, forcing out the last of his air.

The old whale's vision clouded and his enormous brain began to shut down from lack of oxygen. His mind was awash with a hundred images of warm, tropical seas he had hunted, battles he had fought, and offspring he had fathered. He was distantly aware of his body vibrating as huge chunks of flesh were ripped away, but he could no longer feel pain. The last thing he saw was the final remnants of his air bubbling free and heading for the surface, following his son toward the distant light.

Avalanche gave one final shudder.

Then he was gone.

The *Gryphon* was on the hunt.

As he lounged in his oversized captain's chair, crew at his booted feet, and waiting for information to lead them to their next kill, Garm Braddock felt more like a barbarian king on his throne than the commander of an ORION-class Anti-Biologic Submarine. At six-foot-four and a muscular 245 lbs., the twenty-nine-year-old ex-athlete figured he could probably pass for a Viking berserker, even without his dusty rep.

Garm rested his chin on the knuckles of one hand, surveying oncoming seas, the occasional clumps of seaweed and driftwood swatted away by their powerful bow wave. As he spotted an approaching school of *Petrodus enchodus* split apart and scatter, Garm pondered the changes their oceans had undergone over the past few decades. Known to anglers as the "sabertooth salmon," the swift, five-foot predators, with their tiger stripes and sharp fangs, were one of several Cretaceous survivors that had escaped into the sea with the fracturing of Diablo Caldera, some thirty years prior. Like many other "extinct" species the volcanic island preserved in the confines of its stony prison, the salmonids adapted well to Earth's predator-depleted oceans. In fact, their numbers had exploded.

At least they grill up tasty, he mused.

Garm inhaled slowly, holding the air deep in his chest and feeling the pressure build before letting it out. He was weary. Not just from finishing their two-week patrol, which technically ended two days ago, but the Saurian War in general. The government still labeled it a "suppression exercise", but like most prolonged conflicts marked by high body counts on both sides, it was a war. A bloody one, which had been going on for nearly seven years now.

Garm had been waging it non-stop for the last five.

The call to arms began in a most unexpected fashion. He was only eighteen when the first "scout" – as he referred to it – was captured. It was a young male *Kronosaurus imperator*, maybe twenty-eight feet in length, which had gotten entangled in a long-liner's cables. The predator had been cherry-picking tuna off their hooks when it got snagged. By the time the astonished boat crew realized what was dragging their floats under, the frantically struggling marine reptile had wrapped itself up like a mummy. It was completely exhausted and helpless.

The story of the creature's capture hit the airwaves like a lightning bolt. A living pliosaur of any size, twenty years after the shocking Paradise Cove Incident and resultant death toll, was front page news. A bidding war among the wealthiest aquariums in the world promptly broke out, with *Oceanus* ending up the winner and purchasing the traumatized animal at an unheard-of price. It was quite the coup and enabled the struggling theme park to fill its long-abandoned Orca tank with something far more entertaining and lucrative.

With the media frenzy continuing unabated, Oceanus's PR reps milked their pricey captive for all it was worth. Garm remembered watching the parade on TV, gawking like the rest of the world at the size of the military motorcade. No expense had been spared. They had a battalion of rifle-toting marines on foot, armored personnel carriers running point and bringing up the rear, and even anti-tank choppers hovering overhead. All were there to escort the double-wide, extended and reinforced tractor trailer as it crawled past the hushed throngs lining Main Street. The truck's forty-foot Lexan water tank was plastered with promotional banners, leaving only a few, strategically placed gaps, so onlookers could catch a tantalizing glimpse of the prisoner. All the while, loudspeakers blared a prerecorded circus barker routine, going on and on about how dangerous the *Kronosaurus imperator* was and the unimaginable risk to humanity if it should escape.

They made it seem as if the bewildered reptile was going to somehow break out of its indestructible prison, magically sprout legs and wings, and swoop down to devour them all.

Of course, animal rights groups like *Sea Crusade* were right in the thick of things. Lawsuits were filed and the creature's rights under the ESA came under fire. Eventually, and despite heartbreaking testimony from the families of the last pliosaur's victims, its status as an endangered species was upheld. It was decreed illegal to kill, capture, or harass the animals in the wild, under penalty of international law. The current specimen, however, due to its value as a "scientific oddity," and the fact that Oceanus researchers presented expert testimony that it was too distressed to be released back into the wild, was permitted to remain in captivity.

Oceanus's executives wasted no time in making the most of their opportunity. The initial plan had been to put the young *Kronosaurus* on display. But once it recovered from its ordeal, the park's trainers discovered something unexpected. The creature was more than just a crocodile with flippers; it possessed a rudimentary intelligence. After a few days, it recognized its handlers as the source of its food and stopped trying to attack them.

It was also surprisingly agile. It could jump through suspended hoops, swat a ball with its flippers, and even balance one on the tip of its snout if the mood struck it. They found that, with enough patience and given ample rewards, it could be taught to do tricks, just like the killer whales that occupied those same cramped quarters, a decade earlier.

For the park's Board of Directors, the decision was a no-brainer. Why put a sea monster on display for people to gawk at as part of the price of admission, when you could charge them one fee to enter the park, and another to see it perform?

Garm and his family were invited to Oceanus as VIP guests for the grand unveiling. "Chomper", as the juvenile male had been named by the nation's schoolchildren through a masterfully orchestrated publicity campaign, had been well trained. He performed flawlessly during rehearsals, receiving a fresh yellowfin tuna for every trick he completed. With tuna stocks at an all-time low, however, it wouldn't do for the aquarium to showcase their prize predator wolfing down another endangered species. Frozen Crevalle Jacks were substituted during the actual performance.

It was a bad move. Chomper promptly rejected the offerings, spitting them out, and even flung one toward the stands. All the while, the Orca-sized reptile emitted loud snorts to communicate his annoyance. The trainers had no choice, however; the show was like being aboard a jumbo jet during mid-takeoff – there was no way out. A few minutes later, in front of ten thousand in attendance and another half a billion watching on PPV, things went awry.

Chomper refused to perform his big finale – accelerating into a high speed underwater roll before leaping straight up to pluck a fish from a trainer's hand. During practice sessions, they'd perfected the stunt. The saurian's seven-ton body landed with a prodigious splash that, if properly positioned, would shower the first twenty rows of gleeful guests with a deluge of pliosaur-scented brine.

As the head trainer blew her shrill whistle, instructing him to begin, Chomper remained submerged. To encourage him, the whistling was amplified through the amphitheater's loudspeakers. He still refused to surface, laying on the bottom and shaking his head like a petulant child. His angry sonar clicks echoed throughout the stadium. Then, when the annoyed trainer began smacking the surface of the water with her hand, he actually stuck his man-sized jaws up out of the water and hissed at her. The trainer, although understandably nervous, played off his behavior as if it was part of the show. The crowd ate it up.

Finally, after a relentless barrage of noisy whistles and palm slaps, Chomper relented. He went deep, spiraling down to the bottom of his tank, and then turned back. Up he swam, his four flippers pumping like pistons to build up speed, until he exploded out of the water. His target was suspended from the top of a crane: a ten-pound fish dangling from a male trainer's hand, thirty feet up.

The crowd watched, spellbound, as Chomper's glistening form rose in seeming slow motion. His toothy jaws opened as they approached the frozen Jack. At the last moment, his head snapped sideways so fast it was a blur, missing the fish entirely, and clamping down on the stunned trainer's chest instead.

There was a split-second of hang-time – just enough for the astonishment to sink in – before the pliosaur yanked his scaly head back in the opposite direction. The trainer's heavy belt and chain, designed to keep him from being "accidentally bitten" and pulled from the crane's basket, held fast. But they didn't save him. Between the pliosaur's tooth-lined jaws and the irresistible pull, he managed one blood-curdling shriek before he was torn in two. The audience gasped in collective horror as Chomper dropped back down, his gory prize gripped tightly in his mouth.

The front rows of the amphitheater got the deluge the promoters were hoping for. But it was one mixed with blood, brains, and bits of intestines, as Chomper shook his head from side to side, voraciously devouring the trainer's still-twitching upper half.

Garm could still taste the bile in his mouth.

The attack seemed to be a rallying cry for pliosaurs the world over. No sooner had the media storm over what Oceanus deemed a "tragic accident" begun to die down, when the sightings started. Pliosaurs of every size imaginable, from five-foot hatchlings to seventy-five-foot adults, were being spotted in almost every ocean of the world. At first, the reports were dismissed as hoaxes or mass hysteria. But when video clips started popping up all over the web, reality set in. History's deadliest predator was far from extinct.

Kronosaurus appearances increased, with the creatures becoming steadily bolder as their numbers grew. With Earth's oceans virtually emptied of sharks and whales, there were few natural predators to keep them in check. Some experts estimated their population eventually reached over one million. Native, blubber-rich or slow-moving species, like basking sharks, porpoises, mantas, and manatees were among the first to suffer. Unable to match the speed of the ravenous marine reptiles and defenseless against their powerful jaws, they were butchered like cattle. Countless other species were similarly decimated, and as the number of adult pliosaurs increased, even the mighty blue whale came under siege.

With an international panic on their hands, the governments of the world hotly debated the issue. Some recommended implementing a culling program, whereas others wanted to maintain the species' "endangered" status and leave them be. They believed nature would balance itself out. That position changed when the attacks on people started.

As whales were killed off or fled to cooler waters, the number of confirmed human fatalities increased exponentially. Wading into the surf at your favorite beach became tantamount to committing suicide. And being on a surfboard or Jet Ski was no safer. Charter fishermen and their clients were being snatched out of their boats or rammed and devoured as they floundered in the water. And it wasn't just pliosaurs. Other supposedly extinct animals had also escaped the caldera and begun to proliferate, including primeval fish and squid that also viewed people as prey. Native fish stocks crashed worldwide as the expanding presence of Diablo Caldera's former inmates began to alter the ecology of the oceans.

The financial implications were grim. The beleaguered boating and fishing industries went under and the market sank with them. Oil prices and inflation ran rampant. Many insurance companies were forced into bankruptcy and premiums from those that stayed afloat skyrocketed.

Travel by water became almost non-existent and, when unavoidable, it was considered insane to board any unarmed vessel that wasn't made of steel and destroyer-sized or better. The death toll continued to rise, with disappearances so common they hardly made the news anymore. It was estimated that, over the previous ten-year period, somewhere between one hundred and two hundred thousand people had been killed worldwide, with tens of millions more dying from the resultant food shortages and famine as fish stocks dried up.

The media was calling it "Judgment Day".

Finally, an emergency session of the UN was held. It was decided that humanity's needs outweighed those of nature's most efficient killer. The human race would fight to retain its place at the top of the food chain. *Kronosaurus imperator's* protected status under the Endangered Species Act was repealed and an open season was called for on the giant reptiles, with rewards handed out and no size or bag limits. Despite the assorted "police actions" being fought against terrorist regimes and religious fanatics, who used their ideologies as a license to murder and rape, the nations of the world would unify and focus their collective military might on the menace that had all but taken over three quarters of the planet.

For the first time since they survived the asteroid strike that wiped out the dinosaurs, pliosaurs found themselves targeted for extermination. Slogans like "It's them or us!" and "Send 'em back to the Cretaceous!" made the front page of papers worldwide.

The military mobilization was impressive. Old or new, every vessel that possessed suitable capabilities was called into play, from the Navy's old hunter-killer submarines to aircraft carriers and destroyers – even Coast Guard cutters got in on the game. Several military planes were adapted for use and new, specially designed anti-materiel helicopters, like the stealthy GDT Bearcat, took the field.

It was a slaughter. Targeted from thousands of feet up, spouting pliosaurs were helpless against the barrage of cruise missiles and high-speed rounds that tore them apart. The mightiest killer in the sea had no defense against depleted uranium rounds fired from a mile away. The carnage grew and the revenge-hungry public, as always, swayed by the media, reveled in every measure. As the news carried more and more, Hollywood jumped on the bandwagon. Fighter pilots from one carrier, famous for their highly publicized efforts at hunting down and eradicating suspected man-eaters, ended up with their own reality TV show: *Pliosaur Wars.*

Perhaps the most ironic testimony to mankind's fear-driven desire to drive the huge marine reptiles to the brink of extinction and beyond came in the form of a popular kids' breakfast cereal. *"Kronosaurus Krunchies"* consisted of crispy "people" clusters with soft red centers. On top of that, the cereal made tiny squeaks as it was chewed. Hence the company's popular tag line, *"Kronosaurus Krunchies* – they scream when you crunch 'em!"

Admittedly, Garm mused, he'd eaten a few bowls of the stuff. It wasn't half bad and came in handy when circumstances dictated a serious sugar rush was in order. Plus, the galley stocked it . . .

Month after month, the war for earth's oceans raged. Within a year, it was estimated that over 500,000 of the dangerous reptiles had been eradicated. Coastal attacks had been reduced, but were far from eliminated. The siege continued. Then, problems began to crop up.

As *Kronosaurus* numbers dropped, targets of opportunity became less frequent. In addition, the surviving animals appeared to be learning by observing, or perhaps sensing, the deaths of others of their kind. Some compared it to great white sharks fleeing an area after Orcas killed one of their kind. A few researchers promoted the theory that pliosaurs had the ability to genetically pass on knowledge to their offspring. Whatever the case, the creatures grew more cautious, breaching and spouting less often and remaining at the surface for shorter periods of time. To reduce spiraling costs, the President authorized their newest combat drones to finish the job, while special teams of beachcombers were discretely assigned the distasteful task of finding and destroying *Kronosaurus imperator* nests before the young could hatch.

The autonomous drones found their task more difficult than anticipated. The pliosaurs' protective counter-shading made them difficult to spot from the air. When viewed by satellite they blended with the sea, reducing the ability to target them over a vast expanse of ocean. Their body temperature was also problematic. Although they possessed a core temperature higher than that of the surrounding water, their peripheries were a match, making them all but invisible to infrared and thermal targeting systems.

Wiping out the nests was more successful. Tens of thousands of the two-foot, spherical eggs were dug up and crushed or burned, and catching the occasional mother *Kronosaurus* hauling herself out of the surf under the cover of darkness was a nice bonus. But soon, even locating nests grew difficult. The pliosaur cows, as if sensing the threat to their young, did something unheard of among marine reptiles: they changed their nesting sites. Remote and often uninhabited islands were randomly chosen – some so tiny and obscure they didn't even appear on maps. The predators appeared determined to endure.

With aerial surveillance continuing to drive costs higher, and with drone kills only marginally effective, the military decided to increase the role of their submarines. The Navy was given the green light. Their hunter-killers would track the monsters down and bury them in their own backyards. Armed with the latest hardware, the subs were successful, at least according to news bulletins. Their state-of-the-art rocket-propelled torpedoes were lethal. Traveling at speeds no marine life – or ship for that matter – could match, once they locked onto a target's sonar, they stayed on it until detonation.

Unfortunately, cumbersome nuclear attack submarines, designed to hunt and destroy other subs in deep water, were ill-suited for chasing smaller, more agile adversaries around the coastline. The costs associated with each confirmed kill were astronomical and every battle was a game of Russian roulette. Sub commanders soon discovered pliosaurs could turn and attack in the blink of an eye, oftentimes while pursued by the very same sub's torpedoes. Losing a multi-billion-dollar war machine for every *Kronosaurus* put down was a financial equation no Navy accountant could balance.

Inevitably, the Coastal Defense Force, or CDF, with its own breed of anti-biologic submarines, was born. Forged in the fires of humanity's fury and quenched in the blood of untold thousands, the ORION class and its predecessors were the country's ultimate solution to the pliosaur menace. With minimal crews, they tirelessly patrolled the waterways, from the surf all the way to the fringes of the US's Exclusive Economic Zone. Any animal that violated those waters was chased off or eradicated, with confirmed rogues mercilessly hunted down and destroyed.

The moment he'd laid eyes on the *Gryphon* in dry dock, Garm Braddock knew destiny's plan for the remainder of his life. What happened to the rest of the world was beyond his control; they could go to hell in a hammock as far as he was concerned. His course was set. There would be no white picket fence in his future. No wife or children. He would be *Gryphon's* captain, and she his iron mistress. On the bridge of his own command, he would track down the deadliest predators in all of Creation and confront them on their own terms.

He was going to kill every lizard he could find. And when the end finally came, he would leave the world the same way he came into it.

Bathed in blood.

TWO

As the last of the toothy salmon skirted *Gryphon*'s armored nose, Garm surveyed his primary bridge crew. Their stations were situated directly ahead of his position, spread in a tight arc across the twenty-five-foot chamber that occupied the upper half of the sub's bow, and facing the curved, foot-thick transparent titanium barrier that ran the width of the chamber and served as their observation portal. Unless they were in combat mode, the heavy ceramic-composite shielding that covered the observation portal was kept raised. The ever-changing seas beyond made for a pleasant distraction, even if it did make it seem as if they were prisoners inside the world's largest fish tank.

At the helm was Ensign Connie Ho. Even with her conservative hairstyle and aversion to makeup, the diminutive helmswoman was fit and attractive. She was also a formidable cage fighter. As several of her more amorous shipmates had already discovered, once she set foot on a vessel she was manning, she was not to be trifled with.

Ho was a recent addition to Garm's roster. She'd been tossed out of the Navy after she beat the snot out of a drunken officer who thought "Sorry, not interested," translated as "Please grope my ass." When the bouncers pulled her off the guy, she had him on the ground, cradling his mashed testicles, while she unloaded one right hand after another into his face. *Not bad*, Garm thought, *considering the fat bastard was three times her weight*. Once he read that, coupled with Ho's documented ability to guide a Boomer sub safely through falling pack ice, he snatched her up. The Navy may have rejected her, but on *Gryphon* she fit right in.

Next to Ho and manning sonar was her verbal sparring partner, Ensign Adolfo Ramirez. Unlike *Gryphon*'s helmswoman, Ramirez had come straight from the Academy. Tops in his class, he was one of those guys blessed with 20/10 vision and owlish hearing. Surprisingly, and despite his Don Juan mustache and reputation, he hadn't gotten himself into trouble like their new helmswoman had. What he *did* have on his back was a love of the dice, a bitter ex-wife, and, until Garm advanced him an off-the-books short-term loan, pending jail time for being behind on child support.

You couldn't ask for better motivation.

On fire control was Lieutenant Commander Kyle Cunningham. One of Garm's closest friends, Cunningham was a general goofball and the only member of the crew that was married – for the most part happily. Garm and Kyle had gone through basic training and the academy together. Cool under fire, and with the self-described ability to "shoot a torpedo up a dolphin's ass at 500 yards", Kyle was every captain's choice for Combat Systems Officer. As a bonus, his mother-in-law jokes were priceless.

Last, but not least, was Ensign Heather Rush manning communications. Alert and efficient, albeit with a subdued demeanor, the willowy, freckle-faced blonde had followed Garm from ship to ship and assignment to assignment. Although he rarely caught her staring and she'd never expressed any overt interest, it was popular opinion she carried the submariner's version of a torch for her well-built captain. Why else would someone who couldn't even swim volunteer for the most dangerous submarine assignment in the world?

Garm exhaled, running thick fingers through his close-cropped coif. His hair was chestnut-colored like his father's, but he had his mother's pale blue, almond-shaped eyes. Women – and there had been many – said those eyes made him look like an overgrown husky: cuddly and huggable. Men compared him more to a wolf: dangerous and unpredictable. An amalgamation of Irish, Norwegian, and Japanese ancestry, Garm had been blessed with the best possible genes his assorted forebears had to offer. Back in high school, disgruntled linebackers from rival football teams used to call him "The Hybrid" – although never to his face.

Garm closed his opal orbs and listened. If he tried hard, it seemed he could just make out the mercurial rush of seawater, racing along their near-frictionless hull. But that was impossible. With *Gryphon*'s high-tech acoustic cladding, they were all but soundproof. A moment later, his eyes and ears pricked up as his sonar tech sucked in a breath.

"I think we've got one, sir," Ramirez said, removing one of his headphones. He stroked his mustache with his free hand, but his hunter's eyes remained locked on his sonar screens. "Reading is 3,000 yards off the port bow, bearing zero-five-zero. Per SOP, deactivating OMNI ADCAP sonar. Fathometer readings indicate target is a large biologic, holding at two hundred feet. Checking organic profiles."

Garm shifted, sensing his chair's shock-absorbing pneumatics compensate for the strain. He eyed Ramirez's back, watching for the telltale rigidity that inevitably preceded confirmation of one of his sightings.

Ramirez went ramrod straight. "Contact confirmed: designate pliosaur." he said. "Based on the readings, a very large female, sir. Probably the one that killed those fishermen a few days ago. I think she's feeding."

"Nice work, ensign," Garm said. After the ups and downs of their sixteen-day patrol, it would do him and his crew good to finish up with a big kill. Not to mention, if it was a confirmed man-eater that size, it would bring them all a hefty bonus. "Helm, what's our status?"

As Ho turned sideways in her chair, Garm smiled. The feisty helmswoman had this chameleon-like way of looking at him with one eye while keeping the other on her screens. "We're cruising at three hundred feet, sir. Speed is twenty-five knots. Approaching a strong crosscurrent. Setting maneuvering thrusters to compensate."

Garm gave a desultory nod. "Reduce speed to ten, five up to periscope depth and extend photonics mast. Communications, let me know once we've got satellite overview. In the interim, helm, match target's depth and plot an intercept course. Let me know when we have visual. Sonar, rig for silent running, passive only."

Amid a chorus of "aye, ayes," Ramirez cleared his throat. "Deactivate ANCILE, captain?"

ANCILE was their newly-installed obstacle avoidance system. It was equipped with both intruder alert and acoustic intercept, and would not only blanket an incoming threat with active sonar pings, it could lock *Gryphon*'s advanced weapons systems onto incoming targets. The only downside was, when the system went active, the pinging gave away their position.

"ANCILE on standby, POSEIDON fathometer only. Activate SVALINN. If she scans us I want her emissions suppressed with out-of-phase pulses. No bounce-back. I don't want this bitch knowing we're here until we're right on top of her," Garm replied.

Now we'll see once and for all if those fancy new sonar arrays can cancel incoming pings as well as they claim . . .

"Aye, sir," Ramirez replied. He turned back to his board, his hands a blur. From the set of his jaw, Garm could tell his sonar tech disapproved. It was a tradeoff. The POSEIDON M45 Passive Fathometer Sonar System didn't function as a traditional sonar projector; it absorbed ambient sounds generated by wave noise striking the seafloor and used the resultant echoes to create a detailed 3D map of their surroundings. It was 100% undetectable, but it was not without weaknesses. High sediment concentrations reduced its effectiveness and excessive noise generated by biologics like whales or dolphins could confuse the system. Worst of all, powerful active sonar emissions could scramble it altogether.

On the other hand, if it was an adult pliosaur they were approaching, having ANCILE locking sonar pings on every boat or big game fish that passed within range was sure to alert their quarry.

"Fire Control, what's our status?" Garm asked.

Cunningham swiveled in his direction. "REAPER is on standby. We're down to 1,107 rounds of 30 mm and have four fish left." He paused, checking his screen. "Per SOP, tubes one and four are loaded and primed. We are wet and hard and ready to pump. Unless, of course, you want to upgrade to the M66's . . . sir." He winked.

Garm grinned. In addition to her usual complement of NAEGLING M9 ADCAP torpedoes, all ORION class subs were armed with a pair of HARPE M66 UPURS for emergency use – meaning as anti-carrier weapons in the event war broke out. The twelve-foot M66's were capped with nuclear warheads – pure fission implosion devices that packed a two-kiloton wallop – a ridiculous overkill, even for the biggest pliosaur in history. Not to mention, completely illegal without authorization. Garm's CSO loved joking about "accidentally slipping one in there."

"The usual stuff will be fine, LC," Garm drawled. "Set torpedoes to acoustic tracking with safeties off at one hundred yards; we'll use target's own sonar emissions to zero her if we miss and she makes a run for it."

"Aye, sir."

Garm glanced approvingly around the bridge. With her refitting complete and his best people on point, the oldest of the ORION-class AB-Submarines was performing with lethal efficiency. Or, as Cunningham would say, she was one "badass bitch."

At 132 feet in length and a submerged displacement of 435 tons, the *Gryphon* was tiny for a combat sub – at least according to the Navy. Despite that, she was the most highly-decorated ship in the history of the Coastal Defense Force. Initially intended to be a branch of the Coast Guard, the CDF was now under private contract with Grayson Defense Technologies, the company that sponsored her refitting. GDT was aligned with the military, and had emerged as the country's primary undersea defense against the ongoing pliosaur threat. With no bureaucracy to slow things down, getting the ten-year-old sub's overhaul approval had been as simple as the stroke of a pen.

Among the long list of items included in *Gryphon*'s recent modifications was the installation of an AMS-424 high-yield nuclear reactor, powering eight Mako M69 pump jet MHD Propulsors, each generating 1,500 hp. As a result, she was now not only quiet, she could do over 41 knots submerged and possessed an agility beyond compare. Her hull-based maneuvering thrusters were tied directly to the engines, allowing the sleek hunter-killer to hover in place, move sideways, or even make zero radius turns – all while implementing firing solutions.

Gryphon's hull had also been revamped. In addition to applying state-of-the art acoustic cladding, her basic hull design had been upgraded as well. Foregoing the teardrop shape traditional subs used to mimic whales, the ORION class utilized a Mako shark body design to reduce hydrodynamic drag. Compared to the Navy's traditional, tube-shaped military subs that looked like lumbering cigars in the water, the ORIONs were more like Corvettes.

Along with its aggressive stance, *Gryphon*'s new hull was incredibly durable. It had a super-slick outer casing made up of shock-absorbing ceramic, married to a pressure hull of reinforced titanium steel. In addition to their innate high tensile strength, her inner and outer hulls were also widely spaced, giving her very high reserve buoyancy. Finally, her main pressure hull had eight separate watertight compartments.

In submarine terms, she was nearly indestructible.

She needed to be. She hunted sea monsters for a living.

"Captain, I've got satellite overview coming online," Rush announced.

"Show me what we've got."

Rush tapped her screen. *Gryphon's* transparent bow turned opaque and then shimmered. A moment later, it became a twenty-foot wide monitor. The ocean view was that of a satellite, albeit from 30,000 feet or better.

"Zooming in," Rush said.

A second later, they were through the clouds and had a birds-eye view of the seas directly below. White seagulls and dark-colored cormorants swarmed the area, with scores swooping down to scoop up pale scraps of flesh, while others buoyed about on the surface. The image was so clear you could almost smell the salt air and hear the birds' raucous cries.

"I don't see much of a slick," Garm said. "Increase magnification."

The satellite zoomed in until it seemed as if they would plunge into the shimmering water. There was a telltale disturbance – a hint of something big and shadowy moving far below – but nothing definitive.

"Okay, lose it. Where are we with that visual?"

"Distance to target 1,500 yards," Ho announced.

"Acknowledged," Rush said. She tapped a few keys. "Based on water clarity, we should be able to get a clearer image right about . . . *now.*"

"Holy shit!" Cunningham spouted.

"Wow, that *is* a big boy," Ensign Ho muttered. The corners of her mouth turned up. "Hey, Ramirez. You think nailing this sucker will let you catch up with the ex?"

"Hey, *Ho,* why don't you catch up with my nuts?" the sonar tech shot back.

"Big *girl,*" Garm corrected. "And can the banter."

"Sorry, sir. Do you think it's the same one that sank the trawler?" Ho asked.

"SOS said it was bigger than their sixty-foot boat. That's got to be it."

The dark-hued *Kronosaurus imperator* cow was enormous. Her rowboat-sized pectoral fins moved fluidly up and down, the up-stroke working against her buoyancy and maintaining her position as she straddled her kill. Her monstrous jaws, big enough to engulf a rhino, and lined with interlocking teeth sixteen inches in length, gaped wide before crunching down on her prey. Particles of flesh clouded the screen as she bit and the resultant sound was so loud that, even with their acoustic cladding, everyone swore they could hear it.

"Jesus, is that one of them?"

Garm turned in his chair and nodded as Doctor Kimberly Bane entered the bridge. The five-foot-nine, middle-aged brunette-just-start-ing-to-gray was their temporary Independent Duty Corpsman. She'd been flown in by chopper the day before, after their medical officer had been medevacked for acute appendicitis. If she hadn't been en route to base anyway, Garm would have declined. Like many doctors, Bane was overqualified for her position and felt her status as a physician added to her rank. On top of that, she was hardly a seaman. Being onboard a submarine was tough on newcomers initially, but she'd been seasick ever since she got there.

"Impeccable timing, Lieutenant," Garm said. "I understand you've never seen a pliosaur before."

"I prefer *doctor*, if you don't mind," Bane replied, her face pale as she wiped the sheen off her brow. "I'm only on loan until we get to Rock Key. And to answer your question, not alive," She took a hesitant step toward the screen. "My God, it is terrifying." She blanched as she took in the carnage. "How big?"

On the screen, their target began to shake its prey, wrenching loose a four-thousand-pound slab of frilly red meat. Garm appeared unimpressed. "Sonar . . ."

Ramirez studied his screens. "Over eighty feet. Most likely a Gen-1, sir."

Bane shook her head. "What's it eating?"

Garm signaled to Rush, who adjusted the viewer, zooming in on the pliosaur's victim. "Prey item appears to be a very large whale shark, ma'am," she said.

"What's all that red stuff?"

Ensign Ho cleared her throat. "Captain, distance to target nine hundred yards and closing."

"Maintain course and reduce speed to five," Garm replied. He stood up, towering over Dr. Bane, and indicated the screen. "Pliosaurs love shark gills, doc. To them, it's a delicacy. If it was a whale, it would have most likely started with the tongue or the heart. Notice the shark's tail is intact."

"Yes?"

"Whale sharks are filter feeders – defenseless against predators that size. Pliosaurs are smarter than people think. With this shark, it went straight for the kill. But when they go after a potentially dangerous meal, they incapacitate it first. Before great whites were wiped out, I watched a sub-adult attack one. They were about the same size – maybe eighteen feet or so – so I expected a prolonged battle. Instead of going right at it, however, the pliosaur just swam beside the shark, eyeing it up and down. Then it dropped back and, a second later, *BAM!* It came out of nowhere and amputated its tail. End of story."

"I don't see any blood in the water," Bane observed. "Shouldn't there be blood?"

Rush spun in her seat. "Captain, I'm picking up a transponder reading, two hundred yards off our starboard bow, bearing two-two-zero. Signal is stationary. I think it's another submarine."

Garm shot Ramirez a look.

The sonar tech swallowed. "Nothing on the scope, sir. She must be rigged for silent running. And with our search and destroy systems down . . ."

"Communications, give me a visual."

Rush's brow furrowed up as she checked her screens. "Nothing. Whoever it is, she's cloaked."

"Do you want me to go active?" Ramirez asked.

Garm's eyebrows slamming down were like a portcullis dropping over the gates of his eyes. "Rush, get me that transponder code. I want to know who's knocking on our back door. Cunningham, lock LADON onto--"

"Already got it, sir," Rush interjected. "Code belongs to the *Antrodemus*."

Garm stood up straight. *Antrodemus* was their sister ship, and as notorious a pliosaur killer as the *Gryphon* was. She was a few years younger and had gone through similar upgrades. The two subs normally covered different territories, but when they overlapped competition got fierce.

He ground his molars. *Boy, she has got <u>some</u> balls if she thinks--*

"Encrypted message coming in on the digital acoustic link, sir," Rush said. "Shall I read it?"

Garm cleared his throat. "Proceed."

Modern subs like the ORION class used secure links consisting of high speed digital pulses to send either verbal or text messages. The pulses were focused directly on the target, in frequencies that jumped up and down thousands of times per second. No sonar could detect or decipher them, even at point blank range.

"It says, 'Ahoy, Captain Braddock. No interest in stealing your kill. Munitions low. Request permission to accompany *Gryphon* back to base after bag completed. Captain Dragunova, USS *Antrodemus*.'"

Garm nodded. "Tell Captain--"

"Sorry, sir. There's a PS."

"Go on . . ."

"It says, 'Tell Ramirez he's getting sloppy for not noticing big school of sardines shadowing *Gryphon* for last ten minutes.'"

Ramirez flushed under his captain's withering stare.

Garm exhaled. "Rush, please tell Captain Dragunova we're thrilled to have her run backup. And I will take her last suggestion under advisement."

"Aye, sir."

"Ramirez, time to redeem yourself," Garm said, suddenly animated. "Let's show the *Antrodemus* how we do things. Helm--"

Rush turned in her chair. "Captain, we've got an overflight, altitude 3,000 feet. He's circling . . ."

Garm squeezed his eyes shut. *What else can go wrong?* An overflight meant a search plane. And he was pretty sure he knew what kind. "On internal speakers."

The rumble of noisy turbines immediately filled the room. Rush touched her screen, lowering the volume, then glanced at Ramirez.

"Engine noise and intermittent transients confirm a military craft," he said. His index finger ran down one of his screens. "Designate C-88." His eyes met Garm's. "It's a Hedgehog, sir."

"Son of a bitch is trying to steal our kill," Cunningham muttered.

Ramirez shook his head. "Someone must have called it in," he said. "I know a Hog's capabilities. The pilot can't confirm a target at that depth, even with satellites. He's probably hoping she'll spout so he can get a quick lock."

Garm's lips tightened. The C-88 Hedgehog was the Air Force's replacement for the venerable A-10 Thunderbolt, AKA the "Warthog." With its reputation as a lethal flying gun platform, the Thunderbolt had been converted into an airborne pliosaur hunter shortly after the military's campaign against the huge reptiles started.

Of course, as evolution decreed, the C-88 was far more lethal than its predecessor. Bristling with weapons, including an arsenal of acoustic tracking missiles and the same LADON gun system *Gryphon* used, the Hedgehog was also capable of vertical takeoff and landing and could hover while unleashing its full payload. The more immediate problem, however, was that, even when they weren't firing a shot, they were noisy as hell.

"Captain, she's getting twitchy," Rush advised.

On the screen, the giant pliosaur stopped feeding and its head angled up. The water's surface directly above it began to froth as the C-88 passed overhead.

"Rush, shoot a message to that flyboy," Garm snapped. "Tell him we are locked on target and he's about to spook her."

"Aye, sir," Rush said.

"Captain, do you want me to take a shot from here?" Cunningham asked.

"Negative," Garm replied. "An animal that size that's not afraid to approach the coastline is too big a threat to take chances on. I want a sure thing."

Rush touched her earpiece. "Captain, the pilot refuses to relinquish the target. He said, once it surfaces it's his."

"Oh, *really*?" Garm smiled humorlessly. "I'd like to speak with him directly. On speaker, please."

Rush hesitated. "Uh, yes sir." She hit a few keys. A moment later, the plane's static-laden radio transmissions emanated from their internal speakers.

Garm grabbed a mike from Rush's station. "Attention C-88, this is ORION-class AB-Submarine *Gryphon*, please identify."

The pilot's gruff voice came right back.

"Yeah, this is Lieutenant Borkowski, call sign *Big Daddy*. I already told your girl, I'm not relinquishing the target. It's first come, first served, pal. Sorry."

"This is Captain Braddock of the *Gryphon*. We've been stalking the 'target' for the last twenty-four hours and are on attack approach." Any hint of amiability left Garm's voice and his pale eyes became as hard as agates. "That animal has already killed ten people we know of. And if it escapes because of you and all the noise you're making, I am going to hold you *personally* responsible. Do I make myself clear?"

Other than the faint rumble of the Hedgehog's powerful turbines, the *Gryphon*'s bridge was momentarily silent.

"Did you say 'Braddock' as in Garm '*The Gate*' Braddock?"

"Affirmative."

"Uh, well . . . why didn't you say so? In, um . . . consideration of the civilian lives lost and since you guys were already on approach . . . I'll give you the field."

"Thank you."

"*Big Daddy* out."

Garm handed the mike back to Rush, then turned and smiled disarmingly at an obviously tense Dr. Bane. "See, doc? Civility wins every time."

Rush removed one of her headphones. "The Hedgehog has veered off. Target has resumed feeding."

Garm plopped back into his chair. "Excellent. Helm, what's our status?"

"Distance to target 400 yards, sir," Ho replied. Shall I activate the shield?"

"Not yet. Sonar?"

"Target is periodically emitting active sonar scans. I'm able to suppress, but if we alter direction or speed she'll know we're here."

"How long before she spots us, based on water clarity?"

Ramirez wiped his brow with the back of one hand. "Any minute now, sir."

Garm sat up straight. "Helm, lower shield. Sonar, compensate for shield implementation resonance. Once shield is in place, prepare to initiate iridophores."

Bane asked, "What's 'active suppression'?"

Garm studied her. Despite putting on a tough exterior, he could see she was still green around the gills. Being seasick on a submarine sucked. "What kind of doctor are you?"

"My PhD is in epidemiology. Why?"

"Interesting."

A faint vibration ran through *Gryphon*'s heavy hull as the foot-thick ceramic composite barrier that was part of her outer casing slid down, reinforcing the ultra-clear portal that formed the front of the bridge. Garm detested the shield. He preferred looking his opponents in the eye, but it was a necessary precaution. Pound for pound, the modified titanium was stronger than steel and would flex inward, rather than crack, but it wasn't indestructible. The *Gryphon* may have outweighed its quarry by a wide margin, but if 100+ tons of enraged marine reptile impacted on them at fifty miles an hour, it could stave in their hull, crippling or sinking them. As one of Garm's predecessors had discovered.

"Shield in place, sir," Ho announced.

"No reaction from target," Ramirez added.

Garm nodded. He noticed Dr. Bane holding onto the back of Ramirez's chair and got up. "Take my seat, doc. Please."

Bane frowned. "Thank you, captain. But I'm fine."

Garm pointed at the behemoth on their viewer. "I appreciate your notion of independence. But if we miss our first strike and that thing gets past our guard, we may take one hell of a hit. Believe me, you'd much rather be sitting than standing when that happens."

Bane hesitated, then glanced up, just in time to watch the gorging pliosaur bite what was left of the whale shark in half. She swallowed nervously. "Point taken, captain. And . . . thank you."

"I'd click on that restraining harness, too," Garm said as she situated herself. He turned to his crew. "Okay, people. Let's show those mama's boys onboard the *Antrodemus* how it's done. Ramirez: initiate iridophores."

"Aye, sir. Cloaking system powering up."

Bane reached out and touched Garm on the shoulder. "I'm sorry, captain, but what is the 'cloaking system' he mentioned?"

Garm's eyes were like searchlights, fixed on the screen. "Besides their sonar, pliosaurs have keen senses: hearing, smell, and eyesight. We can approach as quiet as a mouse from downstream so she doesn't hear or smell us, and if we're careful, we can hide from her sonar – to a point. But once we're in visual range, the game is up. She'll focus her sonar on us at the highest frequency. Our SVALINN active sonar suppression won't hold up under that intensity. At that point, she'll either make a run for it or attack. I'm betting on the latter."

"Does the cloaking help?"

"All ORION-class AB-subs have electronic iridophores embedded in their outer hull. Even our sonar arrays are coated with them. They're like millions of mirrored projectors that can reflect the surrounding environment. We can also program imagery into the iridophores to camouflage us."

Dr. Bane blinked. "So, we can turn invisible, like in 'Predator'?"

Garm allowed himself a chuckle. "Not exactly. We've tried a lot of options over the years, from appearing as air bubbles to just plain water. Their sonar still IDs us, just like it would in the dark. Our best bet is to imitate something of similar size that won't be viewed as either threat or competition."

Ramirez turned in his chair, "Iridophores active. System recommendations are: floating mass of kelp, mating colony of squid, school of herring--"

Garm smirked. "With the size of the breakfast our CSO had this morning, I'm thinking we're packing too much mass to pull off kelp."

"Said Paul Bunyan, after wolfing down a dozen eggs, half a loaf of bread, and enough bacon to feed that thing out there," Cunningham shot back.

Garm chuckled. "Program us to be a big baitball. Make us . . . anchovies."

"Anchovies?"

"Absolutely. It's her last meal. She should have anchovies on it."

Ramirez grinned. "Aye, sir."

Bane's eyes widened as the room resonated with the hum of the sub's cloak taking effect. She stared at the bulkheads, as if expecting the walls to change shape or disappear. "If we're a baitball, won't it try to eat us?" she asked.

Garm shook his head. "With forty tons of fresh shark meat in front of her, I'm pretty sure she's got enough on her plate."

"Iridophores successfully engaged, captain," Ramirez stated.

Outside, *Gryphon*'s slate-gray hull shimmered then disappeared. In its place, a glittering school of tiny fish slipped forward, moving slowly toward the voracious pliosaur.

"Distance to target, 200 yards," Ensign Ho announced.

"Fire control, charge REAPER." Garm said.

"Really?" Cunningham wore a surprised look.

"Yes, really," Garm replied. "That bitch devoured an entire crew – men with families. I want to be able to tell them we sent her to hell in style. Charge REAPER and prepare to fire. Helm, I want as small a sonar profile as possible. Point us down her throat."

"Yes, sir!"

As Dr. Bane opened her mouth, Garm interjected, "REAPER stands for Rail Energized Armor Piercing Electromagnetic Repulsion. It's the submarine version of a rail gun. Ours fires a 2,000-pound tungsten projectile out of a sixty-foot barrel, using an electromagnetic pulse as propellant. The electricity is drawn from our reactor. Once unleashed, the pulse accelerates the projectile out of the barrel at over 5,000 mph. The kinetic energy released is 600 megajoules." Garm looked her in the eye. "That's the equivalent of a 100-ton locomotive striking a mountain at over 250 mph."

"Irresistible force . . ." Bane muttered. "And the target?"

"If all goes well, there'll be nothing left but flippers."

Bane scanned the chamber. "Wait, a sixty-foot barrel? I've seen pictures of this sub online. I didn't see any--"

"You're standing on it," Garm advised. "The REAPER gun runs through the front half of the sub, starting in front of the reactor. The mouth of the barrel is right under our feet."

"Is that safe?"

"I don't know. Cunningham, what do you think?"

"Hasn't killed us yet," the CSO snickered. "Although we don't get to use it as often as I'd like." A set of glowing crosshairs suddenly appeared on their viewer, and a heavy, rhythmic vibration could be felt building under the bridge's flooring. The acrid smell of ionized air began to permeate the room, and a metallic taste was in everyone's mouth.

As Bane involuntarily latched onto her chair's armrests, Garm hid his smirk. "Helm?"

"Distance, 150 yards," Ho said. She made a barely perceptible adjustment on her steering yoke, lining the pliosaur up in Cunningham's sights.

"Target is locked on," he said, giving her a thumbs-up sign.

"Sonar?"

"Partially suppressing target's sonar emissions to match our image density," Ramirez replied. "Cloak is working. She believes we're a school of baitfish, either huddling scared or waiting to feed on her leftovers."

Garm's wolfish eyes studied the monstrous creature he was preparing to kill. His heart rate began to speed up as he felt the power of the REAPER grow. In mere moments, he would give the command to fire, and watch as a super-heated blast erupted from their bow, slicing a ten-foot swathe of destruction through the surrounding water, and annihilating the beast that had ended so many lives. If there was any justice to be had in this world, it was here and now.

He turned to his CSO. "Fire control status?"

"REAPER at 73% and building, sir," Cunningham said. "Estimated time to fire--"

"Captain, we've got a problem," Ramirez cut in. "Target is gravid."

All heads turned to Garm, their looks of wanton surprise matching his own.

"Are you sure?"

"Yes, sir. Fathometer scan verifies," Ramirez said. His eyes did the ping pong thing across his screens. As the *Kronosaurus imperator* turned sideways, he pointed at the viewer. "Man, you can tell just by looking. She's about to burst!"

Garm's lips compressed as he sucked in a huge breath.

"REAPER at 85% and building," Cunningham advised.

Bane cleared her throat. "Captain, Dr. Grayson's orders are quite specific in this matter. In the event--"

"I am well aware of what our mandate says, *lieutenant*," Garm growled. His jaw muscles began to bunch up.

"Captain, REAPER at 93% and building . . . we can't wait much longer."

"Fuck!" Garm slammed one fist into the opposing palm. Loose objects on the bridge started to rattle. "Shut it down."

"Are you serious?"

"You heard me, CSO. Do it *now.*"

"Aye, sir," Cunningham said. He hawked his gauges while flipping switches. "Reducing electromagnetic buildup . . . initiating thermal management system to compensate."

Son of a bitch! Garm stalked back and forth like a caged lion, angrily sucking air in through his nose and blowing it out his mouth as he fought to get his own energy buildup under control. After a few seconds, he pulled his shoulders back, uncomfortably aware of his crew – and Dr. Bane – all staring at him.

"Rush, send a priority-one message to Captain Dragunova," Garm began. "Tell her target is a pregnant Gen-1 and, per mandate, must be taken alive. We're giving them the honor of bringing her in."

"W-what? We're giving the commission to *Antrodemus*?" Ramirez asked.

"Relax, ensign. You've done well on this patrol," Garm stated. "We can afford to share the wealth."

"But that's like ten--" Ramirez's sea of whining ebbed in his throat as he clocked Garm's cool expression.

"Chill out, Ramirez," Cunningham sniggered. "It's still one less ugly mother running around giving people grief." He let out an exaggerated sigh. "Now, if we could only do something about my *wife's* mother . . . *There's* a reaper you don't wanna mess with."

Garm grinned humorlessly as the chuckles faded. "I'm glad you're all in a good mood. Now, get ready; you've got another chance at a bonus."

Ho's head turned like an owl's. "A bonus for what, sir?"

Garm peered over Ramirez's shoulder, checking his screens. "The demon we've got coming at us in about five minutes."

As the larger of the two sperm whales made good its escape, the male octopus renewed its assault. The bulbous lips covering its mouth peeled back, revealing its lethal jaws. Shaped like an inverted parrot's beak, the four-foot, razor-edged mass of black chitin was as strong and hard as iron – capable of biting through steel cable.

The octopus threw itself back onto the white whale's carcass with a tremendous thud, its maw snapping like shears, ripping through what ribs remained. It began gouging out huge chunks of the cetacean's internal organs. Each bite carved away over four hundred pounds of meat, which the great cephalopod greedily swallowed. The whale's still-warm body and iron-rich blood, coupled with the delicious taste of blubber that flooded the chemoreceptors in the octopus's vast array of suckers, maddened the already voracious beast and it began to savage its meal. Soon, the dark waters around it were glutted with scraps of skin and flesh, around which hundreds of tiny fish and squid swarmed, eager to partake in the gruesome feast.

The battle with the hapless sperm whales had been decided before it even began. The cetaceans simply had no chance; they were outmatched, both in size and speed. A true product of bathymetric gigantism, the coldwater-loving *Octopus giganteus* and its ilk were the largest mollusks in the history of the planet. They had haunted the ocean's abysses since the Triassic – back when marine reptiles ruled the seas. In fact, they had evolved to prey upon them. The modern sperm whales were simply a substitute for the 70-foot Ichthyosaur *Shastasaurus sikanniensis* that was the preferred prey of the cephalopod's distant ancestors. In many ways, the whales and Ichthyosaurs were alike; they were similarly-sized, cumbersome and slow-moving squid-eaters, with relatively weak jaws. Moreover, the whales possessed the same primary weakness the Ichthyosaurs had: they were air breathers.

As the octopus tore another frenzied beakful of meat away and gulped it down, it tasted its own venom. The paralytic saliva it secreted was a weapon that, like the creature itself, had become specialized over the eons. Whereas it originally evolved to deal with struggling 80-ton reptiles, now it functioned to immobilize blubbery, warm-blooded cetaceans. The adaptation served the giant cephalopods well as they lurked in the deep submarine canyons, waiting for their unwitting victims to come to them.

Lately, however, there was little prey to be had. Fewer and fewer sperm whales prowled the icy blackness of the abyss and the great octopi had been forced to rise up into shallower waters in search of them. They had no choice. They were on the verge of starvation.

Feeding with increased urgency now, the male octopus glimpsed the missing half of one of its tentacles moving about on the nearby seafloor. The tendril writhed like a worm on a hook, blue blood oozed from its ruptured end. It was an autotomic response; the severed limb had a mind of its own and would continue to wiggle, attempting to lure whatever predator injured the octopus. The loss of the forty-foot piece was a minor annoyance. It would regenerate over the next few weeks.

A sudden disturbance in the pitch-black water drew the male octopus's attention. Moments later, the reason for its accelerated feeding emerged up the canyon wall.

It was the female.

As the male's mate approached, his body began to change. Thousands of papillae that covered his thick skin sprang to life. In seconds, his relatively smooth hide became bark-like and rough. A series of spiky projections emerged like intimidating horns above his eyes and he swelled himself up, attempting to appear bigger and more imposing.

The *Octopus giganteus* female was undaunted. She was a fourth again larger than her mate, and doubly as massive. With lethal fluidity, her one hundred-foot tentacles with their manhole-sized suckers carried her forward. As she spotted the partially-stripped whale carcass underneath the male she stopped. Her glittering eyes narrowed and her color turned from dullish gray to deepest black. She began to tremble with barely-contained rage. Then, with a bloop-like rumble, she rushed forward, her eight powerful arms a bristling nest of serpents, eager to destroy.

Paling in the face of his enraged mate, the male jetted backwards, wisely relinquishing the meal. A second later, his ravenous mate impacted on the partially-consumed sperm whale and enveloped it. Her eyes glared at him like twin orbs of fire as she began noisily tearing what remained to pieces.

Still hungry, but hardly foolish enough to risk the female's wrath, the male scoured the area for something to nourish his 134-ton body. The yard-long squid and wormlike hagfish that lurked nearby were too small and swift to suffice, and a thirty-foot *Architeuthis dux* he spotted jetted away the moment it sensed him. Finally, he happened upon his own, amputated arm. Without hesitation, he pounced on the forty-foot tendril, seizing it with his tentacles and guiding it toward his waiting beak. The arm fought back, twisting and turning like a worm on a hook as he mercilessly shredded it. Nothing went to waste.

The female, soon finished with her feast, sat like the engorged colossus she was atop the sperm whale's gnawed skeleton. Her body heaved like an exhausted sprinter's as she sucked copious amounts of seawater into her mantle and then expelled it. The male approached cautiously and extended one tentacle, ready to sacrifice it and retreat if either her hunger or anger were unabated.

The female remained calm and allowed her mate to run the tip of his arm across the rough skin of her mantle in a crude caress. A moment later, she hoisted herself off the pile of bones and began to drift upward. The male studied her possessively. Her magnificent body was immense and bloated to the point she looked like she might rupture.

With surprising silence, the female expelled a powerful jet of seawater from her mantle's muscular siphon and began to cruise up the slopes of Ophion's Deep. The male was far faster and, after a moment's hesitation, quickly caught up to her. Keeping pace, he followed, sensing the gradual changes in temperature and pressure as they rose in the water column. Far in the distance, his keen eyesight detected a grayness that he knew would eventually become daylight.

The male octopus was uncomfortable outside his domain. Terrors of the deep though they were, his kind rarely came to the surface. Their natural abode was the frigid blackness of the abyss. But wherever the titanic female went he would follow. Only twice in their hundred-year lifespans had the pair ventured into the shallows, and only because, as now, the whales they fed upon had disappeared. During those occasions, they encountered objects on the surface, some of which dwarfed even them. The warm-blooded bipeds riding atop these objects rarely spotted them, however, and when they did, they gazed upon them with dread-filled eyes.

They had borne many names over the centuries. The 18th century Swedish zoologist Carolus Linnaeus called them *Singulare monstrum*, and the French malacologist Pierre <u>Dénys de Montfort</u>, *Poulpe colossal*. But terrified Norwegian fishermen, who watched their boats ripped asunder and their comrades dragged screaming to their deaths, came up with a far simpler name for the ocean's most horrific predator.

They called them Kraken.

THREE

"Sonar, what's our position relative to both the target and *Antrodemus*?" Garm asked. Around him, the bridge crew was on high alert. Still sitting rigidly upright in his spacious captain's chair, Dr. Bane held her breath.

"We're holding position, 150 yards from target," Ramirez responded. "*Antrodemus* is approaching at seven knots, on intercept course two-zero-zero. Distance to target, 300 yards and closing."

"And the depth here?"

"Around 900 feet, sir."

Garm eyed the gorging man-eater on their viewer, still furious the *Kronosaurus imperator* had to be taken alive. Its feeding had slowed, becoming noticeably less voracious. Soon, the beast would have its fill and abandon its kill to scavengers. They were rapidly running out of time.

"Sonar, how's our cloak holding up?"

"Iridophores are holding firm; no instability detected, sir," Ramirez replied. "We're good, as long as we don't exceed ten knots or make any sudden course alterations."

Garm folded his meaty arms across his chest. He glanced at their fathometer screens, his tactician's eyes studying the surrounding terrain. "Helm, plot course two-five-four, maneuvering thrusters only. Move us 200 yards further from target, then take us to the bottom."

"The bottom, sir?"

Garm moved to Ensign Ho's station and pointed at the glittering 3-D hologram she shared with Ramirez. "You see that 500 yard-long, 50-yard-wide trough carving its way across the seafloor?"

"Aye, sir."

"We can fit in their lengthwise, correct?"

"Piece of cake, sir."

"Good." He patted her on the shoulder. "Lower us inside until we're flush with the seafloor, and hold position." He indicated the creature on their viewer. "Remember: maneuvering thrusters *only*. We're invisible right now. Let's keep it that way."

As Ho started her preparations, a loud *clang* on a nearby bulkhead caused Dr. Bane to jump.

"What was that?" she asked, one hand clutching her heart.

"Swordfish, ma'am," Cunningham said with a snicker. "One of the few species fast enough to benefit from the pliosaurs. They're everywhere. Stupid bastard thought he found himself a nice easy meal of anchovies and ran smack into the hull."

"At least we know our cloak's working," Ensign Rush offered.

"Amen, girl," Cunningham smiled back at her.

Garm rested his hands on the back of Ho's chair, watching their bow viewer as she maneuvered the sub. His stomach registered their rapid descent as the *Gryphon* dropped like a high-speed elevator, seven hundred feet straight down. Directly below, the jagged crack they'd targeted gaped across the rocks like a toothy grin from the seabed.

"Lower us in," he said. "And keep the primary target on our viewer."

As the sub eased into the Sears Tower-sized crevasse, it inexplicably started to wobble. A cloud of detritus obscured their viewer and the floor slanted steeply. There was a loud metallic groan as the boat angled hard to port. They were drifting sideways, heading straight toward the rocks.

Ho's head snapped up and she stabbed two buttons before grabbing the yoke with both hands. "There's a powerful rip current running through the trough, sir," she announced. Her teeth clenched as she held the controls and fought to bring them level. "I can compensate with maneuvering thrusters, but it's going to require a lot of power." The whirring sound of their hull thrusters fighting to hold them in place became noticeable.

Garm cursed on an exhale. "Sonar, can you compensate for the disruption?"

Ramirez shook his head. "Not enough, sir."

Garm chafed. "Helm, bring us up and hover directly over the trough. We'll hold there. It's still better than sitting out in the open."

As the sub rose through the detritus storm and their viewer cleared, Ramirez turned. "Captain, is this like what happened to the *Titan*?"

Garm looked at him and the sonar tech licked his lips and turned back to his screens. With a newbie on the bridge, Ramirez knew his CO's inclined chin was as close as he was going to get to a nod.

"What's going on?" Bane asked.

"Watch," Garm instructed. "The game's afoot."

On *Gryphon's* bridge-wide viewing apparatus, a school of foot-long sardines headed directly for the distracted *Kronosaurus imperator*. If the titanic reptile in any way noticed the approaching baitfish, it gave no indication.

Bane said, "Is that the--"

Garm held up a hand, then pointed at their viewer.

Suddenly, a pair of dark objects with fins, each around eight feet in length, materialized from under the school of sardines. Like sleek phantoms, they began to move off, one to either side. They cruised purposefully through the gloom, silently circling the still-feeding pliosaur at a distance of forty yards.

"Those are LOKI M22 Decoys," Garm said quietly. "Impeller-driven AUVs."

"AUVs?"

"Autonomous undersea vehicles."

"What are they doing?" Bane whispered back. She leaned forward, then reached for the buckle of her restraining harness.

"Stay in your seat, doc," Garm warned. "The decoys are emitting false acoustic signatures – probably appearing as hungry sharks waiting to scavenge what's left of her kill, once she abandons it."

The bridge was pin-drop silent as they watched the pair of tiny craft inch closer to the giant predator. Soon, they were only fifty feet away. The pliosaur, shaking free a meaty morsel, glanced at the nearest LOKI. Her gleaming eyes crinkled up in obvious annoyance and a throaty rumble escaped her flesh-filled jaws, echoing across the seafloor like distant thunder.

Suddenly, a bright strobe light erupted from the other AUV. The *Kronosaurus's* wedge-shaped head whipped toward it, her black pupils contracting into tiny pinpricks against the dazzling display. Then a strobe emanated from the first decoy, confusing the creature. She swelled up with anger and began to emit powerful sonar pulses, her huge jaws whipping from side to side as the annoying lightshow continued. Before she could make up her mind which decoy to destroy first, a disturbance in the water directly in front of the female garnered her full attention. The school of scavenging fish began to shimmer. A second later, they dissolved away and something far more formidable took their place.

Antrodemus had revealed herself.

Facing the monstrous reptile from less than a boat length away, the blood-red hunter-killer stared down its barrels at its prehistoric adversary. Active pinging resounded across the seafloor as the big sub zeroed its target.

The pliosaur cow's crimson eyes blazed with fury at the intrusion. Fragments of flesh spilt from her jaws as she uttered an underwater roar so powerful it caused *Antrodemus* to wobble on its axis. With a massive power-stroke from all four of her flippers, the cow threw herself at the sub.

At that exact moment, the tiny AUVs found their openings and fired.

A pair of yard-long, silvery bolts trailed bubbles as they zipped toward the pliosaur's exposed neck. With barely detectable thuds they struck, burying themselves in its rock-hard scales. The impact, though negligible, had an immediate and profound effect on the behemoth. The moment the barbed projectiles slammed into it, it froze in place. Its eyes rolled wildly in their sockets and its cavernous jaws snapped left and right. Then its movements slowed and its muscles began to spasm. Its flippers drooped and its eyes rolled up inside its head. Like a giant rag doll, it sagged in the water.

"Wow, that was fast," Ho muttered.

"As a good divorce should be," Ramirez said, winking. He held out a hand, smirking as Ho grudgingly handed him a C-note. "I don't suppose . . ."

She smirked. "I'll think about it."

Garm's head swiveled from the viewer as Bane undid her restraining belt and moved next to him. "Is it over?"

He nodded.

"I thought you had to bring it back alive?"

"It's not dead," he said, regretfully. "It's been forced into brumation by 400 mgs of Cronavrol, shot directly into its spine."

"Cronavrol? I've never heard of it."

Garm gave her a look. "I don't expect you would have."

Obviously annoyed, the epidemiologist shook her head. "So, it's asleep?"

"More like hibernating, doctor," Cunningham cut in. "Many aquatic reptiles go into brumation as winter approaches. No movement. No feeding. They wake up occasionally to drink, but that's about it."

On the viewer, a school of several hundred foot-long fish boldly swarmed around the immobile pliosaur, exploring its vast bulk and picking away at the hunks of flesh embedded in its teeth.

"I've never heard of marine reptiles brumating."

Cunningham cleared this throat. "Many *Archelon* fossils are believed to be the result of extended dormancy, courtesy of the asteroid that wiped out the dinosaurs," he said. "The impact winter forced them into premature brumation with insufficient fat stores and they starved. We think--" The gabby CSO paused as he noticed Garm's annoyed look. "Sorry, sir. They, uh . . . had a *Cheers* marathon on last night."

Garm snorted. "More likely the turtles drowned when they woke and found ten feet of pack ice over their heads." He turned to Bane. "Reptiles can't spontaneously grow gills, doc."

Bane's expression turned contemplative. "I never knew pliosaurs hiber-- I mean, brumated. Could that be useful in reducing their numbers?"

"It was," Garm stated. "We used to find them all winter, just lying on the seabed. Killed hundreds that way. But no more."

"Why not?"

He shrugged. "I suspect there are several subspecies; some brumate and some don't. On the brighter side, we don't find them in higher latitudes anymore during--"

Garm's attention diverted to their viewer as *Antrodemus* closed on her downed foe. There was a loud clang, followed by a low metallic groan. Directly underneath the bow, a section of the sub's hull began to split apart.

"What's happening?" Bane asked.

"She's extending her labium," Garm replied matter-of-factly.

"Her *what*?"

Garm's face betrayed nothing. "ORION class subs are equipped with an extending labium – a forty-foot robotic arm with pincers on the end, much like the feeding apparatus of a dragonfly nymph."

Bane studied him through hooded eyes. "I see."

As they watched, the three-pronged claw tipping *Antrodemus*'s robotic arm extended toward the sleeping *Kronosaurus*. The mechanical pincers opened a full twenty feet, before carefully locking onto the titan's girthy midsection. In the background, jet pulses plumed as the sub's hull-mounted maneuvering thrusters fired short bursts, keeping her in position while her engineer manipulated the pliosaur's inert form. The creature was completely dormant, oblivious to what was happening.

Bane checked her watch. "Don't you have to feed it oxygen?"

"No."

"But won't it drown?"

Garm leaned over Ramirez's shoulder, checking his screens. He gave the sonar tech an approving pat on the shoulder. "No." He turned and made his way to his captain's chair, dropping into it and tapping a few buttons on one armrest. "Pliosaurs are like sea snakes. Their skin absorbs almost 30% of the oxygen they need from the water."

"That's why they never surface during brumation," Cunningham ventured. "It also contributes to why they can stay submerged for so long and are such powerful swimmers. The faster they go, the more oxygen they take in."

"Okay, 'Cliff'. Enough." Garm shook his head. "Doc, I suggest you grab that free chair and strap in. It's almost show time."

Dr. Bane hurried to the empty station, her pensive eyes locked on the bridge viewer. As he gauged her expression, Garm ascertained she was looking forward to the safety and security of her pending desk job. He couldn't blame her.

"Alright, people. We're expecting some very unpleasant company," he announced. "Helm, up five. Make our depth six hundred. Set course one-one-zero, right standard rudder. At coordinates, hold position, maneuvering thrusters only."

Cho was already working the controls. "Aye, sir."

"What's the plan, captain?" Cunningham asked.

Garm indicated the glittering, black and gold POSEIDON 3D fathometer screen suspended between sonar and navigation. "The Continental Shelf is flat here – easy to pick up incoming transients, with few places to hide." He pointed at a particularly craggy seafloor section on the sonar display. "Here, where it drops into the Blake Plateau, is where we have to watch. It's a maze of seaweed-filled ravines and rock outcroppings. With all the marine snow, even the fathometer can't read it well."

"At position, sir," Cho announced.

"Good. Point us right at the drop-off with our backs to *Antrodemus*, but maintain depth. Sonar, bring ANCILE online," Garm ordered. "Activate intruder alarm and acoustic intercept and feed all readings to fire control. Unless I'm mistaken, our visitor will be coming in fast and hot."

Cunningham's mouth started to open then snapped shut.

"Shall I maintain cloak?" Ramirez asked.

"Negative. Deactivate iridophores," Garm replied. "Once we move, he's going to know we're here. I'd rather have him focused on us instead of *Antrodemus*. Bring SVALINN online. Suppress any incoming pings. Make him rely on visuals."

"Very good, sir."

"Communications, send a text to Captain Dragunova. Tell her we're going to run interference."

Rush nodded. "Aye, sir."

Bane cleared her throat. "Captain--"

"Fire control," Garm swiveled in his seat. "Activate Ladon Gun System and load tubes two and three. Ultraviolet and infrared homing seekers only. Beyond that . . . you may indulge yourself, Mr. Cunningham."

"Aye, sir!" his CSO said with a smile. As Cunningham's fingers tattooed his screen, he started whistling, "Home on the Range." A moment later, he began belting out an adulterated version of the song.

Oh, give me a home where no buffalo roam,
And I don't have to watch where I sit.
Because nothing is worse, or will cause me to curse,
Than to step in some buffalo--"

"LC, I said you could indulge yourself," Garm said, shaking his head. "Not damage our eardrums or frighten off our quarry."

"Sorry, sir," Cunningham said with a sheepish grin. "Too many re-runs of 'The Voice.'" He tapped one, final button, then checked his screens. "The fish are in place and programmed . . . tubes two and three are flooded . . . all outer doors open. LADON Gun System up and running . . . auto-engage activated."

"Good. You carry that tune much better," Garm said. He put his hands behind his head and relaxed back in his seat, confident in Kyle's preparations. And that LADON would get the job done.

Named after the one hundred-headed dragon from Greek mythology, Grayson Defense Technology's LADON Gun System was the ORION-class's 8-barrelled, 30 mm Gatling cannon. Protruding from a dorsal mounted, SODOME-topped turret, and spitting out 3,000 supercavitating, AP, high-density, depleted uranium penetrator rounds, LADON was lethality epitomized. Although underwater use limited its effectiveness to 200 yards, with its high-speed tracking and auto-engage capabilities, at 100 yards or less, it spat enough death to chew through a battleship.

"Oh, for crying out loud!" Bane wore a beyond-fed-up look. "Captain Braddock, I *demand* to know what is going on."

Garm's eyes crinkled with amusement at the outburst, but otherwise remained locked on their viewer. After a bit of finagling, the *Kronosaurus imperator* female had been successfully situated atop *Antrodemus*'s labium. With a hum, the robotic arm retracted, until the slumbering giant was pulled securely against the sub's bow. One LOKI Decoy continued to hover nearby, shining a powerful spotlight on the prisoner, while the other did silent spirals around both the robotic arm and its captive, tightly securing the saurian in place with a shiny steel cable.

"You were right about there being no blood, doc," Garm admitted. "Once I saw her disruptive camouflage, I should have suspected she was gravid."

"I don't--"

"Pliosaurs feed when they make a kill," Garm said. His tone was instructive and devoid of emotion. "They don't wait. There should have been blood. Something else killed that whale shark and brought it here." He gestured at the screen. "And gave it to her."

"What kind of *something*?"

"Her mate."

"Mate?" Dr. Bane's eyes scrunched up in confusion. "But . . . I thought pliosaurs were solitary."

"For the most part," Garm said. "But after mating, dominant bulls tend to hang around to ensure no other male gets in on the action. Protecting their genes, if you will."

"But the female, does she tolerate the male's presence?"

"Not exactly. Cows are twenty five percent longer than a bull and double their weight, so they're not something to mess with," Garm advised. His eyes flipped from Ramirez's station to his CSO's. "But the male is faster." He pointed at the tightly bound predator. "She might top out at forty-four knots, I know. I chase them. But a healthy bull, with his big flippers, can do over fifty. So, he'll shadow her, maybe from a few miles out, and take off if she comes after him. On rare occasions, some bulls will actually try to placate their mates. Or maybe they just want to ensure healthy offspring. They'll make a kill and bring it to the female."

Bane paled. "Her mate is close by."

"Most likely."

"And when he discovers what you're doing . . ."

Garm chided. "What *we're* doing. You're part of the team, doc, if only for another few hours."

"But if he's miles away, how will he--"

Graaaaaaaar.

Time and hearts froze as they watched the female's jaws part. Her plaintive moan reverberated like a foghorn through the bridge, before pealing across the surrounding water at four-and-a-half times the speed of sound.

"Damn bitch talks in her sleep!" Ho muttered.

Garm did the Captain Kirk thing as he leaned forward in his chair, hands gripping his armrests. "Communications, forget *Antrodemus* for now. Switch our live feed to the viewer and prepare photonics to zoom in on incoming signal."

"Aye, sir." Rush replied.

There was a low crackle as the image of *Antrodemus* and her giant prisoner vanished and was replaced by pitch-black seas.

"Searchlights, sir?" Ho asked.

Garm's face betrayed a hint of annoyance. "No. Rush, switch to infra-red."

With a touch, the on-screen display on the bridge monitor shimmered then took on an eerie glow. Five hundred yards away, the ragged peaks that jutted up like a forest of stone from the seafloor were highlighted in brilliant shades of green and blue. In and around the rocky outcroppings, a starfield of tiny gold specks marking fish and squid twinkled in the darkness.

Garm glanced at Ramirez. "Anything?"

The mustached sonar tech shook his head. "No, sir. Maybe it's--" A sudden ping caused Ramirez's head to spring up. "We've got incoming, sir! Confirmed biologic – distance 700 yards and closing!"

A claxon sounded, coupled with a loud series of pings as ANCILE went live and began targeting the reading.

Garm hawked their viewer. "Helm, prepare to blow ballast. Sonar, talk to me!"

"OMNI ADCAP tracking . . . bearing is two-six-eight," Ramirez replied. He started taking quick, Lamaze-style breaths, as he was wont to do during combat. "No sonar emissions – target is running silent – but organic profiles confirm; it's definitely a pliosaur, sir. Speed is forty-five knots and accelerating."

"Fire control, do you have a lock yet?" Garm asked. The claxon increased in volume and warning lights began to flash.

"Negative!" Cunningham shouted. "I need OMNI's targeting. ANCILE readings are too intermittent." The CSO glanced up from his station at the viewer. "He . . . he's using the ravines and outcroppings for cover!"

"Smart son of a bitch," Garm muttered. The claxon began to annoy him and he snapped his fingers. "Kill that," he ordered. Out of the corner of one eye, he could see Bane gripping her armrests so hard her knuckles were white. "Sonar, distance to target?"

"Six hundred yards and closing!" Ramirez said. "Target is zigzagging . . . still no transmission on the bearing. Changing course to zero-one-zero." His eyes widened. "He's targeting *Antrodemus*, sir!"

"Helm, emergency rise!" Garm barked. His stomach sank into his balls as Ho initiated a full-power ascent. "Hard left rudder! Keep us between them!"

"On it, sir!" Ho replied. Her eyes turned to blackened slits, her teeth bared as she worked the yoke.

Garm growled. The pinging from ANCILE's acoustic intercept had become so fast and loud his head felt like it was going to explode. There was something different about this animal. He could feel it in his bones. It was experienced, almost tactical in its movements. His eyes rounded. *Has it fought a submarine before?*

"Target is preparing to break cover, sir!" Ramirez announced. "Sonar lock is imminent. Whoa . . . this can't be a male!"

"Why not?"

"It's too big!" Ramirez replied, wiping his brow with the back of one hand as he eyed three screens at once. "It must be another Gen-1 female invading this one's turf. Madre de Dios, it's even bigger than the last one!"

Gryphon's sonar pings sounded like machine gun fire filling the bridge. On the screen, the pliosaur's image popped up on the infra-red, exploding out of the blue-green virtual forest it was hiding be-hind. Its body glowed a bright reddish-orange as it emerged into open water.

"Target is in the clear! Systems locking on!" Ramirez yelled.

"I've got a firing solution," Cunningham stated. "Permission to engage?"

On the screen, the pliosaur's image grew. It was swimming in a huge arc, dropping down deep. Then suddenly it changed direction and rose up along the rocky break line, curving toward *Gryphon* at an astonish-ing speed.

"She's trying to flank us!" Garm bellowed. "Helm, hard right rudder. CSO, you are clear to engage!"

"Tubes two and three, firing!"

There was a high-pitched whoosh as the NAEGLING ADCAP tor-pedoes left their tubes, followed by a rumble as their boosters engaged. A modified version of the old Russian Shkval design, the NAEGLINGs were solid-fuel, supercavitating, rocket propelled torpedoes that sliced through the water at 350 mph. Once their infrared/ultraviolet homing seekers were activated, they could travel ten miles tracking a target, and cover that distance in less than two minutes.

"Torpedoes closing!" Cunningham shouted. His eyes reflected his targeting screen as he tracked the two NAEGLINGs.

Now eyeing *Gryphon*'s main viewer, the rest of the bridge crew held their breath, watching the deadly missiles speed toward their target. A series of loud, ratcheting noises began emanating from the internal speakers.

"Target is emitting active sonar, sir." Ramirez announced.

Cunningham started his countdown. "Distance to target: four hundred yards, three hundred, two . . . what the *hell*?"

A split-second before impact, the pliosaur's flippers flared out like wings, altering its trajectory. As it rose in the water column, the onrushing NAEGLINGs zipped harmlessly under it – one missing by a yard. Unable to course correct in time, the two torpedoes slammed into the stone escarpment 100 yards behind the giant predator, detonating in a fiery blast.

The bridge crew shielded their eyes as their infrared screen blazed white. A split-second later, *Gryphon*'s sturdy hull shook from the powerful shockwave.

Cunningham stared slack-jawed at his targeting screen. "I-I don't believe it. I missed! I never miss!"

"Get over it," Ho remarked.

"Rush, restore visual," Garm ordered, blinking rapidly to clear the tiny motes of light that danced before his eyes.

"Already on it, captain," she replied. A second later, the viewer was back to normal. A collective gasp escaped the bridge crew. The pliosaur was coming right at them. Its image filled the screen, its bone-crushing jaws spread wide.

"Target is at 150 yards on direct intercept, bearing zero-zero-zero!" Ramirez bellowed. "She's coming in fast!"

Garm's big hands balled into fists. *So, she wants to play chicken, eh?* "Helm, back full. Communications, lose the zoom."

Rush swallowed hard. "Zoom is already off, sir."

Ho asked, "Order to brace for collision?"

Garm swore under his breath. "Kyle, kill that son of a bitch."

Cunningham's eyes lit up. "With pleasure, sir. LADON engaging!"

Garm watched his crew involuntarily grab hold as their main viewer was about to be enveloped by the pliosaur's ghostly orange maw. A moment before impact, the beast twisted away, swerving hard to starboard.

BRRRRRRRRRRRRT!

The high-speed thrumming of the LADON's Gatling cannon's lethal bursts shook the bridge. On the viewer, tracer rounds marked the gun's underwater swath of destruction as it targeted the fast-moving colossus.

BRRRRRRRRRRRRT!

"Shit, she's looped under us, sir!" Cunningham yelled.

Garm's teeth ached from clenching so hard and he cursed. LADON was a line-of-sight weapon. It was devastating on marks at their level or above. But against a target underneath them it was useless.

"Emergency blow!" he bellowed. "Brace for impact!"

"She's bypassed us, sir!" Ramirez cried, shaking his head. "I think she's after *Antrodemus* . . . or the other female!"

"Helm, swing us around!" Garm yelled. "Fire control, keep on her!"

"Target reacquired," Cunningham announced. "Engaging!"

BRRRRRRRRRRRT!

Garm grabbed his armrests, bracing himself against the inertia as the engines and maneuvering thrusters worked hard to move *Gryphon*'s 435 tons through a quick one-eighty. On the viewer, LADON's depleted uranium shells streamed like laser beams as it continued to track its target, the high-speed turret spinning and firing faster than the sub could maneuver.

"Winged her, sir!" Cunningham exulted as several rounds tore into the fast-moving pliosaur. It was almost on top of *Antrodemus*. Tied helplessly to the other sub's bow, the unconscious cow was oblivious to the larger predator headed for it.

"Time to finish the job," Cunningham said.

BRRRRR—

"What the--?" the CSO's face contorted as the weapon stopped in mid-burst. He checked the round count, bewildered when it showed nearly seven hundred shells remaining.

"It's the new safety," Garm announced, springing to his feet. "You obviously didn't read the manual." He strode toward the main viewer, helplessly watching as the giant *Kronosaurus* closed on *Antrodemus*.

"LADON senses other American subs and automatically disengages to prevent friendly fire incidents."

Ho snorted derisively. "In other words, it just saved you from getting court-martialed, dumb ass!"

Cunningham's wounded expression and subsequent response was drowned out by what sounded like two tractor trailers colliding, as the pliosaur smashed into *Antrodemus's* sail and kept going. Metal fragments exploded out from the point of impact and the big sub issued an eerie groan as it tilted on its axis.

"Jesus, they're hit!" Cunningham yelled. "Preparing to fire tubes one and four!"

"Belay that!" Garm bellowed. His CSO froze, finger literally on the trigger. On the viewer, the wounded pliosaur began to fade in the distance, every stroke of its powerful flippers carrying it further away.

Cunningham's face was a mask of confusion. "Sir, it's escaping! We can kill it with our last two fish! They're set for acoustic tracking. We can lock onto its sonar and--"

Garm leaned in close, speaking low so only the two of them could hear. "Kyle, take a deep breath and listen. It's stopped emitting. If we fire, what sonar projector will our torpedoes lock onto?"

Cunningham stared at him. Then he glanced at the listing *Antrodemus* on their bow viewer. He looked at Garm with fear-filled eyes.

"My God . . . I-I would've killed--"

"No, you wouldn't have," Garm assured him. "You'd have realized in time, or hit the self-destructs, if need be." He rested a hand on his shoulder before turning to the remainder of his crew.

Ho glared angrily at Cunningham but remained silent.

"Communications, that hit may have taken out *Antrodemus's* photonics mast. See if their communications are functional and get me their status."

"Yes, sir!" Rush sprang rigidly upright. As she slipped on her headphones, she cast a sympathetic glance toward Cunningham. A moment later, she cleared her throat.

"Sir, I've got an incoming message from Captain Dragunova," Rush announced. "They're using the transmitter from their Remora. Message reads: 'Lost communications and external viewers. Have sustained outer hull damage to sail. Pressure hull intact. Sonar partially functional. Request *Gryphon* take point. Will follow you in.'"

Garm pursed his lips and nodded. "Tell Captain Dragunova will do. As soon as they've confirmed the package is secure we'll get under way." He turned to Ho. "Helm, pop the shield and plot a course for Rock Key. Engage as soon as they give the green light. *Antrodemus* will be slowed by drag, so match her depth and keep our speed under 25 knots."

"Aye, sir," Ho nodded.

"Stay alert, people." Garm said, folding his arms. "We hurt him, so I doubt the big bastard will be back. But we're not out of the woods yet. Plus, we've got a very unpleasant package to deliver. Let's get to it."

As the rest of the bridge crew went about their business, Garm dropped down beside Ramirez. "Give me everything you've got on the thing that attacked us," he said quietly.

"Of course, sir." Ramirez hesitated. "May I ask why?"

Garm's pale eyes narrowed. "Because I think we just had a run-in with the monster Grayson's been looking for."

FOUR

He was almost there . . .

He couldn't believe he was finally going to do it.

Victory was a foregone conclusion. But when his heart started racing, Dr. Derek "Dirk" Braddock decided he'd better slow his roll. Head down, he braced one hand against the wall of the brightly-lit corridor and sucked in a couple of breaths, steeling himself for the unpleasant task ahead.

There would be no backing down now. This time he was committed. This time there was no reason for him to--

A mere fifteen yards from his mom's office, Dirk's knees locked up. He stood there with a tablet tucked under one arm, a forlorn expression on his face, and all but ignorant of the muttering technician who rushed past, pushing an unwieldy supply cart.

As Dirk wallowed in a self-made mire of indecision he realized that, in addition to his leg cramps, something was wrong with his hearing. Other than the sound of his own ragged breathing, everything was muffled. The ongoing thrum of machinery, assorted human voices, and occasional inhuman grunts and bellows that made up the typical "white noise" in Tartarus were all but indecipherable

Tartarus.

As he stared apprehensively at Dr. Amara Braddock's thick metal door, Dirk contemplated the appropriateness of the facility's name. In Greek mythology, Tartarus was the abyssal dungeon wherein the wicked were tortured for all eternity. It was also where the monstrous Titans had been imprisoned after they were overthrown by the Gods of Olympus. Other cultures and religions had their own names for the place: Gehenna, Hades, Sheol, Perdition, or just plain old Hell.

Tartarus worked just fine.

Dirk's nostrils ached as he snorted a harsh breath. He stared at his size-10 shoes, cursing them for bringing him this far, only to come up with another pathetic excuse to turn away. He was going to take the coward's way out; he knew it the moment he got up this morning. He'd just been deluding himself.

Of course, he *did* have a mountain of projects to catch up on. He had to compare and cross reference all their genealogical records with the results from recent findings, organize the presentation for the incoming envoy, and then there was the new specimen to prep for . . .

Dreading the work that awaited him, Dirk ran a hand through his unkempt hair. The motion told him he was both sweaty and in need of a trim. His locks were glossy black, like his mom's. At five-foot-eleven, he was about the same height she was. He had her 160 IQ, too. Of course, he didn't have her amazing eyes. Those were reserved for his brother Garm, naturally. Garm had it all: the height, the looks, and the godlike physique. At a fit and trim 170 lbs, Dirk was nothing to sneeze at. He had a lean, athletic build, but he was hardly the wide-shouldered, towering Adonis his twin was. Women literally threw themselves at the guy. He'd lost count of how many.

Dirk's brows scrunched down over his eyes. Maybe that was why his mother always doted on him more than his brother. Was it pitying? Despite what people assumed, it was Amara, not Jake, who hung the "Dirk" moniker on him. "*It's the perfect nickname for someone whose daddy is a fencing champion. A 'dirk' is a small sword, sweetie.*" She'd smiled and kissed him on the forehead as she said that. All Dirk heard was "small."

As he raised his tablet to eye level, the unexpected appearance of Dr. Grayson's stern face gave him a start. His aging mentor had these dark, implacable eyes that radiated purpose and vitality, despite being surrounded by a forest of silver. Those same eyes softened the moment he spotted Dirk.

"Ah, there you are, son," Grayson said, smiling. His smile dipped and his brow lines deepened as he glanced down. "Hmm. I see from your tracker you're outside your mother's office again. Did you . . . ?"

Dirk force-fed himself a grin and resisted the urge to scratch at the itchy cybernetic implant embedded in his forearm. "Actually, I was just passing by on my way to see you. I thought we'd confer on today's findings."

"Ah . . ."

Dirk tried not to tense as Grayson studied him. Even remotely, the old man was uncannily good at reading people.

"Good thinking. Come to my office."

Dirk closed out the call and got his sorry butt in gear. As he walked, he realized with more than a little guilt that, the farther he got from his mom's office, the better he felt.

<hr />

As he neared Dr. Grayson's expansive office/quarters, Dirk hesitated. There were two members of Tartarus's private security force stationed outside, instead of the usual one. Dressed from head to toe in black military fatigues, with crew cuts and boots more befitting a state trooper, all the facility's guards came across as big, hulking thugs – the kind you'd avoid on dark, deserted streets.

"Thug" was an apropos description. Dirk had surreptitiously checked their records. Every one of them was some sort of career criminal who was facing life in prison or worse. Grayson called them his "last-chancers". He prided himself on taking men whose lives – admittedly, through their own wrongdoing – were destroyed and giving them a fresh start. Working at Tartarus, they received a clean slate; they got to support the men and women who helped safeguard America's waterways, and were paid a decent salary for doing so.

Although he wasn't as adept as Dr. Grayson, Dirk considered himself a pretty good judge of character. He'd interacted with quite a few of their last-chancers over the years and they were hardly the type to turn over a new leaf. To a man, they were crude, sneaky, and violence-prone. He also knew what their salaries were, and they certainly weren't doing it for the money. No, it was fear of the needle, pure and simple. When given the opportunity to have their sentences commuted in exchange for committing to one of the most dangerous jobs on the planet, they readily agreed.

Dirk suppressed a grin. They must have figured it was the lesser of two evils. Until they arrived at Rock Key, that is, and realized the scope of the evil they'd be guarding. It was no wonder so many of them went AWOL.

"Good morning, Dr. Braddock," the nearest guard monotoned as he approached. Dirk politely flashed the man his ID.

He recognized him. It was Sgt. Bryan Wurmer, the cruel-faced ex-marine with the salt-and-pepper mustache. He'd replaced Sgt. Wharton after he'd put in his time. Dirk did a quick mental check. Wurmer once ran a Cuban refugee camp outside of Miami. He'd been convicted of running an underground sex-trade using the teenage boys and girls under his care, some as young as twelve. Intimidating and violent, he treated his "hoes" like most pimps did.

When he wasn't beating them, he was sexually abusing them.

As the other guard held the door, Dirk was grateful shaking hands wasn't a requirement. Corporal Kevin Griffith was a former farm hand from Oklahoma. At first glance, he came across as an innocent country boy: freckle-faced, rawboned, and sporting a gap-toothed smile. He was also a big animal lover – literally. He'd gutted his previous employer with a pitchfork after getting caught in the barn, engaging in coitus with several of the farmer's prize heifers.

Dirk grimaced; they had plenty of livestock pens in Tartarus. He shuddered, wondering what process Grayson used to screen his candidates.

As he entered his mentor's office, Dirk spotted him leaning over the big saltwater aquarium he kept behind and to one side of his desk. The antique desk, itself, was elevated a few feet above floor level, situated atop a set of carpeted risers, and flanked by an ornate pair of 15th century braziers that must have been seven feet tall. It gave Grayson a nice overview of his well decorated office. The décor was impressive. An eclectic mixture of expensive antiques and state of the art technology, it was as if history was at war with itself, the past versus the present.

One thing Dirk always found interesting was that, despite the fact Eric Grayson was the founder and CEO of a company that made all sorts of pricey military weapons, the eccentric billionaire had none of them on display. Unlike Dirk's dad, who, despite occasional disagreements with his mother, had an entire room in their house devoted to his extensive sword collection.

Dirk noisily cleared his throat. "I'm here."

"Ah, come up, Derek," Grayson responded, still hovering over the ten-foot tank. "Do mind Raphael," he cautioned, as Dirk started up the risers.

Dirk glanced down, narrowly avoiding stumbling over the snoring Neapolitan mastiff behind Grayson's desk. The old man had a pair of the big, foul-tempered canines. Raphael's partner in crime, "Uriel," lay a few feet away. As Dirk moved toward his owner, Uriel hoisted his broad head, his beady eyes sleepily studying him. After having assured himself that the young scientist posed no threat, the brindle-coated mastiff lowered his jowls back onto the carpet and resumed battling his littermate in the world's loudest snoring contest.

"What's with the extra security?" Dirk asked. His nose crinkled up as the heady odor of unwashed dog invaded his nasal passages, and he resisted the temptation to ask how long it had been since the smelly Neapolitans were bathed.

"Oh, just putting on a show," Grayson replied distractedly as he fished noisily around inside a pull-out drawer from the aquarium's ornate wooden stand. "We've got Admiral Callahan and his cronies flying in for the demo, remember?"

"Ah . . . Sorry, I forgot." Dirk said, watching with interest as Grayson emerged holding some sort of multi-colored cube. Despite his seventy years and severe arthritis, his mentor's energy levels rarely waned – especially if there was an experiment afoot. "So . . . how's Einstein?"

Einstein was the old man's pet *Octopus vulgaris*, a common octopus. Except there was nothing "common" about Einstein. Grayson purchased him a few months back from a *Sea Crusade* research vessel, after the yard-long cephalopod exhibited the uncanny ability of climbing the conservationist ship's anchor chain under cover of darkness, prying open their aerated holding tanks, and slipping inside to gorge on their specimens. "*Any octopus that smart doesn't deserve to be served up as sushi,*" he'd announced.

"He's absolutely amazing," Grayson stated. "Although I must say, keeping him mentally stimulated has become something of a challenge."

"He gets bored?"

"'Against boredom, even the gods struggle in vain.'"

"*The Antichrist?*"

"Very good, Derek. Nietzsche would be impressed."

"'One repays a teacher badly if one remains only a student.'"

"And now the pupil seeks to test the professor," Grayson sighed as he peered through the glass at his prize. He glanced up at his protégé and grinned. "*Thus Spoke Zarathustra.*"

The twelve-pound cephalopod sat in a contented pile of suckers, rhythmically sucking in and expelling water through his mantle. Obviously familiar with his owner, Einstein's swirling eyes followed Grayson through the glass, his skin subtly changing hues as he tracked his master's every move. "I believe the theories are correct. Given their intelligence and documented tool use, if they had longer lifespans, the octopus might well have emerged as Earth's dominant life form instead of us."

"And to think we dip them in soy sauce," Dirk chuckled. "What's that?" he asked, indicating the colorful box Grayson held.

"A plaything for Einstein; it's my octopus version of a Rubik's cube," he announced, holding it up proudly. "You'll notice there are only four squares per side." He lowered his voice to a whisper. "I had to dumb it down a bit. After all, it *is* just an octopus."

"He's able to solve that?" Dirk didn't bother hiding his disbelief. As Grayson jumbled the cube's sides, Einstein's eyes lit up. His color changed to a ruddy pinkish hue and his breathing became more rapid.

"Oh, yes," Grayson chuckled. His own orbs gleamed like blue sapphires. "He's a real learner, this one. The first time it took him all night. The second time, around four hours, then one. Now . . . Oh, wait! Hold this."

Dirk caught the tossed cube with his free hand, watching in bemusement as Grayson momentarily disappeared behind the big aquarium. He returned a moment later, carrying a one-gallon jar filled with seawater. In it was—

"A nice, fat, she-crab, bursting with roe," he said, setting the jar and its lively occupant in front of Einstein. Through the double layers of glass, the blue crab was oblivious to the presence of its natural predator. But the effect on the octopus was immediate. As Einstein ogled the well-armed crustacean, his body began to pulse, his chromatophores flashing like a neon sign run amuck. "Pregnant crabs are like cupcakes with caviar frosting to an octopus."

"We've got to get him motivated." He winked at Dirk.

Dirk studied the cube. The scientist in him still believed it was some parlor trick and that the cephalopod had merely learned a set of pre-arranged moves. Impressive, to be sure, but not outside the realm of possibility.

"You're wearing your Doubting Thomas face," Grayson chided. "Why don't you mix it up and give it to him?"

"Really?"

"Would I deceive you?"

Dirk didn't hesitate. As a child, he could solve a Rubik's cube in record time. Even Garm had been impressed; his hands might have been huge, but he could never summon the mental discipline to master it. Dirk's fingers were a blur as he cranked this simplified version to the most difficult starting point he could think of. He approached the tank and, as Grayson unlatched and raised its lid, he dropped it in.

The weighty cube didn't have a chance to sink. One of Einstein's tentacles struck like a rattlesnake the moment it hit the water, and a half-second later he was all over it. Flushing a deep scarlet, he settled to the bottom, possessively cradling the puzzle. Like a child relishing a new toy, Einstein turned the cube this way and that. Then, with surprising dexterity, his clinging tentacles began to maneuver it. Several braced it tightly against his body and the bottom, while others encircled it, exerting steady, opposing pressure.

Click.

The first move surprised Dirk. Not only because it was hard to believe a mollusk could manipulate the cube in the first place, but because it was the same move he would have chosen. As he watched, fascinated, the octopus continued making moves, occasionally stopping to consider, then backtracking and redoing. All the while, its colors shifted to match its growing excitement.

Dirk glanced at Grayson, who stood nearby, beaming like a proud father. He checked the wall clock. Only five minutes had passed and Einstein had already made significant progress. Fifteen minutes later, the last square clicked into place.

"That . . . that was *amazing*!" Dirk sputtered. "I never--"

"Wait, wait . . . this is the best part," Grayson said. "Come here."

As Dirk stood next to him, his mentor once again raised the tank's lid. He gestured for Dirk.

"What?"

"Put your hand here," Grayson said, pointing at a spot just above the water.

"Are you serious?"

"You don't trust me?"

His mind still reeling, Dirk held his hand a few inches from the water's surface. Still sitting on the bottom, puffed up with seawater, Einstein extended two of his tentacles. Up they stretched, until they pierced the surface.

Dirk nearly choked as the octopus handed him back the cube. "I . . . I don't know what to--"

"I don't know what you should *say*, but I do know what you need to *do*," Grayson emphasized, indicating the gallon jar.

"Oh, of course!" Dirk hoisted the heavy container and unscrewed its lid. Directly below, Einstein trembled in anticipation. "Should I . . ."

"Just dump it in."

The blue crab never knew what hit it. The moment it broke the surface it was enveloped. One paralytic bite and it was over. Like the tiny sea lord he was, Einstein sat atop his kill, contentedly munching away as particles of crab meat and pieces of shell spewed out from under him and drifted across the tank's floor.

Grayson wiped his hands on a towel, then tossed it to Dirk. "Good stuff, wouldn't you say?" Before Dirk could respond, he added, "By the way, I think he likes you."

Dirk nodded. "He really is something. I'm impressed, not only by the cognitive ability, but also the dexterity."

His mentor gestured at a pair of chairs situated in front of his desk. "You have to keep in mind, he's got more than one brain focusing on the job." He moved behind his desk and eased himself down into his plush office chair.

"I'm sorry, Dr. Grayson. Cephalopods have never been my strong suit," Dirk said as he seated himself. "Now, if you want to talk Sauropterygians or cybernetics, I'm your guy."

Grayson nodded. "They're not my specialty, either, but I've done my research." He patted a large volume sitting atop the assorted documents and journals piled across his desk. "It turns out, in addition to it having a brain proportionately as large as that of many mammals, an octopus's tentacles have minds of their own. Only one third of its nervous system is in the brain. The other two thirds of its neurons are distributed in the nerve cords of the arms. It can give its tentacles an assignment and then forget it. That'd be like you telling your hands to write an email while you relaxed and watched a movie."

Dirk raised an eyebrow. "So, the tentacles are completely autotomous?"

"If severed, they act on their own, although not doing complex tasks," Grayson emphasized. He leaned wearily back, rubbing the back of his neck with one hand. "The octopus needs to see what a tentacle is doing to continue giving it orders. In Einstein's case, it helps with the cube; while his tentacles are implementing one move, his brain is considering the next."

"Intriguing," Dirk said. He eyed the thick book on his mentor's desk. "All of that is in there?"

"And more. Would you like to . . . ?"

"Absolutely." As he reached for the weighty tome, Dirk's eyes fell on an unfamiliar object, peeking out from under a stack of papers. "Is that an antique French inkwell?"

"Very perceptive," Grayson said with pride. He cleared the area around his latest acquisition. "Hand-wrought bronze, late 19th century. The workmanship is superb. I keep it next to the supercomputer. It reminds me how far we've come."

"She's a beauty." Dirk took in the impressive mound of papers. "You might want to consider getting someone in here to help organize," he said matter-of-factly. "So people could better appreciate it . . ."

Grayson laughed. "Derek, you're as bad as my housekeeper, albeit a bit more tactful." He removed his glasses and looked up as if reading an invisible screen. "How does that go? Oh yes: 'If a cluttered desk is a sign of a cluttered mind, of what, then, is an empty desk a sign?'"

"That doesn't sound like one of your usual quotes."

"Einstein," his mentor instructed. He grinned as his protégé cast dubious eyes toward the octopus tank. "The *real* one."

Dirk smiled. "Good one." He hoisted his tablet. "Current events?"

Grayson nodded. "Let me get these old knees working and I'll come see what you've got." He gripped his armrests, grimacing as he struggled to get up.

"Wait, hang on." Dirk sprang to his feet. Sidestepping Uriel, he put an arm around the old man and helped him.

"Thank you, son," Grayson said with a smile. "I was told they're bringing one in?"

"Yes, sir," Dirk said. His fingers tap danced across his tablet as he brought a series of images up. "It's that big cow that sank the trawler. She's gravid and, as you can see from her stats, she's a Gen-1 for sure. Once we've run a prenatal, we'll know if it's our boy."

"I'm surprised your brother spared her," Grayson remarked. "Don't get me wrong, Garm's got some amazing gifts. But he's not exactly a 'bring 'em back alive' kind of guy."

"Actually, he passed on the capture. Dragunova's bringing her in."

"Ah." Grayson rubbed his eyes before he resumed scrutinizing Dirk's images. "Very good. We can definitely use the specimen. Callahan needs two replacements. But what makes you think 'our boy' is the daddy?"

Dirk gnawed his lower lip. "There's, uh . . . more to the story."

Grayson sighed. "Derek J. Braddock, you are twenty-nine years old and I've known you for the last ten. I think it's high time you stopped your, 'How do I tell him I wrecked the car' routine?' and just spat it out. Now, what happened?"

"One of our 'cars' took a hit."

"Which one?"

"*Antrodemus*. But it wasn't the cow's doing. After she'd been subdued, her mate attacked the subs and, despite taking fire from *Gryphon*, did some damage."

Grayson rubbed his temples. "How bad?"

Dirk brought up an image of the *Antrodemus* and zoomed in on the damage to her sail.

"Their photonics mast was destroyed and the outer hull fractured across a four-square-yard area. On a positive note, the sail's new pressure hull wasn't compromised."

"Time to repair?"

Dirk mentally crunched some numbers. "The outer casing, we can have patched in twenty-four hours. But the photonics assembly is completely gone. If we're going with a replacement, we're looking at three days. If it's a rebuild, more like five."

Grayson nodded. "It could've been worse."

"There may be a silver lining, sir."

On his tablet, Dirk pulled up a scaled-down version of *Gryphon*'s 3D fathometer screen, complete with glowing miniatures of the two subs and the rogue pliosaur. He fast-forwarded to the highlights of the battle. "The bull that attacked the subs was not only huge, according to Captain Braddock's report, it was experienced. It used the terrain to mask its sonar signature and ran silent. The only time it employed its acoustics was when it was under fire – at which point it managed to avoid a pair of Naegling M9's traveling at over 300 mph. Both sub commanders stated in their reports they are convinced this is the same animal that destroyed the *Titan*, two years ago."

Grayson's eyes intensified as he finished reviewing the engagement. "I concur; it's had experience with both submarines and torpedoes. But how big is it? Do we have images?"

"Yes, sir." Dirk closed the fathometer reenactment and brought up individual sonar stills. The glowing, reddish-orange images of the giant reptile were devoid of detail. He tapped a few keys. "Implementing enhanced translation of acoustic images."

With a final tap, the pixilated pliosaur was replaced with a computer-generated approximation of the real thing. The creature was massive and gnarled, its giant head coated with scars from untold battles.

"Ugly bastard," Dirk muttered.

"He's *beautiful*," Grayson breathed. "Size estimate?"

"Ninety feet minimum," Dirk replied. "Could be a hundred. It's hard to say, they were under fire. Of course, it could turn out to be another mutant female, which would compound our problem."

Grayson flipped from image to image. He stopped on one where the creature was broadside to the camera and zoomed in. "Not a chance. You see how wrinkled his skin is? I don't know what caused all that scarring, but it matches the reports. And there's no mistaking that hump."

Dirk nodded. Although he had some concerns as to what this discovery meant for the project, he was as excited as his mentor at the prospect of success after so many years.

"That has *got* to be him," Grayson asserted. "There can't be two males that size running around."

Dirk nodded. "After we finish testing the new female, we'll know for sure."

Grayson rubbed his hands together gleefully. "Indeed, we will, my boy. It's basically a formality, but before we start allocating resources, we want to be sure."

"Yes, sir . . ." Dirk replied.

"Don't be so down-in-the-mouth," Grayson said, clapping him on the shoulder. "You should be excited. Your brother just found *Typhon!*"

Hanging ten miles back, the Ancient one cruised silently. His boat-sized fins flared out to the sides like sails, slowing his forward momentum until he hovered ten feet above the coral-strewn seabed. With gentle, undulating strokes, he held position, listening to the distinctive sounds of the two submarines as they withdrew, taking his mate with them.

The bull pliosaur's sunken eyes narrowed and he uttered a deep rumble of rage that vibrated across the ocean floor at a frequency so low it shook the nearby rock. For a mile in every direction, reef occupants either withdrew into their burrows or took shelter in nearby crevasses. Larger fish, cephalopods, and marine mammals that had no place to hide simply fled.

At a full ninety-four feet in length and weighing 216 tons, the Ancient was the biggest, most dominant predator to prowl the seas. His massive, twenty-foot mandibles were lined with thick-ridged teeth measuring over two feet from root to tip, and powered by the most powerful jaw muscles of all time. His thick hide was covered with rock-hard scales, and further reinforced by layer upon layer of fibrous scar tissue – frayed medals of valor from thousands of battles. Despite the bull's size, he moved stealthily through the deep, propelled soundlessly along by four barnacle-tipped flippers. He was nature's perfect killer and had ruled the oceans, alone and unchallenged, for centuries.

Moving with eerie silence, the Ancient began to rise in the water column, the powerful downstroke of his pectoral fins casting up clouds of silt as he cleared an underwater ridge. Experience had taught him caution and he emitted no sonar as he traveled. Even if he was willing to chance giving away his position, the cow was already beyond the range of his formidable sound sight. He could still hear her intermittent groans, as well as the sounds given off by the noisy thing she was tied to. The female was still alive, although the great bull couldn't understand why. The tiny bipeds usually killed his kind on sight. She was most likely destined to be torn apart on the surface, her remains cast into the sea as they did to the big warm-bloods he and his ilk fed upon.

Eventually, the cow's sounds stopped altogether, followed by the noises generated by her captors. The male could still smell her pheromones, however, mixed in with the scent of leaked oil. The scoop-shaped passages in the roof of his mouth were connected to the most highly-developed underwater olfactory system evolution ever designed. Her blood had not yet been spilled, although it undoubtedly soon would be.

Frustration began to take over, compounding the Ancient's already intense animosity toward both the bipeds and the giant metallic life forms they infested. Except for a handful of times he had been challenged, for untold seasons he had managed to maintain his seclusion. Now, however, the tiny mammals actively hunted not only him, but his entire species.

He had sensed the deaths of thousands; victims of either their warm-blooded foes or the fiery death that rained down from above. The fact the old bull had failed to protect his current mate enraged him even more, and he gnashed his sharp-ridged teeth in ill-contained fury.

Fifty yards off his port side, the Ancient espied the fourteen-foot shortfin Mako that continued to shadow him. Like iron filings to a magnet, the big shark was drawn to the scarlet billows that continued to seep from the ragged seven-foot gash across his dorsal ridge.

He paid the fish no mind. The graze-wound from the submarine was a minor annoyance. The bleeding had already slowed and would soon stop. Once that happened, the shark would move off. And if not, he would encourage it. The bull's lips curled slowly back in what could have been a grin. He considered making a run at the Mako, but then dismissed the notion. He was hungry, but the resultant noise might alert his pursuers to his presence. In addition, the fish was fast and maneuverable and would be very hard to catch.

The wrinkled skin around the Ancient's eyes contracted. He could sense the water underneath his mottled belly growing shallower. The bipeds were bringing the female to shore. His jaw muscles tightened and he shook his monstrous head. To follow them there, away from the protective shelter of the deep, would be a death sentence.

After a moment's deliberation, the futility of continuing the pursuit became apparent. The old male had no choice but to accept the situation. He emitted a low rumble of frustration that sent the Mako scampering away and then veered east.

Accelerating to his normal cruising speed, the Ancient pondered the loss of the gravid cow. The clutch she carried was her last of the season. He had accompanied her from island to island as she laid the previous five – nearly four hundred eggs in all. On one trip, he guided her all the way to the remote island of their ancestors. There, warded by jagged black reefs and a protective fog, their progeny would hatch in moderate safety, before digging their way free from their sandy womb.

As his scarred flippers sped him along, the bull's muzzle contorted into an annoyed grimace. His scarred snout was peppered with rows of fresh tooth punctures that itched like mad. They were the pliosaur's version of love bites, and he had received many during his courtship of the female. Like the god many Pacific islanders worshipped him as, he had scattered her other would-be suitors, interrupting their mating chase with the intention of claiming her as his own. But the big female was intimidated by his size and responded with aggression, snapping at him repeatedly.

Eventually, the cow got over her initial fright and permitted their coupling to take place. Afterward, however, she resumed lashing out at him. It was her right and he did not begrudge her. Her mating hormones had elevated her innate nastiness to demonic levels and he absorbed many bites from her powerful jaws when he drew near, even when presenting her with the gift of food. Whenever possible, he presented his shoulder hump to her, allowing the great mound to bear the brunt of the damage.

As his hump ached from where the female's sixteen-inch teeth had repeatedly buried themselves, the great reptile's mind wandered. He recalled the incident, ages past, when a floating infestation of bipeds had given him that gnarled mass of tissue and nearly ended his life . . .

It was a cool fall day, a hundred miles off the coast of Iceland, and the Ancient was resting on the surface after devouring a pair of hapless Minke whales. With his belly pleasantly distended and secure in the knowledge no living creature could challenge him, the old bull allowed his sense of invincibility to get the better of him. He closed his eyes and slipped into a deep slumber.

It was a slumber that nearly became permanent.

A whale killer's lookout spotted the sleeping behemoth's broad back, awash on the surface, and figured they'd stumbled upon a big blue whale. They puttered in as quietly as possible and then killed their engines, allowing wind and tide to carry them close enough to fire.

The pain as the whaler's grenade-tipped harpoon slammed into his shoulder and detonated was the worst agony the pliosaur had ever known. Only his exceptionally tough tissue and huge shoulder bones prevented the rocket-propelled harpoon from penetrating deep into his chest cavity before it exploded. As it was, it was all the stricken beast could do to wrench himself free from the harpoon's lethal tether and submerge. For fifty yards in every direction, the water around him turned a brilliant shade of scarlet.

Onboard the whaler, its crew cheered.

As the Ancient struggled to right himself, he twisted his head around and took stock of his injury. The wound was horrific; a fleshy crater nearly ten feet across where great gobs of skin and muscle had been sheared away. A huge slab of meaty shoulder bone protruded from the wound site, along with several badly broken ribs. The subsequent blood loss nearly felled the giant predator and he fought not only to retain consciousness, but to drive away the hordes of scavenging sharks that arrived within minutes to plague him.

After thirty minutes passed and no carcass bobbed to the surface, the disappointed whaler's crew assumed that their "Hvalur" somehow escaped and moved on. The old bull was far from finished, however. He clung to life with a tenacity only reptiles were capable of. Despite the near-fatal blow, he locked onto his attackers by scent and sonar and began trailing them. Where they went he followed, hanging back to avoid detection, but always keeping the boat within range of his sound sight.

For the first few days the wounded *Kronosaurus* did nothing except stay alive and fend off the omnipresent sharks. Ironically, the predators that sought to feast upon him became the key to his survival. Too hurt to hunt, he played possum, feigning immobility until a blue shark or great white came close enough to take a bite. And then bite he did.

In a few days, the Ancient's ragged wound had closed over. Within a week, his strength began to return. Still, he kept his distance, following the five-hundred-ton whaler, keeping just out of sight. Twice, the whalers unwittingly provided valuable nourishment for him. Peering over the side, they waited in vain for a stricken Minke whale to rise to the surface, not realizing their blubbery prize was being devoured fifty fathoms down.

Two weeks after he was attacked, just as the whaler's crew was turning in for the night, the old bull retaliated. Wary of the metal vessel's harpoon cannon and props, he struck from below. Over and over he rammed his gargantuan adversary, repeatedly breaching its thin metal hull until the mortally wounded vessel floundered and sank.

Of the whale killer's fourteen-man crew, the first six died in the water. As their comrades struggled into the ship's only lifeboat, their cries of alarm became gurgling screams of terror as, one by one, they were dragged under and devoured. The remaining survivors huddled together, soaked and shivering, scanning the water with hand-held lights and praying their distress call had been heard. A pair of rescue ships arrived within the hour, shining their bright beams upon the water. The lifeboat was gone, as if somehow spirited away.

It had been. The moment the survivors' would-be rescuers appeared on the horizon, the Ancient clamped down on the lifeboat's dangling bow rope and made off with it. The boat's astonished occupants, shrieking en masse as they were hauled away, ended up traveling twenty miles in thirty minutes. When they were finally released, the drenched and bewildered whalers faced the coming dawn with no radio, little food or water, and a vengeful demon stalking them.

Over the next few days, the beast tortured the surviving crew members. He alternated between surfacing nearby and flashing his giant jaws, or spouting beside the boat and spraying them with icy seawater. Several times, he rushed past, nearly swamping the tiny boat and exposing the great mound of fresh scar tissue that adorned him like a hunchback's hump – a hump they had given him.

On and off throughout the day the terrifying ordeal continued. And each night, the Ancient reared up over the side of the boat and took one or two of them.

By the fifth day, only two remained. Knowing their tormentor's habit of coming for them shortly after nightfall, the terrified men took to huddling between the hull ribs in the bottom of the boat, hoping to escape notice.

The creature would not be fooled. Snorting loudly, he bullied the lifeboat, pushing and shoving the twenty-four-foot vessel this way and that, threatening to overturn it. He kept it up until the two men, realizing that there was no escape and at least one of them was going to die, turned on one another. After a desperate struggle, the larger of the two – coincidentally the captain – emerged victorious. Tossing his beaten cook over the side, he screamed for the "djöfullinn" to come and claim its prize.

It did. Rearing silently up behind him, the Ancient pinned the stunned captain in his streaming jaws and, with surprising gentleness, held him aloft like a prize from some county fair. Then, he began to bite. Like a pair of giant vises, his monstrous jaws started to close, his huge fangs sinking oh-so-slowly into the captain's body, piercing him like a battery of swords, while he shrieked and flailed and vomited blood. The terrified cook watched through maddened eyes, struggling to stay afloat in a cloud of his own feces.

After swallowing the dying captain in a single gulp, the creature departed. The cook was left unharmed, at least, physically. Shaking uncontrollably, the shell that had once been a man managed to climb back aboard. For the next thirty-six hours he remained in the bottom of the boat in a fetal position, until a passing trawler found him. Filthy and dehydrated, his incoherent babblings about the "Midgard serpent" were disregarded as the ramblings of a lunatic.

With an angry snort that dismissed both his memory of the whaler and the throbbing ache in his hump, the Ancient considered the possibility he might soon be the last of his kind. It would not be the first time. For eons, he had swum through oceans of time, alone and with nothing to do but feed and hide from the bipeds that prowled the surface. Then one day, to his astonishment, he detected one of his own. It was a potential mate, escaped from the fiery prison that had kept their kind in check since the fall of the dinosaurs.

By the time he tracked her down, however, it was too late. Clouds of blood and fragments of tissue in the water told a sorry tale. Even so, he followed her trail to the bottom of the abyss until he finally found her. Her head was gone, her once mighty remains rent and swarming with scavenging hagfish and sleeper sharks. From the metallic smells emanating from her corpse, it was obvious she'd fallen victim to the warm-bloods and their noisy metal hosts.

To the Ancient's surprise, however, it was not the end. The cow had laid at least one clutch of eggs before her untimely death, and those eggs soon hatched. Within a few seasons, the oceans of the world once more resounded with the calls of young pliosaurs, hungry and growing fast. The old bull reveled in the knowledge their species would not die with him. He kept his distance from the tiny ones, however, keeping any innate competitive or cannibalistic instincts in check as he waited for them to grow. The endless parade of seasons continued and the hatchlings began to develop into adults. Soon, they began to breed and their numbers grew.

Finally, after a seeming eternity, the surviving cows from that initial clutch matured into the apex predators Nature had designed them to be. Stretching seventy-five feet or more in length and weighing over one hundred tons, they were at long last physically, and more importantly, sexually, compatible.

The Ancient managed to mate with several of the big females, and protected them to insure the passing of his genes. As was always the case, however, after the final clutch was laid. no bond remained between the pair. The young cows invariably went off on their own. Innately cunning though they were, they lacked the old bull's experience when it came to stealth and concealment.

Most of the first-batch cows were dead now. And the slaughter continued.

Trembling with pent-up rage, the bull pliosaur sought something to appease not only his growing need for flesh, but his temper. His phenomenal sense of smell soon rewarded him with a fresh blue whale carcass. Most likely felled by a collision on the surface, he could smell the great cetacean's blood permeating the water. It was a scent and flavor he knew well. Chancing a quick burst of sonar, he pinpointed its remains. It was three miles away and drifting with the tide. A mixed bag of sharks, squid, and caldera fish swarmed around it, but had not yet begun to feed.

The reason for their hesitation became apparent. A trio of bull pliosaurs had lined up at the trough and were sharing the enormous meal. They were all mature males, ranging from fifty to sixty feet in length. Normally hostile toward one another, the vast bounty before them had caused any inter-species aggressiveness to be put on hold, letting them feed without risk of injury.

The Ancient's scarred lips snarled slowly back, revealing his well-used arsenal of interlocking ivory fangs. As soundless as the death that would one day claim him, he rose in the water column and accelerated to full speed, heading straight for the whale carcass.

And the young challengers that laid claim to it.

FIVE

Well, so far so good...

Except for some occasional knuckle-cracking, Captain Garm Braddock felt he was doing a pretty good job of maintaining a cool exterior. Not an easy thing, he acknowledged, when you were part of a team responsible for smuggling one of the ocean's most lethal predators into a top-secret facility, while simultaneously trying to make sure you didn't get blindsided by an even deadlier one.

"Sonar, where's my update?"

"Sorry, captain," Ramirez replied. "I just had a quick hit and was triangulating. The sonar signature matches the one that rammed *Antrodemus*."

Garm's head snapped back on his shoulders. "Inbound?"

No, sir," Ramirez rubbed one eye as he checked his screens. "Bearing is two, four, five ... about twelve miles back. Signal is withdrawing." He blinked hard to clear his vision. "Status update: all sonar systems – active, passive, and search-and-destroy – are online and fully operational. ANCILE is engaged at highest sensitivity. In acoustic terms, if someone drops a greenback on the deck of a cabin cruiser five miles away, I can tell you the denomination. There will be no surprises, sir."

Garm grinned. "Good. Helm, what's our status?"

"We're a mile from the fence, captain," Ho replied. "Current speed is twenty knots and we're cruising at seventy-five feet. It's getting shallow, sir, and the bottom's pretty rocky. Recommend we adjust course to intersect Jörmungandr."

"Concur. Give me right standard rudder, reduce speed to fifteen, and make your depth sixty," Garm said. "Communications, extend photonics mast and update *Antrodemus*."

"On it, sir," Ensign Rush replied. She rolled her shoulders back and then shifted in her seat as she tapped away.

Garm frowned. His primary bridge crew was as tired as he was. He couldn't blame them. They'd all been going at it fourteen hours straight. By the book, they should have been relieved two hours ago, himself included, but his team had requested permission to remain at their posts. He wasn't sure if it was because they wanted to spearhead *Gryphon's* triumphant return or if they knew the pickle they were in and wanted to make sure the job was done right.

It didn't matter. As good as his second-stringers were, Garm would take his exhausted primaries over *Gryphon's* well-rested backup squad any day. Personality quirks or no, they meshed better, and he knew he could count on each and every one of them in a pinch.

"Fire control, how's it looking?" Garm asked.

Cunningham swiveled in his seat. "As requested, LADON gun system is trained on our six, with SODOME actively scanning for threats. Tubes one and four remain flooded, per SOP, and outer doors are open. I've adjusted our remaining two fish for infrared/ultraviolet homing only. Anything that tries sneaking up on us is going to be in for a rude awakening, sir." He gave a lopsided grin, more befitting a man who just came from a less-than-respectable Oriental massage parlor than one who'd been in combat for fourteen hours straight.

"Excellent," Garm replied. He envied Kyle's energy. And, he was pleased he appeared to have rebounded nicely from his earlier mistakes. "Rush, send a message to Yeoman Perkins in the galley to bring up coffee and pastries for the bridge crew – make it the good stuff. You guys deserve it."

"Thank you, sir," Rush smiled amidst a backdrop of enthused whistles.

Garm held up a hand. "One second. Dr. Bane, how do you take your caffeine?"

"These days, in an IV," Bane said with a smile. "But milk and sugar will be fine. And, thank you."

"You're welcome."

"So, Captain . . . not that I haven't enjoyed the assorted near-death experiences, but how far out are we?" Bane asked. Still pale from intermittent dry heaves, she got up unsteadily from her seat and moved beside his chair, taking in the swirling waters ahead as a school of brightly-colored Dorado exploded past their transparent prow.

"About twenty minutes," Garm said.

"And are we--"

"Captain, we're approaching Jörmungandr," Ho announced. "The fence is 1,000 yards and closing." She glanced at Bane, "Sorry, ma'am."

The lieutenant nodded, but before she could continue, Garm cut in.

"Eyes front, doc," he said. "You'll find this interesting."

As something big loomed in the distance, Bane squinted hard. She put on her glasses. "What *is* that?"

Directly ahead, the craggy opening of a 100-foot wide trench, cut directly into the seabed, gaped at them like a gigantic wormhole. It appeared endless, a ragged wound in the ocean's bottom that carved through the surrounding reefs like a highway, relentlessly winding its way along. From their vantage point, the dark, seaweed-coated channel looked like an immense sea serpent, resting its coils on the ocean floor.

"That's Jörmungandr, AKA the World Serpent, and our ticket home," Garm announced. "We'll fit with no problem, even toting that oversized lizard."

"Good Lord. You made this?"

Garm grinned. "The Naval Corps of Engineers gouged it out using mining rigs and underwater dredgers. It's seven miles long – winds past Islamorada, all the way to Rock Key. Took them two years to do it."

"Couldn't you have gotten in without it?"

"Not without being seen by every yokel with a camera phone," Garm remarked. "CDF or no, what we do is still clandestine. It's pretty shallow in these parts. And with *Gryphon* drafting twenty feet up top and more than twice that submerged, well . . . let's just say you don't build a multi-billion-dollar submarine and then drag her belly on the rocks."

Bane gestured at the roughly excavated seafloor. "They damaged a lot of coral. I'm surprised you weren't vilified."

Garm shrugged. "We might have been, if anyone knew what was actually happening. But between cleaning up oil spills and building the fence, there were plenty of excuses to cordon off the area," he explained.

"Besides, we've provided enough man-made reefs throughout the region to more than make up for the damage."

"And that justifies it?"

He gave her a dry look. "I think that if people knew what really goes on in Rock Key, they'd be more concerned about that than the tunnel our subs use to get in and out."

"And what, exactly, are these mysterious "goings on" you're referring to?" Garm arched an eyebrow. "Don't you work there?"

"I've only been assigned to deal with a bacteriological issue, captain," she replied. "You *do* know about the infections, yes?"

"Of course," Garm said. You had to have your head under a rock these days to not know undercooked pliosaur meat contained lethal pathogens, or that consumption of it led to cerebral hemorrhaging and death. Many nations with established fishing industries had issued reports of widespread infections. He lowered his voice. "They're abroad, right?"

"So far."

"And you're helping Grayson's pharmaceutical division expedite a cure?"

"Hopefully."

Ensign Ho cleared her throat. "Captain, approaching the fence. Shall I enter access code?"

"Proceed."

Through the bow window, a series of metallic gray towers emerged from the murk like misty phantoms, reaching for the surface. Forty feet or more in height, and running like interconnected telephone poles to either side, they stretched as far as the eye could see. As the *Gryphon* drew closer, the rope-like netting that ran between each anchorage point became visible – a crisscrossing silvery web with mesh large enough to accommodate a grown man walking upright.

"Is that the pliosaur net?" Bane asked.

Garm nodded. "Rust-proof, titanium-polymer alloy. Almost indestructible. There's a couple hundred miles of it, running in and around the Keys. Makes the tourists feel safer and helps keep the local fishing and boating industries afloat."

"How much did that cost?"

"Don't ask."

"Is it effective?"

Garm smacked his lips. "Only against the adults. The big ones shy away for fear of being ensnared. But to prevent our surviving resident manatees, dolphins, and sea turtles from getting entangled, they had to make the mesh holes fairly large. Juvenile pliosaurs – still plenty big enough to kill you – can squeeze through the openings."

"Or jump over it altogether," Cunningham interjected.

"We have access, sir," Ho advised.

At the point where the titanium barrier intersected Jörmungandr, its reinforced framework expanded to form a 100-foot wide gate, complete with a weighted mesh curtain that hung all the way to the seafloor. There was a low rumbling sound as the gate's counterweight system activated and the mesh slid smoothly up, like a gigantic garage door opening. Ho's timing was perfect, and the *Gryphon* traveled through the opening without having to adjust speed. Seconds later, they were past the gate and bulldozing their way through an enormous school of jellyfish before continuing.

"Nice job," Garm said. "Sonar, how's *Antrodemus*?"

"According to POSEIDON, she's two hundred yards back and holding steady," Ramirez replied. He indicated the fathometer screen. On it, a miniaturized version of their sister-sub, complete with a pixilated pliosaur lashed to its nose, trailed behind, moving slowly past the predator-resistant barrier.

"So far so good," Garm muttered. "Helm, distance to Rock Key?"

"Two-and-a-half miles, sir," Ho said.

"Maintain speed and depth." Ahead, the Jörmungandr trench curved between jagged reefs before resuming a straight-line course. He glanced at Ensign Rush. "Extend photonics and transfer forward surface activity to the main. Let's see what's going on up there."

"Yes, sir," Rush replied. She checked her screens. "There's a problem, sir."

"Explain."

"There's a small flotilla of fishing boats cruising around in the immediate vicinity, including one directly above us." Rush touched a key. "I can extend the mast in between them, but it's going to be an up and down affair."

"It's day one of the annual Bulldog Fish Rodeo, sir," Cunningham advised.

Garm nodded as pre-war memories of fishing with his dad popped into his head. Things around Florida were very different now. Their resident population of *Xiphactinus audax* – popularly known as the Bulldog fish – had exploded of late. Another byproduct of the collapse of Diablo Caldera, the fleet, silvery predators were among the largest bony fish known, topping twenty feet in length, and weighing up to four thousand pounds. Their size, speed, and ferocity when hooked made them immensely popular with big-game fishermen who, despite the risk, drooled at the prospect of slugging it out with a behemoth the size of an adult great white shark.

They were also staple prey items for the region's surviving pliosaurs.

For the last seven years running, the Florida Keys had hosted an annual Bulldog Fish roundup. It drew thousands of boats, all targeting the toothy predators as they stalked the region's migrating schools of tarpon. With half a million dollars in prize money going to the crew that landed the largest fish, competition between anglers was fierce. Unlike billfish tournaments, however, the roundup was a no-release competition, with the chrome-colored predators hung up and weighed on the docks, before being cut up with chain saws and sold to nearby restaurants. In the beginning, animal rights groups had tried boycotting the roundup. But with adult *Xiphactinus* being proven man-eaters responsible for hundreds of deaths each year, the activists' cries fell on deaf ears.

There's certainly no shortage of the greedy bastards, Garm snorted. He absentmindedly rubbed at his hip before moving to their transparent prow. A pod of a half-dozen Bulldog fish shot past, their fanged jaws agape as they harried a school of nearly one hundred tarpon. Above, he could make out the hull of a fifty-foot canyon runner, backing down on what looked to be a very large *Xiphactinus*.

Garm shook his head. Even behind the relative safety of the pliosaur net, manning a boat that size with a fiberglass hull, the charter boat's captain had to be either certifiable or packing some serious firepower. He was betting on the latter. You never knew when the tournament's action might attract the attention of something very large and unpleasant.

"As soon as we're past them, extend the mast," Garm ordered. "Sonar, how's it looking?"

"I've got twelve boats within a thousand yards, plus a helicopter scanning the area." Ramirez gnawed his lip. "It's too big to be a news chopper. Based on rotor noise and intermittent emissions, it's got to be military." He tapped a few keys and affirmed. "ID confirmed, sir. Designate: Bearcat."

Probably keeping the network choppers at bay, Garm thought. *As popular as the tournament is, the last thing they need is a major incident showing up on the evening news.* He nodded. "Good call. Their rotor noise should help keep the more cautious lizards at bay."

Rush cleared her throat. "We're past the fishing boat. Photonics and satellites coming online, sir."

Garm rested his arms on his chest and watched as their window to the sea was replaced by a modern submarine's view of the surface. Unlike bulky, old-fashioned periscopes, with their limited fields of view, *Gryphon's* photonics assembly, with its powerful optronics, provided a full 120 degrees of the surface and could swivel 360. On the viewer, an assortment of boats cruised in the distance. Several were anchored up, and a few were backing down as they slugged it out with their monstrous quarry. Above the melee, and maintaining an altitude of 1,000 feet, the heavily armed GDT Bearcat hovered like some enormous black raptor, hungry for a kill.

Garm held up an index finger, moving it in tiny circles. "Rotate view. Let's see what that boat's got on."

The screen's picture swiveled smoothly to port and pinpointed the sleek charter boat, now holding position 150 yards to their stern. As the viewer zoomed in, Garm could make out the name *Prodigal Sun*, emblazoned across its transom. Another jump-cut and the straining angler's bearded face came into view. He looked like a lumberjack seated in the boat's fighting chair, his thick arm muscles bulging as he heaved slowly back on his unlimited-class tuna rod, before leaning forward and cranking for all he was worth.

Ramirez sniggered as he clocked Ho staring wide-eyed. "Hey, Shortstack, I didn't know you were into the Grizzly Adams look!"

The annoyed helmswoman flipped him the bird without looking.

Behind the sweat-soaked fisherman, a mate gripped the back of their heavy-duty fighting chair, swiveling it to match the surging

Bulldog fish's movements. At the rear of the cockpit, another crew-member stood waiting, cradling in his arms the biggest flying gaff Garm had ever seen. The *Gryphon*'s captain smiled as he spotted what he'd been expecting – an additional crewman, situated in the crow's nest with the captain, and armed. He couldn't make out the model of the firearm he was gripping, but whatever it was, it was big.

"Rush, split screen," Garm said. "Show me what they've got."

The primary viewer switched to a pared-down version of the surface, combined with the sub's standard underwater view from below. Through her reflection in their bow window, Garm watched Dr. Bane move from her seat and head to the prow. She took up position at his side.

"Wow, that's some fish," she muttered. On the viewer, the embattled *Xiphactinus* passed directly above them, angrily shaking its head as it tried to break free of the tether that was steadily sapping its strength.

"What do you think, Ramirez? Twenty-one . . . twenty-two feet?" Garm asked over his shoulder.

"Twenty-*five*, sir," his grinning sonar tech replied, incorporating his best "Quint" accent. "Two tons of him!"

"Valuable fish . . . if they land it," Cunningham pointed out.

A school of tarpon rushed past, causing Dr. Bane to jump as one panicked and bounced loudly off the sub's transparent nose. Behind them, three hungry bulldog fish in the twenty-foot range flared their gills and gave way as an even larger hammerhead shark bullied past, its yard-wide jaws snapping in warning.

"Holy shit, it's *Bismarck*!" Cunningham chortled. "Check him out!"

As the five-thousand-pound Great Hammerhead pushed aside its ancient rivals and closed on the fleeing tarpon, Garm gave the old fish a nod of respect. Crisscrossed with scars, "Bismarck" had managed to survive not only decades of shark-finning and competition from hordes of X-fish, but the invading pliosaurs as well. He was a rarity. Possibly the last of a dying breed.

Ho's alarmed voice yanked Garm back from his musings.

"Captain, *Prodigal Sun*'s fish is approaching our sail," she advised. "Risk to the photonics assembly is--"

Garm cut her off. "Communications, retract mast. Switch to sub-surface viewing only. Show me *Antrodemus*."

"Aye, sir," Rush said. "Switching to aft viewers."

Gryphon's forward-facing underwater images dissolved and their sister sub's intimidating form took over. *Antrodemus* followed soundlessly in their wake, matching their speed and depth, with 100+ tons of sleeping monster lashed to her nose. With the comatose pliosaur's positioning giving the ORION class sub an undeniably hammer-like appearance, Garm couldn't help but notice the parallel to old Bismarck.

Last of a dying breed . . .

As *Antrodemus* passed directly under *Prodigal Sun*, Garm stifled a snicker. *If those poor bastards knew what was right beneath their feet . . .*

It was true; some things are better left unseen.

"Captain, I think I detected some movement from the package," Ramirez announced.

Garm wheeled on him. "Are you sure?"

"It was subtle. But I'm pretty sure."

Garm's eyes zeroed Cunningham. He was relieved to see his CSO had already locked LADON onto the *Antrodemus's* bow.

"Incoming call from Captain Dragunova," Rush said. "She's patched a relay through their Remora."

"On speaker. Ramirez, zoom in on the package," Garm said. He started toward sonar, then froze. A quick glance at their viewer confirmed things.

Although its eyes remained closed, the pliosaur was definitely moving. Its wedge-shaped head had twisted to one side and one of its foreflippers was straining against the silvery cable that held it in place.

"Ahoy, *Gryphon*," Captain Dragunova's voice, complete with her too-heavy-to-ignore Russian accent, blared out of their speakers.

"Ahoy, *Antrodemus*. How's the patient?" Garm did his best to sound casual.

"Dee patient ees fine," Dragunova said. "She is just having – how you say – bad dreams?"

Garm glanced at Cunningham, who gave him one of his 'I don't have a clue' looks and shrugged.

"Recommend *Antrodemus* takes point. We're less than a mile from--"

"Nyet. With sonar damaged, ees better we follow you. You can tell base, in case we are, as you say, 'coming in hot.'"

"Can you dose it again, just to be sure?"

"We deployed Lokis already, but dosage eendicators and organic monitors say ees not necessary."

Garm shook his head. "And if they're wrong and she comes to?"

"We have Reaper on standby."

"That's insane. You'll blow your actuators off and cripple your vessel."

Dragunova's voice turned stony. "I will *not* allow dees beetch to escape right off the beach. And damage? Day can fucking bill me!"

Garm sighed. "Understood. We'll lead you in. *Gryphon* out."

As Rush closed the com, Garm noticed Bane studying him. "Something on your mind, doc?"

"An interesting woman," she said. "She certainly has a way with words."

He chuckled. "You have no idea." On the aft viewer, the pliosaur's unexpected shifting ceased as quickly as it started. Its flippers went limp and its head drooped back down to its previous inert position. Tiny specks of detritus swirled around it like dust motes as a pair of LOKI AUVs materialized. They began flanking it, keeping pace and scanning it repeatedly.

Ramirez exhaled in relief. "I think Captain Dragunova's right, sir. The package seems to be settling back down."

"Fine, but from now until we dock, I want you on that thing like pork on a pig. If it so much as farts, I want to know."

"Yes, sir." The sonar tech stroked his mustache. "Does a belch count?"

Garm gave him an appraising look. "That was almost funny. I think our CSO's rubbing off on you."

"God forbid, sir."

"Cunningham, stay on point," Garm instructed. "If Dragunova's wrong and the package starts to come unraveled . . ."

"Pin the bow, sir?"

"You got it. Their shielding won't withstand a sustained barrage, so keep your bursts short." Garm headed back to the prow with Bane in tow.

Ho cleared her throat loudly, "Captain, were approaching the end of Jörmungandr. Tunnel entrance is seven hundred yards and closing."

"Set course and reduce speed to ten knots. Once we're inside, make sure we have plenty of clearance. With her damaged sonar, *Antrodemus* has one serious needle to thread. Let's leave some big breadcrumbs for her to follow."

"Aye, sir."

"Communications, move in tight on the package." Garm said.

The aft viewer magnified the unconscious *Kronosaurus*. The sleeping colossus was completely lifeless. All around it, hordes of hand-sized fish of every hue imaginable explored it like a rainbow-colored cloud, some even entering its cavernous mouth and weaving in and around its giant fangs.

Bane gestured at the spectacle, "Why are all those reef fish crowding around that thing? Aren't they afraid of being eaten when it wakes up?"

Garm chuckled. "Pliosaurs don't eat fish that size. It'd be like you dabbing at grains of salt: hardly worth the effort."

"So, what do the fish get out of it? Safety?"

"And food. They're scouring it, picking off tiny parasites and scraps of dead skin. For the lizard, it's a free facial."

"You have an interesting way of looking at things, captain," Bane said.

"So I've been told," Garm replied. His head swiveled toward Rush. "Kill the underwater view and take me back topside."

"Aye, sir," Rush replied.

A moment later, the bridge crew winced in unison. Compared to the dim depths they'd grown accustomed to, the sudden burst of sunlight filling the compartment forced everyone to shield their eyes.

Garm lowered his hand. "Sonar, stay on POSEIDON all the way in. Understand?"

"Of course, sir," Ramirez said, flipping switches.

Garm gestured. "Rush, roll us around."

Five hundred yards away, the mile-wide, 1000-foot tall stone mound that constituted Rock Key filled their screen. Virtually barren, with but an occasional patch of grass or shrubbery, the island looked like an immense boulder that some Titan had used as a plaything and then abandoned, leaving it sitting half-submerged in the water.

"No boats or watercraft in the area," Garm remarked as he scanned the surrounding sea. "Good to see they're taking the markers seriously."

The big submariner grinned. One of the tricks the CDF designed early on to ensure Rock Key's privacy was the installation of warning buoys ringing the island. The buoys were marked with a swimmer hazarded by a set of toothy jaws, and gave the illusion that the area was safety-net-free, giving pause to even the most brazen of boaters.

A hint of movement to one side caught Garm's eye.

"Swivel viewer to starboard," he said. A moment later, "Hold."

On the surface, a tiny dot bounced along, heading toward nearby Islamorada.

"Enlarge object."

The dot became a high-powered Jet Ski. Aboard, two men wearing red and white lifejackets zoomed along at a full clip. From their stern, under Old Glory, a small red flag with a white hand in its center extended from a yard-long flagpole. The flag flew straight behind the big Ski, shivering in the breeze.

Garm gave the riders a small salute.

"Who are they?" Bane inquired.

"LifeGivers, our resident lifeguard superheroes." Garm said. "When a *Kronosaurus* or Bulldog fish attacks and everyone else is swimming for their lives, they jump on their Jet Skis and try to save people. Assuming there's anything left to save, that is."

"On *that* tiny thing?" Bane's eyebrows practically touched her hairline. "Lord, they must be fearless." She eyed the retreating Jet Ski.

"One of my friends used to be one," Garm said. "Ballsiest guy I ever knew. He said it's like being a firefighter, rushing into burning buildings. Except the 'buildings' try to eat them."

"And here I thought you were the only one with a dangerous job."

"Hardly." Garm signaled Rush. "Kill the main."

"Aye, sir."

Gryphon's bow window cleared and the oncoming sea once again became visible. Rays of golden sunlight stabbed through the turquoise water like iridescent spears, illuminating schools of tiny fish and squid that fled as they drew near. Garm inhaled out of reflex, desperately wanting to breathe fresh sea air.

"So . . ." he gestured for Bane to accompany him. "Besides what we just had on the viewer, have you seen Rock Key before?"

"No, but I'm familiar with its history." She ran one hand across the cool surface of their clear titanium window, then rubbed the condensation between her fingertips. "Due to the sturdiness of its natural stone, during WWI it was used as a military research center for developing high explosives."

"Go on."

Bane cleared her throat. "During WWII, the Navy decided to utilize it for artillery practice – a death knell for the islet's already-struggling resident wildlife. The entire island was shelled a hundred times over and carpet-bombed too. After the war, it was deemed unfit for human habitation and has been closed ever since."

"Anything else?" Garm probed.

"Just the usual online urban legends about clandestine nuclear experiments. A lot of people believe the island is still uninhabitable and that setting foot on it means a slow death via radiation poisoning. Personally, I think it's all bullshit."

"Oh, it absolutely is." Garm winked.

Bane cocked an inquisitive eyebrow.

"My brother Derek was the one who 'leaked' that info."

The epidemiologist's eyes lit up. "Ah, another way to keep nosey people away." She eyed him contemplatively. "You Braddock boys are a cunning lot."

Garm smiled and leaned in close, showing off his opalescent eyes. "I don't know *what* you're talking about."

"Oh, please," Bane scoffed. "Don't even think of batting your sky-blues at me, child," she chuckled. "Although it's been awhile, your mother and I are good friends. She told me all about you and the ladies."

Garm's attempt at feigning offense failed miserably. "You knew my mom?"

"A year after Paradise Cove, I attended a lecture she gave. We got to talking afterward and hit it off." Bane folded her arms across her chest. "Actually, her position as head of research at Rock Key was the reason I accepted the transfer."

Garm's playful expression vanished and he put his hands in his pockets, watching as the water ahead of them grew shallow. Boat traffic was non-existent and the fish they passed steadily decreased in size until all the larger predators had vanished. A hundred yards away, past the end of the ragged Jörmungandr trench, the blackish opening of "The Tube" emerged into view.

Bane glanced over her shoulder at the bridge crew and lowered her voice. "Can I ask you something personal, captain?"

Garm grinned. "Are you hitting on me?"

"What? Hell, no!"

"Then, yes. And, by the way, when we're out of earshot of the crew, you can call me Garm."

"Actually, that's my question."

"Come again?"

"'Garm' isn't exactly a common name. How did you come by it? Your mom would never tell."

"Hmm. Well, I assume you know Derek and I are twins."

"Fraternal twins. I saw pictures of you guys growing up."

"Well, when it came time to name us, my parents disagreed. My mom wanted to name Derek 'Dirk' because of my dad's fencing career. He'd just taken silver in the Olympics."

"That sounds cute."

Garm shook his head. "My dad felt it was too much like a character from some novel. He was adamant, and since they each got to pick a name, he won."

"And you?"

"My mom was royally pissed. She had a foul temper to begin with, so when it was my turn she just snatched a mythology book off a nearby shelf."

Bane gasped. "She *didn't*."

"Yep. She opened the book to a random page and announced that, whatever god or monster's name was on it, that was me."

"Didn't your father have anything to say about it?"

Garm planted his hands on his hips and stared at the floor. "What could he say? After making such a big deal about Derek, he'd painted himself into a corner." He cricked his neck to one side, loosening tense muscles. "Of course, the funny part is, when Derek turned five, mom hung the 'Dirk' nickname on him, anyway. Now everybody calls him that. So, in the end, she won."

Bane smirked. "We usually do. So what does 'Garm' mean?"

"According to the Vikings, a gigantic wolf that guarded the gates of Hel. On the day of Ragnarok he broke free and engaged Tyr, the god of war. They killed each other."

Bane stared at him. "Well . . . it could've been worse."

Garm chuckled. "Hell, yeah. I could've been named Frigg, after Odin's wife!" He gave an exaggerated shudder.

"You're an extraordinary man, Captain Garm Braddock." She gave him an admiring smile. "Your mom must be very proud."

Garm's eyes swept forward. A hundred yards ahead, the hundred-foot opening of the Tube waited. Carved into the dense rock of the island, the underwater tunnel ran over five hundred yards, terminating in the very heart of the complex. In the interest of security, the Tube was unlit from the outside. It appeared as an uninviting hole in the rock, its edges craggy with coral and overgrown with long strands of seaweed and kelp that hung down like a billowing green curtain. The result was like swimming into the black, bearded maw of Poseidon himself.

"Helm, remember: slow and centered," Garm said.

"Noted, sir," Ho replied, one hand gripping her steering yoke while the other stabbed buttons too fast to follow.

"Sonar and fire control, once we're inside, *Antrodemus* is on her own," Garm announced. "Let's pray nothing goes awry."

"Yes, sir," Cunningham and Ramirez replied in unison.

"Communications: update the receiving dock on our status and make sure they've got a transfer rig ready, as well as engineers on hand to assess damage to *Antrodemus*."

"On it, sir," Rush said. "Should I request a medical team?"

Garm nodded his approval. "Good thinking."

He waited a moment, watching his team do their thing, then ground his molars for a moment, before resuming his conversation with Dr. Bane. His mother's friend or no, it was time to test her mettle. And to see if she had any idea what was coming her way. He indicated the fast-approaching submarine tunnel. "It appears Grayson's people weren't exactly forthcoming when they gave you your assignment. Did they tell you what goes on in this place?"

"Other than the names of my teammates and that I'm supposed to be solving a pathogen problem, no," Bane replied. The deck shifted beneath them and her eyes betrayed a hint of fright as *Gryphon's* prow dipped into an oncoming trough and then angled upward. It was aiming for the Tube's mouth. "It's common knowledge that Grayson's parent company, GDT, makes advanced weaponry for the military, and that they acquired your mother's robotics technology firm via a leveraged buyout a few years back. Other than that, Rock Key is pretty much a mystery."

"The base isn't called 'Rock Key,' doc," Garm advised. "That's just the island. You'll be working in Tartarus."

"*Tartarus*? Was that your mother's choice as well?"

"No." Garm grinned mirthlessly. "Tartarus is the CDF's southeast coast base of operations, as well as home to the most advanced bio-weapons technology on the planet."

Bane's eyes rounded. "Bio-weapons? Wait, I wasn't told about any--"

Garm rolled right over her words. "Ironically, in Greek mythology, Tartarus was where the Titans were imprisoned after they were overthrown by the gods of Olympus."

Like a monstrous artillery shell inserting itself inside the barrel of the world's largest howitzer, *Gryphon* slipped soundlessly into the Tube. The sunlit, blue and green sea and all its life vanished, and the sub's prow became a window into a lightless void. Ahead, a series of red navigation lights lining the tunnel walls clicked on systematically. For the bridge crew, the effect was like falling into a pitch-black lava tube, ringed with glowing embers.

Garm took a deliberate step closer and loomed over Dr. Bane. He locked gazes with her, knowing from experience that, bathed in the Tube's navigation lights, his pale eyes gleamed a frightening scarlet. "When you see what's at the other end of this tunnel, I think you'll find the name my mother chose for me ended up being uncannily appropriate."

Although she swallowed nervously, Bane stood her ground. "I'm really looking forward to seeing your mother again, Garm Braddock," she said. "And to finding out about these bio-weapons you mentioned." Her own eyes narrowed. "While I'm at it, shall I tell her how you tried to scare me, just now?"

Garm scoffed and turned back to the bow window. "You won't be telling my mother anything."

"And why is *that*?"

He shook his head and spoke over his shoulder. "It's unbelievable. You really don't know anything."

Bane's eyes flashed angrily. "Apparently not. So why don't you enlighten me, *captain*. Why can't I speak with Dr. Amara Braddock?"

"Because she's dead."

SIX

C'mon, Derek. You're my big boy. You can do it!

As the sound of his dad's encouragement faded into wistful memory, Dirk sagged backward, one hand clamping onto the nearby doorjamb. He shook his head. His dad was gone and he wasn't some baby, walking unaided for the first time. He was a man and it was time he started acting like one. It had taken him six months, but he'd finally found the courage to enter his mother's office.

Dirk had anticipated a sense of relief from walking through that door, but the way his heart was pounding, it felt like the damn thing was chewing through his sternum like some alien parasite. Any second, he expected to feel his rib cage splitting apart. He could picture it in his head; it would plop to the floor like some demonic cephalopod, waving its bloodied arterial stumps like tentacles as it scuttled across the--

Jesus, get a grip, Braddock!

Cursing himself for staying up late watching old horror movies, Dirk forced his imagination back into the closet where it belonged and focused on actualities. It was a smart move. In Tartarus, reality was far more terrifying than illusion. Here, letting your imagination run wild could get you killed.

Dirk drew in a lungful and let go of the doorjamb. His fingers were practically numb, and he grimaced as he shook out his hand. Ignoring the staccato beat of his heart, he turned on the lights.

As the powerful overheads clicked on and forced him to squint, he felt like he'd entered a tomb. In some ways, he had. His mother wasn't buried here, obviously, but this was where she died.

Dirk's eyes ricocheted around the place. Unlike his office, which was, like Dr. Grayson's, situated in Tartarus's lower levels, his mother had chosen a work station high up, overlooking the facility. On one side, her office walls were traditional cement and drywall: a decorator's attempt to add smoothness to rough-hewn rock. On the other, walls of crystal clear Celazole soared nearly twenty feet, terminating against Tartarus's natural stone roof. The transparent sections were segmented and formed a 100-foot arc, giving an impressive view of the lower levels, as well as the facility's huge amphitheater. The durable polycarbonate was installed in ten-foot pieces and braced with interlocking beams of brass-coated steel. Further down, a fifty-foot observation deck curved outward. There, the clear walls were replaced by a four-foot high railing of thermoplastic and steel, allowing visitors to gaze down from a dizzying height.

As he turned left and willed his feet forward, entering the office proper, Dirk felt a mountain of shame press down on him. After waiting so long, he felt like a morbid invader. It was strange, since Amara Braddock had always welcomed visitors with a big smile and open arms.

Dirk surmised his misgivings were most likely a result of the stark contrast between then and now. His mother's office had been her private sanctum: a much-needed refuge in a facility that housed the world's greatest horrors. There, she could focus on what mattered most. Namely, resolving the problems plaguing Earth's oceans and protecting the people that depended on them.

The young scientist sighed. Now, her defunct sanctuary was little more than a shrine. He shuffled past chalkboards covered with marine ecology equations; underneath them were towering stacks of scientific journals and newsletters. On one wall, a huge bulletin board was plastered with pages from magazines.

Dirk felt a tiny spasm of pain as his cheeks contracted into a sad smile. Despite access to unlimited technology, his mom loved pinning physical copies of pertinent articles in plain sight. *"I'm like the 'dinosaurs' we're trying to deal with. I'm too stubborn to adapt to the modern world and determined to make it bend to my will,"* she'd say.

As he made his way to his mother's expansive office desk, Dirk felt himself calm. The sight of the custom-made wood and aluminum behemoth with its extensive system of drawers, all designed to her exacting specifications, brought back a plethora of fond memories.

With what bordered on reverence, Dirk rolled her ergonomic chair back and then eased himself into it. The chair's casters needed oil and it creaked under his weight, but he was relieved when it failed to collapse as the paranoid voice inside his head said it must.

Resting his palms on his mom's desk, Dirk's eyes swept its dusty surface. He started pinpointing familiar objects. There was the yard-wide monitor she'd salvaged from her first mini-sub, a photo of her and her long-dead friend Willie Daniels, his parent's wedding portrait and some family pictures, and the tooth fragment and skin sample from the gigantic cow pliosaur that ravaged Paradise Cove, thirty years prior.

Dirk picked up the weighty chunk of yellowed ivory and examined it before putting it carefully back in place. He shook his head as he pondered just how many deaths that one creature had ultimately caused.

The sight of the smashed alarm clock sitting beside the old computer monitor shook Dirk out of his funk and caused him to chuckle. While honeymooning in Maui, one of his parents had hammer-fisted the thing into a pancake, but neither would ever say whom. It didn't matter. His dad's martial arts training notwithstanding, his mom's foul, early-morning temper was legendary. It didn't take a genius to deduce who the guilty party had been.

Smiling now, Dirk tapped the start key on his mother's computer. While the system booted up, he opened one of her desk drawers and started exploring. His lips did the fish thing as he extracted a plasteresin cast of his and Garm's baby hands. He snorted as he noticed their birth weights, carved into the sturdy material. Him: seven pounds, eleven ounces. Garm: twelve pounds, fifteen ounces.

Dirk blew out a breath. One day – hopefully, without paying off some therapist's mortgage – he'd put his insecurities and jealousies behind him. It wasn't like he didn't love his brother. He did, more than anything. It was just that he hated him too. At least, sometimes.

Setting the cast aside, Dirk logged onto his mother's system. Her wallpaper was a ten-year-old Christmas family photo. He smiled as he studied it, remembering the day it was taken. He and Garm had just turned nineteen: young, eager teens, filled with dreams and hormones, and his dad was wearing that hideous Santa Claus sweater they'd all taken turns knitting. Everyone looked so happy, especially his parents. He'd never seen a couple hit the half-century mark that looked so young, so vibrant, and so in love.

And alive.

It was hard to believe they were both gone. Nearly eight years for his dad now, and his mom so much more recently. She'd never recovered from Jake's death. None of them had. Poor Garm took it the hardest of all, which made sense. He'd always been closer to their dad. With him, it was the opposite. He'd worshipped their mom.

Dirk scanned a score of video shortcuts that decorated Amara Braddock's desktop like apples on a tree. He pursed his lips contemplatively, then clicked on one entitled, "Derek and Garm, 1st."

It was the boys' one-year birthday celebration at the old house. They were playing contentedly with magnetic blocks, when their parents came waltzing in with a lit cake. While his mom sat it on the table and kept on singing, Jake scooped up both boys in one arm and carried them like pillows to their highchairs. Once they were safely imprisoned and the candles blown out, he and Garm were each given a huge slab of cake, which they alternated devouring and using as face paint.

Dirk leaned forward, intently studying the video. He realized he'd never seen this portion. His dad was wiggling one of his thick fingers in front of him, teasing him until Dirk clumsily swatted at it. Then, he pressed his fingertip gently against the tip of his baby son's nose and said, "Doink!" in a playful tone. Dirk giggled hysterically and bounced up and down as if he was on springs, cajoling his father to continue the game. After a dozen more "doinks," Garm grew jealous and started squirming in his own highchair, demanding some "doinking" for himself.

Smiling sadly, Dirk wiped his eyes and closed the video. The whole "doinking the nose" routine was one of his core memories. In his mind's eye, he could see it as if it was yesterday.

A second video labeled, "Karate Lesson" caught his eye and he opened it. This one was from a few years later, and featured their father teaching their mother some self-defense moves. Of course, this "sparring session" ended up the way almost every other one had, with his parents rolling around on the floor in a playful wrestling match that turned into a passionate make-out session.

Dirk chuckled as he closed the video. He was about to open one whose title struck him as odd when a distant crash, punctuated by a loud splashing sound, assailed his ears. He felt a chill creep up his spine on frigid spider's feet and the hairs on his nape pricked up. It was coming from beyond the railing.

That railing.

Rising to his feet, Dirk moved along the polycarbonate wall until he reached the observation deck. He placed one hand hesitantly on the cool metal railing that topped the waist-high barrier. Then he glanced fearfully over the side. He wasn't afraid of heights, just what he might see. Two hundred feet below, technicians were hosing down the reinforced concrete stage of Tartarus's enormous aquatic amphitheater. He could smell the filtered seawater, even from this height.

Dirk breathed a sigh of relief; he'd forgotten about the big presentation scheduled for later that evening. His eyes swung sideways, focusing on the missing section of railing, twenty feet further down. His chest rose and fell as he espied the crisscrossing lengths of red police barricade tape that still adorned it like bloody bandages, and he started forward. He could barely feel his legs. In his mind, it was like that final stretch to the gallows.

Dead son walking . . .

Suddenly, Dirk froze. Flashbacks from the video showing his mother's horrifying death appeared before his eyes and he staggered sideways as if struck a physical blow. He gritted his teeth and fought to shrug off the haunting visual.

When he finally reached the ten-foot breach, Dirk stood there, trembling. His hair pushed back and the usual sounds of men and machines faded into the background. Soon, the only thing he could hear was the snapping sound of a loose piece of tape, fluttering in Tartarus's artificial breeze. He swallowed hard and moved closer, still keeping a good five feet from the edge.

Something crunched underfoot. He lifted his foot and blinked as he caught sight of a small pile of dried flower petals. He dropped to one knee, scooping up a few and kneading them between his fingers, watching dispassionately as they turned to dust.

As Dirk stood up, something touched him on the shoulder. He cried out and spun wildly around. A sigh of relief escaped his lips, and he chuckled nervously at the swaying plant basket, hanging on wires suspended from the sprinkler pipes. There were several of them that once held his mother's prized ivy gardenias. She'd doted on them daily, feeding and pruning them, even talking to them. With their ability to bloom for extended periods, they'd been her favorites, and under her dotage they'd blossomed.

Now, they were dried-out husks, their crumbly vines hanging limply down like the desiccated tendrils of some long dead cephalopod.

Reaching out and gently stopping the plant basket's swaying, Dirk moved carefully around it and back toward the break in the railing. He inched closer.

It is an unnerving thing, to stand on the precipice of a loved one's demise.

Dirk's pain-filled eyes raked the taped-off gap and he shook his head. Just as he was turning to leave, a metallic gleam caught his eye. He moved to the right-side support and dropped down on one knee, gripping the steel and brass post. The scientist in him took over and, for a moment, the horror of standing where his mother died was forgotten. He scanned the metal where the railing had parted, rubbing his thumb along the two connector points and examining where the steel was sheared away.

Actually, it was only shorn at the top, he noted. The bottom connector was torn, as if a great weight had been applied to it. He checked the other side, and it was the same. There were no signs of corrosion or defects in the metal.

Dirk mentally calculated the weight of an inch-thick, ten-foot by four-foot section of Celazole, versus the strength of the connectors. Something was off. Even with the weight of an adult human added to the mix the numbers didn't add—

Baaaaaa! Baaaaaa!

The blare of Amara Braddock's office phone nearly gave Dirk a heart attack. He stumbled toward her desk, his mind still on overdrive. A glance at the caller ID caused him to recoil in surprise and he hit the speakerphone.

"Hi, Dr. Grayson," he croaked, hastily clearing his throat. "Yes, I'm finally here. You spend a lot of time tracking people's locators."

"Only the ones that are important to me, son," Grayson said. "I'm glad you worked up the resolve to face your demons. I know it's hard, but it's a good thing. You'll see."

"Yes, sir," Dirk said. He plopped down in his mother's chair, his eyes unintentionally revisiting the video icon labeled, "Garm fencing lessons." He muted the monitor's audio and clicked on it.

"Derek, if you need a little time, that's fine," Grayson began. "Just keep in mind, *Gryphon* is already in the Tube, with *Antrodemus* and the new cow close behind. The teams are prepped and, frankly, I need you."

On the monitor, Dirk's mother's face appeared. She was wearing glasses and her lab coat and looked tense and tired. This wasn't an old family video, he realized. It was a recent recording, a scientific presentation on--

"Derek, did you hear me? I said I--"

"I'm sorry, Dr. Grayson," Dirk blurted out. "Yes, I heard you." He extracted a flash drive from his lab coat and inserted it, quickly copying the video. As he removed the drive, he spotted the archaic test tube housing the skin fragment from the original Paradise Cove pliosaur. There was a disturbance in the fine dust surrounding it; the sample had been moved recently.

As he put the drive back in his pocket, Dirk's eyes narrowed. The same dust film covering his mother's desk also coated her office floor. As he cocked his head to one side, he spotted footprints – his and someone else's. Judging by foot size, it was definitely a man. The footprints were recent.

"Derek?"

Dirk faked a cough. "I'm on my way, Dr. Grayson."

Giving the room a final, analytical eye sweep, Dirk hurried toward the exit. Inside his lab coat pocket, his hand gripped the tiny flash drive as if it was the only known antidote for a poison he'd just ingested.

"Your mother's *dead*?" Dr. Bane's eyes were wide with shock. "I-I'm so sorry. But when? How?"

"Keep your voice down." Garm glanced back at the bridge crew, relieved that they had the decency to feign acute onset hearing loss. "Amara Braddock's death is officially listed as a 'slip and fall.' Technically, that's accurate."

"That's awful. What a tragedy. She was an amazing woman."

"She was, indeed." Garm nodded.

"But why didn't you tell me sooner?"

"I wasn't sure if you knew. And frankly, it's not my favorite topic."

"I understand." Bane extracted a tissue from her lab coat and dabbed at moistened eyes. "I'm sorry for your loss. Yours and the world's."

"Thank you."

Ensign Ho cleared her throat. "Approaching the Vault, captain."

Garm nodded. "Good. Communications, is everything prepped dockside?"

"Yes, sir," Rush replied. "I just got an update from *Antrodemus*. They're navigating the tunnel slowly. So far, no problems."

"Excellent. Helm, light it up."

"Aye, sir," Ho said.

Like twin flamethrowers, *Gryphon*'s high-powered searchlights lanced through the scarlet-tinged obscurity of the tunnel, illuminating the carved-out stone and the titanium-steel rings bolstering it. Despite the near-dark conditions, the Tube's walls were alive with a thick layer of marine plants and algae, layering the hard rock. The foliage gave the passageway a softer, almost throat-like appearance, reinforcing the sensation of being swallowed.

Some things are better left unseen.

Ho looked up from her screens, "Distance to the Vault, 100 yards, sir. We have clearance, doors are opening."

Garm nodded. "Hold position."

The "Vault" was the 100-foot wide submarine entry gate to Tartarus. Dr. Bane stared, spellbound, as a crack magically appeared in what otherwise appeared to be a fast-approaching dead-end. With a metallic groan that could be heard and felt, even through their heavy acoustic cladding, the Vault's immense doors began to open.

"Now *that* is a serious barrier," Bane remarked.

"Damn straight," Garm chuckled. "Those babies are six-foot thick titanium-steel. Each one is sixty feet high and fifty feet wide. Once they're closed, they're strong enough to withstand a nuclear blast."

"Jesus, who are you trying to keep out . . . *Godzilla*?"

"More like keep *in*," Garm nodded. "Come to think of it, we've never had a *Kronosaurus* invade the Tube. Before they installed chemo-inhibitors in the water filters, some of the big males used to come sniffing around here. One even got tangled in the net. Great press when we put him down. But now, nada."

"Just the bulls?"

"It's a mating response," Garm said. He glanced over at Ensign Ho, who was eyeing her screens and speaking in low tones to Ramirez. He couldn't make out what they were saying. The rumbling of the Vault's portals was reminiscent of an approaching avalanche. "Pliosaur females secrete powerful estrus hormones that a mature bull can detect fifty miles away. It's like Chanel No. 5 for lizards: irresistible."

Bane placed her palms against *Gryphon*'s clear prow and studied the brightly-illuminated framework that surrounded the colossal doors. "Does the Tube, or at least this entrance, have any defenses?"

"Other than the sensors and cameras," Garm said. "Just me." He pointed a thumb at himself. "Garm, Guardian of the Gates of Hel."

Bane smirked. "I'm serious. What happens if one of those big males gets past the net and makes it into the Tube?"

"A pliosaur trying to break through *that*--" Garm pointed at the Vault. "Would be like you banging your head against an armored car. Besides its sheer strength, the outer casing is frictionless. There's nothing to get a grip on and no way to pry it open."

"So, if one *did* come in here . . ."

"It'd be a one-way trip. He'd have to come back out for air at some point. And when he did, we'd cut him to pieces."

"Gotcha."

Ensign Ho announced, "The vault is open, sir. Proceed to dock?"

"One moment," Garm said. "Communications, update on *Antrodemus*?"

Rush cupped one hand over her earpiece. "Everything looks good. The package is 'sleeping like a baby' and they're holding position, 250 yards back."

"Good. Helm, how's the dock?"

Ho checked her screens and nodded approvingly. "Our timing is good, sir. It's nearly high tide. Dock depth is thirty-four feet and receiving crews are on standby on Dock A."

"Excellent." Garm gave Bane a contemplative look before turning back to communications. "Proceed inside. I'll leave the mating to you."

"Very good, sir," Ho replied, easing them forward. Her face darkened as Ramirez tried and failed to stifle a snicker.

"Mating?" Bane asked.

"With the docking ramps," Garm advised. Outside, the water at the top of their bow window began to churn violently as they angled upward. He grinned and started toward the exit. "Come with me. We're going topside."

Bane flushed. "You mean--"

"Topside," Garm repeated, pointing straight up. "You've been throwing up for the last two days, doc. Between that and the lack of info they gave you when they transferred you here, I think you've earned the deluxe tour."

"Okay," Dr. Bane replied warily. She moved to catch up with him. "Lead the way."

A few minutes later, the two climbed the steps leading to the interior of *Gryphon*'s armored sail. Garm stopped at a heavily reinforced, titanium-steel door, resting on huge hydraulic hinges. He signaled to Dr. Bane to wait as he watched a series of red LEDs arranged in sequence above the exit. There was a faint rumble and a loud whooshing sound as the LEDs transitioned from red to orange, then finally to green. Garm waited a second more for a loud beep, then grabbed the door's actuator lever and hauled it from three o'clock to nine. With a grunt, he forced the weighty barrier open.

Dr. Bane gasped as a warm breeze blew her hair back and spritzed them both with cold seawater. Garm moved forward, ducking down to clear the dripping doorjamb, and then took her hand to guide her through. Together, they stood on the sail's tiny conning deck. Dr. Bane sniffed the air, then placed one hand over her nose and the other atop her stomach.

"Well, it definitely *smells* like hell." She said, blanching. "What is that stench; is it filled with actual demons?"

"A few ... mainly the two-legged variety," Garm said with a chuckle. He faced front, resting his hands on the conning deck's armored gunwales as *Gryphon* emerged from the dark tunnel, chugging toward Tartarus's main docking station.

As the brightly-lit docks came into view, Bane gripped the waist-high barrier before her. Her neck craned forward, her eyes popping. "Wow."

Garm watched her with interest. The main docks were huge by any standard – big enough to house six aircraft carriers docked side by side – with a steel-reinforced stone roof that soared two hundred feet above their heads. The brightly-lit, excavated walls were lined with observation decks on each level, giving one the impression of being inside some sort of inverted hotel. Of course, the sub captain mused, there were no sun worshippers lying on those "balconies."

Garm's eyes dropped. Ahead, the 100-foot wide concrete passage they were floating along abruptly widened and divided, splintering into three distinctive canals that ran parallel to one another. From above, they looked like colossal rake marks in the concrete – gouges, left by some Kaiju-sized raptor's claws. Another five hundred feet further, and the canals rejoined one another, reforming into a single channel that terminated in a partially-submerged, 150-foot-wide steel-and-cement disc. In between, and alongside each canal, the sprawling docks were dotted with workers busy maneuvering large carts, inspecting stacks of crates, and manning forklifts, tractors, dump trucks, and assorted other construction vehicles. There was a constant breeze flowing through the complex, and the air, despite a series of ten-foot ventilation shafts that dotted the walls, bore the scent of diesel fumes, saltwater, and something else.

Under Ho's expert touch, *Gryphon* began to turn, inching herself toward the canal on the far right. Ahead, a crowd of nearly one hundred workers and technicians stood waiting. Garm looked them over. There were accountants, mechanics, and inspectors, eager to survey the sub; a reactor crew waiting to check for radiation leaks; and supply engineers in trucks, prepared to replenish everything from foodstuffs to ammunition. Far to the left, at the empty receiving dock, he spotted the medical team Rush recommended, as well as the crew that had been assigned to handle the incoming specimen.

Garm glanced up as a sizzling shower of sparks spewed down and hissed into the water, ten feet from their prow. 150 feet in the air, a section of interlocking steel girders that crisscrossed the airspace above them like an impossibly large spider web was occupied by a team of welders and engineers. They were hard at work, repairing one of the huge hydraulic cable lifts that moved nimbly about above the dock and transported everything from live Naegling torpedoes to fully armed mini-subs.

"It's amazing," Bane said, momentarily forgetting the smell. "What's that huge circle with a channel cut into it?"

Garm followed her gaze, then glanced over her shoulder and blinked as a massive form moved behind the transparent wall to their right. He shook his head and smirked. "That's a submarine turntable," he said. "Like for trains. It lets us spin the boats around so we don't have to back out of the Tube."

"And those machines suspended overhead? How do they--"

With a snort of exasperation, Garm reached over and did the "Jurassic Park" thing. Placing one big hand atop Bane's head, he twisted gently to the right until she was looking at--

"Holy fucking shit!"

Garm's body shook with laughter, as much from the unexpected curse as the look on the epidemiologist's face. A hundred feet to *Gryphon*'s starboard, the bordering concrete dock ran smack up against the paddocks.

The pliosaur paddocks.

Running the length of the docking chamber, a series of gigantic aquariums had been permanently installed, each one braced against the next, with five-foot thick, stainless steel frameworks supporting them. The clear polybenzimidazole windows that faced dockside were each two hundred feet wide and one hundred feet high. Imprisoned within, the ocean's deadliest carnivores cruised restlessly back and forth.

As the nearest of the giant reptiles swam up and pressed itself against the thick PBI, eyeing them, Bane yelped like a frightened Chihuahua and staggered back into Garm. She stayed there, pressing back against him and neither apologizing for the mishap, nor uncomfortable with their sudden closeness.

Garm rested his mitts on Bane's trembling shoulders and said, in a mock Scottish brogue, *"Aye, lassie. Here, there be dragons!"*

Bane's lips tightened and she wheeled on him. "You bastard!" she lashed out, ineffectually punching him in the chest. "You did that deliberately!"

Garm pretended to be cross. "Striking a superior officer? How unbecoming of you . . ."

Bane's nostrils flared angrily. "You deserved it. I could've had a heart attack."

He grinned. "Ah, yes. I forgot, you *are* a mature woman . . . I suppose I should've been more careful."

Bane's fists clenched and her eyes flew open wide, but to her credit, she reined in her temper. She exhaled, low and long, then redirected her gaze to the tanks as they paraded past. "So, these are the 'Titans,' eh?"

Garm nodded. "That's *Fafnir*," he said, gesturing toward a monstrous, battle-scarred female with notched flippers. "*Thanatos* is the dark one with the green eyes and heavy jaw, and those two bulls are *Romulus* and *Remus*."

Bane's head jerked back. "Two males in one tank? Isn't that dangerous?"

"Not with them; they're shell-brothers."

"Shell-brothers?"

Garm pointed as the two sixty-foot bulls passed one another without a hint of animosity. "See their matched markings? They're identical twins – two pliosaurs that gestated inside the same egg. Unheard of, until now."

"That's amazing. So, they get along?"

"Get along?" Garm scoffed. "It's like they share the same brain. They function as a team, and a lethal one at that. Once you're settled in, check the video library. When we captured them, they were in the process of ripping the pectoral fins off a blue whale three times their size."

"What about that one?" Bane asked, indicating a sixty-four-foot pliosaur that swam excitedly back and forth as *Gryphon* hove by. The giant reptile became increasingly animated and pressed its muzzle against the thick barrier, its eyes focused on Garm. "He seems to like you."

"*She*," Garm corrected. "Her name's *Proteus*. She's an adolescent Gen-3."

"You guys and your names," Bane teased. "A female, eh? Seriously, I think she digs you," she said as the young cow eyed the big submariner in a manner that could only be described as covetously.

"She recognizes me because I'm the one who captured her," he said, his pale eyes turning back toward the bow like a swiveling battleship's turret. "*Kronosaurus*'s are like elephants, doc. They never forget. Or forgive."

"I was under the impression you didn't like bringing them back alive," Bane said. "Why her?"

Garm gave the epidemiologist a look. "In five years, I've taken four of those monsters alive. All under orders, and because they were valuable scientific oddities."

"What's so odd about her?"

Garm sighed. "I'll show you." He turned to face the seventy-ton marine reptile. Without warning, he bared his teeth and raised his arms overhead like an angry silverback gorilla. *Proteus* recoiled and her skin color began to change. In seconds, she went from cobalt blue with white undersides to 100% mottled green – a near-perfect match for the light-dappled seawater within her enclosure. The big saurian wasn't invisible, but she was decidedly hard to make out. Then, as she turned on her tail and swam away, she practically vanished.

"Wow, she's like a chameleon," Bane muttered. "I read that a pliosaur's color can shift based on stress and, of course, their hue patterns alter during the mating season, but I never knew they could do that!"

"As a species, they can't. She's some sort of mutation."

Bane stroked her chin. "Is that why you brought her in, because she's too dangerous to leave in the gene pool?"

Garm nodded. "That, and my superiors wanted to study her for weapons research."

"Weapons research?"

"Of course," Garm gave her an amused look. "Where do you think the technology for this sub's iridophores came from?"

Before Bane could reply, all the pliosaurs began to swim excitedly around their tanks. A few submerged or hovered near the bottom, while the remainder did excited loops or surfaced and stuck their huge heads up out of the water. A loud thrum resonated across the docking chamber and one of the cable lifts began to move. Like a giant black widow spider, it zipped nimbly across the network of girders, fifteen stories up, until it was situated above what appeared to be a fifty-yard swimming pool. The pool was warded by a heavy-gauge Cyclone fence that towered twenty-five feet in height.

A warning claxon sounded.

"That must be the 'officers-only' pool," Bane observed.

No sooner had she spoken, when the SUV-sized assembly, complete with a set of hydraulic powered pincers reminiscent of the ones junkyards used to dispose of cars, plummeted toward the pool. It was tethered by thick steel cables and, a moment before it hit the water, the pincers opened wide.

"You wouldn't want to do the breast-stroke in there," Garm remarked.

There was a prodigious splash as the pincers vanished into the deep water. A moment later, the partially lax cables stiffened and began to twitch. Another claxon sounded and the cables started to retract. The water around the lines churned violently. Seconds later, the metal jaws broke the surface, tightly locked onto the tail section of a ferociously struggling, nineteen-foot *Xiphactinus audax*.

"Holy--" Bane nearly choked. "Is that pool *filled* with those?"

"Gotta feed the inmates, doc," Garm said. He watched emotionlessly as the flailing 3,000-pound fish was hauled straight up to a height of one hundred feet, before heading purposefully toward the first pliosaur tank.

Ten feet below the surface, the dark *Kronosaurus* cow labeled "*Thanatos*" remained motionless. Only her glittering green eyes betrayed her as she tracked the approaching fish. As it drew closer, her powerful throat muscles started to spasm and her echolocation clicks resonated through the air. When the pincer assembly hovered fifty feet above the surface, another claxon sounded. The pincers opened and . . . *BOOM!* Like a grenade exploding in the water, the giant predator's fanged jaws struck, seizing the hapless *Xiphactinus* the moment its head pierced the water. There was a ferocious struggle as the doomed Bulldog fish flailed against the grip of its natural predator, followed by a wet, crunching sound. With a low rumble, *Thanatos* shook her misshapen head from side to side, until the waters of her enclosure were clouded with blood and scales.

"Yikes," Bane said. Above them, a series of lift assemblies moved to the Bulldog fish pool, made their drops, and then headed toward the pliosaur tanks with their thrashing burdens. "Note to self: swimming in pool, not advised."

Garm nodded. Alongside, every *Kronosaurus imperator* waited impatiently for its meal, their ratcheting sonar clicks bonding together to form a low-pitched hum that vibrated even *Gryphon*'s heavy hull. Garm rubbed at his forearm as his arm hairs stood on end. Soon, the dock resounded with the sounds of bones being splintered and flesh rent as the grisly feast increased in scope and frenzy.

Bane cast about. "So, is that all they eat, those fish?"

Garm shook his head. "They have a varied diet. We have a series of oxygenated pools containing an assortment of large fish that we breed specifically for them, including bluefin tuna and beluga sturgeon."

"What, no great white sharks?"

"Reproductive rates are too slow."

Bane blinked. "I was kidding." She gnawed her lower lip. "I'm afraid to ask, but is there anything *else* you feed them?"

"Not unless you count the livestock on the lower levels."

"You mean cows and sheep?"

"Cows yes, sheep no. Too small. But we have Bactrian camels, Cape buffalo, American bison, and giant eland, if memory serves."

Bane was aghast. "Wait, you feed them mammals . . . alive?"

"I don't feed them *anything*," Garm said coolly. "Pliosaurs prefer their food bloody and still twitching. And yes, they do seem to relish mammalian flesh."

"Any cetaceans?"

"No. There'd be a pile of lawsuits if word got out. And besides, my brother would never allow it."

There was a sudden vibration as *Gryphon*'s forward maneuvering thrusters fired. "Brace yourself," Garm advised. There was a series of thumps as the hull thrusters continued to fire short bursts. Seconds later, the submarine came to a complete stop.

There was a ten second delay, while waiting dock crews loitered around. Then, with a high-pitched whining sound, *Gryphon*'s hydraulic-powered boarding ramps extended from her flanks like insect legs, locking her onto the platform and providing access for those on it. A final shudder shimmied through the sub's thick hull, punctuated by a loud *thunk*, and then silence.

"Time to disembark," Garm announced, gesturing toward the sail door. "Gather your things. I'll meet you on the starboard dock in ten."

"What then?" Bane asked, looking around at the football field-sized docking station. She gazed apprehensively up at the nearby menagerie of ravenous marine monsters.

"We'll find out where you're supposed to be. In the meantime, try not to get eaten."

Bane's eyes flashed angrily. "You are *not* funny, Garm Braddock!"

"Who said I was being funny?"

SEVEN

"I'm surprised your people aren't ready to mutiny," Commander Jayla Morgan remarked, studying the drawn faces of *Gryphon*'s battle-weary bridge crew as they stood around the dock, waiting on their commanding officer. "After you let Dragunova take their prize . . . *and* bonuses."

Surrounded by bookkeepers, Garm looked up from signing an electronic tablet and cocked a grin. Despite Jayla's habit of flirting with insubordination, he liked his thirty-two-year-old second-in-command. The buxom, dusky-hued, five-foot-nine South African had been with him for two years now, and was one of the few people he trusted to command his vessel during those rare times he left the bridge; usually only to eat, sleep, or use the head. He especially liked how her normally-dormant accent flared up when she became irate or agitated.

His crew, on the other hand, didn't care for her. Jayla was by the book, with almost no sense of humor. That was terrific when it came to keeping things tight and orderly, but Garm had learned early on that men and women facing death on a daily basis needed to relieve stress. In his eyes, if that involved some occasional banter on the bridge, that was fine.

But Jayla didn't see it that way. She hated the camaraderie amongst the bridge crew. Cunningham, in particular, got on her nerves. The friction between them was just one more reason why Garm only left *Gryphon*'s backup team to her tender mercies.

"Really?" he replied, scrawling his name on one digital form and pressing his thumb print to another. "I don't think so, but let's see." He snatched up a nearby tablet and turned to face his crew. "Our tallies for this tour included seven Gen-2s, four Gen-3s, eleven Gen-4s, and that little rat bastard Gen-5 that killed that surfer off Miami." He did some quick fingering on the tablet. "That means you primaries each made a whopping $29,457.00 over the last sixteen days. Anybody unhappy with that – maybe want to string up your captain?"

"No, sir!" came the universal reply. Cunningham saluted sharply and added, "We'd follow you into hell, captain. Even without the money." He gave a lopsided grin and added, "Of course, getting paid *does* help . . . sir."

Jayla's hazel eyes moved from Ho to Ramirez to Rush. "Sure, that's a nice payday, but wouldn't you rather have had the extra ten grand each that bringing in a confirmed Gen-1 man-eater brings?"

"Oh, but they're getting the ten G's each," Garm retorted. He watched Jayla's mouth do the fish-out-of-water thing before he turned to his team. "You heard me. You guys pulled our asses out of the fire back there, so consider your bonuses earned."

"Uh, how are you going to do that, boss?" Ho asked confusedly.

"I'm giving you the money."

As the bridge crew exchanged surprised glances, Jayla shook her head.

"Bridge crew dismissed," Garm said, giving them all a casual salute. "Go get drunk, sleep, workout – whatever makes you happy. And Cunningham, go see that pretty wife of yours. I'm sure she misses you. You guys have three days to kill, with nothing *to* kill. And you've earned them."

As his ecstatic crew shouldered their packs and dispersed, Jayla shot Garm a disapproving look. "Permission to speak freely, captain?"

"Of course, First Officer Morgan."

"You're spoiling them, sir."

Garm accepted one last form to sign, passed it back, and nodded. "Yes, I am. But they deserve it. Besides, you should talk; you and your guys got to sleep most of the last twenty-four hours, and you *still* got paid."

Jayla laughed. "Sleep, with Ho driving the *Gryphon* like she's off-roading in her Jeep?"

"I dare you to tell her that," Garm said, smiling humorlessly. He shook his head. "Enough chit chat, Commander. You're Officer of the

Deck until further notice. I want munitions replenished and the galley restocked by 1600 hours. Have the reactor crew run a full diagnostic and the base engineers do a complete inspection of both hulls. We may not have taken any hits, but between the heavy maneuvering and the ammunition expended, I'd like to make sure we don't have any unpleasant surprises waiting for us."

"Very good, sir!" Jayla said, saluting smartly. "Who do you want on the bridge?"

"Brown and Alvarez will be fine. Skeleton crew only."

"Aye, captain." Jayla smiled jauntily as she turned on her heel and began barking orders at the hapless crew of a waiting munitions truck.

Garm grinned. The woman certainly enjoyed being in charge. He had a momentary vision of her dressed in a leather dominatrix outfit and holding a riding crop and shuddered.

After excusing himself from the remainder of *Gryphon*'s receiving crew, Garm gestured for Dr. Bane to accompany him. She'd been standing around watching the festivities, and waiting to find out where she was supposed to be. They'd walked but a few steps when he noticed her wearing a befuddled expression.

"Something wrong, doc?"

She cleared her throat. "I'm confused about the money. Are you authorized to arbitrarily hand out bonuses?"

"Oh, it's not the CDF's money I'm giving them," Garm replied. "It's mine."

"What? You're giving them forty thousand dollars of your own money?" Dr. Bane shook her head. "That must be half your check!"

"And your point is?"

"Well, can you afford it?"

Garm's easy smile flatlined as they resumed walking. "When my mother died she left all her shares in JAW Robotics to Dirk and me. With the recent buyout by GDT, the value of that stock has more than tripled."

Bane's brow crinkled up. "Wait, so you're--"

"A billionaire? Pretty close, at least on paper."

Her jaw dropped. "B-but if you're so rich, why the hell do you go out hunting rogue pliosaurs?" she stammered. "What is it, some sort of obsession? Do you feel you have something to prove?"

"Only to myself."

"That's . . . that's insane!" she blurted out. "You could get yourself killed out there! Aren't you afraid to die?"

"Only of dying badly," Garm said. He looked up at *Proteus*'s tank. The mutant *Kronosaurus imperator* was eyeing him through the thermoplastic barrier, like some gigantic cat that wanted to play with its food. Their eyes met, then his swung back to Bane's and he winked at her. "Everyone dies, doc. Dying *well*, now *that's* something to strive for."

Bane shook her head and stared at the ground. "You are a strange man. I don't--"

"Head's up!"

Garm's head snapped up as the warning cry echoed from high above. His reflexes kicked in and he grabbed Dr. Bane by the shoulders, yanking her back just in time to keep her from being flattened by the falling head of a *Xiphactinus*. The three-hundred-pound chunk of fish smashed onto the concrete dock with the sound of a soaked bag of cement, spattering blood and brine in every direction.

Bane's protest at being manhandled died in her throat and she stared, stupefied, at the monstrous fish head staring up at her. Alive, a *Xiphactinus* wore a toothy Joker's grin. It was far more macabre in death.

"You okay, doc?" Garm wiped away the streaks of blood that lined her trembling face. A worker climbed hurriedly down from a nearby scaffold, his steel-tipped work boots ringing as he came thudding over.

"Geez, I'm really sorry, lady," the sweating ironworker offered. He eyed Garm pensively, then pointed up at the creaking lift assembly, high above their heads. "The filters take care of most of the scraps, but any heads that are left gotta be removed with the lift. They can clog the impellers."

"I'm fine . . . really, I'm okay," Bane managed dazedly. She shook her head as if recovering from a left hook and straightened up. To the worried ironworker's surprise, she extended her hand. "Thank you for your concern."

The man shook her hand, then glanced at Garm with unsure eyes.

"We're good," Garm said. "Just check your unit's power calibrations. And make sure the incident's noted in your log."

"You got it. Thank you, Mr. Braddock," the man said. He radioed to the lift crew, who began lowering their pincers to retrieve the slippery fish head.

Bane took a few steps and then stopped. She leaned unsteadily against Garm, one hand clutching her heart. "Jesus, I almost died. I've been here fifteen minutes and I was already almost killed. I'm going to die here!"

"Oh, come on. It's not that bad," Garm reassured. "You're going to be in the labs most of the time, not here on the docks."

"Oh, wait. You're right. I'll just be in an enclosed box working on lethal pathogens," she remarked, rolling her eyes. "Gee, that makes everything *so* much better!"

"Yeah . . ." he clicked his tongue. "Speaking of pathogens, you may have gotten some *Kronosaurus* drool in your mouth just now. Everyone here's been immunized, but you should get checked, once you've unpacked."

Bane pointed a trembling finger at her commanding officer's nose. "How many people have been killed in Tartarus over the last year?"

Garm hesitated. "Uh, well, we didn't have the locator implants until seven months ago, so some people were listed as missing or AWOL . . ."

"How many *confirmed* deaths?"

"Forty-two. But I don't see how--"

"Oh, God. What am I talking to *you* for?" Bane scrunched her eyes shut and pressed her hands to her face. "You work on a sub, killing monsters all day, and when you're not doing that, you're *surrounded* by them!"

"Hey, what can I say? Some guys are just lucky."

Bane shot him a look of pure venom then hugged herself as she walked. "I can't believe I'm stuck here. Wait until I get my hands on--"

"Hold on," Garm interjected. His eyes swung upward, focusing on a trio of enormous monitors that hung from the very center of the web-like latticework of girders, fifteen stories up. The monitors were arranged back-to-back in a triangle, so they could be viewed by everyone in the dock, regardless of location. There was a sudden crackle as snow filled the screens. Seconds later, a news bulletin popped up. It was muted, but the images needed no translation.

Footage of a breaching humpback whale dominated the screen. Erupting up under the cetacean and matching its prodigious leap was a similar-sized pliosaur, jaws snapping. As the big whale crashed back down, the marine reptile's fangs were embedded in its throat. The helicopter's feed zoomed in as the two giants thrashed at the surface, the humpback's twelve-foot flukes crashing up and down and the pliosaur's flippers flapping wildly. Within moments, the water around them turned a brilliant crimson and the humpback's struggles ceased.

Garm shook his head as he took in the grim scene. "Whales evolved that breaching behavior to avoid a charging *Carcharodon megalodon*. It doesn't work on *Kronosaurus imperators*, unfortunately."

Bane sighed, but continued watching. The monitors turned staticky again and then a second newscast played. This one was filmed off the coast of British Columbia and showed a super-pod of at least thirty killer whales battling a forty-foot pliosaur. Two of the toothy mega-dolphins had their jaws locked on each of the larger predator's flippers and were pulling hard, holding it spread-eagled, while the other members of their troupe rammed and savaged its throat and belly. The besieged marine reptile got in a few licks, but it was hopelessly outnumbered. Soon, the Orcas began to toy with its tattered remains, pushing its body to and fro and taking turns tearing at it.

"Drawn and quartered. Nice work," Garm said, nodding in appreciation. As Bane threw him a look, he gestured at the screen. "Surviving Orcas have taken to hanging out in communal pods to give themselves numerical advantages. They'll typically flee before they take on a full-grown *Imperator* cow, but when an adolescent male that size comes a-calling, they're not going to pass up an opportunity to eliminate a threat."

As the broadcast concluded and the screens turned black, Bane's eyes swept the platform. Behind them, teams were already busy carrying crates across the *Gryphon*'s ridged metal gangplanks, with Commander Morgan scrutinizing everything they did. A munitions crew sat waiting for their turn, with a full brace of Naegling torpedoes lying in stabilizing grooves on the back of their flatbed.

"Can we get me where I'm supposed to be?" she asked. "I'm tired and I'd like to lie down."

Garm nodded. "I was told you'd be met across the way." He looked around, spotted a six-wheeled MarshCat parked nearby. The rugged, amphibious ATVs were the Tartarus version of a golf cart. He signaled the driver as they approached. "Take us to the receiving dock, please."

"Sure thing, Captain Braddock," the cadet said, sitting up straight.

Garm helped Bane into the back and then climbed in. He made it a point to position her behind the driver, more so the ATV wouldn't dip noticeably when he seated himself than in consideration of her comfort.

As they zoomed along, turning left and passing over the bridge-point of the central canal leading to the disc-shaped submarine turntable, Garm took a moment to close his eyes and relax. He wasn't as exhausted as his co-passenger, but he was pretty tired.

Bane, obviously happy to be off her feet, uttered a sigh of contentment and started looking around like a sightseer on a bus tour. As they approached an enormous pliosaur skeleton, suspended from steel cables, fifty feet above their heads, she tapped Garm on the shoulder.

"Is that the Paradise Cove animal?"

Garm shook his head. "What's left of that lizard rests on the bottom of Ophion's Deep. My parents made sure of that."

"So, then what is it?"

"One of the first Gen-1s ever encountered," he said over the racket of a passing forklift. "She was brought in by the *Titan*, a year before I came onboard."

"The *Titan*? Wasn't that the sub that was destroyed?"

Garm nodded. "She went down with all hands. A shame, her captain was a good man."

Bane looked up and whistled as they drove underneath the preserved skeleton. "Wow, that looks as big as the one *Antrodemus* is bringing in."

"Pretty much."

"Is that as big as they get?"

Garm smacked his lips. "Normally."

Moments later, the ATV's driver stopped with a sudden squeal of brakes, parking alongside an enormous empty tank that stretched a full four hundred feet in length. Around them, dozens of technicians sat inside their vehicles, with a few sitting on the hoods. Overhead, a significantly larger version of the lift assemblies that transported food to the *Kronosaurus* tanks hung poised and waiting. Instead of one set of pincers, suspended from a series of cables, however, this larger unit had a suspended, platform-like base that measured seventy-five by thirty feet and had three separate, significantly larger, grippers protruding from it. Unlike the sharp-edged food transports, the twenty-foot metal jaws on the larger unit were rounded at the tips and encased in some sort of thick, black polymer.

As Garm thanked the driver and climbed out of the MarshCat, a petite redhead wearing a CDF uniform approached and gave him a sharp salute. "Lieutenant Lara McEwan, reporting for duty, sir," she said, then indicated a small troop transport parked nearby. "My team and I have been assigned to assist Dr. Daniels with the specimen transfer."

Garm recognized the girl as he saluted back. "It's good to see you again, lieutenant. This is . . ." he stopped as he realized Bane had wandered off. "Well, at any rate, you've got quite the prize coming in."

"Yes, sir." Lieutenant McEwan's eyes lit up. "We received a message from *Antrodemus* a few minutes ago. They should be hitting the dock any time now. They said they've got a huge Gen-1 female, is that correct?"

Garm nodded absentmindedly as he tracked Bane's movements. The last thing he needed was for her to fall into one of the canals and get swallowed by a stray *Xiphactinus*. "She's an evil bitch," he said. "Possibly the biggest we've ever brought in."

"Except for . . ." she hesitated, her startled blue eyes meeting Garm's aquamarines. "I'm sorry, sir. I--"

"Focus, lieutenant," he said. "Is everything prepped?"

"Yes, sir." McEwan whipped a tablet out from under one arm and checked it. "Given the risk of the specimen emerging unexpectedly from imposed brumation, Dr. Daniels decided to forego the sling. She wants to get the cow sedated and into the holding tank as quickly as possible."

Garm glanced up at the economy-sized lift and nodded. "Very good."

"Yes, captain." McEwan began gnawing her lower lip with pearly-white incisors. "Permission to speak freely, sir?"

"Always."

"Well, um. Putting aside rank for the moment . . ." She swallowed her nervousness and then blurted it out. "Since you're going to be at base for the next few days, I was wondering if you're free for dinner tonight. I've got a portable grill in my quarters, if you're hungry, that is. In which case, I'd love to heat something up for you."

Garm's eyes lit up at the obvious innuendo and he grinned. The girl was cute, he gave her that, and ballsy too – another plus. And it wasn't like he was in what anyone would call a committed relationship. But a dalliance like that could be dangerous for both of them.

Besides, she was so tiny. He'd probably break her in half.

"Lieutenant . . ."

"Lara," she insisted.

"That sounds wonderful, Lara," Garm said, choosing his words thoughtfully. "And I'm not saying no. But given the specimen, the damage to *Antrodemus*, and something else we encountered that may require immediate action, I can't commit to anything. I'm sorry."

"Understood, sir," she said, flushing.

"Call me Garm," he said, winking. "As long as it's just you and I." He looked around then lowered his voice. "I'll take a rain check."

"Yes, sir," McEwan said, beaming. She glanced at the Vault's closed inner doors and then eyed her transport. "Dr. Daniels will be here any minute. I better get my team off their collective asses . . . *Garm*."

He faked a grin as she walked away with a noticeable spring in her step. He hated leading someone on. But considering the job she had to do, he figured it was better she be alert and eager than sullen and dejected.

"Kids," he chuckled. "Speaking of which . . ." He glanced around worriedly until he spotted Bane milling about, ten yards away.

By the time he walked over to her, she was gazing, wide-eyed, at the huge hydraulic lift suspended high above them. Then she started taking in the slew of trucks, men and gear spread out across the receiving dock. Finally, her eyes found the giant tank and swept its considerable length. "Wow, that is one serious fish tank," she muttered. "Why is it so much bigger than the others?"

"Actually, they're the same size," Garm said. He folded his arms across his chest. "The habitats you already saw for our indoctrinated 'inmates' are perpendicular to this one. They're lined up lengthwise to conserve space. This is the holding tank. We use it as a triage pool to pen new arrivals while they're screened and treated for injuries, parasites, and infections."

Bane approached the unoccupied tank and craned her head back. The water was crystal clear, with none of the algae and small fish present in the occupied paddocks. It was also only filled to the fifty-foot mark. As she turned sideways, her eyes focused on the tank's massive, titanium-steel frame. Her head cocked to one side as she studied its shiny welds.

"How thick is the Celazole in these aquariums?" she asked.

"A little over eight feet, from what I've been told. Why?"

Bane took a knee by the corner of the holding tank and ran a hand over its cool metal corner. "This section looks different from the rest . . . newer." She looked at Garm. "Was it repaired recently?"

He gave her an appreciative nod. "Very observant. Last year, in fact."

"What happened?"

"The tank's previous occupant got a little feisty and had to be moved to a more hardened facility."

"More hardened than *this*?" Bane's mouth formed a tiny circle. "I'd hate to see the creature that could do that kind of damage."

"You would," Garm affirmed.

"The water seems much cleaner than the other tanks. Are you having filtration problems?"

Garm chuckled. "You ask a lot of questions, doc."

"An idle mind is the devil's playground," she responded. "And you've got enough devils here already."

"Touché," he said with a grin. "The tanks all have seven-stage filtration systems that keep them fairly sterile." He gestured at the tanks across the way. "In addition, we pump in fresh seawater regularly and mimic marine conditions as much as possible, including sandy bottoms, cleaner fish, and even some phytoplankton."

"So this one is kept barren to eliminate possible contagions?"

"The water's also been treated with a heavy-duty, pliosaur friendly anti-biotic – not that they need it. Immune system-wise, the bastards are pretty much indestructible."

"Sounds like a high level of care for prisoners."

"They earn their keep," Garm said.

Bane stood up as she finished her examination of the tank. She shielded her eyes and squinted at the far-off row of occupied aquariums.

Even though they were two blocks away, the size of the enclosures and their restless inhabitants still stood out.

"They're awfully quiet," she wondered aloud. "I'm surprised you keep them lined up like that. I would think they'd try and get at one another. At least occasionally."

"There are low-grade iridophores in the tank dividers that keep them from seeing one another, except when they're supposed to," Garm said. "But even if there weren't, their behavior inhibitors usually keep them from getting frisky."

Bane did a double-take. "You control them?"

"Did you see any of them ramming the glass or trying to attack the people on the other side?"

"That's amazing. How?"

"You'll see."

"Wait a second . . ." Bane's expression intensified and she started tapping her index finger rapidly against her chin. Garm grinned; he could practically see the wheels whirling inside her head. A second later, her eyes grew as big as golf balls and her head shot up so hard it looked like it hurt.

"Holy crap!" she spouted. "These . . . these *monsters* . . . they're the bio-weapons you were talking about!"

Garm turned to her wearing a Cheshire cat grin. "Bingo."

Fourteen miles off Marathon Key, the *Octopus giganteus* pair floated like phantoms through the darkened depths of the Florida current. Drawing thousands of gallons of saltwater into their mantles and shooting it back out, they rose soundlessly, like lethal dirigibles. To the male's relief, the giant female had chosen a deep crevasse nearly ten miles in length in which to establish her newfound hunting territory. Although the chilly, 2,000-foot depths of the Straits of Florida were hardly the icy abyss he was accustomed to, they were infinitely preferable to the sun-lit layers they were currently heading toward. The two had no choice but to prowl the surface. With the squid-eaters they preyed upon on the brink of extinction, their kind was following suit. Fewer and fewer of the monstrous cephalopods prowled the extreme depths, and those that remained eked out a pathetic existence, scavenging as much as hunting in a desperate attempt to stave off starvation.

The male's horizontal pupils swiveled in their sockets as he changed direction and jetted ahead. In addition to possessing color vision and keen eyesight, his eyes possessed a feature unique among invertebrates. His vision was linked to a pair of mineralized organs in his brain called statocysts. In addition to functioning like ears, the hair-covered masses allowed him to sense the orientation of his body relative to horizontal at all times. It was nature's compass; an autonomic response that kept his pupils parallel to the seafloor, regardless of lighting or any maneuvers he executed.

As they ascended past the three hundred-foot mark, the male's eyes began to narrow, his pupils constricting against the painful day-light. The water was sickeningly warm high up in the water column, but it was also filled with inviting scents and flavors that meant one thing.

There was prey nearby.

Excitement began to build as he gazed hungrily about. Two hundred yards to his right, his colossal mate was also scanning the area. Her time would be upon her soon, and despite their previous feeding, she was once again ravenous. The male was fortunate. Cannibalism was common among their kind, and if it wasn't for their many years together, the female might have turned on him already. Still, they had to find food, and fast. Sooner or later her patience would run out. And his luck with it.

They hunted in earnest now, jetting toward any possible meal with their mighty tentacles at the ready. For predators their size, however, the pickings were sparse. They encountered a school of tiny squid, but those were too small to grasp, let alone consume. Twice, they came upon pods of large pelagic fish, but the fleet predators proved to be fast and nimble and were impossible to catch. With their large eyes, the *Xiphactinus'* spotted the great octopi from far off and scattered, long before the hungry cephalopods could close the distance.

The male ground his beak in frustration. Once, they sensed the appearance of a larger prey item: some sort of carnivorous, whale-sized reptile that emitted noisy clicks like the big cachalots they traditionally fed upon.

The male's instinctive memories recognized the creature as a pre-historic rival from long ago. But it was the same as with the schools of fish. The short-necked plesiosaur sensed its enemies' approach and vacated the area at an impressive velocity. The male and his mate were no slouches in the speed department. She was capable of jetting backwards at fifty miles an hour and him a bit more, but they were incapable of quick course changes and their accelerations were short-lived. They were built for power, not endurance.

Suddenly, a thrumming vibration in the water drew the attention of both octopi. An enormous floating object, as big as an iceberg, was approaching their position. Wary of a potential predator, the two froze where they were, their tentacles hanging limply down, their color and texture changing to match that of algae-coated driftwood. Only their glittering eyes gave them away.

As the mountainous object moved closer, the noise it gave off became deafening. It displaced a wall of water so big, the monstrous cephalopods were tossed back and forth. The water's surface overhead churned like a boiling cauldron and, from the back of the object, twin maelstroms roared with a sound like undersea geysers erupting.

Even without touching the colossal entity, the male octopus could taste it in the water. Its skin was constantly shedding tiny particles of rust, a metallic flavor that was immediately recognizable. The object was not alive. It was a mobile mountain of iron, somehow moving across the surface with a power that defied both wind and current.

As the object passed over their position, leaving them unmolested, the male relaxed. Filled with innate cephalopod curiosity, he began to study the giant thing as it moved steadily away. When the racket it gave off faded, his cool mind refocused on addressing the issue at hand – filling a pair of very empty stomachs.

A sudden change in water pressure alerted him to his mate's approach and he turned to greet her. The huge female drifted closer, her bloated body trembling with ill-contained hunger. Their eyes met and the male octopus experienced a sudden frisson of fear. He was already injured; the stump of his missing tentacle ached non-stop as it worked to regenerate itself. In his weakened state, he would not survive a rush from her. Then, just as he was preparing to flee, she uttered a deep, gurgling summons. Above her mantle, a half-mile in the distance, the male sensed what she'd picked up on.

It was some sort of whale moving along on the surface. Based on its shape, it appeared to be an exceptionally large finback, an animal the giant octopi knew of, but rarely encountered. Finbacks were the fastest of the great whales. They lived in the light, high in the water column, where they fed on schools of plankton and krill. The only time they descended into the depths was at the end of their life cycle. And then, only as putrescent, shark-ravaged corpses.

The male studied the approaching leviathan. He could see its sleek lines as it scythed through the blue-green water. It was moving slowly, traveling in a straight line, and constantly hugging the surface. Its sound sight also seemed different than normal: weak and fragmented. To the huge cephalopod, it meant the finback was wounded or ill, a juicy prize, ripe for the taking. If they could get close enough before their presence was detected, they could bring it down.

The male's eyes gleamed as he reached out and caressed his mate. Their communication was based on sight and touch, rather than sound, and nothing more was needed. They descended to six hundred feet, vanishing into the darkened depths before splitting up. Their plan was simple. The larger female would approach the whale head-on, while her mate closed from the rear. When the moment was right, they would rise from the deep with lethal speed and power, slamming the trap shut before the injured cetacean realized anything was amiss.

As he jetted silently down and then started to arc back up, the male octopus studied the finback's pale belly as it passed directly overhead. He spotted the bow wave cast up by its tapered snout and, toward its tail region, the thick, keel-like caudal fin that helped stabilize the big whale as it maneuvered.

Suddenly, the male's eighty-foot tentacles flared out to the sides. The thick webbing between them billowed like an enormous windsock, creating a braking effect that caused him to stop dead in the water, while quick bursts of seawater helped him hover in place.

The male's eyes widened and he rose another one hundred feet to make sure. His color quickly shifted from a mottled sea-green to a bright reddish-orange, his frenzied chromatophores signaling his excitement.

The finback was more than just ill. Its tail was horribly injured. In fact, its flukes were completely gone. The reason for its slothful speed was now apparent. With its flukes shorn away, the bullet-shaped whale could neither dive nor flee. It was completely helpless and easy to kill.

With an explosive burst, the male octopus lunged violently upward, his huge body displacing tens of thousands of gallons of seawater as he aimed for the maimed whale's belly. Three hundred yards away, his mate surged forward with an urgency only insatiable hunger can inspire. Like a pair of monstrous torpedoes, they hurtled toward the unsuspecting whale, their lethal tentacles trailing behind them like bundled spears. As the distance between him and the finback vanished, the male felt the venomous saliva he secreted flood his mouth in anticipation of the blubber-rich meal to come.

It was time to feast.

EIGHT

Like the leviathan she'd been named for, the 139-foot schooner *Rorqual* sliced her way through white-capped turquoise waters. She was a true queen of the seas, a tri-masted beauty whose snow-colored masts jutted over one hundred feet into the sky. Her broad sails bulged like canvas-coated breasts, swelling with the never-ending power of the wind, while her gleaming wooden decks rose and fell with the rhythm of the waves. She was one with Nature, her timeless design merging with the elements instead of defying them, and deep within her sturdy oaken bosom beat the undying heart of the ocean.

As he paused to bask in the bridge's sunlit portside doorway and felt the breeze press his locks tight against his head, Billy Barnes realized he was having the time of his life. He couldn't help but laugh. Initially, he'd railed against his mom and dad sending him on a seven-day "voyage" aboard the *Rorqual*. Especially after he found out visitors had to work as deckhands during the trip. Or, in his case, as a radio operator. Now, however, he wished he could spend the rest of his life here. The smell of the fresh ocean air, the exhilarating wave spray, watching billfish ride the big sailing ship's cresting bow wave – what more could an eighteen-year-old ask for?

In truth, his parents had given him the gift of a lifetime.

It was one he'd never forget.

"Patience, Master Barnes," Captain James Krieger said as he watched him resume pacing. "You've got only seventeen minutes left on your watch. Then you're free to sunbathe, climb the rigging, or crawl into your bunk and pass out, as you see fit."

"Sleep? Who can sleep at a time like this?" Billy's head shake ended in a broad grin. When he'd first come aboard, he and *Rorqual*'s two-dozen other "recruits" had a tough time. Besides enduring bouts of seasickness, they'd been forced to absorb a deluge of info that the schooner's experienced core crew threw at them during their first and only formal training session aboard the floating classroom. The physical part, however, had been far worse. Their backs and necks were sunburned from long hours spent scrubbing the deck, their hands blistered and raw from working the lanyards and cranking in the ship's three-quarter ton anchor.

That was five days ago. Now, Billy's palms felt like leather, and he was toughening up on the inside, as well. He was developing a new-found confidence, the kind that playing second-string for his high school basketball team just couldn't provide. Last week, he didn't know a beam from a berth. Today, he could tell a cleat from a clew, and differentiate a mast from a mizzen. He felt like a veteran seafarer, one who'd been away from the ocean for far too long and was eager to once again experience everything she had to throw his way.

"So, Cap . . . just how big *is Rorqual*?" Billy asked, peering from bow to stern. With no radio messages to receive or send for the last few hours, he felt if he didn't learn something new he would go mad.

Captain Jim smiled paternally as he adjusted his white captain's hat. Billy grinned. Over the last few days, he'd grown immensely fond of the aging German yachtsman. Certainly, more so than his uncles, who only cared about their cars and stock portfolios. It was more than *Rorqual*'s commander just having so much to teach; he was a genuine person who truly cared about his charges, despite the fact he only had them under his wing for a week.

"Without the bowsprit, this old girl is one hundred and fourteen feet long," Captain Jim began. "Sparred length is one-thirty-nine. She's got a twenty-six-foot beam and – with you well-fed landlubbers aboard – is pushing three hundred tons."

Billy chuckled as he leaned out the doorway, shielding his eyes with one hand as he peered up at the top of the mainmast. He could see his friend Cal in the crow's-nest, pointing at the horizon and whooping it up as he played lookout. *The kid must think he's Blackbeard . . . actually, make that Spiderman*, Billy thought. He shook his head. Although he had no innate fear of heights, the crow's-nest was one place he had no desire to visit. Getting flung back and forth like an inverted pendulum, a hundred feet in the air, was not his idea of a good time. But then, Cal always did have a screw loose – one his parents undoubtedly hoped being onboard *Rorqual* would tighten.

Billy wandered back inside the bridge, peering through the glass at the black metal railing that protruded from the gunnels. The railing looked like the kind you'd see fencing in big suburban properties . . . or cemeteries. It was constructed of interwoven, solid steel posts that extended six feet out. The posts were set three feet apart, and each had a long, lance-like point, jutting outward at a forty-five-degree angle. As he watched, a tern alighted on the hot metal railing and then flapped off, squawking irately.

"Hey, Cap? Is that railing standard on schooners?" Billy asked. "I remember looking at pictures of the old tall ships and I didn't see any of them with it."

Captain Jim nodded. "In the old days, we didn't have sea dragons rearing up to snatch men off the decks. The spikes are a deterrent." He winked. "Can't have some hungry pliosaur making off with one of my crewmen, now can we?"

As he clocked the sharpened steel spears, Billy's eyes betrayed a hint of nervousness. He'd been on the lookout for a *Kronosaurus* since they'd left port. Out here, past the Keys' protective nets, he was sure he'd spot one, but so far, they'd come up empty. Of course, considering the video clips he'd watched, maybe they'd been lucky. *Rorqual* was big, but maybe not big enough.

"So, if a pliosaur came after us, what would happen?" he asked.

"Heaven forbid." Captain Jim raised an eyebrow. "I've been running these 'educational cruises' for five years in these waters. "In that time, we've survived nine run-ins with the scaly bastards, excuse my French. And that's enough for me."

"Nine?" Billy's eyes popped.

"Yep. Five of the mid-sized ones tried sticking their crocodile heads up over the gunwales to grab crewmen, but they got stuck on the rail spikes and changed their minds."

"Wow."

Captain Jim cleared his throat. "And three of them thought the *Rorqual* was a whale and tried taking a bite out of her hull."

Billy swallowed a gasp. "Omigod, what happened?"

"You could feel the hit," Captain Jim said, his expression suddenly grave. "The first two just left tooth rakes in the wood. But that last one . . . he must've been a big boy. He punched a hole in the keel before he took off." The old man patted his belly and chuckled. "I guess he didn't like the taste of tarred oak."

"Were you in danger of sinking?"

"Nah, this old girl's made of hardwood and she's got a blister hull to boot. She's pretty buoyant. We've survived squalls at sea, she and I." He gave the wooden decking under his feet an affectionate thump with his heel. "Take a lot to drag *Rorqual* under, my boy."

As visions of attacking pliosaurs clouded his brain, Billy's mind began to wander. He imagined himself in full pirate regalia, swinging a giant cutlass as he battled hordes of man-eating monsters. *Imagine if a Kronosaurus comes after us on this trip? Now that would be a story worth telling the guys.*

Billy's head shook as he shrugged off his daydream. "Hey, wait . . . didn't you say there were *nine* attacks? What happened during the last one?"

Captain Jim looked down at the floor. "You're sharp, Billy. Not much gets past you." He locked the captain's wheel in place. "The last one was the biggest I've ever seen. Sperm-whale sized, easy. She reared up out of the water and squashed down ten feet of the railing like it was nothing. Took two of the crew in one bite before I could stop her." He shook his head somberly. "Our only fatalities."

"God . . ." Billy breathed. "How did you stop her?"

"With *this*," the old man said, resting his hand on a menacing-looking, black and gray rifle that hung on a nearby bulkhead. "My old Barrett XM500 sniper rifle, a relic from my military days."

"You *shot* it?"

"Right through the eye," Captain Jim said. His eyes narrowed as he relived the attack. "From point blank range, I put a .50 caliber tungsten penetrator round into her brain." He pointed outside. "Killed her right there, thirty feet from where you're standing."

"Wow. You . . . you're a hero!" Billy spouted. "Did they give you a medal?"

"Nope." He rolled up his sleeve, exposing a foot-long indented scar that ran from his elbow to his wrist. "But *she* gave me this little love bite, just to make sure I'd remember her."

"She *bit* you?"

"Just one tooth," he said, rolling the sleeve back down. "It was a reflex bite. Damn thing was already dead; her jaws just didn't know it yet."

"Man, I can't believe you made it."

Captain Jim winked. "You don't survive to my age, kid, without being a wee bit resilient."

Billy rubbed at the goose flesh popping up all over his arms. "You don't think one that size will come after us today, do you?"

Captain Jim scoffed. "Highly unlikely. The CDF's had them on the run for years. Most of them know better than to approach a boat this size. They--"

A loud series of beeps drew Captain Jim's attention to the ship's brightly-colored sonar screen. As his brow lines deepened, Billy moved closer. On the screen, a highly-pixilated reading had popped up directly below their position. The signal was massive but amorphous, as if it was constantly changing shape.

"We've got one . . . make that *two* large sonar readings: one astern, a second dead ahead." Captain Jim's head owled from bow to stern. He turned back to his screen. "They're changing course . . . closing fast." His eyes went wide. "Good God, it can't be!"

BUH-WHUMP!

There was a thunderous impact and *Rorqual* came to a sudden stop, her heavy oak frame shuddering. Outside, a dozen crewmen and guests went flying, along with anything that wasn't tied off or bolted down.

Caught off guard, Billy was thrown hard to the deck and ended up facedown in a heap. As he lay there, he wondered how an iceberg had ended up adrift in the Straits of Florida. His reverie was interrupted by a sudden crash, as a forty-foot spar from one of the masts came hurtling down, embedding itself ten feet into the deck boards and nearly skewering an unconscious mate. Torn rigging and rent canvas cascaded down all around it. As he struggled to his feet, Billy heard a high-pitched shriek, followed by a dull thud. He staggered out of the doorway, his eyes filling with horror. Like a broken doll, Cal's twisted body lay on the deck, along with a good portion of the crow's-nest. All around, men and women were screaming and hanging onto any handhold they could find as the wounded *Rorqual* uttered an unnatural groan and began to move again. The three-hundred-ton ship listed hard to port, then swayed sickeningly back toward starboard.

Billy wiped at some stickiness around his eye, his hand coming away bloody. He was vaguely aware of Captain Jim shouting something at him, but he couldn't make it out. His ears were filled with a loud droning sound, interspersed with shrieks and the sound of cracking wood. He looked up and saw Stephanie, the pretty blonde he'd just met, hanging upside down, thirty feet in the air. Her right foot was entangled in the rigging and she was screaming for help.

He had to do something. He had to--

"Get on the radio!" Captain Jim shouted, grabbing Billy by the shoulders and shaking him.

Billy blinked repeatedly. "W-what did we hit?"

"*We* didn't hit anything," the captain growled. He reached over and snatched his rifle off the wall, removing its magazine and checking it before sliding it back into place and giving it a hard smack. He turned toward the door, his blue eyes hard and dangerous. "Something hit *us*."

"What 'something?'"

"*That.*" Captain Jim pointed. As he spoke, he pulled the charging handle on the .50 caliber Barrett back, loudly chambering a round.

Billy's next words came out as a squeak of purest terror. A series of gigantic tentacles had emerged from the water and were crawling across *Rorqual*'s broad decks, some gripping the wood, others exploring. They were enormous – as thick as suspension bridge cables, and covered with disc-shaped suction cups the size of SUV tires. The suckers gaped wide like a thousand hungry mouths, their ridged surfaces glistening with some sort of viscous, drool-like slime.

Any hope Billy harbored that the ship's protective palisade would deter their monstrous attacker evaporated in seconds. As soon as one of the arms touched the blackened steel spikes the hard metal collapsed as if it was made of rubber. Even the surrounding wood had black, charred drag marks left on it wherever one of the tentacles touched it.

One of the senior crewmen grabbed a boathook and swung it violently at the nearest tentacle. It was like hitting stone and on the second swing the pole snapped. A section of tendril as thick as a barrel lashed out, striking the hapless man and sending him sprawling. As he started crawling away, the tentacle curled back like a hooded cobra, then extended, feeling around for him. As it passed directly over him, one of its serving platter-sized suckers grazed his back and buttocks and he uttered a God-awful shriek. Billy blinked in disbelief. The crewman's clothing and much of the flesh underneath had melted away as if he'd been brushed with acid.

Before the horribly injured mate could draw a breath to scream again, the tentacle struck with astonishing speed. Wrapping around the unfortunate sailor like an attacking python, it held him suspended ten feet in the air before pulling him over the side. As he heard the splash, Billy prayed the doomed man drowned as fast as his screams did.

KA-WHUMP!

A second bludgeoning impact shook the wounded *Rorqual* to its core. Everywhere Billy looked, crewmembers and guests screamed in terror as the monstrous tentacles began scooping them up and dragging them overboard. Captain Jim cursed as the lurching ship caused him to stagger and lose his grip. His rifle clattered to the floor. As he bent to retrieve it, a monstrous tentacle came down over their heads, its weight caving in the bridge's aluminum roof and shattering all its windows. Billy dropped into a protective crouch and watched as Captain Jim grabbed his gun and rose unsteadily to his feet. He saw the old man freeze, his eyes locked forward, his expression utter astonishment.

"Krake . . ." he muttered. He stared at Billy with maddened eyes. "They're *Krake!*" he shouted.

"W-what?" Billy sputtered. "I-I don't--"

Billy lost the power to speak as a second set of immense tentacles emerged from the churning water. Like a wave, they enveloped the bow of the ship, feeling their way around as they began to seize people. There was a painful cracking sound as one tendril curled around the bowsprit and snapped it like a twig. As Billy helplessly watched, a second found and seized Stephanie around the waist as the poor girl fought to free herself. Her muffled screams ended a second after she was engulfed and torn away. Billy gagged and began to vomit; one of Stephanie's legs remained behind, horribly twisted and spurting blood as it hung from what was left of the rigging.

Billy screamed as Captain Jim grabbed him. "Get on the radio!" he bellowed over the cries and crashing. A loud hum shook the boards under their feet. "Send out an SOS to the CDF! Warn them about the Krake! Tell them they need to deal with them!"

Nauseous and dazed, Billy wiped the puke from his chin and staggered a step back. He spotted the radio and saw that it still had power. Outside, a fire had broken out and smoke was beginning to obscure visibility. The shrieking and crashing continued. "What the hell is a Krake?" he yelled. He saw Captain Jim turn to face the carnage, his jaw set. "Wait . . . what are you--"

"I'm saving my ship!" he snarled. "Get that SOS out and then find a place to hide!"

Before Billy could respond, Captain Jim plunged into the white smoke, his shouldered rifle extended out before him. He heard a series of incredibly loud gunshots, followed by a deep, resonating rumble that could have been a roar. There were two more gunshots, interspaced with screams, and punctuated by a violent crash that caused the entire ship to shudder.

Billy gasped. The mainmast had shattered at its base, and the ship's spine along with it.

He waited a moment to see if there would be any more gunshots. There weren't. Outside, the fire was spreading and the screams had begun to die off.

Because there's nobody left! Billy thought frantically. He snatched up the radio mike and mashed the transmit button down, his thoughts barely coherent as he started spouting Captain Krieger's message.

Outside, through the mist-like smoke, he saw row after row of titanic tentacles begin wrapping around *Rorqual* amidships, like overlapping belts. The mortally wounded schooner let out a mournful groan and began to shiver. Billy knew she was dying. There had been no reply from the CDF. He cast about, trying to remember where the lifeboats were, and wondering if he should try and make it to one. He shook his head and grabbed the mike one last time.

"Attention Coast Guard and CDF, SOS, repeat: SOS. This is schooner *Rorqual*. We have been attacked by--"

Billy's words jammed in his throat like a rusty saw blade. Through the obscuring smoke, something moved. He leaned forward, holding the bottom of his t-shirt over his mouth and waving his hand in front of his face.

A moment later, he saw something that caused his heart to plummet into his bowels. One of the behemoth's gnarled tentacles was worming its way toward the bridge. He could see it through the smoke, slithering toward him like a hungry anaconda. As it knocked over a nearby water barrel and reared up, he saw it clearly; its greenish-brown skin bristled with hungry suckers, their surfaces dripping death.

The Krake had heard his distress calls.

And it was answering them.

———————

Dirk Braddock grinned as the elevator door whooshed opened and Dr. Stacy Daniels came bounding in. She was wearing workout tights and sneakers and paused to pluck out one of her wireless ear-buds before she shot him her most dazzling smile.

"Good morning, Dirk."

"Hey, you saved me a call," he said, his chest involuntarily expanding as the familiar scent of jasmine permeated the lift. "I figured you'd be downstairs with Gretchen. You two have been inseparable lately."

"She's shedding," she replied, then added with a wink, "You know how we girls get when we need moisturizing . . ."

Dirk chuckled. Even though they were no longer a couple, the tall, thirty-two-year-old Chinese-Jamaican scientist remained one of his closest friends. He thought the world of her, both personally and professionally. In a place like Tartarus, Stacy was a godsend. During her college days, she'd worked for one of the big marine parks as a cetacean handler/trainer, working with dolphins and killer whales. Now, she held PhDs in both Neurobiology and Robotics and was one of the top neural surgeons on the planet, not to mention a highly respected authority on Thalassophoneans.

Stacy *loved* macropredators of all kinds, and pliosaurs most of all. A decade earlier, she'd been one of their staunchest advocates and campaigned rigorously against the government's planned culling program. When it became heartbreakingly obvious, however, that there was no other recourse and the creatures had to be dealt with, she switched over to studying them.

She'd analyzed how they breathed, moved, mated, and even thought – all in the hopes of developing a scientific solution to the problem, as opposed to wholesale slaughter. Helping Dirk head up the program at Tartarus had been the perfect opportunity for her. It had been his mom's idea, and a damn good one at that.

Complications notwithstanding . . .

"By the way, I saw your appearance on *Pliosaur Wars*," he mentioned. "You looked good. I like the dye job. And that you stuck to your guns."

"Thanks," Stacy said, leaning back. Her amber-colored Asian eyes flashed merrily against a background of soft caramel-colored skin, all framed by a veritable lion's mane of curly blonde hair.

As Stacy straightened up, she intertwined her hands over her head, uttering a moan-like grunt as she stretched, before switching to gyrating at the waist. As her movements "accidentally" showed off her full breasts and the curvature of her toned backside, Dirk swallowed and looked up, focusing on watching the LED elevator floor numbers as they counted down.

Stacy studied him. "So, you must be excited about her arrival, yes?"

Dirk's confused expression turned contemplative. "Oh, you mean the specimen. Absolutely." He turned to her. "You know she's gravid, right?"

"Yes, I saw the preliminary," she said. Her resultant scoff was tail-gated by a frown. "I assume that means we're aborting the entire clutch."

"Probably, but there's bigger news."

"What's that?"

"Her mate managed to put a hit on the *Antrodemus*," Dirk said. "No casualties, thank God, but Garm's guys got some good intel before he got away. He's huge, a giant. We think--"

Stacy's eyes lit up. "It's *Typhon*?"

"The prenatal should confirm it." Beneath his lips, Dirk's tongue ran over his teeth. "If it does, you can bet the farm Grayson's going to mount an immediate expedition to hunt him down. It'll be priority one."

Dirk felt the elevator come to a stop and readied himself.

"Tell me something," Stacy said, standing in his way. "Just out of curiosity, did your mother approve of me?"

His jaw hung like a broken marionette's. "What kind of question is that? After your father was killed she took care of you, your housing, clothes, education, even gave you a piece of her company. She looked after you like you were her own. You know that."

Stacy's eyes softened but her jaw remained taut. "Yes. But I didn't ask you that. I want to know if she *liked* me."

"She *loved* you. With all her heart."

Stacy swallowed and her eyes closed tight, their lids cracking only after she heard the elevator door hiss open behind her. "Well, at least *one* of you did," she muttered, turning on her heel and leaving him standing there.

"Stace . . ."

———

Still shaking his head, Dirk caught up to Stacy – a surprisingly hard thing to do, considering his legs were longer. He speed-walked beside her, pretending the uncomfortable silence was intentional. As they wound their way past the men and machines decorating the receiving dock, he wondered for the umpteenth time if he'd made a mistake ending their relationship. He certainly missed the sex; six months of abstinence was a mighty long time. And it was obvious she was far from over things.

As he spotted Garm towering over a uniformed CDF officer and a second, unfamiliar, woman, he ordered his recriminations into a holding pattern and walked briskly toward them.

"Dr. Derek Braddock," he said to the middle-aged brunette, extending his hand. A quick glance confirmed no name tag on her lab coat.

"Dr. Kimberly Bane," she replied, giving him a surprisingly firm handshake. "I'm your new epidemiologist. And you're Amara's other boy," she added before he could respond. Her face turned grave. "I was very sorry to hear of your loss."

"Turns out she knew mom." Garm's handsome face inclined toward Bane and he grinned amiably. "Good to see you, little brother,"

Dirk's expression flip-flopped as his eyes went back and forth. He finally settled on nodding. "Thank you, Dr. Bane. Oh, uh . . . this is Dr. Stacy Daniels, our chief neural surgeon and behavioral specialist. She'll be assisting with the new specimen."

"Nice to meet you," Stacy said, smiling warmly as she stepped forward and shook hands. "I'm looking forward to working with you."

"Thanks, same here," Bane replied

Stacy looked up at Garm and smiled. "Glad you made it back safe and sound, big guy."

Garm smiled back. "One does what one can."

Satisfied that the pleasantries were out of the way, Stacy turned businesslike. "Lieutenant McEwan, is everything prepped?"

McEwan stood at attention. "Yes, doctor. We are at 100%. It should be smooth sailing."

Dirk turned to Bane. "How was your trip, doctor?"

The epidemiologist's eyes widened. "I wouldn't use the term 'smooth sailing,' that's for sure," she said. "Your brother and his crew are a unique bunch, let me tell you."

Dirk grinned. "So I've been told."

"Actually, if I'm being brutally honest, he saved all our lives," Bane acknowledged. "And mine, one more time, right over there." She pointed across at the row of pliosaur tanks then exhaled heavily. "Frankly, I've had enough near-death experiences in the last forty-eight hours to last me the rest of my life."

"I'm sorry to hear that," Dirk offered. "They did toss you into the deep end."

"The 'deep end'?" Bane ran her fingers through her hair and scoffed. "Let me tell you something, I was *not* this gray when the trip started."

"We'll get you settled in as quickly as possible," Dirk said. "And please accept my apologies."

"It's not your apology that I want, Derek," Bane announced. "I'd like to speak to our mutual employer, your boss."

Garm's eyes shifted and his face split into a huge grin. "Speak of the devil," he said, clicking his tongue at one of the facility's rugged ATVs as it barreled toward them. "Here comes your chance, doc."

As the transport came to a stop twenty-five yards away and its passengers disembarked, Dirk espied Dr. Grayson, accompanied by a high-ranking naval type. From his file photo, he recognized him as Rear Admiral Callahan. The driver was a heavily armed marine, and a second one, practically his twin, hovered around the admiral like his shadow.

Dirk's smile flatlined when he saw Tartarus Security Chief Dwyer and Jamal White, Dwyer's second in command, flanking Dr. Grayson. He'd researched White just the other day. He was a disgraced former

NYPD officer who'd transformed himself into an in-house drug czar. Once his superiors made the mistake of putting him in charge of the evidence locker, he started "redistributing" a good portion of the heroin and crack that came in. He was "giving back to the community," as he said during his trial. White was dangerous – a one-time Golden Gloves light-heavyweight contender – and smart too. But not smart enough to not get caught.

Dwyer was the one who made Dirk nervous. At six-foot-five and weighing at least 280, he was a mean-tempered bastard. But it wasn't his size that gave the young scientist pause. Nor was it his flat, simian-like face or his perpetually bloodshot eyes – eyes that, when he thought Dirk wasn't looking, tossed unfriendly glances his way. It wasn't even the crescent-shaped scar on his lower lip. It was the fact that there was nothing about him in their files. Not even the encrypted ones reserved for Officers of the Company, like himself. It was like Dwyer sprang up out of a bottle or something

Dirk put his misgivings about the man on hold as Grayson and the admiral headed his way. As they drew closer, he fought down a smirk. Despite the old man's age and frailty, the assorted handlers and technicians milling about the receiving dock parted like the Red Sea as he and his entourage approached.

Geez, you'd think he was dangerous . . .

Ten yards out, both the admiral's and Grayson's security personnel hung back and assumed at-ease poses. Dirk played politician and signaled Dr. Bane to be patient, while Stacy headed straight for their employer. A moment later, he and Garm followed in her footsteps.

"We're all set, Dr. Grayson," Stacy said. She pulled her hair to one side and adjusted an ear-mike she was wearing. "*Antrodemus* is right outside the Vault, waiting on us."

"Excellent," Grayson said. He extended his arms out to the sides in an attempt at relieving stiffness and glanced around approvingly. "It's an exciting day." He smiled as he spotted Dirk and Garm. "Hello boys, it's--" he hesitated, then touched his temple as if realizing he'd forgotten something. "Good God, where are my manners? This is--"

"Rear Admiral Ward Callahan," the naval officer replied, stepping quickly forward. He was heavyset, with intense eyes and a pronounced salt-and-pepper mustache. "I'm Admiral Warminster's replacement and head of the Navy's bio-weapons division." He extended a paw-like hand to Stacy first. "Dr. Daniels, I've seen your file. Your credentials are most impressive. And Dr. Braddock," he nodded at Dirk, "It's a privilege to finally make your acquaintance. As you both know, the Navy needs two top-notch replacements. I'm looking forward to seeing your inventory."

Dirk's smile took a vacation when Callahan didn't bother waiting for his reply and headed straight for Garm. "Now, *here's* a guy that needs no introduction." He took Garm's hand with both of his, pumping it vigorously while grinning like a well-fed hyena. "Garm 'The Gate' Braddock: terror of the heavyweight division. I am a huge fan – seen every one of your fights – many of them live."

"Nice to meet you, too, Admiral," Garm said matter-of-factly. "But my boxing days are behind me. That was a long time ago."

"A long time ago?" Callahan echoed. "You know, I'll never understand why you walked away from it. You scored some of the most exciting knockouts in the history of pugilism! I was ringside when you beat the tar out of that seven-foot Siberian guy, what the hell was his name?"

"Ivan Volkov," Garm said quietly.

"Yeah, that's him." Callahan said, his eyes lighting up. "They called him '*The Wolf*,' or some such nonsense." He scoffed. "More like '*The Elephant*.' He kept backing you up against the ropes and laying on you, trying to use his 365 pounds to wear you down while he took breaks. You remember that?"

"Yes . . ."

Callahan's hands clenched and he became animated. "I saw your face in round five as he tried draping those big arms over your shoulders for the tenth time. Man, you were *pissed*. You timed him on the way in, then twisted to the side and dropped down. A second later . . . *boom!* Huge uppercut! Guy's arm practically came out of the socket."

Garm glanced from face to face, obviously uncomfortable with the attention.

"It was all over after that," Callahan said, breathing hard and holding his considerable stomach. "You chopped him down like a Christmas tree."

Garm grinned mirthlessly. "Like I said, a long time ago."

Callahan reached over and gave him a playful tap on the shoulder. "Yeah, right; look at you, still in ring-shape." He put up his hands in an old-school boxing pose, pretending he wanted to spar. "Boy, I'd hate to mess with you!"

Garm played along, his hands palms-out in a placating gesture. But Dirk wasn't fooled. His brother's smile never dipped and his eyes never left Callahan's face, but he could tell he'd already sized up his "man" like an X-ray machine. Callahan's obesity, his clumsiness, as well as the slight limp he exhibited from a bad knee and arthritic hip, had all been recorded in an instant.

Dirk sighed. Garm was just like their father. He was and always would be a fighter. If you were his enemy, look out. But if you were his friend, he could always be counted on: a rock people clung to when disaster struck.

That was Garm, a true guardian. And people loved him for it.

As Callahan stopped to catch his breath, he put a hand on Garm's shoulder and lowered his voice. "I heard about your parents. Your mom's death was a tragedy. Your dad's too. I met him years ago, back when I was heading up the parade for that captive *Kronosaurus.* You know, the one they put on display in *Oceanus.*" He shook his head. "He was a good man, your father."

"Jake Braddock was a great man," Dr. Grayson inserted. "And he left a legacy behind, beyond that of even his amazing sons. Because of his help, our researchers were able to develop the antibodies that kept pliosaur bacteria-borne ailments from evolving into a plague of biblical proportions."

Dirk cleared his throat. "Speaking of which . . ." Using eye movements, he indicated Dr. Bane, who stood beside Lieutenant McEwan with her arms folded. "Our new epidemiologist would like a word. I believe she feels she was misinformed about a few things."

"Of course," Grayson said, "In due time." He turned to Garm and smiled warmly as he reached up and clapped him on one rock-hard shoulder. "I saw the attack footage, son. Your tactics were very impressive. I'm relieved you made it back safely, you and your team. I don't know what this place would be like if we lost you."

Garm shrugged. "It wasn't my time."

"Indeed. So, why did you pass on the Gen-1?"

"With all due respect, Dr. Grayson, I'm not a dog catcher."

"Of course, you're not. But what about the prize?"

"You of all people should know money is not an object to me."

Grayson studied him. "Not that prize, son. I'm talking about the competition between you and *Antrodemus*. You know you don't like to lose."

Garm regarded him from his great height. "Everyone loses. Sooner or later."

"That's what Volkov said," Callahan spouted with a snicker.

Suddenly, a loud claxon pealed across the docks and a bright red strobe light lit up over the thirty-foot portion of the Vault's doors that was visible above the waterline. All conversation on the receiving platform abruptly ceased.

Stacy touched her earpiece. "We're a go," she said. "Incoming."

"Okay, people; it's showtime," Dirk said. He nodded to Stacy, who moved a few steps back and started talking into her ear-mike. A moment later, there was a low rumbling sound and the concrete under everyone's feet began to pulse. In the distance, the water around the Vault's doors churned like an unwatched pot. A black vertical line appeared in the center of their seamless surfaces as the armored portals slowly opened.

"Well, then," Dr. Grayson said, shooting Garm an indecipherable look. "Let's get ready to see the latest addition to our family. And to congratulate our incoming victors."

NINE

Trailing fragments of skin and blubber, the Ancient cruised lazily at a depth of four hundred feet. Like a dark-hued barrage balloon, his immense body hugged the bluish-gray twilight layer that existed between the ocean's sunlit phototropic zone and the forever blackness of the deep.

The great beast yawned, his cavernous jaws spreading wide enough to swallow a hippopotamus. He shifted his girder-like mandibles from side to side, easing the steely adductor muscles that ran through the six-foot temporal openings in his skull, and provided him with the world's most powerful bite. There was an explosive burst of bubbles a hundred yards away, as the revelation of his ridged fangs sent a prowling swordfish swimming for its life. The Ancient ignored the frightened broadbill. His stomach was stretched to the point of bursting from nearly twenty tons of whale meat and blubber.

Appropriating the still-warm blue whale carcass from a trio of smaller males had been all too easy. The rival bulls detected his presence from five hundred yards off by the powerful pressure wave that preceded him. He'd made no pretense at stealth and flew straight at them like a nuclear submarine with teeth. It was an intimidation tactic, pure and simple. There was no need to kill others of his kind. One sonar scan on their part was all it took for the first two to relinquish their kill. The last one was a bit more tenacious, and required the addition of a thunderous grunt from his monstrous jaws before it, too, tucked tail and fled.

Sensing the contentment only a full belly can bring, Lethargy flirted with the old *Kronosaurus*, running her claws in rake-like caresses along his scar-covered back. He uttered the pliosaur's version of a sigh as his deep-set eyes were drawn to the light-dappled waters above. He would have enjoyed basking on the surface; the sun's warmth would ease his aches and speed his digestion, but the waters he traversed were too dangerous to risk lying in plain sight. This far from shore, the smaller entities the bipedal warm-bloods infested were few and far between. But the larger ones were still present, as were the noisy flying things that spewed death from the clouds.

Suddenly, the Ancient cocked his head to one side and began to draw large quantities of seawater into his mouth, funneling it through the scoop-shaped passages in his palate. He recognized the scent in an instant. Not far from his current position, there was blood in the water.

It was fresh, mammalian blood . . . biped blood.

The wrinkled skin around the great bull's eyes contracted as the sclerotic ring that enabled his kind to focus underwater compressed inward. He swept the area, but saw nothing but fish and a few drifting fragments of wood. His jaws closed tightly to reduce drag and he began to accelerate, arcing through a wide swath of water. The blood trail was diffused over a large area and he could not pinpoint the source.

Curiosity made way for frustration and, after a moment's deliberation, his throat muscles started to ripple. He began emitting a powerful cone of sonar that blanketed the surrounding sea. Moving his head back and forth, he spun his body clockwise with powerful flicks from his boat-sized flippers. The deep, ratcheting clicks he produced reverberated in the distance.

A minute later, he found what he'd been searching for. Sitting on the seabed some five miles away, near the drop-off of a ten-mile long crevasse, was the blood source.

The need to replenish his air was upon him, and with a power stroke that would have moved a destroyer, the Ancient made for the surface. He backstroked just before breaching so he remained hidden, allowing only the top of his snout to break the surface. Like a geyser, he spouted twin columns of water vapor that blasted thirty feet into the air before inhaling, slowly and deeply. Moments later, the watertight flaps that sealed his yard-long nostrils closed tight and he sounded.

Faster and faster he descended, ignoring the steadily increasing water pressure, his eyes glittering like polished garnets as daylight's grip inevitably failed. Within seconds, he reached the seafloor, one thousand feet down. There in the darkness, draped across a coral-coated outcropping, was the wreck of a large wooden ship.

The old bull studied what remained of the once proud vessel. Its hull was broken amidships. The gunnels were mashed down and the deck boards cracked and split, as was the ship's oaken spine. Her masts were all but gone. Only two-thirds of one remained: a splintered spire, grasping in vain at the lingering daylight, far above.

As the Ancient scanned the wreck with his sound sight, his glittering orbs narrowed. He remembered something from many seasons past, back when there were many such ships. Back when . . .

Suddenly, the water around him seemed to waver and the great creature snorted loudly in alarm. His vision began to blur and he blinked repeatedly, scrunching his deep-set eyes tightly closed in an effort to bring things back into focus.

When he reopened them, it was two centuries ago, shortly after the escape that nearly cost him his life and left his scaly hide scarred for what remained of it. He was a young bull, traversing a stretch of sea between the coast of Africa and some tiny island. He'd been smaller then – perhaps two-thirds the size he was now – but still an apex predator with few natural enemies.

A thousand yards away, he detected the presence of a large life form traversing his newly-claimed territory and moved to investigate. As he drew near, he scanned the intruder to determine whether it was potential prey or a rival carnivore.

The adolescent bull grew perplexed. The newcomer was quite large, at least twice his size, yet despite moving ponderously along the surface, it had no visible means of propelling itself. It wasn't a gigantic turtle, as he'd assumed at first, nor was it one of his kind; in fact, it had no flippers at all. It also had no tailfin or flukes, just a small ventral fin set far back, so it wasn't a shark or one of the big warm-bloods he'd recently hunted. Still, it changed direction under its own power, and from the constant thrumming and creaking calls it gave off, it was definitely alive.

Filled with curiosity, the bull sounded and cruised directly under the mysterious intruder, scanning it repeatedly with echolocation clicks and scenting the water around it. His lips wrinkled up and he snorted irritably. The creature had a large, hardened belly and gave off a repulsive odor. If it was edible, it would undoubtedly make for a distasteful meal.

Eventually, the young bull decided to examine the intruder from above. Surfacing a hundred yards away, he stuck his scaly head up out of the water and eyed it. It was enormous – even bigger above the surface than below. Its hide was a dull brown color, with a large white band running along its length, and black pock marks marring its flanks. Along its dorsal was a series of tall, spike-like fins that soared straight up, and extending behind them were billowing white membranes, like the sails of a gigantic billfish.

The bull moved closer, circling the entity like a hungry shark as he waited to see what it would do. As he drew to within forty yards, it made no move against him, either defensively or offensively, but rather maintained its speed and direction.

After nearly twenty minutes of the game, the pliosaur began to grow bored. He was about to submerge, when he noticed something strange about the creaking entity. It was apparently suffering from some sort of parasitic infestation. Atop its dorsal he spotted dozens of small bipedal creatures, covered with loose-fitting skin. They skittered about it with impunity, their actions so brazen the bull would have assumed they were its offspring, were it not for the obvious differences between them.

Finally, the young bull wearied of the intruder and prepared to sound. As he filled his lungs, there was a bright orange flash and a sound reminiscent of thunder. A moment later, the water thirty feet to his right exploded and a powerful concussive force washed over him. He was uninjured, but recoiled in alarm. More thunderclaps followed and the sea around him began to erupt as dark-colored objects crashed into it. One eventually came so close it grazed him, and the bull realized what was happening. The two-legged leeches scurrying atop the creature's broad back were hurling its rock-hard feces at him.

Infuriated, he spread his huge jaws wide, baring his lethal fangs and hissing menacingly at both the intruder and the bipeds it hosted. A second later, he sounded. Using great sweeps of his four flippers, he departed as quickly as he'd come.

The Ancient's gnarled head shook violently as he chased away the unpleasant memory and returned to the present. He studied the nearby shipwreck, his eyes narrowing. What piqued his reptilian curiosity was that, despite the floating log they rode upon having been completely destroyed, and all the blood that was diffused into the water, there were no survivors huddled together on the surface. Nor were there any bodies below it.

The old bull rose several hundred feet in the water column, his sound sight scanning the shattered remains of the sailing ship one last time. Still unsatisfied, he swung his gnarled head and swept the surrounding area, his powerful sonar bursts punching away at the rocky ravines that gave the seafloor its unique topography and bouncing back. Other than the resident sea life and the yawning blackness of the barren crevasse to his left, there was nothing.

It was time to depart.

Suddenly, the Ancient paused, his barnacle-tipped fins undulating against the current as he hovered in place. His nostrils flared and he sucked more water into his mouth. There was another scent mixed in with the intoxicating flavor of diluted mammal blood. It was something even he was unfamiliar with. Whatever it was, the scent was strong. It seemed to trigger some instinctive memory in the remote recesses of his brain. It represented something very old, something primeval . . .

The old bull grunted in annoyance when the deeply submerged recollection refused to reveal itself. He felt the need to surface and, with a final shake of his limousine-sized head, ascended, the rhythmic strokes of his flippers powering him toward the waiting air.

Far below, huddled together in the eternal darkness, the ghosts of the *Rorqual* watched him go.

———

"Here she comes!" someone shouted excitedly. As Dirk looked around at the adrenalized faces of the Tartarus receiving crew, he realized the rush brought on by bringing in a rogue pliosaur never waned. Especially if you were intrigued by morbidity, he mused. After all, statistically-speaking, nearly 30% of their captures resulted in at least one dockside fatality.

Five hundred feet ahead, the dark waters between the Vault's wide-open doors and the waiting channel churned violently. There was a watery explosion, accompanied by a chorus of gasps, as *Antrodemus* broke the surface of the canal. Rising up like some scarlet-skinned behemoth, the 132-foot, 440-ton war machine streamed torrents of seawater that gushed down her armored sides and spattered the nearby edges of the receiving dock. She was a mighty warrior, wounded in battle, but returning home triumphant.

And adorning her nose was Death.

Dirk's chest rose and fell as he took in the sight of the slumbering behemoth chained across the ORION-class sub's prow. Even from this distance, he could make out the beads of brine that formed like salty dewdrops on the exposed portions of the Gen-1's armored skin. Coated with heavily overlapped, iron-hard scales, her hide was a deep azure in color with pale stripes, fading to an off-white underside. Her massive, wedge-shaped head was positioned portside, and by Dirk's estimate, measured nearly seventeen feet in length. Even more impressive were her armor-piercing teeth: a gleaming arsenal of ivory, protruding out from under her thick-scaled lips.

One more man-eater to deal with, Dirk thought, shaking his head. He sighed. At least it also meant one less rapacious predator swimming around out there.

To his right, he saw Stacy Daniels and Lieutenant McEwan on their radios, communicating with the technicians that controlled the winch assembly poised one hundred feet overhead. A team of inspectors wearing hazmat suits waited at the dock's edge, while Tartarus's private security worked to keep everyone else at a respectable distance.

"She's a beauty," Dr. Grayson announced to no one in particular. He and Admiral Callahan had taken up position a few feet to Dirk's left. Garm, vigilant as always, remained close by. Dirk wondered if his big brother ever got tired of watching his back.

"She is indeed, sir," Dirk replied. "Definitely a healthy, robust Gen-1 female." He turned to Callahan. "What do you think?"

"Hell, yeah," the stocky naval man snorted. "She'll do nicely. But in case you've forgotten, I need two."

"Relax, Ward," Grayson said. "Have I let you down yet?"

"No, Eric. You have not."

Dirk took a step forward, gesturing for Stacy to join him. Together, they watched as *Antrodemus* chugged steadily forward, then veered

KRONOS RISING: KRAKEN (VOLUME 1)

left before entering the receiving dock proper. As she reduced speed, a chorus of loud grunts and splashes began emanating from the pliosaur tanks across the way. The aquarium occupants had all gathered against their Celazole walls and were eyeing the unconscious new arrival. A few had their heads pressed against the clear polycarbonate, while others spouted noisily. As the sub moved closer, two of the largest breached and then rolled on their sides. They started smacking the surface of the water with their huge pectoral and pelvic fins, sending prodigious splashes of water spraying up and over the sides of their enclosures and making a thunderous racket that echoed throughout the cavernous, dome-shaped chamber.

"What's with them?" Callahan inquired.

"It's a social thing," Stacy said, waving off the pliosaur's antics. "Sort of like what humpbacks do, except instead of 'hello' it's their way of saying, 'I'm big and dangerous and this is my territory, so don't fuck with me.'"

"Dr. Daniels . . . language, please." Grayson admonished.

Stacy pursed her lips and glanced at the floor. "Sorry, sir."

Suddenly, the concrete under everyone's feet began to vibrate and there was a tremendous gurgling sound, punctuated by a watery rumble as *Antrodemus*'s maneuvering thrusters fired hard in reverse and brought the sub to a stop. They fired several more bubbling bursts, stabilizing her. Then a loud hum resonated across the dock as the sub's hydraulic gangplanks extended out from her sides like thick metal oars, mating her to the landing and locking the big pliosaur killer in place. Ten-foot geysers of steam shot out noisily from several points on her hull. Then she went silent.

"Okay, people," Stacy yelled through cupped hands. "Security, please keep everyone back, including the inspection team. Let's make sure this little lady's still in dreamland before anyone gets close."

"You heard the doctor," Dirk directed. He moved toward the creature's scar-streaked snout with Grayson, Callahan, and Garm at his heels, and Dwyer and one of the admiral's aides not far behind. "Keep your distance, people," Dirk warned. As he got to within ten feet, he gestured for Stacy to join him and for everyone else to stay put.

Like church mice, they approached the sleeping *Kronosaurus*. Its immense head, as large as an old-fashioned Cadillac, was cocked at a forty-five-degree angle and suspended a few feet above the dock. As they got close enough to touch it, Dirk could feel his heart trying to crawl up into his throat. It was terrifying, being this close to one of the world's deadliest predators. Exhilarating, but terrifying.

"Holy fucking shit," Callahan muttered. "Man, never been this close to one before. And a wild, unwired one at that." He took a couple of sniffs. "Jesus, what's that stench? Smells like a crocodile farm mixed with rotting meat."

"Probably food particles stuck between her teeth," Dirk said. "We'll deal with that." He glanced at Stacy as she moved beside him. "Well, what do you think?"

"Oh, yeah . . ." she said, whistling excitedly. She held her arms far apart and eyed the unconscious behemoth's immense girth. "She's a big, fat preggo. The test results should be very revealing."

Grayson cleared his throat. "Is the lift ready?"

Stacy touched her earpiece and then signaled to McEwan. "Just about, sir." She eyed the huge hydraulic assembly suspended overhead. Its motor was already running, a powerful system of turbines and hydraulics that, given time, could raise a Union Pacific *Big Boy* locomotive.

Callahan whistled as he continued eying their prize. "Man, look at the battle scars on her . . . and the teeth! That is one wicked-looking bitch."

In Dirk's head, the term "wicked-looking bitch" brought something altogether different to mind. Or rather, some*one*.

With a loud slamming of *Antrodemus*'s heavy sail door, Captain Natalya Dragunova emerged with her crew. She mouthed a curse as she took in the damage to her sub and an irritable look came over her. A moment later, her booted feet hit the landing and she forced her way past the assorted accountants attempting to shove tablets in her direction.

Dismissing her weary crew with the wave of a hand, Dragunova headed straight toward Dirk.

Make that stalked toward him.

If Dirk thought being close to a wild *Kronoscurus imperator* had his heart racing before, it was in overdrive now. Standing six-foot-two and packing 195 pounds of toned muscle on her voluptuous frame, the tawny-haired Amazon heading his way looked more like a hungry lioness than a human being.

KRONOS RISING: KRAKEN (VOLUME 1)

"Easy, there, big boy . . ." Stacy whispered in his ear.

Dirk blinked as if he'd come out of a trance. "W-what?"

Before he could say another word, Dragunova was right on top of him.

"Captain Natalya Dragunova, reporting," she said to Grayson. Her cantaloupe-sized breasts strained her uniform shirt as she pulled her shoulders back and shot the CEO a salute. "Meeshun accomplished, sir."

"Well done, captain," Grayson replied. He looked up at her and smiled.

"Full meeshun report," Dragunova said, handing him a tablet. She gave Garm a nod of professional courtesy, then turned to Dirk as if just noticing him. Her gray eyes seemed to betray some sort of inner amusement and she grinned. "Hello, Doctor Derek Braddock. Ees good to see you again."

Dirk worked hard at remembering how to breathe. For some reason, the way his name rolled off Dragunova's tongue in that thick Russian accent of hers, made it seem as if everyone else had been saying it wrong for his whole life.

"It's good to see you too, Captain," Dirk said, inhaling slowly. It was amazing; even with more than 100 tons of foul-smelling reptile ten feet away, all his nose could detect was her scent. It was damn weird, since as far as he knew the woman never wore perfume. "I've got a repair crew ready to analyze the damage to *Antrodemus*. Just as soon as we've gotten the specimen quarantined."

Dragunova gave the captive pliosaur a sympathetic look. "Da, da. Poor theeng. She ees exhausted." Before anyone could stop her, she rested her hand on the tip of the sleeping beast's snout. There was a collective gasp and even Garm looked shocked.

Dirk felt like he was going to faint.

Is she crazy? Why not just poke a sleeping dragon with a stick?

"Careful there, little lady," Callahan advised. "That's Navy property. Wouldn't want to get sued if that big evil bitch wakes up and makes a meal outta you."

"'Little lady,' eh?" Dragunova's lips pulled back from her teeth in what resembled a smile, but her eyes were storm clouds. She bent at the waist and ran her fingertips over the wet scales coating the pliosaur's colossal head. "You know, *admiral*, you're right. She ees a beeg, evil beetch, and I should know. But, like most of us beeg, evil beetches, when we sleep we look like angels, da?"

Callahan looked confused. "Uh, right."

"Mud k." Dragunova teased the downturned tip of one of the *Kronosaurus*'s Bowie-knife-sized fangs with her finger before straightening up. She flashed Callahan a smile. "Oh, and admiral; kees my beeg, Russian ass."

Dirk's eyes became ostrich eggs and he couldn't move, let alone speak.

For his part, Callahan turned stroke-red and looked like he was about to explode.

"As outspoken as ever, *Captain* Dragunova," Grayson said, grinning and putting a hand on the admiral's forearm before things got out of hand. He leaned toward Dirk and whispered. "'Woman was God's *second* mistake,' my boy."

"*Beyond Good and Evil?*" Dirk hazarded.

"Gotcha." Grayson winked. "*The Antichrist.*"

Dirk smirked. "Captain Dragunova, if you wouldn't mind?" he indicated the waiting Hazmat team.

"Of course not," she replied, sauntering a few steps back.

The four-man Hazmat crew tiptoed forward as if they were traversing a minefield. Once they were in position, three of them began sweeping their noisy scanning wands over whatever portions of the *Kronosaurus imperator* they could reach, while the fourth ran a laser scanner over its exposed surfaces.

Once the scanning was complete, the first three crew members moved back, while the fourth approached the slumbering creature with a heavy pair of bolt cutters. Leaning cautiously over the edge of the dock, he reached down and cut the shiny cable holding it to the sub's labium with a series of loud snips.

As soon as the cable was removed, the Hazmat team's leader approached Dirk, Stacy, and Grayson, and removed his cumbersome headgear. He was middle-aged and stocky, his shaved head and face coated with a fine sheen of sweat.

"No radiation," he said, shaking off his gloves and wiping away some of the perspiration. "Some bruising and scrapes, but no serious external injuries that I can detect. There are a few of those skin parasites we've been seeing lately, so watch yourselves." He winked and signaled his team. Gathering their gear, they trudged off.

Dirk shook his head. "Dr. Daniels, how are her stats?"

Stacy's amber eyes swept her tablet. "Vitals look good. Pulse and heart rate are within acceptable brumation norms and I don't see any spikes that would indicate any 'bad dreams', as was reported." She shot Dragunova a look. "I think she's good to go."

"Okay," Dirk said. He turned to McEwan. "Make sure you have a full load of sedative ready, just in case."

The lieutenant nodded and retrieved a gray rifle case she had resting nearby. Inside was a black and chrome-colored tranquilizer gun that looked big enough to take down a full-grown *Argentinosaurus*. As she checked the bulky weapon, Dirk signaled to Stacy. "Let's raise her."

Stacy touched her ear-mike and started relaying instructions. Moments later, the hovering seventy-foot lift assembly platform began to slide down its suspension bridge cables, accompanied by a deep hum. As it dropped, its twenty-foot insulated steel pincers swung open – a trio of lobster claws, eager to seize.

Callahan looked up at the slow-moving hoist and grunted irritably. "Why don't you just use the sub's robotic arm to lift the damn critter out of the water? Wouldn't that be easier? I mean, it's already sitting on top of it."

"Too much mass at extension, admiral," Dirk responded matter-of-factly, then glanced up at the approaching lift assembly. "This animal weighs over one hundred tons. In the water, we're talking neutral buoyancy; the sub's manipulator can handle it. But in the air . . ." he scoffed. "We'd blow the actuators for sure."

Dirk and the rest of the team took a step back as the lift's insulated pincers gaped wide and then started to close around the pliosaur's girthy neck, chest and hip regions. The oversized hydraulics gave off a high-pitched thrum as they methodically tightened. Dirk glanced at Stacy, who was studying the hoist readings on her tablet. A series of green lights appeared across the top of her screen and she gave him a nod.

Dirk took a deep breath. *So far so good . . .* His eyes sought and found the lift operators, high above, and he signaled them.

Like steely serpents, the partially lax lift cables went rigid and then reversed. A deep revving sound echoed across the receiving dock. Slowly but steadily, the lift exerted pressure, its powerful grippers digging into the pliosaur's thick skin as the saurian's dead weight began to bear down. Then, inch by inch, and streaming rivulets of seawater, it was hoisted up out of the canal. Relieved of the incredible pressure, the *Antrodemus*'s robotic arm let out a metallic wrench of relief and the sub's forty-six-foot-wide bow rose a full two feet.

Dirk's eyes expanded as the *Kronosaurus* cow was carried up and over the concrete and steel lip of the docking canal, moving across to the receiving platform, proper. The tips of its huge fins barely cleared the floor, and streams of saltwater mixed with seaweed cascaded down from its glistening body, drenching the gritty gray concrete below. Denied the water's supportive embrace, the pliosaur's bloated belly and throat folds drooped almost to the floor.

Dirk shuddered involuntarily. Seeing the great creature suspended out of its element like some giant rag doll was unsettling.

As the lift stopped, leaving its burden suspended beside the nearby holding tank, Stacy moved next to Dirk. Her boot heels clicked on the concrete as they walked together. "Vitals are steady and I've got her weight." She touched a key on her tablet. "152.7 tons . . . estimate postpartum around 138."

Callahan whistled as he caught up to them. "That is one serious lizard." Disregarding the creaking sounds the hoist was giving off, he extended a hand toward the pliosaur's armored skin. His alarmed aide spotted the move and rushed over, grabbing the stocky admiral by the shoulder.

"I'm sorry, sir. That could be dangerous," the big marine cautioned.

Callahan wore an annoyed look. He turned to Stacy. "Doctor Daniels?"

Stacy shrugged. "According to our bio-readouts, she's out cold. As long as you don't inflict any bodily harm, she should stay that way. At least until the Cronavrol wears off."

"See? Relax, Sanders," Callahan remarked. He reached up and tapped the pliosaur's flank with a gnarled fingertip. "Man, they weren't kidding when they said these things are resistant to small arms fire. It's like stone!" he gestured to his bodyguard. "Feel this." He turned to Dirk. "Hey, doc. Just how tough is the hide on one of these critters?"

Dirk's lips compressed as he did some quick mental calculations. "On a specimen this size, small arms would be useless." He stepped forward, taking care to avoid the shallow pools of seawater that collected around the still-dripping saurian. "Fifty caliber BMG and under won't even penetrate its epidermis, let along cause internal trauma."

"That's why we go with the big guns!" Callahan guffawed. As Dirk conferred with Stacy and Grayson, the admiral and his aide wandered around the slumbering *Kronosaurus imperator,* with Callahan poking and prodding.

Dirk shook his head. "Okay, let's get her sedated and then--"

"Hey, what's all this milky-white shit dripping out from under this thing's fins?" Callahan shouted. "Is it sick?"

Dirk sighed. "No. It's just a stress hormone," he shouted back over his shoulder. "They secrete it when they're injured or traumatized." He lowered his voice as he turned back to Stacy and Grayson. "Which means we better get moving."

Dirk glanced back, fearful of what trouble the admiral might cause, but then relaxed when he spotted Garm hovering nearby.

"Hey, Gate," Callahan said, ducking under one of the pliosaur's rowboat-sized flippers. "Can you imagine this little lady laying on you in the ring? Now *that* would tire a guy out!"

Garm grinned humorlessly. He spotted Sanders, scratching at his crew-cut while studying something on the creature's neck. The battle-hardened sub commander watched in amusement as the marine reached over and poked a finger at one of its hand-sized scales. He jabbed it harder, then jumped back when it moved. "Fuck!" He turned with fearful eyes. "What the hell is that?"

Garm moved a step closer. The "scale" Sanders had dislocated began to shift from side to side. There was a wet, squishy sound as it settled back in place.

"That's a lizard louse," Garm said, chuckling. "A parasitical isopod. They're translucent, so they tend to match not only the shape, but the color of the scales. They latch onto a host and use their sharp mouthparts to bore through the skin between the scales so they can drink blood."

Sanders shuddered. "That is fucking nasty."

"Yeah. Oh, and make sure you don't get one on you," Garm warned. He caught Callahan's eye and winked. "On human males, they go straight for the genitals and embed themselves in the scrotum. You have to tear them out with vice grips!"

As Callahan laughed uproariously, Garm turned to check on Dirk. Unbeknownst to him, behind his back, Sanders whipped out a black-bladed combat knife and started prying away at the louse. When the tenacious parasite hunkered down and refused to be dislodged, he slid his blade under it and started sawing. Seconds later, the sea louse fell away, leaving an exposed section of raw skin from which blood began to seep.

Sanders spat in disgust as he squashed the squirming isopod under his boot. Then he wiped his blade clean on his sleeve and sheathed it, not noticing the pliosaur's ruby eye opening directly behind him. The football-sized eyeball rolled dazedly in its socket, its oval-shaped black center unfocused and dilated. Then it stabilized, its pupil going perpendicular and contracting into a tight slit.

A shrill beep emanating from Stacy's tablet caused all conversation to stop. Everyone froze . . . everyone, except Garm. His head whipped around just in time to see the beast come to life. At first, its blood-colored orb was focused on Sanders. But as Callahan moved closer, it turned its attention to him. The admiral was only ten feet away with his back turned.

Dirk watched in slow-motion horror as the pliosaur's huge neck muscles contracted like steel cables beneath its thick skin. It's formerly limp head raised and began to arc to the left, and a creaking sound signaled it testing the tensile strength of the pincers restraining it.

A second later, hell's gates were torn asunder.

With a frightful hiss, the *Kronosaurus* whipped its huge head to the right, its slavering jaws gaping wide. Dirk froze, watching what came next in horror. Against a backdrop of alarmed cries, his brother Garm made his move. Powerful legs pumping, he dove completely under the beast's wedge-shaped mandible, clearing it by inches, and tackled Callahan like a linebacker. The admiral's face was a Kabuki mask of astonishment. The impact of Garm's 245 pounds sent both men flying. They skidded into the shallow pool of water under the creature's huge belly, causing it to miss them completely and overshoot its mark.

And grab Sanders instead.

The hapless marine let out a blood-curdling shriek as he was scooped off the floor and tossed into a prehistoric meat grinder. Gleaming ivory fangs the size of a man's forearm sank into his chest and groin. Bright red arterial blood began to spurt, then sprayed for a hundred feet in every direction as the behemoth shook him like a terrier does a rat, mercilessly savaging its victim.

There was a momentary pause, followed by a loud chomp as the pliosaur bore down, incorporating the full power of its crocodile-like jaws. Sanders' already mutilated body flew apart like lunchmeat struck by a chain saw. Severed limbs and pieces of organs struck horrified bystanders and bounced off the nearby holding tank, leaving crimson streaks that trickled down the clear thermoplastic.

Its blood-foaming jaws spread wide, the pliosaur cow let out a deafening roar that pealed like a ship's horn throughout the canyon-sized docking chamber. Then it started to heave against its bonds. The panicking receiving crew took one look and ran for their lives, tripping and falling over one another. Flailing side-to-side like a fish out of water, the infuriated beast pitted its titanic strength against the steel grippers keeping it in check.

Panicking in the face of the creature's assault, Dirk staggered back. His heel caught on a fleeing tech's toolbox and he lost his footing, landing painfully on his rear end. Through a montage of pushing, shoving bodies, he witnessed Garm dragging a dazed and soggy Admiral Callahan out from under the belly of the berserk *Kronosaurus*. Still on his ass, Dirk's gaze swung left and right. He saw Dragunova rush to his brother's side and, together, they carried the semi-conscious naval exec to safety. Behind them, he spotted several members of Tartarus's security force, fleeing like everyone else. Dr. Grayson alone stood his ground, standing barely twenty feet from the monster's snapping jaws, while a river of fear flowed around him like water around a rock.

Dirk clamped his hands over his ears as the thrashing pliosaur let out a second, thunderous bellow that could have cracked stone. He pushed up with his hands and made it to his feet. Thirty feet to his left, Stacy was on the ground. Her teeth were clenched and she was cradling one knee. Dirk uttered a grunt of pain as a black-clad figure pushed roughly past him. It was Dwyer. The hulking security chief wore a murderous look and was cradling one of the laser-guided, 10-gauge shotguns that were standard issue. Dirk heard the familiar "clack-clack" as Dwyer chambered a shell before leveling the weapon at the pliosaur's face.

"No!" Without thinking, he barreled into Dwyer, knocking the bigger man off balance and forcing the scattergun's muzzle straight up. The weapon's booming discharge was barely noticeable over the beast's roars and its sabot round vanished into the stone ceiling, high above. "No guns!" Dirk bellowed, shoving a warning finger in Dwyer's pumpkin-like face. The ex-con's red-rimmed eyes became blackened slits of hatred, but he closed his mouth and said nothing.

Dirk screamed at Stacy. "You've got to dose her, now!"

As Stacy fought to retrieve her weapon, a high-pitched creaking forced Dirk's attention back toward the hoist. The creature's struggles were beginning to wobble the lift's seventy-foot cradle, causing the array of thick steel cables that supported it to rub noisily against one another. Dirk gasped in alarm. If even *one* of the cables kinked up . . .

Far across the docks, Tartarus's resident pliosaurs had all surfaced. Like rubberneckers watching a burning car wreck, their heads rose from the water, their gleaming eyes blinking as they took in the spectacle. Despite all the excitement, the beasts remained uniformly silent, almost as if they were waiting for something.

Dirk grimaced as a painfully loud wrenching sound assailed his ears. He realized to his horror that the gripper encircling the pliosaur's neck was beginning to fail. Already it was partially opened and the behemoth, sensing it, started struggling more ferociously than ever. Once one gripper went, the rest would fall like dominoes. Assuming the pliosaur was uninjured from the five-foot drop onto unforgiving concrete, the berserk titan would find itself loose in their canal system. Beyond the sheer chaos and inevitable loss of life, it could cause immeasurable damage – possibly even taking out one of the docked subs before they could put it down.

Dirk cursed as he slipped in a shallow pool of blood. Down on one knee, he saw Lieutenant McEwan helping Stacy to her feet. In her hands, Stacy held the tranquilizer gun. Dirk cupped his hands like a bullhorn and yelled. "Stacy, the hoist's going to go! You've got to--"

His words were cut off as the *Kronosaurus* wheeled savagely in his direction. Twisting hard against its shackles, it lunged at him. Snapping shut like the world's biggest bear trap, its monstrous jaws came together only five feet from his face. Dirk staggered back, wiping at the viscous drool that ran down his cheeks. He could feel panic grab hold of his shoulders, its sharp raptor's talons digging in. A few feet away, Dr. Grayson spoke calmly into a handset, while Garm and Dragunova half-walked, half-carried, Admiral Callahan in his direction.

Frustrated at having missed its mark, the berserk monstrosity shook its head from side to side, trying to force the pincers around its neck open just a bit more. It began to shake with rage at being denied its freedom and sucked in a noisy breath, opening its bloody jaws to bellow once again.

It never got the chance.

The startled beast's cry died in its throat as a sound equivalent to an atomic bomb blast reverberated across the docks. So loud was the unexpected roar, and so low in frequency, it vibrated the water in both the canals and pliosaur enclosures like a 6.0 aftershock.

Dirk felt the blood chill in his veins. Across the way, the resident pliosaurs were as still as statues, their blinking ruby eyes the only parts still moving.

"Good God . . ." Callahan breathed. He rose unsteadily and turned and stared at the billowing black curtain that cordoned off a huge section of the far end of the docks.

The sound had originated from behind it.

"Was that *her*?" he asked. He wiped at the blood trickling from his nose and mouth. Behind him, Garm and Dragunova stood ready for anything.

Dirk tried to speak, but his throat was so tight he could only nod.

"Jesus, look at that . . ." Callahan muttered.

The moment the deafening roar hit, the pliosaur's frantic struggles had ceased. Its eyes were wide and it slumped in the hoist carriage, freezing like a frightened fawn that relies on camouflage and immobility to stay alive.

"Out of the way!" Her jaw set, Stacy pushed past Dirk and the admiral. Shouldering the big tranquilizer rifle, the athletic Jamaican fired three .50 caliber darts straight into the immobile saurian's face. It neither moved nor reacted to the shots. Seconds later, the traumatized beast's eyes closed and it sank into a drug-induced coma.

As Dirk breathed a huge sigh of relief, Callahan sought about for Grayson. The old man was already headed toward the admiral with

Dwyer in tow. With surprising dexterity, the CEO weaved past injured people, taking care to avoid stepping on what looked suspiciously like a human spleen.

Trembling with excitement, Callahan ran up to him. "When do I get to see her?"

Grayson frowned. "In due time." He signaled Dwyer. "Get a medical team in here ASAP." The security chief nodded, eyeing Dirk as he talked into his radio.

With a heavy exhale, Stacy handed McEwan back her dart gun and limped to Dirk's side. "Nice shooting," he said. He eyed her injured leg and knelt to check on it. "Is it bad?" he asked, carefully squeezing and massaging her knee.

She smiled at the unexpected attention and shook her head. "It's just bruised. One of our fearless security officers trampled me as he ran like a frightened sheep."

Grayson scoffed. "Wonderful. How about you, Derek? Were you injured?"

"I'm fine, sir," Dirk managed.

Grayson scrutinized his face. "You've got saliva on you. Better get down to medical and get checked out. You may need a booster."

"Yes, sir." Still in a fog, Dirk timed a lengthy exhalation to calm himself. He turned to Garm. "How many did we lose?"

"From what I saw, we've got nearly a dozen injuries, but the only fatality was Sergeant Sanders." The big sub commander turned to Callahan. "Sorry about your man, admiral."

"Hey, Sanders knew the risks," Callahan remarked.

Dirk's eyebrows lifted and he saw Garm and Dragunova exchange looks.

"You were very impressive out there, son," Grayson told Garm. "Your reflexes are incredible."

"You're telling me," Callahan interjected. He shook his head, wincing as he touched a badly bruised hip. "Man, Gate. That was like getting hit by Denver's front four! You saved my ass for sure. Thank you!"

"Just doing my job, sir."

"Your job?" Callahan snorted as he adjusted his torn uniform. Suddenly, his eyes lit up. "Hey . . . would you consider a position on my staff? I could use a man like you watching my back."

Garm grinned. "With all due respect, sir, I don't think you can afford me."

"And don't attempt to steal any of my people," Grayson added.

Dirk took in the carnage. It felt like he was waking up from a bad dream and part of him hoped he was still in it. He glanced at the sedated *Kronosaurus* and then turned to Stacy. "How is she?"

Stacy scooped her tablet up off the floor. The screen was cracked and it was spattered with blood, but it still functioned. She touched a key. "In dreamland. I hit her with enough dope to OD a herd of elephants. She should be out for hours."

"Good. Let's get her into the holding tank until we can get all this cleaned up." Dirk studied the bloodied crowd of employees, muttering to one another as they loitered a safe distance away. "Then we'll do her physical and prep work. We'll hold off on the procedure until tomorrow."

Stacy nodded. "Do you want to leave the hoist on her?"

"Only until the auxiliary unit is brought up." He glanced at the immobile *Kronosaurus imperator* and shook his head as he addressed it directly. "You caused a lot of problems," he said. "I hope you turn out to be worth it."

Dr. Grayson moved next to him, shamelessly admiring the sleeping predator. "Oh, she will, my boy. Trust me, she will."

As Dirk stepped sideways, a sudden squishiness underfoot caused him to look down. To his disgust and horror, he realized he was standing on several feet of Sanders' small intestine. He paled. "Oh, God . . ."

Grayson turned to Dwyer with an annoyed look. "Where the *hell* are the cleaners with those body bags?"

Dwyer's face darkened. "Sorry. They're already on the way, sir."

"Well, hurry it up!" Grayson snapped. As Dwyer jumped back on the radio, the old man turned to Dirk and rested a hand on his shoulder. "Relax, son. We'll get this mess cleaned up in a jiffy. Everything will be fine. I promise you."

As he looked around the steaming charnel house that was the receiving dock, Dirk wasn't so sure about that.

TEN

Try as she might, she couldn't handle the screams.

Dr. Kimberly Bane winced as she extracted her incisors from her hand. Her first knuckle and index finger were bruised to the point of bleeding from biting down so hard, but it was the only way she could keep from crying out.

Watching a man die was not an easy thing.

Especially when it was someone you knew and cared about.

She hit pause and grabbed a Kleenex. As she dabbed her eyes and blew her nose, she looked around, breathing in the cold sterility of her new laboratory. She shook her head and chuckled sadly. The irony of the bleached-whiteness of her surroundings, juxtaposed to the horrific reds, browns, and puce greens on the video she'd pulled up, was far from lost on her.

After a few furtive breaths, Dr. Bane hit the resume icon on the eight-year-old file marked "Subject M-223." The "*Oh God*" that slipped from her dry lips echoed Amara Braddock's as she rushed to her dying husband's side.

Jake Braddock was in the final stages of what the papers called "Cretaceous Cancer." Technically, it wasn't a malignant neoplasm as the public believed, but rather, a particularly virulent strain of pathogenic bacteria that simultaneously attacked the circulatory and nervous systems, causing excruciating inflammation, followed by cerebral hemorrhaging, madness, and finally, death.

Twenty-two years prior, there had been a dozen such cases, all in the wake of the Paradise Cove incident. Every one of the infected had managed to survive close contact with the creature that razed Harcourt

156

Marina. Following its elimination, the CDC swept in and isolated them all. They couldn't save them, however; every one of the infected died an agonizing death. But the outbreak everyone dreaded was contained and no additional cases popped up.

Until fifteen years later, that is. With bacteria-laden pliosaurs running rampant, inevitably, the disease reemerged. Most of the locales were remote and linked to the ocean: ports, marinas and fishing villages. Coastal communities in Third World countries which subsisted on the sea's bounty were hit the hardest. The meat from any fish that survived a wound from a *Kronosaurus imperator* was invariably tainted. But the worst outbreaks, by far, took place when one of the pliosaurs, themselves, was killed and cut up for consumption.

The problem went beyond the individuals who inadvertently consumed the diseased flesh. The bacteria propagated throughout the host's body, especially in the salivary glands. A single infectee could bite scores, even hundreds of people before succumbing to the disease, and those hundreds could infect thousands more.

Bane blew out a breath. Until she'd settled in and gained access to Tartarus's classified data, she had no idea how bad things had gotten. The news networks were either in the dark or they weren't discussing the disease, but it was running rampant. There were besieged coastal communities in Okinawa, Taiwan, and the Philippines, where entire towns had been overrun. Their governments had had no choice but to send in troops to wipe out every living thing in an effort at containment.

It was Jake Braddock who had turned the tide. He'd helped develop a vaccine that stopped the contagion's spread. Not by direct action, nor even by aiding in research, but by being a Guinea pig. His blood was the key. During his encounter with the "Monster of Paradise Cove," he'd ingested the beast's saliva. Yet unlike everyone else who'd been exposed, he developed no symptoms.

After being poked, prodded, scanned, X-rayed, and bled repeatedly, the answer finally came to light. Jake's body had developed its own defense against the lethal bacterium that called a *Kronosaurus imperator* home. The next question was "how?" The answer turned out to be barotrauma. Before the bacteria in Jake's body had the chance to multiply to lethal levels, he'd been subjected to submersible dives as low as 5,000 feet. The resultant pressure (and subsequent failure to decompress properly) had somehow neutralized the pathogen. What started as an infection ended up as a vaccine. Jake's body started manufacturing its own antibodies and had been doing so ever since.

Grayson Pharmaceuticals began immediate development and marketing of their own, patented curative, and Jake Braddock and his family were handsomely rewarded for his contributions. Unfortunately, the reward was short-lived. A few years later, the saurian bacteria mutated in his system, and Jake's immune system could no longer contain it.

Bane swallowed as she continued viewing the result. In addition to the "normal" side effects exhibited by victims of Cretaceous cancer: oozing skin pustules, blood dripping from the ears, nose, and eyes, uncontrollable drooling, and maniacal tendencies, Jake's body itself had mutated. There was no other explanation for it. As the camera moved tight on the 50-year-old former athlete, she almost vomited.

His skin was the color of a week-old bruise. His eyes had turned red, like a snapper's, and pinkish pus seeped from their corners. As his mouth gaped wide, she saw his tongue. It was swollen and coated with some sort of awful whitish thrush. His lips were crusted over, his hair was falling out in patches, and his forearms and shins were covered with scabrous folds of skin that looked like scales. It was like something from a horror movie.

Despite her husband's nightmarish state, his wife remained steadfastly by his side, talking calmly, trying to soothe him, while someone in the foreground – it sounded like Derek – kept screaming for a doctor. It was useless. Even with the love of his life holding his hand, Jake was beyond reason. The infection had warped his mind and left the ex-lawman dangerous. For his safety, as well as the safety of others, they had no choice but to tie him down.

The medical restraints were ill-received. Jake heaved at them like a madman, and when they failed to break, he kicked and twisted, trying to tear the bed apart. An inhuman growl rose in his chest and he lunged at Amara like a rabid dog. She had to pull away to avoid being bitten, and when she pressed her hands against his chest to hold him down, what remained of his shirt sloughed away, along with most of the skin underneath. The cold hospice air hitting exposed nerves sent what was left of Jake's mind over the edge.

Unable to take anymore, Amara spun toward the camera. Her attractive, angular face was a puffy wreck and she held her blood-and-pus-drenched hands up, gaping at them. She was too horrified to move and it was obvious she was going into shock.

All of a sudden, Derek was there, pulling his mother back as his father's violent struggles converted into full-fledged convulsions. A whitish fluid began to spew from his nose and mouth and his body thrashed as if he was being electrocuted.

Thirty seconds later, with Derek restraining his mother despite a litany of curses, Jake Braddock flatlined. As if on cue, a resuscitation team in full hazmat gear burst in. They tried everything, including an array of injections and repeated jolts from the defibrillator, all to no avail. Five minutes later, they called it.

As orderlies pulled the covers up over the body and solemnly wheeled it out, Bane saw the world through a veil of tears. She watched Amara bolt hysterically from the room with a distraught nineteen-year-old Derek following her. As the obviously detached cameraman spun around to film their exit, standing in the back of the room, his face an ill-fitting mask of grief and shock, was a young Garm Braddock.

"He took it hard."

The unexpected man's voice made Bane jump. She'd been so engrossed in the on-screen nightmare, she hadn't heard the door whoosh open. Now furious, she froze the video and wheeled around. Job or no, after what she'd just seen, she was in no mood for any of Grayson's lackeys.

"Look, I already *said* I'd get the damn implant, so *leave* me the--"

Bane's voice shrank to a throaty whisper as she spotted Derek Braddock standing there. His eyes were fixed on the screen behind her, studying his brother's face.

"Oh my God . . ." she managed as her eyes followed his back to the monitor. "I-I'm so sorry. I--"

"Harder than any of us," Derek finished. He sounded surprisingly calm and composed, although from the look in his eyes, Bane could tell he was like a ceramic doll, teetering on a shelf's edge. One good nudge and he'd fall and shatter.

"Dr. Braddock . . . *Derek*--"

"My friends call me Dirk," he said, looking at her now.

Come to think of it, she noted, he wasn't looking *at* her as much as *through* her. There was a lot of his mother in him. He was highly intuitive.

"I didn't know it was your father on the video," Bane said, sounding lame and hating herself for it. "It wasn't marked and until I saw your mom . . . I'm very sorry."

Dirk lowered himself onto a nearby stool. "It's okay. You had to watch it at some point. Actually, I've never seen it. Well, until now."

"But you--"

"Living it was enough."

"You've suffered many losses," Bane said quietly.

Dirk sat up straight. "My mom used to say loss comes with life. But you shouldn't let it stop you from living."

Bane nodded. "She was a good friend. Now that I'm here, I miss her even more."

"Me too, doc," Dirk said.

Bane smiled sadly as she dabbed at her eyes with one fingertip. "Your brother calls me that, even though I got all haughty about it," she sniffled.

"It's a Braddock family tradition," Dirk said, trying to smile back. "Maybe my mom told you about it?"

Bane laughed as a fresh flood of tears streamed down her cheeks. "Yes . . . yes she did."

Dirk gestured at Garm's pixilated face, his shattered expression still locked in stasis on the monitor. "Would you mind?"

"Oh, of course not," she replied as she hastily hit stop. She stared at the blackened screen. "You said he took his father's death hard?"

Dirk exhaled. "He tried not showing it, but everyone could tell Garm wasn't, well . . . *Garm* after that. He and our father were inseparable. I mean, dad loved us both. But those two, they had a special connection."

"They were both warriors," Bane hazarded. "At least, that's what your mom told me."

"Something like that," Dirk nodded. He folded his lean arms across his chest as he sat back on his stool. "Garm was always a fighter. In school, if someone tried to bully me he'd fold them in half and slam-dunk them in a trash can."

"Wow." Dr. Bane smiled. "I guess not too many kids messed with you."

Dirk chuckled. "He really took to boxing. My dad taught us both, but Garm thrilled to it – the crowds, the spectacle. It was like he'd been a gladiator in a past life. When he was seventeen, he won the Golden Gloves. He took silver in the Olympics a year later, and became a pro heavyweight the year after that."

"I remember. Your mom was so proud; she sent me clips from his Olympic bouts." She shook her head. "He should have gotten the Gold."

Dirk nodded. "He would have, if the Turkish guy hadn't been--"

"Playing patty-cake while running for his life?"

Dirk's eyebrows did the Mr. Spock thing. "Wow. You two *did* talk."

Bane grinned as she made a show of batting her eyelashes. "Well, you know how we girls are."

"That's not how he does it," Dirk said with a smirk.

"Who?"

"My brother."

"Oh, you mean--"

Dirk checked the doorway, then leaned closer. "When Garm wants to show off those fishing lures of his, he looms over a woman, like *this*, and fixes her with a steely gaze. Then he blinks twice." He chuckled. "It's like watching a snake hypnotize a bird. By the second blink, they're completely in his power."

Bane laughed aloud. "Oh my *God*, did you know he tried it on me?"

They both burst out laughing. "I can imagine."

For some reason, Bane felt like she was missing a drink in her hand. "You know," she intimated. "He *is* very impressive. I mean, I don't want to sound like a horny cougar or anything, but c'mon. *Look* at the guy."

"Been suffering it my whole life, doc."

"Yes, but in truth, you are *far* more interesting," she said. "Has no woman ever told you that?"

Dirk grinned. "Listen, if you're trying to get out of your locator implant by buttering me up--"

"Oh, fiddlesticks," Bane said. "I already said I'd do it. I just don't see what the big deal is."

Dirk hesitated. "In a place like this, sometimes people go missing."

Bane wore a confused look. "You mean, like, they go ashore for the weekend and never come back because they've gotten into something?"

"Yes. Or sometimes they don't leave. They're still here, but they've ended up *in* something . . ." He stared at her meaningfully.

"Ah. And the locators let you know--"

"*Which* something they ended up in."

Bane smacked her lips loudly. "Yep, just another fun day here in Tartarus!"

Dirk grinned. "By the way, Dr. Grayson said he spoke with you about the whole 'misunderstanding' thing?"

She scoffed. "That's a funny thing to call it. Especially after what I went through. But yes, we sat down and he told me something that made me decide I was okay with things."

"Really?" Dirk's head angled to one side. "And what was that?

"*I'm doubling your salary, Dr. Bane,*" she said, impersonating Grayson's gravelly voice.

Dirk nodded. "Nothing wrong with that."

"It's hard to argue with a man who has everything," Dr. Bane stated.

"Don't I know it."

She stood up, rubbing her palms on her lab coat. "It's been nice chatting. Before I get back to whatever it is I'm being overpaid to do around here, is there anything you need from me?"

Dirk sighed. "Now that you mention it: yes. I was at the dock earlier and got a faceful of *Kronosaurus*. Dr. Grayson thinks I might need a booster."

Bane sucked in a breath and nodded. "Thankfully, I was touring my lab when it happened." She shook her head ruefully. "I heard about that poor man . . . Okay, I already treated everyone else, so let's get you taken care of."

As she extracted a vial from a nearby fridge, followed by a needle that seemed better suited for horses, Dirk balked. "Wouldn't it make sense to run a workup first, just to see if there's anything to worry about?"

"Nah," Bane said as she turned the vial upside down and inserted the syringe. "Better to act preemptively, rather than chancing an infection taking hold."

Dirk eyed the dripping needle tip and swallowed. "Are you sure that's not reserved for one of our--"

"Lizards?" Bane chuckled as she held the needle up and tapped it. "The injection's intramuscular. You know that."

Dirk's brow creased up and she realized he was replaying his past inoculations in his head.

"Let's go, kiddo. Pants down and assume the position," she said. "I promised your mom I'd take care of you, no matter how much it hurts."

Bane's jaw muscles ached from maintaining a straight face, but she managed to keep from guffawing. She felt a momentary twinge of embarrassment as Dirk bent unenthusiastically over the counter, but it vanished as she took in his athletic, 29-year-old buttocks.

"I really wish we could discuss this," Dirk muttered as she swabbed one cheek with a prep pad.

Bane smirked. "Oh, just relax. What is it you guys are so fond of telling us girls? Oh, yeah. 'C'mon, baby. It's not *that* big!'"

<hr />

"Grayson, your boy, here, is a world-class pain-in-my-ass," Admiral Callahan said, giving Dirk a decidedly unfriendly look. "I've lost two units in a month, and now you expect me to pay full price for replacements?"

I'm *'a pain in his ass?'* Dirk thought. A malicious idea came to him and he smirked. *I should send him to Dr. Bane.*

Callahan's heavy footfalls echoed across the concrete docks as Dirk and Dr. Grayson paraded him past the pliosaur tanks with a stern-faced security officer and the admiral's surviving aide in tow.

"Actually, the losses you're referring to had nothing to do with the reliability of the units in question," Dirk asserted. "Nor the efficacy of our technology." Grayson had remained tight-lipped since the tour began, which wasn't surprising. His mentor was usually content to let him handle these discussions.

"Says you." Callahan paused to adjust his belt's positioning around his substantial midsection. "Two units in two months is a hard pill for the Navy to swallow. And frankly, until I'm satisfied that the 'improvements' you've boasted about are legit, I'm not shelling out another penny."

Dirk fought to keep a straight face. The way Callahan made it sound, you'd have thought it was *his* money he was flapping about, instead of the United States government's.

"Now, when do I get to see the big girl?" the admiral pressed.

Dirk sighed. "The presentation is scheduled for tomorrow at 0800 hours. You'll see everything you've asked for and more, guaranteed."

"Bah. You "guaranteed" me those two critters you sold me would get the job done. You didn't say anything about them getting done *in*."

As Callahan started gnawing on one of his thumbnails, Dirk remembered from his file that he was a heavy smoker. Being in a tobacco-free environment like Tartarus was undoubtedly driving him nuts.

Dirk exhaled through his teeth. "Fine, let's get the deceased units out of the way first." He glanced up, pulling the info he needed out of his head. "The first unit lost was index 17A, code name: *Grendel*, a ninety-seven-ton Gen-2 cow we certified November 14th of last year. She was lost on May 11th of this year, approximately six months later, when she attacked a boatload of insurgents attempting to approach the guided missile destroyer *USS Crusader*, under cover of darkness. When the terrorists were picked up by SODOME passing the ship's defensive perimeter and refused to heave to, *Grendel* was directed to intercept. Per programming, she struck from below. The instant she stove in the attacking boat's hull there was a tremendous explosion, which was, according to the report, '*Sufficient to cripple, if not sink, Crusader.*' Both *Grendel* and the insurgents were killed instantaneously."

Callahan spat irritably. "So, you're trying to tell me the stupid lizard died in the line of duty and I should be grateful?"

"I'm saying you sacrificed a half-billion-dollar bio-weapon to save a fifteen-billion-dollar ship-of-the-line, not to mention God-only-knows how many of her crew." Dirk replied. "The *Kronosaurus imperator* did what she was programmed to do. She sacrificed herself to save lives."

"And the other one – that bull that bought it?"

"That was your fault."

"Excuse me?" Callahan shot back. "How so?"

Dirk swung his tablet up and swiped his finger across the screen. His almond-shaped eyes swung back and forth. "June 4th, unit 24A, a sixty-ton Gen-2 bull pliosaur, code name: *Goliath*, was running point for task force 77 – *your* task force, to be exact." He turned the tablet so that

Callahan could see the data. "Despite the fact sonar reported a huge cow pliosaur approaching on an intercept course, *Goliath* was ordered ahead, directly into the female's territory."

Dirk shook his head. "As expected, the two animals clashed. *Goliath* fought back, but was eventually killed by a lethal skull bite from the significantly larger female."

"And how is that my fault?" Callahan inquired.

"This *unredacted* version of the report states that the go-ahead order was issued by CTF Callahan, Ward C., personally," Dirk said. He gave the admiral a look that bordered on disgust. "Even with his implant, *Goliath*'s instincts should have kicked in and he would have given the female a wide birth. But you overrode his self-preservation protocols. You *wanted* them to fight, like some sort of sick MMA contest."

"How was I supposed to know your boy was gonna get his clock cleaned?" Callahan snapped. As his blood pressure rose, his mustache stood out like a graying bristle brush on a ruddy background.

"My boy?"

Dr. Grayson exhaled heavily before joining the conversation. "Ward, these animals are among nature's most lethal hunters. They are not chess pieces for your amusement." He folded his arms. "We patented our cybernetic implants with the notion of using them to keep others of their kind at bay – to safeguard America's beaches and coastline. It was Washington that elected to convert them into hardware for military applications."

Callahan scoffed. "Yeah? Well, I don't see you turning down any of our big, fat checks, now do I?"

Grayson sighed and interlocked his hands behind him before he resumed walking. "Derek, please continue."

"Very well," Dirk stopped beside the tank of a huge, battle-scarred bull pliosaur. The placard on the tank frame read-- "*Polyphemus*, the largest male *Kronosaurus imperator* we've ever documented. A full seventy feet long and pushing ninety tons, he is a beast. His--"

"No way." Callahan shook his head so vigorously you'd have thought his hair was on fire. "After what happened to the last bull, I'll pass. Sorry."

Dirk and Grayson exchanged glances. "Admiral, mature male pliosaurs have the most testosterone on the planet, topping even the bull shark. Besides their utter aggressiveness, they're also faster and more agile than the cows. You, of all people, should know that speed kills."

Callahan studied the mottled behemoth cruising above him but was obviously unconvinced. "He's a big boy, I'll give him that." He squinted as he studied the huge bull's misshapen head. "*Polyphemus*? Wasn't that the Cyclops in Homer's *Odyssey*?"

Grayson turned and smiled for the first time. "I'm impressed, Ward. I didn't expect you'd be so well read."

"Required reading at the Academy. Personally, I thought it was garbage."

Dirk aggressively cleared his throat. "Like Ulysses' *Polyphemus*, ours is also minus an eye."

"What?" Callahan's lips curled back, exposing his tobacco-stained teeth. "You're trying to sell the Navy – trying to sell *me* – a beat-up lemon? No fucking way!"

As Polyphemus spun on his tail, Dirk pointed at his rebuilt right-side orbit. "Actually, we've upgraded his cybernetic implant to support a state-of-the-art ocular bionics platform."

Callahan's eyes narrowed as he scrutinized the battle-worn pliosaur's luminescent red orb. "Can it see normally?"

"Better than normal," Dirk announced. "His implant sweeps the entire spectrum, including X-rays, and with full digital processing. He's also got a 500X zoom, and a high-speed camera that runs up to 200K FPS."

"Is there a direct feed for all that?"

Dirk nodded. "Of course. Anything he can see you can record. And you can beam the results anywhere you want. His readouts are completely untraceable. He's the ultimate underwater spy and he'll never let you down. As long as you don't send him on any suicide missions, that is . . ."

Callahan's eyes took on a wicked gleam. "Oh, you don't have to worry about *that*. Assuming tomorrow's demo is satisfactory – hey, wait a minute. How much more is that eye costing me?"

Dr Grayson replied, "Not a penny. It's the least we can do for our brothers in the Navy."

"What about battery life with that fancy eye? Does it drain faster?"

"No. All the new implants, regardless of add-ons, last twice as long as the older models – nearly three years."

Callahan rubbed his thick hands together in anticipation. "Sweet. With this beast on the payroll running recon and that behemoth you just brought in--"

"Actually, we have a third unit you may want as well," Dirk said.

"A third? I've only got authorization for two."

Dirk made a show of sucking his teeth. "Gee, that's too bad. She's *very* special."

"'She?' Is she as big as the Gen-1?"

Dirk didn't answer right away. Instead, he moved briskly past the old bull's tank, stopping at the one situated next to it. He gestured at a dark gray pliosaur that hovered motionless near the bottom of its habitat. "This is *Charybdis*."

Callahan wore an unimpressed look. "Doesn't move around much. And it looks the same size as 'Old One-Eye' over there."

"She is," Dirk affirmed. Inwardly, he was starting to wonder about the admiral's obsession with size. "That's because she's a Gen-2 female, probably twenty-four years old."

"I'm supposed to be impressed because she's younger?"

Dirk grinned. "No, but you *will* be impressed with what she can do."

"And what's that?"

Callahan jumped as the big cow swam so close its flippers scraped noisy grooves in the algae coating the other side of the eight-foot Celazole. Dirk gestured at the saurian as it swam away from them. "You see all those scars on her back?"

"She's taken small arms fire. So what?"

"Pliosaurs possess a rudimentary intelligence, admiral," Grayson interjected. His patience with Callahan was obviously wearing thin. "They're highly adaptive." He turned to his protégé. "Show him."

Dirk unclipped a radio from his belt and pressed the talk button. "Tower three, can you drop a burger in number seven for me, please?"

"Will do, boss," came the reply.

Thirty seconds later, one of the overhead hoists rumbled to life. It moved rapidly sideways along the web-like network of girders before coming to a halt and plummeting downward. Jaws spread, it disappeared into a large, open hold, and then reemerged, its grippers securely fastened around the midsection of a frantically struggling, 1,300-pound. Holstein cow. The black and white ruminant's plaintive mooing grew steadily louder and more frantic as she was pulled high into the air and then carried toward *Charybdis*'s tank.

"You see," Dirk said over the mooing. "This particular pliosaur was so traumatized by its gunshot wounds that it changed its hunting strategies."

As the hoist rumbled directly overhead, Dirk lunged forward, extending his arms and ushering Dr. Grayson and Callahan back just in time to avoid a shower of hot manure. There was a loud mechanical thump as the lift stopped abruptly over the pliosaur's tank. Suspended fifty feet above the tepid green water, the cow creaked back and forth on her steel tether, her widened eyes staring apprehensively downward.

Then her mooing stopped.

A loud claxon sounded and the hoist's pincers sprang open. Plummeting downward, the terrified Holstein uttered a bawling cry that became a drowned gurgle as she landed with a tremendous splash.

Over a hundred feet from the bovine's point of impact, Admiral Callahan watched with interest. Despite the fact that the cow's flailing legs hung invitingly down directly above her, *Charybdis* didn't respond. The granite-colored behemoth hovered silently in place, her fourteen-foot flippers gently undulating against the current generated by her enclosure.

"I don't think she's hungry," Callahan remarked.

Dirk said nothing. He just pointed.

Like a Phalanx anti-missile battery targeting an incoming, *Charybdis*'s rowboat-sized head swiveled on her thick neck, her toothy muzzle angling upward. Her deep-set eyes contracted as she studied the swimming mammal and her echolocation clicks reflected off her tank walls. A few seconds later, she was on the move.

Dirk read the confusion on Callahan's face as the 90-ton reptile discarded the traditional attack method its kind favored – coming straight up under a target and either breaching or yanking it under. Instead, *Charybdis* suspended at the fifty-foot mark and began to circle the terrified ruminant like Apache warriors stalking a wagon train. Rather than rushing in to attack, she maintained her distance and began to accelerate. With all four of her thick paddles pumping in unison, her speed steadily increased.

Churned by the movements of the pliosaur's massive body, the displaced water in the tank began to swirl. The loudly mooing cow kicked frantically as her body was irresistibly drawn into a wide spiral. Below her, still five stories down and moving ever faster, *Charybdis* continued swimming. Her jaws were closed tight to reduce drag, her neck straight and her body narrowed. Above her, a powerful whirlpool formed – a huge, sucking vortex that drew the helpless bovine in ever tightening circles.

Callahan's jaw went slowly slack as he watched the contents of the pliosaur's habitat transform from a calm aquarium into a raging maelstrom. The polybenzimidazole walls of the tank began to creak from the increased water pressure and the admiral jumped when pressurized seawater burst like a fire extinguisher from a nearby joint.

Suddenly, *Charybdis* made her move. With the half-drowned cow nearing the eye of the storm she'd caused, she descended. Still circling at nearly forty miles an hour, the behemoth dropped toward the bottom, fifty feet below.

The effect was instantaneous. *Charybdis's* sudden descent caused the sucking power of the whirlpool to increase geometrically. The exhausted ruminant barely had time to utter an astonished grunt before it was yanked under.

Trailing the last of her air, the Holstein spun in dizzying circles, a flailing black-and-white ball of legs that was carried powerlessly toward the bottom. She was a child's toy in the spin cycle of an out-of-control washing machine.

A split-second before the cow's hooves touched the tank's sandy bottom, *Charybdis* altered her trajectory, changing from a tight circle to a straight-line rush. Jaws agape, she pierced the eye of her own personal storm and enveloped the drowning ungulate in a vice lined with fifteen-inch fangs. As her mouth closed, the sound of pulverized bone shook the tank wall nearest to Callahan and the admiral blinked in astonishment.

Relishing her kill, the big female swam right up to him, holding the dead cow in her maw like a dog showing off a chew toy. The clear, nictitating membranes that protected her garnet-colored eyes slid closed and her steely jaw muscles bunched. Billows of blood spewed from her crocodile-like jaws, diffusing into pinkish clouds as she shook her prey.

Dirk watched with grim satisfaction as a pair of severed hooves struck the panel in front of Callahan's face, causing him to recoil. *Charybdis* appeared to enjoy his reaction, as she moved closer. Her sedan-sized head touched the polycarbonate and her protective membranes slid back, allowing her to study him in detail. Her jaws continued to move up and down, forcing the macerated cow's body further back into her gullet. Like rubber, the thick-scaled skin of her throat stretched to accommodate her meal and, with an audible gulp, she swallowed it. She gave Callahan a final glance, then uttered a low rumble of satiation and spun off, cruising toward the far reaches of her enclosure where she all but vanished into the gloom.

Callahan swallowed as he watched her go. "Is this how she usually feeds?"

"Always," Dirk said. "She never breaches or surfaces, stays down most of the day, and when she spouts, exposes only her nostrils before submerging once more. And feeding, well . . . you just saw her technique."

"I'll take her."

Dirk blinked. "Just like that? Don't you have any--"

Callahan waved him off with one hand while the other wiped at the condensation on the outside of the tank wall. He squinted hard, trying to catch another glimpse of *Charybdis*. "I have all the funding I need," he intimated. "And this bitch is going to be my ultimate assassin."

"How so?"

Callahan looked at him in surprise. "Are you kidding? Do you know how many thorns I can pluck while holding her leash?" He gestured at the water before him. "Let's just say there's going to be a marked increase in certain undesirables vanishing at sea, courtesy of sudden, inexplicable weather anomalies. Real Bermuda Triangle shit." He winked at Dirk.

Grayson folded his arms across his chest. "We don't need to know the details, admiral. Suffice to say, the fact that you're pleased with any acquisition is music to our collective ears."

"Damn straight." Callahan's lips disappeared as he mulled something over. "Say, I know the scheduled demo's not until tomorrow, but what about the procedure on the Gen-1?"

"You're interested in attending?"

Callahan turned to Grayson and grinned. "You know, Eric. For a genius, he's remarkably dense."

Dirk frowned as he checked his watch. "Actually, we're starting in just over an hour. I should get prepped." He looked at Grayson for possible input before turning back to Callahan. "Are you sure you want to be there? I mean, it gets a little messy and I wouldn't want to spoil your dinner."

Callahan chuckled and rested a beefy hand on his shoulder. "Derek, my boy, as much as I enjoy slapping on the feedbag, seeing what goes on with these dragons of yours is far more appetizing."

"Well, if you're sure . . ."

"Absolutely. Besides, I could skip a meal or three," Callahan said, patting his belly. "Wouldn't want one of your pliosaurs to mistake me for some fat, juicy steer and try to make a meal out of me!"

"Heaven forbid," Grayson intoned.

ELEVEN

It was near-dusk when the *Octopus giganteus* pair departed the inky depths and returned to the ocean's sunlit upper layer. For a mile in advance, the Gulf Stream emptied of life as its denizens sensed their approach and fled. As before, the giant female took the lead, expelling powerful gushes of water from her mantle and propelling her 140-foot body up the slopes of the crevasse the two now called home.

The male octopus hung back, keeping pace with his mate, but also keeping his distance. He was more worried about the female's foul temper than any discomfort he might incur from being near the surface. The twilight conditions surrounding them were far more bearable than the blazing sunlight they had faced the last time, and the brown bands decorating his gnarled skin reflected his improved mood.

Although they were far from satiated, the two had fed well during their recent hunt. What they had assumed was an injured whale turned out to be some sort of floating construct. It was a vessel, like the hard shell of their tiny cousin, the Nautilus, but made of dry, coarse cellulose – completely inedible, as an investigatory bite had shown. Luckily, a quick exploration of the floater revealed it to be infested with dozens of warm-blooded prey items. They were small, most little more than a beakful. But they were also blubbery rich and nutritious, like seals, only much easier to catch.

Together, the two octopi had thoroughly explored the vessel's shattered frame, stripping it bare of every morsel they could find before they pulled it beneath the waves and dragged it to the bottom. It was a valuable learning experience for them. There were many such vessels; the surface was littered with them. They had inadvertently discovered a prolific food source that required them to do little more than surface whenever they needed to access it.

The key was stealth. As they'd discovered shortly thereafter, most of the floating constructs were propelled by the same noisy geysers that moved the iron iceberg they'd observed a day earlier. They were capable of speed – enough to escape unless taken unawares. The trick was to stalk them under cover of darkness and strike while they rested. Once the titans of the deep had immobilized a vessel with their steely tentacles, the succulent mouthfuls hidden within were theirs for the taking.

As the female stopped to explore a seventy-foot hole gouged into the rocky slopes, the male's thoughts diverted from his stomach to the impetus behind their current search. Although his monstrous mate was as hungry as he, at the moment she wasn't hunting. At least, not for food.

The male's eyes gleamed as he watched his bride squeeze her massiveness inside the ragged cave. No sooner had she entered, when thousands of colorful reef fish occupying the tiny grotto came swarming out. Like a rainbow-hued wave, they swirled around the outside, waiting for the mammoth mollusk to either settle down or abandon their abode. The female's bark-like skin blackened at the sight of the tenacious fish and she lashed out with one of her well-armed tentacles. Several fish were maimed or killed by the strike, but the rest danced away, unharmed. Hovering nearby, they returned like a cloud of locusts, fearlessly exploring the length of the female's sucker-lined arm and feeding on their dead and dying brethren.

The cow octopus's eyes narrowed and she hoisted herself upright. Her writhing tendrils carried her bloated body like spider's legs as she exited the cave, one of them snapping off a ten-foot stalactite that hung in her way and crushing it into fragments as she flowed back outside. She looked around before emitting a watery rumble of frustration – a loud bloop that echoed up the nearby slopes.

The male drifted back, carefully gauging his irascible mate's mental state. She was understandably frustrated. Everywhere they checked it was the same – each cave or chasm was swarming with tiny fish or squid. They were too fast to catch, too tiny to eat. But they were a serious threat. Not to the male or his mate. That would have been ridiculous.

The danger was to their offspring.

The female octopus was heavy with young. She was due to birth soon, and her need to find a suitable nest, free of predators and parasites, was pressing. Unlike other cephalopods that lived only a few years and died shortly after spawning, *Octopus giganteus* were a long-lived species. The female reproduced seasonally. Moreover, the pair worked together to protect their nest until the eggs hatched. They took turns guarding their clutch – often 200,000 strong – with one acting as sentry while the other left to feed.

The problem with this cave was the same as with all the others. Even working in concert, the pair could not fend off thousands of tiny egg thieves. They would die from exhaustion and their larvae would be stripped until none were left. Back in the abyss they had, on occasion, faced similar conditions. But that was before the whales vanished, and then there had been many of their kind. By sheer volume, enough of their young survived to adulthood to ensure the continuance of the species. Now, however, with their numbers so reduced, they could no longer afford to take chances.

They must either find a suitable nest or risk perishing.

The male watched as the female's eyes turned upward. They had reached a point where the rocky slopes of their crevasse turned completely vertical; a crumbly, anemone-infested wall of stone that soared over a thousand feet straight up. At the summit was the beginning of the Continental shelf. The water there was shallow and teeming with life. Food was plentiful, but the warmer temperatures would make life uncomfortable for the great cephalopods. The copper-rich proteins in their blood transported oxygen best under cold temperatures and low oxygen pressure. Their bodies were designed for the void of the abyss. Still, where the female went . . .

As his mate unexpectedly jetted straight up, the male's tentacles bunched up and then drooped – an almost human shrug of frustration. He ground his beak, then filled his mantle with seawater and sped after her. Up she soared, with him following in her swash. High above them, the gray surface light grew less dim by the minute.

Suddenly, the female's progress came to an abrupt halt. So fast was the male traveling, he had to unfurl his arms like a parachute to avoid ramming her. He stopped barely a dozen yards away and then pulled back. They had reached the summit, a gnarled edge of seaweed-dotted stone and coral, bordering the vertical drop into darkness. Beyond, lay the shelf's inexorable rise. Twelve miles up that slope was the roaring surf. And beyond that, dry sand.

The male studied his mate. Her golden orbs were wide with excitement. As he peered over her vast bulk, past the edge of the precipice, he understood why. A hundred yards away lay the rusted remnants of some metal monstrosity. It was huge, more than twice the female's length, and draped along the very edge of the drop-off.

The object had an almost whale-like shape to it. It was partially buried in the sand and had been there for many seasons. Its nose was badly crushed and its tail twisted and bent, but it was its body that attracted the female. In the center of the ancient iron construct was a crack – a break in the unyielding metal. It started from the dorsal and ran all the way to the seafloor: a ragged, rusticle-draped gap measuring forty feet in height and thirty feet in width.

Strangely, inside there were no fish to be seen.

The female wasted no time. Brushing aside a warning touch from one of the male's tendrils, she rushed forward to investigate the site. Arcing up and then coming down directly on top of it, her tentacles poured over the exterior like a mating ball of anacondas, tasting, testing and probing. Brownish clouds of rust particles mixed with sand billowed up as a result of her explorations, but to the male's surprise, no marine life was disturbed.

Content with the construct's exterior, the female made for the opening. His body tensing, the male flew to her side. Experience told him the wreckage was devoid of life because something – perhaps one of their kind – had already laid claim to it, and he was prepared to do battle. But when his mate inserted one of her tree trunk-like tentacles into the opening and probed inside, she found nothing. The wreck was uninhabited.

Moving boldly forward, the female began to insert herself into the jagged gap. Like liquid metal, her tentacles flowed inside, followed by the rest of her. The narrow entrance was easily bypassed, even by her thirty-foot mantle. Except for her beak, the only hard portions of her body were segmented links, a vestigial shell that formed a sort of internal armor. The protective shell segments were easily compressed and did not detract from either her flexibility or ability to squeeze into tight spaces.

Once fully inside, the female coiled up, her gold-colored eyes swiveling as she measured the space for comfort and studied its interior. From her body language, the male could tell she was content with the find. He moved to the entrance and peered within. The space was suitable. It could hold their entire clutch of eggs and allow at least one of the adults to squeeze inside while the other stood guard or hunted.

As the male explored the sand-strewn bottom of the wreck, his probing arms uncovered two things of interest. The first was a small skeleton. He knew at once it was the remains of one of the tiny warm-bloods they targeted as a food source. The bones were old and incredibly fragile; they crumbled to dust the moment he grazed them.

The second find was more intriguing. Under several feet of sand, he came across the rotted remnants of several wooden cubes. They were small – barely the thickness of the base of one of his arms, and broke apart when touched. The contents of the boxes were far more interesting: mounds of black, crystalline powder that had lain concealed beneath the seabed.

The male touched one of the piles of black powder and recoiled. The chemoreceptors on his suckers detected an acrid, unpalatable taste. Moreover, the granules left his body tingling where he'd touched them. Alarmed, the male reached for his mate, encouraging her to leave. She steadfastly ignored his repeated entreaties, even snapping at him when he persisted. She was satisfied with her nest and would not give it up. This was where she would birth their clutch. And from this place, their offspring would spread into the seas beyond.

Frustrated with the female's stubbornness, but knowing better than to press, the male did the only thing he could; he used his tentacles to scoop sand over the piles of black particles, covering them as best he could. This accomplished, he signaled to his mate. The sun was going down and it was time to hunt.

While she wormed her way back out from her pending nursery, the male scanned the surrounding sea. A few miles away, perched atop the surface over deep water, was another of the floating constructs. It was similar in size to the last one they'd encountered. This one was immobile, yet even at this distance it gave off a litany of discernible sounds. It was heavily infested.

With food.

The female wasted no time. The need to gorge her gigantic body on fresh, warm meat was overpowering. This was her last chance to feed before she laid her eggs and she was not about to miss it. Expelling high-pressured seawater from her siphon, she shot toward the target at maximum velocity.

His mouth awash in anticipation, the male hurried to catch up.

———

Thank God, it's a short drive . . .

Dirk's nose wrinkled like a desiccated prune as he sat in the rear bench seat of one of Tartarus's diesel-powered ATVs, wedged between Dr. Grayson and Admiral Callahan as they sped past the seemingly endless row of pliosaur habitats. He compressed his shoulders and overlapped his arms to avoid getting squished, then focused on breathing through his mouth. Callahan may have held the keys to the Navy's bank vault, but the heavyset naval officer's deodorant had given up the ghost a long time ago, and he absolutely reeked of cheap cigars and cigarettes.

Smoking was a vile and disgusting habit, Dirk thought. He turned his face from Callahan and shook his head. Even sea air mixed with the pungent odor of pliosaur couldn't overpower the man's stench at this range. At least Grayson was sharing his misery, albeit more stolidly. Knowing all his mentor's aches and pains, there was no one better at suffering in silence.

As a reminder ping emanated from his tablet, Dirk took a quick breath and leaned forward, talking around Callahan. "Dr. Grayson, I forgot to mention, it looks like we've got another locator on the fritz."

Grayson's eyes stayed focused front but he nodded. A "locator on the fritz" was their code for an employee going AWOL. "Whose locator is it?" he asked quietly.

"Security officer McHale's, sir," Dirk replied. "I ordered a scan, but the signal is off grid. I suspect it's a transponder issue."

Grayson sighed, then leaned forward and addressed their driver. "Phillip, drop me off here, please." As the ATV came to a stop, he climbed carefully out. "Admiral, Derek will take over from here. I'm afraid I have some technical issues to address."

"No problem," Callahan said, thumbing his mustache. He glanced around. They were at the far end of the pliosaur tanks, past the submarine turntable and within walking distance of the fenced-off rear portion of the complex. To the far left hung the ominous, three hundred-foot black curtain that cordoned off a heavily-guarded area marked "Restricted" from the rest of the docks. To the right, an SUV drove slowly past, towing a trailer loaded with bales of hay. Callahan grinned and clapped Dirk on the shoulder, unintentionally spraying spittle in his face, "I'm in good hands."

Dirk greened but managed to keep smiling. "If you can't make the procedure, sir, I'll email you the video and data files."

Grayson nodded and shuffled off, heading toward a nearby elevator.

"Phil, we'll get out here, too," Dirk informed the driver. He hopped out, waiting as Callahan hoisted himself from the other side. Judging by the way the MarshCat's stiff shocks noisily rebounded, Dirk calculated he outweighed Garm by a stretch. No small feat.

"What the hell?" Dirk's eyebrows lifted.

"Something wrong, sport?" Callahan asked.

"Yes . . . and no," Dirk muttered. He touched his wristband to the lock on a gate leading past a twelve-foot chain-link fence. The lock popped free and the gate swung open. "Close it behind you, please," he said over his shoulder as he walked briskly through.

Four hundred feet away, past a pair of canals and a huge, gated pool, lay the heart of the facility's surgical center. A smaller, hundred-foot healing pool formed its core. Around one side of the pool, arranged in a semi-circle, stood a series of heavy-gauge shelving units, stocked with a vast array of scalpels, hemostats, and assorted medical devices – all constructed on a colossal scale. Looming high above everything else stood a battery of searchlights. They were like those used during nighttime baseball games, their fifty-foot towers arranged around the pool in an oval, their powerful halogen lamps angled downward. The lights were dimmed at the moment, but the SUV-sized generators and comparably-scaled compressors the generators backed-up, that handled everything from IVs to transfusions, were already powered up and running.

Directly adjacent to the pool, and anchored deep into the gray granite walls of Rock Key, was a three-hundred-ton, fifty-foot wide lift system, connected to a pair of ten-foot-thick, stainless-steel shafts that towered over a hundred feet in height. The lift was part of a recently upgraded system of high-capacity hydraulics and pneumatics that raised and lowered the *Colossus* neural interface system. The enormous, arm-like manipulators, with their powerful titanium-polymer actuator muscles, were currently deactivated, sitting in repose on the surgical deck's scrubbed and polished concrete floor.

What surprised Dirk wasn't the sight of all their equipment, activated and on standby. It was the fact that their patient, the recently delivered Gen-1, was already on the operating table. The tenacious beast had been prepped and was securely strapped to the floating gurney they used for procedures. Dirk noted that several feet of the creature's muzzle and tail hung past the edges of the near-eighty-foot platform. Judging from its inert state, and the intravenous tubes hooked up to it, the pliosaur was fully anesthetized. Of course, that didn't seem to matter to the one-dozen obviously nervous security officers who ringed the sedated colossus, their weapons at the ready.

Of course, Dirk noted, they should have been facing outward. Their job was to keep unauthorized personnel away from the operating area, not to corral the *Kronosaurus imperator* if it came to. Their 10-gauge shotguns could stop a charging lion, but to an adult pliosaur the sabot slugs they fired would be nothing more than annoying spitballs.

Dirk looked around, trying to locate Stacy. She'd obviously been busy while he was doing Grayson's sales pitch, but why she wasn't here and on top of things baffled him.

"Something wrong?" Callahan asked as he locked the gate behind them.

"No," Dirk lied. "I was just wondering where--"

A loud claxon drowned out his words. This alert was different: longer and lower in tonality than the ones that signaled a food drop or the Vault opening. His head swiveled toward the far-off row of *Kronosaurus imperator* tanks. All the mammoth predators were submerged and watching intently through the dockside windows of their enclosures. Judging by their body postures, they were waiting for something.

Then the music started.

Dirk shook his head and grinned as the Cranberries hit single *"Dreams"* suddenly blasted from the dock's overhead speaker system.

It was so loud everyone in the complex could hear it – including the pliosaurs.

"What the hell is going on?" Callahan yelled, trying to be heard over Dolores O'Riordan's airy vocals.

Dirk pointed at the *Kronosaurus* enclosures. A series of deep thuds reverberated across the tops of the tanks, followed by low whirring noises that steadily increased in pitch. Moments later, the flow of water inside each habitat changed, building up from what started as a gently circulating current until it was the equivalent of a powerful rip tide. The sand and algae inside each tank was churned up, reducing visibility. The pliosaurs resisted the watery onslaught, their flippers pumping hard as they held position. It soon became obvious the great beasts were enjoying a sensation like that of an onrushing tide. In fact, they were reveling in it. They torqued and spiraled as they paddled, casting sideways glances at one another as each tried touching their noses to the glass in front of them.

"It's one of their daily exercise intervals," Dirk shouted.

"Like in prison?"

"Exactly!" Dirk gestured at the powerful current generators attached to the top of each habitat. "The only way to keep them fit and not going stir crazy is to exercise them and their predatory natures. The turbine system we installed creates an adjustable current that flows straight at them. If they don't fight it, they get pinned to the far end of their habitat. It's like putting them on a treadmill and forcing them to run."

Callahan's thick-jowled head angled to one side. "They look like they're racing. Can they see one another?"

Dirk nodded. "During their exercise interval, we deactivate the iridophores that keep them isolated. Seeing one another spurs their competitive instincts."

"What's with the music?" Callahan remarked. "Seems a bit inappropriate."

"Damned if I know why, but they seem to like that particular song," Dirk said. "They get a new mix each day, but she always opens with that track. It lets them know what time it is."

"Who opens?"

"I do," Stacy announced.

Dirk spun around as his ex popped out of a nearby booth, wiping her hands on a dry rag. She was wearing a full-body neoprene swimsuit, like the kind used in marine theme parks. "Geez, you scared the--"

"Shit out of you?" Stacy finished, smirking. "Good. And good to see you, too, Admiral. To answer your question, I program everything for our captive Thalassophoneans, from their diet to their medications. Music-wise, I like to vary the current to match the tempo of each song. They learn very quickly to anticipate speed shifts the moment they hear a familiar track. It's fascinating."

"Thalasso-what?" Callahan asked.

"Thalassophoneans." Stacy repeated. "It's a term we use to refer to a select group of extinct and, of course, extant macropliosaurs. It means 'Sea Slayer.'"

"Gotcha." Callahan's confused frown curved up into a smile as Bruce Springsteen's *"Born to Run"* began to radiate from the overheads. "Now *that's* better! Love the classics!" He looked around and made a show of cracking his knuckles. "So, when's the performance going to start?"

Stacy nodded. "Ah, yes. I was told you'd be attending the *procedure*. We'll be live in about forty-five minutes."

Dirk gestured at the sedated Gen-1. "Why is she already prepped? Shouldn't you have waited for me?"

Stacy gave him a look. "Because I needed to take care of Gretchen. I saved us time by setting everything up in advance. Is there a problem?"

"Uh, no," Dirk said, knowing he'd pay for that later. "I was just wondering who's monitoring her anesthesia." He indicated the ratcheted-down behemoth. "After what happened during the unloading, we don't need any more complications."

Stacy sighed. "Relax, Doctor Braddock. I've got Lieutenant McEwan inside *Colossus* in case of emergencies, and the specimen's anesthetics are being monitored by the new system." She indicated a small monitor on her wrist and then pointed at a matching, 10-foot screen situated above the healing pool. The pliosaur's vitals were clearly indicated on both. "If anything goes awry, I'll know it before she does." She gestured at the IVs running to and from the mammoth predator's neck. "I can dose her remotely at any time."

Dirk gave a hesitant nod. "As long as you've got everything under control."

"Don't I always?" Not bothering to wait for his reply, Stacy bent and picked up a long-handled scrub brush, then headed to a nearby push cart, loaded with ice and several five-foot tuna. "Now, if you'll excuse me . . ."

"So, how's she doing?" Dirk ventured.

"Almost done shedding," Stacy said. She grunted, her toned triceps flexing as she gave the heavy cart a push and started it rolling. "I'm going to hose her down and clean her up a bit. She's been irritable lately. I think she might be going into estrus."

"Wow, her first cycle. That should be interesting," Dirk said. He pondered for a moment, then moved to catch up with her. "Do you mind if we join you?" he asked, then added. "I mean, if you think *she* won't mind."

Stacy hesitated, her lips pursing as she looked Callahan up and down. She pulled a spare controller from her belt and handed it to Dirk. "Put this on him and make sure yours is active." She resumed rolling the cart away from the surgical pool, toward the larger, fenced-in one, two hundred feet away. "And *no* sudden movements."

Dirk carefully checked the settings on both controllers, then turned to Callahan and handed him one. "Keep this clipped on your belt at all times, and don't muddle with the settings."

Callahan was befuddled. "What is it, some sort of pager?"

"Life insurance," Dirk said. "Come on."

Callahan slipped the palm-sized white device onto his belt and hurried after him. As they neared the big inground pool's restrictive barrier, the concrete became noticeably wetter. Ahead, Stacy had reached the only gate and buzzed herself in. "Where are we going?" the admiral asked.

Dirk looked back at him and winked. "You'll see."

They had just made it through the gate and closed it behind them, when Garm Braddock and Natalya Dragunova pulled up in a solid black MarshCat, right beside the fence.

"Hey, it's Captains Courageous," Callahan chuckled, elbowing Dirk good-naturedly.

"What's going on, little brother?" Garm asked as he and Dragunova exited their vehicle and approached the chain link barrier.

"Shh!" Stacy hissed, casting them all a dour look. She parked her pushcart fifteen feet from the pool's reinforced concrete edge and turned to Dirk. "Tell them to keep their voices low," she said. "And unless they've got their own controllers, make sure they stay the hell behind the fence."

"Will do," Dirk said. He turned to Garm, who signaled he understood.

Stacy zippered up the front of her neoprene swimsuit and walked to the water's edge. The inground pool was sizable, a full two hundred feet in length. A fifty-foot-wide canal was connected to one end, but was cordoned off by a heavy titanium steel barrier. The water inside the pool was quiet and clear, but it was deep and dimly lit. The poor lighting and shadows cast from nearby structures gave it a dark, foreboding look. Every so often, large bubbles would rise from its depths and make a loud "bloop" sound as they popped. The bubbles appeared to be traveling, coming closer.

In the background, Wagner's *Ride of the Valkyries* played.

"What the hell's going on?" Callahan asked. The atmosphere was starting to get to him, and he gnawed his thumbnail as he gazed around. He looked frightened; as if he was worried some demon was going to lunge up from the pool's darkened depths at any moment and spring for his throat.

He wasn't far off.

Stacy leaned forward, her hands on her knees, and peered into the water. Then she straightened up and clapped her hands loudly together, before taking a quick step back. A second later, the water in the center of the pool frothed up as if a stick of dynamite had gone off.

"Holy fucking shi--"

Callahan's curse died in his throat as *Gretchen* broke the surface. Loudly spouting twin, twenty-foot columns of compressed water vapor, she shook her massive head, her thick scales shedding seawater. Dirk shook his own head and whistled as he took in her mass. The mottled Gen-6 cow was even bigger than the last time he'd seen her – probably fifty feet from nose to tail now and weighing nearly as many tons.

Without warning, Gretchen surged powerfully forward. One flick of her ten-foot flippers was all it took. She chose her target, angled her wedge-shaped head in its direction, and then rapidly closed the distance.

She was aiming for Stacy.

Dirk swallowed the growing lump in his throat. He could feel his own fear building, but he had the presence of mind to grab Callahan by one lapel and slap a hand over his mouth before the frightened admiral barked something that got someone killed. Pushing a yard-high wall of water before her, Gretchen loomed over Stacy. Her deadly jaws were parted, her banana-sized teeth bared. Dirk barely had time to mouth a prayer before the pliosaur made contact.

To her credit, Stacy stood her ground as Gretchen's wake slapped into her, inundating her from mid-thigh down and nearly knocking her over. A split-second later, the cow's ten-foot jaws impacted on Stacy's hip and thigh. The blow was surprisingly gentle, nudging the girl just enough to knock her off balance and forcing her to catch herself on the marine reptile's armored skull.

"There's my good girl!" Stacy said, beaming as she ran her nails over the top of the whale-sized beast's muzzle, her fingers deftly exploring and scratching at the tough folds of skin around one eye. "How's my baby?" she cooed as if she was talking to the family dog. "How's my precious little angel?"

Dirk had to blink as Gretchen uttered an elephant-like rumble of pleasure and angled her armored head so Stacy could reach a spot she'd missed. He'd witnessed scenes like this a few times over the past twelve months, but it never ceased to astonish him. Nowhere near as much as it did Callahan, of course. From the way he was clutching his chest, the red-faced admiral looked as if he was about to suffer a coronary.

"You okay?" Dirk asked softly.

"Are you fucking shitting me?" Callahan yelled. "Holy mother of--"

GRRRRRRRRHHHHRRRRR!

Dirk's eyes opened so wide they hurt. At the sound of Callahan's voice, Gretchen's fanged muzzle ripped free from Stacy's grasp and wheeled in their direction. Her scaly lips peeled back, revealing rows of razor sharp teeth, and a deep hiss spewed from her jaws. She studied the two men with her soulless red eyes; first Dirk and then the admiral. The forearm-long nostrils on the top of her muzzle flared and she reared her head back, sucking in long, rasping breaths through the scoop-shaped openings in her palate.

"No movements," Stacy emphasized, one hand extending in warning.

"Does a bowel movement count?" Callahan whimpered.

Stacy snickered and resumed soothing Gretchen. "Easy girl . . . easy . . ." She waved her hand, drawing the adolescent cow's eyes back to her. Gretchen uttered an affectionate grumble, deep in her throat, but seemed disinclined to turn away from Callahan. Dirk, she appeared fine with. He was a known entity. But the admiral was not. Her black pupils narrowed as she looked him up and down and she began to growl again.

Dragunova wore a smug look as she pressed her face against the chain link fence. "Hey, admiral, I theenk she likes you!"

Stacy shot her a "shut-up-bitch" look, while a disapproving Garm placed a hand on the tall Russian's shoulder.

"Now might be a good time to quit smoking," Dirk offered. Based on experience, he was pretty sure Gretchen wasn't going to attack. But he wasn't about to do an Irish jig to prove it.

"Ya think?" Callahan breathed. Sweat streamed down his forehead and hung from his mustache, but he managed to remain still.

"It's okay, little girl," Stacy said, reaching under Gretchen's chin and tugging at the hard folds of skin. "Hey! Is my baby hungry? *Is she hungry?*"

As Stacy smiled and enthusiastically slapped her thighs, Gretchen forgot all about Callahan. Her white tongue lolled from her mouth and she wagged her crocodile-like head back and forth. Water mixed with saliva streamed from her partially-open jaws, and the movements of her heavily muscled neck and body continued to cause the top portion of the pool to flow unchecked over its edge.

Stacy went to her pushcart and extracted what must have been a 120-pound tuna. She grabbed it by the tail and half-carried, half-dragged it toward Gretchen. The pliosaur's eyes gleamed with excitement. As she started to reach for the fish, Stacy waved an admonishing finger at her, stopping Gretchen cold, then put her palms together and made a motion similar to a mouth opening.

Gretchen complied instantly, her ten-foot jaws yawning wide. With an impressive display of strength, Stacy heaved the yellowfin tuna over her shoulder like a sack of grain and walked the remainder of the way to the pliosaur's beckoning maw. She paused two feet away, then glanced back and gave Dirk a calculated look.

"Watch this," she said. With a grunt, she heaved the big fish squarely atop Gretchen's thick tongue. As the pliosaur's taste buds sampled the tuna, her crimson eyes rolled back in their sockets. She was literally drooling, but to Dirk's amazement she didn't close her mouth. Like a dog with a treat balanced on its nose, the giant marine reptile was waiting for her master to give her permission to eat.

Stacy wiped her fish-slimed hands on her chest and stomach. She walked around the massive, dripping jaws while Gretchen waited, the bleeding tuna still lying on her tongue. She leaned forward and stuck her head inside the pliosaur's mouth, intently checking her charge's ridged teeth, even tugging hard on one to see if it was loose. All the while, the great reptile remained motionless, watching Stacy with its glittering ruby orbs, but otherwise not moving a muscle.

Dirk's heart climbed into his throat as a mischievous look came over Stacy. He held out his hand. "Stace, no," he hissed as loudly as he dared.

Stacy looked Gretchen square in one eye and held up a stern finger. "*Stay*," she commanded. Then she turned back to her audience, gave Dirk a wink and, using two of Gretchen's thick fangs as handholds, climbed inside her mouth and lay down.

"Fuck me . . ." Garm muttered from the fence.

Dirk thought he was going to have a stroke. He could feel the blood pounding in his temples as Stacy made a show of getting comfortable, pushing the similar-sized tuna to one side, and then trying to move Gretchen's heavy tongue as if it was a comforter. The marine reptile was so ravenous, three inches of saliva had collected in its mouth, but Stacy paid it no mind. After another ten seconds of splashing, she climbed back out, shook the drool from her arms and legs, and then bowed.

As hesitant claps echoed around her, Stacy turned to Gretchen and put her hands in the same, open-mouthed pose. She counted down from three, and at one, loudly closed her hands. The snapping sound of Gretchen's jaws slamming closed sent a tremor through the concrete under everyone's feet, driving the point home like nothing else.

"Sweet Mary's virgin ass," Callahan sputtered. Dirk could see he was dying to rush over to Stacy, but common sense and the crunching sounds Gretchen was making kept his feet firmly anchored. "That was absolutely amazing," he said. "You're the bravest woman – hell, you're the bravest *man* I've ever seen in my life! It is an *honor* to know you!"

"Thanks," Stacy said. Her caramel complexion pinkened from the unexpected praise. "There's nothing like emerging from the jaws of death to remind you you're alive." She gave Dirk her most winsome smile before grabbing a nearby pressure washer. She checked its settings, hit the start button, and then wheeled it towards Gretchen.

"What's that for?" Dirk asked.

"I've been using it to keep her mouth clean!" Stacy yelled over the noisy compressor. She signaled Gretchen to open wide again and started blasting away at the insides of her gaping maw, her gum line and ridged teeth in particular. "It's the *Kronosaurus* version of a water flosser!"

"Does it help with her breath?"

"What do you think?"

Dirk couldn't help but smile at the ingenuity as he watched Gretchen being put through the equivalent of a car wash. After Stacy finished cleaning hunks of meat from the marine reptile's mouth, she had her point her wedge-shaped head toward the ceiling and started hosing down her chin and throat regions, stopping periodically to pull stubborn hunks of dead skin free by hand.

Callahan wore a surprised look as Dirk moved closer. The admiral cleared his throat noisily, but remained where he was. "So, Dr. Daniels, how is it you're able to interact with this beast without getting killed? Is this part of the 'new tech' I've been hearing about?"

"One second," Stacy said as she turned off the pressure washer and picked up a long-handled scrub brush. Using hand signals, she waved Gretchen forward, until her head and neck extended over fifteen feet past the pool's lip. She followed up with a palms-down gesture that resulted in the pliosaur lowering her mandibles gently onto the concrete. With quick sweeps of her brush, Stacy started scrubbing the reptile's massive neck and shoulders. "I raised her from an egg," she announced, breathing heavily from her exertions. "I was the first thing she saw when she hatched and, as a result, she imprinted on me. In her eyes, I'm her mother."

Callahan scratched the back of his neck. "But I thought these things never see their parents; don't they just hatch and crawl down to the sea?"

"Normally, but . . . I'm sorry, hold on," Stacy said. Backed by a chorus of shocked inhalations, she hopped boldly onto Gretchen's hard nose.

Walking over the predator's muzzle, head and neck, and then moving onto the exposed portions of her ten-foot wide back, she turned, her toned legs braced apart. "I think you'll agree; the bonding instinct's still there." She indicated her charge's relaxed state.

"So it would seem." Callahan worked up the nerve to take a step closer. "Tell me, has she ever come after you?"

Stacy leaned forward at the waist, working the scrub brush like a push broom as she cleaned exposed scales. "Would I be here if she had?"

"Not once?"

Stacy straightened up and pushed her hair back from her face. For her part, Gretchen's eyes were closed and her respiration noticeably slowed. She seemed content to lay still and wait for her spa treatment to resume.

Stacy leaned on her long-handled brush. "Once, when she was three months old, she nipped me as I was feeding her."

"Nipped?" Callahan echoed. "What did you do?"

Stacy shrugged. "I screamed at her and then hauled back and cold-cocked her as hard as I could."

"And that did it?"

"Oh, yes. She's never stepped out of line since."

Callahan turned to Dirk and indicated the white controller on his belt. "So what the hell are we wearing these for? Do they even work?"

"Absolutely," Dirk said. He pointed at the top of Gretchen's thick skull. "See that Y-shaped scar? Every one of our resident pliosaurs has the same cybernetic implant. Besides the basic control features that allow you to program them as sentries, there's a built-in failsafe." He plucked his own unit free and held it between his thumb and index finger. "When this switch is flipped to blue, the wearer is designated off limits. The animal's security protocols tell it you're something unpalatable, so it doesn't attack you."

"'Something unpalatable?' Like what?"

Dirk hesitated. "Well, usually . . ."

"Excrement," Stacy interjected with a malicious grin. She finished her scrubbing and hopped nimbly off Gretchen's shoulders, landing in a squat position on the hard pool deck.

"Excrement?" Callahan shook his head. "So, she sees me as a piece of . . ."

"Exactly," Dirk said. Over the admiral's shoulder, he saw Garm slap a hand over Dragunova's mouth. The muscular Russian broke free and wheeled angrily on him, her teeth bared and eyes ablaze.

"You're shitting me," Callahan said.

"Technically, yes," Dirk said with a smirk. In the background, he could see the two sub captains bickering, but couldn't make out what they were saying. It was probably just as well. Dragunova had taken a serious dislike to Callahan and wasn't exactly the type to hold back. He could only imagine what colorful expletives his brother kept from escaping that truck driver's mouth of hers.

Stacy had finished brushing Gretchen and was back on the pressure washer. Switching it to a softer setting, to not risk damage to the pliosaur's sensitive eyes, she teased it with the pressurized water jet. Gretchen responded like a captive alligator, waiting to be fed. Her jaws yawned wide and she lunged this way and that, making loud snapping sounds as her teeth closed repeatedly on air and water.

Callahan was emboldened and moved closer. "So, basically, with this thing on my belt, I can get as close as I--"

He froze as Gretchen's head whipped in his direction. All playfulness had vanished and the humpback-sized beast eyed him with pure hostility.

"Stay back, admiral," Stacy advised. "The controller only works when you're motionless. As soon as you move, the illusion is broken." Her hand raised, she stood directly in front of Gretchen, putting herself between the pliosaur and the object of its enmity. Dirk noted that, although the huge reptile's lips wrinkled up in annoyance, she lowered her head submissively.

Behind the fence, Dragunova scoffed loudly. "Bah, this theeng is not dangerous," she said. "Look at it . . . ees just a щенок; a big puppy dog. I bet she feeds it pliosaur chow!"

Stacy's amber eyes were hard and glittery as she stared down *Antrodemus*'s muscular captain. "A puppy, eh?" She plucked the radio from her belt. "Tower three, this is Dr. Daniels. Besides the usual X-fish, what's the most unpleasant thing we've got on the menu?"

There was a moment's hesitation before the lift crew chief radioed back. "It'd have to be that big Nile croc they brought in yesterday – the man-eater from that zoo that closed down. Nasty bastard. The thing must weigh close to a ton."

Stacy's eyes were locked onto Dragunova's. "Perfect. Drop it in Gretchen's enclosure."

"But, uh . . . I can see you from here," the operator responded. "You're pretty close to the edge."

"So, drop it at the other end. *Now*, please."

"Will do, boss."

All heads turned as one of the hoists' engines sprang to life. Moving smoothly toward a distant pool, it descended to within fifty feet before dropping. After two failed attempts, the lift broke the surface with a thrashing, eighteen-foot *Crocodylus niloticus* locked in its powerful pincers. The hoist made a thrumming sound as it shot straight up, leveling off at one hundred feet. There was a loud, shifting noise, followed by a hum, as it moved laterally toward them across the complex network of girders that spread above the dock like a gigantic drop ceiling.

As soon as the crocodile realized how high up it was, it stopped struggling. Dirk could see its rough, olive-gray hide and pale underbelly as it drew steadily closer. When it got to within fifty feet of Gretchen's habitat, the croc sensed something was amiss. It began to struggle wildly, its thick body bucking and its powerful tail flailing back and forth as it fought to break free.

Callahan snorted amusedly. "Now, *this* should be interesting."

Dirk said nothing. He noticed Gretchen was eying the approaching hoist with what looked like a mixture of hunger and curiosity. *She's probably never seen a crocodile before.* As the hoist reached the opposite end of her habitat, the young cow shifted position. Using quick flicks of her four, kayak-sized flippers, she swiveled in the water until her triangular head was pointed at the precise spot the lift was heading for.

With the hoist nearly in position, Stacy walked briskly along the pool's edge, clapping her hands loudly and drawing Gretchen's attention back to her. She held up her index finger as she walked, stopping when she was perpendicular to the pliosaur's huge head. A moment later, the lift's light flashed red and its claxon sounded. The pincers sprang open and the still-flailing Nile crocodile plummeted fifty feet down, landing with a splash.

One of Dirk's eyebrows crept upward. The moment the one-ton croc hit the water Gretchen's entire body tensed, but she held her position. Her eyes were opened wide and focused on Stacy. All the while, Dirk could feel her ratcheting sonar clicks, tickling the concrete under his feet as she targeted her pending meal. Two hundred feet away, the Nile crocodile surfaced. Picking up the presence of a much larger predator, the big reptile froze, hoping to escape notice.

Stacy remained still except for her hand – the one Gretchen was eyeing. Dirk was fascinated. He could both feel and hear the pliosaur's hunger building; its near-empty stomach was growling like a lion. It blew his mind that one index finger was holding fifty-tons of ravenous carnivore in check. As Stacy's hand formed a sword-like blade, pointed toward the ceiling, Gretchen tensed. She was like a monstrous racehorse, waiting for the starting gun. The water around her swirled as she readied herself, and she watched Stacy with unblinking eyes, waiting . . .

The Nile crocodile began to panic. It started swimming rapidly along the pool's far end, rubbing its nose along the rough concrete as it desperately sought a way out. Suddenly, Stacy's hand flipped downward, her fingers directing the strike.

Gretchen exploded into motion.

With a power thrust from all four flippers, she rocketed forward, accelerating from zero to thirty in less than a second. Her backwash completely inundated the rear pool deck, soaking Dirk's and Callahan's shoes. A split-second later, the voracious beast slammed into the hapless crocodile, enveloping it, but also overshooting its mark and striking the pool wall with impressive force. There was a sound reminiscent of a tank shell impacting on a bunker and the reinforced concrete floor around the pool shook violently.

"Jesus Christ!" Callahan spouted as he staggered to one side.

Dirk covered his ears as Gretchen uttered a deep, vibrating growl that resonated through his bowels. She shattered the water's surface, the doomed Nile croc pinned in her jaws. Its head and forelegs protruded from one side, its tail from the other. As the crocodilian twisted about, desperately trying to sink its teeth into the face of its attacker, the cow shook her ten-foot head. Red-tinged seawater sprayed for a hundred feet, coating the surrounding fence and concrete.

The crocodile was already dead. Its head hung limply, its jaws streaming blood like a broken faucet into the pool's frothed-up waters. There was a wet, crunchy sound as Gretchen brought her fangs together, cutting it in two. Ignoring the tail portion, she hoisted its mangled upper half aloft and began shifting it in her jaws. Once she had it properly positioned, she let gravity do the work and gulped it down.

Dirk grimaced as Gretchen's white tongue emerged from her mouth and ran along her blood-caked lips, like a dog licking its chops. The pliosaur was still unsatisfied, however, and began casting about for the croc's bottom half. She spotted it a few yards away and snapped it up, her jaws giving off loud, crackling sounds as her ridged teeth crushed the tail section's bones into mush.

A smile migrated across Dirk's angular face as he observed Stacy standing with her arms folded across her chest, proudly watching her colossal "daughter" choke down another eight hundred pounds of meat. She swiveled at the hip toward Dragunova and said loudly, "You're right, look at her!" Then she added in a mocking Russian accent, "She's just a beeg puppy!"

Dirk rolled his eyes as Stacy shook her head and muttered the word "сука." His high school Russian was all but forgotten, but he still recognized the word "bitch" when he heard it. *Thank God Dragunova didn't.* That was all he needed . . .

"Okay, people," Dirk said, backing away from Gretchen's pool, his hands extended before him. "Show's over. Anyone who's attending the procedure, please get to your designated seats." He checked his watch. "Stacy and I will be scrubbed and ready to proceed in approximately thirty minutes."

Callahan nodded and then turned to Garm. "Hey, Gate. You got room for an old man in that buggy? I know it's close, but my hip ain't what it used to be."

As Garm opened his mouth to reply, Dragunova muttered something unintelligible and walked off, making tracks away from the surgical center. Probably off to the gym, Dirk mused.

"We appear to have an opening, admiral," Garm said. He moved some small items from the front seat. "Come on down."

Dirk watched Callahan hobble over and clamber into Garm's ATV. He wasn't even fully seated before he started gabbing away. Something about boxing, from the sound of it . . . His brother just sighed and put the vehicle in gear. Dirk chuckled. Garm was going to be much happier when the admiral's visit was over.

Through the fence, Dirk studied Dragunova's body language. From her gait and the set of her shoulders, she seemed irritated. It must have had something to do with Callahan, he figured. She was the type to hold a grudge. With Led Zeppelin's "Rock and Roll" jamming in the background, he watched her muscular legs flexing as they carried her across the docks. His sigh of longing changed to a startled yelp as Stacy unexpectedly appeared beside him. He hadn't heard her approach over the steam-engine sounds of Gretchen spouting.

"You're jumpy," she said.

"Could it have anything to do with fifty tons of feeding pliosaur breathing down my neck?" Dirk said, annoyed. He glanced over his shoulder, just to make sure. A hundred yards past the fence, he could still make out Dragunova's silhouette as she moved past a tech team.

Stacy's eyes narrowed as she followed Dirk's line of sight. "I still can't believe you broke up with me for that juiced-up piece of Eurotrash." She snorted irritably.

Dirk nearly gave himself whiplash as he turned toward her. "What are you talking about?"

"You know *exactly* what – and who – I'm referring to," she said icily. "Stalin's wet dream over there, shaking her 'beeg Russian ass.'"

"Stace, that's ridiculous," Dirk said. He smiled carefully. "There is nothing between Captain Dragunova and me. We've never even--"

"Oh, I *know* that," she said. "But it's not for lack of desire on your part."

Dirk felt a pliosaur-sized surge of panic and faked a chuckle. "That's crazy. Where would you even get such an idea?"

"Oh, please," Stacy scoffed. "Do you think I'm stupid? You broke up with me three days after she got here! We women have instincts for such things. I've seen the way you look at her. The way you're looking at her right *now*."

Dirk's lips tightened and he looked Stacy straight in those tiger eyes of hers. "And how exactly is that?"

"Like you're a hungry-but-underrated jockey, and she's a world champion thoroughbred you've dreamed of riding your entire life."

"Well, she's certainly *built* like a racehorse, I'll give you that," Dirk chortled. "But just because a guy admires a girl's physique doesn't mean he wants to play hide the--"

"Omigod, are you really that blind?" Stacy's face contorted with un-contained anger. "She's a *killer*, Dirk," she snapped. "That's what she is, that's what she does, and that's why she was hired – to *kill* things. Understand?"

Dirk hesitated. "Stace . . ."

"Look, she's nice to look at. I get that. And you're a red-blooded guy. It's only natural," Stacy said, forcibly calming herself. "But she's got ice water in her veins. You heard her joke about Gretchen being a puppy, right?"

"Yes."

Stacy held up her index finger as if she was talking to her pliosaur. "You're a great guy, Dirk Braddock; you're smart, kind, and sweet. But to Natalya Dragunova, *you* are a puppy. And if you're not careful, she'll treat you like one."

"I'm a puppy?"

"Yes. And your stupid male pride won't let you see it." Stacy shook her head. "Never mind. Let's get prepped."

Dirk felt his face flush with a combination of embarrassment and annoyance and a spiteful notion slithered into his head. "You're right. And speaking of prepped: after that bath you took in Gretchen's mouth, I think you better go see Dr. Bane."

"What for?"

"A booster shot," Dirk announced. A tantalizing vision of Stacy bend-ing over for one of those horse needles appeared before his eyes and it took every ounce of willpower he had to keep a straight face. "She's been administering the new formula to anyone who's been exposed."

"Oh, *that*." Stacy waved her hand dismissively. "I had one, earlier."

Dirk's jaw dropped. "You did?"

"Yes, see?" She unzipped the front of her wetsuit and pulled one side down, exposing the red needle mark on her shoulder and a healthy portion of one caramel-colored breast.

Dirk's face darkened.

"What's wrong?" Stacy asked, smiling innocently as she covered back up.

"Oh, nothing," Dirk grumbled. When she wasn't looking, he discretely rubbed his painfully sore ass cheek.

Why that sneaky cougar bitch!

TWELVE

Moving with a grace that belied his 200-plus tons, the Ancient scoured the borders of the Continental shelf, directly adjacent to the drop-off. He was near the spot where his mate had recently been overpowered, and with barely four hundred feet of water in which to conceal himself, the apex predator moved with caution. He cruised at a depth of three hundred feet, oft-times hugging the seafloor, and surfaced only once every forty minutes. If it wasn't for the added security of a moonless night, he would not have ventured so close to shore. But the concealing darkness, combined with the unusual scent that continued to tug at him, had tempted him into taking a chance.

He had followed the trail for many miles; a hunt that started far at sea, eventually leading him here. The scent was unusual – another that his experienced olfactory system was unacquainted with – and he was intrigued. For the last few seasons he'd detected it. always in this same area, and coinciding with the new moon. Although he'd been repeatedly frustrated at his inability to pinpoint the source of the scent molecules, the tantalizing smell continued to waft about in the water, popping up here and there, and he continued to find himself drawn.

After thirty minutes of weaving back and forth, the giant bull finally uttered a cantankerous grumble and gave up. He swung westward and accelerated, following the jagged, coral-tipped edges of the drop-off. Twelve miles to his right lay breakers, a quarter-mile to his left, the precipice, and a two-thousand-foot descent into darkness.

Suddenly, the male's deep-set eyes crinkled up. Directly ahead, the decaying remains of a fallen colossus materialized out of the murk. The whale's hardened carcass was a familiar sight to the old bull, and remained as it had for the last century, draped across a rocky ridge and parallel to the drop-off. Despite the ravages of time, its gray, anemone-dotted skin was still smooth. The only exception was the gaping wound that adorned its broken back, its rusted ribs jutting out for all the world to see.

The sclerotic ring encircling the Ancient's eyes compressed as he studied his fallen adversary. Despite the moonless night, his thermal vision was able to filter enough light to see. From three hundred feet out, he circled the behemoth. It was as huge as he remembered: more than three times his current length and many times heavier. He could see its shattered snout where it was embedded in the rock and sand of the seabed, as well as its twisted tail. Its thick conning tower angled upward like the dorsal fin of some primeval shark, still dangerous, and along its back, ahead of the dorsal, was the rusticle-draped spike that once spat fire.

As he eyed his long-dead nemesis, the old bull found himself un-expectedly sucked back into a moonless night just like this one, only a hundred years prior. He'd been a much younger beast then. Bigger than when he escaped his stony prison, but nowhere near the size he would one day attain. Still, at eighty feet in length, his mass and power made him a match for even the largest females of his kind. Or they would have, if there had been any. He had been alone for more seasons than he could remember, and had adapted to his loneliness to keep from going mad.

One of the tricks he'd acquired over the last thirty years was accom-panying the huge, armored whales that prowled beneath the waves. Not just for company, but for sustenance. The first time he came across one of them had been by accident; he'd been drawn to a series of pain-fully loud shock waves that resonated for hundreds of miles. When he reached the source, he encountered a giant, noisy beast. It was far larger than he, and in shape appeared to be some sort of cetacean.

Except that it never surfaced. And it was made of metal.

It turned out that the iron whales were newcomers to Earth's oceans. Like the Ancient, they were predators. Part of Nature's way of balancing things, they preyed on the titanic surface constructs that housed the tiny warm-bloods, stalking them as they floated about. The "neo-whales" hunted from below, tracking their prey with sonar, much like the great pliosaur and the sperm whales he sometimes battled.

By comparison, the neo-whales' fledgling sound sight was clumsy and loud, but it was still effective. Once they'd locked onto a prospective victim, however, the whales did something unusual. Rather than rushing in to attack, they spat younger versions of themselves at it. The first time he'd seen this, the Ancient was baffled. He'd watched as the small, tube-shaped newborns sprang from their mother's mouth and raced away. Curious as to what they would do, he'd followed them.

The chase had proven exciting. The younglings were as fast as he was, propelled through the water by the same underwater geysers that powered their prey. With an effort, he managed to catch up to one and prepared to mouth it. It was a decision that was nearly his undoing. Only the realization he was fast-approaching one of the surface colossi caused him to veer off.

That innate caution saved his life. A moment later, the tiny metal whale impacted on its target. There was a fiery burst, followed by a powerful concussive blast that sent him tumbling snout over tail, disabling his sound sight and rupturing one of his eardrums.

He swam away, hurt and disoriented, and watched from afar to see what would happen next. The neo-whale parent regurgitated more of its cylindrical offspring. There was a series of fiery explosions and the stricken vessel began to ooze body fluids and list. Its vast infestation of bipeds quickly abandoned their mortally wounded host, crying out in terror as it was drawn beneath the waves. Many of them lay in the water, dead or dying, and around them, their blood formed tantalizing clouds.

The Ancient was intrigued. After the neo-whale sent its offspring to attack it kept its distance, ignoring both the dying host and any surviving parasites. The attack must have been a territorial one, as the parent was not interested in feeding. He, on the other hand, had no such reservations. He moved closer, and when the steel-covered cetacean failed to react to his presence, began to eat. Weaving in and out of the debris field, he swam open-mouthed. Like a blue whale ingesting clouds of krill, he inhaled dead and dying bipeds by the dozen. They were small – seal-sized at best – but meaty and nutritious, and consuming a hundred was comparable to eating a full-grown basking shark, only without the struggle.

After he finished feeding, the Ancient went on his way. A few days later, however, more of the underwater explosions drew him back. He began to associate the deafening sounds with food and came running whenever he heard the dinner bell. Eventually, he took to following the metal whales, albeit at a safe distance. As big as they were, they were slow and clumsy, and without their sound sight, apparently blind. As long as he stayed behind them, following silently in their swash, he was invisible.

Eventually, he came across the biggest neo-whale he'd ever seen. He was fascinated by its mammoth size and for weeks pursued it, starting in Europe and then crossing the Atlantic. The whale was undoubtedly migrating, as it spent most of its time submerged and kept moving, stopping only occasionally to make kills. Still, feedings were plentiful when they took place, so the pliosaur continued the game, pacing the noisy behemoth like a scale-covered shadow and, in between meals, supplementing his diet with nearby sea life.

One moonless night, the neo-whale surfaced and moved into the shallows, a risky move, as it occupied a depth not much greater than it was long. It remained there, silent, immobile, and hovering a dozen miles from shore. After several hours of this inactivity, the Ancient, hungry and impatient, rose in the water column. From only fifty yards out he watched, his binocular vision piercing the water's surface as he spied on the inert whale.

He was shocked to discover the hard-shelled titan was infested with the same warm-blooded bipeds as the huge constructs it hunted. There were dozens of the tiny creatures, slinking out of holes in their host. Some crawled over its wide back, cleaning it of other, less noticeable parasites, while others perched atop its massive dorsal fin and stood guard.

Then, something odd happened. It turned out the neo-whale had an eye situated in, of all places, its fin. There was only one such eye, and it gleamed a phosphorescent yellow. Two of the bipeds were annoying the whale by touching its eye, causing it to blink repeatedly.

When, far in the distance, another such eye began to blink back, the Ancient deduced the truth. The iron-hided behemoth had, indeed, been migrating. It had sought out its mate and was now communicating with it.

A sudden hunger pang began to assail the bull pliosaur's empty stomach and he ground his teeth in frustration. The need to surface was also upon him, and he succumbed to the combined stimuli. Slipping stealthily closer, he approached the neo-whale perpendicular to its dorsal fin, with the intentions of plucking a few parasites from its back. If he was subtle enough, he was sure the colossal beast wouldn't mind.

Spouting loudly twenty-five yards out, the great reptile made for the nearest cluster of bipeds, his monstrous jaws opened, his red eyes gleaming. To his amusement, the defenseless mammals sprang into action the moment they spotted him. Screaming cries of alarm, they scurried this way and that, with several rushing forward and twisting at a vestigial fin that protruded, spike-like, in front of the neo-whale's great dorsal sail.

Then, something astonishing happened. The bipeds spun the spike-like fin toward him and one of them uttered a loud squeak. A blinding burst of light lit up the darkness and the fin spat fire and thunder. The blast came right at him, striking the water a few yards to his right and causing it to erupt. A powerful shock wave slammed into him and he felt a sharp spasm of pain as one of his pectoral fins was ripped open.

The Ancient snorted in alarm and sounded. As he did, the spiked fin spat fire again, causing the water above him to explode, and tearing a network of foot-wide holes in the thick skin of his back.

Furious at being injured, the great bull submerged to a depth of two hundred feet and sped in a wide arc. He heard a series of loud clangs and thumps emanating from within the neo-whale, coupled with the dampened cries of its mammalian parasites as they moved around inside its digestive system. He realized the creature was preparing to sound.

As the iron-hided whale descended to one hundred feet and began emitting active sonar, it occurred to the Ancient that perhaps the bipeds were more than just parasites. Perhaps a symbiotic relationship existed between the two, like that between him and the small fish that cleaned leeches from his skin and food particles from between his teeth.

His ponderings evaporated as the great metal beast matched his depth and swung slowly in his direction. The familiar ringing sounds that preceded it spewing forth its young told him everything he needed to know.

The neo-whale wanted to fight.

The Ancient's mighty chest cavity expanded with unfettered fury at the thought of an intruder challenging his eons-long reign. He uttered a thunderous roar and rushed forward. The neo-whale spun to meet his charge. Seconds later, two of its lethal young erupted from its mouth. The Ancient slowed, watching as the tree-trunk-sized creatures raced toward him. His lips snarled back, and with a power stroke displacing a hundred thousand gallons of seawater, he accelerated straight at them. The distance between them vanished in seconds. Then, at the last moment, he flared his fins and dove downward, causing the fast-moving younglings to speed right over his broad back, missing him completely and continuing impotently on out to sea.

Having dodged his adversary's first strike, the enraged pliosaur wasted no time. Using his superior speed and maneuverability, he weaved around the cumbersome behemoth, before coming up under it and slamming headfirst into its lower jaw and throat. Although he'd never seen the neo-whale bite, he wasn't taking any chances. Like a thunderclap, his armored skull impacted on the whale's vulnerable underside, caving in its thin metal skin.

For the pliosaur, it was a costly maneuver, one that left the interlocking scales covering his head bleeding and badly lacerated. But the effect on the wounded cetacean was far more devastating. Oozing oil, it broke off its attack and turned to flee. The Ancient was far from finished, however, and pursued. Spiraling around his oversized opponent, he slashed repeatedly at it, cutting painfully noisy grooves in its hard flanks with his sixteen-inch teeth as he searched for a vulnerable spot.

As the neo-whale reached its top speed and made a run for the nearby drop-off, the pliosaur turned away from it. Trailing blood, he retreated. A thousand yards out, he turned back. His crushing jaws were agape and there was murder in his eyes. Gone was the notion of systematically dismantling his adversary. He was going to stop it and its nest of parasites before they escaped into deep water.

He was going to destroy them.

Hurtling straight toward the steel cetacean's flanks, he broadsided the brute at a speed exceeding fifty miles an hour. The impact echoed across the submarine canyons for twenty miles, as an explosive blast of shattered metal and pressurized air was released. With a horrendous groan, a huge rent appeared in the stricken whale's side, quickly lengthening and expanding. As its nose dipped and it plummeted toward a nearby underwater ridge, the Ancient realized he had broken the thing's back.

Seconds later, the paralyzed whale impacted headfirst on the sand-coated rock of the seafloor and collapsed, its thunderous impact creating a rapidly expanding cloud of sand, oil and blood.

Still not assured of his victory, the giant bull circled his fallen adversary, scanning it with powerful pulses that penetrated the obscuring debris. He could both "see" and hear water flooding the dead whale's insides, along with the muffled screams of surviving parasites as they drowned. A few minutes later, there was silence.

The Ancient held his position, offsetting the current with occasional flicks of his fins. He continued to eye the fallen giant, watching as the tide cleared away the billows of blood and blackish oil that seeped from it. A wave of dizziness suddenly came over him and he shook his head. When his vision cleared he was back in the present. The wreck of the neo-whale was transformed. Its once shiny hull was overgrown with seaweed and algae, its bow and tail section partially concealed beneath the shifting sands. Even the cavernous rent in its side had changed; its once sharp edges were draped with reddish rusticles, giving it the appearance of an infected wound.

As the current picked up, causing the sand in and around the downed submarine to swirl like a miniature dust storm, the Ancient began to blink. His nostrils flared and he drew in snoutfuls of seawater, sampling it. Suddenly, his football-sized eyes opened wide.

There was another scent.

He had been so intent on tracking the elusive smell that had drawn him here he failed to notice a second one, mixed in. It was the same alien scent he came across when he scouted the wreck of the wooden sailing ship.

The Ancient swung his limousine-sized head back and forth, tasting and testing the water. The foreign smell had an unusual effect on him. He could feel his pulse racing and his muscles contracting as he analyzed it. The scent was far stronger now, its source most likely close by. He looked around. Suddenly, his gaze fell on the giant wound in the neo-whale's side.

The scent was coming from there.

Wary of using his sound sight this close to shore, the old bull moved closer, his garnet-colored eyes zeroing what was, effectively, a pitch-black cave behind the forty-foot gash. Unable to see inside from his current vantage point, he dropped down until he was suspended less than ten feet above the seabed. Then, he began to creep forward.

Closer and closer he crept, his nostrils feverishly studying the unfamiliar smell. It grew more pungent the nearer he got, and although he couldn't place it, an alarm began to sound in the furthest reaches of his primitive mind. There was something . . . *primordial* about the scent. Something he needed to be wary of.

As he stole to within fifty feet of the rusticle-spewing entrance, the Ancient readied himself. Caves were often inhabited by unpleasant things. His flippers began to undulate, casting up vast clouds of sand, and his car-sized heart beat faster and faster, pumping blood to his rock-hard muscles, readying them for action.

The smell grew steadily stronger.

From twenty feet out, the old pliosaur lunged savagely forward, thrusting his battle-scarred jaws directly into the opening. His armor-piercing teeth were bared and he was ready to fight.

Beyond its rusted steel ribs and a network of decaying wiring, however, the interior of the gutted neo-whale was barren. There was nothing except sand, coral, and some rotting pieces of wood. Confused, the Ancient looked left and right, then withdrew, backing away. His lips wrinkled up and he shook his monstrous head. He had pinpointed the source of the unusual smell – the scent was stronger inside the wreck than anywhere else – but whatever left it was long gone.

With a dismissive shrug of his barnacle-dotted fins, the old bull turned on his tail. He was beginning to feel the need for oxygen and angled his snout toward the surface. Like the rippling fins of a colossal manta ray, his flippers propelled his massive body upward. As he pierced the water's topmost layer and filled his cavernous lungs, his predator's mind switched from pondering mysterious smells to something more pressing: his next kill.

His growling stomach reminded him that it had been too long since he last fed. He rested on the surface for a moment, reveling in the warm night air and listening to the sounds of bats and insects flitting overhead. Far in the distance, he spotted the lights of a passing luxury liner. He watched it glimmering on the horizon until it faded from view. Finally, with nothing to maintain his interest and a cavernous belly to fill, he sounded and sped toward the beckoning deep.

———

Dirk Braddock waved a gloved hand in front of his face. His eyes were tearing up and he was trying not to gag into his surgical mask, as the sickeningly sweet stench of pliosaur amniotic fluid filled the air. He checked the 100-foot healing pool at his feet. The tepid water, with its powerful antibacterial and regenerative additives, was a dull scarlet from all the blood streaming into it, and he could hear the filtration system's powerful pumps straining as they fought to cleanse it.

"What's the count?" he asked a nearby technician. He surveyed the huge mound of eggs, piled high atop a nearby flatbed. The five-man team had been busting their collective asses for the last twenty minutes, lugging the blood-streaked, thirty-inch eggs from their progenitor to the disposal truck.

The tech leaned forward, gazing apprehensively inside the gaping, ten-foot hole that had been incised through layers of scales, skin, adipose tissue, and muscle, exposing the sedated Gen-1 *Kronosaurus imperator*'s uterine cavity. The mammoth beast had been rolled onto its side atop the healing pool's floating gurney and was held in position by both *Colossus*'s gigantic arms and a pair of yard-thick restraining belts. An esophagus vacuum tube was inserted into its mouth, past its arsenal of machete-sized fangs, and IV lines as thick as fire hoses were embedded in the folds of its fifteen-foot neck. "Looks like this is the last. I count eighty-four altogether, Doctor Braddock," the tech replied. Grunting, he hoisted the weighty ivory globe up on one shoulder and staggered toward the truck. It was hard work, Dirk acknowledged, as he watched him totter along. He could see the side of the man's face through his translucent faceplate. Even with a full-body, climate-controlled hazmat suit, he was sweating like a pig.

Dirk wiped his blood-soaked goggles and glanced around. Other than the facility guards, who had moved to the outer perimeter and were focused on keeping unnecessary personnel at bay, it was just him, the surgical techs, and Stacy. She was seated inside *Colossus*'s reinforced steel cab, manning the controls and waiting for what came next. The only witnesses were Admiral Callahan, his remaining aide, Gibbons, and Garm, omnipresent and overprotective, as always.

To Dirk's surprise, the big sub commander seemed more concerned about Callahan's capacity for causing mischief than he was about guarding his sibling from potential harm. It was a pleasant change of pace, he had to admit.

Dirk squinted up at the blazing hot halogen overheads, then wiped his brow with his gown sleeve before talking into his chin mike. "Resuming analysis and indoctrination of newly captured Gen-1: designate: *Goliath*. Specimen is an adult female *Kronosaurus imperator* approximately 30 years old and measuring 81.3 feet LOA. Initial mass was calculated at 152.68 tons." He paused to glance up at the ten-foot screen protruding from a nearby wall. In addition to the giant saurian's pulse and blood pressure, its vital statistics and an ongoing real-time sonogram were vividly displayed. "Uterine contents have been excised. Post-partum mass is calculated at 137.43 tons."

Dirk paused as the lead tech waved his arms to get his attention. Behind him, two of his subordinates had climbed into the flatbed containing the pliosaur eggs and were sitting there with the engine idling.

"Yes, Mr. Jones?" Dirk asked, clicking off his recorder.

"I'm sorry, Dr. Braddock," Jones apologized. He glanced down at his e-pad and shook his head. "How do you want these disposed of?"

Dirk resisted the urge to glance up at *Colossus*'s nearby control booth. He knew how Stacy felt about aborting unborn animals, even dangerous ones. If his ex had a flaw, it was that she allowed her maternal instincts to overshadow sound judgment at times. The partially developed embryos had no scientific value. They'd done in-uterine scans of the eggs and none of them qualified for preservation. And from both practical and ethical standpoints, they couldn't allow them to go full term. The oceans simply couldn't handle another eighty-four hungry pliosaurs on the prowl.

"Take them to tank four," Dirk said, sounding far less assured than he intended to.

As the tech nodded and turned away, Callahan raised his hand like he was back in grade school. "Hey, uh, sport. Isn't tank four the one housing all those big-ass fish – the ones with the teeth?"

"The *Xiphactinus*. That's right."

"Holy shit!" Callahan chortled. "You're feeding those behemoths the babies of one of their natural predators? Now *that* is ironic."

Dirk shook his head. "Although we've never had boots on the ground in Diablo Caldera, admiral, it's a safe assumption that the lesser predators the pliosaurs fed on helped keep their numbers in check by consuming their young. As did the adults of their kind, I'm sure."

Callahan gave him a thumbs-up sign. "Gotcha. Carry on."

"Thanks," Dirk remarked. Behind him the truckload of doomed pliosaur eggs shifted into gear and pulled slowly away.

"Resuming re--" Dirk sighed as he saw Callahan's hand go up again. "*Yes*, admiral . . ."

"Sorry." Callahan pointed at the sedated pliosaur's partially-opened eyes. "So, uh, does it know any of what's goin on? I mean, is it aware you just killed its babies?"

"*She* is probably distantly aware of what is occurring around her, but is, obviously, unable to act," Dirk replied.

"Isn't she gonna be pissed off when she comes to?"

"All the more reason for us to follow procedure and install her implant." Dirk glanced down at his patient's scarred head and grinned. "Besides, in case you haven't noticed, she's looking at *you* right now. And since she'll be leaving here *with* you, once she's recovered, if she *does* have any vestigial memories, well . . . good luck with that."

Dirk reined in a smirk as he studied his screens. He tapped his radio. "Lab, this is Dr. Braddock. How's the breakdown coming? Over."

There was a moment of static before the reply came through. "The prenatals you sent down are being compared to known profiles. Results will be ready in twenty to thirty. Over."

"Thanks, Jim. I'll wait on you. Braddock out."

Dirk changed frequencies and fired a transmission at Stacy inside *Colossus*. "Dr. Daniels, I'm going to need your help closing."

"Roger that," Stacy said, perking up. She was situated in what was effectively the "head" of *Colossus*: a reinforced steel cube about the size of a powder room. Through the curved thermoplastic window that formed the upper half of the cab's face, he watched her lean forward, her arms inserted in the neural interface ports that allowed her to control the world's largest manipulators.

Mounted on its ten-foot thick, stainless steel shafts, the twenty-year old, two hundred-ton robotic lift system was an early brainchild of Amara Braddock's robotics company. Originally designed for use in construction, the retired *Colossus* system had been overhauled and upgraded to handle captive pliosaurs inside Tartarus.

In truth, Dirk mused, the admittedly obsolete bionic arms were a godsend. Their regular hoists could do the job, to a point, but manipulating unconscious saurians that exceeded one hundred tons sometimes required a bit more muscle.

Colossus certainly lived up to its name.

With a loud, hydraulic hiss, the fifty-foot, stainless steel arms that gripped the sedated Gen-1 female around the neck and hips came to life. Standing at the pool's edge, between a pair of hands that could each envelop a Mini-Cooper, Dirk wondered if this was how Fay Wray felt in "King Kong."

With impressive dexterity, Stacy worked the controls. Shifting her grip on the huge reptile, she held it stable with one four-fingered hand and loosened its restraining straps with the other. This accomplished, she lifted the pliosaur like it was a child, carefully manipulating its unconscious form until the behemoth ended up flat on its back.

Out of the corner of one eye, Dirk saw Garm tense and chuckled. His big brother – a tenuous title, as he was only seventeen minutes older – was inherently paranoid that he'd either get squashed by the manipulators or eaten by a prematurely revived specimen.

It hasn't happened yet.

"Okay, she's in position," Stacy said, her voice emanating from her cab's speakers. "Are you ready?"

Dirk nodded and accepted a five-foot, articulating surgical stapler from a nearby tech. He checked its magazine, pulled the activator handle back, and then hopped across the yard-wide space between the gurney and the pool edge. He moved nimbly around the immobile *Kronosaurus*, shifting the stapler to his dominant hand. He was glad they'd upgraded to the latest model. It was still no picnic, but its unwieldy predecessor had weighed as much as an Olympic weight bar.

Stepping carefully onto one of the pliosaur's boat-sized flippers, Dirk felt like a Lilliputian walking across its gigantic body. His knee-high latex boots made squeaking noises as their specially designed soles adhered to the reptile's thick scales.

Dirk signaled to Stacy and then ducked, allowing one of her manipulators to pass directly overhead before it reached inside the creature's incision. With surprising gentleness, she pulled the membranes of the pliosaur's reproductive system back together, holding each layer firmly between stainless steel fingers while Dirk ran the surgical stapler smoothly along each cut. He could hear the characteristic "*k-chak*" sound as each self-dissolving polymer staple shot out and took hold.

Within ten minutes, the last suture was in place and the yawning opening in the pliosaur's tough belly scales had been sealed as tight as a drum.

Dirk climbed down off the drugged beast and wiped the sweat from his brow before surveying his handiwork. The stitches looked good and the animal's vitals were strong and steady. Between the medications they'd administered and the species' inherent regenerative capabilities, it would recover in record time.

Puffing out a breath, Dirk crossed over to a nearby table and put the stapler down. He removed his stained mask, goggles, and elbow-length gloves, tossing them into a medical-waste bin, then put on fresh ones. He wiped his brow once more, then picked up a nearby tablet and hopped back onto the gurney.

"Okay, Dr. Daniels," he radioed. "Let's turn her dorsal-side up and continue with the evaluation."

Stacy nodded and Dirk stepped back as the giant arms on either side of him bent at the elbows. Their industrial grade pneumatics kicked in, whining as *Colossus* hoisted the 137-ton pliosaur straight up and then flipped it carefully back over. Replacing it on the floating gurney, Stacy used the manipulator's fingers to reattach the restraining straps over its neck and mid-section – more a stability precaution than a security concern.

As Stacy's shiny robotic arms pulled back, coming to rest on the platform directly behind him, Dirk skirted the sedated marine reptile.

"Okay, admiral, since this girl is going to be 'hooking' for you, let's get down to business." He tapped his recorder. "Finishing statistics: specimen, code-name *Goliath*, has a skull length of sixteen feet, ten inches. Mandibular beam peaks at seven-foot-six. The teeth are large and sharply ridged, with trihedral cross-sections." He glanced down at his tablet and touched a key, then spoke into his chin mike. "Dr. Daniels, I'm bringing Fenris online."

"Roger that," came the reply.

While *Colossus*'s arms lifted back up off the platform and extended forward, hovering overhead, Dirk signaled to a team of nearby medical techs. Wordlessly, the three men approached what looked like an ornate, fourteen-foot thermometer with an enlarged, rubber-covered end, resting on a pad near the shelving units. A heavy-gauge electric cable attached to the narrow end of the unit was connected to a nearby generator. Two of them hoisted the heavy device and checked its settings, while the third guided its lengthy power cord to avoid entanglements. Inching carefully forward, the men moved toward the head of the *Kronosaurus imperator*.

"Fenris?" Callahan asked. "What's that?"

"It's our bite-gauge, admiral," Dirk replied. He walked toward the techs, his fingertips tapping his tablet. "We like to calibrate the bite force of every specimen we bring in. I'm sure you'd like to know what kind of power this little lady is packing, yes?"

"Absolutely. How hard does *Polyphemus* bite?"

"Forty-seven tons per square inch. He can bite a minivan in two."

"Wow. You know that off the top of your head?"

"Of course."

Callahan leaned back in his chair, nodding his appreciation as Dirk reached the pliosaur's snout and moved alongside its fanged jaws. He extracted a laser pointer from his lab coat and began to direct it over the drugged marine reptile's skull.

"A quick lesson in pliosaur anatomy, admiral," he began. "Notice the large bulges on the top of the skull; these are the animal's adductor muscles. They're responsible for closing its jaws."

Callahan nodded.

Dirk continued. "All pliosaurs have enlarged supratemporal fenestrae to anchor these immense muscles." He swept the red dot down the animal's muzzle. "When you combine the triangular-shaped head, the deeply-rooted, sharply ridged teeth, and a deep mandibular symphysis, you're basically looking at history's most lethal bite."

Dirk focused his pointer on the *Kronosaurus*'s ivory fangs. "Unlike its smaller relative, *Kronosaurus queenslandicus*, which had rounded teeth and was forced to twist feed like a croc to tear chunks from large prey items, an *Imperator*'s jaws are like giant shears. If something's too big to swallow whole, they just bite it into manageable portions."

One of the techs holding the big bite gauge signaled Dirk. "Fenris is prepped, Dr. Braddock."

"Thanks." He touched his chin mike. "Dr. Daniels, are you ready?"

Stacy's response was a hum of giant actuators as she directed her bionic arms toward the pliosaur's head. Accompanied by a clicking sound, a nub-like electrode protruded from the tip of each of *Colossus*'s index fingers. With amazing precision, Stacy maneuvered the hands around to the back of the animal's skull and pressed her fingers against its rear jaws, one electrode on either side.

"In position," Stacy radioed.

"Okay, shock her," Dirk said.

There was a loud buzz as a powerful jolt of electricity shot through the sedated *Kronosaurus*. The results were instantaneous. With eerie silence, the creature's seventeen-foot jaws began to open, stretching until a buffalo could have fit inside. The white insides of its mouth became visible, and thin strands of gooey saliva hung from its sharp-edged fangs. Dirk suppressed the urge to gag as its foul breath hit him – a delightful combination of rotting meat and the hordes of bacteria that fed on it.

"Okay, hold her," Dirk said, breathing through his mouth. He signaled the tech team. "Insert force transducer."

There was a collective inhalation from everyone in attendance as the rectangular, rubber-coated end of the gauge was inserted into the pliosaur's jaws, toward the rear of its mouth. Dirk checked his tablet, confirming the positioning. He watched the gauges on his screen, waiting for a confirmation of system readiness.

"Hold her there . . . hold her . . ." he held up a gloved hand, waiting. "And . . . now!"

As Dirk's hand swung down, Stacy dug her electrodes in deeper and increased the voltage. The pliosaur's jaws slammed shut, sending an impact tremor through the concrete floor that could be felt forty yards away.

Dirk's eyes lit up as he caught the readings. "Okay, got it. Cut it!" he yelled.

Stacy pulled back, causing the marine reptile's jaws to spring back open, just enough that the nervous techs could extract the crushed end of the bite gauge. They backed carefully away and carried the device back to its station.

"Fenris figures coming up," Dirk said. He touched a tab and sent the information to the monitor directly above the healing pool. "Bite force is approximately seventy-six tons, admiral."

"Holy shit!" Callahan sputtered. "Is that a record?"

Dirk shook his head. "No, but it's strong enough to crush a pickup truck or bite the head off a sperm whale."

"Hey, now there's an idea . . ."

Dirk shook his head and moved back to his previous station. Above him, Stacy guided *Colossus* back to a resting position.

He cleared his throat and resumed dictating. "Continuing examination . . . Besides evidence of feeding and competition-related injuries, there are scars running along the specimen's dorsal region indicative of old puncture wounds. Scars are numerous – I count nine – and run in a jagged, strafe-like pattern. Date of injury is impossible to ascertain, estimate eight to ten years. Scar gradation indicates specimen dove on impact. Positioning and size of impacts suggests automatic weapons fire, most likely armor-piercing rounds of .50 caliber or higher." Dirk glanced over at Callahan. "Looks like your boys missed one, admiral."

"Humph." The admiral got up from his chair and stood on tiptoe as he scrutinized the strafe pattern. "Looks like it's from one of the old Apaches. Wait until you see the new BladeHawks we've got coming off the line. They're beyond deadly. Counter-rotating rotors, fast, whisper quiet and armed to the teeth. If radar can't pick 'em up, no pliosaur will, either!"

Dirk sighed. "Continuing analysis . . . There are large, recently-healed bite marks on the nape region of the specimen. Assume copulation and post-copulation damage."

Callahan cleared his throat. "Jesus, they bite even when they fuck?"

Dirk shook his head and prayed for strength. "As you know, bull pliosaurs tend to be smaller than their mates. Therefore, in an attempt to exert dominance during mating, the male immobilizes the female by biting the back of her neck, like a tomcat. You can see how much thicker the scales are in that region to compensate for this 'affection.'"

"That's one hell of a love-bite."

"The female gets even." Dirk pointed to the unconscious cow's snout and continued his analysis. "Specimen exhibits evidence of numerous, recently-healed abrasions on the muzzle, in particular on and around the gum line." He glanced at Callahan. "In what is considered to be unusual reptilian behavior, the male sometimes remains near the female, post-copulation. Post-mating behavior by bulls varies, but has been known to include driving other males from the area, as well as making kills and surrendering them to the impregnated cow. Behavior typically continues until the female lays her initial clutch of eggs."

"Initial?"

"Initial . . . as in first."

Callahan rubbed his chin. "And the scratches on her nose?"

"Sometimes, males get brazen or try to claim a share of a kill before the cow has had her fill. They end up getting driven off by the female."

"The price of love."

Dirk held his tablet at arm's length and tapped the screen. A moment later, a blue laser emanated from its underside and began sweeping up and down the *Kronosaurus* cow's neck. "Scanning nape region now." His eyes bulged as he checked his readings. "Assuming standard gape formulas apply, and presuming the absence of any pathologies, the male that inflicted these injuries was substantially larger than the female . . ."

Dirk paused his recording and clicked his radio. "Jim, where the hell is that fetal report?"

There were a few seconds of delay before the lab tech responded. "Boy, you're impatient today. Coming through now. You might want to sit down for this."

Dirk swore under his breath as he skimmed the data. "Well, it's confirmed. Test results of fetal amniotic fluids indicate hatchling's DNA scans are inconsistent with any plotted profiles."

Callahan shifted in his seat. "English would be nice, doc."

Dirk faked a smile. "Popular opinion is that all pliosaurs are descended from the original adult female that attacked Paradise Cove, thirty years ago. That she laid at least one clutch of eggs before she was--"

"One clutch? Wait, they can lay more than one?"

"Absolutely. Once impregnated, cows have the ability to store the bull's sperm and produce multiple clutches over a 6–9-month period, like sea turtles. Clutches typically range from 60–100 eggs, with 80 being the average."

"Fuck . . . Well, that explains how--"

Dirk folded his arms irritably. "How eighty hatchlings could multiply into millions of ravenous monsters that ran unchecked and unchallenged, until they tipped the ecological balance of the world's oceans and decimated marine life on a global scale?"

"Doc, if you're insinuating that--"

"A seventy-eight percent survival rate back in the beginning didn't hurt them any, that's for sure," Dirk announced. "My mother was right. With most of our apex predators – sharks, whales, billfish, and giant tuna – practically wiped out, our depleted oceans were defenseless. At five feet, even a newborn *Kronosaurus imperator* has few natural enemies. Once they reach eighteen feet or more – a yearling, in case you didn't know – they're virtually untouchable."

"Thanks for the history lesson, doc. But I think we've managed to put a dent in their numbers. And when I say 'we,' that includes you and your research."

"Yes, 'we' have. And expanding populations of the predators they shared the caldera with has slowed them as well." Dirk looked down, clearing his tablet with a quick swipe. "Back to the DNA profiles . . . To date, almost every pliosaur we've studied has been descended from that original clutch."

Callahan scoffed. "So, they're guilty of in-breeding. Big deal."

"Reptiles aren't mammals, general," Dirk said. "At any rate, that all changed a few years back. We started finding specimens, usually Gen-3s or younger, that had additional DNA mixed in, but never a Gen-1. The specimen you see here is no exception. Her DNA matches our original profiles. Her *offspring*, on the other hand . . ."

"What about her offspring?"

Dirk's eyes sought and found Garm's. "The clutch she carried was fertilized by an animal we have listed as an anomaly. His designate is *Typhon* and we've been tracking him for years. His genetic profiles are outside anything we've mapped. He's our mysterious sperm donor."

Callahan snorted annoyedly. "Are you telling me you've got a rogue *Kronosaurus imperator* running around out there that was around before the original animal was killed? Its mate or some such thing?"

Dirk's brow tightened. "Its mate . . . I don't think so. In fact, no. Definitely not." He checked his data again. "This creature is older. We suspect he's been around for a long time."

"How long?"

A shrill beeping sound from the overhead monitor yanked Dirk's attention from the conversation. "What the hell?" He adjusted the settings via his tablet as Stacy's voice emanated from his radio.

"What've you got?" she asked.

"Something's not right," Dirk advised. He adjusted the system, gradually increasing the volume while filtering out background noise. The pliosaur's heartbeat grew steadily louder as it was funneled through the monitor's speakers – a slow, methodical bass-drum beat, typical of a dormant reptile. As he made a few more adjustments, a second sound became audible; it wasn't as loud, but it was synchronized to the sedated saurian's pulse.

It was another heartbeat.

"What is that, an echo?" Callahan asked.

Dirk shook his head. His head inclined toward the monitor and he eyed the rapidly-updating sonogram.

"Do you think they missed one of the eggs?" Stacy radioed. She was on her feet inside *Colossus's* booth, her nose pressed against its protective Celazole barrier.

"No." Dirk's jaw muscles bunched up as he started to grind his molars. "It's something else . . ." He swiped his fingers down his tablet screen in swift, repetitive strokes. Above him, the sonogram began to do high density cutaways, stripping away layer after layer of the pliosaur's body, like slices from an MRI.

Suddenly, his fingers froze and his eyes tightened. Out of the corner of his eye, he saw what looked like a tumorous lump appear and then vanish along the pliosaur's flank. He turned toward his brother.

"Garm, you'd better get over here."

THIRTEEN

As soundlessly as a pair of lethal blimps, the male and female *Octopus giganteus* rose from the depths to close on their quarry. They had discovered its plow-shaped anchor embedded in a deep-water reef over a thousand feet below, then followed the anchor chain links like a trail of rusty breadcrumbs, all the way to the surface.

The vessel they'd chosen was sizable, easily as long as the gigantic female was from mantle to tentacle tips, and far heavier. Despite the fact it lay at rest under darkened skies, an ongoing barrage of deafening rhythmic pulses resonated through the ship's steel hull. The vocalizations of prey items rang out as well, and the gnarled skin of both cephalopods flushed pink at the prospect of a pending meal. They had developed a taste for the small, air-breathing warm-bloods, and grew increasingly aroused as they prepared to attack.

They were still four hundred feet from their target when a sudden roaring sound caused them both to freeze. Their luminous orbs exchanged a pensive stare, fearing they'd been spotted and their quarry was about to flee. Relief shot through their mammoth bodies a moment later, however, followed by anticipation, as they realized the loud noise had been caused by a smaller vessel, pulling up alongside to mate with the bigger one.

More prey was arriving.

The male octopus extended one of his tentacles, entwining it around the females nearest arm, as they communicated. Tactile creatures that they were, a quick gaze or a rippling touch of suckers was all it took to cement their plan. Their huge bodies inflated slowly in agreement and the pair broke apart. Sucking enough water into their respective mantles to inundate a two-car garage, they jetted silently upward. They stopped a few feet beneath the surface, one on either side of the target as they held position, seventy-five yards out.

Despite the pitch-black conditions, the male could see his mate clearly. His keen underwater vision was aided by a series of tiny suns, ringing their objective. Directed at the water, the lights were agonizingly bright and lit up the surrounding sea in brilliant shades of green.

Wary of being spotted, the male remained out of range of the spotlights. He steeled himself before peeking above the waves. The great mound of his mantle rose like a six-foot high reef and he studied the hunted through narrowed eyes.

The vessel they'd chosen was white, like a giant beluga whale. It had multiple layers and was topped, here and there, with what looked like white jellyfish mantles, suspended atop stalks. In and around the levels were dozens of the tasty morsels they craved, standing and communicating with one another. Some had darker exteriors and faced outward. They carried black, metallic objects that the male associated with the fire-stick they faced during their previous feeding.

It was of no matter. Although painful, the sticks were ineffective against their dense, rubbery tissues, a minor irritant at most.

Sinking below the waves, the male performed a slow spiral to signal his mate. Then, with a quick jet of water, the pair glided downward in long, tight arcs, passing one another like a pair of tongs at the six-hundred-foot mark, before jetting back up. Accelerating to full speed, they closed rapidly on their target.

Seconds later, their combined weight smashed full force into the anchored luxury yacht.

Dirk's eyes were darkened slits as he hawked the surgical sonogram, high above Tartarus's healing pool. His brother Garm was by his side, arms folded, while an operating tech hovered close by. On the screen, the virtual image of the sedated Gen-1 had been sliced lengthwise, with the current visual showing a cross section two-thirds of the way through and displaying the behemoth's heart, ribcage, and lower digestive tract.

Inside its abdominal cavity, something moved.

"Do you see it?" Dirk asked. The sound of the bloodsucker's throbbing pulse, synced to the pliosaur's heartbeat, gave him the creeps. He *hated* parasites.

"Yeah," Garm remarked. His lips curled up. "It's a big fucker, too. Fifty feet, easy."

"What's a 'big fucker'?" Callahan asked. He was up off his bench seat but being kept away by his aide and another surgical tech. "What did you find?"

Dirk ignored him and radioed Stacy inside *Colossus*. "Dr. Daniels, are you seeing this?"

"Roger that," Stacy replied. "I've got it on my screen. You're going to have to remove it. At that size, and based on its location, it will eventually kill the host."

"Remove *what*?" Callahan demanded. He pushed past Gibbons and the tech, only to freeze as the thing on the sonogram came to life. Like an anaconda undulating, it began crawling around inside the pliosaur's digestive tract. "Jesus, what the fuck is that?"

"*That*, my dear admiral, is a *Vermitus gigas*." Dirk waited for the inevitable befuddled expression and added, "The Cretaceous version of a tapeworm."

"A tapeworm?" Callahan echoed. He pointed up at Stacy. "She said it was killing it. Are you selling me a dying animal?"

Dirk sighed. "Wild pliosaurs often carry parasites, admiral, including ones in their digestive tract. But their immune systems and stomach acidity usually keep them in check. This particular cow, unfortunately, has a worm that has grown outside of its stomach and is embedded in its abdominal wall."

"Is that common?"

Stacy's voice blared loudly from her speakers. "Only when some hotshot flyboy misses his mark and punches holes in the poor animal," she remarked, "Allowing the parasite to grow unchecked."

Callahan's expression soured and he waved his hands at the slumbering *Kronosaurus imperator*. "So, this stupid thing's gonna die?"

Dirk clucked his tongue. "Not if we can help it."

"And how do you propose to do that?"

"We're going to remove the *Vermitus*, of course." Dirk answered. He turned to Garm. "You'd better suit up."

His brother nodded. "You got it."

Dirk brushed aside Callahan's next question. Under protest, the naval officer retook his seat. Meanwhile, Garm moved to a nearby set of shelves and, with assistance from two team members, started climbing into an economy-sized hazmat suit.

"Dr. Daniels," Dirk said into his mike, watching as his twin was zipped up and shouldered an oxygen pack. "We're going to need an ass-lift from you, if you don't mind."

"Always happy to back it up for you," came her chipper reply.

Dirk failed to hide his smirk as *Colossus* resumed moving under his ex's masterful touch. With a loud hum from its actuators, the lift system's enormous arms rose up off the concrete deck behind them and reached for the drugged pliosaur. Undoing its hip belt with practiced ease, Stacy grabbed the behemoth's lower pelvic region and tail base in one huge hand and hoisted it smoothly up, exposing the creature's pale underside and vent.

"Better go with the electro-vac," Dirk recommended as Stacy directed *Colossus*'s free hand over him, heading for the heavy-gauge steel shelving units that housed their oversized surgical tools and medical devices. "That thing's not going to come willingly."

"Roger that."

With a pneumatic hiss, the ten-foot robotic hand closed around an ornate, eight-foot long, stainless steel and ceramic wand, roughly the thickness of a fire hydrant. On the wand's distal end was a lined, metallic bulb. It was shaped like a watermelon, only twice as large. Gripping the wand, *Colossus*'s hand swung down and to the side, hovering three feet above the pool deck. A pair of operational techs in full surgical garb and wearing arm-length latex gloves stepped forward to meet it. Eyeing the machine that could squash them into paste, one attached a six-inch thick hose/cable combination to the wand's receiver end, while the other lathered thick gobs of petroleum jelly on its bulb.

"What's with all the goop?" Callahan asked, watching the prep work.

"Lube, admiral," Garm announced as he strode past. He grinned from behind his suit's clear faceplate. "There's always time for lube."

Callahan's jaw dropped as he met Garm's gaze. Not from the bulky protective suit he was wearing, which made the big sub commander look even more massive than he was. But because of the enormous Scottish claymore he had casually slung over one shoulder. Combined with his hazmat suit, he looked like some enormous, post-apocalyptic highlander, ready to do battle.

"Shit, Gate," Callahan sputtered. "What's with the antique meat cleaver?"

"It's actually from my dad's collection," Garm mused. Holding the weighty, five-foot sword in one hand, he hefted it at arm's length and twirled it around like it was made of Styrofoam. "One of the few pieces we keep on site. Five hundred years old and still sharp enough to cut the head off an ox." He glanced toward the Gen-1's elevated rear end, then back at Callahan and winked. "Or other things . . ."

Dirk cut in before the admiral could respond. "Let's get this done, people." He turned to face the nearby techs, "Everybody except Garm and I are to keep back." He radioed Colossus's cab. "Dr. Daniels, we're ready when you are."

He saw Stacy nod, then stepped back as Garm moved beside the prostrate pliosaur, their dead father's sword at the ready. With a loud whirring, the car-sized, stainless steel hand holding the electro-vac began to move forward. Still holding the sedated Kronosaurus by the rear end with its other hand, Colossus moved the log-sized surgical probe toward the creature's yard-long vent. With practiced strokes, Stacy wiped the lubed tip on its cloaca, prepping it.

"You're going to remove the tapeworm rectally?" Callahan asked from a safe distance away.

Dirk nodded. "Shock it and suck it right out."

"And the meat cleaver?" he asked, indicating Garm's claymore.

"Some creatures respond hostilely when forcibly removed from their place of residence," Dirk replied.

"Man, that is something." Callahan turned to Garm. "Gate, I do *not* envy you this job!"

"You should have seen it in the old days," Dirk remarked. "Before the probe, we had to send a man in a suit up inside to deal with the worm."

"Up its ass?" Callahan blinked in disbelief. "You're shitting me!"

Dirk's almond-shaped eyes crinkled with amusement. "Didn't we cover that already?"

With a loud *splurch*, Stacy had *Colossus* shove the first four feet of the electro-vac deep inside the pliosaur's rectum. To everyone's relief, and despite the considerable violation, the giant predator remained inert. A loud chugging noise started and the probe began to vibrate, its bulb-like end extending like a plumber's snake as it traveled up inside the creature's body, searching for its target.

On the overhead sonogram and through the feed from the electro-vac's integrated camera, Dirk tracked its progress. He could see the colossal tapeworm on the screen. It was lying dormant, probably taking advantage of the cow's lack of movement and feeding, he mused.

Through the probe's lens, thick layers of pale-colored tissue were pushed aside as the mechanical device crept stealthily forward. Eerily silent, it wound left, then right, its infrared camera lighting up the darkness of the pliosaur's bowels. Within seconds, it was past the huge reptile's colon and worming its way through the partially digested food occupying its upper intestines.

Seconds later, it contacted what Dirk calculated was the tail end of the tapeworm. On the sonogram, he saw the bulb-like end of the electro-vac spring open, its sharp-edged petals spreading like a lethal flower. A microsecond later, it sprang forward, latching onto the tail section of the *Vermitus gigas* and simultaneously unleashing a powerful jolt of electricity.

The results were impressive. On the sonogram, the parasite's bulbous body lashed violently back and forth as it fought back against the unexpected assault. The probe's camera provided an additional worm's eye view of the battle, and Dirk could see a wall of talon-like projections raking the lens. Even without the dual electronic images, the effects of the struggle were physically evident, as the unconscious *Kronosaurus*'s flanks bulged repeatedly from the violent impacts of the tapeworm's thrashing coils.

"I can't see enough of the monitor!" Stacy radioed. "Should I reverse it?"

"Negative," Dirk replied, eyeing multiple screens. "It's not coming free; I think it's anchored into the abdominal wall. You'll have to increase the voltage."

"Are you sure?"

"I'm sure; hit it again!"

As the amperes unleashed by the surgical probe increased dramatically, the pliosaur's four huge paddles became as rigid as blades and its 137-ton body started to twitch. Although sedated, its muscles bunched beneath its thick restraining belts, as enough electricity to power a trolley car lit up its insides. Dirk swallowed as he eyed the saurian's flickering life readings. Even for a creature its size, the jolts it was receiving were approaching defibrillator levels, and he was worried its couch-sized heart might stop.

A muffled wrenching sound from inside the *Kronosaurus imperator*'s rib cage drew Dirk's head back down. His eyes met Garm's, then ricocheted back to the sonogram. The *Vermitus* had torn loose.

"We've broken its grip!" he yelled to his brother, then clicked his radio mike. "Stacy, reverse now!"

"Roger that."

Dirk checked the life readings, breathing an audible sigh of relief as the pliosaur's heart rate stabilized. He could hear a low pulsing noise coming from inside it as the electro-vac reversed course. With its metallic jaws tightly clamped onto the tapeworm's thick coils, it was dragging the immobilized creature backwards through the marine reptile's digestive tract, heading for its cloaca and the light beyond.

A nostril-singing whiff of pliosaur excrement hit Dirk between the eyes as *Colossus*'s steely grip tightened around the probe's handle and pulled backwards. A second later, the looped end of the *Vermitus gigas* emerged from the saurian's gaping vent.

Dirk's eyes popped behind his goggles and he heard a collective gasp of astonishment from everyone watching. The tail section of the worm was massive – as thick a full-grown reticulated python. It was a disgusting olive-green color, with a thick layer of mucus covering it. Finger-sized, greenish-brown tendrils ran in lines up and down its length, and undulated in gelatinous waves as Stacy kept up the pressure. Bit by bit, yard by yard, the parasite's body was wrenched from its host.

It was gigantic.

Dirk looked up in amazement as *Colossus*'s fifty-foot arm fully extended. The worm's bloated body was draped across the end of the gurney and extended far beyond, all the way to the surgical center's polished concrete floor. It was the demonic version of a *Titanoboa*, Dirk imagined. Its coils were nearly three feet thick at the widest point and the entire creature must have weighed five tons. He could see rows of backward-curving, blackish teeth lining the worm's flanks like segmented hooks. The epidermal fangs had evolved to embed themselves in the tissue of its victims and prevented the parasite from being forcibly removed.

The worm began to thrash, despite the repeated jolts it was receiving. Its foul-smelling mucus sprayed in every direction and a fresh wave of fecal odor mixed with ammonia filled the air. Despite breathing through his mouth, Dirk gagged into his mask, and it was all he could do to keep from vomiting. He spotted his brother, sword in hand and standing on the other side of the *Vermitus's* coils, and envied him his hazmat suit's integrated oxygen supply.

Suddenly, three bad things happened simultaneously: Garm was struck by a spiky coil and went flying, the worm's huge head popped free from the pliosaur's vent, and the electro-vac lost its grip.

With a thud reminiscent of a soggy sandbag, the *Vermitus's* boneless maw hit the gurney. It lay there for a moment, coated with a vile layer of slime and feces, before it began to move. Sightless, yet somehow aware of its surroundings, it raised its tree-trunk-sized neck eight feet off the deck and swelled up like some nightmarish cobra.

Dirk gasped involuntarily and instantly regretted it. The worm wheeled in his direction, its tentacles writhing. Looking straight into his eyes, its mouth began to split open, its tooth-lined layers peeling back like some hellish lamprey's. Ring after ring of teeth and suckers were exposed, all backward-curving and designed to rip loose and swallow not only blood and body fluids, but flesh and bone as well.

As it slithered toward him, horror flooded Dirk's face. He tried not to breathe and focused on listening to the sounds of his heart pounding for what would undoubtedly be the last few times. He was beyond terrified as he stared up at the giant nematode's horrid head. It was enraged at being wrenched from its host and ravenous, its meat grinder maw gnashing in spiky ripples as it sought about for something to latch onto.

In the recesses of his mind, Dirk could hear the cries of terrified techs as they ran for their lives, as well as the alarmed shouts of security personnel as they came charging, weapons in hand. There was a metallic creaking, followed by a crash, as one of the tower lights was toppled by the worm's thrashing coils and hit the ground, unleashing a hissing shower of sparks.

The *Vermitus* was not distracted by the ruckus. Dirk knew it was locked onto him and he found himself wondering whether the colossal creature possessed some form of thermal vision.

The worm was only three feet away now, its putrid odor washing over him, and as his heels touched the end of the gurney, Dirk realized he had nowhere left to go. His legs would barely respond and, even if he could force himself to run, it would be on him before he turned around. He heard the sounds of several shotguns being pumped, but knew the guards would be hesitant to fire for fear of hitting him.

"Hey, gruesome . . ."

Out of nowhere, Garm's deep voice cut through Dirk's paralyzing fear. The *Vermitus*, distracted by the sound, twisted its loathsome head around. Its dripping, yard-wide mouth swept eagerly toward its target, but it was too late. Jake Braddock's 500-year-old claymore was already in mid-swing. Like a machete striking a celery stalk, the five-foot, razor-edged hunk of Scottish steel, backed by his firstborn son's powerful arm muscles, sliced clean through the worm's boneless neck.

The *Vermitus*'s foul hiss was cut off, along with its head. Its tooth-lined maw dropped to the gurney with a loud splat, before oozing off its edge and splashing into the pool. Spewing foul ichor, the decapitated tapeworm's body began to coil, undulating in S-shaped patterns as it flailed this way and that, railing against its unexpected demise.

With his father's weighty sword still gripped in gloved hands, Garm approached the nearest section of coils and went on the offensive. Swinging the big claymore with uncanny accuracy, he hacked at it, chopping the worm's spike-bristling body into ten-foot sections that writhed and spasmed and spouted greenish gore. The guards joined him in his assault, their 10-gauge shotguns unleashing a lethal fusillade, and Dirk could hear the gunfire. It was faint at first, but grew steadily louder as he began to regain the ability to move.

He sucked in a huge breath as if he'd been trapped underwater and staggered a step forward, taking care not to trip over a seven-foot hunk of *Vermitus* whose cilia-like tendrils continued to twitch. Around him, his brother and the security team worked to make sure the sixty-foot worm's remaining segments didn't cause any mischief. Aided by

Stacy wielding *Colossus*'s enormous arms, they started collecting its assorted pieces and tossing them into a huge pile, shooting or slicing any that continued to move, while one of the techs called into a radio for a flatbed.

Sweating profusely, Dirk moved past an array of scattered surgical gear to a bench the giant parasite hadn't upended and collapsed down onto it. He pulled his goggles up over his head and slid his surgical mask down, all the while focusing on getting his runaway heart rate under control. He saw Callahan and his aide heading in his direction and cursed under his breath.

"Never a dull moment in Tartarus, eh, sport?" the admiral said, grimacing as he dropped down next to him. His aide, Sergeant Gibbons, hovered a few yards away, his hand on the butt of his Glock as he nervously surveyed the scene.

Dirk cleared his surprisingly dry throat. "Yeah . . . you can say that again."

"Glad you made it," Callahan said, clapping him on the shoulder. "When that thing started making googly eyes at you, I thought your goose was cooked."

"Not on my watch," Garm remarked as he walked over. He had his gore-caked claymore shouldered and his hazmat headgear tucked under one arm, looking for all intents and purposes like some demon-slaying knight, fresh from the battlefield.

Which, technically, was an apropos description, Dirk mused, rubbing his aching temples with his fingertips.

Callahan placed his thick hands on his thighs and pushed hard to get himself upright. "Boy, you saved his ass for sure, Gate! If you--"

"Yours too, as I recall," Garm said coolly. He sat his sword and helmet down on a nearby table and sat beside Dirk. "You okay, little brother?"

"Thanks to you," Dirk replied. He smiled ruefully. "You'll always be there when I need you, won't you?"

"Probably not," Garm admitted, his pale blue eyes perusing the filth-coated debris scattered around the anesthetized pliosaur. "But for as long as I have, you know you can count on me."

Dirk frowned at the fatalistic tone his twin was exhibiting and stood up, refusing the proffered hand. He looked around and made a face.

The unconscious Gen-1, the floating gurney, healing pool, and the concrete deck for twenty yards in every direction, looked and smelled like a sewer. Fecal matter, combined with the dead nematode's mucus and bodily fluids, covered just about everything. In addition, one of their light towers was down, and the damage to their gear was substantial.

A heavy sigh escaped Dirk's lips. Grayson was going to flip. He dismissed his concerns and straightened up as he spotted Stacy running toward him. She had a look of dread in those amber eyes of hers, one he'd never seen before.

"Hey, are you o-woof!" Dirk's words were cut off as the athletic scientist knocked the air from his lungs. His yelp of surprise died in this throat as she threw her arms around him and he glanced uncomfortably around, realizing they were adrift in a sea of stares. There was no help for it, and with discretion out the window, he hugged her back, grunting as she squeezed him tight.

"Omigod, I thought you were going to die," Stacy spouted. As she eased up on the bear hug he realized she'd been crying. "It all happened so fast and it was so close, I didn't know what to do!"

"Hey . . ." Dirk cupped her chin with his thumb and forefinger and tilted her head up so he could see her eyes. "I'm fine. Garm was there." He gave her a meaningful look to remind her where they were.

Stacy's eyes widened and she sucked in a quick breath before pulling herself away. She made a show of straightening her oil-spattered lab coat, then turned to Garm. "Thank God you were," she said, faking a chuckle. "I would have been forced to finish the procedure without him, and you know how Grayson feels about overtime . . ."

"Absolutely," Garm said, winking at her. "Maintaining your schedule was foremost on my mind, doc."

Callahan sawed a finger back and forth, scratching at his mustache, and snorted irritably. "Yeah, yeah, yeah. This is all very touching, but what happens now?" He gestured at the mess.

Dirk eyebrows drooped. He glanced at Stacy, who was still staring like she was ready to have his children. "What do you think? Is it safe to keep her under?"

Her lips scrunched to one side. "We'll need to lower her back in the pool to keep her from being asphyxiated by her own weight, but as long as we keep her dosage constant and feed her, I don't see why not."

"Okay, let's get her rinsed off first and insert a food tube while the pool's filtration does its thing," Dirk said. "We'll lower the gurney and keep her at neutral buoyancy while the cleanup is done and then reconvene in an hour."

Stacy looked down and gagged as she realized she was standing on a yard-long strip of worm guts. "We're going to need the entire center sterilized, the equipment included."

Dirk nodded his affirmation and turned to a nearby tech. "You heard the doctor. Get a steam crew down here to assist. I want a complete inventory of all gear, a list of anything that's suffered even cosmetic damage, and replacement components on site within thirty minutes."

"Yes, Doctor Braddock."

As the man spun off and started chattering into his radio, Dirk turned back to Stacy. "Dr. Grayson is going to need a report." He looked down at his badly-stained surgical garb. "I'll zap up to my quarters and get cleaned up and shoot it to him. Meet you here in forty-five?"

"Sounds good," Stacy said. "I'll keep an eye on the patient."

"Thanks."

Dirk spotted his fallen tablet lying among the debris. He bent down to retrieve it and wiped at the gunk on its screen. Amazingly, the thing still worked. As he weaved his way around a nearby security guard, his brother fell in beside him.

"Come on," Garm said. "I'm playing chauffeur already. I'll give you a lift."

"Sounds good," Dirk said, realizing his feet felt like they were embedded in buckets of cement. It was amazing how coming so close to dying sucked the life out of you. He felt like crawling into bed and sleeping for a week.

They had barely taken a step when Stacy called out. "Hey, Captain Braddock."

Garm shot her a quizzical look.

"Take care of our boy, okay?" Stacy said.

Garm grinned as he gave his twin a friendly nudge. "Always."

They wandered off, the sounds of men and machines struggling to remove quarter-ton hunks of man-eating worm fading behind them.

Garm leaned back in his MarshCat, one muscular forearm draped across the six-wheeled vehicle's steering wheel and watching as Dirk entered Tartarus's nearest elevator. He waited until the doors closed before he exhaled with a hiss, trying to dispel some of the tension he had locked inside.

He cursed through clenched teeth, furious at himself for what happened with the monstrous tapeworm. Getting knocked off his feet like that was amateurish. If he'd been a split-second slower in regaining his footing, Dirk would be dead.

He put the ATV in gear and started forward, weaving around the occasional technician or janitor as he moved past the line of pliosaur tanks. It was late, and the dimly lit submarine slips and vast expanse of concrete docks were nearly deserted. He scoped out *Gryphon*, sitting in her berth and ringed by a half-dozen security personnel. The sleek warship was illuminated by overhead spotlights, her iron-gray sail jutting up from her armored hull like a monstrous Orca's fin, amplifying her already formidable appearance.

Across the way, he clocked *Antrodemus*, similarly attended, but with the addition of a team of welders and engineers working to repair her fractured outer hull. He could see the bright sparks from their acetylene torches, streaming like gold-colored sparklers as they worked through the night. Even with rotating shifts, it would be days before the crimson-hued sub was seaworthy, let alone battle-ready.

Garm glanced wearily toward the far-off surgical area, obscured by towering columns and a series of fences. His lips compressed as he considered skipping the implant procedure and hitting the gym or, better yet, the rack, but he dismissed either notion. After what just happened, he wasn't letting his little brother out of his sight.

Garm slowed his ATV to a crawl and chuckled. Dirk really hated the "little brother" routine, but after nearly three decades, it was a hard habit to break. Besides, as he'd pointed out innumerable times while they were growing up, he *was* technically older. And he was certainly the larger of the two.

Suddenly, Stacy Daniels popped into Garm's head and he pursed his lips. Now *that* was a touchy situation. He was one of the few people who knew that Dirk and she had been an item – at least, before that display of obviousness – and that they had ended things. It was a shame; Stacy was a great girl: smart, sexy and athletic, and their families had a long history. If her father, Willie, hadn't taken a bullet for their mother on-board the doomed *Harbinger*, all those years ago, he and Dirk wouldn't even exist.

Of course, obligation wasn't the best reason to stay with someone, but the family dynamic did have a poetic ring to it. It was almost as if karma had decreed they would end up together. He shrugged. Maybe they'd work it out. Stacy was certainly willing. She was obviously still in love with Dirk.

Garm grinned at the irony. His brother had gone through some amazing women over the years: doctors, physicists, even an astronaut. Each one was good-looking, intelligent and dedicated, yet for some reason he was never satisfied. Why, Garm had no idea. He'd have given his left testicle to latch onto one of Dirk's exes. Instead, he ended up with the same type of woman he always did – an aggressive Amazon who had just one thing on her mind: raw, animal sex, and plenty of it.

Oh well, I suppose there are worse things.

As he passed *Proteus*'s enclosure, Garm slammed on the brakes. Something was wrong. His wolf's eyes swept the two-hundred-foot aquarium, trying to pinpoint the mutant pliosaur. He couldn't see her. Of course, with her adaptive camouflage and the low-lighting conditions that maintained Tartarus's inmates' internal clocks, the adolescent cow should be difficult to spot. Difficult, but not impossible . . .

Peering intently through the thick Celazole, Garm threw the ATV in park and got out. His heavy boots ground loose concrete dust as he moved closer, one hand shielding his eyes against the reflection of the overheads on the dense polycarbonate.

As he reached the enclosure wall and wiped at the condensation, he frowned. It was impossible, but except for mounds of sand and a school of small fish, the tank was empty. Disbelief was pushed aside as reality shouldered its way in.

Proteus was gone.

Garm's mind raced, wondering if Grayson had decided to sell one of his prize specimens or maybe moved her to a different paddock. It didn't make sense. They couldn't have moved her. All the enclosures were occupied. He reached for the compact radio on his belt and--

"Holy shit!"

The radio clattered from Garm's astonished fingers as he staggered back. Like a demon materializing from a wisp of smoke, the monstrous predator appeared before his eyes and slammed into the eight-foot thermoplastic barrier. There was a thunderous *THUMP* and the walls of her enclosure vibrated from the impact.

"You evil fucking bitch!" Garm snarled, his hand closing on the butt of the Smith & Wesson .50 caliber pistol hanging from his belt. Cursing under his breath, he released his grip on the weapon and stepped forward, his eyes opaline slits of fury as he glared at the seventy-ton marine reptile.

Proteus remained where she was, her rippling, thirteen-foot flippers grazing the bottom of her enclosure, her toothy muzzle pressed against the PBI wall. Her crimson eyes seemed to dance as they bored into Garm's and, from the set of her jaw, he could swear the damn thing was chuckling.

As their stare-down continued, Garm had a flashback of their first encounter. It had ended much like this: the wily marine reptile, already half-paralyzed from shocks received from a trio of LOKI AUVs, slamming into *Gryphon*'s transparent prow in a final show of defiance, before succumbing to the combined voltage. Her teeth were bared and her gleaming eyes locked on Garm's, holding his gaze even as she was bound and packaged for transport. She was beaten, but defiant to the end.

"Yeah, I remember . . ." Garm muttered. He placed his right palm against the cool polycarbonate barrier, feeling its moisture. To his astonishment, the huge reptile lowered her crocodile-like head and pressed the tip of her scarred snout against the spot where his hand was. She stayed there, hovering above him like a passenger jet with fangs, eyeing him with what bordered on possessiveness.

"You two should get a room."

Proteus's head arched back and she uttered a throaty rumble of annoyance. Garm wheeled around, his own irritated expression mirroring the adolescent pliosaur's.

It was Oleg Smirnov and Kevin Griffith, two of Grayson's "jack-booted thugs," as Dirk called them. Garm stared disapprovingly as they approached. The CEO had scores of the former inmates skulking around Tartarus. They came and went, with few lasting more than a couple of months. Personally, he doubted any of them would fulfill their contract.

"I theenk she likes you," Smirnov said with a smirk. He hesitated, watching nervously as the pliosaur cow spread her jaws in a threat display and then backed away. Her colors shifted, and in seconds she vanished back into the murkiness of her cage.

"Seriously, you guys need a room," Griffith reiterated.

"Let me guess. You two are lost and looking for the lady's room, right?" Garm replied, grinning humorlessly. "Or, in your case, Griffith, the cattle pens? I mean, it *is* Friday night."

Smirnov cleared his throat to cover up his partner's grumbled response and held out a slip of paper. "Actually, vee have a message for you."

Garm accepted it with a nod. Oleg Smirnov, he didn't have a problem with. Besides the fact he was a convicted murderer, that is. He knew the man from his boxing days, back when the big Ukrainian had been one of his sparring partners. At six-two and two-thirty, Smirnov was strong, fast, and could take one hell of a punch. But any chances he had of making it as a prizefighter ended when he caught his wife in bed with another woman and beat them both to death.

"Grayson said to hand this to you, personally," Griffith stated, his bloodshot eyes discretely sizing up the big submariner.

Kevin Griffith, on the other hand, Garm actively disliked. Dirk had shown him the files on some of their CEO's "Last-Chancers" and it was like a tour of an insane asylum. Murderers, rapists and drug czars: there wasn't one of them worthy of redemption, including the freckle-faced farm boy standing before him.

"The schooner *Rorqual* called in an SOS a few hours ago," Garm said, reading the printout. "According to Captain Krieger, they were being attacked by creatures called 'Krake.' Before more info could be gathered, the radio went dead." He continued reading. "Coast Guard arrived on the scene and found nothing except debris and a few life preservers. There were no survivors."

Garm put the paper in his pocket. "What the hell is a Krake?"

"It's an old Norwegian word. It means a malformed animal."

An unfamiliar voice emanating from the dimness of a nearby corridor startled the three men, causing them to spin around as one. "In modern German, Krake is the plural for 'octopus.' In its singular form, it can also refer to something far larger, i.e. the mythical sea monster known as the Kraken."

Garm's stunned expression morphed into a huge smile. Ten feet away and belted into one of those high-tech, fully-automated, robotic wheelchairs, was a lean-faced, light-haired man in his early thirties. He was tanned and unshaven, and sporting a wry smile. With his angular features and green eyes, most women would have considered him eminently desirable.

That is, if he had arms and legs.

"Sam Mot, you crazy son of a bitch!" Garm spouted. "What the hell are you doing here?" With the two black-clad security guards in tow, he walked up to the quadruple amputee, his right hand extended before him.

"Garm 'The Gate' Braddock," Sam replied, his gel-cushioned seat elevating on its pneumatics as one of his chair's robotic arms came to life and shook Garm's hand. "You haven't changed a bit; you're the same big, ugly bastard you were the last time I laid eyes on you. Still driving the ladies wild?"

Garm grinned, taking his hand back as the bionic fingers released their grip and the limb whirred back into a reposed position. "One does what one can," he said, winking.

"Nice chair," Griffith remarked.

"Thanks, your mom likes it," Sam replied seamlessly.

Garm shot the security guard an icy look. "I'm sorry. You'll have to excuse our security personnel. They weren't hired for their manners." As he realized Sam was accompanied by a pensive-looking medical technician, loitering in the background, he gave the nurse a smile and a nod.

"Hey, she's with me," Sam said, chuckling. His chair did a quarter-turn toward the nervous brunette, "Sorry, doll. This guy's the biggest pussy hound I've ever met. He never quits."

Garm winced and cast the girl a sympathetic look. "I apologize, miss. Mr. Mot caught one venereal disease too many, back in the day, and his brain's never been the same."

Sam cackled. "Hey, do you remember those twins? The tall cheerleaders, the blondes with the boobs – the sister, she gave you a dose of--"

"*So*, you were saying something about a Kraken?" Garm interjected. "And what *are* you doing here?"

"The ship's captain was German," Sam said. "The word 'Krake' was probably just slang for a big *Kronosaurus imperator*. Maybe there was more than one of them."

"Pliosaurs aren't pack hunters," Garm said. His gaze swiveled to *Romulus* and *Remus*, cruising slowly back and forth inside their shared tank. "Well, not normally . . ." He pulled the missive from his pocket and turned to Smirnov and Griffith. "Where's Captain Dragunova?" he asked. "Has she seen this?"

"Last I saw, she was een the gym, punching holes een the heavy bag," Smirnov said. "But Dr. Grayson said the information was for you alone."

Garm nodded. *Antrodemus* would be out of commission for three days, minimum. If they did, indeed, have another rogue pliosaur on their hands, *Gryphon* would handle it. He hoped, however, that the schooner sinking turned out to be the result of an unfortunate accident. He and his crew were exhausted and in desperate need of some R&R.

"So, seriously, what brings you to Tartarus?" Garm asked, turning his back on Smirnov and Griffith as he walked with Sam. He guided the wheelchair-bound amputee and his nurse beside *Proteus*'s tank and away from the guards. Once they were out of earshot, he paused. "Don't get me wrong, I'm happy to see you, I just want to know the *why*."

Sam made a face and shifted uncomfortably in his seat, twisting his neck from side to side. Frustration set in, and he willed one of his chair's bionic arms to reach up and adjust the neural interface headband that allowed him to control the unit.

"There, that's better," he said. "Sorry, damn thing was itching the shit outta me," he said, grinning. "They didn't tell you I signed on?"

Garm blinked. "Wait . . . what? You joined the CDF?"

"You got it, old friend. Can't let you have all the fun."

"I-I don't get it." Garm indicated Sam's chair. "I mean--"

Sam smirked. "I know . . . I'm half the man I used to be."

"What?" Garm's face dropped. "No, that's *not* what I meant. You know--"

"I found a way to fit in, big guy," Sam said, cocking his head to one side. "I just needed a niche. And I got one."

Garm felt a chill that had nothing to do with the facility's reduced evening temperature. "Oh, Sam, you didn't . . ."

"Hey, wasn't it you who requested one of the new AWES suits in place of your old Remora mini-sub?"

"Jesus . . ."

Sam flashed him a Cheshire cat smile. "You need a pilot who can 'fit the bill,' as they say, and I'm your man!" His chair's arms sprang to life and struck a bodybuilder's double-biceps pose.

Garm rubbed his eyes. He felt a headache coming on. "I wish you'd reached out to me before you did that. Except for the proving grounds, those suits have never been tested. Anything could go wrong. It's insanely dangerous."

"More dangerous than my last job?" Sam cocked an eyebrow.

Garm hesitated. "Uh . . . good point."

"Hey, cheer up." Sam winked. "It's going to be a blast, just like old times."

"Right . . ."

Sam nodded as his nurse noisily cleared her throat. "Sorry, brother. I just flew in. Let me get checked out and settled and I'll come find you."

"That'll work," Garm said. He turned to the nurse. "You'll take good care of him, right?"

"Excuse me?" Sam cut in. "I think you mean *I'll* be taking good care of *her*. Let's go."

The nurse shook her head as she trailed Sam toward the nearest elevator. Garm stood there, listening to his old friend talk the girl's head off until the hum of the wheelchair's servos was cut off by the closing doors.

"So, who's the doorstop?" Griffith asked, moving to stand beside him.

As his words sank in, Garm's eyes narrowed into icy slits. He felt the predator inside him waken and start rattling the bars of the psychological prison keeping it in check. He decided to let it peek outside.

"You know, Griffith, there are fourteen bones in the human face . . ." He turned and locked gazes with the gap-toothed zoosexual. "And if you ever say anything like that ever again, I'm going to break every one of yours."

Griffith's eyes peeled wide and he choked on a cocktail of rage and fear. His neck muscles twitched as he resisted the urge to turn and see where his partner was. Garm was unconcerned. He'd already clocked Smirnov, standing twenty feet away. Judging by his stance and the way he was hanging back, the husky Ukrainian had no desire to get involved.

No honor amongst thieves . . .

"Do I make myself clear?" Garm asked, his big hands twitching.

Griffith paled and his lips trembled. After a tense moment, his eyes drooped and he nodded.

"Good." Garm walked to his MarshCat and climbed inside. He gave the brutish guard a disdainful look. "I'm glad we had this conversation."

Then he put it in gear and drove off.

Fourteen

A groan escaped Dirk Braddock's lips as he moved through his quarters. He paused, rolling out stiff shoulders one by one, before heading for his desk. Halfway there, he decided he needed a pick-me-up and detoured into the kitchen. Programming an insta-mug of coffee, he tossed in a splash of half-and-half and two tablespoons of sugar as he watched it brew.

With the steaming mug sitting on a coaster of petrified wood, he eased himself into his ergonomic chair and glanced at the clock. His expression turned to disgust when he realized it was past midnight. He flipped on his intranet, took a long draught of Kona and sighed. A hot shower and the chance to change into a clean t-shirt and sleep-trousers had helped, but the stress of the last few days would not be denied its due.

Dirk ordered his quarters' overheads to full and grimaced as the combination of the potent illumination and the glare from his five-foot monitor forced him to squint. As his eyes adapted, he scanned his fastidious workstation. Everything was neat, clean, and organized, including his expensive set of marine predator teeth.

He had acquired an enviable collection of museum pieces over the years – an easy thing to do, once money was no longer an object. He had a *Mosasaurus* fang measuring eight inches, a *Megalodon* tooth pushing nine, a ten-inch *Deinosuchus* tooth, a similar-sized *Spinosaurus* fang, a thirteen-inch *Physeter* tooth, a fifteen-inch *Livyatan* canine, a sixteen-inch *Liopleurodon* canine, and his biggest tooth to date, a seventeen-inch impact tooth from a cow *Kronosaurus imperator*. It was a gift from Garm, pulled from the still-twitching remains of one of the biggest Gen-1s ever killed.

Of course, most of the valuable pieces of dentition were fossilized. Only the sperm whale and *Imperator* teeth were recent, and the *Physeter* was pre-ban ivory, cracked and yellowed with age. But that came with the territory. He was thinking about getting a nice *Tyrannosaurus* tooth to round out his set. It wasn't a marine predator, of course. But no carnivore collection would be complete without a curved, serrated fang from a huge bull *Rex*.

Dirk reached for the massive *Kronosaurus* tooth, hoisting it from its wooden stand and hefting it. It was razor-sharp and heavy, over eight pounds, and he examined it respectfully before replacing it. Suddenly, the tooth fragment from his mother's office popped into his head, along with the sample of pliosaur skin that someone had moved.

The same someone who'd left footprints behind . . .

Dirk opened his desk drawer and eyed the flash drive he'd copied his mom's last journal entry onto. He'd watched it on a secure line earlier. The contents were disturbing. He considered telling Grayson, but worried the recording might prove upsetting for the old man. He slid the drawer closed. He had to think about that. The other things he found in his mother's office, however, needed to be addressed as soon as--

Dirk's eyes bugged out as he saw Eric Grayson's incoming video chat. It was amazing; the guy must have ESP or something.

"Good evening, Dr. Grayson," he said as he accepted the call.

"Derek, I'm surprised you're still awake," Grayson stated, his head dominating most of the big HD monitor. He loomed closer, his face a Gulliver-sized mask of concern. "I got your report about the incident with the *Vermitus*. My God, the parasite's size was shocking. And what happened . . . are you okay?"

Dirk nodded into his coffee mug. "Garm was there." He tapped a key, reducing his mentor's window and image size to reasonable proportions.

"Thank the Lord." Grayson nodded gravely. "I saw the surveillance footage of him doing his Conan thing with your dad's old sword. Even when he's not in command of a warship he's quite the warrior, a veritable godsend."

"It's not the first time he's pulled my bacon out of the fire," Dirk acknowledged. "And I'm sure it won't be the last."

"By the way, I've been checking around. I haven't been able to find your brother or Captain Dragunova, for that matter."

Dirk pursed his lips. He knew it irked Grayson that both of his ORION-class submarine captains had refused to be implanted with locators.

"Beats me, sir," he said. "I haven't seen Dragunova since this afternoon, and Garm looked pretty beat when he dropped me off. I assume they've both crashed, along with their respective crews. They've certainly earned a break. They were all on extended patrols, working nonstop. Remember?"

"Yes. Well, I'm afraid they may have to go back out."

"What? Why?"

"You've seen the genome mapping. *Typhon*'s definitely in the area. This may be our chance to finally capture him."

"Yes, sir," Dirk acknowledged. He pulled up a map window on his monitor and traced a line around the Florida Keys with his index finger. "Based on our admittedly scattered reports, he makes repeat appearances in this region. Given how shallow the water is, I don't understand why; it's perplexing."

"He's a nomad and doesn't hold down a set territory." Grayson shrugged. "That's why he's so hard to pin down. He's a smart, big lizard." His eyes dropped as he surveyed something on his desk. "There's something else. I sent your brother a private message. A big schooner went down with all hands off Marathon, a few miles past the twelve-mile limit. It's within our patrol range."

Dirk sat his coffee down. "You think *Typhon* sank it? It doesn't fit his profile. He usually avoids ships."

"I'm not sure. All we've got is a confusing distress call." Grayson said. "There have been no satellite hits yet, but we have to get both subs prepped. Once we get a confirmed sonar signature, they'll need to launch at a moment's notice."

Dirk licked his lips. "But Dr. Grayson, even if we discount the fact that both sub crews are exhausted--"

"Their secondary crews can hold down the fort while the captains and primaries rest en route."

"Yes, sir." Dirk exhaled. "But *Antrodemus* is still damaged. The hull plates should be repaired within twenty-four hours, but the photonics assembly will take two days at least."

Grayson frowned. "That's right . . . damn. Can they sail without it?"

Dirk was alarmed that his mentor had forgotten about the damage sustained by one of his ORIONs. "I wouldn't recommend it. *Antrodemus*'s recent upgrades included ANCILE's sonar arrays being partially integrated into the optronics assembly."

"Yes, but isn't everything else functional?"

"OMNI ADCAP and POSEIDON are, sir," Dirk said. "But without ANCILE's obstacle avoidance pinging and acoustic intercept, they're vulnerable. *Typhon*'s destroyed one anti-biologic submarine that we know of and crippled this one. We can't risk losing *Antrodemus*, not to mention Dragunova and her crew."

"No, of course not," Grayson concurred. He blew out an exhale and ran a hand through his silvery hair. "Maybe we should increase the repair crew shifts?"

"Already done, sir," Dirk said. "They're working round-the-clock."

"Of course. Good boy . . ." Grayson looked down, checking his notes. "So, how did today's implant procedure go?"

"Excellent," Dirk said. "I was about to send you the files."

"Good. And the patient?"

Dirk touched a key and opened a window he shared with Grayson. A dockside video feed opened and an overhead camera zoomed in on the receiving dock's huge holding tank. Inside, the eighty-foot Gen-1 christened *Goliath* rested quietly on the surface, breathing easily through her blowholes. On the opposite side of the eight-foot Celazole barrier, Admiral Callahan and his aide, along with a black-clad member of Tartarus's security, kept vigil over the dark-colored marine reptile.

"Her hyper-regenerative abilities have kicked in and she's recovering nicely," Dirk said, directing the camera with his finger as it panned across the immobile predator. He stopped when he reached its wedge-shaped head and moved in close. The pale, Y-shaped scar on the top of the Gen-1's skull was plainly visible. "As you can see, her incision is nearly healed. As anticipated, there is no sign of tissue rejection."

Grayson nodded. "And her readings?"

"Her pressure is normal." Dirk scanned his tablet before continuing. "Brainwave readings via the implant are excellent with no sign of neuron interference. She's exhibiting increased alpha activity, as expected. Her hormone and neurotransmitter levels are good and, despite the trauma she's been through, her norepinephrine and dopamine levels are currently stable. Her beta-endorphin levels are . . . within acceptable norms."

"Excellent." Grayson eyes shifted sideways as he studied the video feed on his end. "What about Callahan, how's he looking?"

Dirk pulled tight on the admiral. Based on his facial expressions and body language, the stocky naval man appeared to be in a terrific mood. He was gesturing excitedly to his aide, clapping him on the shoulder repeatedly while rambling non-stop.

"I'd say he's a wee bit excited about his pending purchases," Dirk observed, grinning as he spotted the exasperated look Gibbons wore when his superior turned his back. "Sales-wise, I don't anticipate any problems. In fact, after tomorrow, I'm betting we'll be getting purchase orders out the yin yang."

"That's wonderful, Derek," Grayson said. "Is everything prepped for the demo? I don't want any snafus. We've got billions riding on this."

Dirk felt his stomach muscles start to tighten and he forced himself to relax. "I've been over every aspect of the presentation, sir, down to the minutest detail. And Dr. Daniels and I rehearsed it on the simulator a dozen times. It should be a cakewalk."

"Good to hear. Are you going to be okay, handling things?"

Dirk's chin lowered to his chest. "I'm fine, sir."

"You're going to be close to *her*," Grayson pressed. "If you want someone else to do it, it's perfectly--"

"I said I'm fine, sir," Dirk said curtly.

"I see." Grayson's expression turned clinical and he focused those implacable eyes on his youthful protégé. "What about Dr. Daniels, is she mentally prepared for this? I've seen her psych reports. They're not convinced she's fully recovered from last month's post-implant incident. They say she's developed chronic claustrophobia, among other things."

Dirk hesitated. "Stacy's fine, sir. It was an understandably traumatic experience. But if anyone can shrug it off, it's her."

"Are you *sure*? Look . . . I know how much she means to you."

"Sir?"

Grayson snorted irritably. "Derek J. Braddock, do you regard me as some doddering old fool?"

Dirk was horrified. "Of course not! You've been like a father to me. I--"

"Then as a *father* let me say that, despite all these wrinkles, I was a young man once," Grayson said, "And I understand how it is. But as your CEO, I'm also very much aware of everything that goes on within this facility. You're my pride and joy, and I cut you more slack than anyone, but don't ever assume that I'm ignorant. Do I make myself clear?"

Dirk swallowed. "Yes. And thank you for your tact, sir."

"She's a good woman, Derek. I hope it works out for you."

"I, uh, don't know about that, sir," Dirk said, trying to recover his poise. "But I believe Stacy is fully capable of doing her job."

"Very well. I trust you," Grayson said. He shifted his head from side to side, grimacing as he sought to loosen stiff muscles. He popped a pill and chased it down with a sip of water. When he looked back, his eyes softened. "I don't think we can afford another personal loss – you more than anyone."

"I agree, sir." Dirk said. His lips compressed. "Dr. Grayson?"

"Yes, Derek . . ."

"There's another matter we need to speak about." Dirk sat up straight, knowing his sudden rigidity would be picked up on. As expected, Grayson's demeanor shifted on the monitor, his expression concerned, almost paternal.

"This sounds serious, Derek. What is it?"

"I found something in my mother's office."

Grayson's brow furrowed up. "What kind of 'something'?"

"There was evidence someone was in there. And that old skin sample – the one from the Paradise Cove specimen – had been moved or removed from her desk."

"That's absolutely true."

Dirk felt his eyebrows hike up. "Wait . . . you *knew* about this?"

Grayson sighed. "I sent one of the guards in there to bring down the sample. He was told not to disturb anything and he obviously didn't follow instructions. I'm sorry. I'll make sure he's spoken to."

"But you promised me nothing in there would be touched until I--"

"We needed to run a new DNA profile prior to the prenatal on *Goliath*. Our previous samples were degraded and, with the new system in place, well . . . it was necessary."

"But why didn't you just ask me to go get it?"

Grayson closed his eyes and rubbed his temples. "I've watched you on the security cameras. Before today, you couldn't get within ten yards of Amara's door. How could I ask you to go in there?"

Dirk looked down, feeling foolish. Then his lips tightened and he looked back up. "There's something else, sir."

"There always is."

Dirk licked the insides of his lips. "When I was in there I looked at the break in the railing. The spot where my mom . . ."

" . . . fell." Grayson finished. "And?"

"I looked at the connectors where the section gave way and something doesn't jibe."

"What do you mean?"

"Well, I haven't done exact calculations," Dirk admitted. "But I'm confident the railing wouldn't have given way on its own."

"How so?

"The metal should have held up. Even considering the mass of an adult human female weighing . . ."

Grayson seemed to age fifty years as he leaned wearily back in his chair. "Son, we went over this ten times in the weeks following your mother's death. She leaned on the railing and it gave way."

Dirk shook his head vehemently. "The numbers don't support that. And the bottom part didn't snap. It was torn, indicating gradual pressure was applied to it."

"That makes sense." Grayson acknowledged. "She fell almost two hundred feet into the amphitheater pool. And the steel-framed PBI section hit five seconds after she did. It's confirmed by the ground-level security footage – the one not interrupted by the blackout."

"So, you're saying that the weight of the--"

"That slab must have weighed four hundred pounds. The connectors at the base are designed to withstand vertical shearing force, not lateral. The load must have caused the bottom connectors to tear as it hung down. Isn't that what you saw? They're torn, right?"

"Yes," Dirk acknowledged. "But the top portion shouldn't have given way in the first place. The connectors should have held."

"Maybe there was a defect in the metal."

"I don't think so. I didn't have a metallurgical scanner with me, but there were no flaws I could see."

"That you could *see*." Grayson emphasized.

"A defect big enough to cause a steel bolt that thick to snap would be visible to the naked eye," Dirk said, feeling more confident, "And for *both* to fail at the same time? The odds against it are astronomical."

Grayson rested his weathered chin on the knuckles of one hand. "When a loved one is tragically taken from us, it's inevitable we want someone to blame, to focus our rage on, some . . . *boogeyman*, for want of a better word. Have you considered that, perhaps, it was just an accident?"

"What kind of accident?"

"Maybe she was watering the plants she kept in those hanging baskets and slipped and fell, striking the railing and causing it to collapse. The accident report showed a stool in that exact area."

Dirk shook his head. "Impossible. She would have impacted on a downward angle. She might have broken some ribs or cracked a vertebra, but the railing would have held up. The breaks indicate the railing was subjected to lateral pressure, and a lot of it."

"Maybe she slipped sideways?"

"Slipped on what?"

"I don't know, Derek," Grayson said, obviously exasperated. "Water from the plants or a mop, maybe? Stranger things have happened."

"I don't think so . . ."

"So what do *you* think happened?"

Dirk hesitated. "I don't know. Something doesn't add up. First the railing fails, then there's the blackout and resultant power surge, then the current cycle activating. It's just too much to swallow."

Grayson shook his head. "It does seem like a lot. But those are all known and explainable phenomena. We were having rolling blackouts due to reactor problems for weeks prior to Amara's accident, remember?"

Dirk railed at the use of the word "accident." He was still dissatisfied with the discussion but knew he was beating a dead horse. "I suppose . . ."

"Son, you need to get some rest," Grayson advised as his protégé battled back a yawn. "Tomorrow's an important day and the demo is not without risks. Get some sleep. After things settle down here, if you want to run a metallurgical study on the connectors, I'll happily look at your figures." He nodded. "Hell, I'll even assign our best mechanical engineers to do one for you. Believe me, if anything unusual took place, we'll find it. Okay?"

"Thank you, Dr. Grayson." Dirk said, feeling somewhat better. "I'm glad I've got you in my corner."

"Where else would I be?" Grayson posed. "Now take a muscle relaxer or something if you need to, but get some rest! I need you and Dr. Daniels in good form tomorrow."

"Yes, sir," Dirk said. "Good night, sir."

"Good night, Derek."

As the video feed closed, Dirk sat there, tapping his index finger on the handle of his coffee mug while his incisors dug a trench in his lower lip. He decided to chance a call to Stacy to see how she was feeling about the demo. He glanced at the time. It should be fine. She was a night owl.

He sent the call, sipping still-hot Kona as he waited for her pickup. When she didn't answer, he shrugged. She must've turned in early, he thought. Still, Stacy was a light sleeper. The ringer should have woken her. Maybe she was in the shower . . . On a whim, he turned on Tartarus's personnel directory and ran down the list. His finger hovered over the scan button next to her name.

Dirk hesitated, realizing he felt like a stalker. Then he thought about Dr. Grayson's habitual checking up on people and used it to push the creepy feeling aside. After all, he was on the Board of Directors with GDT. He was well within his rights to make sure a performer in an upcoming presentation was resting properly.

He jabbed the scanner and frowned when the results popped up. Stacy's locator indicated she was not in her quarters. He watched as her beacon materialized on the grid overlay and started to pulse in place. She was down by the docks, past the surgical center . . .

Dirk's head recoiled on his neck. She was by Gretchen's tank.

Dirk stroked his chin – a habit he knew he'd picked up from Dr. Grayson. He placed his hands on his desk, his fingers tapping the smooth wood polymer like piano keys. Stacy was certainly spending a lot of time with her reptilian charge. To an extent, he could understand her maternal feelings toward what was, essentially, a wild animal. But to be down there with it at 1 AM, while the rest of the world slept? That bordered on bizarre. Hell, it crossed the border like an illegal and brought its friends along for the ride!

Dirk grabbed his keyboard and started tapping, his lean fingers a blur as he cued the security cameras to Stacy's locator. It wouldn't hurt to see what she was up to, just to make sure she was safe.

Seconds later, he found her. She was walking past Gretchen's dimly lit enclosure, outside the protective fence that prevented unauthorized employees from getting too close to the pliosaur's saltwater pool. He zoomed in and spotted the fifty-foot reptile. She was on the surface, pacing Stacy as she walked and ogling her master through the tall, chain-link fence.

People could say what they wanted about the efficacy of the implants, but Gretchen certainly knew who her "mama" was. There was never any doubt about that.

As Dirk watched, Stacy glanced around, making sure no one was watching before she opened the door to a nearby storage shed. She slipped inside, closing the door behind her.

That was odd.

Dirk zoomed in tighter, focusing on Stacy's face as she reemerged. She was carrying a large bucket of some kind. She set it down and glanced about once more, before moving toward a cottage-sized concrete building, set right into the dock floor. She looked left and right, then produced a key and unlocked the door before disappearing inside. Dirk leaned closer to his monitor, his expression intensifying. Unlike the big storage sheds situated across the docks that housed a variety of materials and supplies, that structure was a utility room. It housed the high-powered circuit breakers for a good portion of the docks, including emergency shutoffs for the pliosaur tank filters and pump systems, most of the dock lighting, and the . . . security cameras?

As his video screen went dark, Dirk's expression morphed from befuddlement to disbelief to outright suspicion. He grabbed his keyboard and attempted to revive the feed but the power was gone. He tried several other locations and got nothing as well. A quick check of the grid confirmed it. All the dock cameras were down. Additional scans showed that the turbines powering the current generators for the pliosaur tanks had kicked on, producing an impromptu exercise session for their denizens.

It was bizarre, Dirk thought. Like a reemergence of the rolling blackouts they'd had six or seven months ago. It was the same thing that happened the night--

His heart jumped in his chest. The cameras shutting down, the current generators kicking in . . . it was identical. Maybe the power surges weren't caused by a reactor transference problem after all. Maybe they'd been caused deliberately.

Dirk stood up. His head was pounding and he sucked in air like an exhausted sprinter. It was impossible. Stacy would never hurt anyone, let alone a member of his family. The very thought was ludicrous.

Still, the cameras were down and the current generators were chugging away. Something was amiss and he intended to find out what. He thought about alerting security – maybe having them meet him down there – but dismissed the notion. The fewer interactions he had with those "men" the better. Besides, if he was wrong, keeping the assured confrontation to a minimum was a smart move. Stacy would never forgive him as it was. No sense in making matters worse.

Snatching up his shoes, Dirk hopped into them en route to the door. Without a backwards glance, he ordered his quarters sealed behind him and headed for the nearest elevator. As the doors hissed closed, he glanced down at his tablet. On it, Stacy's locator pulsed like a tiny, beating heart. According to the grid, she was inside Gretchen's quarters now and she wasn't moving.

Dirk's jaw muscles tightened as he steeled himself for the unpleasant task ahead. For some unknown reason, his ex had deliberately disabled an entire floor of security cameras and activated systems that weren't programmed for use until the following morning.

She was up to something. And he was going to find out what.

As the final beats of *Satisfaction* by the Rolling Stones faded in the background, Stacy Daniels moved wearily along the docks, heading back toward the nearby storage shed. Her task was complete and she shifted her weight to one side to offset her lopsided burden. As she walked, she felt Tartarus's artificial breeze kick up, the cool burst of air striking her from behind and penetrating her soggy neoprene wetsuit. The chill permeated her core, causing her to shiver. She shrugged off the familiar discomfort and focused on another, more incessant one. With each step, she tried to wiggle her hips. When that failed, she stopped and reached down, tugging hard at the rubbery material around her crotch. She hated the thick thermal suits she was forced her to wear, especially when they rode up like that.

As she reached the shed, she resisted the urge to glance around again to see if anyone was watching. She checked her waterlogged sports watch and scoffed. It was past 1 AM and she was bone tired. The combination of long hours and the ongoing subterfuge was weighing on her, but she had no choice. A life was at stake and she was committed.

Stacy switched her burden to her free hand so she could grab the door handle. A grunt escaped her lips; despite her physique, she was so fatigued the five-gallon bucket she carried made her arm feel like it was going to pop from its socket. She swung the thick wooden door open and tottered inside, closing it behind her as she reached for the light's pull cord.

She blinked as a trio of bright LED bulbs lit up the disorganized mess inside the shed. Rows of shelves, laden with everything from cleaning compounds to thick slabs of tile, ran down the structure's thirty-foot interior, and she worked her way between two rows as she made her way to her locker.

The place was a disaster area, she acknowledged as she pulled the padlock and swung her locker door open. Her exhalation was a nasal chuckle. She could only imagine what that neat freak Dirk would say if he saw it.

Dirk . . .

Stacy's full lips tightened and she snorted through flared nostrils. It aggravated the shit out of her that she couldn't get the neurotic son of a bitch out of her head. After six months, she'd thought she was over him, but that incident with the tapeworm . . . God, he'd nearly gotten his head chewed off. She shuddered and tried convincing herself it was her soggy suit, not the fact Dirk had come so close to dying before she had the chance to tell him how much she--

She shook her head angrily, her tight blonde curls swirling about as she hoisted the heavy pail inside her locker and slammed the metal door closed.

"What's in the bucket?" Dirk asked, his lean face materializing in the darkened space the locker door had just occupied, like a shocker shot from some horror movie.

"Jesus fucking Christ!" Stacy shouted. She staggered back, one hand on her bosom as her rump bounced painfully off a nearby shelving unit and knocking over most of its contents. Her eyes blazed with fury. "You asshole, you scared the shit outta me!"

"I bet I did," Dirk said. His dark eyes were unusually cold and analytical. "What's in the bucket?" he repeated. His gaze was fixed on the closed locker.

Stacy managed to regain her composure, despite her heart pounding in her chest. Dirk was in a foul mood. A thought came to her and she hesitated. Had he seen her?

"It's adhesive," she said, with the confidence of someone who knows they're telling the truth. "Why?"

"Adhesive for what?"

"For one of the tiles near Gretchen's enclosure," Stacy said. She hated lying but decided to go with an aggressive defense. "It was coming loose so I repaired it. Is there a problem?"

"Show me the adhesive," Dirk demanded.

Stacy eyed him coolly. "Fine." She swung open the locker door and pulled out the fifty-pound bucket, dropping it perilously close to his toes. "See for yourself."

Dirk dropped to one knee and grasped the bucket by its lid, pushing it back on edge so the light shone on the label. "Super caulk, eh?" He set it down and touched a finger to the white-colored gunk that clung to the outside rim, rubbing it between his fingers. He stood up and smeared the remainder of the caulk on the side of her locker.

"I'm sure you don't mind," he remarked, indicating the ramshackle contents of the shed. "I doubt anyone will notice."

"That's out of character for you," Stacy retorted irritably. Her amber-colored eyes narrowed. "You're the only guy I know who folds his dirty laundry."

"There's nothing wrong with being organized," Dirk replied. "It helps to make sure nothing escapes notice."

"Look, Braddock. If you have a problem with me, why don't you just say it?"

Dirk sported a less-than-amiable grin. "Let's step outside."

"Lead the way," Stacy replied, confused by his uncharacteristic stiffness. As she followed him, she felt like she'd been challenged to one of those after-school dust-offs she'd engaged in a few times in Jamaica, back in junior high.

As they got outside the breeze hit her again, but she stopped herself from shivering. Now was not the time to appear weak or frail. The music had stopped and, over Dirk's shoulder, she could see Gretchen's scaly head. The saurian was peeking up from her darkened pool, her crimson eyes observing the two of them from twenty yards away.

"Look, I'm cold, I'm wet, and I'd like to shower and rest up before tomorrow's show, so can we make this quick?" she asked.

"Always to the point, eh, darling?" Dirk said. "Okay. Let me be equally direct. And for the record, this conversation is between us – for now."

"Okay . . ."

"You initiated an unauthorized exercise interval for our resident Thalassophoneans. Why?" Dirk demanded.

"They needed it," Stacy replied. "Their recent muscle mass and vascular scans indicated a . . . hey, wait a minute. What do you mean 'unauthorized'? I'm the one who designs and schedules their workouts!"

"True." Dirk's almond-shaped eyes contracted as he mulled over what he was going to say. "So, giving them an extra workout was purely for the health and well-being of our stock."

"That's right," Stacy said, realizing she was being interrogated. She felt a sinking sensation in the pit of her stomach. She'd never seen Dirk like this. He was like a teapot ready to blow. She had a bad feeling about what was coming next but there was no help for it. "They needed it."

"I see." Dirk clasped his hands behind his back. His voice increased in volume and took on an accusatory tone. "And it had nothing to do with concealing the sudden power spike that would have shown when you disabled the security cameras for the entire dock?"

Stacy felt her mouth go slack. "I . . ."

"You *what*?" Dirk demanded. His hands dropped to his side and he took a step toward her.

He stopped in mid-step as an ominous grunt split the air.

Dirk spun around and his eyes went wide. Behind him, Gretchen reared up out of the water, her scales streaming water like some sea serpent of old. The fifty-ton pliosaur's toothy jaws were agape and her ruby orbs studied him with undisguised interest.

"You're upsetting her," Stacy warned. "Keep your voice down."

Dirk swallowed nervously, and she could tell he was trying to calculate whether Gretchen was capable of dragging her substantial bulk up out of her pool paddock and flattening the ten-foot fence that separated them.

Dirk lowered his voice. "Look, I saw you go into the utility room. Seconds later, the power got cut to every camera down here. And it's been that way ever since. I *know* you were responsible. So, before I present the evidence to Grayson, I'm asking you *why*."

Stacy felt a pain, deep in her chest. To have the man she loved believing she'd gone rogue, and be so quick to turn on her on top of it, was like a vampire getting a stake to the heart.

"I . . . I can't tell you," she said, her eyes dropping to the floor. She shook her head sadly then looked up at him. "But it's nothing bad. Can't you just believe me and forget it, please?"

"Believe you?" Dirk echoed mockingly. His expression turned ugly and he moved closer, only to gnaw his lower lip in frustration and back off as a growl vibrated the concrete under their feet. "Why should I?"

"You *know* why."

When he just stood there with a stupid look on his face, Stacy shook her head in disgust. She turned to leave, then uttered a yelp of fear and surprise as Dirk grabbed her by the shoulders and spun her roughly back around.

"You're not going anywhere! I want to know what you're up--"

Dirk froze as Gretchen's bellow shook them to their bones. His hands were still gripping Stacy's shoulders as he held her at arm's length.

They both turned to look. Before their astonished eyes, the infuriated Kronosaurus threw one of her ten-foot flippers over the side of the pool and raised a third of her massive back up out of the water. She glared menacingly at Dirk. Her head was cocked at an odd angle and she started drawing deep, shuddering breaths.

"What's she doing?" Dirk asked. He seemed stunned that something so heavy could hoist itself up like that.

"She's scenting us!" Stacy shouted, alarmed and a bit frightened that Gretchen could and would ever consider leaving her pool. "And deciding whether to attack!"

"Deciding based on what?" Dirk appeared unable to move, his hands glued to her shoulders as he locked gazes with the infuriated marine reptile.

"On what's happening! She's not sure whether you're attacking or trying to mate with me!"

Dirk's jaw dropped. "Trying to . . . *what*?"

As his fingers continued to dig into her deltoids, Stacy caught a whiff of his aftershave. It was the one she'd given him for his birthday. The familiar, manly scent, combined with his sudden assertiveness, was a huge turn-on. She found herself wishing he'd always been like this, instead of a wishy-washy--

Suddenly, Stacy had an epiphany.

"Kiss me," she ordered. "Quickly!"

Dirk's head whipped toward her, his expression one of pure incredulity. "W-what did you say?"

"You heard me. Do it!"

There was a tremendous splash as Gretchen's other pectoral fin emerged from the water. It came down with a thunderous slapping sound, flattening a nearby wheelbarrow and spraying brine in every direction. A low rumble echoed from the pliosaur's cavernous throat and the muscles that powered her broad flippers began to bunch up.

Stacy grabbed Dirk by the front of his t-shirt and pulled him close. "She thinks you're harming me, and I'm *not* wearing a controller. If you don't want to die, be a man and fucking kiss me!"

His panicking eyes scrolled down her face, along the slope of her nose, until they hovered above her parted lips. A second later, he yanked her towards him. Their mouths merged and Stacy felt herself melt. Six months of deprivation were washed away in an instant. The floodgates weren't opened, they were inundated.

She gave a purr of delight as she felt Dirk's passion resurface, too, his ardor matching her own. Their embrace was that of long-lost lovers, their kisses increasing rapidly in urgency. As he tried coming up for air, Stacy pulled him down again, pressing herself tightly against him. His groan as her body melded itself to his aroused her even more. She breathed hotly in his ear, her tongue lapping at his earlobe, her teeth gnawing the side of his throat in ways she knew drove him wild.

Twenty yards away, Gretchen froze. Like a colossal snake, she continued to scent them, her eyes blinking repeatedly as she took in the heated exchange. Her growl began to reduce in volume.

"Jesus . . ." Dirk panted. His eyes were closed and his breathing became more and more ragged as Stacy continued to writhe against him. When she saw his incisors cut a groove in his lower lip, she knew he was as turned on as she was. She started grinding her pubis against his in circular movements.

"W-what's she doing?" he gasped. "Is she still . . . ready to attack?"

Stacy extracted her pearly whites from Dirk's neck long enough to give Gretchen a sideways glance. She frowned as she realized the pliosaur had calmed. Her jaw tightened and she extended her free hand in her charge's direction, signaling her. A split-second later, the beast spread its slavering jaws and uttered a deafening roar.

"I-I don't think she's buying it!" Stacy cried. She grabbed the collar of Dirk's V-neck and ripped it from throat to navel. Her nails raked his sweat-soaked chest and she began pinching his nipples. As he rocked back on his heels, she grabbed the zipper front of her own bodysuit and yanked it all the way down. She saw his jaw drop as her perfect, caramel-colored breasts sprang free.

Dirk sucked in a gasp and stammered. "Wait . . . what are you--"

"Shh!" she hissed. "We have to convince her!" With Gretchen's growl still reverberating, she grabbed Dirk's thick, black hair at the crown and, despite his sputtered protests, forced his head down onto her nearest nipple.

Any complaints from her now-aroused ex were silenced. Stacy emitted a throaty wheeze of delight as his hot mouth began to do the Devil's work. Soon, she could hear her own breath coming in quick pants and felt her heart booming inside her chest.

She signaled Gretchen to growl once more and then, taking advantage of the resultant distraction, thrust her hand down inside Dirk's khakis. His mouth yawned wide and he uttered a wail of purest ecstasy.

Fearing the young scientist might somehow find the willpower to break her spell, Stacy seized his hair once more and lifted his mouth free from her saliva-soaked chest. She guided him back up, toward her waiting lips.

"Is she . . . c-calm?" he managed, swallowing hard as his body swayed hypnotically as a result of her handiwork.

"Let me check," she whispered, her amber eyes locked onto his. She squeezed him hard, watching with amusement as he hissed like a serpent through clenched teeth.

"Oh, God! You've . . . got to . . . stop!" Dirk moaned. His eyes were saucers, rolling around in his head. He was obviously worried they'd be caught but seemed disinclined to pull away.

"Relax, stud. Somebody killed the cameras, remember?" she said, smiling wickedly.

"B-but somebody might see us!"

Stacy licked her lips and leaned close, her breasts jutting proudly out. "You wanna go somewhere?"

Dirk's head flung itself left and right, then targeted the nearby shed.

"Are you serious?" Stacy asked, still gripping him.

"Why . . . why not?" Dirk said, his labored breathing synched with her movements.

"But it's so messy in there . . ."

A predatory gleam appeared in his eyes, one Stacy hadn't seen in a long time. He reached out and grabbed her tightly by the hips.

"It's about to get a whole lot messier," he growled as he guided her inside and shut and locked the door.

Outside, Gretchen relaxed back into the water, her scaly chin resting on the pool's edge. Her breathing had slowed, but her half-closed eyes remained focused on the shed.

Like a silent sentinel, she continued to watch and listen.

FIFTEEN

The hunt was on.

Slipping forward under cover of darkness, the Ancient continued to track his prey. Like the olfactory range-finders they were, the scoop-shaped nasal passages in his palate repeatedly sampled the surrounding sea, causing him to alter direction until he pinpointed his unsuspecting quarry.

Descending to a depth of five hundred feet, the giant predator departed the Gulf of Mexico and continued on, invading the tepid waters of the Caribbean Sea. The nutrient-rich basins all around him abounded with marine life and were among his favorite hunting grounds. He gazed about. To his left, lay the sandy coastlines of Cuba, to his right, the craggy cliffs and beaches of the Yucatan Peninsula.

All of a sudden, the bull's deep-set eyes crinkled up. Whenever he traversed this stretch of ocean, he felt the same strange pull. He had no way of knowing it was submerged memories – instincts that harkened back all the way to the Cretaceous. Nor could he comprehend that those same, migrational blueprints in his brain had been rendered obsolete, along with a good portion of the planet, by the impact of a billion-ton asteroid that struck not far from where he swam.

He did, however, have a vestigial recollection of the world killer's fiery impact. It was a gift bequeathed to him by his ancestors – the same forebears who were imprisoned in a nearby caldera and survived the subsequent cataclysm that claimed both the dinosaurs and most of Earth's marine life. They and their progeny had remained there as captives, history's deadliest predators, held in stasis for over sixty-five million years. They stayed until Nature saw fit to shrug her seismic shoulders and unleash them once more upon a ripe and unsuspecting world.

As the fragrance of fresh whale spoor called to him, the Ancient accelerated. He had scented the group of cetaceans from thirty miles off and was closing steadily. It was a pod of sperm whales. He could sense the movements of their sausage-shaped bodies as they lumbered along. They were a mile ahead now, moving at less than ten miles an hour. Although he refrained from utilizing his sound sight out of instinctive caution, based on their individual scents he could tell he was pursuing a large group. It was a fortuitous find; there were plenty of adults and calves, assuring him of bountiful feeding.

Suddenly, the Ancient's lips curled upward, revealing the tips of his palisade-like fangs. He could feel wave after wave of the sperms' noisy echolocation clicks washing over him. The pod had been alerted to his presence and were pinpointing his position. He inhaled the heady aroma of fresh whale urine, listening to their frightened squeals as they sped up.

There was no more need for stealth. Ascending the water column like some humpbacked harbinger of doom, the pliosaur revealed himself to the frightened sperms. His ruby orbs reflected the moonlight and, even without his sound sight, his keen eyes could make out their fleeing forms a thousand yards ahead. Their squarish flukes pumped frantically as they increased speed in a desperate attempt to outdistance him.

Accelerating to his top velocity of just over fifty miles an hour, the Ancient arced effortlessly around and ahead of the fleeing whales, passing them at a distance of five hundred yards. As he cut them off, the pod stopped dead in their tracks and started milling about. They were obviously stunned that their pursuer had gotten ahead of them. The sound of their combined sonar clicks was indecipherable, an annoying broadband barrage as every member of the group focused their echolocation on him.

The Ancient wheeled about until his scarred muzzle was pointed directly at the pod. Two hundred feet below the surface he hovered in place, his enormous body offsetting the tide's pull with sinuous flicks of his barnacle-tipped flippers. Knowing his sonar emissions would be masked by those of his prey, the marine reptile began to scan his hapless quarry, his fanged jaws agape in anticipation of the pending meal.

The pod numbered twenty-four in total. There were twelve large cows ranging from thirty-five to nearly fifty feet in length, six sub-adult males and females in the thirty to forty-foot range, and three calves ranging from eighteen to twenty feet. Being the youngest, and hence the most tender, the calves were the pliosaur's first choice, meal-wise. As anticipated, their mothers began to bunch up in a circular formation around the helpless youngsters, their flukes pointed at the center and their toothed jaws directed outward.

The Ancient's glittering eyes shone as he studied the augmented defensive tactic. The sperms had learned from previous encounters with his kind. In the past, they tried defending themselves with their tails pointed out, attempting to utilize swatting strikes from their powerful flukes. Against a sub-adult pliosaur, the technique was marginally effective. But against a full-grown adult, it was useless. In fact, it made extracting a cow from the formation that much simpler; one devastating strike to the peduncle, right past the flukes, would cripple the chosen female, leaving her flailing helplessly as she bled out. Eventually, the rest of the pod would have no choice but to abandon her to save themselves.

Now, however, the whales sought to fight back with their teeth. Any predator trying to attack a member of the pod had to risk being bitten on the way in. A grunt echoed from the marine reptile's massive jaws – the pliosaur equivalent of a chuckle. He had been on the receiving end of hundreds of sperm whale bites over the centuries. In the beginning, when he was smaller, they had been painful, even damaging. Now, they were little more than a nuisance. The big squid-eaters simply lacked the sheer size and power to inflict significant damage. Moreover, their narrow jaws and relatively blunt teeth were designed to grasp soft-bodied cephalopods; they were incapable of piercing his thick-scaled hide.

But it wasn't the female sperm's Marguerite formation the Ancient now had to contend with. Since his species had reappeared and spread throughout the seven seas, the big cachalots had altered their social structure. Whereas before, large, dominant males led solitary lives, joining up with groups of females only for mating purposes, now things were different. One or more bulls typically traveled with cows and their offspring now, as protectors.

As it turned out, there were three huge males functioning as sentries for this particular group. Their size made them easy to discern, and as they broke off from the rest and advanced toward him, the Ancient sized up his opponents.

The trio consisted of full-grown bulls in the prime of their lives, ranging in size from sixty-two to seventy feet in length, and weighing from seventy-five to one hundred tons. As they hastened toward him in a flying wing formation, his throat muscles began to ripple. A moment later, he started scanning them with his own, powerful sonar emissions.

He took the biggest bull – the one spearheading the charge – as the leader. It was a monstrous beast with a massive, gnarled head that was peppered with plate-sized, circular scars and tiny eyes that blazed with fury. Its body bore the marks of numerous other battles, including tooth marks from at least one *Kronosaurus*.

The Ancient began to move, his boat-sized paddles propelling him fluidly forward. Despite his tremendous size, he moved with eerie silence as he prepared to attack. He had no doubt as to the outcome of the battle. His speed and maneuverability were far superior to that of his outsized opponents. In seconds, he was six hundred yards away and accelerating.

As he closed the distance, he felt the inevitable pummeling of the three bull sperms unloading their powerful sonar beams on him. Even from four hundred yards, the sound weapons packed a punch. Against the fragile nervous systems of squid and octopi, they were lethal. He knew. He had observed them in action, thousands of feet down. Against him, however, they were mere fin-slaps; they stung, but little more.

The Ancient waded through the ongoing sonic barrage, relying entirely on sight and smell. The moment the fusillade began, he had closed his jaws tight and stopped using his own sonar sight. He knew from experience that his own sound-imaging senses could be temporarily disabled by the assault. It didn't matter. Here, near the surface, with the light of the full moon to aid him, he didn't need echolocation. The cows' guardians would never abandon the pod by diving to escape.

The bulls had no choice. They had to fight.

The Ancient's jaws flexed as he targeted the leader. His intention was to cripple him and put the others to rout. At the three-hundred-yard mark, however, the big bull suddenly slowed down. It was a tactically sound move; the sudden deceleration allowed the wings of the attack formation to arc forward, like a set of bull's horns. The whales' intentions were obvious; they intended to engage him from three sides at once, hoping to use their numerical advantage and combined mass to offset his superior size and strength.

The Ancient uttered a cantankerous grumble. In his youth, he might have given in to the temptation to prove his superiority by pitting his strength against that of his challengers. But now, however, the wily predator was far more experienced.

Speeding forward at maximum velocity, the pliosaur closed to within one hundred yards of the lead whale, then veered off. He skirted the snapping jaws of the bull sperm on the far left – an infuriated, sixty-seven-foot beast with a twisted jaw and prop scars on his back – before looping around his cumbersome opponent and turning back. The marine giant's scaly body was a spiraling mass of fins and teeth as he executed a figure eight that put him exactly where he wanted to be: on his opponent's flank.

There was a tremendous crash, coupled with a distinctive crunching sound, as the Ancient slammed into his unfortunate adversary. His twenty-foot jaws snapped like giant shears, slashing into the big sperm's chest cavity, slicing through skin, blubber, and muscle, and grating against bone as his ridged teeth cut grooves in the whale's thick ribs. Blood and hunks of blubber spewed into the surrounding sea, an expanding cloud of scarlet.

It was a devastating strike, but hardly fatal. The whale, sensing its speedy attacker closing by the pressure wave preceding it, torqued its huge body in an effort to shield its vulnerable belly. Having survived the initial hit, and despite the larger predator shaking its eighty-ton body back and forth, the bull sperm went on the offensive. Spreading its fourteen-foot jaws, it clamped down on the pliosaur's nearest flipper and bit down hard, its eleven-inch teeth sinking deep into the fibrous tissue.

The Ancient felt the painful bite but ignored it. Still gripping the thrashing whale in his powerful jaws, he tried maneuvering it into a position where he could finish it. The whale was experienced, however, and kept twisting its mammoth body in an attempt to keep its thickly-muscled shoulders and scarred dorsal section facing its attacker.

As the other dominant males drew near, the Ancient realized what the tenacious cachalot was doing. Despite the severity of its wounds, it was attempting to immobilize him long enough that its teammates could arrive and inflict enough damage to either kill or drive away their would-be predator.

The thought of being hamstrung and helpless sent the pliosaur into a rage. Jolts of adrenaline flooded the old bull's bloodstream, permeating his dense musculature. Unable to twist himself into a position where he could either disembowel his foe or amputate its clinging jaw, he went for a more direct approach. Backed by a bellow that sent shock waves reverberating throughout the surrounding sea, the Ancient bared his gigantic fangs and struck at the clinging sperm whale's most fortified spot – the base of its mammoth neck and skull.

The planet's most powerful jaws closed with a force sufficient to shatter granite. Like steel machete blades, his trihedral teeth sank deep, over and over. Ragged hunks of blubber and bloody fragments of bone spewed into the murky water, creating a grisly cloud that surrounded the two opponents.

The stricken whale began to cry out in pain, and its comrades flew forward with the speed of desperation. Only one hundred yards out and closing, their toothy jaws opened as they prepared to engage their primeval enemy.

They were too late.

With a final, devastating bite, the Ancient's mammoth jaws split the mortally wounded sperm whale's skull, reducing the largest brain in the world to pulp and completely severing its nervous system. The dying whale began to spasm. Its air supply spewed out of its blowhole in a thick stream of bloody bubbles and its body violently convulsed. Seconds later, its jaw went limp.

Freed from the eighty-ton chain that had restrained him, the Ancient threw himself forward with a power thrust that displaced hundreds of thousands of gallons of seawater. Speeding between the two onrushing bull sperms, he ignored a grazing strike to his humped shoulder and struck with rattlesnake speed as he hurtled past, slashing left and right with his mighty jaws. The larger bull suffered a raking bite that nearly blinded it and left ten-foot gashes in its thick skin, and the smaller one had its right pectoral fin chopped to ribbons.

The Ancient continued past the stricken sperms some five hundred yards, before spewing forth the ratcheting sonar emissions of his species. His huge head swung back and forth as he took in the situation.

The pod of cows and younglings had taken advantage of their guardians' sacrifice and slipped away during the battle. Of the three dominant males, the two wounded bulls were withdrawing. All that remained was the hemorrhaging remains of the dead bull sperm, its jaw hanging flaccidly as it rolled belly-up. The scent of its blubber and blood spread rapidly throughout the water, an irresistible dinner bell that resonated through the hungry pliosaur.

With a quick scan to make sure there were no more surprises lurking nearby, the Ancient approached the carcass, eyeing it covetously. The big sperm's tough skin and iron-hard sinews were hardly as tender as that of the young calves it warded, but it would suffice.

Ignoring the bothersome engine noise of a military destroyer that suddenly passed overhead, the Ancient began to feed. His monstrous jaws opened like a toothy bear trap and he lunged forward, his armor-piercing teeth carving multi-ton hunks of flesh and blubber from the belly of the whale's still-warm carcass. A huge rent appeared in the sperm's abdomen, and hundreds of feet of snaky intestines spilled out, infusing the nighttime waters with blood and body fluids. Nearby, a horde of sharks and caldera fish gathered, hungrily eyeing the vast bounty, but wisely keeping their distance.

The Ancient gazed upward, his garnet-colored eyes studying the moonlit silhouette of the retreating naval vessel as he swallowed another gullet-full. Although the warship didn't appear to be searching for him, he took no chances and remained submerged and out of sight. He had no need to surface as he fed. Unlike a crocodile, which evolution had gifted with a wedge-shaped head design similar to his own, the pliosaur was not reliant on a palatal valve to keep water out of his lungs. His esophagus connected solely to his stomach, and he breathed entirely through separate nasal passages that culminated in a pair of muscular blowholes. He was Nature's supreme killer and perfectly adapted to his pelagic lifestyle.

As the sounds of the destroyer faded into imperceptibility, the Ancient resumed feeding. Shearing off a huge mouthful of intestines with quick snaps of his jaws, he greedily swallowed them. His mouth design was different than that of the circling sharks. Instead of taking cookie-cutter bites from his prey, his huge mandibles, with their interlocking, trihedral teeth, functioned like a pair of gigantic shears. When he encountered prey too large to swallow whole, he simply cut it into manageable portions and then gulped down the pieces via his widened posterior gape.

Swallowing a three-ton hunk of blubber and muscle, the giant pliosaur paused. He raised his scarred muzzle to a forty-five-degree angle and scented the surrounding sea. The surviving sperms were already long gone and the course they had taken was far from his chosen migration route.

It mattered not. For him, from the surface to the darkness of the abyss, food was always available. He went where he wanted and when he wanted. He was the ocean's undisputed monarch; nothing could challenge him.

And anything foolish enough to try was simply added to his menu.

Garm Braddock was tense and tired as he approached his quarters. Between the physical and mental drain of *Gryphon*'s extended patrol, having to spare the life of, and escort back, yet another known maneater for indoctrination, followed by the stress of nearly losing his brother to a sea serpent-sized lamprey, he was spent. He shook his head. He needed the release of a good training session: some mitt and bag-work, maybe even some sparring – if he could find a suitable volunteer – to take his mind off things. But any workout was going to have to wait until tomorrow. At least he'd made sure any members of his crew still on base were asleep in their beds before he headed to his accommodations. It was tough being the Papa bear for those characters. He leaned on the doorjamb and slapped his palm against the biometric lock panel, his heavy sigh matching the swooshing sound of the thick metal door as it slid smoothly open.

Garm entered his dimly-lit quarters, his pale eyes adjusting to the amber-hued nightlights. The heady scent of lavender mixed with pine told him Tartarus's maid service had recently been by. He didn't bother ordering the overheads on; he had no plans on being up that long. He clicked open his gun belt, sitting the weighty S&W semi-auto on a nearby dresser, then headed toward the bathroom. Stripping off his shirt and trousers on the way, he kicked and tossed them toward a nearby hamper and was bare-assed by the time he got there.

Outside the bathroom, he paused and glanced longingly at his nearby king-sized bed. She was a big girl and a real beauty: one of those body-formatting, temperature-regulated, therapeutic numbers. Damn thing cost as much as a car. Dirk bought it for him last Christmas after he hurt his back and, after the first night, he fell in love with it. He named her Bertha, and if she hadn't been so huge, he'd have taken her with him on patrols. The tall submariner sighed again as he slid open the bathroom door. Brushing his teeth and heeding the call of nature was pretty much all he was capable of before collapsing into the loving embrace of his well-padded mistress.

Inside the near-dark bathroom, Garm brushed and flossed at light speed, his calloused hands relying more on muscle memory than his cat-like vision. He grabbed a bottle of mouthwash and took a swig, swishing it around before spitting and rinsing like a champ. He wiped his mouth and grinned as he put the cap back on. Not using a Dixie cup was a foul habit he'd picked up from his dad. He had more than one memory of his parents arguing about Jake sipping directly from the bottle.

"How can germs survive inside?" his dad insisted. *"It's all alcohol!"*

In the end, they ended up using "his and hers" bottles . . .

Garm smiled sadly as he stashed the mouthwash and took a moment to study his naked physique. He ran his fingers across his toned midsection and frowned. Although he hadn't lost any size, his vascularity was definitely down. He could tell by his abs; they lacked that stony hardness they usually had. A grunt of annoyance escaped his lips. Sitting in a captain's chair for days on end was the surest way to not only losing one's edge, but to gaining weight as well. He'd bet serious money that if he stepped on a scale right now he was pushing 250, as opposed to his usual 245.

As Garm's eyes scrolled down past his groin, they settled on a series of two-inch scars that peppered his right thigh and hip like machine gun rounds. He had a brief recollection of the awful hakapik mark that graced his mother's hip: the result of a near-fatal wound she received trying to protect baby harp seals from hunters, back when she was just eighteen.

She never tried to hide her disfigurement, not even when wearing a bathing suit. Garm's eyes lowered to half-mast as a wave of sadness washed over him. He missed her more than words, and the fact that her killer had eluded his vengeance haunted him day and night.

He poked the gnarled white surface of one of his scars with a hardened fingertip. The skin was tough and numb to the touch, much like the rest of him. Unlike his mother's selfless act, however, his own wounds were, admittedly, received under far less noble circumstances. He remembered first the drinking and carousing, then the waves and water, and finally, all the blood and screaming.

Garm looked up and gave a start as he realized Sam Mot's grinning face had replaced his in the vanity mirror. Dizzy and disoriented, he pitched forward, catching himself on the sink, and scrunched his eyes tightly closed. When he reopened them, he discovered he'd somehow gone from his bathroom to a sleek flats boat, motoring off the coast of Key West. It was nine years prior. The *Kronosaurus* phenomena was just starting to heat up and, from beachgoers to boaters, everyone was excited about it. On top of that, resident anglers were going nuts about the possibility of hooking one of the huge, primeval fish that were prowling Florida's waterways.

Garm had accepted his dad's recommendation and taken a much-needed break from boxing. He'd accepted an invitation to chill out and go fishing with his old high school buddy, Samuel Mot. Sam was a daredevil by nature, as well as a founding member of the recently formed LifeGivers: the lifeguards who skyrocketed to fame by risking their necks rescuing the victims of pliosaur attacks. Sam had bragged incessantly to his pugilist pal about the trolling opportunities in Key West – both the scaly kind in the water and the softer, two-legged variety that rubbed sunscreen on themselves and lay basting on the island's warm, sandy beaches.

"I'm telling you, Garm, these beach bunnies love big, athletic guys, and the braver the better. Between your bloody battles in the ring and me dragging terrified surfers from the mouths of hungry monsters, how can we go wrong?" Sam said. "We'll clean up. And in between scoring with the babes, maybe we'll even catch a fish or two!"

Sam was right. Once Garm perfected the "hypnotic stare" he taught him, making the most of his imposing height and wolfish eyes, they'd been inundated with ravenous females. The girls were relentless. In fact, after five days of non-stop depravity, they had to "borrow" Sam's dad's boat *Idle Worship* and hit the water to escape them. Now, the two friends were trolling for slightly more dangerous prey. In fact, they were in pursuit of the biggest, nastiest fish around.

They were going to try to hook a *Xiphactinus audax*.

At the time, fishermen had just starting learning about the Bulldog fish; the annual roundup for them didn't even exist. A few of the smaller, man-sized ones had been caught by local anglers, but one of the big adults that devoured full-grown tarpon had yet to be brought to gaff. Few had tackle strong enough to deal with them and nobody had a clue as to how many of the toothy things were really out there, let alone how dangerous they were.

Things were about to change.

The fishing started off slow. They were trolling a mile or so offshore and, after two hours of putt-putting around, hadn't had a nibble. So, when the starboard rod bent like a drunken letter U and started screaming off 300-pound test line, the two buddies began jumping for joy.

As Sam's guest, Garm got the nod to take the first fish. Strapping a fighting belt and harness around his muscular frame, the athletic 20-year-old wrestled the rod free from its stainless-steel holder and went to work. The 130-pound class stand-up rig they'd mated to a super-wide reel was designed for giant tuna, so they were confident that, whatever they'd hooked into, their gear could handle it.

The Bulldog fish that fell for their lure was sizable. They spotted it as it breached, fifty yards back, its chrome scales flashing like a mint condition 50's car bumper as it went airborne. Sam estimated it at nearly ten feet in length and over six hundred pounds. It was a powerful swimmer too, and, despite the heavy drag, made determined runs, repeatedly stripping backing in one hundred-yard sprints and even pulling the boat with it. Garm kept at it, however. Pushing the reel's lever drag to its maximum setting, he hauled back with his powerful arms and pumped like a madman. After twenty grueling minutes, he finally turned the tide. Inch by inch, yard by yard, he started bringing the weary fish to the boat.

Sam was steering with one hand and recording with his cell phone with the other. He was ecstatic. The give-and-take battle had ended up taking them close to shore. In fact, they were within eyeshot of the beach. Once they hauled the giant fish to the docks to be weighed and photographed, they'd end up on the evening news for sure.

Then, seventy-five yards out, something went wrong. There was an abrupt cessation of pressure and the line began to shake. Powerful vibrations shimmied up the heavy braid, causing the rod's industrial-grade roller tip to wobble.

"Something's got your fish!" Sam cried. He climbed atop the nine-teen-foot flats boat's sunlit poling platform, one hand shielding his eyes. "I don't know if it's a shark or another bulldog, but I saw its wake and it's fucking huge! Get ready. If it hooks itself you're in for it!"

Sam was more right than he knew. A few seconds later, the larger predator – having swallowed its victim whole – took off like a cruise missile. Garm stared at his smoking reel in disbelief as the high tensile strength braid peeled off at an astonishing rate. In seconds, his nine hundred yards of line was down to five hundred, then three . . .

"Shit!" Sam jumped down to start the main engine but shook his head. "You better brace yourself!" he shouted. "There's no time to chase her! We're gonna get spooled!"

Garm was reaching for a fillet knife to cut the line when the well ran dry. The spool locked up and he uttered a grunt of surprise as he was pulled sideways. He let go of the rod and tried to grab the poling platform, but his feet slipped on the wet deck. A second later, his hip hit the gunnels hard and he was yanked headfirst over the side.

Fortunately, Garm had the presence of mind to suck in a quick breath before he was jerked under. Whatever was on the other end of their line was huge; he was dragged ten feet beneath the surface and towed forty yards from the boat in seconds. Then the fish sounded and started to go deep. He could see the sunlight fading as he was pulled down. The pressure was incredible, but with a Herculean effort he managed to unclip the rod from the fighting harness seconds before he would've lost his air and been dragged to his death.

He surfaced with a monstrous inhale, waving his arms and shouting wildly. He saw the relief on Sam's face as he stood on the bow platform. He'd been looking in every direction, ready to dive in to save his friend. "I lost the rod!" Garm yelled as he started crawl-stroking toward the boat. "I'm sorry . . . I couldn't cut the line!"

Sam laughed aloud. "Don't sweat it!" he yelled back. "Let me get on the trolling motor and I'll come get you!"

"Sounds good," Garm replied, stopping to spit out seawater and catch his breath. He realized he was still wearing the cumbersome fighting belt and bucket harness and the added resistance was exhausting. He began to tread water, watching as Sam stepped on the foot pedal of the bow-mounted electric and started inching toward him. Garm laughed and splashed atop a swell as he waited for his ride. "Some fishing trip," he chortled. "But hey, at least I got to cool off!"

Sam's amused reply was lost and Garm realized he could no longer hear him. His sight, hearing, sense of smell and touch . . . all his senses were suddenly focused elsewhere as a chill ran up his spine. He'd felt an unmistakable shift in the nearby sea, a pressure wave generated by something moving through the water. Whatever it was, it was directly underneath him. And it was big.

As the hair on the back of his neck pricked up, Garm decided freestyling it back to the approaching *Idle Worship* was a good idea after all, heavy gear notwithstanding.

He was twenty yards away when Sam spotted the fish's shadow.

"Jesus . . ." he said, his eyes bugging out of his head. "Garm, there's something following you. Whatever it is, it's gigantic! Swim faster, brother!"

"What the hell do you think I'm doing?" Garm panted, snorting irritably as he stroked with all his might.

Ten yards away, Sam abandoned the trolling motor and moved to start the boat's big outboard instead. He mouthed a prayer as he turned the key. "Come on, Braddock!" he shouted. "Move your overgrown ass!"

With a surge of adrenaline, Garm reached the boat and threw one arm up over the gunnels, looping it over the low railing and holding on for dear life. The wind kicked up and the swells caused *Idle Worship*'s hull to roll up and back, yanking him half out of the water and preventing him from grabbing on with his other hand.

Sam wasted no time. In a second he was there, reaching down and latching onto the waterlogged bucket harness that cradled Garm's buttocks, with the intention of hauling him over the side like a gaffed fish.

"For the record," Sam grunted as he heaved upward. "This does *not* count as me grabbing your ass!"

Garm's chuckle became a pain-filled grunt as he felt the bite.

It was a sharp stabbing sensation, like someone jammed a drawerful of steak knives into his thigh, coupled with so much pressure he swore someone parked a Buick on his leg. He had a brief glimpse of Sam's stunned face; reflected in his horrified eyes was something huge and silvery. A moment later, Garm was torn violently away and pulled under.

This time there was no opportunity to take a breath. His world became a churning azure canvas, choked with bubbles. Water flooded his lungs and he clamped his jaw tight, desperately trying to hold onto what air he could. His chest burned and he felt himself being flung helplessly back and forth, his limbs trailing like a stuffed animal's. The pain in his leg increased exponentially as the bite tripled in force and he started to panic.

Then he saw the fish.

It was a full-grown *Xiphactinus*, a big male, judging from the hump that decorated its misshapen head, and measured over twenty feet in length. Except for the captive pliosaur on display in *Oceanus*, it was the largest marine predator he'd ever seen in the flesh, the size of a full grown great white shark.

Garm caught a glimpse of the Bulldog fish's ivory teeth and its amber-colored eye before it shook him and bit down once more. Waves of agony enveloped him and he fought to remain conscious. He could hear panic pounding on his door as a wave of epinephrine flooded his bloodstream. Everything started moving in slow motion and his supercharged mind switched to survival mode. Then, with surprising calmness, he took stock of the situation.

The *Xiphactinus* had hit him from the side and had his right hip, buttocks, and a good portion of his thigh sandwiched in its two-foot-wide maw. He could feel its blade-like teeth, up to six inches long, embedded in his flesh. The fish's eyes blazed with fury as it felt him struggle, and it shook him like a terrier shakes a rat. It was trying to drown its prey before swallowing it whole.

Despite the searing pain that shot like spurts of electricity through his ass and leg, Garm realized he'd been lucky to not discard the bulky standup harness and belt. The padded material from the bucket harness had done little to stop the X-fish's formidable dentition; its fangs were buried to the hilt in his muscular rump. But the metal plate and padding of the sturdy fighting belt had prevented its dagger-like teeth from slicing open his groin and pelvis. It could easily have punctured his femoral artery.

Or worse, castrated him.

As the ravenous fish adjusted its grip, Garm realized his luck was running out. Dark blood was spurting from his wounds, forming an ugly crimson cloud that obscured his already blurred vision. His right leg was in agony – undoubtedly broken – and the water that invaded his lungs was slowly killing him. He couldn't hold his breath much longer; once he opened his mouth he was a dead man.

Still, Garm refused to give up. The warrior in him got up off the canvas and started to fight back. With a snarl of defiance, he lunged for the fish's monstrous head. His hands impacted on its hard, slimy skull as he punched, clawed and gouged. He managed to graze one of its luminescent eyes, but any damage his fingers did to the thick-walled orb was summarily ignored.

Garm's furious attack was short lived. His arms began to grow heavy, increasing in weight until each seemed to weigh a ton or more. Soon, he could no longer lift them and his struggles began to fade. He gazed upward. The water's surface was so close, the shimmering daylight but a few feet away. He reached for it, his unfeeling fingers following the twisting paths of his escaping air bubbles. It was useless. He could feel the darkness welling up to claim him.

A bloodcurdling cry and a lean shadow sailing overhead distracted Garm from the encroaching blackness and his eyes struggled to refocus. There was a tremendous splash a few yards away and he gaped in astonishment.

Sam had come to the rescue. Hefting the six-foot aluminum and steel harpoon they kept onboard like a spear, the fearless LifeGiver had perched on the bow casting deck, waiting for his chance. When he saw it, he'd done the Tarzan thing. Springing into the air above the feeding *Xiphactinus*, he brought the harpoon down with all his weight and strength, driving it through the shallow layer of water that separated them.

And plunging it into the Bulldog fish's back.

The skewered *Xiphactinus* went insane. Its fanged jaws opened wide and it spat out its pending meal. Flailing back and forth, it snapped furiously at the shiny metal rod that had been driven clean through its barrel-shaped body. A moment later, the stricken predator sped off, its six-foot tail churning the water behind it into froth and sending both Garm and his would-be rescuer spinning head over heels.

Expert swimmer that he was, Sam recovered quickly. In the blink of an eye, he righted himself and was at Garm's side, pulling him to the surface through an ever-widening patch of scarlet and dragging him toward the boat.

"C'mon, Garm . . . breathe, man! Breathe!" Sam encouraged, holding on with one hand and shaking his nearly comatose friend with the other as they reached the rolling edge of *Idle Worship*'s hull.

At the sound of his voice, Garm's eyelids winched themselves upward. He opened his mouth to speak, but nothing but a gurgling sound came out. A moment later, he pitched forward and started vomiting uncontrollably, his battered body heaving as it expelled the seawater from his inflamed lungs. As the retching gradually subsided, the bloodied fighter's eyes came into focus.

"Man . . . that fucking sucked," he groaned.

Sam snorted amusedly. "Oh, c'mon. Don't be a wuss. I got you, didn't I?"

Garm managed a weak laugh as he draped one arm atop the flats boat's gunnels, his forearm resting on its smooth deck. "You're lucky I'm too . . . fucked up to throw you a beating . . ." He took a moment to catch his breath then looked Sam in the eye. "Thanks, man."

"Anytime, Big G. Now, do you think you can make it aboard, or do I have to rig a block and tackle to hoist your ginormous ass out of the water?"

Garm chuckled and shook his head, a mixture of seawater and blood streaming from his chestnut-colored hair and running down his face. He stuck his tongue out and tasted the salty combo. "I changed my mind . . ." he said with a grin. "I am *so* kicking your butt."

"Licking my *what?*" Sam made a show of appearing horrified, but then his eyes turned serious as he took in the reddened water all around them. "All jokes aside, you're in bad shape." He grabbed onto the top of the bucket harness. "Let's get you out of the water so we can slap a pressure bandage on those wounds. I can't have you bleeding out on me. Your dad will kill me."

"Sounds good . . ."

Sam's lips tightened as he saw how pale Garm was. "Okay, grab hold and on three. One . . . two . . . and heave!"

In unison, they wrestled Garm's heavily muscled frame up out of the water and onto *Idle Worship*'s foredeck. The big fighter lay on his side, drawing in deep breaths before clambering painfully to his feet. He tried putting weight on his wounded leg, winced and shook his head. If his right femur wasn't shattered, it was hanging by a thread. Worse, blood was streaming in thick rivulets from under the badly gouged fighting belt and running down his shin. It showed no sign of stopping. A trip to the ER was definitely overdue.

"Let me help you," Garm said wearily. Gripping the steering wheel for support, he leaned forward and extended a hand to Sam, only to stagger back as a powerful wave of wooziness nearly toppled him.

"Just stay put," Sam instructed, reaching up with both hands. "I got this."

Garm watched his wingman grab hold of the boat's railing and prepare to hoist himself out of the water.

"Man, can you imagine how many babes I'm gonna hook up with when I tell them I saved a heavyweight contender from becoming fish food?" Sam smirked, his triceps jutting out as he effortlessly powered himself into a vertical position, leaving just his legs in the water. "But don't worry, old buddy. I'm sure I can send a sympathetic nurse or two to your room to--"

Garm stared in confusion as Sam stopped talking and his eyes flew open wide. A moment later, he was yanked down with astonishing force, his chest bouncing off the hard edge of *Idle Worship*'s deck with an impact sufficient to splinter bone. The LifeGiver's grin was a distant memory, his expression one of pain and shock as he desperately wrapped his arms around the boat's thin aluminum railing.

A second later, he choked in a huge breath and screamed. It was one of those piercing, high-pitched shrieks – the kind a dying animal makes.

As the boat's portside began to dip, Garm realized what had happened. Sam's weight alone couldn't upend the heavy, 19-foot flats boat. Something sizable had gotten ahold of him.

"It's got my legs!" he screamed.

Ignoring the dizziness that threatened to overwhelm him and the blood gushing from his wounds, Garm staggered to the gunnels. What he saw sent a tidal wave of fear cresting up his spine.

A *Xiphactinus* had grabbed Sam's dangling legs, engulfing them to mid-thigh. He could see the silvery fish through the algae-stained water. It was smaller than the one that had attacked him, but at a solid twelve feet still tipped the scales at over one thousand pounds. It was on its side, just under the surface, its spiky teeth embedded in its terrified prey.

"You gotta help me!" Sam shrieked. "Get it off me!"

Garm cast about, desperately searching for a means to dislodge the aggressive Bulldog fish. As he snatched up a nearby gaff, Sam's body began to convulse. The fish started shaking its huge head from side to side, attempting to dislodge him. Sam screamed again and again as its powerful jaws tore huge rents in his quadriceps and hamstrings, cutting him to the bone. In an instant, the water around them churned a bright red.

"Get the fuck off!" Garm bellowed. Fighting to stay focused, he dropped to one knee and started swinging the four-foot aluminum tool like a war hammer. The sound of his powerful blows resounded off the surrounding water, but did little to deter the thick-scaled carnivore. Even when the gaff's five-inch steel hook sank deep into its head, the tenacious fish shrugged it off.

"I can't hold on much longer!" Sam cried out. As if on cue, the X-fish began to thrash powerfully to and fro. Pulling backwards, it nearly tore Sam's hands from the railing.

Garm cursed and tossed the useless gaff aside. He spotted the fillet knife he'd dropped on the deck nearby and his eyes lit up. *That* was what he needed. As he started hobbling toward it, however, he heard a sound that stopped him cold.

Idle Worship's railing was giving way.

With an eerie creak, the shiny aluminum tubing buckled, the screws holding it to the portside deck popping free one by one. Garm forgot the knife and spun back around. Crouching down and wrapping his arms under Sam's, he grabbed him in a bear hug and held on, just before the railing tore free.

"Oh, no you . . . don't!" Garm snarled as the Bulldog pit its power against his. Despite the waves of pain radiating through his own, horrifically injured leg, he dropped into a full squat, his friend clutched tightly to his chest. The hungry fish was furious at being denied its meal and resumed tearing away at its victim. Sam screamed piteously as his thigh muscles were repeatedly shredded by the creature's blade-filled maw.

"Don't let it take me!" he pleaded. Tears streamed down his face and his arms flailed helplessly.

"No fucking way!" Garm swore as he waged a tug-o-war against his oversized opponent. He gave a mighty heave and realized that what remained of his considerable strength, combined with the X-fish's neutral buoyancy, gave him a momentary advantage. He had Sam's entire torso up over the gunnels and a section of the fish's massive head sticking out of the water.

As he felt the LifeGiver's blood stream onto his sandaled feet, however, Garm panicked. Fatigue hit him like a brick over the head and waves of nausea began wracking his powerful frame. Soon, only dogged determination was keeping him conscious. He spotted the damage to Sam's mutilated thighs and averted his eyes. His friend's wounds were even worse than his own. If they didn't get medical attention soon, they'd both bleed to death. Not that that was their most immediate concern. The fish that clung to Sam was at least four times Garm's weight and showed no indication of letting go.

Bulldog . . . the damn thing was certainly living up to its name.

Garm resisted the urge to scream in frustration. He knew if he couldn't kill or dislodge the *Xiphactinus*, it was just a matter of time before he lost consciousness and Sam was pulled under and swallowed.

Then he remembered the knife.

He could see it with his peripheral vision. It was barely three feet away, the sun glinting off its ten-inch stainless steel blade. If he could bury it in one of the Bulldog fish's big amber eyes, *that* would surely discourage it.

"Hang on," Garm croaked. As he leaned toward the fillet knife, tiny motes of light swam before his eyes. He was almost out of time. Sitting back on his haunches, he kept one arm wrapped tightly around Sam's chest and reached for the weapon. It was just a few inches away. He gritted his teeth, his wounded hip and back screaming as he continued to bend. Just a few inches more . . .

Garm's lips curled back in a defiant snarl as he wrapped a meaty hand around the knife's black rubber handle. He hauled back, intent on driving it into the *Xiphactinus*'s brain.

He was in mid-strike when the other fish surfaced.

Like chrome-colored torpedoes, a pair of ten-foot Bulldogs exploded up and out of the water, their fanged jaws gaping. With wet, chomping sounds, they engulfed Sam's dangling arms almost to the shoulders and bit down hard. If the lifeguard's screams of pain and terror were loud before, they were nothing compared to now, as a trio of toothy terrors feasted on his flesh.

Garm nearly lost it as the resistance he'd been battling doubled. The arm he had wrapped around Sam began to buckle, and he had no choice but to drop the fillet knife and resume bear-hugging him. He leaned back and held on for dear life, watching with disgust as the knife skittered along the off-angled deck and vanished into the water.

"Jesus . . . they-they're killing me!" Sam screamed.

Garm gasped as his feet suddenly slipped out from under him and his ass hit the deck hard. Waves of agony shot up his spine until his skull felt like it would explode. He hissed in pain as he felt the shorn railing cutting into his calves and his heart plummeted into his stomach. They were both sliding down the bloodied deck, heading straight for the sea of jaws waiting to tear them to pieces.

"Just . . . just let me go!" Sam cried weakly. "Save yourself! I'm done!"

Garm gritted his teeth, "Like hell you are."

Fighting through a haze of pain, he gave the nearest *Xiphactinus* a savage kick and then braced both heels against the two-inch lip at the edge of the boat's wildly swaying deck. He uttered a guttural roar of defiance and pulled back with all his strength. Sam's screams were starting to subside as blood streamed from all four of his limbs, spraying across the already-soaked deck and trickling into the sea. Garm glanced at the wine-colored water and spotted the fins of at least a half-dozen other Bulldog fish circling nearby. The smell of blood had driven them into a feeding frenzy.

As the trio of fish clinging to Sam like pit bulls continued to lash from side to side, Garm found it was all he could do to hang on. He was running on pure adrenaline and it wouldn't last. His strength was already beginning to fade. Once his grip broke it was over. He growled angrily and looked around, frantically trying to find a way to keep his best friend from being ripped apart before his eyes.

A boat horn drew Garm's eye and he uttered a throaty cheer. Miraculously, salvation was on its way. A thirty-six-foot canyon runner was chugging toward them, accompanied by a pair of industrial-size Jet Skis running red flags.

It was the region's resident LifeGivers, rushing to save one of their own.

"Hang on, Sam!" Garm wheezed, ignoring his own, half-butchered leg as he adjusted his feet against the slippery deck. "Help is on the way!"

Sam was incapable of responding. Half-blind and deaf from pain and blood loss, he could do nothing but wail incoherently as the three fish tore at his lacerated limbs, intent on swallowing them.

Suddenly, the *Xiphactinus*, perhaps sensing the larger boat bearing down on them, redoubled their efforts. All three began twisting their thickly muscled bodies into S-curves and yanked savagely backward, their dagger-like fangs buried to the hilt in the warm, pulsating tissues of their victim.

Garm cursed as the colored motes of light floating before his eyes turned to big, crimson blobs. A moment later, he was wracked by a brick wall of nausea that collapsed squarely on top of him. He felt himself start to pitch forward and wrenched back with whatever he had left. His tendons cracked and his muscles tore as he resisted the combined strength of all three fish. But it was too much for him. He gagged from the effort and began vomiting all over himself and Sam.

Through a veil of suffering, Garm squinted at the approaching rescuers. They were only fifty yards away and closing fast. A glimmer of
hope clung to him and, despite all the misery, he hung on.

Just a few seconds more . . .

Out of nowhere, the horror he was experiencing escalated
to nightmarish proportions. Sam uttered a shrill shriek of agony,
drowning out Garm's horrified gasp. The efforts of the two smaller
Bulldog fish had borne fruit. There was a horrific squelching sound as
Sam's muscles succumbed. Their jaws tightly closed, the fish pulled
smoothly backward and vanished into the sea, taking with them almost all the flesh that covered his arm bones, and leaving behind a
ravaged mess of exposed nerves and torn tendons. Blood spewed everywhere, spraying into Garm's mouth and eyes, and he dry-heaved
in response.

His mind reeled, trying to process the horror he'd witnessed. Before
he could, however, there was a moist, cracking sound, like a waterlogged tree branch snapping in two. A second later, the fish still clinging
to Sam's legs bit clean through his savaged quadriceps and the femurs
underneath, amputating them both in mid-thigh.

Garm fell back from the sudden cessation of pressure and crashed
painfully to the deck, with what remained of Sam lying on top of him.
Mercifully, the mortally wounded teen had finally lost consciousness.

Garm's mind began to shut down to preserve his sanity. He could no
longer smell or feel as he sat up in a daze and tried to administer first
aid. His fingers were barely functional as he undid his shoelaces. His
world was now the raw meat of Sam's arms, and the bloodied stumps
that had been his legs. As he pulled the shoestrings free he heard muffled voices, like from a distant radio. He was vaguely aware of the big Jet
Skis motoring noisily alongside and their riders' shocked cries of alarm.
He stared blankly at them, blinking repeatedly as they screamed into
their radios for a medevac.

Garm's body finally failed him and he collapsed to the deck. The
impact of his head striking a nearby cleat was but a dull vibration, and
he was only distantly cognizant of the thuds of footsteps as rescuers
climbed aboard the floating charnel house known as *Idle Worship*. He
felt his own life's blood continuing to spit out in dark-colored gouts as
he lay on his back, each spurt of merlot matching the beat of his dying

heart. His head turned to one side and his glazed eyes remained open, his dilated pupils fixed on what was left of Sam. His cracked lips opened and he tried to speak.

"T-t-tourniquet . . ." he mumbled, his trembling, blood-caked hands still gripping a sticky shoelace. "Must . . . apply . . ."

Then the swirling red that had become his world was banished and blackness took the field.

Sixteen

When Garm Braddock pried open his eyes, the first thing he noticed were the spasms of pain radiating through both hands. He looked down and realized he'd latched onto the edges of his bathroom sink so tightly his knuckles were white. He released his grip, as well as the breath he'd been holding, and stared blankly into the empty basin. As his pulse and breathing returned to normal, he studied himself in the mirror, shaking his head at how pale he was. He wiped at the trickles of sweat running down his forehead with the back of one hand, then grabbed a washcloth and pressed it firmly to his face, breathing into the soft terry cloth as it conformed to his features.

As Garm pulled the towel away and studied his visage in the crinkled-up cotton, he got a momentary vision of the Shroud of Turin. He burst out laughing. It was ironic; Grayson *did* have an annoying habit of calling him a "godsend." He scoffed as he scrubbed at the sheets of perspiration that coated his chest and stomach before tossing the dampened washcloth into a nearby basket.

Not hardly.

Resting one hand on the sink, Garm blew out a breath. He remembered the PTSD incidents that plagued his dad, back when he and Dirk were kids. It took years, but Jake's issues eventually disappeared – a recovery he credited to the love he got from his family. In Garm's case, and despite all the trauma he'd experienced, he'd never had a flashback in his life. That is, not until seeing Sam again after so many years, when a mountain of submerged memories surfaced and ran him over like a freight train.

He snorted irritably. That was one ride he could've done without.

He moved to the toilet, flipping the seat up with one foot, then cricked his neck to one side and reached for himself as he prepared to urinate.

"May I .... *help* you with that?"

"Holy fuck!" Garm bellowed. He whirled around and caught sight of Natalya Dragunova's reflection in the vanity mirror. Her muscular frame was propped against the doorjamb, her arms folded across her chest as she looked him up and down. He wheeled on her. "What the hell is your problem, woman? Ever hear of knocking?"

"Relax, Wolfie," she said with a grin. "I said hello but you deed not respond. You were staring een the mirror with these crazy eyes and sweating like a peeg. Are you okay?"

Garm cleared his throat, embarrassed that she'd seen him like that. Then he remembered he was naked and holding his dick in his hand. "Yeah, I'm fine." He indicated the raised toilet lid. "Uh ... do you mind?"

"Not at all," Natalya said, her soles clicking on the ceramic tiles as she walked toward him. Before he knew what was happening, she'd come up behind him. Even through her spandex top, he could feel the heat from her cantaloupe-sized breasts pressing against his back. Next thing he knew, she was reaching around and feeling for his crotch. "I've always wondered what ees like for a man to pee," she said. "May I?"

Garm's jaw dropped, but for some inexplicable reason, he did nothing to stop her. "What, you wanna *hold* it for me?"

"Da," Natalya said. He stood there gaping as she explored his privates. It took her a moment to figure things out. Eventually, she settled on gripping his manhood with her left hand and everything else with her right. Garm felt fresh drops of sweat form on the back of his neck and tried to imagine the ugliest, most repulsive woman he could think of to avoid getting hard.

It wasn't working.

"Uh oh," she breathed in his ear. "I think we better hurry. Ees starting to grow and I don't want too much elevation to spoil my aim."

Garm swallowed nervously. "I can't believe you're doing this," he muttered.

"Oh, just shut up and pee for me."

He fought down his anxiety, sucked in air as if getting ready for a big lift, and then managed to get things flowing. Out of the corner of one eye, he watched Natalya with amusement as she skillfully directed his unnaturally loud stream of urine. She had her tongue tip pressed against her upper lip and a devilish look in her granite eyes.

"What do I do now?" she asked as his stream sputtered and stopped.

Garm chuckled. "You shake it a few times to make sure there's nothing still in the . . . *Ouch!*" he exclaimed, giving her an angry sideways glance. "Damn it, woman; that's attached!

"Sorry," Natalya snickered. She released her hold and pulled away, swaying out of the bathroom. She was wearing one of those sleeveless, black catsuits she liked working out in, and the material clung to her considerable backside as she moved.

Garm shook his head as he reached for a nearby bathrobe. "You know, these surprise visits of yours need to stop. I'm starting to regret adding you to my biometric lock."

He walked into his living room to find her lounging on the arm of his sofa with a coquettish look on her face.

"Oh, hush, dahling." She pouted when she noticed the robe. "We are to practice discretion, da?"

"That's a given. But besides the fact that you nearly gave me a stroke, what if I'd mistaken you for an intruder? I could have injured you."

She repressed a chuckle as she stood up. "Really, Wolfie? I am so scared!" She wore an amorous expression as she started toward him. "Ees that what you want to do? You want to *hurt* me?"

"Whoa, easy there," he said, extending his hands in a half-hearted effort at keeping her at arm's length. He knew where this was going, but after his little foray down memory lane, he wasn't exactly in the mood. "Can I get you something to drink?" he asked, backing toward the fridge.

Natalya frowned. "Just some ice water, please."

He grabbed a pair of drinking glasses from the cupboard, held one under the icemaker until it was full, split the contents, and put both under the dispenser.

"I got a private message from Grayson," he said, handing her one.

"Spasiba," she said, clinking hers to his before taking a sip. "A 'private' message? How mysterious. About what?"

Garm took a long draught, relishing the sensation of cold water sliding down his esophagus. "A big schooner was attacked, earlier today. At least, that's what the report indicates."

"By a pliosaur?"

"Apparently. Grayson thinks it was *Typhon*."

Natalya's eyes narrowed. "And that bastard ees going to send you back out after heem, alone?"

Garm sighed. "I don't know. Dirk won't admit it, but Grayson's completely obsessed with capturing the damn thing. It wouldn't surprise me."

She sat her glass down hard on the kitchen counter. "That's suicide. You saw what that theeng can do."

He shrugged. "If I have to go, I go. It's my job."

Natalya scrutinized him through hooded lashes. "Oh my God . . . You *want* to go after heem on your own! For what, the challenge?"

Garm frowned and waved her off.

"You know, I watched you when you were zoned out." She moved closer, her stormy eyes locking onto his pale blues. In bare feet, she was six-two. In shoes, she was easily his height. "I know the look of a man fighting for hees life. Who were you fighting, Wolfie?"

Garm turned away. He started slugging his water like it was bourbon and he an alcoholic who'd just fallen off a very tall wagon. He turned back. "It wasn't my life I was fighting for."

"Then whose?"

His jaw muscles bunched as Natalya stood next to him. With his peripherals, he watched her reach out to touch him on the shoulder, but then pull back.

"You can trust me, Garm," she said. "We may only be 'fuck buddies,' as they say, but I have my dignity. I do not – how you say een this country – blab?"

He nodded. "Okay. You've seen my scars."

"Da. Buckshot?"

"Bulldog fish. I was nineteen."

She gave a low whistle. "You are lucky to be alive."

Garm exhaled hard. "I'm alive because my best friend sacrificed himself saving me."

"He died?"

"Partly."

"Partly?"

"A school of them tore his arms and legs off while I watched. I . . . I couldn't do anything."

Natalya's face turned solemn. "I am sure you tried."

Garm nodded lamely. "Well, now he's here."

"Here in Tartarus? Why?"

"He's signed on for *Talos*."

"Ah . . ." Natalya nodded slowly. "And he's joining you on *Gryphon*."

"Yes."

She turned contemplative. A moment later, she took Garm by the arm and directed him to the couch. "Come."

"What for?" he asked.

"Just seat," she instructed. Once he complied, she hopped on the sofa next to him and started rubbing the thick trapezius muscles that adorned his upper back. "My God, you are tense. You need deep, relaxing massage. I geev you."

Garm sighed as he felt her hands skillfully working his weary muscles. "It's okay," he said, halfheartedly attempting to rise. "I'm fine."

"I deed not say you had choice," Natalya warned. Her grip tightened as she forced him back down.

"Nat, I don't need a massage," Garm complained. His hands shook as they balled into fists. "I need to *do* something. I need to *hit* something."

She wore an expression of mock fear. "You want to beat something? Perhaps you mean me?"

"What? No, don't be stupid. I'd never – *ow!*"

"What deed you call me?" she said, her iron fingers pinching a nerve on the side of his neck.

"I didn't mean that. It's just--"

"Good. I was about to beat your ass, Wolfie."

Garm's body shook with laughter as he pictured Sam's patented: '*You were about to eat my <u>what</u>?*' reply to a statement like that.

"That actually sounds like fun," he said.

Natalya smirked as she increased the intensity of her massage, her long fingers kneading the muscles of his upper back like pizza dough. Soon, it was all he could do to keep his eyes from rolling up inside his head. He was in Elysium.

"You like dees, da?"

When he swallowed and nodded, she breathed in his ear. "Good. Eef you seat like good boy until I am done, perhaps I let you heat me."

"Hit you? I don't--"

"Weeth your rampaging battering ram of love, silly," she purred. "You can batter down my castle gates to save me, da? I need saving *so* badly."

Between the heat of her breath and her scent filling his nostrils, Garm was instantly aroused. He cleared his surprisingly dry throat and immediately relaxed. "Well, if you feel *that* strongly about it . . ."

"Absolutely." She pulled open his bathrobe and slid it down, exposing his wide shoulders, then ran her fingertips deftly across his chiseled upper back, her touch so light it made his skin tingle. "I love all your muscles . . . such a beeg, strong man."

"Flattery will get you everywhere."

Natalya chuckled. "I know, Wolfie."

"You know, one day you're going to slip up and call me that in front of my crew and we'll be outed."

She scoffed. "So what? Dare are no regulations against two captains fucking. What can they do?"

Garm shrugged. "Grayson won't be happy. He could make trouble."

She stopped her massage. "Trouble for you? What can he do? You are – how you say – officer of company, da?"

Garm's lips formed a tight line. "True, but he could transfer *you*. Or come up with a reason to void your contract and just fire you."

"Bah, let heem try." She snorted derisively. "I wade through his black-booted convicts and break my foot off in hees wrinkled, old ass!"

Garm laughed aloud. "Damn, I like your style, woman." He reached back, his big hands cupping her hips.

"Seat still," Natalya warned, prizing his mitts off the top of her buttocks. "I tell you when finished."

"Man, you're tough." Garm grunted amusedly. "You're quite the fighter, aren't you?"

She ignored him and started running her hands down the muscles straddling his spine, digging in deep and causing waves of pleasure to radiate up his back, all the way to the base of his skull. He leaned into the pressure, relishing the welcome release of tension and wondering why the hell they didn't do this all the time.

"Speaking of fighting, you never tell me why you become boxer," Natalya pointed out. "You're smart, come from good family. Why you choose to fight?"

Garm exhaled slowly. "Probably because it's the only thing I was ever really good at."

"Was your dad boxer?"

"No. He was a competitive swordsman, a fencing champion, believe it or not, and an accomplished MMA fighter. When I was little, he taught me tons of stuff. Actually, I got to use some of it against that *Vermitus*, earlier. In fact, come to think of it, that's the biggest thing I've ever killed with my own two hands."

"Good." Natalya nodded her approval. "A swordsman, huh?" She arched an eyebrow. "Sounds like a man from another time."

Garm nodded, leaning his head to one side as she began working on his thick neck. "Yeah, if you'd seen my parents together, back in the day, you'd have thought they were straight out of some fairytale. Him, the knight in shining armor, her, the damsel, always ending up in distress and needing saving."

"Don't forget dee dragons," she reminded. "We have plenty of them swimming around, just waiting to snatch up little . . ." Her hands froze as she felt his muscles turn to stone. "I'm sorry, Wolfie. I--"

"It's okay," Garm replied, forcing himself to settle down once more. "Maybe if my dad was still alive, six months ago, she'd be, too."

Natalya cleared her throat. "Can I ask you personal question?"

He grinned. "If I said no, would it stop you?"

"Nyet. I was curious, so I went online and researched your boxing career."

"Ah . . ."

"How ees eet a man goes from being top-ranked heavyweight contender to fighting illegal underground fight clubs?"

"Wow . . ." Garm's eyes widened and he drew slowly back from her. "You know, you'd make a good boxer, Nat. You don't pull punches."

Natalya sat back sideways, eyeing him. Her physique and outfit gave her the appearance of a resting panther. "Ees not my way. So . . . why?"

He frowned and faced forward, his hands in his lap. "You went digging. You already know."

"Because you killed those two men een the ring."

Garm's jaw muscles tightened. "I killed *one* fighter in the ring. Jenkins – didn't die. He just ended up . . ."

Natalya's eyebrows went up. "Retarded?"

He chuckled. "I was going to say a vegetable, but I'll go with that."

"Ees not, how you say, politically correct term?"

"Nat, there are people who are mentally handicapped, and there are people who are just plain retarded. Jenkins was one of them. He was an asshole. And he was brain-dead long before I tried removing his head from his shoulders."

"Ah . . . so eet was not accident. You beat heem so badly on purpose."

Garm turned to face her, his feral eyes gleaming. "Damn straight, I did."

"Why?"

"Because that cockroach sent his 'posse' to terrorize my girlfriend, right before the fight. They caught her in the hallway outside the locker room, said they were going to gang rape her."

Natalya's lips curled back from her canines. "Assholes. Why they do that? They think to screw up your head before fight?"

Garm shrugged. "If so, they made a mistake. I saw her in the audience crying, right before the opening bell, and my trainer told me what happened."

"What did you do?"

"I did something I shouldn't have. I let the beast out of its cage." He interlocked his fingers and extended his arms straight out in front of him, his thick knuckles cracking one by one. "Our game plan was forgotten. I went out there with the intention of beating Jenkins to a pulp, and that's exactly what I did. In fact, if the ref and his trainers hadn't jumped in and stopped me, I'd have killed him."

Natalya scoffed. "He deserved it. What about other man? What hap--"

Garm stood up, shrugging his robe back up over his shoulders. "Look, I can see where this is going. So rather than playing 'Twenty Questions,' how about if I give you the Cliff's Notes version of my boxing career, okay?"

"Da . . ."

He blew out some tension. "Three months after Jenkins' boys lost their meal ticket, I watched my dad die from Cretaceous cancer. It was a nightmare. My mom was destroyed. Dirk and I were walking around in a fog, everything was just chaos. I tried backing out of my next fight, but my manager and the promoters wouldn't let me. It was a setup for a title shot, so the fight ended up going ahead as scheduled. And I killed the guy."

"Lopez. I read about dees. Een second round you break hees skull, da?"

"No. I shattered his jaw and the fragments punctured his skull and severed his brain stem."

"Same theeng. Was that on purpose, too?"

Garm's muscles tensed. "Per my lawyers, I don't go into the particulars of that fight. It's not a 'topic for discussion.'"

"I already told you, I don't blab. I--"

"I *said* I don't talk about it," he snapped.

Natalya stared at him. "Okay, fine. Go on."

Garm got up and started pacing the room. He could feel himself getting worked up and rubbed the hardened knuckle portions of his fists together, trying to let off steam. "After Jenkins and Lopez, nobody would fight me. I was branded a killer – too dangerous to be in the ring with."

"No surprise. What about MMA? You could've switched to cage fighting," Natalya offered.

"Not my style. I don't want some guy crawling all over me; I'm a standup fighter," Garm said. He moved laterally back and forth as he spoke, as if he was in the ring, stalking someone. "When I die, it'll be on my feet. You get me?"

She licked her lips and nodded.

"Anyway, I couldn't get a fight. And I really needed one . . ."

"Why? For money?"

"No, I . . . I don't know. I needed to--"

"To improve your record? To get title shot?"

Garm scoffed. "It had nothing to do with money or titles. I needed to be in the arena. I needed an opponent, one dangerous enough to make it worthwhile." He felt himself growing agitated, like a covered pot bubbling. "But nobody here would face me, and even if someone was game, the 'powers that be' publicly stated they wouldn't sanction my bouts. So, I went overseas."

"Ah . . . dees is when you started putting up purses."

He nodded. "It was the easiest way to attract challengers. I put up a half-million bucks in cash, and offered anyone who could match it a straight-up bet. The money was put in escrow: winner takes all."

"As it should be," Natalya said.

"Yeah, well, it didn't work out very well," Garm replied. "Quality opponents were hard to find and after I beat down the first two guys, word got around. We had to start shrinking the purse to keep things going. Pretty soon it was just 50K and open season."

"Open season?"

"Washed up or wannabe fighters, no drug or steroid testing, basically a big fiasco," he said. "It got to the point where juice-heads from area gyms – guys with no boxing background whatsoever – were just showing up ringside with bowling ball bags filled with drug money, hoping to make a name for themselves. One night, I sent three of them to the ER."

Natalya chuckled. "Sounds like boxing in the 19th century."

"More like prison," Garm remarked. He realized he was getting worked up and slowed his roll, standing in one place until he got his breathing back under control. "Anyway, after a while it just wasn't worth it. So I came back to the states and started hanging out. A few months later, I hooked up with these sleazy promoters and ended up hitting those underground fight clubs you read about. For the next year, I did nothing but bust heads and live on booze and broads, until Dirk and my mom finally tracked me down and dragged my sorry ass back home."

"They saved you," she stated. "Healed you and brought you back."

Garm laughed aloud. "I don't know about the 'healing' part. My mom sure as hell tore me a new one. But Dirk *did* get me treated for a really nasty case of the clap!"

He froze as Natalya's eyes became limpid pools of fire.

"That was, uh . . . ages ago."

"Whatever. So, you joined the CDF so you could fight again?"

"To fight the monsters that destroy people's lives," Garm clarified. "And the disease they spread that helped ruin mine." He gestured at an imaginary horizon. "Out there, I'm in command. I can face my demons on their terms. There are no refs, no rules, and most importantly, no rounds. None of that bullshit. It's winner takes all and combat is to the death – as it should be."

"Except when you have to bring them back alive," Natalya pointed out.

Garm snorted irritably. "Yeah . . . Grayson and his money-grubbing science experiments. It's never enough for that guy."

"You don't like heem," she observed.

"Dirk does. He thinks the sun rises and falls on his 'mentor.'"

"I deed not mention Derek," she said. "I said *you* don't like heem."

"Obviously. Why, do you?"

She shrugged. "He ees nothing to me. Just a means to an end."

"As are most men, I think," Garm said. He turned to her, his pale eyes latching onto hers.

Natalya stiffened. "What the hell does *that* mean?"

"You've been doing a lot of research on me," Garm said. He leaned back on the kitchen counter, his muscular arms crossed. "Pretty invasive stuff for a 'fuck buddy.' So, what's *your* story?"

"My story?"

"You heard me," Garm said. "I'm no stalker, to go prying into someone's personnel records, but I want to know. Why did you enlist? Not to sound sexist, but you must've blown the roof off their aptitude tests to end up a sub commander."

"I have an 'innate grasp of three-dimensional combat skills,'" Natalya said. "And, according to them, I have . . . balls?"

He smirked. "You do. At least, metaphorically. But what made you decide to join and claw your way up the food chain? It couldn't have been easy."

She hesitated, her eyes considering the door like a trapped animal, searching for a way out. "I had . . . nothing better to do."

"Oh, no. No running away, Nat," Garm said, following her gaze. "I really want to know. What makes a woman forego raising a family and spend her days risking life and limb, slugging it out with prehistoric predators?"

A look of weariness suddenly draped itself over Natalya's toned shoulders and she sat back. "I owe you apology, Wolfie," she said with a sigh. "Eef you invaded my privacy, like I deed yours, you would already know the answer to your question."

Garm felt like the Spider approaching Little Miss Muffet as he sat down beside her. "I'd rather you tell me."

She looked him in the eye. "Okay . . . When I came to thees country to find surviving member of my family, I was only fifteen. I was not as you see me now," she said, indicating herself. "I was tall, but not so athletic or . . ."

"Magnificent?" Garm offered.

She smiled warmly as she reached over to touch his face. "You are good man, Garm Braddock."

"That's what my urologist tells me when I strip down for her." He smiled back at her. "So, you were saying?"

She sighed. "When I was twenty, I met nice American man: a plastic surgeon. He was not so beeg and strong, but he was smart and successful, and he worshipped me. So, I end up marrying heem."

"So far so good."

"Da. But story does not have happy ending."

"Most don't."

"A few years later, we were vacationing een Keys. Duck Key, ees not far from here."

Garm nodded. "Nice place. We went there a few times, back when Dirk and I were kids."

"I like the bond between you two," Natalya said.

"What do you mean?"

"Most people would say, 'When *I* was a child.' But you don't. You mention Derek, too. I like dees."

Garm grinned. "Funny, I never noticed that. So, go on."

Natalya took a deep breath, let it out slow. "We had a rental boat weeth some friends, a beeg sailboat we would snorkel on."

"Sounds like fun."

"Eet was. Then one day we were een the water and a--"

"*Kronosaurus* took your husband . . ."

"Eet was much worse than that." She breathed through her nostrils. "I lost much that day."

Garm cocked his head to one side. "I don't understand."

"I lost my faith een men and . . ."

As she quieted and her eyes fell to the floor, Garm was taken aback. In the six months since they met, he'd never known Natalya Dragunova as anything other than an oversexed, untamable tigress that brooked no nonsense from anyone. Seeing her small and vulnerable was jarring and he hesitated, not sure how to proceed.

He cleared his throat. "Hey . . . if it's tough to talk about, it's okay. I didn't mean to make you uncomfortable."

Natalya looked sideways at him, gauging his sincerity. Garm swallowed, despite himself. In the ring, he'd stared-down some of the scariest human beings on the planet and never batted an eye. But with her, he felt totally out of depth.

"Ees okay, Wolfie," she said. "Eet was a long time ago."

"Would you like some more water?"

"Nyet, spasiba." She hugged herself as she spoke. "Paul and I were een the water when the creature came. We saw eet surface fifty meters away and knew right away what eet was. Eet was small one, maybe seven meters, but very fast. The boat was close, so we swam like crazy peoples. I got there first and started to climb the ladder. That's when I found out I married a . . ."

"A what?"

"A coward."

Garm was confused. "Wait, what happened?"

"Paul was so terrified, he grab me by the heeps and pull me off the ladder so he could climb out instead."

"What? Are you fucking serious?"

"Da."

Garm shook his head in disbelief. "You're telling me the chickenshit yanked you off the ladder? He tried to sacrifice you, his wife, to one of those monsters to save his own skin?"

She nodded.

"W-wait, I-I'm having a hard time with this," Garm stammered. "Did he at least *try* to help you out of the water?"

"He never got the chance," Natalya said. "Hees plan, how you say . . . backfired?"

"How so?"

"When he yanked me off and threw me back, the pliosaur was right behind us. I fell over eets jaws and landed on eets neck as eet struck."

Garm's mouth slackened with the realization. "So, it ended up grabbing--"

"Paul," she affirmed. "I saw the jaws close and heard heem scream like little girl as he was torn from the ladder. Blood everywhere."

"So, trying to sacrifice you cost him his own ass," Garm remarked. "Good. That's justice, the goddamn coward." He noticed she'd grown quiet again. "What happened then?"

"While eet was eating Paul alive, I struggled to climb back up. I was screaming for help. Our friends were below deck and came running up to pull me out of the water. I was bleeding badly."

"You were bitten?" Garm was confused. He knew her body well and she had no bite marks he'd ever seen. In fact, other than that tiny scar on her throat and the callosities on her knuckles, she had no marks of any kind.

Natalya shook her head. "No, I was having . . . miscarriage."

"Oh, God."

"God not help me," she stated. "I was five months pregnant when dees happen. The impact on the creature's head, plus stress . . . eet was too much."

"I'm so sorry, Nat. There was nothing anyone could do?"

"No. I lay on the deck, losing my baby, while my *pussy* of a husband meets the fate he deserve."

"Wow." Garm shook his head. "It's ironic. If it wasn't for his cowardice, it might have gotten you instead. In a way, he kinda saved your life."

"I lost my baby," she emphasized. "I rather be dead, too."

He hesitated. "I understand. If it's any consolation, I'm glad you're not."

Natalya studied his face, her gray eyes doing his X-ray thing before she hoisted herself up off the sofa. She walked around the room, rolling her shoulders out one by one, the taut muscles of her upper back and arms rippling. "So, Wolfie. Now you know why I am how I am. And why I choose man like you as my playmate."

Garm stood up, a confused look on his face. "A man like me?"

She planted her feet shoulder width apart, her arms folded as she looked him up and down approvingly. "Da, you are not like Paul," she said, scoffing at the recollection of her dead husband. "You are, how you say, 'real man'?"

Garm chuckled. "Why, because I'm an athlete?"

"You *are*, and then some. You like beeg grizzly bear. Nothing scares you."

"And that's what you like?"

"What every female likes," she said. "Not just humans. Ees nature's way, attraction to strongest of species, da?"

"I suppose so." He grinned teasingly. "So that's what you're into, the natural order of things?"

Natalya's eyes softened then hardened. "Oh, believe me; I will never be with weakling again. But ees more than that. I like that you are strong on inside, too. You take care of people you care about. Like your brother, da?"

"Dirk?" Garm shrugged. "I guess so. I mean, I've always kinda looked after him, ever since we were kids."

Natalya nodded. "He ees nice man, your brother. But een thees place, with these people, he ees small feesh in beeg feesh pond. He ees lucky to have you."

Nice man. Garm mulled over her words before giving her a curious look. "Some think so. So, tell me, Nat. Do you like my brother?"

"Do I . . . like heem? As a person?"

"As a man," he pressed, irritated that she was stalling. "Come on, I've seen the way Dirk looks at you. It's like he's a mountaineer and you're Everest. You know he's dying to climb you."

Natalya moved close to him, her lips bunching as she tried to read him. It was a wasted effort. Garm was wearing his lizard face, the one he used in-between rounds to conceal injuries or fatigue. She wasn't getting anything from him.

After a moment, she turned away, laughing. "I can't tell eef you're jealous or not, Wolfie," she said with a chuckle. "But, I'll be honest weeth you."

"That's considerate."

"I do like your brother," she said. "He ees funny man, da?"

"He has a wry sense of humor," Garm acknowledged. He felt a sudden pang of jealousy and wondered whether it was just his maleness coming under fire, or if he'd actually grown attached to this tawny-haired lioness as a side effect of their biweekly sexathons.

"Deed you know he asked me out on date, my first day here?"

Garm's jaw dropped. "Are you serious? You never told me that."

Natalya grinned and nodded. "Da, ees true. And I have to say, I was very eempressed."

"How so?"

"Because I was a mean, nasty beetch," she said with a snicker. "And I gave heem hard time."

"So, what happened?" Garm asked, annoyed that he cared to know. "Did you blow him off?"

"What?" Natalya's cool eyes turned to fire. "Did I . . . *blow* him? Nyet! What ees *wrong* weeth you? I--"

"Whoa!" Garm exclaimed, trying not to laugh and failing miserably. "Blow him *off*, not *blow* him. That means to give him the brush off, to tell him to get lost, to--"

Natalya snorted dismissively. "Da, da, da, I understand." She shook her head. "Nyet, I deed not 'blow heem off.' I respected that he had balls."

"I see. Um . . . so what happened?"

"I agreed to eat weeth heem."

Garm's head recoiled on his shoulders. "You guys went out to dinner?"

"Not exactly." Natalya lounged back against the kitchen counter, her tongue running over her strong, white teeth. "I wanted to get eet over weeth, so I meet heem in cafeteria, late at night."

"I don't understand."

She sighed. "I told you, I won't be weeth any man unless he ees at least my equal. Understand? And Derek ees . . ."

"Not?" When she nodded, he asked, "So, what went down?"

She shifted position as if uncomfortable. "I try to lower heem down easy, but he was very . . . how you say, tenacious?"

Garm grinned. "Sounds like Dirk."

"I finally had to resort to direct approach."

"Meaning what?"

Natalya shrugged. "I challenge heem to arm wrestling match. I tell heem eef he beat me, I go out weeth him. Eef not, nyet."

"Yeesh. So, uh . . . who won?"

She looked at him like he was an idiot. "Are you serious?"

Garm's whistle sounded like a WWII bomb falling. "Wow, what an ego crusher. Was, uh, anybody else there to see this 'contest?'"

She shook her head. "I looked around and made sure. I deed not want to embarrass heem."

He shook with laughter. "I think you might have failed on that one."

Natalya shrugged. "Eet was necessary. Otherwise, he would be following me around like beeg puppy dog."

"So that was it?" Garm asked. Despite the perceived rivalry, he felt a strong urge to defend Dirk. "I mean, just because you're taller and stronger than him, you couldn't give him a chance? He's got a lot of great gifts. He's incredibly intelligent, loyal to a fault, and--"

Natalya turned on him, her eyes lightning bolts slicing through storm clouds. "You know, I told you *twice* now, Garm Braddock, and you not listen; I need a *man* in my bed and by my side, not a boy."

"Dirk's not a--"

"A man who ees strong and fearless. One I can count on eef sheet heats the – how you say?"

"Fan. When the shit hits the fan."

"Da, *fan*," she fumed. "Your brother ees nice guy. But he ees scared of own shadow. He's had you protecting heem all hees life. Trust me, Wolfie, he ees *not* for me."

"Okay, take it easy," Garm said, his hands extended outward in a calming gesture. "I get it. Sorry, I guess I was just making sure."

She glared at him. "Making sure what? That I not fuck someone else? That your brother wasn't going to steal me from you?"

He felt himself getting annoyed. "I don't know about all that. I just wanted to make sure I wasn't stepping on the poor guy's toes, that's all."

"I see." Natalya threw the door a hard glance. "Good old Garm. Always looking out for baby brother. Like I said."

He followed her gaze. "Are you thinking of leaving?"

"Hmm?" she looked back at him, her lips pursed. "Da. My coming here was not the fun and games eet usually is."

Garm frowned as disappointment banged on his door. Despite the state Natalya found him in when she first barged in and the heaviness of their subsequent conversation, there was no avoiding the fact that his fellow sub captain looked amazing in her tight, curve-hugging workout attire. In addition, he realized that, for some reason, he found her unexpected show of vulnerability a tremendous turn-on. A sea of horniness suddenly inundated him and he decided to try and do something about it.

"Yeah, you're right," Garm said, feigning agreement. "All this emotional stuff is too much for you. I understand."

"What does that mean?"

"It means that, when push comes to shove, you're kind of a cold fish, Nat. You're uncomfortable discussing things that matter, and you'd rather run away than engage in a serious conversation."

When Natalya's jaw muscles bunched like steel balls, Garm realized he'd made a mistake taunting her. The woman had a vicious temper and an overhand right to match, and it would be a shame if the only interaction between them turned out to be an impromptu slugfest. Especially since he'd inherited his father's chivalrous nature when it came to members of the opposite sex and was bound to get the worst of it.

He decided to apply the brakes before things skidded out of control.

"Chill out," he placated as she stalked toward him. "I'm just fucking with you."

"You're *fucking* weeth me?" she snarled through clenched teeth. He could see she was sizing him up. "You make beeg error in judgment."

Garm became conscious of the loosely tied bathrobe he was still wearing and shifted position, putting the heavily-padded couch between them. It was a barrier he knew wouldn't last, so he decided to change tactics. "Look, I didn't mean to upset you. It's just that you look so goddamn hot in that catsuit and I thought, I don't know, *maybe*, if I got you all 'outraged womanhood,' you might forget about our depressing talk and start thinking about more pleasurable ways to relieve stress."

Natalya abruptly stopped pursuing him around the room and instead targeted him with angry eyes. "You use stupid manipulation tactic on me? You play dangerous game."

Garm shrugged. "You're right. I'm an asshole. Sorry."

"Da, you are a beeg mudak. A stupid, childish one."

He made a face. "Yeah. Thanks for agreeing with me."

"Ees no problem."

Garm sighed. Although he knew his chances of getting laid had evaporated, at least the two of them wouldn't end up in the infirmary. Again.

Natalya observed his crestfallen expression with amusement before turning and walking toward an ornately framed, antique wall mirror.

She stopped in front of it and studied her reflection in the silvered glass, her gray eyes roving up and down her face and figure. Her expression altered, becoming analytical, almost critical.

Garm's jaw dropped as she suddenly reached up, grabbed the top of her black, micro-fiber bodysuit, and pulled down hard. Twisting from side to side, she worked the clingy material past her broad shoulders, exposing and then freeing her perfectly formed breasts. They spilled up and out from their restrictive home like a pair of triple-D honeydews, her pink nipples standing at attention in the cool air.

As he watched Natalya move closer to the glass and hoist her breasts, examining each in turn, Garm swallowed nervously. His immediate instinct was to pounce on her, but he knew better.

"Tell me, Wolfie, have you ever thought about why women have only one set of breasts?" Natalya asked, squeezing her "girls" together like a pushup bra and staring curiously down at them.

"Uh . . . what?" Garm felt drops of sweat soaking into the underside of his bathrobe and his heart became a trip hammer in his chest. He was beyond aroused, but a healthy dose of caution mixed with paranoia kept him rooted in place.

Natalya studied him in the mirror and snickered, pleased that she'd already achieved her desired effect. "Theenk about it. Dogs, cats, peegs, cows . . . so many mammals have like, what, three pairs of boobs? Why not women?"

Garm stared like a bird transfixed by an approaching serpent as she turned in his direction, cupping one of her huge mounds in each hand and bouncing them enticingly up and down.

"What do you think?" She grinned wickedly. "Would you like eef I had three sets of teats instead of just one?"

Garm struggled to clear his suddenly parched throat. "Are you kidding? I get confused dealing with just two. With six, I'd be there all day, trying to make heads or tails of things!"

As Natalya's little strip tease continued, a feeling of ballsiness came over the big submariner and he threw caution to the wind. He started toward her, his manhood pushing eagerly against his robe, his chiseled face even more strongly carved by the intensity of his arousal. He'd taken just two steps, however, before the object of his desire extended a hand, palm out in warning, cooling his ardor with an unseen wall of ice.

"I deed not say you could touch me," she advised. "You have behaved badly and don't deserve the privilege of fucking me."

As Garm stood there, neck-deep in a mire of consternation, Natalya turned her back on him and began to work her sleeveless, one-piece suit even lower, pushing down on it and wiggling her hips from side to side, until it lay in a dark heap at her feet. She turned to face him then, an Amazonian goddess, her feet spread apart and arms raised overhead in a tension-relieving stretch that caused her breasts to jut proudly outward.

Garm's eyes swept hungrily up and down his lover's naked frame, eyeing her muscular legs, her flat, hard stomach, and the silky-smooth mound of perfection that resided between her thighs. His heart started doing the subwoofer thing in his ears, booming louder and louder until it was all he could hear. He cursed inwardly. If this was any other woman, he'd know sex was a foregone conclusion. But Nat was such an unpredictable, spiteful creature. It would be just like her to drive him to the brink of insanity, only to storm out of his quarters buck naked and walk calmly back to hers, her clothes draped over one forearm.

"Do you *want* me, Garm Braddock?" Natalya asked, running her hands slowly up her thighs. Her lithe fingers arced gracefully inward, her fingernails just grazing the outermost edges of her pubic region before traveling upward. She smiled naughtily at him as she began tweaking her nipples. They protruded like giant pencil erasers, their tips pointing in his direction.

Garm choked down the huge lump in his throat. "I think that's the mother of all rhetorical questions," he muttered.

"I can see . . ." she teased, eying the bulge in the front of his robe that gave new meaning to the term, 'pitching a tent.' "But you are very naughty boy. I theenk you owe me for getting me upset."

"I, um, I couldn't agree more. What did you have in mind?"

Natalya made a pouty face as she considered. "I theenk I weesh to receive oral pleasures from you," she began. "Perhaps that standing sixty-nine position we deed before. Then, I want doggy style – fast and deep. I want you to bite me while you do me, and you must pound me so hard you make me scream. You can do thees, da?"

As he did the bobblehead thing, Garm wondered if she'd lost her mind. He started toward her, only to be reined in once more by a look.

"Also, no ass today, and none of that meessionary position. You know I don't like. You agree, da?"

Garm nodded so vigorously his head nearly flew off. She really was nuts. He was so aroused at this point, he'd have signed over half his shares in the company, just to have her.

Natalya checked her watch. "Humph. I don't want to be up too late. You have one hour to do your job. Then I--"

Her words became a throaty squeal of delight as he barreled into her, scooping her up in a massive hug and carrying her toward the bed.

In Garm's sex-charged mind, a familiar bell rang out.

Round one was about to begin.

SEVENTEEN

Creeping stealthily along the coral-strewn seabed, the male *Octopus giganteus* gazed upward, his gleaming golden eyes studying the moonlit surface five hundred feet above. He paused, his amorphous body twisting like a monstrous piece of rope as he swept the nearby water column. His search for additional victims had proven fruitless. Ahead, the nutrient-rich waters of the Straits of Florida became a veritable wasteland as sharks, whales, and even a huge bull pliosaur, all detected his presence and fled.

Dawn was still a spectral flicker on the horizon as he approached the downed submarine his mate had chosen as their midden. Still 150 yards out, the male stopped. His tentacles writhed like a nest of angry vipers as he waited for the contractions to cease. His hunger pangs were growing stronger, to the point his empty stomach growled like some ravenous beast that senses food is within reach. It was, but his burgeoning paternal instincts, combined with a healthy dose of fear, prevented him from giving in.

As he closed to within seventy-five yards of the wreck, the male adjusted his grip on the prey item he'd kept hidden beneath his mantle. As he did, the chemoreceptors in his suckers detected the intoxicating taste of blubber and transmitted it to his hunger-warped brain. He examined his kill. It was a dead Orca, a decent-sized bull measuring twenty-seven feet in length and weighing nearly eight tons. He'd surprised a pod of the aggressive pack hunters as they passed over what appeared to be a harmless stone outcropping, seizing the nearest one with his tentacles and wringing its neck while its panicking brethren swam for their lives. The toothy cetacean was small – hardly enough to satiate the female's boundless appetite – but it was the only thing of respectable size the male had been able to catch, and he knew better than to return to his mate empty-handed.

Not in her current frame of mind.

Outside the entrance to their lair, the male hesitated. He contemplated the lightless opening. Many of the reddish brown rusticles that draped the forty-foot rent in the century-old submarine's hull had been broken off or shattered by the pair's repeated comings and goings. In the blackness that welled beyond, he could see his mate's eyes: twin globes of fire that shone like embers in the darkness.

As he studied her, the male's own eyes glittered and his giant body swelled with pride. His mate had given birth in his absence. He could make out the strings of gelatinous eggs that hung suspended from the sub's rusted ribs like translucent grapes. There were tens of thousands of them, each one containing a rapidly-developing larva that writhed within the confines of their foot-long wombs.

The female *Octopus giganteus* hovered protectively over her brood, her powerful gills sucking in tremendous quantities of seawater which she expelled slowly from her siphon. She directed it gently over the eggs, keeping them clean and oxygenated. Mixed with the water, the male octopus's keen eyes espied more of the black, crystalline granules that littered the nest's floor. The dark-colored sand mingled with the eggs, caressing them before drifting harmlessly back down to the seabed.

Spotting his approach, the female sprang to life. Her gigantic body swelled to twice its normal size and she curled her lethal arms about her clutch. Her luminescent, yellow orbs narrowed into slits. Like any mother, she would defend her offspring with her life.

The male froze, fearful that the cow, blinded by maternal instincts, would attack him on sight. Then he remembered his gift and extracted it from between his tentacles. The female's eyes widened at the sight of the fresh whale carcass and she shifted position. Unwilling to relinquish guardianship of her brood, she extended one of her bridge cable-sized tendrils over one hundred feet from the nest and demanded the offering.

Not willing to chance her temper, the male gave the dead Orca a healthy push. Backed by a burst of seawater from his own siphon, he sent the still-warm cetacean spiraling flukes over fin in the female's direction. The tip of her tentacle curled gently around the killer whale's remains as it neared the bottom, her suckers sampling it.

The taste was obviously to her liking. A split-second later, the Orca was snatched back into the nest with astonishing speed and enveloped.

The male octopus remained motionless, his body wracked with hunger, listening to the sounds of maceration as the female's five-foot beak shredded the bull killer whale like a meat grinder. Starting at the whale's snout and working toward the flukes, its flesh, blubber, and bones were ground to pulp and greedily swallowed.

In less than three minutes, the body of the once-proud cetacean vanished as if it had never existed. The cow octopus sucked in a few deep breaths and sat there, the gnarled skin covering her immense body slowly changing hues. A moment later, she began to cast about.

She wanted more.

As her gaze fell on him, the male paled and retreated a safe distance away. He settled down into a clump of tentacles, his 134-ton body draped atop a seaweed-choked hillock as he waited to see if his mate's hunger would subside. When she continued glaring at him with those malevolent eyes of hers, he knew it would not. Rising, he gave the cephalopod's version of a shrug before turning toward the nearby abyss.

The surface had stopped being productive. He would try hunting the extreme deep instead. Perhaps he would be fortunate enough to catch a prowling sperm whale off guard. If so, he would be able to not only appease his mate, but also stave off his own pending starvation.

As he jetted down into the lightless depths, the male accepted with cool, mollusk deliberation that his own fate was inconsequential. Only the survival of his brood mattered. It was evolution at its most basic. They were the future, not him. He would nourish his mate and protect both her and their clutch until his strength was gone.

It would not take long for their eggs to hatch: a few weeks at most. Once they did, there, in the safety of the shallows, away from the hordes of rapacious squid that swarmed the deep-water trenches, their offspring would survive in far greater numbers. They would grow and multiply, feeding off the plentiful warm-bloods that occupied the fragile surface constructs, until they reached adulthood and could tackle more imposing prey.

When that day came, and their numbers had rebounding suffi-
ciently, even the sunlit portions of the sea would be theirs for the taking.

———

"So, basically, you screwed around with an *entire floor* of security cameras, just to stop Grayson from finding out your pet pliosaur got its period?" Dirk shook his head as he walked through his quarters' kitchen,
flipping on the coffee maker and ordering the overheads to full. He
frowned as he adjusted his nametag in a nearby mirror. He'd heard
Stacy's bizarre story once already, albeit while the two of them were
entwined in a post-coital embrace, but he wanted to listen to it again
under less distracting circumstances.

"Hey, is this the same bed you bought your brother last Christmas?"
Stacy called out from the bedroom. Out of the corner of his eye, Dirk
saw her bend forward, deliberately sticking her butt out as she dug both
palms into the expensive mattress. She wore a huge smile. "Because it's
awesome!" she exclaimed.

"Yes, it's the same bed . . ." he drawled. He turned back to the mirror and allowed himself a schoolboy grin. In truth, their unexpected
tryst had been just what the doctor ordered. After six months of self-
imposed celibacy, he felt like a new man. Now, however, he had to deal
with the fallout. He liked Stacy; he always had. But he knew in his bones
she wasn't "Miss Right." And he did *not* want to use her as a "Ms. Right
Now." That left the two of them holding a harsh reality check – one she
wasn't going to be very happy with, once she discovered she was the
one paying it.

"Dirk, I know last night started out rough," Stacy called out. A moment later, she came bouncing out of the bedroom, checking her hair
and adjusting her lab coat. Judging by the bounce in her step, last night's
lovemaking had obviously buoyed her spirits as well. "But I want to
thank you for listening to me." She reached into one coat pocket and
smiled as she came out with a name tag. "I'm glad you still had some
of my stuff here." She walked up, her tight blonde curls bouncing, and
kissed him.

"Let's get back to the listening part," Dirk grumbled. It bothered
him that Stacy was so happy. It made letting her down easy that much

harder. He sighed as he watched her parade around his place, her head swiveling as she looked to see what had changed over the last six months. He extracted a silk tie from his pocket and looped it around his neck, then blew out an annoyed breath. He should've paid closer attention to his dad's instructions for tying a Windsor knot. He grunted irritably as he fumbled with it. He hated wearing a tie; it made him feel like he was being choked. Normally, he wore a polo shirt under his tech garment, but with the importance of this morning's demonstration, appearances counted.

Dirk checked the wall clock as Stacy poured the coffee. They had plenty of time to get prepped for the presentation and, if they hauled ass, might even manage to sneak out of his quarters before someone spotted them. At least, he hoped so. The last thing he needed was the rumor mill getting started again. "So, last night's drama was all about concealing the fact that Gretchen is in estrus? Why? I don't understand what the big deal is."

"You know how Grayson is," Stacy said, walking over to him and handing him a steaming cup of Colombian. One whiff told him she'd brewed it just the way he liked. "He might decide to weaponize her, which would include sterilization," she said, "Or pair her with *Polyphemus*, before he ships out. Or even worse, the twins." She shuddered at the thought.

Dirk sipped his coffee and nodded. Stacy had a point. Although he couldn't imagine Grayson queuing Gretchen for sale, it was official policy to neuter any implanted pliosaur before delivery to a vender. He stood ramrod straight as she reached up and adjusted the mess he'd made of his tie. "What would be so wrong with that?" he asked. He grimaced as she pulled roughly on the tough silk. "The mating thing, that is. I mean, she's a *Kronosaurus* cow. It's kind of her purpose in life."

"I know you think Gretchen is big and scary, Dirk. But in human terms, she's a thirteen-year-old girl." Stacy explained. "She's inexperienced, not to mention too young and small to copulate with adult bulls." Her eyes widened like a pensive parent's, watching their child board the school bus for the first time. She shook her head vehemently. "She's not like them," she insisted. "All she's known is people. She could be injured by our brood stock, even killed."

"Is that why you keep her in the training pool instead of the empty paddock?"

Stacy finished his tie and nodded. "That, and it's easier for us to interact."

Dirk sucked on his teeth contemplatively. He checked his tie in the mirror, smiled, then hooked an arm around Stacy's waist and pulled her close. "You know, between deejaying the demo, overseeing repairs to *Antrodemus*, trying to track down *Typhon*, monitoring *Goliath*'s recovery, and a hundred other things I've got going on, it's distinctly possible that updates on the menstrual cycle of a sub-adult pliosaur won't make my list of newsworthy events."

Stacy looked down, her hands on his chest. "Are you sure?"

He gave her a huge grin. "Are you kidding? After last night's performance, I might lose the list altogether!"

She leaned back against his grip, pressing her pelvis playfully against his. "Me? What about that crazy position you pulled last night?"

"You mean the missionary one where I held you, suspended, over the bed?"

"Yes! Omigod, you somehow supported all your weight – *and mine* – on your forehead and the balls of your feet. That was amazing!"

"Yeah, that was '*Bridge Over Troubled Water*,' like the song."

"Seriously?" Well, it was unbelievable. It felt like I was floating weightless as you ravaged me." Stacy's expression suddenly downshifted. "Where exactly did you pick that up?"

Dirk smirked at the unfamiliar green in her eyes. "Actually, my brother told me about it a few years back. I just never had the guts to try it until last night."

She nodded. "Garm, eh? Wow. No wonder the ladies are beating down his door. Any other sex secrets he told you about that you've been holding back? Because I'm looking forward to--"

Dirk's teeth dug into his upper lip. "Yeah . . . Listen, Stace. Last night was great and all, but, uh . . ."

She clocked the familiar look and exhaled heavily. "Relax, stud. I know, 'It was fun and we were both overdue, but it doesn't mean we're back together,' yada, yada, yada . . ." She gave him a smug look. "Look, if we're being 100% truthful, I should tell you I have no interest in resuming a relationship with you, Derek Braddock."

He did a double take. "You don't?"

"Nope." She smiled sinfully. "You're nothing but a hot piece of ass to me."

"I am?"

"Yes. Is that a problem?"

Dirk thought it over. Then a wry smile crept across his face. "Actually, no. Not at all."

"Good," Stacy moved to Dirk's workstation, sitting her dried neoprene bodysuit in a neat bundle on his desk. She spotted his assortment of fossil teeth and whistled. "Wow, your collection's getting better all the time. I love the *Livyatan* tooth."

"Thanks," he said, pleased she'd noticed his latest acquisition.

"Imagine one of them taking on an *Imperator*?" She clicked her tongue. "Now *that* would be a fight worth watching."

Dirk chortled. "Don't let Callahan hear you say that. You'll give him ideas. You should've seen how excited he got when I demonstrated *Charybdis*'s sneak attack. I swear, the gabby bastard had wood."

Stacy's amused grin faltered as she ran one finger up the side of his big pliosaur fang, stopping when she reached the tip. "You know, it would be great if, one day, we're finally able to mount an expedition to Diablo Caldera. Boots on the ground, so to speak. See where it all began."

Dirk nodded. "It could happen. I've spoken to a few people, and I know Grayson's in ongoing negotiations with the Cuban government, trying to get approval."

"Negotiations?" She snorted amusedly. "C'mon, Dirk. We've been hearing that for years."

He shrugged. "Hey, with all the political turmoil they've got going on these days, who knows? Maybe if the old man greases the right palms at the right time, he'll pull it off."

Stacy's gaze swung upward, sweeping the neatly maintained shelves of a nearby bookcase. Suddenly, she espied the ornate samurai swords, sitting up top and resting in a black lacquered stand. "Wow, are those your dad's?"

"They were." Dirk nodded. "After he died, my mom donated most of his stuff to the Smithsonian. She kept those. They're her side of the family's hereditary swords. Pretty much all that's left from his collection,"

"That and the giant meat cleaver we keep down by the surgical center."

Dirk shook his head and grinned. "Oh, yes. The Scottish Claymore. I forgot."

Stacy walked over and rested her forearms lightly on the bookcase's top shelf, gazing in wonder at the antique weapons. "They're gorgeous. Are they valuable?"

"Incredibly. They're almost a thousand years old," Dirk advised. He indicated the ancient swords with a flourish. "The historical katana and wakizashi of the Nakamura clan. According to mom, 'they claimed many lives on the field of battle.' A few years ago, a big Japanese conglomerate offered her a couple million bucks for them, but she wouldn't sell, not for any price."

Stacy whistled. "I don't blame her. It would be like pawning her family's history." She winked and gave him an exaggerated bow. "*Your* history, my young samurai."

"Imagine me dressed in armor and walking around with those in my belt?" Dirk chuckled. "That would make Grayson what, my warlord?"

"He'd settle for nothing less than *Shogun*," she giggled.

They stopped talking as the North wall of his quarters let out a deep groan, like something heavy was pressing against it. There was a loud thump and the wall shuddered, jostling everything in Dirk's apartment.

"Jesus. Is that *her*?" Stacy asked, wide-eyed.

"Yeah." Dirk felt his stomach tighten as the wall was bumped again.

Stacy studied the thick aluminum slab covering it. "Does she do that often?"

"Only when she knows someone's here."

"She can hear us?"

"Oh, yeah," Dirk said. "Dampeners or no."

Stacy's eyes widened and she flushed. "Wait, so that means she heard us last night while we were . . ."

"Oh, I don't doubt it. She probably sat there eavesdropping all night, like some prehistoric voyeur."

Stacy started to approach the wall, but retreated as it shuddered again. She shook her head. "She shouldn't be able to do that. Not with the new implant. She's fighting her inhibitors, somehow. We need to put the demo on hold and report this display of aggressiveness."

"She's not being aggressive, Stace," Dirk said. "She's being a bitch."

"Say what?"

"This is a game. She's not attacking her containment walls. She can't and she knows it. If she *was*," He indicated his wall clock and mirror. "Everything in here would go flying, us included. She's just 'accidentally' brushing the edges of her paddock."

Stacy shot him a worried look. "But why?"

"So I know she's there," Dirk surmised. "And to let me know she knows I'm here, too."

Stacy headed deliberately toward a keypad on the adjoining wall. "I've got to see this for myself."

"No, don't!"

She froze in midstep, caught off guard by the fear in Dirk's voice. "God, how long has she been tormenting you?"

"Six months."

"And you've kept your shield down all this time?"

"Pretty much."

Stacy hesitated as the wall behind her groaned once more. A second later, there was a low whooshing sound and then silence. "Is she gone?"

Dirk nodded, then headed toward his workstation with a bemused Stacy following close behind. He plopped down in his office chair, his thoughts on the flash drive he'd secreted in his desk. He considered showing it to her but dismissed the thought. There would be time for that later.

"Wow, I'm sorry. I had no idea you were dealing with this. Maybe--"

A chime emanated from Dirk's monitor, interrupting Stacy and distracting him from his ponderings. It was a video call. He checked the ID and frowned. It was Dr. Bane – his newfound pain-in-the-ass.

Dirk signaled Stacy to stay quiet and out of camera range before he keyed the call. "Good morning, Dr. Bane," he said, reaching for his coffee mug and doing his best to appear nonchalant. "A little early, don't you think?"

Bane's head was huge on the big HD monitor. She looked pale and drawn and had dark circles under her eyes. She had to be exhausted, yet somehow, she was alert, even excited. "I'm sorry," she said, making it a point to glance offscreen as if checking the time. "I just pulled an all-nighter and didn't realize the time."

"What can I do for you?" Dirk said, gingerly sipping his still-hot coffee.

"I haven't been able to get ahold of Dr. Grayson to show him my findings," Bane said. She formed a steeple with her hands, her fingertips bouncing again and again off one another.

From the look of things, Dirk figured she'd had way too much caffeine. That, or she was highly agitated.

"I've gone over all the epidemiological files in Tartarus's data banks and drawn some fascinating conclusions in terms of methodology for both curtailing the spread of Cretaceous cancer and treating existing sufferers." Bane's eyes grew larger as she leaned closer to her webcam. "After our previous discussion, I figured you'd be interested. How soon can you come to the lab?"

As he listened, Dirk's spine went stud straight. The fact that Bane had reviewed all their lab reports and findings in the brief time she'd been there was, in itself, impressive. Of all the researchers he'd known, only his mother was capable of such a feat. But for her to have drawn up theories on containment and curative measures as well? Astounding.

"I'm intrigued," Dirk admitted. He blinked hard as a frightening image of his father's corpse popped into his head. "We should meet."

"Kimberly, please."

Dirk cleared his throat, pretending not to notice the look Stacy was giving him over the top of his monitor. "Okay, Kimberly. I definitely want to review your findings. But I've got the military demo in an hour, with a follow-up shortly thereafter. Can we convene at, say . . . 1200 hours?"

Bane nodded vigorously. "I'll have everything prepped."

"Excellent." Dirk studied the epidemiologist on his monitor, especially her eyes. "You look tired, Doc--Kimberly. Why don't you rest for a few hours so you're more refreshed? I'll need you firing on all cylinders; this is important stuff."

Bane's brow crinkled up. "Yeah. I'm pretty stoked, but I can try. Thanks. I'll see you at noon."

"Will do."

The inquisition started the moment he closed the video chat.

"She has you calling her by her first name?" Stacy asked. "That's rather informal."

Dirk's look of incredulity needed no reinforcement. "Are you serious? Many researchers refer to one another by first names in a work environment."

"Yes, but *you* don't"

His jaw draped down. "Stace, the woman is old enough to be my mother. In fact, she *knew* my mother. Are you *really* going to go there?"

Her lips formed a tight line then relaxed. "Sorry. I guess I'm still recovering from riding you like a stallion for an hour."

"It was forty minutes," he chided. "Don't exaggerate."

"Close enough."

Dirk checked the time as he stood up. His eyes turned pensive and he focused on his shoes, noting a lace that needed replacing. "Uh, we've got to get set up." He finally began. "I just . . . uh, need to know if . . ."

"If what?"

"If you're sure you can handle it."

Stacy's eyebrows took the express elevator up her brow. "Of course I'm up to it. It's my job, my life, in fact."

Dirk didn't bother masking his dubiousness. "You're forgetting; I was there for her post-implant testing. I saw what you went through. I know how terrifying it was. And I've seen your subsequent psych report."

"Derek, I'm fine," she monotoned.

"Are you?" he asked. "You wanted the shower curtain open last night, the bedroom door ajar while we slept, and you kept throwing off the covers in the middle of the night."

"I was hot!"

"Hot?" Dirk scoffed. "It was freezing and you clung to me like a koala bear all night. Just a minute ago, you were dying to raise the shield wall, in my opinion not just to see what was going on, but to open things up in here."

"I do *not* have claustrophobia," Stacy insisted. "I'll admit I do have infrequent flashbacks of what happened. I just need to face my fears and conquer them, okay?"

"Face your fears?" Dirk echoed. "By experiencing the same thing, only a hundred times worse?"

"If that's what it takes, yes."

Dirk's eyes narrowed as he tried to gauge Stacy's resolve. Any hint of nervousness had vanished, and in its place was the steely determination that was one of her greatest assets. It was one of the things he loved . . . make that *liked* most about her.

He looked her up and down. Even in lab garb, with that liquid caramel skin and those amber eyes, standing out like tiger-eye gems from beneath a mane of tight, blonde curls, she was stunning. Of course, he much preferred her in the figure-hugging neoprene wetsuits she typically wore. Which was good, he mused, because she'd be back in one shortly.

Dirk sighed. "Well, as long as you're confident . . ."

"Don't worry. We're going to knock Callahan's socks off."

"Oh, God. Please don't. The guy stinks as is. Can you imagine what his feet smell like?"

Stacy giggled then looked around. "Shall we get going? I've got to get geared up and you've got diagnostics to run."

"Yeah." He looked around, his hands fidgeting inside his pockets. "Are you *sure* you had your booster shot?"

"Absolutely." She looked him in the eye. "Jesus, will you stop worrying? It's like you're afraid I'm going to die or something."

Dirk cleared his throat as they made for the door. "We're all going to die, Stace. It's one of those little certainties of life. I'd just prefer to have you not do so writhing and screaming in agony."

"You're a hopeless romantic, Dirk Braddock."

He ginned as he activated the door's release. "That's what the ladies tell m--"

Dirk's cocky expression turned to dismay as the door whooshed open and he came face to face with black-clad Security Chief Angus Dwyer and his second in command, Jamal White. The two hulking ex-cons smirked and exchanged knowing glances. Then they looked Dirk and Stacy up and down, grinning.

Great, we haven't even made it out the door yet and we're busted.

"Well, well, well . . ." Dwyer said, staring down at them from his great height. "Doctor Grayson asked me to check on you both to make sure you were ready for the demonstration. I didn't expect to find the two of you together. It's fortuitous. Saves me a trip."

"Two fish on one hook!" White chortled.

"Can it," Dwyer snapped. His ape-like jaw tightened and the crescent-shaped scar on his upper lip flushed as he gave his subordinate a nasty look. He turned to Dirk. "I apologize for my officer, Doctor Braddock," he said, his red-rimmed eyes intense. "I'll address the issue. In the interim, we're here to escort you and Dr. Daniels to the amphitheater and to assist as needed in any preparatory work that's to be done."

"Okay. That sounds good," Dirk replied. He eyed the six-wheeled MarshCat the two security officers had waiting outside with trepidation. Dwyer's words may have sounded professional, but there was something about the way he stared that made the young scientist uncomfortable. Still, there was nothing to be done about it. At least, not now.

Dirk waved the door closed behind him, slapped his palm on the biometric lock, and then guided Stacy toward the diesel-powered ATV. "We'll sit in the back," he announced, a little annoyed by the way Jamal White was unabashedly ogling her. He took Stacy's hand, helping her in before seating himself.

"That'll work," Dwyer said, signaling for White to drive. "I'll take shotgun," he said, hoisting his 6'5" frame into the front passenger seat, while his comparably-sized underling hopped behind the wheel.

Dirk noticed the rugged MarshCat dipped markedly as the two guards got in, its shocks straining under an additional quarter-ton of weight. He made a mental note to look into the load rating of the facility's vehicles to see if they needed upgrading.

"Everyone ready?" White asked. He glanced back at Stacy and smiled, his pearly white teeth standing out in stark contrast to his mahogany-colored skin. "You good, sugar?"

"We're good," Dirk replied.

"Well then, I guess we're off," White said, putting the ATV in gear and gunning it. "Hang onto your drawers, folks. This ride could get bumpy!"

White accelerated rapidly, weaving left and right and dodging an occasional, cart-toting technician as he sped through the concrete corridors of Tartarus. One glance at the speedometer inspired Dirk to fasten his lap belt and he motioned to Stacy to do the same. He had a feeling that, as close as the amphitheater was, with one of Grayson's "Last Chancers" behind the wheel, they'd be lucky to get there in one piece.

Eighteen

Almost there . . . just a . . . bit . . . more!

Leaning precariously over the edge of the bed, Sam Mot craned his neck so hard it hurt. He had his mouth open and his jaw jutting forward as he strived to clamp his teeth onto the padded edge of his neural interface headband. It was so close . . . inches away, sitting there in plain view on the gray-colored nightstand. But like most things in his life, it was just beyond reach.

The former LifeGiver shifted position, wiggling his hips and pushing down on the mattress with his chin, striving to shift his center of gravity forward. It was infuriating; having no arms and legs made even the simplest of tasks physical and mental torture. Sam shook his head in exasperation. He was sweating like a pig, but he refused to quit. He needed that headband. It was his only means of controlling his high-tech wheelchair. Without it, he was just eighty pounds of meat being carted around in a wheelbarrow.

Sam glanced sideways at the robotic chair. The LJ-3000 sat ten feet away, its gleaming mechanical arms hanging limply at its sides, the faceless countenance of its cervical pad glaring mockingly at him. He stopped and stared longingly at the expensive contraption. Equipped with state-of-the art bionics, it helped make life bearable. But bereft of his neural-cranial headband, he may as well have been staring at a 20th century lawn mower and yelling at it to make him a sandwich.

Sam took a couple of quick, yoga-style breaths, in through the nose and out through the mouth, trying to dispel his frustration. He had only himself to blame for his debacle. Rather than keeping his headband on the mattress next to him, as was the norm, he'd left it on the nightstand to give himself room. He started to curse, but stifled himself as the impetus for his lack of foresight shifted in her sleep.

He took a moment to admire the soft skin covering Mariela's considerable curves, before refocusing on his task. His dalliance with the demure Dominican nurse had been the unexpected highlight of his day. He wasn't sure if it was his charm, his association with some of Tartarus's higher-ups, or just the fact that she was scared to death of sleeping alone in a place crawling with monsters that inspired her to spend the night with him. Whatever the case, he wasn't about to complain.

A frown creased Sam's face. He considered waking the girl so she could hand him his controller, but stubborn male pride quickly relieved him of any such notion. Oh, it was the sensible thing to do, and would've taken all of three seconds, but one way or another, he was going to do it himself.

Elongating his neck once more, Sam leaned further over the edge of the bed. *Just a tiny bit more . . .* When he stuck his tired tongue out, he realized he could just about reach it. He smiled. Now all he had to do was shift the neural band onto its side so he could bite down on the damn thing.

Sam's cry of alarm as he tumbled off the bed was cut short by the painful thump of him hitting the floor. He had plenty of experience with falls and instinctively bunched his shoulders and tucked his chin to his chest to protect his neck. He lay on his side, his eyes closed and cheeks flushed with shame, waiting for Mariela to peek down over the side of the bed wearing that all-too-familiar look of pity that made him want to vomit.

To his astonishment, the girl remained dead to the world.

Grinning ear to ear at his luck in ending up with a snooze-monster as a bedmate, Sam looked around. His headband had flipped off the nightstand as he fell and lay halfway between him and his wheelchair, barely six feet away. Rolling onto his stomach, he did the mortifying caterpillar thing, contracting his chin, hips, and stomach muscles in waves as he wormed his way toward it.

Grabbing hold of the device with his teeth, Sam twisted his head to upend it against a nearby wall before deftly working it over his crown. He felt the itchy tingle permeate his scalp as enough of the poorly-aligned neural connections fired to give him control. A moment later, he willed the LJ-3000 to life.

The fully-charged chair hummed as it powered up, its banks of blue LEDs lighting in series as it swiveled in Sam's direction. Its thick pneumatic wheels turned as it approached his prostrate form. Concentrating hard, he directed the device's bionic arms to extend, picking him up and placing him gingerly in the driver's seat. Sam was glad he'd gone for all the bells and whistles, including the most powerful actuators available. If the need arose, he could pick up a refrigerator with the damn thing. Hoisting his torso was nothing.

Once he was properly situated, Sam used the 3000's dexterous robotic fingers to adjust his headband and the harness that held him in place. It was tempting, but he resisted the urge to reach over and give Mariela an affectionate pat on the rump before heading into the bathroom. Grayson's big military demo was less than an hour away and he wasn't about to miss it.

As Sam increased his chair's height to mannish levels and used his pseudo-limbs to brush his teeth, he studied his reflection in the mirror. He grimaced as he took in the scarred stumps where his arms had been. It was a decade since his world went to shit. He'd never regretted saving Garm's ass. Not once. But he could feel the searing pain of the flesh being stripped from his bones as if it was yesterday. Being reduced to half a man was a trigger that never stopped firing, and no amount of time or therapy could dull the psychological ache. Nothing could: not booze or broads or any drug he could think of. And he'd tried them all. Even going out on his boat every day for a year and slaughtering Bulldog fish by the hundreds didn't make a dent.

Revenge wasn't the key. He wanted his body back. And with it, his life.

Ironically, in exchange for something as paltry as a lien on his used-up soul, Eric Grayson was willing to give him both.

Sam willed his chair to bend at the waist and spat a nasty wad of toothpaste into the sink. He shook his head. For years he'd agonized over getting cybernetic limb implants. Although bulky, they were a proven technology, sturdy and reliable. Not to mention, irony of ironies, Garm's mom's company made the best in the world. But he had no desire to be a cyborg. He'd feel like a robotic Pinocchio. He wanted *real* arms and legs. And if he had to sup with the devil to get them, then so be it.

Actually, Eric Grayson was far from demonic. Despite his media-driven reputation as a ruthless corporate raider, Sam found the elderly CEO both up front and likable. When they'd spoken online, Grayson empathized with him. And when he found out about Sam's lengthy friendship with Garm during their first phone conversation, the offer came easily.

Sam felt their arrangement was more than fair. All he had to was operate their prototype AWES *Talos* system for just one season and they were square. Grayson would have the geneticists at GDT bypass the anti-cloning laws via the test-subject loophole and craft him new limbs from his own DNA. They'd do the transplants, provide the requisite rehab, and even pick up the tab for periodic post-op PT as part of an all-inclusive package.

Sam had no idea how much the out-of-pocket cost for all that would've been, but he knew he couldn't afford it. Not even if he cashed out the trust fund his parents had left him.

'Why don't you just ask Garm and Derek to fund the transplant?' Grayson had initially suggested. *'I'll happily okay it, and I'm sure they'll jump at the chance to help an old friend.'*

Sam wore a disgusted look as he rinsed and reached for the floss. That was never happening. He'd followed the corporate takeover of Amara Braddock's robotics firm in the news, as well as the subsequent public offering that turned her two sons into billionaires overnight. He was happy for them, but friendship or no, he wasn't about to go hat-in-hand to Garm and ask for anything. No fucking way. He may have had no limbs, but he had his balls. He was still a man, and he was damn sure going to act like one. He'd earn his own way back to being what he once was.

Maybe then, after he was back on his *own* two feet, he and that big galoot could focus on spending money on good times.

Sam smiled at the thought, then rinsed his face and grabbed a towel. As the whirring sound of his actuators faded, a stirring from the bedroom told him Mariela had finally roused herself. He checked the time and grinned. Still forty-five minutes before the demonstration. His grin upgraded to a mischievous smile as he wheeled his chair out of the bathroom.

He had just enough time to show his favorite nurse what his bionic "other half" was capable of.

Dirk vacillated, a few feet outside the entrance to the amphitheater tunnel. The gateway towered over him, an intimidating twenty-foot maw, gouged through craggy gray granite. He peered inside, studying the rows of eight-foot-thick pilings that jutted from the floor like giant molars, reinforcing the passageway's rough-hewn sides and buttressing its roof.

He exhaled slowly. The fortified stone hallway that served as the facilitator's entrance to Tartarus's stadium was considered the ultimate in durability – rated to withstand a nuclear blast, or so they claimed. But to the young scientist, traversing its dimly-lit length to face what lay on the other side was like a one-way trip into the belly of the beast.

120 feet away, Dirk could see the corridor's arch-shaped end. It was brightly-lit and inviting, but the non-stop flow of tepid air that swept through the tunnel, laden with the smell of seawater and the rank stench of something else, did little to relieve his fears.

"It's not going to bite you," Dr. Grayson's disembodied voice pointed out.

Dirk jumped, then glanced back over his shoulder and faked a smile. He hadn't realized the CEO was still there, standing next to his chauffeured ATV, those omniscient eyes of his boring into his youthful protégé.

"Are you all right?" Grayson asked.

"Yeah . . ." Dirk cleared his throat. "Sorry, sir. I guess I was just--"

"I understand, son." Grayson's visage mirrored Dirk's concern. "Trust me. But sometimes we need to let sleeping dogs or, perhaps, in this case, sleeping *ghosts*, lie."

"Yes, sir. You're right, as usual."

Grayson nodded. He placed one hand on the MarshCat's rugged frame and raised a hand to signal his driver, but then stopped. "Are we good to go, Derek? Seriously. I'm supposed to be with Admiral Callahan and his cronies, but if you need me beside you for emotional support--"

"No, no." Dirk shook his head vigorously. "I'm good. I've got this."

"And Dr. Daniels?"

"Already on her perch and waiting, sir."

"Very well." Grayson gripped one of the ATV's padded roll bars and struggled to clamber inside. He grimaced as he put too much weight on one leg and nodded to salt-and-pepper haired Sergeant Bryan Wurmer, who rushed over to help him. Once he was situated, the old man took a moment to adjust his seatbelt before glancing back at Dirk. "If today goes well, it will make our budget for the next five years. So, knock 'em dead!"

God willing, not a prophetic choice of words, Dirk thought. He nodded and gave his employer a thumbs-up sign as Grayson's vehicle pulled smoothly away and vanished around a nearby corner.

With a heavy sigh, he turned and entered the corridor. The dankness embraced him and his footfalls echoed off stone and steel, his pupils contracting with the approaching brightness. Moments later, he reached the towering archway.

Stepping into the light, Dirk glanced up, blinking at the stadium's powerful solar arrays, several hundred feet above. Unlike the rest of Tartarus, with its comparatively weak LED overheads, the theater and its surrounding pools basked beneath the glow of an artificial sun. Saying it was bright was an understatement. You needed sunglasses for any prolonged visit, and sunscreen, too; in addition to emitting equatorial levels of heat and light, the powerful solar simulators could dish out one hell of a burn.

Of course, in Tartarus, succumbing to malignant melanoma was usually the last thing on one's mind.

Dirk swallowed hard and put on a confident face before crossing the sixty-foot stone and steel dock leading to the nearby stage. Around him, the illuminated waters of the amphitheater pool splayed out like a vast, saltwater lake; a semicircular body of water over one thousand feet across.

Like the dockside *Kronosaurus* tanks, the stadium pool's transparent Celazole walls extended 100 feet above sea level. But unlike the rectangular paddocks, its curved sides dropped another 200 feet straight down into Tartarus's stony core. The sturdiness of its construction was also far removed. Its exposed thermoplastic partitions were far stronger than those used for the pliosaur enclosures. At the top, they were a full ten feet thick, at the bottom, more than twice that. In addition, there was a network of riveted, titanium-steel struts, each up to twenty feet thick and strong enough to support a tank battalion. They arced up from the stone floor like curved talons, reinforcing the arc-shaped polycarbonate barrier every one hundred feet.

It was the biggest, strongest man-made aquarium in the world. And the ultimate display case for the comparatively tiny group currently occupying several hundred of the stadium-style seats arranged on the other side of the pool's indestructible walls.

Of course, the colossal saltwater tank was empty now, Dirk contemplated as he moved briskly toward the podium. He looked around. Despite the attendees, it was surprisingly quiet and his shoes clicked loudly on the hard stone. In the distance and above the pool's crystalline edge, he spotted Eric Grayson. Accompanied by two of his security personnel, the CEO was hobnobbing with Ward Callahan and the rear admiral's entourage of at least two dozen naval officers, *attachés*, and accountants. They were gathered center-stage and situated high enough in the tiered seats to have an unparalleled view of the pending festivities. In addition to the military personnel, there were hundreds of Tartarus employees, also waiting. Dirk could see a dozen guards, an assortment of technicians, CDF officers and enlisted men and women, and what looked to be the full complement of both *Gryphon* and *Antrodemus*. Everyone who wasn't on duty was there for the show.

Make that almost everyone. As he studied his pending audience, Dirk noticed his brother Garm was conspicuously absent.

His twin had informed him last night that he wouldn't be attending. *"I'm sorry, little brother. I wouldn't be able to help if something goes wrong and, besides, you don't want me there anyway. If you put me that close I might do something stupid."*

Dirk understood. Frankly, he didn't want to be there, either, but it wasn't like he had a choice. Besides, it was good Garm wasn't present. After that last, harrowing patrol, his brother needed to take his mind off things. And, as Dirk looked around and noted that Natalya Dragunova was also coincidentally MIA, he figured the big submariner was busy doing just that – by burying his disgustingly handsome face in his fellow submarine commander's considerable charms.

He was glad for him. Jealous as all hell, but glad, nonetheless.

As he reached the reinforced concrete podium, Dirk turned to his right. His dark eyes scaled the shorn rock wall that formed the rear bulwark of the amphitheater, its pool included. He pinpointed Stacy, adorned in one of her form-hugging blue bodysuits, and situated fifty feet up on a narrow platform overlooking the water. He couldn't see her face well enough from this distance to gauge her mindset, but she seemed okay. At least so far.

Dirk smirked at the irony. Stacy may well have been right about him having the hots for Dragunova. Then again, what man, or woman for that matter, wouldn't? But as intuitive as his on-again-off-again play-mate was, she didn't have a clue that the object of his affection and his overprotective brother had been playing "hide the pliosaur" for the last five or six months.

In fact, as far as Dirk could tell, nobody, not even super-sleuth Dr. Grayson had figured it out. The two brothers hadn't discussed the matter, but they didn't need to. Dirk knew Garm better than he knew himself. It was obvious.

It wasn't that, despite their well-known rivalry, the two captains were often seen together. Nor was it their occasional bickering that told the tale. It was the subtle nuances. Like the almost imperceptible air of rigidity Garm gave off when Dragunova was around, or his unchar-acteristic professionalism when a snide remark might otherwise come out. And, of course, there was his seeming obliviousness to her consid-erable sex appeal. *That* was the clincher. You'd have to be a corpse not to find the curvaceous Russian desirable.

Heck, she could probably give a cadaver an erection! And for someone as oversexed as Garm to not even notice her? Oh, please . . .

Dirk shook his head and scratched his nose to conceal a chuckle. Oh, no. Mr. and Mrs. America may have thought they were slick, but he knew better. Those two were fucking like lions in heat: probably right now, matter of fact.

That lucky bastard.

Dirk snorted angrily. He hoped their relationship meant more to Garm than his usual hit-and-run routine. Dragunova may have been tall and built, with the tact of a charging Panzer, but he could tell, deep down inside, she had a vulnerable side. She just needed someone to en-tice her into exposing it.

319

Dirk herded his covetous thoughts back into their primordial cave and refocused on business before mounting the podium steps. The amphitheater's dais was situated ten feet back from the edge of an eighty-foot wide, oval-shaped platform of steel and reinforced concrete that, seen from above, extended from the end of the dock like the top of a gigantic letter T. Around the structure, seawater fanned out for over four hundred feet in every direction.

Placing a hand on the podium's biometric scanner, Dirk extracted an earpiece from his lab coat pocket and waited for the system's hybridized keyboard and monitor to emerge. As they activated, he leaned forward, his fingers tap dancing across the board's polycarbonate keys. He began by accessing Tartarus's powerful neural interface program, systematically bringing its collective servers online, their assorted backups included. Once that was accomplished, he did a scan of the reactor to check for anomalies and checked the status of their emergency generators.

Dirk was taking no chances. He wanted full and uninterrupted power, topped by every reserve he could think of. There would be no glitches.

"How are you doing, Stace?" he asked, one hand cupping his earpiece. At this distance, nobody in the stands could hear him, but out of paranoia he kept his voice low and his mouth angled downward.

"Oh, you know me," she quipped. "Always ready to dive into danger!"

Dirk nodded. "How's the CCUBA? Any issues?" He could tell from the hollowness of her voice that Stacy had already donned one of GDT's compact, military-issue *Thunnus* rebreathers, or Closed Circuit Underwater Breathing Apparatus, as was the official designation. The form-fitting headgear, with its motion-sensing integrated lens system, was barely the size of a dirt bike helmet, yet allowed the wearer to see underwater like a swordfish and remain there, sans bulky tanks, for nearly an hour.

"So far so good," she radioed. He could hear her sniffing. "Phew. Smells like someone used this one already, but beyond that, no issues. Seal is perfect and oxygen readings are showing 98% with all circuits clear."

"Roger that." Dirk said. At least she wouldn't drown. He hesitated. "I know better than to ask if you're okay."

"Then, why are you?"

He chuckled. "Okay, let's get things started."

Reaching down, Dirk extracted what appeared to be a high-tech skullcap from the podium's lone drawer. He donned it, then touched a small side panel on the right temple that caused it to compress silently inward, its padded interior conforming to the shape of his cranium. That accomplished, he tapped a series of buttons on the left temple, causing the unit to power up, and then started running diagnostic checks on his now-synched computer's interface control system. All the while, the cap's thousands of neural connectors fired in waves. The sensation as the device melded itself to the corresponding nerves in his scalp was practically unbearable – comparable to a column of hungry driver ants foraging through one's hair – but he dismissed it. He was used to the discomfort.

Besides, his job was far easier than Stacy's.

Dirk eyed his monitor screen, his fingers a veritable blur atop the illuminated keyboard as he checked and rechecked the system. Finally, when he realized he was past the point of redundancy and was stalling, he gave Stacy a quick thumbs-up and keyed his microphone. Half the people in the audience held their ears, with the rest grimacing as a painful barrage of feedback erupted from the stadium speakers. Dirk's own face contorted as he reached down and adjusted the amplifier.

With every other task completed, he paused to bring the paired, forty-foot LCD screens hanging directly overhead online. With a hum, their pitch-blackness dissolved, replaced by two different underwater views of the amphitheater pool, courtesy of the dais's submerged video system. The new cameras had incredibly powerful zooms. Even given the considerable distance from the podium to the tiered seats on the opposite side of the aquarium wall, he could pull in tight on individual people in the audience, even if they did come out assorted shades of blue and green.

Dirk tapped a finger on his chin before reaching down to hit a key. A moment later, one of the monitor's feeds switched to a view from one of the stadium's high-powered roof cameras, giving the audience an overhead shot of the entire pool.

As he reviewed his mental list one last time, Dirk looked around, rapping his knuckles on the podium's hard surface. He exhaled heavily.

He had forgotten nothing. It was time.

His eyes swept the calm surface of Tartarus's artificial lake and the expectant throng outside of it. He angled his head to one side, giving Stacy a final glance. As he did, something bright and ephemeral caught his eye. He craned his head back until it hurt, his sharp eyes seeking the source of the unexpected movement.

Dirk felt the equivalent of a fist burying itself in the pit of his stomach. What he'd spotted was a yard-long piece of red barricade tape. It was hanging from the section of broken railing outside his mother's office, two hundred feet up, fluttering like a bloody kite's tail in the breeze.

His eyes lowered and he found himself focusing on the spot where Amara Braddock died, not two hundred feet away. On cue, the video of her awful demise began looping inside his head, a never-ending cycle of horror. He felt cold and he could hear his breath growing louder as a wave of nausea swept through him.

"Dirk? Hey, Dirk . . . Earth to Dirk . . . *Hello!*"

He cleared his throat noisily as Stacy's voice continued to blare from his earpiece. He touched a hand to it, reducing the annoying device's volume. "Yeah, I'm here," he said, shivering.

"And you were worried about *me . . .*"

Dirk's jaw muscles tightened as he watched her shake her head disapprovingly. He could do little to mask his irritation, but at least they were on a secure channel.

"We can talk about it afterward," Stacy offered.

Dirk clamped down on his headshake. "I'm good," he growled. His dark eyes intensified as he reached for the stadium microphone switch. "Let's do this."

He exhaled and queued the mike.

"Ladies and gentlemen," he began, pausing to gauge the intensity of his magnified voice as it rebounded across the cavernous chamber. For some bizarre reason, he found himself wondering, if there *was* a "god," whether his voice sounded like that. "Thank you for coming to today's presentation."

Dirk's gaze traversed the water's surface beyond the podium, hurdled the ten-foot Celazole lip extending above it, and swept the faces of those in attendance, until he zeroed his mentor. When he espied Admiral Callahan, yakking away in the old man's ear, he chuckled. The loquacious naval man and his newbies had no idea what they were in for.

"On behalf of Dr. Eric Grayson, myself, and the entire Board of Directors of Grayson Defense Technologies, I welcome you to Tartarus!"

Dirk activated the background music, causing it to rumble from the stadium's ten-foot speakers like an approaching thunderstorm. It was his personal favorite: a dramatic track, reminiscent of scores from the old "Jurassic Park" movies. It was certainly apropos, he thought. He touched another key, causing an exterior feed to merge with the music. This one was nothing but a deep, pulsing sound that cycled every two seconds.

Boom . . . boom . . . boom . . .

Dirk detached the wireless mike from the podium and held it as he walked to the water's edge. As he gazed into its foreboding depths, he imagined that, with his neural-cranial skull cap on, he must have looked like some reject from "Flash Gordon." He raised the microphone to his lips. "For those of you that have never been here before, or seen what you're about to see, please keep two things in mind. The first is the non-disclosure agreement that every one of you signed. Any violation of your NDAs will result in *stiff* penalties." He grinned like a game show host mugging for an unseen audience. "And if you think Uncle Sam is good at giving you the shaft, you don't want to know what we're capable of."

Boom . . . boom . . . boom . . .

Dirk smiled, waiting for the nervous chuckling to die down. Despite the breeze it was warm, and he was dying to remove his lab coat and tie. "The second is to remain calm. Although this is a military demonstration and what you are about to see may be frightening, you are perfectly safe. Every possible precaution has been taken to ensure your safety."

As opposed to Stacy and me, who get to do the Texas two-step in the lion's den.

Dirk moved laterally along the beveled concrete edge of the platform, working his way back toward the podium. "I'm sure many of you know the name 'Tartarus' comes from Greek mythology. For the uninitiated, it was the Ancient Greeks' version of purgatory or hell. Where the wicked were tormented for all eternity, and where the enemies of the gods of Olympus – in this case, the monstrous Titans – were imprisoned."

Boom . . . boom . . . boom . . .

Judging by the eerie silence that ensued following any pause on his part, Dirk could tell he had his audience right where he wanted them. Mike in hand, he stood beside the podium. On its top was an illuminated red knob, like a panic button, covered by a clear acrylic shield. He reached up and flipped the cover open, taking care not to touch the knob.

In an attempt at giving off an air of casualness, Dirk rested one elbow against the podium. "During your respective tours, you've seen some of our very own 'Titans,' the monstrous *Kronosaurus imperators* that wreaked havoc on the world's oceans, and which we have incarcerated here. Unlike traditional prisons, where the inmates' savage impulses are held in check by walls, guards, and barbed wire, we tolerate no 'rage against the cage' here. We keep our monsters on a tight leash, no matter how horrifying they may be."

Boom . . . boom . . . boom . . .

As he shot a quick glance at Dr. Grayson, waiting for his nod of approval, Dirk noticed Security Chief Dwyer seated at the CEO's right. It was hard to tell from his vantage point, but the young scientist got the unmistakable impression that the intimidating ex-con's eyes were fixed on him.

He shuddered. Dwyer really gave him the creeps.

Dirk's grip on his mike tightened. "You've seen some of our more impressive specimens, all successfully implanted with our latest technology and completely under our control. This includes *Thanatos*, whose name means 'Death,' as well as *Surtur*, *Fafnir*, and *Romulus* and *Remus*. A few of you have even been treated to a visit with our latest addition, the former murderess known as *Goliath*." Dirk held up an emphasizing finger, "*Goliath*, along with a few of our other prized specimens, is slated to join the Navy's burgeoning bio-weapons division." He paused to give Admiral Callahan a perfunctory nod and received an enthusiastic thumbs-up in response.

Boom . . . boom . . . boom . . .

"But a few of you distinguished guests have been asking about something else. Something . . . *more*." Dirk surveyed the bleachers, catching and holding quite a few pairs of eyes, a few of whom looked quickly away. "You've been listening to or spreading rumors of an entirely different class of predator that's being housed here. Something bigger, something *badder*, something that cannot be controlled."

Dirk's brother Garm popped into his head and he grinned. Just then, a glimmer of light caught his eye and he realized his image was emanating from one of the giant overhead monitors. One of the ceiling cameras was following his every move and he played to it. "You are *correct*," he said. His grin broadened and he added. "At least about the bigger and badder part."

Boom . . . boom . . . boom . . .

With a final check on Stacy, Dirk reached for the big, red button atop his podium and gave it a smack. The sound was picked up by his microphone and echoed across the coliseum. It dissipated quickly, absorbed and overpowered by a much louder rumbling as a pair of sixty-foot titanium-steel doors along the amphitheater pool's rear wall began to split apart, exposing another body of water in an adjacent chamber. Sliding noisily into their stone housings, the yard-thick barriers separated foot by foot, until they vanished completely and locked in place with an audible thump.

Forgetting about his audience for the moment, Dirk focused on the 120-foot seaway the twin portals had just created. He could see the aquarium's surface swirling from the sudden influx of seawater. But when nothing beyond that happened, the spectators in the stands began conversing in hushed tones.

Dirk slid his finger down the keyboard's touchpad, causing the background music to fade. The deep, pulsing sound, however, remained, pumping ominously from the speakers and echoing across the stadium's tepid waters. The people in the stands gradually took notice of the sound, with the more astute among them realizing what it was and excitedly telling everyone around them.

It was a heartbeat.

Boom . . . boom . . . boom . . .

Dismissing the murmuring of the now-pensive crowd, as well as the pitter-patter of his own heart, Dirk focused his will through the cybernetic skull cap. There was an intense tingling sensation, followed by a moment of pain, and then he was through. It was impressive. The new cortical implant was far more advanced than its predecessors. It allowed a virtual bond between host and controller.

He felt her presence almost immediately – a dark and wrathful entity. He started to push, pinpointing her location. She was down deep and hugging the northern side of her enclosure, presumably trying to put as much distance and as many walls between them as possible.

You're very smart, aren't you, bitch? Dirk sent. *You think putting a few layers of stone and a couple hundred yards between us will shield you from me. But you're wrong.*

Focusing hard, he exerted his willpower. He could feel the connection taking place, the neural impulses from his controller pulsing like tiny lightning bolts inside his head. The barrage of stimuli he got back via her cranial implant was overwhelming. Soon, he could see through her eyes. It was surreal. He experienced the full spectrum of her vision, like a transparent hologram overlaying his own sight. Her amazing olfactory system was his as well. He could "smell" the brine, bovine entrails, and an assortment of other scents wafting through her paddock. His senses soared, as he experienced water flowing over the cracks and crevasses of her rough skin, and he could feel both her rugged heartbeat and the blood coursing powerfully through her veins.

Suddenly, she started to resist. He could feel her primitive intellect lashing out at him. She was strong but clumsy. He bore down, mercilessly hammering at her, overwhelming her simple defenses. Within seconds, he had her subdued, like some gargantuan dog on a leash. And, like a dog, he made her turn in his direction and cruise docilely underwater, through the canal that separated her pool from the amphitheater. Despite the lethargy of her approach, her sheer size caused the waters at the far end of the stadium to boil, and those in the audience sat stock-still, their eyes riveted to the gate.

Boom . . . Boom . . . Boom . . .

Reaching down, Dirk switched off the feed from the underwater cameras, letting one of the giant monitors revert to static. He flipped the conversion switch and the screen shimmered. A moment later, a collective gasp escaped the crowd. The monitor's viewpoint was no longer that of a camera. They were seeing things as he did, through her predator eyes. Despite the fact that she was still concealed within the furthest shadows of the pool, with her acute underwater vision she had a clear view of everything around her: the pool's rough-hewn depths, the sturdy pilings supporting the dock and dais, and the heavy polycarbonate barrier that separated her from her audience.

She was looking right through it. And she was looking at them.

With interest.

Dirk grinned at his viewers' reactions as they began to realize they were the ones being studied. "Fifteen years ago," he began, "GDT purchased the dilapidated remnants of what was once the world's largest fallout shelter and converted it to the modern research facility you see before you. Shortly thereafter, and long before the military started their suppression exercise against aggressive pliosaurs, our scientists began capturing specimens with the intentions of discovering their weaknesses. She was one of the first to be taken alive, and with good reason. She was a Gen-1, but she was different than her brood brothers and sisters. She was a mutation so huge and lethal she could not be allowed to roam free. But she was also too valuable to be destroyed."

Dirk paused for effect. As he did, he sensed her desire to spout and willed her to the surface. Not wanting to ruin the surprise he had planned, he kept her in the shadows, allowing just her blowhole and the crown of her huge head to breach the surface. There was a tremendous hiss as twin geysers of compressed water vapor exploded to a height of over forty feet. The sound resonated across the stone chamber and, in an instant, everyone in the stands except Dr. Grayson was on their tiptoes, striving for a better look.

As he directed her away from the stone portion of the pool and her silhouette materialized beneath him, Dirk's stomach tied itself up in knots. He swallowed a breath and fought to man up. He'd known her proximity was going to be psychologically problematic, and not just for him. Throughout the amphitheater, people began to yell and point as her shadow coalesced in the distance. The flashes from scores of camera phones went off, the bursts of light like white-hot bullets, ricocheting off the thick PBI walls.

"We brought her here," Dirk announced, raising his voice over the growing tumult. "Where she has continued to feed and grow."

BOOM ... BOOM ... BOOM ...

With the amplified sound of her enormous heart now so loud it was deafening, Dirk had no choice but to kill the feed. He peered down from his podium, watching as she reached the center of the pool, directly adjacent to the audience. He drew another breath deep in his chest and blew out the exhale through bowed lips.

The time for buildup was past. The unveiling was at hand.

With detached deliberation, Dirk directed her toward the stands, some four hundred feet away. Her fins rose and fell like monstrous wings, displacing hundreds of thousands of gallons of seawater as he aimed her straight for Admiral Callahan. He could see the Navy's stocky Bio-Weapons Director clearly. He was on his feet, one hand shading his thick-jowled face as he peered through the dense thermoplastic.

Dirk snorted in amusement. Callahan was familiar with pliosaurs. Just the other day, he'd seen *Goliath* up close and personal. Hell, any closer and he'd have been a meal. But he'd never seen anything like this.

Like a living monolith, *she* emerged from the gloom, her flippers undulating as she crept stealthily forward. Dirk watched the admiral's face as she hove into view and grew larger and larger. Intense curiosity give way to surprise, then to astonishment, and finally, to fear.

When her scarred snout bumped thunderously against the tough Celazole barricade separating them, Dirk's gawking spectators let out a collective yelp of fright. For a moment, he gave her free rein, just to see what she would do. With occasional flicks of her fins to stabilize her, she remained suspended, fifty feet below the surface, studying her audience of tiny primates like a god does insects.

The comparison wasn't far off, he thought. She was as long as the biggest blue whale that ever lived and nearly three times the weight. But she was no plankton-feeding cow. As her mini-bus-sized head swiveled from side to side, her thick-scaled lips curled back, revealing rows of ridged teeth the size of machetes. She gazed imperiously downward, her glittering orange eyes with their depthless black centers blazing like twin orbs of fire.

Not willing to chance what might happen next, Dirk reasserted control. To his surprise, she came willingly. He directed her back toward the surface, one of her twenty-five-foot pelvic fins scraping noisily along the slick thermoplastic barrier as she turned on her tail. A second later, she breached, her nine-yard wide back streaming water. Her titanic head broke the surface and her wrinkled muzzle lifted up and over the edge of the pool wall as she gazed imperiously down at her jailers. The crowd fell back in their chairs and stared back in aston-ishment. Unlike most pliosaurs, with their typical bluish-gray or dark indigo hues, her rock-hard scales were as black as pitch.

Suddenly, her twenty-four-foot mandibles split apart, exposing her full arsenal of thick ivory fangs. A deep, vibrating hiss escaped her mouth, and her spellbound audience sucked in a collective breath.

Despite his degree of control, Dirk could feel her muscles flexing like giant steel bands. A wave of what he interpreted as the *Kronosaurus* equivalent of satisfaction shimmied through her and he realized she was reveling in her power. She was enjoying the fear she generated, but her "feelings" were jagged and disjointed; they formed an ever-thicken-ing emotional wall he had to breach again and again to keep her at heel.

His voice trembled as he spoke into the microphone. "Ladies and gentlemen, I give you the deadliest predator in the history of the planet. I give you our resident Queen of Pliosaurs . . . I give you . . . *Tiamat!*"

Dripping a mixture of drool and brine, the queen's armored snout arched upward, high above the astonished crowd, until her fearsome muzzle was nearly fifty feet above the pool's churning surface and pointed toward the heavens. Dirk glanced toward Dr. Grayson and saw him smile in anticipation of what came next.

A moment later, Dirk directed *Tiamat* to suck in a huge breath and spread her giant jaws wide.

Then he had her roar.

NINETEEN

As his powerful frame bucked, riding out a climax so intense it would have incapacitated most men, Garm Braddock viewed the world through rose-hued lenses. When his passion finally ebbed, the ex-fighter's eyes were rolled up inside his head like a doll's. He blinked repeatedly to bring them into focus and sucked down oxygen like an athlete who'd just completed a hyperbaric Ironman competition. As he spiraled back down to Earth, Garm raised his eyes toward the ceiling in a mixture of awe and gratitude.

Atop him, Natalya Dragunova wore a sinful look on her sweat-streaked Valkyrie's face. Her gray eyes remained locked onto his, gauging the borderline-pained expression he wore as she continued to tease and titillate him.

Garm's teeth gritted from something other than his groin-oriented sensory overload and he looked down. He realized, with some bemusement, that his lover had her fingernails embedded in the skin covering his thick pectoral muscles – almost to the point of drawing blood. He reached up to gently prize them out.

"Ouch . . . ouch!" he winced. "Shit. Okay, that's enough of that."

Natalya made a pouty face and stopped her gyrating. "Aw, poor baby! Are my dull, little nails too much for you?"

Garm cleared his dry throat. "No. I'm just not into pain."

"I theenk you should worry more about my koshka's *bite* than her claws," she taunted. The muscles coating her lithe frame flexed as she rotated her hips in slow, counter-clockwise motions.

He reached up, pulling her down onto his chest, and kissed her passionately. "You know, you're spoiling me for all other women."

"Ees a good theeng," Natalya replied, smirking. Her thoroughly pleased look flatlined, however, when Garm torqued to the left, rolling them sideways toward the center of his king-size bed, until she ended up on her back. When he gripped her by the shoulders and tried climbing on top, she tensed, then became genuinely annoyed. "Wolfie, how many times I have to tell you . . . I don't like--"

Her temper flared as he persisted in attempting to pretend-mount her, missionary style. A brief wrestling match ensued and, when he wouldn't stop, she hauled back and cracked him hard across the face.

"Damnit!" Natalya snarled. "I said *no!*"

Garm's head recoiled from the force of the blow and he flushed red, a combination of anger and embarrassment. "Jesus, Nat," he cursed, pulling away as he touched a hand to his stinging cheek. "What the hell?"

"Five hundred fucking *times* I tell you," she hissed. "No meessionary positions, never!"

"What is the big fucking deal?" Garm shook his head then froze as he clocked her volatile expression. Her lips were drawn back over her teeth, her eyes dark cumulus clouds, ready to unleash their fury. It was a dangerous moment; the kind that, mishandled, could end a relationship, even one as casual as theirs.

"Okay, okay . . . I-I'm sorry," he said, sucking at his lower lip. He detected the familiar taste of blood in his mouth. "I was just being playful, you know? I mean, c'mon. You kinda put me in a good mood after giving me the ride of my life."

Natalya continued to stare daggers at him, but her ire gradually faded. She looked away, her brow crinkling up, then the corners of her mouth curled upward into a smug little smile and she laughed. "I forgeeve you. But only because you have the sense to admeet I am greatest lover you've ever known."

"As if there was ever any doubt," Garm chuckled. He flopped back down next to her and pulled her close, kissing her tentatively at first, then gradually more insistently. She started to respond, but then withdrew a few inches, staring into his aquamarine eyes. He gave her a quizzical look, then reached up, his fingers tracing the toned muscles of her jaw and neck, pausing briefly on the quarter-inch scar that decorated the side of her throat like a mole on a model.

"So, what *is* it with you and missionary positions?" he hazarded.

Natalya growled irritably. "My god, you are like beeg, hungry baby, I swear! I do all sorts of crazy things with you – even give you ass sometimes – and you are never satisfied!"

Garm shrugged. "No, it's not that. I mean, I'm not complaining. Far from it. It's just . . . I don't know. It's such a mundane position, yet we never--"

She pushed herself away and sat up. "Ees very easy to explain. I don't like having man on top of me. Period. Understand?"

"Of course. But, can I ask why?"

"No, you may not," Natalya said. She swung her feet over the side of the bed. "And please don't ask me again. Ever."

"Where are you going?" Garm asked.

"I have to pee." As Natalya rose to her full height, a wave of dizziness hit her. She staggered to one side but managed to catch herself on the nearby dresser. She shook her head to clear it then laughed aloud. "Whoa, I am eempressed! You got me deek-drunk, Wolfie. Too many orgasms!"

Garm smiled, staring covetously at her ass as she regained her poise and made her way into the bathroom. After she disappeared inside, he lay there quietly, staring up at the ceiling. His body was immobile, his hands clasped atop his broad chest. Even his breathing was virtually imperceptible, and if it wasn't for an occasional blink, he could've been mistaken for a reposing corpse.

He was still ruminating when she popped back out a few minutes later, naked as a jaybird. Her gleaming white teeth shone as she gave him a huge smile. "Deed you mees me?" she purred as she sat down on the end of the bed.

"I'll take the fifth," Garm said, winking.

Natalya's eyes swept his quarters, finally focusing on a framed parchment print that adorned a nearby wall. She read the title aloud. "*The Kraken* by Lord Alfred Tennyson."

"It's an antique – a gift from my mom," Garm replied, watching as she became engrossed in the classic poem. "She joked that it should be required reading for all CDF captains."

"Ees very impressive," Natalya said. "A beet on the dark and morbid side, I theenk. But, as you say, appropriate for such as us."

She finished reading and turned back to him. Her nipples were perked up and, as she leaned in close, she ran her nails playfully across his chest, tactfully avoiding the angry indentations she'd left.

Garm could see she was getting in the mood again and glanced at the wall clock. One of the advantages of being a woman was you never had to worry where your next erection was coming from. He, on the other hand, was still encumbered by one of those annoying refractory periods, so some stalling was in order.

"What shall we do now?" Natalya asked huskily.

"How about a game?" he ventured.

"A game? I love games! Like pin my tail on your--"

Garm smiled and shook his head. "No, I meant a real game."

"Oh." Natalya frowned. "What kind of game?"

His eyes bored into hers. "Let's play '*Truth or Dare.*'"

"Ah, I remember thees game . . ." She ran her fingertips absentmindedly down her collarbones as she spoke, her hands eventually cupping her heavy breasts. She glanced sideways to make sure he was watching, gauging his level of readiness, then turned and nodded. "Okay, why not? Eet will be fun. But we must have rules."

"Go on . . ."

"Eef player refuses to tell truth, dare they do must be crazy but possible. And not too dangerous – no sweeming naked in *Kronosaurus* cage, for example."

"Agreed."

She regarded him intently. "And no asking me about meessionary position."

Garm nodded. "Of course."

Natalya sat up straight, a gleeful look on her face. "Wonderful. So, what ees dare to be?"

"Ladies first," he said through a lopsided grin.

"Very well . . ." She glanced upward, her mind wandering. A moment later, her face lit up. "I have eet! Eef you refuse to geev truth, you must go to cattle pens on lower level and geev, how you say, reem job to one of the bulls?"

Garm made a face. "Ugh, that is absolutely *awful*. Where do you come up with this stuff?"

Natalya chuckled. "Ees a fantasy of mine."

"You fantasize about me eating a cow's ass?"

"Why not?" she teased. "Half the time you're full of sheet, anyway."

Garm frowned. "Okay, fine. Now it's *my* turn."

She gave him her most dazzling smile. "Take your best shot, lover boy."

"Oh, I will. If *you* refuse to tell the truth, you have to get down on your knees and give Admiral Callahan head."

"What?!?"

Garm chuckled. Natalya's look of revulsion was the kind you wore when you rushed into a seedy gas station, desperate to drop a deuce, only to find the toilet clogged and filled to the rim with a viscous foulness that defied description. "I'm not done," he said with a malicious smirk. "You have to finish the 'job.' And, you must let him record it, *and* he gets to keep the copy."

As she shook her tawny locks, Natalya reminded him of a pissed-off lion, scattering a swarm of flies. "You know, you are one warped, tweested son of a beetch, Wolfie. I thought I was bad, but you . . . neveroyatno!"

"Thanks, babe," Garm said with an amused grin. He reached over and, despite her stiffness, drew her close. "You're pretty unbelievable, too."

Natalya nearly succumbed to his charms, but then pulled back. She sat up straight, completely at ease in the raw, then took his hand and shook it. "Very well, Captain Braddock. We have deal. But since you are such a gentleman, we shall do, as you say, ladies first."

"No problem." Garm leaned back on the pillows, his big hands clasped behind his head. "Bring it on, darling."

"Oh, I am going to, *dahling* . . ." She rubbed her hands together in anticipation as she mulled over her choices. A moment later, she did a Ramirez, her neck straightening like a piece of rebar. "Ah, I have eet. You remember that boxer you keeled in the ring, da?"

"Yes." Garm did his best to appear detached, but his molars ground together. He knew where this was going.

"I watched the fight online," Natalya confessed. "At first you were like zombie during staring contest, your head down, just looking at canvas. He must have thought you were scared because he began taunting you." She held up a finger. "But just before you break to go to corner sometheeng happened . . . you looked up at heem and your eyes, they meet. Your expression changed. Eet was like a crocodile: cold, dangerous, not human. Your opponent saw eet, too." She nodded. "He was scared, realized he make mistake. Then bell rang and . . ."

Natalya folded her vascular arms across her chest. "I want to know what happened. Not during fight, but *before*. Tell me what make you snap. What make you become a monster that keels a man with bare hands?"

Garm hesitated as the memory did roadwork through his mind. He could see it all; moreover, he could *feel* it. Finally, he sighed resignedly. Short of shoving his head up a steer's anus, there was no getting out of this.

Oh well. It's not going to be pretty. But it's what she wants.

Garm tried unsuccessfully to clear his throat, then reached for the glass of water on the nightstand. He took a slow sip, swishing the cool liquid around in his mouth before swallowing.

"The Lopez fight should never have happened," he began, setting the glass back down. His head did the inverted pendulum thing, trying in vain to dislodge some of the regret. "I told them, but nobody listened. I was . . . not myself, Nat. You know what I mean?"

Natalya nodded. "You know that I do."

"Seeing my dad go out like that, trussed up like a maniac: the blood, the pus, the screaming . . . I've never seen anything like it, before or since. Not in real-life, not even in a horror movie." Garm hunched forward and let slip a mournful breath. "He was a great man. He deserved better."

He formed a steeple with his fingers and peered into the center of it. In his mind, it was the tiny ship's chapel where they held his dad's service, shortly before his burial at sea. He could see it as if it was happening here and now.

"When they sent me into the ring, I was still reeling." He took one finger and poked an impression in the mattress between them. "My feet should never have touched the canvas that night."

"I understand," Natalya said. Her gray eyes shone with a mixture of empathy and curiosity. "But what deed you *feel* before the opening bell? We all have an animal inside us. What set yours free?"

Garm's gaze became a "thousand-fathom-stare", as his mind struggled to embrace emotions he was ill-equipped to process.

"When you experience the death of a loved one, it doesn't just leave with the pallbearers," he began. "It stays, it drapes itself over you and you wear it like a hooded garment. People can see it in your eyes and, when you've lost something so great, life itself loses all meaning. Things like fear of imprisonment or death vanish temporarily and, when people look into your eyes, they can see death staring back at them."

Natalya licked her lips and nodded. "So, when Lopez taunted you, he--"

Garm's eyes latched onto hers. "He wasn't a bad guy. He was just doing what fighters do – trying to psych out an opponent. But by provoking me, he unwittingly gave me an outlet for all the rage I had bottled up. And in the ring--"

"Men die and eet is legal."

Garm exhaled slowly. "Even if it wasn't it wouldn't have mattered. At that moment, I just didn't care. Lopez was what I needed, an adversary I could unleash my fury on. And he paid the ultimate price for it."

"Ees that why you gave a beeg chunk of your purse to hees family?"

He wagged a finger at her. "Tsk-tsk. Only one question per turn, my nosey, 'leetle' Siberian tigress. And you had yours."

Natalya chuckled. "I don't know wheech I find cuter, you trying to eemitate my accent or that funny nickname." She lay naked on her side on the bed, her head propped up off one elbow. "Okay, you played fair. Now ees your turn to ask me question. Go on, geev eet your best shot."

Garm leaned forward and ran his fingers over the soft curves of her hip and ribs, stopping when he reached her muscular shoulder.

"How did you get that scar on your throat?"

Natalya's reaction was far from what he expected. Her face turned paper white and the gasp that escaped her lips was a mouse-like squeak. A second later, her athletic body tensed and she jolted upright. She retreated to the far end of the bed and sat there, glaring at him like a wild animal caught in a snare.

"You . . . bastard!" she spat, her face contorting with barely-contained fury.

"Oh, c'mon," Garm said, trying to defuse things. "It can't be that bad."

"It . . . it . . ."

"Hey, I told you *my* truth," he reminded.

Natalya contemplated him with eyes like the dark slits in a knight's helmet before looking away. "You are smarter than I thought, Garm Braddock. Very well, we shall feenish what we started. Or rather, what *you* started."

She pursed her lips, drawing in a deep breath, and then started talking. "My family was from a Russian fishing village called Kaliningrad, located between Poland and Lithuania on the Baltic Sea."

"I'm not familiar with the area," Garm confessed.

"Ees a very old settlement, of Prussian ancestry," she said. "Eet was once called Königsberg, and was named for a fortress built by the Teutonic Knights during the Northern Crusades."

Natalya's jaw tilted proudly up as her head swiveled in his direction. "I am descended from those knights."

"Really?" Garm sat up straight. "Now, that's interesting."

"Maybe not," she said, shaking her head. "When the Red Army overran the town at end of WWII, the German population fled for their lives. Those who deed not were slaughtered. My great-great-grandmother's husband was keeled een the battle. She was taken prisoner by Russian general. He . . ."

"Fell in love with her and asked her to marry him," Garm finished.

"Da." Natalya nodded. Name of town was changed to Kaliningrad and life continued. They stayed on and their descendants became feeshermen who spend their days drinking beer and trawling the Pregolya River and Baltic for cod and herring."

"Sounds like an idyllic life for some."

"For my parents, eet was," she concurred. "But one day their trawler disappear, vanish without a trace. I become, how you say . . . orphan?"

Garm nodded and, as she ran her tongue over dry lips, he reached for his water glass and offered it to her. She took a quick gulp and held onto it.

"Eet was bad time. Insurance company said eet was no accident and refused to issue payment for either boat or life insurance policy. I was only fourteen. I had no money for rent or clothes, not even food."

"Didn't you have any family?"

"I was told of uncle, here een United States, but I deed not know how to find heem. I was on my own."

"Man, that's rough. So, what did you do?"

Natalya licked her lips and swallowed. "I took job working for local man. He buy and sell feesh. He was a . . . feesh-monster?"

"Fishmonger," Garm corrected. His grin faded fast. Judging by the way she avoided his gaze and her sorrowful expression, he was beginning to regret the need to satiate his curiosity.

"He was beeg, gruff man, but nice," she said. "At least at first. I spend my summer loading and unloading feesh and ice een storerooms and working store. Eet was hard work, but kept my mind off losing my family."

A scary thought began to loom on the horizon of Garm's mind. He tried and failed to dismiss it; he had a bad feeling about what came next.

Natalya stopped talking. Her eyes went blank as she peered back into her past – a past she obviously wanted to forget. Goosebumps pricked up all over her body and she reached for a nearby comforter. Wordlessly, she draped it over her shoulders, a cotton chrysalis to cover her nakedness.

Garm cleared his throat. "Look, maybe this was a bad idea. I--"

"Be quiet, Wolfie," she warned.

Natalya swallowed the lump in her throat and then waded into it. "One night, after close of shop, feeshmonger approach me in back room. He grab me and throw me onto pile of crates . . ."

Oh fuck.

"I was skeeny fourteen-year-old girl, but I knew what he wanted," she said. "I beg heem to stop. I fight back, yell and start to scream, but he pull a beeg fillet knife on me and tell me he cut my throat if I make any noise."

"Jesus, Nat . . ."

Natalya silenced him with a look. "He . . . cut my clothes off and push me down on crates. Then he climb on top of me and . . ."

Garm could feel her dread and shame welling up. It oozed from her pores and pervaded the room, a dank cloud of misery. He wanted to say something, to reach out and comfort her, but he could tell if he so much as twitched she would explode.

Natalya hesitated. She closed her mouth and started breathing through her nostrils, her breath coming in quick pants.

"He stank of stale beer and feesh and rotten onions. I could not breathe. He put the knife to my throat and push the point in far enough to make me bleed," she managed. "He tell me, '*If you move or make sound, I keel you.*' Then, he pulled down his filthy trousers and start to rape me."

Garm felt a murderous rage spring up within him. His own breathing became slow and labored and he saw a trip to Kaliningrad in his immediate future.

"I feel thees burning pain and wetness as he force himself een me," Natalya said. Her voice and body both started shaking, but to her credit, her eyes remained dry. "I couldn't move. The pain, the stench, the humiliation . . . and the knife stuck een the side of my neck. I was powerless."

She stopped talking and stared sorrowfully downward, studying her calloused hands. She grasped the edges of the comforter tightly, hugging herself with it.

"I was virgin . . . I not even had my first period yet."

Garm didn't know what to say or do. His hands trembled as he started to reach for her, but he hesitated. "Nat . . . I . . ."

"He make beeg mistake, Wolfie," Natalya said icily, her head snapping upright. Her forlorn eyes were now as cold and hard as agates, and the unexpected transformation froze him where he sat.

"I suffer much as he rape me, but I wait for heem to feenish."

"W-what do you mean?" Garm asked, shaken and confused.

"As he orgasm, hees body start to convulse, shooting hees deesgusting semen een me," Natalya said. Her lips curled back, exposing her canines. "I waited and watched for hees greep on the fillet knife to relax . . ."

"And then?"

"I snatch eet from hees hand and bury eet in his ear."

Garm jolted upright. "Holy shit! Are you serious?"

"Da."

"You . . . you killed him?"

"Oh, not right away," Natalya said with a grim smile. "I had no experience weeth keeling men then, only feesh. But I must have damaged something een hees tiny brain. He was steel alive, but could not move. He was, how you say . . . paralyze?"

Garm nodded. "Paralyzed."

"Da. So I went to work."

"I-I don't--"

"First, I get up and make sure store was locked. Then I clean myself up," she said. "I take shower in back, change my clothes, throw old stuff een furnace, and take all money from register and safe."

Garm was astonished. "Wow. And the fishmonger?"

"I deal with heem last," Natalya stated.

"What did you do?"

"What you theenk I do?"

"I'm afraid to ask," Garm admitted. "But whatever it was, he deserved it."

"I like the way you theenk," she said with a wan smile. "I pulled the knife out of hees head and cut hees balls off, one by one. Then I make heem chew and swallow them."

"How?"

"I stuff each one een hees mouth, peench nose closed, and put hand over mouth," she said, matter-of-factly. "To breathe, he have no choice but to eat hees own nuts."

"Ah . . ."

"I save penis for beeg finale," Natalya said, relishing the memory of what she'd done. "Eet was pathetic leetle theeng, but symbolic. I push in mouth and smother heem while he choke on eet."

"Wow, good for you," Garm said. He exhaled some of the tension he was feeling, glad that the girl had avenged herself.

"The last theeng that peeg saw before he die was my face," she announced. She shrugged and sighed simultaneously. "Eet was better than he deserve."

"Then what?" Garm asked.

"Then I leave country," Natalya replied. "I make my way to Europe. Eventually, I track down my uncle here working in Naval Intelligence, of all places, and come to United States. The rest, you more or less know . . ."

Garm nodded. "Wow. I-I'm really sorry you went through that. Not to mention, losing the baby, years later."

"Spasiba." She raised the water to her lips, took a long draught, then got up and placed it back on the nightstand. She stood up straight with the comforter draped down like a cape and cricked her neck from side to side.

"So, now you know why I not like meessionary."

"Uh, yeah," Garm said. "Don't worry. I . . . I won't ask again."

"Good. Eet would take great trust on my part to let man get on top of me again. You understand?"

Garm said nothing.

"Deed you know female pliosaurs are very jealous?" she asked.

"What? They are?"

"Da," Natalya said. "During courtship and even after mating, eef male *Kronosaurus* even *looks* at another cow, she bite hees genitals off and eats them!"

She smiled, but her eyes had a feral glow.

Garm shook his head. "That's bullshit. You forget who you're talking to."

"You're right," she admitted. She rolled her shoulders back and allowed the comforter to cascade down to the carpet, exposing the splendor of her physique. "Now, I tell you some theeng that is *not*."

"Okay," he said, unabashedly ogling her.

"Up here," Natalya said, moving closer and snapping her fingers to draw his eyes up from her breasts. "I am not pliosaur. And I am not stupid."

"What do you mean?"

"Although we are just 'fuck buddies,' I do not theenk you would be foolish enough to screw another woman behind my back."

"Go on," Garm drawled.

"Eef you do, eet shall be your loss," she said, flipping her hair to the side and allowing her tawny locks to drape fetchingly down over one toned shoulder. Then, her head came back up and her eyes locked onto his like iron-gray rifle sights.

"But eef I find out you ever breathe a word of what I told you about my past to anyone, the next time your beeg, beautiful cock ees in my mouth I weel bite it off and swallow it, right in front of you."

Garm shook his head vehemently. "There's no need for that. You know I would never."

She leaned close and kissed him wetly, then whispered in his ear. "I know, Wolfie. I know."

Then she sauntered over to the nearby dresser and bent over it, her round ass sticking invitingly out and legs spread wide.

"Now . . . who wants to fuck?"

TWENTY

It was one of those sounds you never forget, Dirk realized. Around him, the roar of the pliosaur known as *Tiamat* boomed like a thunderclap through Tartarus's huge amphitheater, reverberating off its iron walls. Even with his hands clamped tightly over his ears there was no escape; the beast's bellow was so deep and powerful it shook the marrow in one's bones.

Dirk wasn't the only one affected. Across the 1,400-foot chamber's stadium-style seats, the majority of the four hundred spectators gathered together for GDT's presentation covered their eyes and ears and screamed like children hiding from an imaginary monster. But there was nothing make-believe about *Tiamat*. Even those who dared behold the *Kronosaurus* queen's terrifying visage cringed and cowered, from the toughest submarine gunner to the surliest of guards. Only Dr. Grayson, who sat staring at a shrieking Rear Admiral Callahan with a mixture of bemusement and disdain, appeared unaffected by the behemoth's appearance and subsequent bellow.

Dirk chuckled. He figured it was a mixture of the elderly CEO anticipating what was to come, and having wisely turned down the volume on his hearing aid.

Focusing hard, Dirk bolstered his mental control over the monstrous predator. The latest innovations in GDT's cortical controllers were light years ahead of their previous models and enabled the wielder to not only physically control the implanted subject, but utilize its myriad senses as well.

Of course, with the queen, the young scientist realized he was hitting a few speed bumps. All Thalassophoneans had a rudimentary intellect of sorts, honed by 65 million years of incarceration. *Tiamat*'s mind, however, was superior to that of her brethren. She was capable of basic problem solving and he could tell she was actively, albeit clumsily, searching for loopholes in her implant's control factors. She was trying to resist the program, if not shake it altogether.

It was impossible, of course. The cortex-based implant's neural filaments were integrated into both her parietal and occipital lobes. Resistance was, as they say, futile.

Still, it was disturbing.

In order to give his audience a brief respite, Dirk had the giant cow submerge and back away from the aquarium's protective Celazole wall. Trailing bubbles, she sank to a depth of one hundred feet and withdrew until she occupied the center of the one-thousand-foot pool.

Dirk raised his hands for calm and spoke with authority.

"People . . . please, calm yourselves." He indicated the shadowy form submerged at his feet then tapped his skull cap with one index finger. "There is absolutely no danger. I promise you, the queen is under my complete control."

Gradually, the cries of alarm ceased and people regained enough composure to return to their seats. Dirk spotted Security Chief Dwyer and Sergeant Wurmer on their feet and adjusting their uniforms, trying to act as if they'd been unfazed by *Tiamat*. Admiral Callahan, on the other hand, had no problem admitting he'd been scared to death. Dirk saw him jabbering in Grayson's ear, one hand on his heart and laughing good-naturedly. It was a good omen.

"My apologies for alarming you," Dirk continued. He nodded sagaciously. "We were going to pass out adult diapers to everyone on the way in, but we felt people would interpret it as some sort of publicity stunt." He grinned as nervous laughter rippled through the crowd. "Still, if anyone feels the need to get up and use the restroom, now's the time."

Glancing down, Dirk keyed a quick code into his board, allowing Tartarus's internal media system to tap directly into *Tiamat*'s neural interface program and linking it to her optical outputs. He hit a key and looked up. Instantly, the twin monitors above his platform shimmered. The one on his right continued to show what the queen perceived – mainly her nervous audience, huddled behind ten to fifteen feet of indestructible thermoplastic.

The one on Dirk's left, however, went dark. Not black, as if the power had been cut, but amorphous shades of black and gray, like the waters of a pond on a moonless night.

"Now, for you Navy types," he resumed. "Our recent advances in cybernetic implants put GDT's biologic controllers so far ahead of any so-called 'competition' it's no longer funny; it's ridiculous." He plucked the microphone from its stand, stepped forward and walked to the edge of the dais's platform. "With our previous technology, using pliosaurs for coastal sentry duty or fleet defense consisted primarily of maneuvering the creature into a set course of action, i.e. patrolling a designated waterway or engaging a target. But beyond that, the animal was more or less left to its own devices. And the controller – the one pulling the strings – was unable to discern the fine points of what was actually happening, beyond their mother vessel's sonar readings."

Dirk paused as he saw Admiral Callahan stand up and raise a hand. "I'm sorry admiral," he said. "But we're not set up for Q&A. That will be at the post-demo briefing. However, odds are I know what's on your mind, so let's keep going. Anything I miss we can cover later."

As Grayson coaxed Callahan back into his seat, Dirk wandered the platform. "For the navy to appreciate the capabilities of these new--" *and many times more expensive* "--units, it's imperative you understand the degree of management you will have over your subjects. We're talking mind-to-mind communication, people. If I wanted to," he gestured at the giant form lurking below. "I could bring *Tiamat* to the surface and have her lay on her side, doing the 'Hi there!' flipper-waving routine they used to have killer whales do, back in the day."

He stopped at the center of the oval-shaped concrete platform, less than a foot from the edge. "But I don't think you came here to see the world's mightiest predator acting like some stir-crazy dolphin, now did you?"

As the now-enthusiastic crowd responded with a resounding chorus of *"No!"* Dirk nodded. "I didn't think so." He gestured upward as Stacy stepped out of the shadows and into the spotlight, fifty feet up. "Then, at the risk of sounding like some magician in a traveling circus, allow me to draw your attention to my lovely assistant, perched high above us."

Dirk paused, allowing the crowd to make whatever mental leaps they might as to what would happen next. Meanwhile, Stacy adjusted her CCUBA mask and moved to the edge of her platform, one hand grasping a bolted-on steel handle as she waved. "For the record," Dirk announced. "Dr. Daniels is far from just an 'assistant.' She is a leading expert in the fields of neural and maritime robotics, as well as the premier authority on *Pliosauridae*." He turned to face the audience. "That said, she is far more than a pretty face."

On cue, Stacy lost her grip and her balance and, backed by a chorus of alarmed cries, tumbled from her perch. In mid-fall, she twisted her body head-down and interlocked her hands, performing a near-perfect rip-entry and cutting into the water with hardly a splash. She surfaced a few seconds later, powerfully free-styling her way away from the wall and moving purposefully toward the podium platform, some seventy-five yards away.

Despite the impressiveness of Stacy's stunt dive, the pensive crowd, fully cognizant of what was in there with her, was on its feet, pointing and crying out. Seemingly oblivious, she continued to swim, her strokes smooth and steady as she made for the safety of the nearby dock.

All of a sudden, Stacy stopped and started treading water. Like a giant cauldron coming to a boil, the pool's surface around her began to swirl across an area over one hundred feet across. Her head swung back and forth, the mirrored lenses of her Thunnus rebreather reflecting her frightened audience as she peered anxiously about. Then she dove underwater and disappeared. The water around the spot where she was last seen churned violently and went deathly still. Soon, panicked murmurs began propagating throughout the stands.

Moments later, *Tiamat* breached the surface like a scaly battlecruiser, twin columns of compressed water vapor exploding whale-like from her blowholes. And clinging tightly to the gnarled skin of her ten-foot thick nape was Stacy, alive and unharmed.

The crowd cheered wildly. Adding fuel to the fervor, Dirk directed the giant pliosaur to perform a slow oval around the edges of the amphitheater, giving his audience an appreciation of the captive behemoth's true size, compared to the tiny life form affixed to it. For her part, Stacy primarily focused on maintaining her grip, but she managed a quick wave at one point, generating an additional round of applause.

Dirk touched a tab on his keyboard and focused hard into his skullcap. It was time to move to the highlight of their performance. On command, *Tiamat* swung obediently toward him, her speed gradually increasing. As she reached the center of the pool, still two hundred feet from the dock's terminus, she sounded, washing Stacy off her back and vanishing into the depths with a violent splash.

Stacy flailed as she bobbed to the surface. Her alarmed audience uniformly relaxed when they saw she was okay. With the CCUBA on, she wasn't at risk of drowning, but Dirk could tell the strain of being dragged under had left her disoriented. She took a moment to get her bearings before beginning a slow crawl stroke toward the podium.

On the monitor above, her tiny form could be seen flailing on the surface. The viewpoint was from directly below, transmitted via *Tiamat*'s binocular vision as she eyed Stacy hungrily.

"You've seen the degree of control we exert over earth's mightiest predator," Dirk announced. "However, to appreciate the impact of the military applications for the more advanced GDT-ADCAP implants, I believe a different type of demonstration is in order."

He gave Stacy the go-ahead and, with a tiny salute, she dove underwater and began to power steadily downward, her arms pumping and legs kicking until she reached the fifty-foot mark. She remained there, breathing easily through her CCUBA. *Tiamat* had retreated into the shadows by the aquarium's far wall, but on the monitor, the crowd could see she remained fixated on the miniscule mammal that had invaded her territory.

Dirk drew in a breath and brought the giant saurian's hunting instincts to life. A deep, ratcheting sound, like a rusted portcullis being raised, echoed throughout the amphitheater, as the queen focused her powerful sonar on Stacy. It blasted forth, a giant cone of fast-cycling broadband clicks that enveloped not just the suspended scientist, but the entire thousand-foot aquarium.

The potent sound waves bounced off its stony depths and thick polybenzimidazole walls and reverberated beyond, spreading ever wider until they encompassed the entire coliseum, blanketing everyone and everything. The sonar was like a CT scan; you could feel it penetrating your flesh, your bones, even your teeth.

High above, the amphitheater's second screen suddenly came to life. On it, Stacy appeared as a tiny, illuminated figure. She was a glowing target in the crosshairs, her entire body flickering against a background of purest black.

Dirk spoke into the mike. "Any naval vessel utilizing our system has full access to anything the host unit detects. This includes echolocation, visual, audio . . . even olfactory components." He stepped away from the podium and indicated the first screen. "The monitor on your left is, as you've undoubtedly realized, the view from *Tiamat*'s eyes. This is how she sees her underwater world, in color and with a hint of thermal overlay. Her sub-surface eyesight is phenomenal, as one would expect from a pelagic huntress. She can see in all but complete darkness." He moved along the podium platform, indicating the remaining LCD screen.

"The monitor on the *right*, however, is even more impressive," Dirk continued. "Pliosaurs can see underwater, under optimal conditions, out to maybe three hundred yards. With their echolocation, however, they can track targets from a mile or more away, and with astounding accuracy. And *you* will now be able to perceive and document everything they can."

Judging by the anticipatory look on Admiral Callahan's face, Dirk would've bet everything he owned they'd not only be getting a slew of new orders from the Navy, but requests for upgrades on all their existing in-service models as well. GDT's stock prices were going to rocket through the roof, and Eric Grayson would soon be one of the richest men in the world.

"As you can see," Dirk resumed. "*Tiamat* has zeroed Dr. Daniels with her active sonar. She can see her human target clearly and can differentiate her against any and all background matter, even under zero light conditions." He increased his focus, willing the queen to zoom in on Stacy. As she did, the sonar clicks the pliosaur emitted increased in intensity, becoming an almost painful barrage. Stacy's body enlarged on the screen, the intense stream of echolocation cutting through her like an MRI. Every one of her organs – most notably her frantically beating heart – was visible as she fought the pool's circulating current.

"It's interesting to note," Dirk said. "That when using her broadband clicks to target a kill, *Tiamat*'s mid-range sonar emissions are higher than normal. In fact, right now she's cycling at a frequency of around 3,000 hertz." He pointed at the monitor. "This just so happens to be the same frequency whalers discovered many years ago – the one that panicked cetaceans into coming to the surface and made them easier to kill." He turned to his audience. "Whether this is an indication that whales have had encounters with macropliosaurs before and their reaction to this frequency is some sort of innate fear response, remains to be seen."

"Regardless, pliosaurs' advanced sonar capabilities are what enable them to hunt in the darkness of the abyss," Dirk said. "These same abilities will now allow shipboard controllers to pick out and detect isolated targets, both above and below the surface, with unparalleled accuracy. You want to scour a shipwreck? No problem. Search for survivors of a sunken vessel? Piece of cake. There are no limits. You'll know exactly what you're facing, long before you send one of these things in, and you'll be able to exert precise control over each host, in real time, and under real-world combat conditions." Dirk folded his lean arms across his chest. "The world's deadliest and most versatile bio-weapon just became a thousand times more so, with the added bonus of reducing the chances of losing expensive units due to errors in judgment or reliance on misinformation to near zero."

He pointed back at the overhead screens. On it, *Tiamat* continued to target Stacy. The athletic scientist was hovering at the forty-foot mark, her arms and legs working. "Now, in the unlikely event anyone still has any reservations, I'm going to have the queen perform a closer inspection of Doctor Daniels. This will allow us to showcase just how effective a pliosaur's assorted tracking and targeting capabilities are."

Everyone in the stands sat quietly as Dirk ordered the captive *Kronosaurus* up from the depths and had her close on Stacy. Like Death's menacing shadow, she emerged muzzle-first from the darkness. She was two hundred feet down, her gleaming orange eyes visible through the tank's murk as she executed a slow circle directly beneath her quarry.

Suddenly, something went wrong. Dirk touched a hand to his helmet, an alarmed expression on his face. Far below, *Tiamat* was on the move. Circling away and then turning back, she began to curve gracefully upward, her angled flippers causing her monstrous body to climb higher in the water column.

On the monitors, the giant predator's view of Stacy changed as it shifted position. *Tiamat*'s monstrous head swiveled in her direction. In seconds, the beast was on the same level she was – and on an intercept course.

With the crowd's cries of alarm ringing in his ears, Dirk rushed to the podium keyboard and began typing frantically. He didn't have the spectators' view through the tank's walls, but he didn't need it. One poorly angled glance up confirmed their combined fears.

Tiamat was going after Stacy. And he couldn't stop her.

Ignoring the audience's screams of panic, Dirk continued typing like a maniac. Sweat ran down his face as he pressed one hand to the side of his helmet and grimaced. On the screen, the queen was moving in for the kill.

Having realized the seriousness of her situation, Stacy made for the surface. Her arms and legs pumped frantically to outdistance her monstrous pursuer, but it was useless. Like a Mako shark going after a crippled herring, *Tiamat* closed with but a flick of her fins. Her attack was presented in full color, on two screens, and from three different vantage points, for four hundred pairs of eyes to see.

She was barely one hundred feet away when her giant jaws began to yawn.

Then sixty . . . Then twenty . . .

With a powerful surge, *Tiamat* rushed forward, enveloping Stacy in one gigantic bite. Dirk's blood turned to ice as he witnessed the attack through the queen's eyes; it was as if *he* was doing it. He saw Stacy turn toward her attacker, her hands outstretched in a desperate but futile attempt to fend off her approaching doom, then the look of absolute terror on her face as she was swallowed. Then she was gone and the heartless beast continued relentlessly forward, its jaws methodically closing as it gulped down its tiny meal.

Dirk staggered back like a drunkard. The realization that one of the world's most brilliant minds could just vanish like that, could be sucked down like an hors d'oeuvres, and that to her killer, her beauty, her education, her accomplishments, her entire *life* was of no consequence whatsoever . . .

In the tiered stands, the amphitheater's viewers were in a panic. Everyone was on their feet, pointing, screaming and yelling, with most of them pushing and shoving their way toward the exits. The seated security guards sprang to life, desperately trying to quell the stampede and restore calm. Dirk caught a glimpse of Dr. Grayson through the crowd. Even he looked shocked.

Abandoning the keyboard, Dirk rushed to the edge of the podium platform, his eyes gazing forlornly into the foreboding depths where a woman – technically *his* woman – had just been devoured. A moment later, the waters all around him began to violently churn. Dirk stepped hurriedly back. He of all people knew what a displacement boil that size meant.

With an explosive burst that sent five-foot waves up and over the edge of the platform, inundating Dirk to mid-thigh, *Tiamat* erupted up out of the water. Her cottage-sized head reared forty feet in the air, blotting out the chamber's artificial sunlight. She glared menacingly down at him, her streaming maw a terrifying mass of shiny black scales, bristling with rows of fangs the size of a Roman gladius.

Dirk staggered back, his eyes as big as saucers as she loomed over him. Her gleaming orange orbs burrowed into his, riveting him with her rage, freezing him into immobility. Soaked from the waist down by the wall of water that slammed into him, he stood his ground, shivering. His heart was beating so hard he was certain he'd suffer a heart attack, but there was no point in running. Even if he could will his legs into motion, there was nowhere to go.

A deep rumble emanated from *Tiamat*'s mighty chest as she lowered her monstrous head. Her scaly muzzle moved downward with deceptive slothfulness, her scarred snout heading straight for Dirk. He could smell her rancid breath washing over him, a nauseating cocktail of blood and rotting flesh, and he started to gag. Her slavering jaws were only ten feet away and closing.

Then, to the amazement of the frenzied crowd, *Tiamat* did not attack. Instead, she rested her chin on the edge of the podium platform. The reinforced concrete groaned under the fifty+ tons pressing down on it, but the structure held. Although she didn't strike, the *Kronosaurus* queen's baleful eyes continued to bore into Dirk's and he felt cold sweat streaming down his neck and back.

Tiamat began to growl, a throaty rumble that shook the ground like a city subway train running underneath your feet. Waves of primal fear shimmied through Dirk and it was all he could do to keep from soiling himself.

He'd never been so scared in his life. He swallowed hard, trying to maintain his composure. Then, for some inane reason, he found himself focusing on the fact he'd also never been so close to the captive colossus. Looking closely, he could see a network of gray, fibrous scars decorating the beast's immense rostrum. Some were circular, some irregular, evidence of past battles with assorted meals and, perhaps, a few rivals. He could see the layers of rock-hard callosities that coated the terminus of her battering-ram lower jaw, the crocodile-like sensory pits that dotted her thick-scaled lips, and even the rippling muscles that held her yard-long blowholes open. As they expanded, water vapor wafted from her gaping nostrils like steam from a dragon's maw.

This creature . . . this *thing*, was to Dirk Braddock, death incarnate. She'd ruined his life. He should've been filled with horror and revulsion – and he *was* – but the scientist in him was fascinated.

Shrugging off such distractions, Dirk focused a quick command through his synaptic skullcap. To his amazement, *Tiamat* resisted. He blinked in disbelief, then gritted his teeth and brought the full power of his intellect to bear. He could feel the giant pliosaur's cool reptilian brain raging against the intrusion, against being bullied into submitting to the tiny creature before her.

The struggle was intense but brief. Within moments, Dirk battered through her clumsy defenses and forced her into submission.

A second later, and with the terminal ten feet of her mandibles still pressing down upon the podium platform, *Tiamat*'s jaws split apart, her maxilla raising up like a basking crocodile's as she opened wide. Then, amidst a collective gasp of disbelief from the crowd, Dirk walked brazenly up to the fang-encrusted cave that gaped wide before him and placed one foot inside, resting it on the end of the behemoth's couch-sized tongue.

"You okay?" he asked, leaning down and extending a hand.

The feed to the amphitheater's paired overhead monitors switched to that from a pair of ceiling cameras. They zoomed in tightly. There, laying facedown atop the drool-soaked mound of whitish flesh, was Stacy Daniels.

"Yeah . . ." she said weakly. "So, I've got a pretty face, huh?"

"I figured you'd like that," Dirk chuckled.

Releasing her death grip on the *Kronosaurus*'s slippery mouthparts, Stacy accepted his hand and tried regaining her feet. "Get me out of here, Dirk. It stinks like death. If I don't get out now--"

"I got you," Dirk affirmed. Stepping completely into the colossal mouth, he bent at the waist, then gripped her under the shoulders and pulled. The saliva helped as he slid her carefully forward and struggled to hoist her up.

Stacy looked up at the darkened cave roof suspended above them, huge teeth draping down from its edges like razor-edged stalactites. Suddenly, the pliosaur's jawbones shifted from side to side, causing them to stumble and nearly lose their footing.

"Are you sure you've got her?" Stacy asked worriedly.

"Yes." Dirk cocked an eyebrow as he glanced thoughtfully up at *Tiamat*'s streaming palate. The idea that he was standing inside the maw of his nemesis was so surreal, his mind couldn't begin to accept it. He shuddered. "It was a little strange, just now. When I ordered her to open she put up a struggle. I think she's trying to resist the program, I . . . oof!"

Dirk grimaced as Stacy slipped and he barely caught her. He tried straightening his legs to gain leverage, but then grunted as she extended a hand up over his shoulder, pressing firmly against the moist tissue directly above them.

"Careful. You need to watch her pterygoid teeth . . ." she warned.

Dirk glanced up, his eyes widening as he saw one of *Tiamat*'s twelve-inch pharyngeal fangs hanging down, right above his head. Like a mosasaur, she had two rows of them in the roof of her mouth, designed to keep prey moving down her gullet. They were lethal hooks, ready to rip into her prey. Or his scalp.

"Thanks, that would've sucked," he acknowledged. Stooping now, he half-carried, half-dragged Stacy out of the pliosaur's dripping jaws and onto the safety of the platform. Outside, the crowd was already on its feet, cheering like fans whose team just pulled off a Walk-off Win in Game 7 of the World Series.

Dirk helped Stacy a few steps until she felt she could walk. Then, at her insistence, he let go. With *Tiamat* still mentally restrained and lying there, her jaws spread wide enough to admit a good-sized elephant, he bent down and picked up his discarded microphone. Despite having been inundated, the waterproof device still functioned.

He indicated Stacy as he spoke into the mike. "How about that, folks? Let's have a round of applause for our very own Jonah – or make that *Joan* – of Tartarus . . . Dr. Stacy Daniels!"

Dirk was impressed that four hundred people could applaud so loudly and clapped his own hands enthusiastically as Stacy wrestled off her rebreather. She dropped it and exhaled hard before waving feebly to the audience. He studied her. Her hair was matted down, her face pale, and she was drenched with sweat, but considering she'd just survived the most horrifying death imaginable, she looked damn good.

He leaned over and whispered in her ear. "So much for claustrophobia. Do you want to say anything?"

"Hell, no," she said through a forced smile. "Just get me the fuck out of here. I'm barely hanging on."

"What do you mean?"

"I mean I need to puke, okay? And then I need a big-ass bottle of aspirin, a long, hot shower, and a couple of really stiff drinks."

"You got it," Dirk replied with a grin. He placed one arm around her waist as they posed for the crowd. After a few rounds of photos had been taken, he brought the microphone back to his lips. "Thank you very much for attending our little demonstration and please keep in mind, any pictures or videos taken today are for your respective, interdepartmental usage *only*. Remember your NDAs; I don't want to see anything on Facebook or YouTube. Lastly, for those who are attending the post-demo meet, Dr. Grayson and I will see you this afternoon. For everyone else, please follow our security officers to your appropriate destination. And thank you again for coming."

As the applause gradually diminished and the audience started to break up, Dirk turned to Stacy. "You ready to go?"

She scoffed. "Now *there's* the mother of all rhetorical questions." She shifted her weight, then glanced nervously back over her shoulder. "Uh . . . aren't you forgetting something?"

Dirk turned around to find *Tiamat* less than twenty feet away. The giant pliosaur was still locked in place. Her mouth remained open, her lower jaw resting on the concrete platform. She was like some

Draconian statue. Only her eyes moved and they stayed locked on Dirk like luminescent rifle scopes.

He let go of Stacy and moved a few feet to the right until he met *Tiamat*'s gaze fully. He looked into her narrowed, red-tinged eyes.

There was a lot of hatred there.

Suddenly, Dirk's hand went to his forehead; he could feel a headache coming on. Was it his or hers? It was hard to tell. Through his helmet, he could sense her pent-up frustration at being forced into immobility. She was like a lion, trapped in a cage so small it can barely move and desperate to break free.

Dirk gave a perfunctory wave, ordering her back into the water. She blinked, uttered a thunderous snort, then raised her monstrous head and sank beneath the surface so smoothly she barely left a ripple. As she powered toward the bottom, he sent a follow-up message. She was allowed to remain in the amphitheater pool for the moment, but was ordered to avoid the podium and its connecting dock, as well as its curved Celazole walls.

Given the scope of the new implant's behavioral inhibitors, that last order was unnecessary. But with recent developments, Dirk wasn't taking any chances. The last thing he needed was Grayson's prize specimen figuring out some loophole in her restrictive parameters and snatching up some hapless technician as a late-night snack.

Lord knew she'd killed enough people already.

———

The Ancient was frustrated. The calories he'd consumed following his slaughter of the bull sperm whale were nearly depleted, and the ravening hunger brought on by his high-speed metabolism was already starting to plague him. His stomach burned and writhed like a thing alive and his temper grew fouler by the minute.

He'd been on the hunt for the last six hours, scenting his way along the lightless mid-layer of the Cayman Trench. Except for ascending once an hour or so to spout and replenish his air supply, he'd remained at the 12,000-foot mark the entire time. Below his pale, armored belly, the yawning transform fault zone also known as the Bartlett Deep continued down to over twice that depth, its frigid bleakness cloaked in forever night.

For most creatures, the Midnight Zone was a hostile, alien environment, its innate deadliness eclipsed only by that of the airless void of space. But to the Ancient it was home. Insulated by a foot-thick layer of blubber and warmed by the heat of his exertions, neither the coldness of the abyss nor its crushing embrace were a threat to him.

With deceptive ease, the bull *Kronosaurus imperator* continued soundlessly along, his boat-sized flippers using smooth, rhythmic strokes to propel him and conserving the bulk of his energy for the kill. His paddle-like flippers were the ultimate in marine locomotion, an ultra-efficient means of propulsion his ancestors perfected over 200 million years ago. Unlike modern-day pinnipeds, that pushed themselves through the water with only one pair of flippers, he utilized two sets, pectoral and pelvic. His fins operated through myriad planes of motion to control pitch and yaw, as well as velocity. Changing direction or speed was as simple as altering the amount or angle of thrust.

Under normal conditions, such as patrolling or migrating, the fore and rear flippers moved slowly, with the front pair pushing against the water below the creature, and the rear encompassing water more parallel. This enabled each pair of flippers to work simultaneously, moving the maximum amount of seawater with the minimum amount of effort.

During high speed maneuvers, however, such as evading a rival or closing on prey, the flippers' full power was brought to bear. The broad rear flippers took advantage of the suction the pectoral flippers provided on their return stroke to aid them in theirs. Both sets reached maximal extension at the same time. Then, both sets pushed powerfully backward through their respective planes of motion.

In such a manner, macropliosaurs took full advantage of their quad-propulsion system, using all their flippers simultaneously to generate twice as much thrust as a seal of similar size could. Moreover, they could alter direction at will and on the fly. The result was a whale-sized predator with incredible speed and unparalleled maneuverability.

The Ancient's throat muscles rippled in waves as he emitted bursts of long-range broadband clicks, designed to locate prey. This far from the surface, the tiny warm-bloods and their dangerous metal constructs were no longer a threat and he was unconcerned about his sound sight being tracked. Unfortunately, so far he had found nothing.

With a loud snort of irritation, followed by a sudden burst of power that displaced enough water to fill three Olympic-sized swimming pools, the great beast angled sharply upward. Accelerating rapidly, he reduced his depth to 10,000 feet in a matter of minutes and remained there. His internal clock told him that, two miles above his wedge-shaped head, night had come and gone. Cloaked as he was in perpetual blackness, he had seen none of it.

Maintaining his depth, the bull pliosaur increased his speed. He was three hundred miles past the Cayman Islands, traveling between Jamaica and Cuba and heading for the turbulence of the Windward Passage. Beyond, the sparkling waters of the North Atlantic waited with their rich hunting grounds. There would be bountiful feeding then, but right now that mattered not. His need was too pressing to wait.

He needed flesh. And he needed it now.

As he passed worthless schools of miniscule fish and a foot-long, deep-dwelling octopus, the Ancient's glittering scarlet eyes suddenly widened. His sound imaging had detected the presence of a potential prey item: something sizable, at the very periphery of his sensory field. It was high up in the water column, barely 3,000 feet from the surface, and too far to make out in detail. Rather than spook whatever it was, he ran silent, relying on his phenomenal sense of smell to get him within striking distance.

Hurtling through the chilling blackness at nearly fifty miles an hour, the scaly titan was two hundred yards away when he wrapped his target in a blanket of sonar. His thick-scaled lips contracted as he realized he'd detected nothing more than a prowling billfish, feeding on a tightly-packed school of squid.

With a groan that was the saurian equivalent of a sigh, the annoyed beast increased his speed to maximum and threw himself at his prey. It wasn't much, but if he could catch the speedy, fifteen-foot fish it would go a long way toward taking the edge off his growing hunger.

Of course, catching it was the problem.

Despite being caught at the feeding trough, the 1,100 lb. Atlantic swordfish was far from defenseless. Used to battling Nature's cruise missiles – Mako sharks – it was equipped with an array of senses that made it both an efficient hunter and an elusive prey item. In addition to its lateral line, special organs on the sides of the fish's head heated its huge eyes and brain, giving it unparalleled underwater vision, even in complete darkness. It picked up the pliosaur's sonar the moment it was pinged and spotted the fast-approaching mountain of teeth and muscle long before it felt the powerful pressure wave that preceded it.

With frantic stokes of its four-foot tail, the frightened *Xiphias gladius* abandoned its feeding run and took off. Angling steeply upward, it accelerated with astonishing rapidity. With a top speed of over sixty miles an hour, the broadbill was one of the fastest fish in the sea. Its powerful musculature and sleek, fusiform design, culminating in the five-foot razor-edged sword for which it was named, made it incredibly fast and agile. It would not be taken easily.

Like an onrushing nuclear submarine, the Ancient barreled toward the fleeing swordfish. Jaws yawning wide, he plowed clean through the school of defenseless squid, enveloping several hundred of the foot-long cephalopods and gulping them down as he continued toward his primary target.

Its streamlined form gleaming like a polished rapier, the *Xiphias* darted to and fro, with the ravenous pliosaur less than three body lengths behind it. Twice, the Ancient thought he had his meal and powered hungrily forward, and twice he ended up disappointed. The second missed strike was particularly frustrating, as he ended up with nothing but a mouthful of disgusting kelp.

Unable to shake its dogged pursuer, the terrified swordfish banked steeply upward and made for the surface. Its crescent-shaped tail pumping frantically, it sped toward the beckoning sunlight, hoping to lose the giant predator amid the glare and noisy surface traffic.

Although he preferred the comforting shelter of the deep, the Ancient refused to abandon the tasty morsel and stayed glued to the broadbill's tail. The *Xiphias*'s top end speed was more than a match for his and he couldn't begin to compete with its maneuverability. But stamina was his forte. If he could wear the billfish out, it would be his.

Hurtling upward like the battleship *Yamato*, arisen from the grave, the voracious *Kronosaurus* closed on his meal. His shearing jaws were closed tight to reduce friction, his four barnacle-edged flippers pumping hard to send him rocketing upward. The distance to the surface began to disintegrate: 1,000 feet, then 800, then 600 . . .

As his crimson eyes registered the painful sunlight lancing through the ocean's phototropic zone, the Ancient felt his body's dramatic response to the sudden decrease in pressure. His compressed lungs expanded and his heart rate increased, the Volkswagen-sized organ pumping blood away from his body's dense core and back toward its periphery.

The beast ignored the intense physiological changes and continued the pursuit. If he'd been a whale, the rapid ascent and onrushing nitrogen spewing into his bloodstream would have crippled him. But the 65 million years his kind spent prowling Diablo Caldera's 10,000-foot depths had served them well. Over the countless millennia, their bodies had adapted more and more to the crushing pressures associated with deep-water hunts. Unlike their Mesozoic ancestors, whose bones still possessed a spongy core vulnerable to sudden, rapid decompression, modern-day pliosaurs had skeletons like an Emperor Penguin – solid bones that were all but immune to mechanical barotrauma.

They were the ultimate deep-sea killers.

With a vicious power stroke that propelled him up into the dazzling daylight, the Ancient closed to within a few yards of the rapidly-fading swordfish. He could sense the chase was almost done and his enormous jaw muscles began to throb in anticipation.

A moment later, a loud, jarring noise struck the gigantean hunter like a physical blow. He snorted in alarm, his four flippers flaring out like the air brakes on a B-52 bomber, bringing him to a sudden and complete stop. He lay motionless in the water, less than two hundred feet from the surface. His sound senses were inert and his eyes, ears, and nostrils worked feverishly to analyze potential threats.

Three hundred yards away, a large ship passed overhead. It was emitting passive sonar only and didn't appear to be actively seeking him, but that could change at any time. Worse, however, there was a trio of noisy flying things passing overhead in a wedge-shaped formation.

They were close to the surface.

Close enough to detect his huge, shadowy form.

Gnashing his teeth in silent frustration as the swordfish made good its escape, the Ancient played dead, allowing his huge body to sink back into the darkness. Once he'd reached the 1,000-foot mark and was confident his movements could no longer be detected, he started forward.

His flippers resumed their rhythmic stroking and he began to cast about.

Unwilling to chance using his sound sight, he scented the surrounding seawater, drawing it through the scoop-shaped openings in his palate. His powerful nostrils were chemically-enhanced fish finders, and could track wounded prey across many miles of ocean.

A grumble of frustration escaped the old bull's scarred lips as he picked up the swordfish's fading scent. The broadbill was long gone. Still hungry, he shifted in the water column, his flippers undulating as he spun like a colossal sundial, scanning the sea one quadrant at a time.

Suddenly, the Ancient's triangular skull twisted sharply to one side, his humped body spinning to follow it. He hovered in place and continued to taste-test the surrounding seawater. Then his gleaming eyes narrowed. He had detected another possible food source. Unlike the lightning-fast *Xiphias*, this one appeared to be injured and in distress – an easy kill.

The scent was faint. It came from the surface and far off, near the termination of the Cayman Trench and approaching the Windward Passage, between the islands of Cuba and Haiti. The old bull knew the region well. The water was warmer and shallower, but still close to 6,000 feet deep. There was plenty of room for him to maneuver and numerous places to hide if the need arose. He would come in from the deep and survey his target from below, before moving up to snatch it.

Accelerating to his top cruising speed, the Ancient moved rapidly along – a monstrous, dark-hued hunchback, filled with insatiable hunger. At his current speed, he would reach his target long before the great burning eye reached its highest point in the sky.

He would finally find the sustenance he needed. And woe to any creature that came between him and his kill.

TWENTY-ONE

"So, Ward, I take it you were satisfied with our little demonstration?" Eric Grayson offered. The tapping sounds his Barker Blacks made were easily overpowered by the clopping of Admiral Callahan's size-thirteen Oxfords as the two men walked side by side across Tartarus's stone-gray amphitheater floor. They were at the far end of the cavernous underground stadium, moving along the base of the towering PBI wall that made up the aquarium's curved, 100-foot high, see-through window.

"Are you kidding me?" Callahan spouted. He glanced over his shoulder at the black MarshCat ATV that sat idling, forty yards away. In it, his aide and Security Chief Dwyer quietly conversed. "After seeing that ballsy girl come out of your juggernaut's mouth in one piece? Shit, sign me the fuck up!"

Grayson sighed and continued several paces more, stopping finally after they'd passed one of the massive steel buttresses that curved up from the rocky floor like a colossal tendril, its riveted length reinforcing the twenty-foot-thick thermoplastic barrier. "So, we should anticipate receiving future orders from you?"

"Hell, yeah." Callahan paused abruptly, his brow furrows contracting. "Hey, wait a minute . . . do my current purchases come equipped with those advanced control units?"

"Of course. Just like you saw."

"Sweet!" Callahan rubbed his thick hands together like a child surveying a treasure trove of toys on Christmas morning. "What about the older models, the ones we've already got in the field? Can they be upgraded?"

"Absolutely," Grayson said with an easy smile. "But keep in mind, each one will have to be brought in and receive a full overhaul – implant upgrading, synaptic reconditioning, the works. It's not going to be cheap. In fact, I'm afraid the final cost will be almost as much as a new purchase. Is that an issue for you, budget-wise?"

Callahan scoffed. "No worries. When it comes to guarding our sovereign waters, Uncle Sam's got deep pockets."

Both men stopped talking as *Tiamat*'s shadow suddenly passed over them. With a silence reminiscent of the inside of a tomb, the scaly behemoth swam slowly past, ignoring them. She was on their level and less than two hundred feet away, yet Callahan still had to take five steps back to take all of her in. His jaw dropped and he whistled, low and long.

"Mother of God, she is a *beast*! How old is she, a hundred? Two?"

Grayson pulled a tablet from his lab coat and combined checking *Einstein*'s feeding schedule, running a remote reactor scan, and inspecting GDT's real-time stock positions as he responded. "She's a Gen-1, one of the hatchlings from the initial clutch produced by the Paradise Cove cow. That makes her around thirty years old."

Callahan shook his head in bewilderment. "B-but, why is she so big? She must be a hundred feet long, easy."

"Per our last bio-scan, she's 119.8 feet exactly, and weighs just over 445 tons," Grayson corrected, his eyes still on his screen. He smiled.

Excellent, the market's down. Just wait until news of the new Navy contracts leaks . . .

"Holy shit!" Callahan sputtered. "But how come she's so ginormous?"

"I detest that bastardized word," Grayson said. "And to answer your question, Cope's Rule postulates that life forms increase in size over the course of their evolutionary history. However, I'm afraid *Tiamat* is too large to be just a single step up on the evolutionary ladder. That makes her a bona fide mutation – a genetic anomaly that caused normal growth inhibitors to be bypassed, resulting in an animal of unheard of size."

"She's a mutie, eh? Like in the comic books and stuff?"

Grayson fought down the upchuck of disdain that sought to spew from his mouth. "Not exactly."

"So what made her get so huge?" Callahan persisted. "I mean, *look* at her!"

"The prevailing theory is she's the byproduct of a normally dormant gene – some sort of evolutionary response triggered by environmental pressure."

"In layman's terms," Callahan said. He tugged at his medal-laden uniform's lapels for emphasis.

"Of course." Grayson nodded. "In simple terms, it's the law of supply and demand. Our queen was designed to prey on something – something too large for a normal-size pliosaur to take down. That would be the supply." He gestured up at *Tiamat* as she arced gracefully past. "And, *voila*. There you have the demand."

"So she's bigger. Is that it?"

"She possesses a few other peculiarities. I'm sure you've noticed her eyes, and then there's her skin color. We've had *Imperators* ranging from midnight blue to battleship gray." He turned sideways and gave the gigantean beast an admiring smile as she circled in the distance, a lethal shadow, constantly on the move. "But we've never had one the color of polished obsidian. Not until we captured her, that is."

"How long has she been here?"

"Almost ten years." Grayson's eyes scoured the reactor readings on his tablet before glancing back up. "And before you ask, yes, she was smaller then. Around ninety feet. Of course, even then we knew she was quite the prize."

"She is indeed," Callahan breathed. He moved to the thick polycarbonate barrier and wiped away some of the condensation with his palms. "She's obviously bigger than the others. Hell, she makes even *Goliath*, whom I was told is also a Gen-1, look like a midget. Is she smarter than the rest, too?"

"Oh, yes . . ."

"Really? How much smarter?"

Grayson finished his system checks and stashed his tablet. "According to our research, in terms of brainpower the average *Kronosaurus imperator* is about as intelligent as an elephant. They're no slouches. They're emotional creatures and they're also capable of rudimentary problem solving. And, like Proboscideans, they have phenomenal memories. You'd do well to remember that."

"Yeah, yeah, yeah." Callahan pointed a thumb at the tank wall. "What about this bitch?"

"That 'bitch,' as you put it, is killer whale smart," Grayson said. As he regarded the admiral, he couldn't help but wonder if Annapolis offered a formal class on tactless buffoonery. "She's crafty, calculating, and treacherous, too. So be careful. Implant or no, don't ever turn your back on her. She'll kill you if she gets the chance."

Callahan licked his lips and smiled. "Tell me, Eric. Are there any more of these giant mutie bitches out there?"

"Why?"

"Because I want one."

Grayson's frown flatlined as the radio in his pocket squawked. He didn't bother hiding his annoyance as he reached for it. "This is Dr. Grayson, go."

"Security Chief Dwyer, sir. I'm sorry to interrupt."

Grayson turned and gave his distant employee a quizzical look before nodding and speaking back into the unit. "Yes, Mr. Dwyer. Go ahead."

"You asked if was possible to accelerate the queen's morning feeding. I was just informed that we have a viable meal loaded and ready. That is, if you'd still like to proceed."

"By all means, Mr. Dwyer. Please do."

"Roger that. Thank you, sir."

Grayson pocketed the slim walkie talkie and gave Callahan a grin. "Well, Ward. It appears you're in for a treat."

"Breakfast time at the zoo?"

"Indeed."

Callahan stroked his salt-and-pepper mustache as he glanced up, scanning the domed ceiling, twenty stories overhead. "Hmm. I don't see any of that conveyor system you've got going on in the dock area. How do you feed her?"

Grayson indicated the nearest set of stairs, leading up alongside the amphitheater's tiered seating. With the stocky navy man at his six, he led the way up to the halfway point. A moment later, there was an earthy groan and a dull vibration that could be felt in the soles of their feet. *Tiamat* sprang to life immediately. Accelerating, her giant body curved back and away, then headed straight for the rear bulwark of the stadium's thousand-foot pool, not far from where the Celazole barrier emerged from a vertical section of the island's granite core.

Grayson drew Callahan's attention to a thirty-foot section of wall, immediately adjacent to the pool and ten feet above it, which began to grind noisily open. In the distance, the pliosaur queen rose soundlessly from the depths. Easing her ascent, she stopped fifty feet back from the lightless opening and remained there, fifteen feet below the surface of the water, her shimmering eyes alert and unblinking.

Callahan was busy squinting and shielding his own optics, trying hard to see into the lightless interior of the distant chamber. His nose crinkled as a pungent odor escaped its confines and enveloped them. There was a sudden, boisterous grunt, like a bull's lowing mixed with a snort from a primeval pig, and a bulbous, whiskered snout emerged from the darkness.

The admiral gaped. "What is that . . . a hippo?"

Grayson nodded. "A *Hippopotamus amphibius*, to be precise. Over six thousand pounds of him." He leaned closer and intoned, "For some reason, she prefers warm, mammalian meat."

Callahan watched, transfixed, as the fourteen-foot bull hippopotamus gazed pensively down at the saltwater lake that lay less than a body length beneath his columnar legs. His beady eyes blinked and his impressive nostrils flared as he scented the air. Suddenly, the big water horse bared his tusks and uttered a braying bellow of alarm, before fleeing back inside the confines of the thirty-foot compartment.

He found no refuge there. Inside, the chamber's far wall began to slide forward on well-lubricated tracks, pushing the hapless herbivore inch by inch toward the edge, and the horror that waited below like some monstrous spider in its web.

There was a plaintive wail, punctuated by a tremendous splash, as the three-ton bull tumbled sideways over the concrete wall and crashed into the seawater below. On impact, the hippopotamus went completely under, his blubbery body suspended like a plump sausage, floating in a soup pot. His eyes widened as he spotted the giant pliosaur not thirty feet away, grinning at him. Surfacing with a gurgled bellow, the terrified creature swam for his life.

Tiamat wasted no time. Moving smoothly forward, her twenty-four-foot jaws flew apart. Like a bass inhaling a sunfish, she sucked one hundred tons of water into her enormous gullet, along with the writhing hippopotamus.

Rather than swallowing her victim whole, however, as she was quite capable of doing, the giant predator deliberately closed her jaws, catching the unfortunate ungulate in mid-torso. Callahan's jaw descended as he saw the hysterical mammal's tusked head and forequarters protruding from between black-scaled lips. The bull's burbled shriek of agony echoed across the amphitheater, as the *Kronosaurus imperator* queen's sword-like teeth plunged into his body like forks penetrating meat loaf. There was a wet crunch and the front half of the dying hippo twirled away from the pliosaur's mouth like a carrot top, spewing blood and intestines as it spun end over end.

"She did that on purpose," Grayson informed him, watching as the mammoth predator's wedge-shaped snout turned sideways and she casually snapped up the hippo's other half. "She seems to enjoy biting into her prey, as opposed to simply engulfing it."

"Impressive," Callahan replied. He watched with undisguised fascination as *Tiamat* looked around, then spun on her tail and retreated back into the shadows to digest her meal. "So how does her bite force compare to the rest?"

"We haven't been able to accurately rate it," Grayson said. "She destroyed our previous *Fenris* system, but the preliminary readings were off the charts. All I can tell you is, substantially higher."

Callahan shook his head in wonderment as billowing clouds of hippo blood dispersed into the surrounding water. "I gotta tell you, Eric; your pliosaurs are impressive. I used to think they were just giant crocodiles with flippers, but that jaw power? It blows a shark bite out of the water. How do they do it?"

"Well, for starters, the mandibular symphysis--"

"Fuck. English, *please* . . ."

Grayson chafed inwardly. 'Dumbing things down' for military types was tedious work. "Very well, Ward . . . sharks actually generate relatively weak bite forces. We've tested seven-foot tiger sharks and, on the average, they packed only about thirty pounds of actual pressure."

"Wow, that's kinda wimpy."

"It's the jawbones. They're made of soft cartilage. Sharks have a dangerous bite because of their needle-sharp teeth," Grayson said with a shrug. "Think about it. If I embedded a bunch of razor blades in a foot-long hunk of two-by-four and dropped it on your thigh with a thirty-pound weight on top, what would happen?"

"I'd be cut?"

"Exactly," Grayson chuckled. "Back in the day, crocodiles were rated as having the world's most powerful bite – and they are impressive. If you take a great white shark, for example, and match it against a saltwater crocodile of similar mass, the saltie packs four times the punch. Literally."

"Holy shit."

"A pliosaur's jaw structure is similar to a croc's," Grayson continued. "Except the enlarged temporal . . . the *jaw muscles* . . . are even bigger and the teeth in those jaws aren't intended for gripping and holding, as they are in crocodilians. They're designed for cutting."

"Like a sword," Callahan offered.

"More like giant shears," Grayson said. "The teeth interlock and have sharp edges that slide against one another as they close. On top of that, the . . . ends of the jaw bones are solid, fused masses, as thick and as strong as steel girders. Instead of gripping prey, with the intention of doing a death roll and tearing a chunk out, when a *Kronosaurus* slams its jaws shut it--"

"Chops the victim in half?"

"Pretty much. And, as you witnessed, if the prey item struggles it makes the pliosaur's job even easier. Flailing actually helps those armor-piercing fangs cut deeper."

Callahan studied the vast aquarium's gloomy depths, focusing on the section where the giant predator had vanished. His lips and eyes formed tight lines as he blew out a breath. Then he turned back and blurted out, "I want her."

Grayson cocked an eyebrow at the borderline lustful tone. "Excuse me?"

"Her majesty, the queen bitch, *Tiamat* . . . whatever the fuck you want to call her. I *want* her."

"For what? To be one of your task force's guard dogs? I don't think so."

"That *thing*, running point for the fleet?" Callahan snorted derisively. "Fuck no. That would be a waste of talent. Oh, no, my friend. She's going to be my personal submarine destroyer. She'll stave in boomer pressure hulls like they're made of tin foil!" He clapped his hands together loudly. "Man, the Russians are going to shit bricks!" Ignoring the dubious look Grayson was giving him, he rambled aloud. "Come to think of it, they've lost quite a few subs over the years to so-called 'accidents.' I wonder if--"

"*Tiamat* is not for sale, admiral," Grayson announced.

"Ha! Everything's for sale."

"Not *this* thing." The CEO shook his head. "I'm sorry. But she's one of a kind and I can't afford to lose her."

"I see." Callahan flushed and his face scrunched up like he'd just chewed a lemon. "Well, can you make more of her? You know, like some sort of in-house breeding program?"

"I'm afraid not." Grayson clasped his hands behind him and began to descend, with Callahan hustling after him. "*Kronosaurus* cows are like any other female; they accept their mates based on worthiness and genetic desirability, and we don't have a bull anywhere near the size and strength it would take to tickle that lady's 'fancy.'"

Callahan hit the ground floor and paused to catch his breath, resting one hand against the tank's impenetrable PBI wall and wiping his brow with the back of the other. "Have you *tried*?"

Grayson sighed. "Actually, we have. Last year, we captured a Gen-1 bull, assumedly one of *Tiamat*'s brood mates. He was a powerful brute, built like a tank and every bit as huge as *Polyphemus*. We assigned him the code name *Hyperion*."

"And you tried mating them?"

"Not at first. Initially, we presented *Hyperion* to two of our other captive cows and they were both receptive," Grayson said. "He was quite the 'stud,' as they say. After some deliberation, we decided to take a chance and gave him a shot at his sister."

"His *sister*?" Callahan made a face. "Oh, yeah . . . so, what happened?"

Grayson hesitated as *Tiamat* suddenly reemerged. Her flippers spanned a full eighty feet from tip to tip as she cruised straight toward the two men, stopping just a hundred feet away. Then, with eerie silence, she curved sinuously sideways and continued past. Her jaws were slightly parted, revealing ragged hunks of hippo blubber clinging to her teeth, and her eyes blazed like sunlit amber.

"Let's just say we didn't have to bother feeding her for the next few days."

Callahan nearly choked. "Holy shit, she *ate* his ass! Are you serious?"

"Incredibly. The resultant mess clogged the impellers on three of her enclosure's filtration units. It was a very expensive lesson."

"Well, what about artificial insemination? Would that work?"

"No." Grayson suddenly felt very tired. "We haven't been able to isolate the how or why, but without the adrenal stimulation the female receives from bonding with a prospective mate, cellular mitosis doesn't take place. The cells of the fertilized egg don't begin to multiply and, for whatever reason, we haven't been able to induce it. It's like she has to *want* to get pregnant."

Callahan ground his heels in frustration. "Shit. Have you considered--"

"Cloning isn't an option, either," Grayson interrupted. "Her reproductive system is different than that of her sisters. It's just . . . it's complicated."

"Okay, I get it. So, is there any chance you can find a mate for her?"

Grayson smiled. "We're working on it. We--" His lips stopped moving as his eyes fell on Garm Braddock. Now *that* was interesting. Amara's oldest was the last person he expected to see in the amphitheater. The big submariner was far away, several hundred feet downwind, but there was no mistaking that face and frame. He was standing by the tank walls. And he appeared to be sizing up *Tiamat*.

Grayson turned toward the distant ATV and signaled his driver. In seconds, Dwyer had the six-wheeled MarshCat in gear and was cruising smoothly toward them, with Callahan's aide, Gibbons, sitting rigidly upright in the front passenger seat. The big marine's face paled as he eyed the swirling water beside them.

"Mr. Dwyer," Grayson began. "If you'd be so kind as to keep Admiral Callahan company, I'd like to speak with one of my sub commanders."

"Uh, yes, sir," Dwyer responded, throwing the MarshCat in park.

"Oh, shit. It's Gate." Callahan's eyes lit up as he espied the former heavyweight contender in the distance. "Hold up, Eric. I'll join you."

Grayson held up a hand. "Actually, I need to talk to this particular employee in private. It's a . . . corporate thing. I'm sure you can understand."

Callahan opened his mouth as if to protest, but caught the older man's expression and changed his mind. "Okay, sure. I'll be right here."

"Excellent." Grayson turned and began the long march to Garm. His knees ached from being subjected to too much concrete, but he preferred to converse with Derek's enigmatic twin alone and on equal footing.

He'd traveled barely a third of the distance, however, when he heard heavy footfalls thudding up behind him. He sighed and drawled over one shoulder. "Yes, Mr. Dwyer?"

"I'm sorry, sir, but I just got a call," Security Chief Angus Dwyer blurted out. He took a moment to catch his breath. At six-foot-five, with his reddish-brown hair, rangy arms, and flat face, the brutish ex-convict bore more than a passing resemblance to an enormous orangutan. "It's kinda pressing, and definitely for your ears only."

Grayson turned and looked up at him. "I'm listening."

"We got McHale, that missing guard; he never left Tartarus. He was hiding out in the lower levels all this time, by the pens."

Grayson's eyebrows rose involuntarily. "What about his tracker?"

"He took it out himself and trashed it," Dwyer said, then added quietly. "Rather messily, I might add."

"I see." The CEO ruminated on the unexpected development. "That's rather depressing. McHale showed promise. I didn't expect him to turn on us. Was he taking his medication?"

"I'm not sure, but he definitely lost it when they found him, sir. Resisted the guards, injured one. They had to juice him twice to put him down."

Grayson's lips tightened and he tapped his fingertips contemplatively together. "Well, we can't have that. Alert the appropriate parties and have him shipped out immediately." He lowered his voice. "And Mr. Dwyer . . ."

"Sir?"

"Not a word of this to the others. It would be bad for morale."

"Of course, sir," Dwyer said. As Grayson turned to go, he reached out a catcher's mitt of a hand to touch the elderly scientist on the shoulder, but then pulled back.

Grayson pegged him with a look. "Is there something else?"

Dwyer eyes shifted up and over his employer's head, finding and focusing on Garm Braddock. "Actually, yes there is, sir. Do you think it's wise, you . . ."

"I *what*, Mr. Dwyer?"

"You talking to him all alone? I mean, Braddock's kinda unpredictable. And given the situation . . ."

"Oh, rubbish," Grayson said, laughing quietly. "I'll be perfectly safe. Captain Braddock is a man of honor and integrity."

"Those are the most dangerous kind," Dwyer said, his bloodshot eyes still targeting the distant sub commander.

"Are you sure you're not just jealous, Mr. Dwyer?"

"W-what?" Dwyer's head shake was so violent it was near-injurious. "Of course not, sir. I just think he's bad news and is gonna cause problems. He's a *rōnin*, after all."

"A masterless samurai?" Grayson was intrigued. "I see you've been reading, Mr. Dwyer. That's very good. I'm impressed."

Dwyer started to respond, but found himself stifled by a wagging finger. "Garm Braddock is many things, my boy. But a rogue, he is not." He folded his arms across his chest, studying the subject of their discussion from afar. "I like to think of him as more of a . . . Messianic warrior of sorts. He has an aggressive, crusading spirit. And, as such, he has an important part to play in things to come."

"Say, *what*? Wait . . . are you considering that hybrid bastard for the program?" Dwyer asked, patently affronted. He growled angrily. "You don't need him, you've got me!"

"Lower your voice and stow that, mister," Grayson warned. Despite the security chief's size and reputation, the older man moved threateningly close. "Be careful. I am not some *child* that you would play with, Angus Dwyer. In fact, there *are* no children in Tartarus." His dark eyes were jacketed hollow points, primed and ready to fire. "Look around you and remember where you are, and how you came to be here."

The cold fire behind Dwyer's eyes dimmed and he turned deathly pale.

"*I* made you what you are." Grayson hissed. "I pulled you from that cesspool and gave you life and purpose. Do I make myself clear?"

Dwyer stared unsurely down at his size-sixteen boots. His nodded response was more a shudder than anything else.

"Good," Grayson said, calm and congenial once more. "Now, if you don't mind, I'd like to have a conversation with another one of my people. Is that okay with you?"

Dwyer bowed his head like a scolded first-grader and turned to leave.

"Oh, Mr. Dwyer," Grayson said, yanking back on the leash. "On your way, please get on the radio and have the McHale situation dealt with." He fixed him with a stern-but-appraising look. "I'm assuming I can still count on you."

"Of course," Dwyer professed, standing so straight and rigid he could've been a member of the Queen's Guard. "I'd give my life for you, sir. You know that."

Grayson gave him an indulgent smile. "Oh, well, there's no need for that." He turned his back and continued walking.

At least, not yet . . .

Ugly . . . murderous . . . bitch!

Garm Braddock may have appeared calm as he studied *Tiamat* through the amphitheater's reinforced walls, but his jaw ached and his molars were on the verge of cracking. His chest still stung from where Nat's nails had punctured his skin, but the pain of her marking her territory was nothing compared to the heartache that throbbed below like an open wound. He sighed, focused on keeping it together. Then, as his peripherals scoped out Eric Grayson approaching from his three, a bubble of annoyance formed inside his head. It was a big, red cherry, topping a sundae of suppressed rage.

"'For that the superman may not lack his dragon, the super dragon that is worthy of him,'" the smiling CEO quoted as he drew near. He stood alongside the tall submariner, focusing his gaze on the pliosaur queen as she slipped silently past.

Garm inhaled hard through his nostrils. The normal saltiness of the stadium's air was tinged with an unsavory blend of hippopotamus blood and pliosaur stench. "'How many things are now called the worst evils, which are only twelve feet wide and three months long?'" He said, then gave Grayson a look and added. "'But some day, greater dragons will come into the world.'"

"Ah, you know your Nietzsche, marvelous!" the older man quipped. He touched a deductive finger to his chin. "You must have aided Derek with his studies. Of course, that was years ago, yet you've retained a portion of it. Intriguing . . . You're an intelligent man, Garm Braddock. And to think, many regard you as little more than a washed-up prizefighter."

"We all have our crosses to bear."

"Indeed." Grayson regarded him with those dark, probing eyes of his. "You're a hard man to track down, commander."

"It's called a well-earned shore leave, sir," Garm remarked. "But it seems you found me, anyway. What can I do for you?"

Grayson's head swiveled to the side as *Tiamat* swam by. The 120-foot behemoth was closer this time. So close, that one of her pectoral fins made a low, squeaking sound as it grazed the smooth Celazole, like a giant's finger rubbing against a wet, pool-sized dinner plate.

"Magnificent, isn't she?"

"Not the word I'd use," Garm scoffed. "She's a monstrosity, an aberration of nature. She should be destroyed, not admired or studied."

Grayson half-bowed his head. "I empathize with you. You know, come to think of it, I've heard at least one person call *you* an 'aberration of nature.'"

"Not to my face."

Grayson wore a sphinxlike expression as he tried to read Garm. "You're not afraid of her?"

"No. But then, I'm not in the water."

"You know what I mean," Grayson said. "Don't pretend you're obtuse."

Garm grinned mirthlessly. "Who's pretending?"

"You know, I love you and Derek like sons. But the two of you are astonishingly different."

"Yes. I'm taller and better-looking."

Grayson shook his head. "I'm talking about fortitude. Derek does his job, even gets close enough to touch *Tiamat* if he must, but he's terrified of her. You can tell."

Garm looked at him. "Dirk was always the smarter one."

"You've both got great gifts," the older man persisted. "His are mental, yours are physical and spiritual. You've also both got more money now than a man could spend in a hundred lifetimes. Yet *you* insist on commanding an ORION and risking your life, day in, day out. Why, for some misguided vendetta?"

"Why?" Garm had to admit, getting under the normally resolute CEO's skin was giving him a perverse sense of satisfaction. He decided to stoke the fire and invoked his best Clint Eastwood accent. "'A man's got to know his limitations.'"

"But why don't you settle down? Maybe pass on some of those great genetics?" an exasperated Grayson persisted.

Garm's head whipped back toward the amphitheater pool wall. *Tiamat* had crept quietly to within ten yards of the glass – as close as her programming allowed – and was now staring. Not at Grayson. But at him.

Like one of the monstrous Titans from Greek mythology, gazing down upon its worshippers, the *Kronosaurus imperator* queen's maleficent gaze targeted Garm. Her orange eyes were like embers the size of serving-trays. He could feel them penetrating all the way to the back of his skull as an inter-species stare-down ensued.

Despite the ridiculous size difference, Garm glared coolly back up at her. He'd never backed away from a confrontation in his life and he wasn't about to start now – especially with her.

Grayson adjusted his restrictive lab coat and folded his arms knowingly across his chest. "She knows what you want," he said. "As you know what *she* wants. And that's the problem."

Garm broke off from the battle of wills and turned impatiently to his employer. "With all due respect, can I get the Cliff's Notes version of this?"

He studied Grayson's face as the CEO absorbed the blatant insubordination. If he'd pulled a stunt like that in public, there would have been consequences. But here, man-to-man, they were equals. It would've been self-emasculating for the old man to pull rank.

He didn't. Instead, Grayson nodded. Then he went on the offensive.

"Very well, captain," he began. "Let me be direct. I want *Typhon*, and I want him alive."

"I'm quite aware of that, sir," Garm said. "What's your point?"

"My *point*, my dear boy, is that if we're successful in capturing him, he's destined to mate with that lovely lady staring over your shoulder."

Garm didn't have to turn around to know *Tiamat* was still watching him. He could feel her gaze, just as he could her sonar; a damp electric blanket draped across his shoulders. "And?"

"Let's not mince words," Grayson said, looking up at him. The overheads glinted off his silver hair as he got in the younger man's grille. "She killed your mother. Killed her and ate her. Right here, in this room."

Garm's muscles tensed, and he felt his inner beast slam violently against the bars of its cage. In his mind, he saw himself knocking Grayson's head off his shoulders with one blow. "Thanks for the refresher course," he said robotically. "Again, what's your point?"

"I need *Typhon* quite badly to keep this company moving in the right direction," Grayson said. "And I want your personal assurance that you won't let your feelings get in the way of taking him alive."

Garm frowned. "If you're asking me to swear on a stack of bibles that I won't destroy your precious behemoth, I can't." He held up a hand as he saw an indignant look coalesce on the old man's face. "Anything could happen. *Typhon* is unpredictable, the most dangerous adversary we've ever faced."

"You're not a god-fearing man, are you, son?"

"I'm not your son."

"No, you're not. And you didn't answer my question."

Garm cocked his head confusedly. "I don't see what religion has to do with this discussion."

Grayson folded his hands before him in a prayer-like pose. "You referenced bibles and I find that curious, given your well known . . . proclivities."

"A figure of speech. I'm sure you've been in court before."

"Yes, I have. So, then, it's safe to say you're not a believer."

A 'believer?' Garm glanced over his shoulder up at *Tiamat*. He studied her massive jaws, lined with sharp-ridged fangs that hung down like a bevy of icicles. Those same jaws had closed on his poor mother and, despite her screams, no one, mortal or divine, had come to help her. He felt a searing cold in the pit of his stomach, like he'd swallowed a bowlful of frozen razor blades, and he loomed over the old man. "I don't believe in your god. And he sure as hell doesn't believe in me."

"I see." Grayson gazed fearlessly up at him. "Then how am I to trust you – a man with no faith?"

"Oh, but I have faith in plenty of things: duty, honor, integrity . . . even karma, at times. Although sometimes the 'K' needs a little help," he said, winking.

"So, your sense of duty will see things through."

Garm shrugged. "Like I said, anything could happen. I can't make any guarantees. But barring being stuck in a kill-or-be-killed situation, I'll do my best to bring *Typhon* back in one piece."

Grayson contemplated his response, then nodded and extended his hand. "I guess that will have to do, captain."

As they shook, Garm grinned. "Oh, cheer up. Have I let you down yet?"

"Not yet."

He watched as Grayson turned on his heel and began hoofing it back toward his ride. A minute later, he saw him mutter something into his radio and the distant ATV sped forward to meet him halfway.

Garm waited until he was out of earshot. Then he turned back, only to find *Tiamat* still peering down at him with unconcealed interest. His eyes became hardened slits and he bared his teeth in a predatory smile.

"Guess what, bitch?" he said quietly. "It's your lucky day. You're going to have a lover soon, and once you're nice and knocked up, you'll be released back into the wild. Once that happens, Grayson can go fuck himself, because *Gryphon* and I are going to come find you. It doesn't matter where you are or where you go; I'm going to hunt you down like Ahab from Hell, and I'm going to blow that cold, black-blooded heart of yours clean out the other side of your misshapen chest."

A hint of movement in the distance caught his eye and he looked back the way he'd come. He spotted Sam Mot in the distance, sitting forlornly in his cybernetic wheelchair by the stadium exit, and obviously waiting for him.

Garm waved to Sam and started toward him. As he turned away from the pool, he could feel *Tiamat*'s hateful stare still boring into his back. He glanced back over his shoulder at the giant predator, scoffed and flipped her the bird. Then he loped soundlessly toward his old friend.

TWENTY-TWO

Dirk sat back at his desk, contentedly sipping what was a damn good cup of Joe. Despite all the risks and rigors of the demo, it had ended up being a pleasant morning. He and Stacy had enjoyed a long, hot shower together, followed by a late breakfast and a couple of well-deserved shots of Wild Turkey. Once the powerful bourbon had kicked in and helped calm her nerves, she'd headed back to her quarters to prep for the post-demo meeting, while he took advantage of the brief respite to catch up on the spin of things outside of Tartarus.

He needed to, if for no other reason than to remind himself that there was some semblance of life and normalcy outside the hellish place he called home.

Dirk put the self-heating mug carefully back on its stand, his free hand toying with the tiny flash drive that contained his mother's final report. Actually, he thought glumly, other than the security video of her death, it was probably the last footage of her, period.

He contemplated the portable drive and frowned. The memory of how he'd found the report on her desktop materialized in his mind like a popup. It seemed strange for her to conceal it like that – under a file name that would attract only his or his brother's attention. Outside immediate family, no one would know Garm never took fencing lessons.

Dirk exhaled heavily and turned his attention back to his monitor. On it, the networks were reporting on the conflict currently taking place in Cuba. It was frontline news; what had started as minor skirmishes had escalated in size and intensity over the last twenty-four hours. Now, the place was a veritable warzone, with fighting taking place on a scale the tiny island nation hadn't witnessed since the 1950's.

As he took in footage of burning bodies, strewn around the smoldering ruin of what was once a Russian tank, Dirk shook his head. Rebels, freedom fighters, revolutionaries, *counter*-revolutionaries . . . whatever they called themselves, in the end it was all horseshit. Like most wars, it was about money and power, with those that had it taking it from those that didn't and dispensing it as they saw fit.

He reached for his coffee, watching as an entire platoon of guerillas got caught in the open and were mowed down by automatic weapons fire. He pursed his lips and blew a gentle breath across the surface of the hot beverage, watching the tiny ripples traveling across the confines of the cup. Perhaps the fledgling regime that managed to seduce a portion of the Cuban navy and gained a foothold in Havana would be more amenable than the current establishment toward fulfilling his parents' dream – allowing a team of scientists to explore and document Diablo Caldera, the volcanic prison that had housed pliosaurs and an assortment of other prehistoric life forms since the Cretaceous.

Dirk licked his lips and put his coffee back. With a dexterity bordering on the mystical, his hands drifted across his keyboard. As a member of Grayson Defense Technology's Board of Directors, he'd invoked his authority and utilized GDT's vast network of paramilitary contacts to reach out to the leader of the resource-poor Cuban opposition. His hope was that a substantial gift of dollars would lubricate the wheels of progress. Or at least leave the door propped open for future discussions.

Ten million dollars was a tidy sum. He'd personally put up the money, partially because he had little faith in the outcome, but mainly because he didn't want to bother Eric Grayson with his plan. His aging mentor was critical of such things and would have regarded it as a bad investment. *'Save your money, Derek. Let's allow the political process to run its course,'* he'd say with that paternal, yet frustratingly condescending, tone of his.

He clicked open his email and sighed. No reply yet.

Oh well. It was only money.

Dirk jumped as his doorbell buzzed loudly. A glance at the monitor showed it was Grayson. It figured. He stashed the flash drive in his lab coat pocket and hopped to his feet.

"Enter," he said, causing the door to whoosh open.

"Ah, there you are, my boy," the silver-haired scientist said with a grin.

Dirk indicated the three news channels, all showing highlights of the Cuban conflict. "Have you been keeping tabs on this?"

"Of course," his mentor said. "We've been selling to both sides."

"We have?"

"Naturally. No worries, all outdated stuff. And, yes, I know what you're thinking. This could be the break we've been waiting for. And yes, once the dust settles, we'll certainly negotiate with the battle-weary victor. Lord knows they'll need food, medicine, weapons--"

"Money . . ."

"Absolutely." Grayson glanced around Dirk's impeccably clean quarters, then lowered his voice. "We're alone, correct?"

Dirk nodded, hating that his and Stacy's comings and goings were so transparent.

"Excellent." Grayson gave his protégé an appraising look. "First off, that was some stunt you and Dr. Daniels pulled off. Why didn't you warn me you were planning to run a resurrection gambit like that?"

Dirk cleared his throat. "To be honest, sir, we only came up with it the day before. We did a dry run, literally, but we weren't sure if we were going to go through with it until the last minute. I was concerned about Stacy, as you were. Plus, we wanted it to be a surprise. You know, for added shock value."

"A surprise?" the old man chortled. "Are you kidding? You made half the crowd piss themselves, guards included, and I'm fairly certain I caught the scent of fecal matter coming from Callahan's direction!"

"I'm surprised you could tell," Dirk replied. He cursed silently, regretting the inordinate slip. He recovered quickly. "So, it was a success?"

Grayson snorted amusedly. "Let's just say everyone's holiday bonus will be very plump this year. *Tiamat* is going to be very good for us, son. In fact, all the money we invested--"

Th-th-th-thud.

"Speak of the devil," Dirk remarked and meant it.

Grayson stared at the thick aluminum slab that formed the far wall of his charge's living quarters. "Is she still doing that?"

"First time today. But then, she was just ordered back into her paddock."

"Open it," Grayson ordered.

"Uh . . . yes, sir," Dirk replied. Rather than walking to the wall switch, he said aloud, "Raise shield."

There was a loud hum as the painted wall that served as a privacy guard slid smoothly upward. Directly outside, an immense swirl of bubbles obscured visibility as *Tiamat's* monstrous body moved past. The obsidian-colored beast continued on, then turned on her tail and swept back, her glittering, flame-like eyes peering into Dirk's quarters. She backstroked, hovering less than a head's-length from the hard PBI barrier. Holding her position, she studied the two men through her depthless black pupils, like some monstrous crocodile eyeing a pair of baby antelope.

"Fascinating." Grayson's silvery eyebrows lowered as he approached the clear polycarbonate. "It's like she's deliberately harassing you."

"Oh, it's deliberate, alright," Dirk said. "Watch this."

He reached over and tapped the shield button. The *Kronosaurus* queen uttered a thunderous grunt of displeasure and changed position the moment the wall began to lower. Dirk signaled for Grayson to join him by his desk. "Check it out."

On the bottom left corner of the monitor, a window popped open showing the paddock directly outside. On it, *Tiamat's* giant muzzle was so close, all that was visible was her scaly lips and a fang or two. Then she twisted about, adjusting herself with flicks of her fins until one of her luminous eyes was glaring directly into the camera. On the monitor, her menacing orb filled the window, like the "Eye of Sauron" from "*Lord of the Rings.*"

"Is that on auto-feed?" Grayson asked.

"Yes," Dirk said. "When she sees the camera's red LED come on, she glares directly into the lens. And when I say glare, I mean *glare.*"

"Turn it off."

Dirk touched a key, killing the connection and closing the window on his monitor. Outside, there was a low rumble, followed by a sudden swirling sound. Then silence.

"Intriguing," Grayson said. "She's learned to connect the LED with your being able to see her, even with the shield down. Perhaps due to the color she associates it with the opened eyes of one of her kind."

"My thoughts exactly," Dirk agreed. "She can't see me anymore and her behavioral inhibitors won't allow her to keep bumping the wall 'by accident,' so she heads straight to the camera to continue her little game of 'cat and mouse.'"

"That must be very disturbing for you. What happens at night, when you're trying to sleep?"

"She used to keep me up, pulling her stunts," Dirk advised, "until I went online and cut the size of her virtual paddock by two-thirds as punishment."

"Hmm, she learns fast," Grayson muttered. The crinkles around the corners of his eyes tightened as he stored this new information. Suddenly, his head snapped upright. "Oh, I almost forgot. We need to move the conference to 4 PM."

"How so?" Dirk asked. He'd have to move his meeting with Dr. Bane to after dinner. Or maybe make it a dinner meeting. She'd probably go for that. In between, maybe he could hit the gym and squeeze in a much-needed workout.

"Strictly between us, I'm having some issues with a few of my Last Chancers," Grayson admitted.

"What kind of issues?"

"You're already aware of the intermittent AWOL problem. Recently, Officer McHale disappeared. No word, nothing on the scope. He was just found, days later, hiding out in the lower levels."

"What about his tracker?"

"He chewed it out."

"Jesus," Dirk muttered. An exciting idea popped into his head, but he managed to ask, matter-of-factly, "Have you considered terminating the program and bringing in paid professionals instead?"

"Lord knows I have." Grayson paused, grimacing as he rolled out stiff shoulders. "But we've got a binding DOC contract that obligates us for another eighteen months. We'll just have to hang in there and see how it plays out."

Dirk nodded, disappointed he'd be stuck spending the next year-and-a-half surrounded by murderers, drug dealers, and rapists. Frankly, he preferred the company of their resident pliosaurs. Sure, sauropterygians were dangerous, but at least there was no dishonesty in them.

"By the way, although we don't have sonar signature confirmation, I think we've got a lead on *Typhon*," Grayson announced.

"What kind of lead?"

"You already know about the *Rorqual* – that big schooner that went down off the coast of Marathon, correct?"

Dirk nodded. "Yes, but other than that mysterious, partial SOS, we've got nothing to go on. No survivors, no--"

Grayson cut him off, "No witnesses, I know. Well, we just got a message relayed from a luxury yacht that claims to have been attacked less than five miles from there. It's a foreign vessel and a touchy situation. But it's well within our Economic Exclusion Zone. Which gives us every right to investigate."

"When you say a 'message,' you mean a distress call, right?"

"No, it was a text message from someone's cell – a guest on the yacht, apparently. No distress call was sent. And any radio transmissions from the Coast Guard or from us have gone unanswered."

Dirk pursed his lips. "That's odd. It could have been a practical joke, or a misidentification by some girl who had a few too many and thought she saw a sea monster."

Grayson's head bobbed once. "Could be. According to our satellites, the ship appears intact, and we've got no echolocation readings in the area, not even whales. But we know *Typhon*'s a cunning codger. He could be running silent, like before. So let's cross our fingers, because maybe, just maybe . . ."

"How do you want to proceed?"

"How far along are we with the repairs on *Antrodemus*?"

"If we cut a few corners, thirty-six hours."

Grayson drew in a lungful and let it out as a sigh. "I can't risk losing an ORION. The plan is to hold Dragunova's boat back until repairs are completed. I spoke to your brother a little while ago, and he's ready to start the hunt."

Dirk's head yanked back hard on his shoulders. "You're sending Garm out alone? I thought we agreed a tandem attack was in order?"

"Relax, it's just for reconnaissance," Grayson reassured. "If he gets target confirmation, the decision to engage is his. Hell, if he can just nail that SOB with a locator so we can track him once *Antrodemus* is functional, we'll be halfway there."

"I see," Dirk said. His hand lingered in his lab coat pocket, feeling the flash drive. He considered telling Grayson about it, but once again decided to hold off. "I have a question, sir."

"Of course, Derek."

"Assuming we find *Typhon* again, and if we capture him--"

Grayson raised a corrective finger. "Not if, my boy, when."

"Okay. *When* we capture him, and after he succeeds in impregnating *Tiamat*, you do realize we can't keep her here for the gestation process, correct?"

"Of course," the old man said, nodding. "We don't have the facilities for her to spawn properly. Probably not even for proper prenatal development."

"So, you're prepared to release her?" Dirk could feel his right eyebrow doing the dubious Spock thing.

Grayson walked over and hit the nearby shield button, his dark eyes following the smooth partition's edge as it retracted back up into the ceiling. "Release is hardly the word I'd use," he said. Two hundred yards away, *Tiamat* picked up the familiar sound of the barrier being raised and turned immediately back toward them.

"With our current implant technology, we can track the two of them anywhere in the world," he said, watching in apparent enthrallment as a 445-ton engine of destruction swam toward him, stopping less than twenty yards away. "We can give them free reign to do as they please – keeping them out of mischief, of course – and once she's produced her first clutch, we'll sweep in to gather up the offspring."

Dirk folded his toned arms across his chest. "And you're not at all worried about the possibility of losing your precious pet?"

"Losing her how?"

"Oh, I don't know. To the military or maybe to some other carnivore . . ."

"The military?" Grayson scoffed. "We *are* the military! And another carnivore?" He shook his head as he turned back around and gestured with widespread arms at the humungous titan lurking right outside the window. "Don't be ridiculous, Derek. You and I are the guardians of the most powerful predator on the planet. What could possibly challenge her?"

Thirty miles off the coast of the Dominican Republic, in the bowels of the Hispaniola basin, the gray-hued female prepared to feed. Like a giant bear trap, her ten-foot jaws yawned wide, her scarred lips peeling back to expose batteries of triangular teeth up to eleven inches in length. Her maxillae extended up and out, increasing her reach, and she powered her torpedo-shaped body forward with a flick of her two-story tail. There was a tremendous thump, reminiscent of a wrecking ball striking a concrete wall, as she rammed her maw into the dead humpback whale's side.

Although much of the cetacean's caloric-rich blubber and musculature had already been stripped away by smaller scavengers, the humpback bull's nutritious internal organs were still available, encased deep within its protective rib cage. And she would have them.

A sickening cracking sound split the water as she brought the full power of her jaws to bear. Powered by massive mandibular muscles that exerted a bite force exceeding forty tons, her finely-serrated teeth functioned like sharp-edged chisels, smashing clean through the whale's heavy ribs.

Shaking her thick-jowled fourteen-foot head from side to side, the ravenous behemoth wrenched a five-ton mouthful of rib chunks, stomach, and liver from the fleshy crater she'd excavated in the whale's flank. Ragged gobs of flesh and bone the size of a human head spewed forth from between her broad-based teeth as she gulped it down. She pushed greedily forward, past a viscous cloud of blood and tissue fragments, and carried on with her gruesome feast.

As she continued to savage the fifty-foot humpback's remains, the female was rewarded with a second mouthful, this time consisting of the cetacean's huge heart and lungs. Like a curtain of pile drivers coming down, her toothy jaws closed again and again, macerating the fibrous masses of tissue into pulp before they were summarily inhaled.

Pausing suddenly, she swung her blunt snout from side to side, surveying the surrounding waters. Age and experience had taught her to err on the side of caution, and her black, basketball-sized eyes rolled in their sockets as she scanned the deep for potential threats. Although her sense of smell was her greatest asset, her eyesight was equally keen. Two thousand feet down, the seas were shrouded in perpetual blackness. But her eyes were designed to master the abyss. Her retinas were backed by a layer of mirrored crystals that defocused light, reflecting it back and allowing her to better perceive objects. For her, complete darkness was as twilight for the giant mammals she fed upon.

The female saw nothing – nothing except the bright red light. Each time it flared, it registered in the corner of her eye; a tiny setting sun. She had no idea where it came from. It first appeared several weeks before, after a parasite affixed itself to the top of her right, foremost gill plate. Despite the initial sting as it penetrated her rough skin, it was hardly injurious. But it was annoying. Unfortunately, she couldn't reach it with her jaws, and after several failed attempts to dislodge it, she pushed it from her mind.

The dead marine reptile was another story.

Unlike other predators, which wisely gave way when she moved in to appropriate a carcass, the fifty-foot saurian had come at her like a demon. Fast and maneuverable, it dodged her powerful rushes, slashing at her flanks and belly with its crocodile-like jaws. Her body and fins bore the marks of its many teeth. Unable to inflict significant damage, however, the smaller predator eventually grew frustrated and tried for the kill. Sweeping in past her guard, it struck with phenomenal speed, burying its fangs in the thick skin of her throat and hung on.

The tactic proved to be its undoing.

Although its bite was surprisingly powerful, the saurian lacked sufficient size to inflict a fatal wound. The two combatants rolled this way and that, slashing and thrashing. Eventually, with a tremendous head shake, the female managed to close her powerful jaws on her undersized rival's neck and shoulder. A single, crushing bite was all it took. The decapitated pliosaur's body spun away like a leaf and sank into the void.

All that remained were its wedge-shaped jaws, clinging like a pitbull to her heavily muscled throat. Even in death, she could feel its sharp, conical fangs clamped down, the wound itching and burning.

Finally, the irritation caused by her weighty albatross became too much and the female began to shake. Thrashing her gigantic body from side to side, she whipped her gaping jaws up and down. Finally, centrifugal force did its job and her teeth closed on the severed neck. Biting down, she yanked her head savagely in the opposing direction, tearing the dead reptile's jaws free in a cloud of their combined blood.

Angered by the gaping rents the saurian's teeth left behind, the female lashed out. Engulfing its severed head in one bite, she brought her teeth together repeatedly until she'd reduced the armored skull to an unrecognizable mass. A moment later, her lips crinkled up and she spat the distasteful remains out. She watched dispassionately as it twirled end over end before sinking, ghostlike, into the darkness, a phantom head, searching for its body.

Still hungry, she surged forward and re-attacked the humpback's ravaged remains, gnashing through its thick vertebrae and devouring whatever soft tissues she could find. When she finished, she shoved the butchered remnants of the once-proud bull aside and moved on. Her senses stretched forth like a net, tasting and testing the waters far in advance, scanning for potential meals and rivals.

For the moment, there were none.

Her throat wounds began to throb and a feeling akin to cold fury welled up within her prehistoric breast. Between dwindling food sources and environmental changes, her species had been vastly reduced in number. If nothing changed, they would soon face extinction. Until then, however, they would remain monarchs of the sea, with few rivals. Their traditional adversaries, the sperm whales, had shrunk in size over the last two centuries, and no longer possessed the power to withstand them. On the other hand, the packs of pugnacious Orcas that roamed the coastlines of the world remained a threat. Fortunately, the wolves of the sea were shallow divers and easily avoided.

As evidenced by her recent battle, however, a new enemy had appeared on the horizon, in the form of a species of monstrous marine reptile. The scaly giants' sudden arrival was unprecedented and they were adversaries not to be taken lightly. She'd seen the first one decades earlier, watching with fear-filled eyes as it disemboweled her mother, moments after her birth. Even as a pup, she recognized her ancestral enemy. During the Cretaceous, pliosaurs and their ilk had all but annihilated her forebears, and all the while grew bigger and deadlier.

In the present, they were even worse. As their numbers exploded, they did more than just alter the food web; they shattered it. The whales, whose drifting remains were the primary source of sustenance for the adults of her genus, were nearly wiped out, with the survivors fleeing to colder climates. Her species fared no better. Territorial brutes that they were, many of the more dominant adults stood their ground, only to find themselves outmatched by their wily, cold-blooded foes. One by one, they were killed off.

Too small to even consider facing her primeval nemeses, the young female had followed the relocating whales all the way to the chilled waters of Antarctica. There, fortune smiled upon her and she found not only a wintry sanctuary, but food in abundance. The Norwegian, Russian, and Japanese whalers that hunted the region's big baleen whales unwittingly provided an unlimited buffet for her, and she grew rapidly in size and power. Eventually, she reached titanic proportions, dwarfing even the largest of her kind.

Now, nothing could challenge her. Not even the great sea dragons of old.

Two weeks prior, shortly after she'd whelped her last litter of pups, and right around the time the annoying parasite attached itself, the female experienced a sudden and irrepressible desire to return to the seas she'd forsaken. She succumbed to the strange urge and began the arduous journey back from the Antarctic Circle. She followed the coldwater Falkland Current up past Patagonia and continued on, traveling along the Eastern coast of South America and spreading terror as she went. Banking into the South Equatorial Current, she traversed thousands of miles of the North Atlantic, until ending up at her current location.

The female's primitive brain was incapable of understanding why she continued to respond to the pull. She traveled day and night, with it directing her relentlessly onward. Most of the time she remained deep, surfacing only when swathed in darkness, and feeding as opportunity permitted. During the day, she preferred the blackness of the ocean's depths. Not because of an aversion to the sun – her vision was ten times better than a human's in bright light – but rather, for the temperature. She was descended from a coldwater-loving species and, as she moved further into the tropics, the chilled temperatures of the abyssal plains consistently beckoned to her.

With an adjustment of her limousine-sized pectorals, the female rose gracefully in the water column, powered by rhythmic strokes of her towering caudal fin. She ascended to the nine-hundred-foot mark and remained there, soundlessly scenting her way along the thermocline. The twin nares on the underside of her scarred snout flared, drawing saltwater into her sensitive olfactory sacs as she sniffed the surrounding sea. Combined with her superior eyesight and the electroreceptor pores that dotted her head, she had an array of long-range senses at her disposal.

Accelerating to her normal cruising speed, she hurtled along, dispersing frightened schools of fish and squid. For no apparent reason, a sudden burst of adrenaline shot through her and she struck a belligerent pose, her back arching, her fins extending like blades. At a full eighty-four feet in length and weighing 210 tons, she was a flesh-eating machine the size of an adult blue whale. Nothing could threaten her, and anything foolish enough to try quickly found itself added to her bill of fare.

Relishing the cold water rushing through her gills, the monstrous female continued on, secure in her power. Her species had worn many guises over the millennia. To the ancient Fijians, who trembled at the sight of their gigantic dorsal fins, they were *Dakuwaqa*. Among pre-colonization Hawaiians, who worshipped them as gods, they were known as *Kauhuhu*. And, most recently, to infuriated Norwegian whalers, whose kills she repeatedly purloined, she was *Tyvaktige Tispe* – "thieving bitch."

But to the rest of the world, she was something more. She was a terrifying force of nature, one that had been vilified in book, film and fable for the last fifty years. She was also a notorious whale eater, and to many, a mythical devourer of men. More than anything else, she was the largest carnivorous fish in the history of the world.

She was *Megalodon*.

"How's her depth?" Kat asked, glancing up from her portable electron microscope. Her eyebrows were hiked up and she had one of those pensive-but-proud expressions on her freshly scrubbed face. It was the kind of look that made you want to reassure her, even though you knew you'd end up regretting it.

"Still holding at one thousand feet," Jude replied, eyeing their in-dash fathometer screen. "You can stop worrying. I've got her beacon programmed into ANCILE. If she turns territorial again the program will override our auto-pilot and take evasive."

"I'm not worried, Sharky," Kat said. She extended her lower jaw and blew her shoulder-length red hair away from her face with a snort. "I'd just like to know if my station's going to get tossed to hell again."

"I think we're in good shape," Jude said. He pushed his frameless glasses up his nose with one finger as he scanned another screen. Despite his casual tone, he was grateful they'd invested in top-of-the-line engines and a military-grade obstacle avoidance system.

Obstacle ...

Jude chuckled at the word's irony, then leaned back into his padded captain's chair and extended his arms up over his head. He'd been doing that more and more lately, both to relieve boredom and some of the stiffness a fifty-year-old frame acquired after being at sea too long.

Dr. Judas Cambridge, or "Sharky," as his outspoken colleague and partner, Dr. Katerina "Kat" Feaster called him, was one of the world's leading elasmobranchologists – a field of study that specialized in sharks and rays. His other passion was ichthyologic-based cybernetics, a field of robotics he virtually pioneered, back when it was in its infancy. At five-foot-ten and a wiry 160 pounds, Jude was your stereotypical marine biologist nerd: pale, unkempt, and unassuming-looking. He was the kind you'd expect to find hovering over a fish tank or with his bespectacled nose buried in a lab book. Of course, when inspiration was upon him that all changed, and a fire sprang up behind the Harvard grad's hazel-green eyes that could light up a room.

Or, in this case, an expensive cabin cruiser.

Jude checked the feel of *Insolent Endeavor*. The refitted fifty-foot Monte Carlo MC5 represented his life savings. His and Kat's, come to think of it. The modified motor yacht, with its wave-cutting hull, was a marvel of maritime technology. Even more so after they'd stripped away most of her luxury features and converted her into a floating lab and tracking station, cramming everything possible inside her fiberglass hull with the exception of a CT/MRI scanner. And then, only because the scanner's addition would have necessitated them sleeping on the cold, comfortless deck.

Endeavor was speedy, too. Upgraded to twin 1,400 horsepower Cummins marine inboards, she could hit nearly fifty knots before going into the red. More than enough for their purposes.

"How did she respond to the epinephrine surge?" Kat asked. Her blue eyes lowered as she became more engrossed in her work.

As he watched her tuck a rogue lock of crimson behind one ear, Jude smiled. Kat called the habit "battening down her hatches." The spunky ichthyologist-turned-geneticist had been with him for five years now – since the day his contract with GDT had been revoked, in fact. Since then, she'd been his best friend, trusted confidante, and a savvy business partner. Hell, she'd even loaned him a shoulder to bawl on when his bitch of an ex-wife did the "desperate housewife thing" and ditched him for some horny muscle-head.

He'd gone through an entire box of Kleenex that day.

He flushed at the memory. It wasn't exactly his finest hour.

Jude looked away and sighed. He liked Kat, a lot more than he cared to admit. But given that she was a hard-core atheist and a professed lesbian, the chances of any spontaneous shipboard romance developing between the two of them was slim to--

"Knock, knock! Anybody *in* there?"

Jude cleared his throat and focused on his readouts. "Sorry, I zoned out for a second. The, uh, result was textbook perfect. She went into an immediate threat display. The implant is functioning perfectly."

"How about the locator? Is it secure?"

Jude reached for the swing-arm LCD monitor, suspended a foot above his head. On it, the locator's infrared camera lit up the darkness, showing a foreshortened profile of the *Megalodon*'s head as the huge shark powered its way through a blizzard of marine snow.

Up by one corner of the screen, he could see the edges of the cranial implant that they'd sacrificed a million-dollar ROV attaching to the top of the fish's head. Every so often, a flash of pure black lit up the screen, interfering with the infrared lens and obscuring his view until the system reset itself.

The addition of the locator, with its brilliant red strobe, had been an afterthought, but a wise one. The four-foot-wide external implant that clung to Ursula's cranium like a Facehugger, penetrating her thick skull and sending stimulating feelers into her cortex, gave them only limited control over the massive carnivore. They could affect her mood and migrational path, but little more. A bigger problem was that she was now aware of *Insolent Endeavor* and had exhibited the disconcerting habit of charging them when they least expected it.

Fortunately, their ANCILE system saw her coming and responded accordingly. The system was a godsend. Even if it did mean being occasionally tossed out of one's bunk in the middle of the night or thrown off the toilet.

"Looks good," he said, zooming in. He could see a few of the ragged lacerations the *Megalodon*, or "Ursula," as he'd named her after his ex, had sustained during her recent battle with an outgunned, but surprisingly aggressive, bull pliosaur. "Based on her BP, I think the strobe is annoying the shit out of her, but at least she's stopped trying to dislodge it."

"Thank God she doesn't have the brains to just rub it off on something," Kat muttered. "An Orca would've done that in the first five minutes."

Jude ground his teeth. It irked him when someone insulted one of his fish, especially an animal as huge and majestic as Ursula. He gazed at the monitor and pictured the rough-skinned behemoth cruising along, a mere skyscraper's length beneath their fragile hull.

His mind wandered back to the moment he'd first laid eyes on her and goose bumps popped up all over his body. The reports they'd gotten from the region's frustrated whalers didn't do her justice. When she materialized through the obscuring Antarctic murk, she looked like a U-boat with teeth.

She was everything Jude could've hoped for, and more.

He allowed himself an anticipatory smirk. Primordial brute that she was, the huge *Megalodon* was his ticket to the big time. She and her pups were going to bring him wealth and power beyond his most feral fantasies. And a boatload of revenge, too.

Yes, he was going to show them all.

Jude plucked his course calculator from his shirt pocket, then threw *Insolent Endeavor* into autopilot and got up. The seas outside were rough and he compensated for the sway of the big boat by press-ing one hand up against the low cabin ceiling as he walked toward Kat's station. Behind him, the blaze of the mid-morning sun fought to peek its way through the bridge's heavily-tinted windows.

"How's the tissue sample coming?" he asked. He picked up a nearby cup of coffee, gave it a sniff, and then put it down with a grimace.

"Not bad," Kat said, not deigning to look up. "I've just about com-pleted a bio-scan combined with all of last week's diagnostics, and then I'll start her blood work." She reached over to a nearby ice bin and hoisted the huge impact tooth they'd retrieved, several days earlier. Hefting it in both hands, she admired the eleven-inch hunk of ivory be-fore setting it carefully down. At well over eight inches across the root, it pretty much covered a standard-sized sheet of office paper. "Risky or no, going back to that blue whale carcass to check for a recently-shed tooth was a stroke of genius," she conceded. She picked up a pair of for-ceps and poked at the mushy meat clinging to the root. "This fresh gum tissue has been invaluable for my research."

"Excellent." Jude nodded. "It's also a good thing I listened to you and had ANCILE up and running. Otherwise, I doubt we'd have had time to withdraw before she came charging back to defend her kill."

Kat cocked an eyebrow. "Her 'kill?'"

"You know what I mean."

"Hmm. By the way, how's the course plotting coming?"

"Done." Jude held up the tablet. "Taking into account the presence of potential food sources, our best bet is to maintain our current head-ing until we're past the Windward Passage. We're about one hundred miles out."

"And from there?"

"We'll make a run through the Great Bahama Bank, past Andros Island," he said, scrutinizing his map. "She's been holding deep during the day, so there's little risk. From there, we'll swing southwest into the Straits of Florida, and then it's straight on toward Rock Key. And some long overdue payback."

Kat frowned at his spiteful tone. "Listen . . . do you think it's pos-sible you're getting a little carried away with the whole 'revenge' thing? I mean, it's just business, you know? Once we get the contracts, justice is served."

Jude's head rebounded as if he'd just caught a stiff jab. "I gave Eric Grayson five years of my life, Kat. The foundation of his cybernetic implant technology is based on my work. And he tossed me out like yesterday's garbage and stole my designs."

"That's SOP with any big company. You sign your intellectual property rights away the moment you walk in the door."

Jude took a calming breath and adjusted his glasses. "Okay, you're right. But the project was geared toward using Elasmobranches to safeguard swimmers, not convert Pliosauridae into war machines."

"And that was the CEO's decision," Kat said. Now she took a breath. "Did you ever consider that, maybe, if you'd just towed the company line, you might have been able to win him over?"

"I tried," Jude stated. He leaned against a nearby bulkhead, his arms folded across his chest. "When I found out Grayson was looking for something big enough to weaponize, I got proof that *Carcharodon megalodon* was still alive – photographs, videos, even a tooth fragment I bought from a whaler. Do you know what he told me?"

She shook her head.

"He said, 'Those fish aren't predators, they're scavengers.'" Jude wore a disgusted look. "What was the term he used? Oh, yeah. 'The garbage trucks of the sea.' Can you believe that shit?"

Kat licked her lips, then reached over and ran a gloved fingertip along the hacksaw-like serrations that formed the edges of the enormous shark tooth. He could see her choosing her words. "Look, we both know that as they become bulkier and less maneuverable, adult *Megalodons* have a tough time catching prey and end up converting from active hunters to carrion consumers. That's why they're so dependent on whale populations – to sustain their brood stock. But that doesn't make them any less impressive."

Jude scoffed. "Well, my sharks can do something Grayson and his precious pliosaurs can't. They don't have to surface to breathe, and that's going to be a big selling point with the Navy." He wore a smug look. "You know how they like to keep things clandestine."

"I agree." Kat cleared her throat. "Look, we've put everything into this. It can pay off big. I just hope this presentation you've been so 'clandestine' about knocks the buyer's socks off. Because with the external implant, it's not like we can make Ursula turn somersaults."

Jude rubbed his hands together. "Oh, I've got something in mind that's right up the military's alley."

"And what's that?"

"Bloodshed. A fight to the death, winner takes all."

Kat blinked twice. "Excuse me? Are you telling me you're planning to--?"

"I'm going to knock on Grayson's proverbial door and challenge him to a fight: my monster versus one of his."

"You never said anything about this. What, you think he's going to just throw down with you, like two kids in the schoolyard?"

"That's precisely what I expect. And, in base terms, I'm gonna kick his ass."

"That's insane. Why don't we just do the presentation we initially planned? Once the Navy's onboard, we can use their facilities to sedate Ursula, do a full implant, and then--"

"Fuck that," Jude snarled. "My way is faster. And far more poetic."

Kat gave an exasperated headshake. "You're crazy! Ursula's no match for *Tiamat*! She'll be killed and we'll be wiped out, both financially and reputation-wise!"

"You're wrong. Grayson won't risk his queen. Not on my chessboard," Jude asserted. "But the head of the Navy's Bio-Weapons Division is in Tartarus right now. Grayson will have no choice but to send out one of his captive *Kronosaurus* cows – probably that evil bitch *Thanatos*. Once we destroy her, the Navy and all their resources will be ours."

Kat placed the back of one hand against her brow, like she did when she felt a migraine coming on. "Shit. Have you even . . . I mean have you considered how shallow the water in that region is?"

"Of course."

"So, what, then? You don't actually think they're going to give you access to Jörmungandr, so you can trash it in some Kaiju-style cage match, do you?"

Jude's hazel eyes turned to slits and he smiled humorlessly. "We're not going to get that close. We'll hold position by the drop-off, where there's plenty of room to maneuver, and make them come to us."

"Make them how?"

"I think a live video call to Admiral Callahan, overlaid with the footage of that bull *Kronosaurus*'s head being squashed like a grape, will do the trick."

"And if it doesn't?"

Jude shrugged. "Who knows? Maybe Ursula will 'accidentally' knock over one tower each hour from their expensive pliosaur fence until Grayson comes out of his hole. I'm sorry, Kat, but we've come too far to be denied."

She got up muttering something about them both ending up as somebody's bitch and brushed brusquely past him. When she reached the helm, she pointed at the monitor image of Ursula's ragged head. "Look at that. You see how messed up she got fighting a fifty-ton bull pliosaur? How do you expect her to take on a cow three times that weight?"

"Those wounds are superficial. And besides, weight is the key," Jude replied. He'd worked out all the combat variables and was confident of the outcome. "Our *Megalodon* is significantly heavier than anything they can throw at us."

"And, because she's got a fat ass, that's going to win the day?"

"Along with the fact that, like most marine animals, macropliosaurs lose mobility as they grow larger."

Kat shook her head doubtfully. "I don't know about that. I've seen them in action; they're much more maneuverable than similar-sized sharks. And a lot nastier, too."

A sardonic grin swept across Jude's angular features. "Agreed. But Grayson will have to maintain control over whatever specimen he chooses, limiting its effectiveness. Whereas we're just going to let Ursula off her leash and let her innate aggressiveness take over."

"And that's going to be enough?"

"Why wouldn't it? She's got more mass, she's durable, and, most importantly, she doesn't have to come up for air. You'll see. In a protracted battle, she'll win."

"I . . . really don't know," Kat said, staring at her feet. "I've got a bad feeling about this." As she looked up at him, both her eyes and jaw muscles hardened. "You know, I wish you'd told me about your evil master plan before we left port."

"Why, so you could try talking me out of it?"

"No, so I could beat the shit out of you."

Jude chuckled and reached out, resting his hands reassuringly atop her slim shoulders. "I know it sounds crazy, Kat, but sometimes you've got to take risks. But trust me. I've got it all worked out."

He spread his arms wide and gave her a winning smile. "You'll see; in thirty-six hours, we're going to be celebrating. And on some damn expensive bubbly, too, courtesy of the US Navy and Dr. Eric Grayson!"

TWENTY-THREE

Dirk Braddock sat upright at his desk, his lean fingers tapping out a Fred Astaire number on its polished surface. His eyes flitted past his prized collection of macro-predator teeth and back to his oversized monitor. On it were the results of the metallurgical torque and tension tests he'd programmed the day before. His tongue teased his upper lip as his nostrils drew in the enticing scent of fresh Columbian, wafting in from the nearby kitchen. He inspected his empty coffee mug then shook his black-maned head. A refill was tempting, but he'd been sucking down way too much caffeine lately.

In an attempt at relieving tension, Dirk reached for the pair of four-inch, black rubber squares he had resting nearby. They were part of his gym ensemble. Knurled free-weight bars wreaked havoc on unprotected palms and he preferred his free of calluses.

Gripping the squares between a thumb and index finger, he slapped them absentmindedly against the palm of his free hand while resuming reading. The report told him no more this time than last time. What he'd told Dr. Grayson held true; barring some unforeseen fault in the metal used to construct the handrail in his mother's quarters, the sturdy barrier should not have collapsed under her weight. Moreover, the computer simulation he constructed indicated that, even if Amara Braddock had run full bore and thrown herself against it, it was 88% likely to have withstood the impact.

Dirk zeroed his ratty gym bag before flipping his grip guards at it like a pair of flaccid Frisbees. He leaned back and sighed resignedly. His mentor was right. They needed to assign a team of materials engineers to conduct a formal study of the banister steel, to discover if there were any inconsistencies or concealed stress cracks. If there were, it would go a long way toward allaying his omnipresent suspicions. He could stop dwelling on his mother's death and try putting it behind him, like the old man suggested he--

The blare from Dr. Bane's video call nearly gave him a heart attack.

"Hello, Doctor Bane," Dirk drawled. Both his rump and his pride were still sore from the intramuscular booster she'd given him the day before.

"I told you before. Call me Kimberly, please," Bane insisted. "I'm just confirming our three o'clock meeting." Her face grew huge as he switched her to a full-screen panel. He had to admit, despite pushing fifty, the tall epidemiologist looked good. Even under high-res magnification.

She wasn't his type, of course. Not hardly. But Garm would probably do her.

Hmm . . .

Dirk's eyes danced with hidden humor as the thought of enlisting his twin for some adolescent payback teased its way into his frontal lobe. He fought to keep from laughing aloud. *That* would teach the old cougar a lesson. Of course, the big guy probably wouldn't go along with it. He couldn't blame him. If Natalya Dragunova found out Garm was banging another woman, the results would be . . . *yikes.* Of course, if the two of them broke up as a result--

Dismissing such selfish and self-serving thoughts, Dirk leaned forward in his chair. "Actually, I need to push our meeting back, if you don't mind. Did you get my email, that Grayson moved the post-demo conference? It's at four now."

Bane shook her head. "I'm sorry, I've been buried in research. Can we convene afterward, maybe half-past-five?"

"I was thinking more like six," Dirk said. He checked his tablet as he talked. "If you'd like, I'll pick up a couple of dinner trays from the cafeteria and meet you at your lab."

"That's fine," Bane said, nodding. "You'll want a full stomach for what I'm going to show you."

Dirk's eyes swung up from his screen. "Really? What have you found?"

"It's a bit more complicated than I initially thought. I don't want to get into too much detail over the intranet," she said. She licked the inside of her lips. "As you know, Dr. Grayson hired me to evaluate the efficacy of GDT's new serum, SMA-9002, set to be shipped out to fight recent outbreaks of Cretaceous Cancer."

Dirk nodded. "I've seen the distribution reports, including the global listings of known pockets of infectees."

"Yes. Well, rather than just reviewing and signing off on the clinical trials, something a monkey could've done, I decided to familiarize myself with the intricacies of the disease. I began with a rundown of the initial Paradise Cove infectees, before moving through all the containment and curative procedures the CDC implemented, and then, finally, the R&D done by Dr. Wilkins, my predecessor. I reviewed every development, from start to finish, including your father's repeated antibody contributions."

Dirk cleared his throat. "I see."

"I know I've said it before. But I'm very sorry for your loss."

"Thank you, Doc—I mean, Kimberly. Wow. That must've taken some time."

She chuckled. "No worries. The combination of chronic insomnia and an IV coffee drip helped."

Dirk allowed himself a grin. "So, is there anything you want to share before our meeting?"

"Maybe some of the more mundane stuff." Bane's tired eyes exhibited increased alertness as she hacked away with one hand at a nearby keyboard. With her free hand, she rotated a monitor mounted on an articulating arm into camera view, then hit a key. "The first thing that stood out to me, and to Dr. Wilkins, apparently, is that as virulent as *Kronosaurus imperator* bacteria is, as a species, they appear to be immune to it."

On the screen, footage ran of a pair of bull pliosaurs engaging in mating combat. Like grappling hippos, the two behemoths interlocked jaws and tore relentlessly at one another.

"A known commodity," Dirk pointed out. "Their immune systems are amazing, as are their hyper-regenerative capabilities."

"Indeed. Given their ability to repair tissue at such an astonishing rate, I suspect their lifespans may be preternaturally long."

Dirk shrugged. "It's possible. One of the perks of being imprisoned in hell for sixty-five million years."

Bane tapped a key. "Let's look at these two specimens."

Enlarged on the monitor, two vertically-mounted blood sample slides appeared side by side. The cellular activity on the first was obvious, on the second, virtually non-existent.

"Specimen 'A' is a sample of live pliosaur blood," Bane announced. Dirk could hear her flipping pages as she spoke. "It was taken from one of your captive specimens: *Fafnir*, to be exact. The cells were maintained under optimal systemic conditions and injected with a heavy dose of the microbial soup present in the saliva and bloodstream of a different, on-site specimen, number zero-two-eight . . . *Surtur*. As you can see, the invasive pathogens, although inactive, are attacked immediately and aggressively by the host's assorted lymphocytes. Natural killer, thymus, and bone-marrow cells are all present, and in tremendous numbers. The body's defensive response is similar to that of the immunological components found in the blood of the Komodo dragon; the foreign bodies are confronted head-on and implode instantly on contact with the correlating auto-immune cells."

Dirk's eyes narrowed as he watched the oddly-shaped saurian bacteria pop like compressed bubble wrap. He'd seen this type of microbial combat before, but the efficiency and lethality of it never ceased to fascinate him.

Bane continued. "Specimen 'B' is also interesting, primarily because the interactions between the invasive antigens and the host's leucocytes are far less antagonistic."

She was right, Dirk saw. As in the first sample, the injected bacterium remained predominantly inert. Moreover, they stayed so as the host's less numerous and more lethargic white blood cells advanced, tackling and destroying them one by one.

"Are the antigens also from *Surtur*?" he asked.

"Yes."

"What about the host blood? Based on the nucleated erythrocytes, I assume it's reptilian, but I can tell it's not from one of our pliosaurs."

"You are correct. It's a run-of-the-mill *Alligator mississippiensis*."

"Fascinating." Dirk touched a finger to his upper lip. "The invasive cells appear dormant, almost like they're hibernating."

"Yes," Bane agreed. "They just sit there, neither moving nor multiplying, and allow the gator's auto-immune system to envelope and incapacitate them." She clicked on another key. "Now, watch *this*."

A third vertical window opened, parallel to the first two and splitting the screen in three. Unlike the first two specimens, the bacteria in the final sample moved in a highly energized and excited matter, enveloping and infecting every cell they encountered, including the host body's lymphocytes. Within thirty seconds the entire sample had been contaminated.

"That was from a human host, wasn't it," Dirk remarked.

"No one you know."

"Why the extreme difference? Is it the alligator's immune system? They are remarkably resilient."

Bane swiveled the monitor back off camera and leaned in close. "It's more a matter of reptilian physiology. Most of the microbes in a pliosaur's jaw are temperature sensitive and remain more or less inert when exposed to the carrier's typical core temperature of around seventy-eight degrees Fahrenheit. They function and multiply best when exposed to an iron-rich, aerobic environment and maintained at a temperature around--"

"Mammalian levels," Dirk finished for her. "So, the inference is what – that reptiles are immune to Cretaceous Cancer?"

"Pretty much," Bane said, licking her lips. "At first, I thought lowering infectees' body temperatures would be worth investigating, but after crunching the numbers I realized, at best, it would only slow the spread. And the temp needed to be effective would end up being terminal for the host, so . . ."

"So, keep at it," Dirk said, encouraged. "Maybe there's something to it you haven't figured out yet."

"We'll talk about that when I see you." Bane brushed a stray lock of hair from her face. "Oh, there is one other point that, although medically irrelevant, is rather intriguing. At least from a paleontological perspective."

"What's that?"

"Well, it requires a bit of assumptiveness, but, if land-dwelling Cretaceous theropods like, oh . . . dromaeosaurs, for instance, packed a variant of the same infectious slobber that pliosaurs do, it may have had an impact on mankind's evolutionary history."

Dirk's head angled to one side. "How so?"

"Think about it. If a primitive mammal suffered a near-miss from a raptor attack and ended up infected . . ."

Dirk's lips did the "Ah-ha" thing. "They could've developed the same aggressive traits infected humans do when succumbing to the bacteria and spread it to others of their kind."

"Or other mammals, period," Bane offered. "It could've been transmitted like rabies, spreading from bite to bite and infectee to infectee. That is, until the carrier, or carriers, came across a hungry dino and got snatched up."

Dirk chuckled. "So, you're theorizing that the common cold kept mammals in check, preventing them from growing bigger and vying with dinosaurs for control until K-T?"

"More like a very uncommon *plague*," Bane replied. "And hey, you never know. Sometimes, it's the tiniest things that kill us."

"Good point. Thanks, Kimberly. I'm looking forward to your presentation. I'll see you around six."

She grinned at him. "Sounds good. I'll chill the wine."

As Dirk disconnected the call, his smile faded. He leaned back in his chair, his hands sweeping across his keyboard, maneuvering the system's shimmering cursor until it hovered above a non-descript file on his desktop. His jaw muscles bunched and he hesitated, his finger suspended over the tab.

It'd been weeks since he watched the clip. He hoisted an eyebrow as the computer screen in his mind highlighted the exact date: Three weeks, five days, and a little over eleven hours. He'd stopped looking because every time he suffered through it he'd wake up in the middle of the night, screaming and flailing so violently he was at risk of injury. Still, if there *was* something in there that might help with his investigation . . .

Steeling himself, Dirk speed-sucked breaths like he was doing Lamaze on amphetamines. Finally, he clamped down on his last inhalation and jabbed the button.

As the black and white security footage went active, Dirk's exhalation became a wheezy death rattle. The screen was filled with a worm's eye view of the amphitheater pool, filmed from the narrow landing along the northwest wall. The antiquated ground-level camera was one of those old-fashioned, timer-based infrared swivelers. He checked its counter; a little after ten PM.

At first, there was little to see. It was fairly dark and, as it panned left, the lens showed nothing except the rippling surface of the pool, extending far into the distance. When it swung right, however, it was close to shore and took in the pool's thick concrete lip, the walkway bordering that section, and a heavy steel door. Other than the podium landing, the old maintenance entrance was the amphitheater pool's only access point from ground level, the remainder being warded by resilient Celazole walls or towering granite ramparts. The four minutes of grainy footage was all there was and, if the camera hadn't been a generator-powered auxiliary unit Amara Braddock installed as a backup, it wouldn't even exist. All the rest of Tartarus's high-tech surveillance equipment was shut down as a result of the rolling blackout that disrupted the entire facility that evening.

Dirk clocked the video footage counter and held his breath. He knew the drama that was slated to unfold frame by frame – not that the feeling of dread ever lessened. His eyes ached as he watched the camera arc left, just in time to catch the explosive splash of his mother crashing feet-first into the pool. Amazingly, she'd survived the twenty-story drop by twisting her body into an impromptu dive, a moment before impact.

He watched as she regained the surface, her raven-haired countenance a darkened dot in the dimly-lit vastness of the amphitheater. Judging from her jerky movements, she'd broken a few ribs on impact, but she was alive and mobile. At least for the moment.

On the screen, Amara looked up, then recoiled and made a desperate dive. A second later, the ten-foot section of steel and PBI barrier that had sheared off came down like a guillotine, slashing into the water and missing her by less than a yard. She surfaced ten feet away, gasping for breath and cradling her right side as she made for the nearby shallows. She tried employing a traditional crawl stroke, but switched to a slower, more laborious dog paddle when free-styling proved too painful.

For the fortieth time, Dirk watched his mother fight her way toward him. Arms and legs working, she drew gradually closer, the counter clicking away and the camera panning as it seemingly followed her progress. He could see her clearly now, her mouth open as she struggled to breathe. Then, suddenly, barely forty feet from the pool's edge, she hesitated. A look of alarm swept her pain-wracked face and she started treading water. She was looking up at something, or perhaps, *someone*. A moment later, she turned back and headed for the deep-water.

In the distance, some two hundred feet away, lay the big amphitheater dock with its raised dais and podium.

Dirk leaned forward in his seat, his eyes intently following the camera's POV as it reached its zenith and began swiveling back. He froze the video and scanned the image of the maintenance walkway as he had a hundred times before, searching for some plausible reason why his mother turned away from that guaranteed sanctuary and returned to the 300-foot depths of Tartarus's manmade lake.

But there was nothing to see. No villain or threat. No land-dwelling predator or supernatural terror. There was nothing but cold concrete and tiles and the dim, orb-shaped emergency lights that ringed the huge saltwater pool's edge.

Dirk hit play and swallowed the tumorous lump in his throat as the image suddenly shimmied. Something was causing the camera to vibrate and he knew what. For whatever reason, the paired, sixty-foot titanium-steel gates that separated the amphitheater pool from *Tiamat's* paddock were opening.

The young scientist's fearful gaze was reflected in his mother's eyes as she abandoned the dais dock and turned back toward the shallows. Buoyed by adrenaline-inducing terror, she ignored the pain of her injuries and swam frantically.

Dirk could feel his heart banging like an out-of-control pendulum inside his rib cage as the camera swung left, causing him to temporarily lose sight of her. By the time it moved right again the vibrations had ceased. The yard-thick gates were open.

At this point, Amara had covered half the distance back and was swimming like an Olympian, with no signs of slowing or stopping. The 200-foot disturbance in the water behind her made the reason for her impetus abundantly clear.

Tiamat had entered the pool.

The *Kronosaurus* queen was coming.

Whatever had caused Amara to abandon the safety of the maintenance landing, moments before, was either gone or she simply no longer cared. She was coming on strong and in seconds would reach the safety of the rebar-strengthened concrete walkway and its nearby maintenance door.

Dirk's eyes moistened and his vision began to cloud as the pool's bright main lights clicked on. Like a passing eclipse, the rolling blackout was gone and the electricity was back. There was power to the air conditioning, power to the filtration systems, and power to the amphitheater pool's . . . current generators.

The camera was jarred as an unscheduled exercise interval for Tartarus's captive pliosaurs began. You couldn't hear the music, but the water at the shallow end of the amphitheater pool started to churn wildly. A moment later, it jetted away from the lens and the thousand-foot impoundment was transformed into a colossal swim spa. Dirk winced as the powerful artificial current slammed into his mother, pushing her back. She spun helplessly out of control, moving further and further away, toward the deepest parts of the enclosure.

Dirk felt hot tears burn his cheeks as he gripped the edge of his desk. On the monitor, he watched as Amara flailed. She'd realized the futility of fighting the current and changed direction, angling herself back toward the dock and its sheltering pilings. She was obviously hoping to escape the giant pliosaur's notice amid the rush of gurgling water.

It was a calculated gamble. But a bad one.

By the time the strike came, Dirk had closed his eyes. He'd suffered it the first six or seven times, but now could no longer handle it. It was too passionless and insignificant for him. There was no watery explosion. No rising from the depths to inflict a devastating strike. *Tiamat* knew her tiny target was a slug in terms of speed, and injured to boot. She simply reached out, like a partygoer plucking an hors d'oeuvres from a passing tray, and swallowed his mother whole.

And unlike Stacy, there was no coming back.

Dirk buried his face in his hands, hating himself for having run the video again. He made no sound. He just sat there, waiting for his heart rate to return from the stratosphere. Finally, after what seemed like years, he licked his lips and looked back at the screen.

The last ten seconds were the same as always. The camera continued on its predetermined cycle, swiveling away from the spot where Amara Braddock just died and focusing on unfeeling concrete and the illusory refuge of the walkway. Dirk could see the water rushing by at the bottom of the screen, proving the current generators were still running, but beyond that there was no movement. Nothing was amiss. Everything on the recording was the same as it was every other time he'd viewed it.

Yet something seemed different. He just couldn't put a finger on it. It was subtle, like a butterfly whispering in his ear; a tiny, soft-spoken voice, telling him to look again. Open his eyes and look harder and he would see it.

He tried. He looked and stared and looked again. He squinted so hard he saw colored motes, but still there was nothing. Nothing but stone and water: everything looked the same.

As a curtain of lightheadedness began to lower his world to white, Dirk blew out the breath he'd been holding and sucked in another. A growl of frustration escaped his lips and he heaved himself back in his seat, cursing quietly. He wished they'd never come to Tartarus and that his mom had never accepted the position GDT offered. If she hadn't, he'd still have his parents and his family. They'd be alive and in love and he--

Dirk snorted in disgust and sprang to his feet. Heading to the kitchen, he swung open the fridge and snatched up a bottle of spring water. He needed to relieve some stress and, as enticing a prospect as heading to Stacy's quarters for some impromptu nookie was, a workout was by far the smarter choice. The two of them had been going at it like jackrabbits the last few days and, as compatible as they were between the sheets, Dirk's heart just wasn't in it. There was nothing wrong with his ex – the beauteous Jamaican scientist was a catch and then some – but his feelings were caught on someone else. And even though the chances of them ending up together were in the slim to not-a-chance-you-loser category, hope, like Old Faithful, did indeed spring eternal.

Tucking his t-shirt inside his loose-fitting workout pants, Dirk retied his sneakers, scooped up his gym bag, and headed out the door. He had a spring in his step as he hopped in the elevator and headed toward the facility's nearby fitness center. Lifting weights was hardly as pleasurable as ripping Stacy's clothes off and reducing her to a quivering pool of jelly. But crude as it was to say, the gym's assorted dumbbells wouldn't bury him under a landslide of recrimination when he decided to stop pumping them.

Twenty-Four

Something stinks in Tartarus. And it's more than just the damn pliosaurs.
S Dr. Kimberly Bane's eyes were cold and clinical as she hoisted her hefty "Nobody spreads it like an Epidemiologist" mug and gulped down some disgustingly cold coffee. She made a face as she walked to the sink and dumped what remained, then reached for the nearby pot and "slapped in a fresh mag." It was a figure of speech she'd picked up from her Marine Corps veteran ex-husband. One of the more endearing things he used to say when he caught her pouring a late-night refill.

Heading back to the counter that served as the lab's kitchen island, Bane climbed back onto her high-backed stool. She tucked her bangs behind her ears as she surveyed her computer screen. Her headshake was involuntary. The evidence was overwhelming. Before she'd gotten there, things had gone way far south with the GDT lab's research – to the point she needed to raise one hell of a red flag. She scoffed as she imagined what Derek's reaction would be to her news; she couldn't even imagine their mutual boss's response.

Bane tapped an index finger against her incisors as she started to initiate a video call, but then canceled it. After a moment's deliberation, she settled for an interdepartmental email, addressed to Eric Grayson. It was impersonal, but given the sensitive subject matter and the CEO's apparent lack of availability, she felt more comfortable leaving a message via text format. It also created a paper trail, so to speak, and at least she could edit it, prior to sending.

"Dr. Grayson," she spoke aloud as she typed. "Please contact me at your earliest convenience. Have made potentially alarming findings re vaccine SMA-9002. Dispersal of same appears contraindicated.

Recommend a recall on all scheduled shipments, pending review. Respectfully, Dr. Kimberly Bane, ScD, PharmD."

Bane clicked send, then leaned forward and wrapped her lips around her coffee cup's rim. She sipped slowly, relishing the feeling of the near-scalding liquid as it flowed down her esophagus, warming her insides and filling her with that familiar jolt of caffeine that, at times, was the only thing keeping her going. She studied the old ceramic mug and grinned sadly. It was one of the few things Gary gave her that she hadn't tossed, donated, or smashed over the course of their bitter divorce. It reminded her of him: hard, chipped, and worn around the edges, and badly in need of a good washing.

She chuckled as she sat the heavy mug down. She missed him at times, but usually only when the mood struck her. And then, as was often the case, the randy old goat wasn't around when she needed him. It was the story of their marriage.

Thank God it was a short story, and not some 600-page novel.

Of course, nowadays, when she looked around and remembered where she was, she felt like she was in a novel – a *horror* novel. With a shrug, Bane opened her video log and cleared her throat as she prepared to record the day's findings.

"Dr. Kimberly Bane, research log entry dated November 20th. Follow-up from last night's entry. After completing my review, I find myself with no alternative but to call into question the methodology and ethics of Dr. Stanley Wilkins, my peer and predecessor, here at Tartarus."

She glanced down at her tablet before continuing.

"The CDC's initial analysis and subsequent evaluation of 'Cretaceous Cancer' as multiple strains of pathogenic bacteria, versus the malignant neoplasm the media has made it out be, was accurate. In addition, a review of the control groups treated with the prototype serum GDT's offsite pharmaceutical division developed from the barotrauma-induced antibodies found in the bloodstream of Specimen . . ." Bane stopped and grimaced. "Developed from *Subject* M-223, Jake J. Braddock, proved to be nearly 100% effective at neutralizing the invasive microbes, effectively containing their spread and reversing relative symptoms."

She hit the pause button and took a moment to gather her thoughts.

"Preliminary assessment of test subjects treated with the first batch of antibiotics developed from the prototype serum – designate SMA-8996 – indicated high degrees of success. Recipients showed substantial systemic improvements, complete with reversals of primary and secondary symptoms."

"However, after accessing and reviewing portions of lab reports that Dr. Wilkins, for some reason, coded off limits, it is obvious that improvements in the test subjects were greatly exaggerated. Microbial spread in all subjects was not reversed, but rather, forced into remission. Once antibiotic treatment was discontinued, per infusion protocols, the infection reemerged as a significantly more virulent version of itself, resulting in the untimely death of all host subjects."

Bane's jaw tightened as she glanced off-screen at her notes. "It should be noted that both the reemergence of the pathogens, and the subsequent deaths of those treated, were redacted from both audio and video records. This includes those presented to both Grayson Defense Technology CEO Eric Grayson and the company's Board of Directors. Molecular analysis of SMA-8996 points toward a watered-down derivative of the prototype serum, a design flaw that meant it could only suppress, versus treat, the infections. Given that the capacity to develop an efficient serum was readily available, logic indicates that the drug was deliberately engineered to slow the spread of the bacterium instead of killing it outright."

Bane licked her lips. "As is common with infections, failure to neutralize invasive pathogens in their entirety results in the surviving microbes becoming more resilient and eventually developing full-fledged immunity to the prescribed cure. Given the particularly virulent strains of primeval bacteria carried by extant pliosauridae, I can come to but one conclusion – that this was an anticipated result."

"Furthermore, my appraisal of serum SMA-8996's results indicate the surviving pathogens not only grew stronger, per blood samples taken from subjects from both Okinawa and the Philippines, but also that, when permitted to reestablish themselves, they began to mutate rapidly inside their human hosts."

As her eyes scrolled across her notes, Bane mouthed a curse.

"Additional serums, designates SMA-8997 and SMA-8998, were developed based on cultures derived from the aforementioned test subjects. Once again, the 'cure' that was mass produced and distributed was insufficient for the task, and the pathogens continued to mutate. Eventually, the disease became so virulent that infectees themselves began to suffer mutagenic effects. These mutations went far beyond the extreme inflammation, mental instability, and cerebral hemorrhaging that killed off the initial subjects from Paradise Cove."

"My investigation indicates that Dr. Wilkins was hands-on throughout the developmental process of all derivative serums, even to the extent of determining recommended dosages. An assessment of his personal notes points to him being, at best, guilty of extreme bungling, at worst, depraved indifference coupled with criminal intent. Furthermore, from an economics perspective, Wilkins' 'lapses in judgment' have, in my opinion, left GDT vulnerable to class-action suits from the surviving families of all those who received inadequate treatment. Given the thousands of documented deaths to date, the scope of said suits could well bankrupt the company."

Bane hit the pause button with a trembling hand. She sat back in her seat, eyes wide, chest rising and falling. She was no fool. This was a boatload of dynamite she was handling: The kind that, when it blew up, resulted in you either testifying before a congressional subcommittee or spending the rest of your life rotting in solitary confinement in some off-the-grid prison.

She summoned her courage and pressed "resume."

"Additionally, a more pressing problem exists in terms of current infectees. According to my calculations, with Cretaceous Cancer modifying itself at an ever-escalating pace, and given its high transmission rate, within the next twelve months the disease may become so resistant to existing treatments that it reaches pandemic proportions. Once that happens, it will be virtually impossible to curb." She swallowed hard. Then her jaw tightened and she spoke directly into the camera. "The general population must be protected at all costs. I recommend immediate implementation of existing government omega-protocols, including emergency containment and/or neutralization procedures for all infectees."

"Lastly, based on my review of case subject Jake Braddock's file, I have concluded that his acquired immunity to Cretaceous Cancer was compromised due to repeated exposure to systematically upgraded, mutated versions of pliosaur bacteria during R&D, ultimately resulting in his death. After--"

Bane paused as her laptop froze up. An annoyed look came over her and she checked her tablet. It was locked up, too. She moved her cursor around on both screens, trying to free them up, then gasped aloud as both devices suddenly went black.

Seconds later, she uttered a huge sigh of relief as her systems came back online. After a few moments spent confirming her settings were still in place, she resumed her log entry.

"Well, that was annoying," Bane muttered. "As I was saying . . . after reviewing Dr. Wilkins private logs, along with lab video files and records, I was able to confirm this. Jake was informed that he was receiving injections of the original bacteria solely to stimulate more antibody formation when, in actuality, he was being injected with high doses of mutant pathogens, derived from the bodies of victims that had already been treated with serums SMA-8997 and SMA-8998. It's as if their sole purpose was to develop a pathogen too strong for his immune system to handle." The epidemiologist's upper lip curled up. "This goes far beyond questioning lab security protocols. We're talking some serious Dr. Frankenstein shit."

Bane's head lowered and her eyes drooped. When they lifted she wore a determined look. "Amara Braddock was my friend. Her death may have been an accident, but her husband's certainly wasn't. It is my professional opinion that my predecessor, GDT Senior Epidemiologist Dr. Stanley Wilkins, is guilty of an array of human rights violations, including multiple counts of murder, if not genocide. To facilitate his arrest, once formal charges are brought, I attempted to locate him. I was unsuccessful. The contact information we have on file is either incorrect or outdated and he appears to have no online footprint of any kind. Not on Facebook or Twitter, nor any other social media platform. Even Google has no information on him. It's like he virtually scrubbed himself clean."

Bane folded her arms across her chest. "Derek and Garm Braddock, both members of GDT's Board, lost their father because of Dr. Wilkins' 'research.' I recommend the authorities be contacted forthwith and that full charges be brought against him. Regardless of the fallout, we need--"

Bam! Bam! Bam!

Bane stopped talking when she heard the knock. Actually, calling it a "knock" was an understatement. It was a loud banging, like someone was slamming a baseball bat against her lab's heavy outer door.

A quick glance at the video monitor showed nothing. In fact, her security cameras indicated the hallway outside was deserted.

Bam! Bam! Bam!

Bane shook her head. Unless ghosts could knock, there was definitely someone pounding on her door.

"One minute!" she yelled. With nimble fingers, she saved her video log entry and closed her laptop. Halfway to the door, she hesitated. The possibility dawned on her that it might be Dirk stopping by, unscheduled. She paused to check her look in a nearby mirror, then stopped and berated herself for being a horny, premenopausal bitch.

Bam! Bam! Bam!

"I said I'm coming!" she screamed. Stifling a curse, she put on her most intimidating scowl as she moved to the door. Smacking her hand hard against its pneumatic release, she watched as it whooshed open with a serpentine hiss.

"What the *hell* is your--"

Bane's heart caught in her throat as she found herself staring up at two of Tartarus's hulking, black-clad security guards. They were huge, at least half-a-head taller than she, and twice her weight. Far more worrisome; they radiated barely-contained malevolence, like a pair of junkyard dogs chewing their way through their tethers. The bigger of the duo – the one with the gap-teeth and freckles – glared coldly down at her.

"Doctor Kimberly Bane?" he growled.

"Uh . . . yes?"

"We'd like a word with you," he announced, pushing past her and entering the lab.

As she sized up the two intruders, Bane's mind started screaming silent alarms. She felt a powerful fight-or-flight response pulse through her. Instinct told her to run, to get the hell out of there, but one of them was standing in the doorway, barring her way.

She was trapped.

Bane's mind ran a losing race against panic. She tried thinking of ways to bluff the guards, but she was too scared to move. Her world began to collapse inward and she experienced tunnel vision. At the end of that blurry, dark-bordered passageway, all she could make out was the freckle-faced guard's stained teeth, bared in a sinister leer as his comrade closed and locked the lab door.

———————

Oh my God, would you look at that . . . is she trying to kill me?

As good as it was to take his tired mind off things and get a good pump on, the moment Natalya Dragunova walked into the gym, Dirk Braddock felt his already-elevated heart rate spike into the aneurism zone. Not wanting to get caught staring, he looked away as the voluptuous Russian sub commander headed for the nearby free weights. He pretended to catch his breath, resting his forearms on the sweat-streaked arms of the Mook Yan Jong he'd been practicing on.

"Shit, who needs the gym . . . I could just *watch* her workout and I'm good," Dirk whispered. "You know what I mean?" He grinned at the non-responsive wooden dummy, leaning on it and adding. "You know, I like you. You're a good listener."

Drawing in a few more breaths, he resumed his Wing Chun training, practicing the offensive and defensive skills his dad taught him. Weaving rapidly between and in and out of the dummy's arms, his lean hands moved like lightning-fast blades, blocking imagined blows with quick movements and then retaliating with an assortment of strikes.

Dirk loved kung fu. Ever the doting father, Jake Braddock had instructed both his sons on how to defend themselves, starting at age six. *"It's a man's duty to not only be able to take care of himself,"* he said, *"but his loved ones, too."* Whereas Garm, with his size, strength, and natural aggressiveness, preferred the direct onslaught of boxing, Dirk gravitated to the circular sleekness of Wing Chun. It played to his strengths and offset his weaknesses.

Peering through the dummy's obscuring limbs, he gazed surreptitiously around the gym. There were dozens of employees either on break or off shift, squeezing in their routines. He spotted Garm's second-in-command, Jayla Morgan, fifteen yards away. The buxom, dusky-hued South African's biceps were popping like apples as she banged out an intense set of dumbbell curls, while facing a nearby mirror. A few yards further down, Ensign Ramirez, *Gryphon*'s sonar tech, was spotting helmswoman Connie Ho as she worked the bench press.

Tartarus's fitness center was huge, rivaling the scope and scale of many high-end health clubs, back on the mainland. The central training room alone was a full half-acre of resistance and cardio equipment, complete with dozens of the most advanced selectorized weight machines on the market, not to mention enough free weight plates, bars, and dumbbells to construct an old-fashioned M1-Abrams tank.

Given that the base was technically a military facility, there was also an array of boxing and MMA equipment, including three heavy bags in assorted weight classes, a speed bag, top-and-bottom bag, and even a full-size boxing ring. Out of the corner of one eye, Dirk spotted two of the guards in there, sparring. From his vantage point, it looked like Security Chief Angus Dwyer and Lieutenant Jamal White going at it, with a third officer, most likely ex-heavyweight prospect Oleg Smirnov, overseeing things.

White, as Dirk recalled, was the ex-cop-turned-drug-czar, and a one-time Golden Gloves light-heavyweight finalist. It was obvious from his superior hand speed as he moved around the ring, peppering his lumbering superior with jabs. Unfortunately for him, Dwyer shrugged off his blows like they were snowflakes and kept after him, throwing bombs every so often that, although telegraphed, landed with such force they echoed throughout the gym. Dirk could literally feel them through the floor.

Of course, all the punching, taunting, and cheering faded into obscurity when Natalya started her routine.

Dirk knew her on-site workout by heart. Once a week, she did a mixed martial arts routine, her powerful punches and kicks leaving permanent dents in the bags and, once, even shearing the speed bag from its platform. Another day, it was an upper body resistance and plyometrics regimen, the next, a full core and gymnastics routine. But today was his personal favorite: lower body.

As he paused for breath and pretended he wasn't ogling her in a nearby mirror, *Antrodemus*'s captain headed to a nearby squat rack. After a quick warm-up with "just" a 45-lb plate on each side of the Olympic bar, she proceeded to work her way up, slapping on more and more iron and doing high-rep sets with first 225, then 275, and finally 315 lbs.

She usually stopped with three plates on each side. Not because she couldn't lift more – for a woman, her strength was prodigious – but because she preferred high reps and a full range of motion. The first time he'd seen her squatting he had, strictly out of concern she might injure herself, spoken to her about her form. He remembered it well. It was the day before their lunch date in the cafeteria and the subsequent (and thoroughly emasculating) arm wrestling match that ensued. She'd explained with her intoxicating accent that, unlike many athletes, who did squats and stopped when their thighs were parallel to the floor, she preferred to go all the way down. It was most natural, she felt, and reduced the chances of knee injury or joint instability, when done properly and consistently.

Then or now, Dirk wasn't about to argue with her. Dressed in a sleeveless, skin-hugging black catsuit, with her substantial chest jutting proudly out and her muscular arms looking like they should be gracing an anatomy chart, in his eyes, she was a Viking goddess come to life. And when she *did* one of her thirty-rep sets, her legs spread apart, and squatting so low her incredible ass almost touched the floor, he got lightheaded.

Probably because you keep forgetting to breathe, you idiot . . .

Dirk whistled low as he snatched up his nearby water bottle and guzzled a third of it. He was tired of doing the wooden dummy. He'd noticed there was a suitable heavy bag open that he could work on. Unfortunately, as luck would have it, it was near the boxing ring, where those two troglodytes were sparring. But it was also ten feet from where Dragunova had paused between sets and was currently doing a straddle split on the rubberized weight room floor.

Looks like I'm doing the bag! Dirk thought, nodding vigorously.

As he headed that way, it occurred to him that he was basically lusting after his brother's girlfriend like some hormonally-imbalanced adolescent. Of course, if Garm had been asked, he'd have vehemently denied the two of them were involved. But that didn't change things. Dirk realized now that Stacy Daniel's assertion was spot-on. He was a love-sick puppy and there was no denying it. He didn't want to hurt Stacy. She was fun and smart – a great girl – but he wasn't in love with her. And he couldn't make himself be. He had it for the six-foot-two Amazon he was drooling over, and bad.

It was so infuriating! That big lunkhead Garm didn't know what he had, and what he was, undoubtedly, taking for granted. Dirk snorted irritably. If they broke up and he was given the chance, he'd ask Dragunova for her hand and sixteen kids. But for now, he had to settle for casting furtive glances her way as she exercised that unbelievable body of hers.

Dirk moved to the heavy bag and dropped his gym pack on the floor. He had just put on his bag gloves and was starting to warm up his jab when the trouble started.

"Dr. Braddock! I see you got gloves on. You wanna spar a few rounds?"

Dirk looked up to see Angus Dwyer gazing down at him from the nearby ring. The overgrown security chief had his anthropoid-like forearms resting on the top rope and a hungry look on his flattish face.

Dirk tried to contain the incredulity that crept across his countenance. Dwyer must be out of his mind. Even ignoring the fact that Dirk was effectively his boss, or that he could go to Dr. Grayson and have the ex-con fired and sent back to prison in a heartbeat, the brute was six inches taller and outweighed him by a hundred pounds. He either had an overinflated opinion of the young scientist's pugilistic prowess or he was looking to hurt someone.

Although Dirk hadn't been able to find anything on Dwyer, given his fellow "Last Chancers" less-than-illustrious rap sheets, he was betting on the latter.

"Thanks, but I've only got my bag gloves," he diverted, turning back to the nearby punching bag.

"That's okay," Dwyer said. "You can borrow Jamal's. He won't mind. Right, Jamal?"

"Whatever you say, boss," the sweat-soaked ex-cop replied with a toothy grin, his strong white teeth standing out against his ebony skin.

"That's okay, I'll pass. But thanks, chief."

A frustrated look came over Dwyer and he hoisted the top rope high with one hairy arm, before climbing down from the ring. Dirk saw an "uh-oh" look come over Oleg Smirnov, as his superior started forward.

Dirk stood his ground as Dwyer approached. Using his peripherals, he could see all the nearby gym-goers stop and tune in. Jayla Morgan shook her head and walked out, whereas Dragunova remained where she was, resting her hands on her racked barbell and watching in the mirror. She had a disinterested look on her face, like a well-fed lioness watching a Cape buffalo intimidate a passing leopard.

"*Chief*, eh?" Dwyer mimicked. "Yo, this ain't about rank, pal. Just two dudes in the gym, engaging in a friendly sporting match. So, how about it?"

"I'm not interested," Dirk said. Despite the head guard's formidable size, for some insane reason, he wasn't afraid of him.

Maybe insane was the appropriate word.

"What's the matter? You afraid I'll kick your ass?"

Dirk faked a bewildered look. "Wait . . . did you say 'kick' or 'lick'?"

Dwyer's face contorted angrily as his cohorts' chuckles echoed throughout the gym. He moved closer, incensed by Dirk's defiant expression and his inability to intimidate him.

"That's very funny, nerd. I bet you'd like that, wouldn't you? I think--"

"Why don't you leave heem alone?"

Dirk's eyes popped as Dragunova wandered over and placed herself between them. To say he was shocked would have been an understatement. He opened his mouth to say something, but froze as the tall sub commander held up a cautionary finger.

"I theenk you have some problem weeth Doctor Derek, da?" Dragunova announced. Her eyes shone like carbon-steel blades as she stared up at Dwyer. At six-foot-five, he was three inches taller and substantially heavier, but she was unafraid. To Dirk, she looked like a big she-panther, protecting her cub.

"This is none of your business, butch," Dwyer snarled. His jaw muscles twitched; a combination of ill-contained fury and surprise at the woman's unexpected and unwelcome interference.

Dragunova raised an eyebrow. "You call me 'butch?'"

"Or bitch. Either way, butt out. This is a conversation between men."

"Then, I theenk you are one short."

Dirk stood there, stunned, watching as Dwyer's face turned tomato-red. As the ranking officer, he should have interfered. In fact, protocol stated he *had* to. But he was so bemused and, admittedly, strangely keyed-up by the unexpected turn of events, that he found himself staring, transfixed, as the bizarre stare-down continued.

"That's very funny," Dwyer remarked. He threw Dirk a nasty look. "You got big, bad mama bear protecting you now, eh?" He turned back to Dragunova, his red-rimmed eyes boring into hers as he tried to gauge both her fortitude and level of commitment. "You know, I read somewhere that women blink twice as often as men."

"I doubt that."

"No, they do."

"I meant that you can read," Dragunova retorted. Her eyes danced with merriment as Dwyer's fury continued to build.

From inside the ring, Jamal White decided to chime in. "Hey, chief. Is it just me, or do you smell pussy?"

Dwyer smirked, then leaned in and made a show of sniffing. "Matter of fact, yeah, I do. Hey, I guess you really *are* what you eat!"

Dirk started angrily forward, but Dragunova restrained him with a palm pressed tightly against his chest. Her storm cloud eyes continued to zero Dwyer's.

"Then I guess that would make you and your girlfriend beeg deeks, now wouldn't it?" she said smugly.

Dwyer looked like he was going to explode. His eyes grew as big as teacups, bulging from their sockets. Suddenly, his gaze shifted past Dragunova. His enraged expression changed to one of hesitancy and he gave ground.

Over her shoulder, Garm Braddock came into focus.

Dirk hadn't said a word as his brother approached. Although the big submariner wore a look of vengeful fury, for the moment he appeared contained, like a racecar, approaching the starting line with its superchargers rumbling, waiting for the flag to drop.

Wordlessly, Dragunova stepped back, allowing him to take her place.

"Mr. Dwyer, I am shocked," Garm said humorlessly. His elevated chin swiveled as he took in both White and Smirnov, in the background. "You guys threw a Tupperware party and I wasn't invited?"

"Whoa, count me out," Smirnov announced. He backed away, his big hands extended, palms out. "I am not part of thees."

Garm gave his old sparring partner a polite nod as he turned and departed the gym, then looked Dwyer in the eye.

"And then there were two . . ."

"This ain't your concern, Brad--"

"Oh, but it is," Garm said. His eyes shone like dry ice as he moved closer. "And when you're picking on my little brother, I am *very* concerned."

As Dwyer licked his lips, Garm studied the structure of his face, pinpointing its weak spots. "That's an interesting scar you've got on your upper lip," he said. His eyes intensified as he looked closer. "Oval-shaped, kind of like a human bite mark. But it's too small. A child's bite, perhaps?"

Dirk and Dragunova exchanged uncertain looks. Judging from her semi-relaxed body posture, at this point, he figured *Antrodemus*'s captain was content to let Garm handle things, with her getting involved only if it became necessary. Or, perhaps she had simply been playing for time all along, figuring he'd show up.

Dwyer's nostrils flared at the unwelcome scrutiny. Then his upper lip contracted into an ugly sneer. "You know, 'Gate,' I've always wanted to try you."

"Try would be the operative word."

"We'll see about that." Dwyer snapped his finger. "Jamal, get down here."

"You got it, boss."

Dirk watched as Jamal White hopped down from the ring, his sparring gloves still on. At six-foot-three, he was an inch shorter than Garm and thirty pounds lighter. He slipped forward, an unfriendly smile creasing his face.

"You want me to teach this cracker a lesson?"

"Go for it," Dwyer said, steeping a few paces back.

White sniggered. "Yo, Braddock. You in serious trouble." He made a show of dancing in place while firing a series of punches in the air. "You don't know who you messin' with."

"Oh, yeah?" Garm chuckled. "What are you going to do, change your tampon in front of me?"

"What? I'm about to kick your ass, white man!"

Garm's amused expression evaporated, replaced by a blend of boredom. "As you and your fellow racists are so fond of saying behind my back, I am not a 'white man.' Nor am I, technically, an 'Asian man.'" He shrugged. "I'm just a man. Something you should try sometime."

"Why y-you . . . you a *dead* man, mother-fucker!"

Dirk inhaled sharply as White flew at his brother, firing punches. Garm waited patiently, then twisted at the waist, melting from side-to-side as he calmly weathered the anticipated assault. Suddenly, he weaved to the left and, as his foe's next jab missed its mark, slipped the follow-up and grabbed the ex-cop by the face with one big hand.

White's startled cry was muffled as Garm torqued his huge body and extended his arm, tossing his off-balance opponent ten feet, right on his ass. His wolf's eyes were already on Dwyer, absorbing his telltale shocked expression and giving him a 'come hither' look.

"Get up!" Dwyer snarled at his subordinate.

White shook his head and dusted himself off as he regained his feet. As he did, he latched onto one of his gloves with his teeth and tore it off, followed by the other one. In seconds, he was back on the offensive.

"No, man!" he brayed through an erratic headshake. "I ain't going down like wet biscuits!"

As White rushed in like an angry bull, Dirk saw the set of Garm's jaw and took a quick step back. He extended one arm between his brother's broad back and Dragunova, instinctively trying to shield her. He'd seen too many of Garm's fights, both in and out of the ring, to not know what came next. That initial smush had been a playful, "You're too little to play in my sandbox," kind of thing. But now, the former heavyweight contender was all business.

Garm's eyes narrowed as he took a half-step forward. As he moved, his muscles flexed like titanium-steel bands, transforming his 245-pound body into the fighting machine that, years earlier, wreaked havoc on the heavyweight division.

Dirk watched his brother's feet with interest. Garm had taught him ages ago how, even when backpedaling and throwing a jab, he could incorporate his body's full power. He just dug his toes into the ground like a raptor's talons and did an instant reverse, pushing himself – and all his weight – forward. Just a two-inch hop did the trick. The lesson was never as apparent as it was today.

Garm smiled as White came right at him. The former drug czar was fast and furious. And predictable.

Instead of slipping his jab or slapping it aside, Garm timed it perfectly and met it – with his own. With both of them bare-knuckled, it was a risky move. But a calculated one. Unlike most fighters who, for sparring or bagwork, wrapped their hands religiously to avoid injury, he eschewed such measures. He felt it set him up for injury and used wraps only when mandated. As a result, his carpal bones and knuckles were as hard as iron.

Garm's left fist was an interceptor missile, targeting his adversary's. There was a thud as they collided, punctuated by a cracking sound and White's high-pitched shriek. The Last Chancer stared in disbelief at his shattered hand. A split-second later, Garm's overhand right caught him smack on the left cheekbone, practically knocking his head from his shoulders. He dropped as if he'd been poleaxed.

Dwyer wasted no time. Mouthing vile curses, he launched himself at *Gryphon*'s commander, catching him with a cheap shot to the temple, followed by an uppercut to the groin. Not wanting to give Garm a chance to recover, the infuriated ex-con kept up his assault, grabbing his opponent and hurling him against a nearby column, before unleashing a brutal barrage of power punches.

Dirk felt panic spike up his spine as he saw his brother cover up against the unrelenting fusillade. Things looked bad; Garm's adversary was bigger and heavier. Out of the corner of his eye, Dirk saw a dark-colored officer's uniform come into view and realized it was Admiral Callahan, accompanying Oleg Smirnov.

A moment later, Dwyer's flurry started to wind down. He was running out of steam and the two antagonists ended up in a clinch. There were a few seconds of struggle, like two brown bears grappling, then Dirk saw his brother's lips move. He couldn't make it out, but Garm muttered something.

Then he smiled.

A moment later, Angus Dwyer uttered a bellow of pain as an uppercut of unbelievable power lifted him clean off the floor. A gasp of astonishment escaped the lips of everyone watching. Before he touched down, a looping left hand followed, catching him on the bridge of the nose and driving him to his knees. He stayed there, his pale face a bloodied mess.

Teeth bared, Garm hauled back to finish off his disabled opponent. Dirk saw his expression and cold fear filled his lungs. His brother wasn't fighting by the rules this time. There would be no standing eight-count, no throwing in the towel. He planned on putting Dwyer down, once and for all.

"Cease this insanity!"

Eric Grayson's shrill cry of fury resounded through the fitness center like the shriek of a wounded baboon. Everyone froze, even Garm, as the old man came charging over with Admiral Callahan and Oleg Smirnov in tow.

Dwyer was still on his knees, dazed and gasping for air and wobbling like an axed tree, the moment before it falls.

"What the *hell* is going on here?" Grayson yelled furiously as he took in the scene.

Garm said nothing. His anvil-like jaw was set, his eyes teeming with uncharacteristic loathing as he glared at his downed foe. Nearby, an unconscious Jamal White remained where he had fallen.

"It was the guards, sir," Dirk began. "Dwyer was trying to bully me into boxing with him and then--"

"WHAT?" Grayson's face turned beet red as he tried and failed to contain himself. He stalked toward his incapacitated guards, gesturing for Smirnov's help, then latched onto Dwyer's blood-spattered t-shirt with a trembling hand. "You stupid, ungrateful, insolent--"

The semi-conscious security chief tried talking as the beefy Ukrainian guard grabbed him under one arm and started hoisting him to his feet. "W-we, uh . . ."

"Just shut up, mister," Grayson spat as he jammed a finger in his face. "Not one *word*. Do you hear me?"

As Dwyer turned the color of cream and meekly nodded, Dirk's jaw dropped. He'd never seen Grayson furious before. He was far removed from the fragile sexagenarian he'd grown accustomed to.

"Derek, are you alright?" Grayson asked, his dark eyes softening as he turned and studied his protégé. "Were you injured?"

"Uh, no . . . I'm fine, sir," Dirk said. "Actually, I wasn't even involved. The two captains intervened on my behalf."

Grayson's silver-coifed head bobbed up and down as his eyes shifted from Dragunova's cool countenance to Garm's bloodied face. The big pugilist was breathing hard and had crimson trailing from his mouth and one nostril.

"How are you, Captain Braddock?"

"Better than those two idiots," Garm remarked, wiping at his mouth with the back of one hand. He gave Ward Callahan a look as the heavy-set naval man came over to stand beside him, a huge smile on his mustached face.

"What's the story?" Grayson asked Oleg Smirnov, as he dropped down on one knee and examined Jamal White.

"Thees one is steel out," Smirnov said, flipping White onto his side and gripping his chin in one hand. "Left cheekbone might be broken . . ." He shifted the ex-cop's head from side to side, studying his badly swollen face. "Da, entire orbit ees crushed like beet." He glanced up at Garm and gave him an admiring nod.

Grayson exhaled hard through his nostrils and walked up to a still-shaky Angus Dwyer. Reaching up, he yanked the big man's face downward, then pulled his eyelids open, one by one, and scrutinized his reddish eyes in intense detail.

"Your nose is broken, Mr. Dwyer," Grayson muttered. He gripped his chin and twisted his head hard, left and right, eliciting a gasp of pain and causing him to stagger to one side. If Smirnov hadn't lunged forward to grab him, he'd have toppled. "And, you've got a well-deserved concussion," he added.

"I'll . . . I'll be fine," Dwyer mumbled, leaning on his underling for support.

"I'll be the judge of that," Grayson said, turning his back and wiping the blood and spittle from his hands. "You and Lieutenant White are suspended, effective immediately."

"Suspended? Are you serious?"

"I am, indeed. Officer Smirnov?"

"Yes, Dr. Grayson?"

"Kindly escort these two men to the infirmary," Grayson said. He glanced down at White and shook his head. "Have them send up a gurney for this one."

Dwyer shook off Smirnov's support and forced himself erect. "How long is this 'suspension' going to last?"

"For as long as I deem necessary," Grayson replied, turning back to face him. "We'll start with three weeks. Your pay will be docked retroactively and it goes in your file. In addition, I want you off the island, pending reinstatement."

"Three weeks? What the--"

"Pray I don't make it permanent," Grayson warned. The unspoken threat was apparent.

"Yes, sir . . ."

"Officer Smirnov, you are to complete the necessary paperwork. You're also promoted to Acting Security Chief, until otherwise notified."

"Da, sir," Smirnov replied sharply. "Thank you, sir."

Grayson turned back to Dirk and Garm and the small crowd of onlookers gathered about. He looked weary as he raised his hands. "Okay, people. The excitement is over. Please accept my apologies for the disruption and go on about your duties. I assure you, this type of thing will not happen again."

The remaining witnesses to the impromptu brawl turned away, a few resuming their workouts, but the majority heading for the locker rooms. A gym porter knelt next to Jamal White, cradling his head and checking his vitals, while a second one spoke into his radio. Dirk saw his brother casting baleful eyes at Dwyer as the disoriented ex-chief made his way outside, with Smirnov accompanying him and talking into his walkie talkie.

As Garm started in Dwyer's direction, Grayson reached out and touched him on the forearm. He wore a knowing look. "Captain Braddock, a word with you."

"Sir?"

"I know what you're thinking, Garm. But I don't want any more trouble," he said. "It's over. You taught him a lesson and it's done. I'll handle things from here. Do I make myself clear?"

Garm's lips were a seamless crease on his rugged jaw. He inhaled slowly and let it out as a sigh. "You're the boss."

"Good. I'd hate for you to miss the meeting, as well," Grayson said. He turned to Admiral Callahan, who continued to hover beside Garm, a huge grin still on his face. "Ward, shall we go?"

"Uh, you go on outside. I'll catch up with you," Callahan said. "I wanna talk to Gate for a minute."

Grayson hesitated, but then acquiesced. His keen eyes studied the faces of those still present before focusing once more on his fallen officer. He snorted amusedly. "Very well. But make it quick, please." He reached over and placed a hand on Dirk's shoulder. "I'll see you this afternoon?"

The young scientist forced a smile. "Of course, sir. And . . . I'm sorry about all of this."

"Not your fault, son," Grayson said. "I'm really looking forward to the meeting." As he walked off, Dirk overheard him muttering, "There are lots of exciting things happening. Lots of exciting things . . ."

TWENTY-FIVE

"Gate, that was goddamn amazing," Admiral Callahan declared, his bulldog-like head's enthusiastic nod underscoring his words.

Garm Braddock sighed. The head of the Navy's bio-weapons division had been following him around like some star-struck groupie ever since his brief-but-brutal brawl with two of Tartarus's security guards.

"Seriously, if asked, I'd have paid good money to be front and center for that," Callahan said. He scoffed. "You dropped White like he was a used condom. And when your uppercut lifted Dwyer's fat ass right off the floor? Unbelievable!" The thickset officer's eyes lit up as he lobbed a clumsy blow at some imaginary opponent. "It was like watching a modern-day Foreman-Frazier – something to tell the grandkids about!"

Garm's hunter's eyes scanned the curved concrete corridor where Security Chief Dwyer and Oleg Smirnov had vanished, mere moments before. He was inwardly alarmed by the hostility Dwyer was directing at Dirk as he walked up on them. It was far more than two gym guys razzing one another. It was personal, like the sadistic ex-con had some deep-seated grudge against his twin that had built up over time. That kind of enmity didn't fade. Worse, Dwyer was treacherous – a threat not to be taken lightly.

A whirlpool of unease inundated the big submariner and he shook his head. Eric Grayson could give all the mealy-mouthed speeches he wanted about disciplinary action and "docking pay." The aging CEO was far from a boots-on-the-ground kind of guy. In fact, he had no combat experience whatsoever. Garm, on the other hand, had spent most of his life facing down dangerous foes. And his pugilist's instincts told him Angus Dwyer was a problem that had to be dealt with.

As he surveyed the empty passageway, nodding occasionally in response to Callahan's incessant rambling, Garm realized his options were frustratingly limited. Grayson had effectively put him on notice, so claiming self-defense was now no longer an option. If he put Dwyer in a body cast now, as he was very much inclined to do, he would undoubtedly be brought up on charges. And if he didn't seize the moment and teach the sadistic creep a lesson, he would lose his chance. *Gryphon* would be back on patrol soon. Either way, whether he was rotting in a holding cell or imprisoned in his captain's chair, his little brother would be left alone and defenseless.

Garm ground his molars. The only silver lining was that, with a three-week suspension in effect, Dwyer would be thrown off-base temporarily. *Gryphon*'s next patrol would be completed by then, allowing him plenty of time to get back and deal with the issue, if it was still necessary.

"C'mon, Gate. I gotta know!" Callahan demanded.

Garm snapped back to the here and now. He realized, with some embarrassment, that the admiral had been prodding him about something. What, he had no idea. Although he found the boisterous, cigar-munching naval man annoying, he was the key to Grayson and GDT's ever-growing profits. It would be career suicide to upset him.

"I'm sorry, know what?"

"What you *said*," Callahan replied. His big salt and pepper mustache drooped atop an uncharacteristic frown. "Weren't you listening to me?"

"I'm sorry, admiral . . ." Garm said, faking disorientation. "I caught a cheap shot in there, left me a little loopy."

The admiral nodded. "Yeah, I saw that. Frankly, I was stunned you didn't go down. But, still, I gotta know what you said."

Garm was confused. "Said to whom? White, Dwyer . . . Grayson?"

"No." Callahan's eyes brimmed with excitement. "Do you remember the Angelo Rubino fight?"

"Remember it?" Garm chuckled. "I should. I was *in* it."

"You sure were. I was ringside, and you were in command the whole time. You were using that guy's head as a bongo drum. Then, outta desperation, in the fourth, the big meatball low-blowed you when the ref couldn't see. Right in the balls." Callahan's face contorted and his fists balled up as he recalled the moment. "He bulled you into the corner, kinda like Dwyer did, today."

"Ah, yes. I remember now."

Callahan started breathing hard as he moved around with his hands up. "He was trying to pummel you and you were doing your cage thing, your guard up and leaning back while he kept firing away."

Garm's head snapped to attention. "*Ah*, you mean--"

"Yes! He was throwing all these bombs, trying to finish it before you could recover . . . but he got winded and you guys ended up in a clinch. I saw your head come up and you wore an evil smile, just like you did today. You whispered something in his ear and then proceeded to take him apart like a bunch of Legos."

"So, all you want to know is what I told Angelo that night?"

Callahan did the bobblehead thing. "Fuck, yeah! I couldn't make it out and it's been driving me nuts for years. Even tried hiring someone to read your lips on the video, but the angle is no good. I'm positive it's the same thing you muttered to that juiced-up orangutan, a few minutes ago."

Garm nodded imperceptibly. "Now that you mention it, I think you're right. It must be force of habit or maybe a jogged memory." He looked at Callahan. "Guys like Dwyer and Rubino are cut from the same cloth. They're big, clumsy sluggers who can't win fair and square, so they go all street, figuring they can overwhelm you."

Garm snorted. "I've dealt with their kind many times. They're like rhinos: no staying power." He shrugged. "Don't get me wrong. Rubino messed me up pretty good before I bounced back. He split my lip, busted my nose, and caught me with a hook to the side of the neck that hurt me. But then he ran out of steam. And I ran out of patience."

Callahan reached out with trembling hands. He was so wound up, he wanted to grab the front of Garm's bloodstained shirt and shake him. But he managed to stop himself a few inches shy. "Gate, *please* . . . the anticipation is killing me. I gotta know. I just *gotta*."

Garm angled his head to one side. "Geez, I didn't realize it was such a big deal. Okay, fine. I told Dwyer the same thing I told Angelo. The same two words I'd say to anyone who tries to take me down and fails, right before I drop a world of pain on them."

"And they are?"

"My turn."

As he saw a huge, "that's-one-off-the-bucket-list" smile make its way across the admiral's expectant face, Garm winked at him. Then he turned and started off.

"Where are you going?" Callahan asked.

"To the showers," Garm replied. He gave him an apprehensive look. "You're not going to follow me, I hope."

Callahan grinned and shook his head. "No thanks, Gate. You've shown me enough for one day. For a lifelong fan of the sweet science, it means more than you could know."

"Good. Then let's leave it at that."

Anticipation of the hunt began to well within the Ancient's cavernous breast as he closed on his unsuspecting quarry. They were less than three miles ahead now and heading right toward him. As they traveled, their plaintive calls resounded like dinner bells through the water column, combining with their blubbery scent to entice him hungrily forward.

Although the seafloor lay five thousand feet beneath his hard-scaled belly, he maintained a cruising depth of only six hundred feet. Lurking in the dark, just below the ocean's phototropic zone, he was shallow enough to make spouting easy, yet deep enough to be able to disappear into the embracing blackness of the abyss at will. Behind him lay the termination point of the Cayman Trench, to his left and right, the islands of Cuba and Haiti.

As he spiraled back down from replenishing his air supply, glittering bubbles danced along the Ancient's scaly flanks. His twin blowholes were clamped shut to ensure no oxygen was lost. There would be no more spouting. He had stalked the pod of gray whales for hours, his four boat-sized flippers using reduced power strokes to conserve energy as he traveled soundlessly through the choppy waters of the Windward Passage. Eventually, he had managed to get ahead of them and cut them off. Within minutes, he would be within striking distance.

As the grays' communication clicks permeated the surrounding sea, the Ancient closed his deep-set eyes and relished both the welcoming sound and the sensation of tepid water rushing over his rough skin. The layers of fibrous scar tissue that coated much of his body itched like mad at times, and the Passage's warm embrace was a much-needed spa to the old bull. As huge and powerful as he was, and despite his regenerative abilities, he had his share of aches and pains.

He was far from indestructible. Nor was he immortal.

A sudden squeal of alarm caused the giant pliosaur's ruby-red orbs to snap back open. He had been approaching the gray whales from the southwest, staying downstream to minimize giving away his position. Once he drew close enough to ID the member of the pod whose blood trail he'd picked up on, he planned on accelerating to attack speed, broadsiding his hapless victim and killing it instantly.

But something was amiss. From two miles away, he could hear the pod's high-pitched calls growing louder and more frantic. Soon, their sonar clicks echoed throughout the region. The Ancient's ivory fangs interlocked as his titanic jaws closed and flexed. It was an unforeseen aggravation. Unlike the toothed sperms he fought and fed upon, the big baleen whales were not active hunters that relied on their sound senses to target prey. As a result, what echolocation abilities they possessed were far less sophisticated. Their sonar was used mainly to pinpoint distant clouds of krill, or at night to navigate. During daylight hours, they relied on their sensitive hearing and keen eyesight to show them the way.

Now, however, the entire pod was on high alert. Their cries grew more and more raucous, and clumsy broadband clicks began to radiate from every member. Soon, cones of sound spread out like a spider web, covering every direction at once. It was just a matter of time before they managed to--

The Ancient uttered a grumble of frustration as he felt himself being pinged by active sonar. A second later, a uniform squeal of terror split the water and the entire pod turned and took off at breakneck speed. Shaking his huge head, he immediately switched to full-power strokes and threw himself forward. His speed increased rapidly, from the slothful twenty miles an hour he had been maintaining until he was doing more than twice that.

As he closed the distance between himself and the fleeing cetaceans the bull noticed that, for some bizarre reason, the whales had stopped running. Like a besieged wagon train, they began forming up until they took on the appearance of a giant baitball.

The Ancient slowed his approach. Although his primeval brain was capable of only limited problem solving, he had centuries of experience to draw upon. The gray whales were far from mindless cows. They should have scattered in every possible direction. If they had, they'd have lost only one or two members of the pod. But instead, they were huddling together like fish in a barrel, their squeals of terror traveling far and wide.

The old bull's football-sized eyes contracted inward as a strange scent wafted into his nostrils and through the scoop-shaped sensory organs in his palate that broke down smells. A moment later, he realized why the whales had stopped running.

Something was in their way.

Throwing caution to the wind, the *Kronosaurus imperator* scanned both the whales and the ocean beyond with a quick burst of his powerful sound sight. The mile-long cone of sonar he emitted lashed out at four-and-a-half times the speed of sound and reverberated back. As his gigantic mandibles absorbed the incoming broadband clicks and sent them to his brain for analysis, he got a detailed picture of the surrounding sea.

In a heartbeat, he knew there were exactly eighteen members of the gray whale pod – all adults. He had pinpointed their location, as well as their current speed and depth. He could tell their approximate age, size, and even their physical condition. And he also knew what was hunting them.

He could see it clearly now as it rushed forward, five hundred yards behind the terrified cetaceans. It was herding them along, its ten-foot-wide jaws opening and closing as it sought an opportunity to sink its teeth into a vulnerable member of the pod.

The notion of another predator appropriating that which was his sent a jolt of adrenaline lancing into the great bull's sofa-sized heart. When it came to competitors, only the big females of his kind were tolerated, and then, only during the mating season. At all other times, he reigned supreme. He would not allow another carnivore to challenge him for a kill. Or even to scavenge what remained of one, unless he had abandoned it.

A black rage descended over the Ancient's vision as he began to accelerate. With his front and rear flippers pumping at full power through their respective planes of motion, he increased his velocity to maximum. Foregoing his usual caution, he began to emit powerful sonar pulses, his eyes crimson slits and his battering ram jaw clamped shut as he hurtled forward. As he rocketed through the oncoming seas, his pulse rate quickened, pumping more and more blood to his muscles, and increasing his body's already formidable ability to rend and destroy. He was, for all intents and purposes, a living engine of death.

And his target was the invading *Megalodon*.

Dirk stood in a gym shower stall, his hands resting against one tiled wall as the hot water beat down on his painfully tight trapezius muscles. He gritted his teeth and cricked his neck from side to side, both hearing and feeling vertebrae pop as he worked at relieving tension.

He was lucky Garm showed up when he had. Angus Dwyer was obviously out of his mind.

What the hell is that guy's problem? And what was Natalya thinking? She could've gotten bruised up or even lost some teeth, and for what?

Dirk stuck his head under the showerhead, blowing an exhale through the sheet of water that cascaded down his face. He had to admit, witnessing his Amazonian love interest defending him like that was an absolute turn-on. She was like a tawny lioness, getting in Dwyer's face like that. Unbelievably brave, and those thighs . . . *God, she looked good today*. Of course, her sticking up for him also meant, in her eyes, that he was a child who needed protection, instead of a man who could handle himself.

He shook his head ruefully under the spray. *That's just great . . . as if being Garm's "little" brother wasn't emasculating enough.*

"Dirk, you in here?"

Speak of the devil. "Back here," Dirk replied, poking his head out as his twin hung his comforter-size bath sheet up and jumped into the next stall. He'd already tossed his bloodstained shirt and was looking to rinse away the final vestiges of his fistfight with the guards.

"So, um . . . thanks for intervening like that," Dirk offered. "It was looking pretty hairy there."

"No worries," Garm said. He kept to the front and started rolling his shoulders out as he waited for the water to heat up. "But stay away from that Dwyer creep. There's something wrong with that guy."

"I think there's a lot of things wrong with him."

Garm snorted in amusement. "Yeah, you never found anything?"

"No. In fact, other than a standard employment file with his picture and salary, he's got no personal info whatsoever. Not even on the DOC servers. There's no contact number, former address, or next of kin. Not even a DOB. It's like he doesn't exist."

"That's bizarre. Have you asked Grayson?"

"Not yet. But I guess I'll have to." Dirk made a face as he caught sight of the nasty bruise gracing Garm's temple. "That was one hell of a punch you took. You okay?"

"Oh, please. Those guys hit like first graders."

Dirk faked a grin and started soaping up. A thought came to him out of left field. "Hey, Garm?"

"Yeah?"

"Speaking of first graders . . . you never told me what you did to Billy Balconis and his goon friends, to keep them from pounding on me every day."

"Wow." Garm's chuckle echoed around inside the adjacent shower. "You're time tripping. That really *was* in first grade!"

Dirk nodded. "Actually, I kinda know what you did to his two wingmen. I saw you grab Jimmy D'Angelo by the throat, behind the playground building. And Andrew Lawrence was sporting one hell of a mouse, the next day."

Garm chuckled. "I heard he fell down."

"That's what he said in homeroom. Neither of them would say a word."

"What can I say? Fear is a great motivator."

Dirk stopped scrubbing for a moment and cleared his throat. "So, are you gonna tell me or what?"

"What is this, memory lane day?" Garm asked, amusedly. "Tell me the truth; did Callahan put you up to this?"

"The admiral? What are you talking about?"

"An inside joke, Dirk. Never mind. So, you want to know what happened to poor little bully . . . I mean, Billy, eh?"

"*Duh.*"

Garm stuck his big head out of the shower, glancing around to make sure nobody else could hear. He caught and held Dirk's gaze. "After I caught up with his buddies, I couldn't have Billy-boy staggering around with his face all busted up. Even if he didn't fess up, you know that would've been a green mile straight to the principal's office. And let's not even dwell on the beating I'd have gotten when I got home."

Dirk's eyes widened at the thought. "Shit, you're right about that. Mom would've thrashed your ass, big time."

Garm laughed aloud at the shared memories. Their dad had been physically imposing – a dangerous guy, to be sure. But when it came to disciplining his two sons, Jake was a complete mush. Amara, on the other hand, was like a mama wolverine with PMS when it came to doling out punishments.

Garm kept his voice low. "Anyway, so what happened is, I grabbed a couple of bananas from the cafeteria and waited for him in the boy's bathroom."

"Bananas? I don't get it."

"When he came in, I locked the door. And before he could call for help, I punched him in the stomach so hard he vomited."

Dirk winced. "Jesus. Why, so there were no visible marks?"

"Exactly. Then I yanked his shirt up over his head so he couldn't see and dragged him into a nearby stall."

Dirk was confused. "For what? A swirly?"

Garm wore a shit-eating grin. "Nope, I made him stick his hand in the bowl and squeeze the--"

"Holy shit! You peeled the bananas?"

"Yep. He was crying like a little girl the whole time."

"Wow, that's messed up. Funny as all hell, but messed up."

Garm nodded. "Then, I pulled his shirt back down and let him see it was just fruit he was holding." He glanced toward the door then added. "But I told him, if he ever bothered you again, the next time it would be the real thing. And he wouldn't just be grabbing it. I'd make him *eat* some!"

There was a moment of silence. Then they both burst out laughing.

"I'm glad to see you boys are having a good time een here," Dragunova remarked.

As if by magic, she appeared right outside the showers, her hands on her hips, and studying them both through those timber wolf's eyes of hers.

"Holy shit!" the brothers yelled simultaneously.

"Nat, what the fuck are you doing?" Garm snapped. Unlike Dirk, who was busy trying to hide his manhood behind a woefully inadequate bar of soap, his brother was quite comfortable being nude around *Antrodemus*'s captain.

"Dr. Grayson asked me to . . ." Dragunova's eyes lit up as she looked Dirk up and down. "Bozhe moy! You two really *are* tweens!"

Garm's face darkened. "Nat . . ."

"Oh, fine, you beeg baby," she pouted. She turned her back to them, her defined arms folded atop her chest.

Dirk desperately wanted his towel, but he wasn't about to go get it. "Uh, Captain Dragunova, maybe we could just see you out--"

"Sorry, boys. But Dr. Grayson eenstructed me to tell you at once," she replied. "Wolfie, the Talos Mark VII suit for *Gryphon* has arrived from JAW Robotics and ees seeting een a crate at the loading dock. You need to sign for eet and oversee delivery and installation."

"And that couldn't wait until we got out of the shower?" Garm remarked.

"Also, Dr. Derek . . ." Dragunova's head swiveled on her toned shoulders and she smirked as she threw him a sideways glance. "Dr. Grayson wants to start the meeting early. You two need to come at . . . oof!"

Genuinely annoyed by the way she was leering at his brother, Garm stormed naked out of the shower and grabbed her by the upper arm. Cursing under his breath, he half-pushed, half-dragged her toward the exit, with her glancing back the entire time.

"I guess eet's not true what they say about guys weeth small hands, da?"

As they vanished around the corner and started squabbling like an old married couple, Derek stood there with his jaw drooping. After pondering what just occurred, it was all he could do to keep from doing a victory dance, right there in the shower.

———

A half-mile behind the pod of foraging gray whales, the *Carcharodon megalodon* female maintained her pursuit. Several hours earlier, she'd picked up the scent of blood oozing from a member of the pod and had been doggedly following them ever since.

As the migrating cetaceans altered course yet again, the female's myriad senses strained to keep pace. Moments earlier, the grays had swung southwest, entering the turbulent depths of the Windward Passage and heading for the nutrient-rich waters of the Caribbean Sea. Unseen and undetected, she hung back, trailing them like the deadly shade she was.

The huge shark was irritated. When she first entered the passage, she experienced a powerful urge to break off the hunt and maintain her original heading. It was the same mysterious summons that had drawn her from the frigid waters she called home and started her on her epic journey. The pull was strong, but for the first time she resisted. The writhing of her empty stomach outweighed the nagging stimulus. Eventually, the desire to redirect vanished and she found herself in full command of her senses. The bizarre internal conflict had reawakened her hunger, however. She needed to feed soon, and the mobile mountains of flesh she was pursuing were, by far, the best prospect.

As the whales continued obliviously onward, the *Megalodon* felt the temperature of the surrounding sea inch upward. She knew it would soon be outside her comfort zone and spread her twenty-foot pectoral fins wide. With a powerful thrust from her sail-like tail, she glided silently downward, causing a football field-sized school of squid to simultaneously dump their ink as she parted them like the Red Sea. Descending to six hundred feet, she leveled off and held position, relishing the comforting coldness of a deep-water current.

Suddenly, a familiar odor enveloped the female and she drew copious amounts of seawater into her watermelon-sized nostrils. The infusion was a heady combination of gray whale urine mixed with estrus hormones from the adult cows. It was like a drug to her and she relished the pungent aroma, her mammoth jaws reflexively parting.

Despite the distance between them, she could sense the whales' bodies shifting, their muscular forms moving sinuously up and down as they feasted upon the region's omnipresent clouds of krill. Even though the pod was too far off for her basketball-sized eyes to lock onto, she sensed the compression waves they gave off, even from a thousand yards away. Although she possessed no external ears, her coarse skin was dotted with tiny, soundwave-sensing pores that sent incoming signals to her cilia-coated lateral line. The linear-shaped sensory organ was an evolutionary masterpiece that ran from the tip of her bulbous snout to the termination of her crescent-shaped caudal fin. It effectively enabled her to "hear" with every inch of her mammoth 84-foot body.

As the taste of fresh whale blood once again infiltrated her mouth, the *Megalodon* became aroused. She shook her massive head from side to side, her broad-based, triangular teeth gnashing together in avaricious anticipation. At an astounding 210 tons, she was a ponderous beast – too slow to match the speed and agility of a healthy gray whale. But a birthing cow or an old or injured one was a different story.

Although she was predominantly a carrion feeder who made a living appropriating carcasses from more active predators, she was, above all else, a consumer of flesh. Given the chance, she would catch, kill, and devour anything she could, as slow-moving prey like sea turtles and walruses often discovered. But a fresh whale kill, coated with still-warm blubber and spurting hot blood into the surrounding sea, was a rare opportunity.

And she was on the trail of just such an opportunity.

It was an old cow, judging by the scent, and a badly injured one at that. Its dorsal was shredded by a series of ragged wounds – undoubtedly a passing ship's prop – and the wounded baleen whale struggled to keep up with its pod-mates. The strain was beginning to tell, and every so often its wounds would reopen, unleashing a torrent of crimson that stained the nearby water a bright red and put every shark in the area on alert. But the honor of the kill, when the cetacean deteriorated to the point she could finally catch up to it, would be hers and hers alone.

Relaxing as the blood trail faded once more, the *Megalodon* resumed her silent stalking. Her twenty-four-foot caudal flukes swung fluidly from side to side, each stroke displacing enough saltwater to fill an Olympic-sized swimming pool. All the while, her forward-facing eyes swept the darkened seas ahead, scanning for food or foes. She was an eating machine whose forebears had survived the dinosaurs and tenacity was her forte. She was hungry, but she was calculating. Most importantly, like all successful scavengers, she was patient.

The scabbed-over wounds she'd sustained during her brief battle with the bull pliosaur began to itch once more, and the irritated female bared her teeth. Her twelve-foot gill slits flared wide as she yawned, her mighty jaws stretching wide enough to engulf an elephant. The sudden influx of cold, oxygen-rich water invigorated her, and her protective, nictitating eye membrane blinked several times as she tore through an approaching cloud of krill.

Although she was comfortable in deep water and saw well in the dark, the giant shark and her kind were primarily a shallow water genus. There was a sub-species of *Megalodon* that split off from their lineage during the last Ice Age, and that now inhabited the ocean's extreme depths. However, they were a far different animal. With more limited food sources, they tended to be smaller, reaching a maximum length of around fifty feet, and had lost much of their mottled gray pigmentation. Pale ghosts of the deep, they eked out a living scavenging descending whale carcasses and preying on, or falling prey to, the titanic squid whose hunting grounds they shared.

Unlike her deep-dwelling relatives, who relied on anti-freeze proteins in their blood to survive the freezing temperatures of the abyss, she was basically a gigantic version of her more modern cousin, the salmon shark. Warmed as they were by vascular counter-current exchangers in her circulatory system, she was one of the few fish in the world that could regulate her body temperature. As a result, she was a far more active predator than her abyssal brothers and sisters and could prowl both the surface and the icy waters of the deep.

Or in her case, the Arctic waters she called home.

A sudden noise drew the female's attention. It wasn't coming from the gray whales, however. Instead, the sound emanated from far behind her and high up – from the surface, in fact. Recognizing it, the great fish's jaws closed, her thick teeth pressing tightly together in frustration.

The racket the surface vessel gave off was annoyingly familiar to her. For weeks, it had plagued her like an overgrown pilot fish, following her at a distance and shadowing her every move. Several times, she attempted to drive it off, but each time the thing came back.

The female swung sideways and glanced briefly at it before turning away. Her body shook with the shark equivalent of a shrug of futility. The boat was too fast for her. As long as it kept its distance, she had no choice but to tolerate its presence.

Turning her nose back onto the whale pod's trail, the *Megalodon* continued the pursuit. Based on its movements, she could tell the injured cow was beginning to fade. Bit by bit, the distance between them gradually lessened. Soon, it would be too weak to continue and the pod would stop to let it rest. At that point, she would make her presence known. Rising into the light, she would launch her attack while the gray whale's pod-mates fled for their lives. Then, she would have the two things she desired most: the delicious, calorie-rich blubber that she was so often denied.

And the chance to kill.

TWENTY-SIX

"How's Ursula doing?" Dr. Katerina Feaster asked as she got up from her station and moved toward the helm. It was midday, and *Insolent Endeavor's* twin 1,400 horsepower Cummins inboards were purring like gigantic kittens as the upgraded fifty-foot Monte Carlo MC5 kept pace with the slow-swimming *Carcharodon megalodon*.

"She's fine," Dr. Judas Cambridge replied, his bespectacled eyes locked onto an overhead monitor. On it, the temporal region of the giant shark's living room-sized head could be seen as it continued tirelessly along, passing through a half-mile cloud of plankton and detritus and bumping aside the occasional jellyfish. A couple of *Flagorneur* fish suddenly appeared on the far side of the screen, suspended a few yards away and mirroring Ursula's every move.

Jude made a face. He despised the yard-long Diablo Caldera escapees. They were upsized Cleaner Wrasse that latched onto large predators like sperm whales, pliosaurs, and sharks, and fed off them. Actually, not off *them*, per se, but off their fecal matter. They hung around their host like tilapia crowding around a hippo, waiting for it to excrete. The moment it did, they attacked the cloud of nitrite-rich excrement like hungry piranhas, burying their faces in their host's cloaca or rectum as they gorged themselves. Once, he saw one swim completely inside Ursula's anal cavity – not that the great fish seemed to notice.

It was, after all, a symbiotic relationship, he mused. *She fed them and they tongued her ass.*

Jude chuckled at the visual, then blinked as the screen went momentarily black and the Wrasse scattered. It was the blinding flash of the locator's bright red strobe, momentarily overloading the sensitive infrared lens. He looked down and checked their sonar. "We're five hundred yards back and she's holding at six hundred feet . . . speed is ten knots."

"Did she finally stop fighting the implant?" Kat asked.

Jude shook his head. "I gave up and put it in sleep mode. She's locked onto that wounded *Eschrichtius robustus* cow and refuses to give up the hunt." He swiveled his captain's chair until he was facing his partner-in-crime and shrugged. "I guess there's no fighting hunger."

Kat's blue eyes contracted, the edges of her mouth dipping down into an uncharacteristic pout. "How badly is this detour going to set us back?"

"Not much." Jude touched a toggle switch, activating the zoom on Ursula's locator's integrated camera. He pushed it to maximum. A second later, the rising and falling flukes of the nearest members of the gray whale pod came into view. The one bringing up the rear was obviously struggling. "With the wounds that cow sustained from colliding with the freighter, she can't last much longer. We're only twenty miles into the Windward Passage. Ursula will make her kill soon and we'll document it. Once she's got a full belly, she'll be easier to influence. We'll reactivate the program and get her back on track. It'll cost us a couple of hours at most."

"Good." Kat leaned forward at the hip, arching her back and resting one hand on the console as she eyed the locator's monitor. "I see her lacerations have scabbed over nicely."

As his business partner's baby powder-scented perfume permeated his nostrils, Jude shifted in his chair. His hazel eyes widened at the unexpected closeness. As was her habit, Kat had showered and changed after breakfast, and was dressed in a skimpy tank-top and loose-fitting sweatpants. They were the low-ride variety, and between the bright pink thong that shamelessly delved into the exposed portion of her ass and her fresh scent, he was having a tough time focusing on science. At least, any kind pertaining to marine life. "Uh, yeah . . . she's definitely going to look good. On camera, I mean."

Kat gave him a sideways glance and grinned. "You're planning on using the footage as part of your pitch, I assume."

"The footage?"

"Of her making her kill. I get it. It makes her look much more fearsome – a good selling point. That way, if Grayson throws the whole 'carrion feeder' angle at the Navy, you can offset it. What the hell do those guys know, right?"

Jude's jaw hung partially open. "Um, how did you know I--"

"C'mon, Sharky. Give me some credit," she said with a chuckle. "Who knows you better than me?"

Jude nodded in appreciation of Kat's astuteness. He'd been dreading unveiling his "evil master plan" to her. Challenging one of his estranged former employer's pliosaurs to a battle to the death was a bit unorthodox. In fact, to a scientist, it was borderline crazy. He'd half-expected her to freak out and demand they call the whole thing off. But to his relief she'd not only handled it, she agreed to go along. He couldn't have been more grateful.

As Kat pushed herself erect and held up the tablet she had stashed under one arm, Jude worked hard at not noticing she wasn't wearing a bra. It was obviously cold in there and he made a mental note to check the boat's air conditioner settings.

"I've got good news," she said.

"Let's hear it," Jude replied, clearing his throat.

"I finished my comparative and genetic profiles of both our fish and the abyssal *Megalodon.*" She handed him the tablet, beaming proudly as he started scanning her findings.

Jude licked his lips as he scrolled down the screen with one finger, speed-reading as he went. "Fascinating . . . Ursula's gum tissue confirms it. They're separate species that separated from the original chronospecies."

She nodded. "A response to evolutionary pressure from climatic changes, I assume. Darwin theorized that two distinct populations of the same species, isolated from one another for only ten thousand years, could evolve down divergent paths. I'd say this proves it."

"Yes, but with a Lazarus taxon? It's remarkable."

Kat moved closer, resting her hand on his shoulder as she leaned down. "Forget the DNA sequencing for a moment. Read the implications of the hematology and anatomical reports. The interspecies divergence is far more extreme than anticipated."

Jude's eyes did the old-fashioned typewriter thing, ratcheting back and forth at high speed as he read on. After a moment, he looked up at her, his expression one of marked surprise.

"They're . . . they're completely different."

"Night and day."

"So, the smaller albino variety we tracked last summer, we already knew they were more sluggish--"

"Like giant six-gills, adapted to life in the deep-water trenches."

Jude glanced down, focusing on a particular paragraph, then eye-balled the corresponding chart. "Their circulatory system is completely unlike Ursula's. Instead of internally warming cold, oxygenated blood coming from the gills and cooling it via vascular heat, the abyssal sub-species uses . . ." He paused and looked at her. "Is this correct?"

Kat nodded. "That hunk of skin we got from the bait cage confirms it. Their blood is clear and saturated with natural antifreeze glycopro-teins, most likely manufactured by the pancreas."

"So, they don't have to rely on movement-generated body heat like Ursula does. They can exist in sub-freezing temperatures indefinitely, using the ice-inhibitors they carry in their blood – like an Antarctic no-tothenioid fish?"

"Exactly."

"But in a shark? I've never heard of such a thing."

Kat shrugged. "Convergent evolution. The Arctic cod evolved antifreeze proteins in its blood and it's completely unrelated to notothenioids."

Jude's lips tightened and he drew a deep breath. "Well, sharks have been around since the dawn of time. If any fish could develop it, they could."

"Of course, this means that the two species are incapable of interbreeding."

Jude glanced up at her, realizing her hand was still on his shoulder. "Well, that goes without saying."

Kat reached onto his lap to retrieve her tablet. She hesitated as she clocked the contemplative look on his face. "What's on your mind?"

Jude felt a sudden surge of excitement. "We can use this," he an-nounced. "As a sideline, once we acquire those Navy contracts."

"Use what?"

"The anti-freeze proteins," he said. He stripped off his glasses and stood up, his eyes running wild as his mind raced to catch up. "For cryogenics technology. I've seen the current research. They've been trying to develop a preservative based on notothenioid glycoproteins for decades, but they've gotten nowhere. The ice fish's evolutionary gap is too wide. But with the *Meg*--"

"I love it," Kat interjected. She wore a huge grin as she hugged her tablet to her chest, like a geeky high-schooler with a favorite textbook. "And I *love* how your mind works. Do you really think you can do it?"

"Do I really think *we* can do it." Jude wagged a corrective finger at her. "And the answer is *yes*." Awash with anticipation, he reached out and gripped her firmly by the shoulders. "Just think: we'll pioneer food that can be kept frozen indefinitely. And, eventually, we'll find a way to suspend astronauts for deep space travel. My God, we are going to do some amazing things together!"

As he saw her cock an amused eyebrow up at him, Jude realized he was still holding her. He released his grip and stood there, wallowing in waist-high doubt. Finally, he ran a nervous hand through his sand-colored hair. "I'm sorry, Kat. I, uh, got a little worked up."

She smiled. "That's okay. I liked it."

"You did?"

"Absolutely. I love when all your cylinders start firing and you get assertive like that. It shows me what you're made of."

Jude nodded. "Uh, thanks. I'm really glad we're together on this."

"Me too." She pursed her lips, her eyes flitting about. "And for the record, I think your ex-wife is an asshole."

He chuckled. "That's something we have in common."

As Kat headed toward her station, Jude found himself drawn to the bright pink thong, peeking out from the top of her sweats. A second later, he realized she had glanced back over her shoulder to say something and caught him red-handed.

"Are you checking out my ass?"

"What? Uh, no! The, uh . . . color of your underwear inadvertently drew my gaze, like a brightly-hued bass lure does to a passing fish."

She turned back around, an entertained expression on her face. "Wow, I pray to God you never have to take the stand in my defense. As a liar, you suck!"

Jude stared a hole in the ground. "Sorry. I . . . it won't happen again."

"Why not?"

He blinked and did a double take. "W-what?"

Kat gave him an appraising look. "Initially, you caught me off guard with the whole, 'I'm gonna kick Grayson's ass' routine. But after thinking it through, I've decided it's very ballsy."

Jude didn't know where she was going with this and decided to play it safe and just stand there. Kat stared deductively at him, like he'd seen her do a hundred times as she was weighing the pros and cons of a new discovery.

She walked over to a nearby porthole and glanced outside, shielding her eyes against the bright sun. "You know, I like men, too."

Jude tried to speak, but discovered he had the Gordian knot lodged in his throat. She glanced back at him and smirked.

"Not often, mind you. Usually, there's an issue."

"What, uh . . . what would that be?"

She pinned him with a look. "In purely clinical terms, most guys don't know how to eat pussy. And, not to sound mean, but I hate giving lessons."

Jude nodded slowly. He felt like a deer staring into an oncoming tractor trailer's headlights; he was scared to death, but too fascinated to get out of the way. He frowned as Kat turned back to the portal, eyeing the calm seas beyond. Beneath their feet, *Insolent Endeavor* continued to cut through the waves like a scythe through wheat, smoothly and efficiently.

She glanced up at the low ceiling, studying the rugged big game fishing rods they had suspended directly overhead. "I've been thinking about it for the last few days and I've come to a decision."

Jude swallowed the painful lump in his throat. "And what's that?"

"I have decided to have sex with you."

Omigod.

He couldn't believe it. Just like that, she'd thrown it out there. No discussion. No 'would you like to?' or any such nonsense. She just made the announcement, as if his compliance was a given and it was the most natural thing in the world.

Jude hesitated, trying to make sure his ears weren't playing tricks on him before responding. "Okay . . ."

Kat started walking around the cockpit, observing things as if she had just arrived and not been there 24/7 for the last two weeks.

"If you like it and you want us to continue having intercourse, that's great. And if you don't, or if you think it's bad for our relationship and you want to stop, or even if you decide you never want to see me again, that's fine, too." She moved closer, eyeing him up and down as she tucked a stray lock of scarlet behind one ear. "I don't care."

Jude stared at her with a dazed *'Where have you been all my life?'* look. Over the last few weeks, he'd fantasized about being with her dozens of times. And now it was going to happen. He felt a heatwave start to build in his toes. It moved rapidly upward and nestled in his groin. "I'm sure it will be great. So, uh . . . what do we--"

"There is one condition, however," Kat interrupted.

"Oh, sure. What is it?"

"I get to pick the position."

Jude's eyes lowered to half-mast as a depressing thought shot through his head. Despite her words, it was obvious his prospective lover was into women only, and the thought of sleeping with some hairy male was anathema to her. He imagined she couldn't stomach seeing a man's face while she had sex.

"Let me guess," he hazarded. "You want to do it from behind."

She chuckled. "No, silly boy. I don't have my strap-on with me. You're perfectly safe."

"*What?*"

Kat burst out laughing as she spotted his bewildered expression. "I'm kidding, Sharky. Relax. I just prefer to be on top . . . at least for starters."

Jude felt himself begin to perk back up. "Wait, you mean you're going to do all the work and all I have to do is lay there?" He scoffed. "Are you kidding? I am *so* your guy!"

"Good."

"So, uh . . . what do we do now?"

"We get naked."

By the time her words had registered inside his head, Kat's tank-top was tossed and her thong and sweats lay in a pile around her ankles. He stared, unabashedly ogling her nakedness. His eyes ranged hungrily downward, starting at her slim throat, then over her perky breasts, down her tight stomach, and around her immaculately waxed pubic region.

Oh well, so much for strawberry-flavored carpeting.

He started to fumble with his belt, then stopped as she turned, bare-assed, and headed for the controls. "What are you doing?"

"Putting us on autopilot, silly," she said with an evil smirk. "I don't want any excuses when I'm riding you like Secretariat and the finish line is in sight."

"Oh, well . . . that makes sense," Jude said as he started wrestling out of his shirt. He wasn't sure what she meant by that, but he was dying to find out.

"Let me help you," Kat said. Reaching down, she pulled his t-shirt up and over his head, her lips meeting his even before his arms were free.

Jude felt his adrenaline kick in as her nipples pressed against his chest like the hot little hitchhikers they were. As his shirt fell to the floor, he wrapped his wiry arms around her and drew her close, their mouths merging in a kiss that started off hesitant, but then increased rapidly in urgency and intensity.

BING! BING! BING!

"What the hell is that?" Kat breathed as they broke apart. She licked her lips and glanced worriedly around the cockpit, her breasts lifting as she pressed her palms over her ears.

Jude's ardor cooled as he rushed to the nearby helm. His already adrenalized eyes swept their monitors. "It's ANCILE's proximity alarm!" he yelled over the shrieking claxon. "Ursula's slowed down for some reason and we're closing on her fast – less than three hundred yards!"

"Is she coming after us?" Kat asked. Despite her pensive eyes, she didn't bother to retrieve her clothes. Instead, she bent over and scanned a nearby monitor, then jabbed a key, silencing the alarm.

"No," Jude said, checking their sonar systems. "It's the whale pod. They've stopped swimming." He checked ANCILE once more. "Weird. They're just milling around. I don't think they know she's following them yet."

Kat clicked her tongue. "Good. The cow must be dying. She can feed and then we can get back on course."

"Most likely. Which will be good because--" Jude's head hauled back hard on his shoulders. "What the hell?"

On ANCILE's screen, the signals marking the giant *Megalodon* and the gray whale pod grew convoluted, the readings bunching up. Despite Kat disabling the claxon, warning signals flashed on the screen. Shirtless, Jude plopped down in his chair and leaned forward, his slim fingers attacking the keyboard.

Beside him, Kat stood with her feet spread apart and her arms folded atop her breasts. She was watching all the monitors at once, most especially Ursula's. "What's with the whales?"

"I don't know," Jude fretted. "Something weird's going on. According to the system, while we were . . . busy, the pod turned around and started heading straight toward Ursula. Then they stopped cold. Now they're all bunched up and acting very skittish."

Kat frowned, then reached over and hit a switch, turning on the ship's external hydrophone array. A moment later, the squeaks and squeals of frightened gray whales filled the cockpit.

"Listen to that racket!" she exclaimed. "They must have spotted her."

"Definitely," Jude said, tapping keys and activating their recording equipment. "You can even hear their sonar clicks as they--"

He stopped talking as a rumbling groan spilled from their internal speakers. It was a low-pitched sound that shook their hull like an approaching train. A second later, the sound stopped.

"What the hell was that?" Kat asked. She hugged herself as goose bumps pricked up all over her arms, legs, and stomach.

"I don't know," Jude said. He saw a red warning signal flash on the SVALIN monitor and studied it, his eyes narrowing. Suddenly, the screen came alive with movement. "Holy shit, the whales are freaking out! They've definitely spotted Ursula, but it's like they don't know which way to run." He zoomed in with the locator's infrared lens and then switched on the ship's integrated hull cameras. He checked them all, then shook his head in exasperation. "The water clarity sucks. I can't see anything, but there's something else out there!"

"What kind of *something*?"

Jude pointed at the sonar screen. "ANCILE's showing a mobile, non-cetacean biologic on the other side of the pod. Whatever it is, it's got the whales trapped between Ursula and it. Look, now the entire pod's breaking away at full speed!"

Kat swallowed nervously. "What is it? What's out there?"

Jude shook his head and swore under his breath. "I don't know. But whatever it is, it's *big*."

TWENTY-SEVEN

"**D**r. Grayson, with your permission, we're ready to get started," Dirk Braddock announced, looking down toward the far end of the conference room's expansive mahogany table as he addressed his silver-haired mentor.

"By all means, Derek. Please proceed." Eric Grayson replied, sitting back and relaxing in his executive chair. Although the nine remaining seats lining the conference table were roomy and comfortable, the CEO's Galuchat leather seat was so massive and luxuriously appointed, it looked like a throne by comparison. Next to him, Admiral Ward Callahan sat rigidly upright, scratching at his salt-and-pepper mustache and gripping his coffee mug as he waited for the festivities to begin. Dirk thought it was ironic that, affixed to the wall directly behind the verbose and, at times, insensitive naval man's head, was a plaque inscribed with one of his and Dr. Grayson's favorite Jean-Jacques Rousseau quotes:

"Nature never deceives us; it is we who deceive ourselves."

Dirk gave Callahan a polite nod and then gazed around the room. The post-demo meeting's itinerary included more than just a follow-up sales pitch for the Navy. There would be a call to arms, so to speak, and as he swept the brightly-lit chamber's forty-foot length, he took note of everyone else in attendance.

First around the table, moving clockwise, was Dr. Stacy Daniels, his off-again-on-again paramour and head of Tartarus's pliosaur program, followed by Captains Braddock and Dragunova, commanders of the base's ORION-class Anti-Biologic Submarines. Seated across the table from the two captains were their seconds-in-command – Jayla

Morgan from *Gryphon*, and Javier Gonzalez from *Antrodemus*. Morgan was a familiar face to Dirk. She was notoriously tough, but steadfast and dependable. Gonzalez, on the other hand, was a relative newbie. Dirk didn't know him well; he'd been with the CDF for only six months. An Annapolis grad that transferred over, the dark-skinned Cuban's combat record showed him to be a superb tactician with a hard-earned reputation for coolness under fire. At just over six feet in height, he was two inches shorter than his imposing captain, but with his raw-boned and rugged physique and intense eyes, he cut an impressive figure, nonetheless.

Besides, Dirk thought, if Natalya approved of him, the SOB *had* to be tough.

Last, but not least, standing two yards behind Grayson's chair, stood Acting Security Chief Oleg Smirnov, garbed in his traditional black fatigues and boots. The big Ukrainian's presence was a formality – his duties at the meeting basically amounted to helping the aged CEO in and out of his chair and fetching coffee.

Dirk stood up and cleared his throat. "I'd like to thank everyone for coming on such short notice after the meeting was moved up." He glanced down at the array of tablets he had propped up before him like a poker hand, his eyes taking in his notes. "Our first order of business is to follow-up on this morning's demonstration." He reached for a glass of water and held it up. "I may be premature in my evaluation and, please forgive the pun, but I think things went *swimmingly*. That said, I'd like to propose a toast to my fearless colleague, the one and only Dr. Stacy Daniels."

A chorus of cheers and some surprisingly loud clapping resounded throughout the conference room. Even Grayson joined in.

"I saw what you deed on video afterward and eet was the most courageous theeng I ever saw," Dragunova admitted, raising her glass and giving Stacy a sincere nod of respect. "You are a credit to all womankinds."

"Uh, thank you. Thank you, all," Stacy said, flushing under the unexpected praise. She glanced fondly up at Dirk. "We were just doing our jobs."

Callahan hoisted his coffee mug and chimed in, "And a damn fine one, the two of you. Man, that performance sure stirred my sweetbreads!"

"I assume that means you're satisfied with our new implant technology?" Dirk implied.

The admiral angled his head in Grayson's direction. "I already told your boss, kiddo. I'm not only buying every new unit I can get my hands on, I'm having all the old ones upgraded, as well."

"Excellent. Then let's move on to our next two points, which are updates on the global pliosaur population estimates and the Cuban political situation, as it pertains to Diablo Caldera."

"Derek," Grayson interjected. "The admiral has requested a report on *Typhon*. Let's focus on him, please."

"Damn straight," Callahan said. "After seeing your *Kronosaurus* queen *Tiamat* in action, I won't rest until I have a whole fleet of those fang-faced, four-finned death-dealers at my beck and call. And for that to happen, we need that big bull pliosaur to breed that bitch and make lots of little sons of bitches."

"Very well," Dirk said, pursing his lips. "We don't have a ton of data, but I'll answer any questions I can. What would you like to know, admiral?"

Callahan rubbed his thick hands together in anticipation. "Well, first off, where is he now? How soon can you get your subs into the area and how long will it take to capture him? Last, but not least, how big is he really and why is he so big? Will he fit in the Tube? Is he another mutie, like *Tiamat*? And do you think they'll mate?"

When Callahan finally stopped and came up for air, Dirk exhaled and touched a tab on his center tablet. The conference room lights dimmed and there was a low hum. A section of ceiling in the center of the room, directly above the table, opened, and what looked like a white tile, about two feet square and six inches thick, became visible. It began to glow and pulsate.

"What's that?" Callahan asked.

"Those were a lot of questions, admiral," Dirk pointed out. "And *this* is a civilian version of the holograph projector used in our POSEIDON 3-D fathometer screens." He grinned. "It's a step up from the old 'PowerPoint' presentation days, wouldn't you say?"

Dirk waved his hand over one tablet, causing the projector to spring to life. Shimmering dots of black and gold descended from it and swirled around, like fairy dust, writhing in the wind. The sparkles began to coalesce directly above the conference table, eventually forming a five-foot translucent sphere. A moment later, the sphere shimmered and vanished. In its place was the computer-generated image of a gnarly-looking pliosaur, its fanged jaws frozen in a pixeled grimace.

"This is a graphics reconstruction of *Typhon*, based on the combat footage recorded during his confrontation with our submarines," Dirk began. He noticed both sub captains and their seconds intently studying the hologram. "Even with our satellites, we have not been able to pinpoint his exact whereabouts, which means timetables are meaningless. I can, however, enlighten you as to what we've ascertained so far. As you can see, he's a bit on the battle-scarred side."

"What's with that big hump on his back?" Callahan asked. "Is this guy like Quasimodo or something?"

"Based on what the system interprets as a mound of bone and scar tissue, I'd lean toward the disfigurement being caused by trauma, versus pathology," Dirk replied. He moved his finger around, causing the three-dimensional image of the bull pliosaur to slowly spin. "I'll move on to current mass estimates, but please keep in mind these reconstructions and the accompanying data are all approximations. First, we'll switch over to a graphic of your typical bull pliosaur."

As he spoke, *Typhon*'s image vanished in a burst of light and was replaced by a 3-D reconstruction of a sleeker, less robust *Kronosaurus imperator.*

"This animal represents a sexually mature male, and at sixty-two feet in length and approximately seventy tons submerged displacement, he is considered large for the genus," Dirk said. He touched his keypad and a second pliosaur image appeared next to the first. The new animal was significantly bigger. "This is an atypical cow pliosaur. I say atypical because it is what is traditionally considered to be the species' maximum size." He glanced down at his notes, then at Callahan. "In fact, admiral, this particular reconstruction is based on our computer scans of your new acquisition, *Goliath*."

"Nice. She is a big beast, isn't she?"

"Yes, admiral," Dirk replied. "Now let's bring *Typhon* back, put to scale with the other two."

"Son of a bitch," Callahan whistled aloud as he saw the three pliosaurs lined up in size order.

"*Typhon* dwarfs the average male," Dirk stated. "He's fifty percent longer and three times the weight. In fact, except for the queen, he is both longer and heavier than the largest cows of his kind. If *Tiamat* is going to accept a mate, he's by far your best bet." He held up a finger for emphasis. "That's assuming, of course, that she finds him both viable and genetically desirable."

Dirk heard Garm mumble something along the lines of, "Poor bastard's gonna need a serious makeover," but ignored it.

Dragunova cleared her throat. "How much larger ees thees animal than the one we captured?"

Dirk experienced a brief flashback of her size comments after she'd seen him naked. "Uh . . . computer estimates put him at thirteen feet longer than *Goliath*. Around ninety-five feet."

Garm's hunter's eyes narrowed. "Shit. How much does he weigh?"

Dirk licked his lips. "Our best guess is big blue whale range: between 210–220 tons."

Everyone jumped as Callahan slammed his palm loudly on the table. "Now *that's* what I'm talking about!" he shouted. He turned to Grayson and pointed at the shimmering holograms. "You said it right, oh pal-o-mine. That boy is *exactly* what we need!"

"Calm down, Ward," Grayson said quietly. "Derek, please continue."

"Yes, sir." Dirk rechecked his notes before resuming. "In terms of why *Typhon* is so huge, admiral, there are myriad possibilities. As you stated, he could be just like *Tiamat*, a--"

"Mutie?"

Dirk faked a smile. "The term is mutation. And, yes, it is possible. We theorize that an anomaly like *Tiamat* hatches once every hundred years or so – probably in response to environmental pressure such as availability of prey or competition from another predator. Conversely, we know that, during the Pleistocene Epoch, a steady increase in cetacean size contributed to the decline of the shark *Carcharodon megalodon* – an example of prey items outgunning their predator."

Callahan wore a confused look. "Wait a minute. So, if these things have been trapped in that caldera for all those millions of years, how come we haven't seen more mutants? The one that trashed Paradise Cove was regular, right? If they're so big and tough, how come the only ones left in there weren't mutants?"

"Because the survival rate for *any* creature in an enclosed, predator-rich environment like Diablo Caldera would be dismally low," Dirk advised. "Although we haven't had a team in there to confirm it, we can logically deduce that Diablo's huge saltwater lake is teeming with the same giant squid and fish that were released during its fracturing. Plus, adult pliosaurs are notoriously cannibalistic. I would estimate only one in two hundred hatchlings survived their first year. And less than one in five hundred made it to adulthood."

"Well then, thank God we killed off most of our sharks and whales before the eggs hatched from that last one, right?" Callahan snorted. "Otherwise we might not have all these big, scaly beauties swimming around!"

"Yes, 'thank God' . . ." Stacy remarked without looking up from her notes.

"So, tell me, doc," Callahan said. "Is *Typhon* one of these 'mutations' or not?"

Dirk felt a headache coming on and started rubbing his temples. "Dr. Daniels, would you mind? This is more your area." Like his twin, he had limited patience when it came to Callahan, and what he did have was exhausted.

Stacy's tight blonde curls jiggled as she threw him a compassionate nod and stood up. In the center of the room, the hologram containing the three pliosaur images continued to slowly rotate.

"We've run genealogy profiles based on the DNA from a variety of *Imperator* specimens, including the original Paradise Cove female," Stacy began. She reached down, took a sip of water, and then set her glass back down. "We've also done profiles of *Typhon*'s DNA by isolating it from that of two of the pliosaurs he's fathered. From the look of things, his chromosomes were removed from the caldera gene pool centuries ago."

Garm inhaled sharply. "Did you say *centuries*?"

Amid a litany of surprised murmurs, Dirk saw Grayson's approving nod. Beside him, Admiral Callahan grew agitated. He shook his head and waved his hands to draw attention to himself.

"So, what does that mean, exactly?"

"It means, admiral, that the pliosaur we're about to hunt is a superannuated individual," Stacy advised. She stared at him, masking her amusement as she waited for the inevitable question.

"And that means . . ."

"He's very old, hence his great size."

Callahan blinked. "Wait, you said centuries." He pointed at the black and gold hologram. "You're telling me this thing's a couple hundred years old?"

"Apparently."

"That's impossible . . . isn't it?"

Stacy shook her head. "Reptiles are like fish, they're indeterminate growers. Given enough space, as long as they keep eating they keep growing."

Callahan's head bobbed up and down. "I know that. It's the immortality part I'm not buying."

She frowned. "Why not? Bowhead whales are mammals and live over 250 years. Greenland sharks can reach over 400 years. And many reptiles have notoriously long lifespans."

"Okay, fine. I get what you're saying, little lady," Callahan said. "But this guy is ginormous. Wouldn't someone have spotted him if he's been swimming around for the last two hundred years?"

"I suspect he's been seen many times," Stacy replied, tactfully ignoring the sexism. "Most of the time, I imagine he's mistaken for a whale. But we have documented sea monster sightings going back to the 18th century, many of which could be attributed to *Typhon* or a creature like him."

Callahan shook his head. "But in more modern times, with radar, sonar, and satellites . . . he's never been spotted or tracked?"

"As his battle with our subs demonstrated, *Typhon* is both experienced and crafty," Stacy said. "We are not dealing with a stupid animal, admiral. He's learned over the centuries. He knows what sonar is, knows how to run silent, and knows how to use structure to conceal himself. He's quite the tactician."

Callahan was obviously unconvinced. But when he opened his mouth to say so, Stacy ran right over him. "Just to give you an example . . ." she said, holding up her tablet and reading from it. "On November 11th, 1972, warships from the Norwegian navy detected a 'fast moving, submarine-like object' in Sonja Fjord, off the west coast of Norway. They tracked it with sonar for two weeks, using a fleet of surface ships and sub-hunter helicopters. On November 20th, 1972, the object was seen for the first time. It was described as a 'massive and silent, cigar-shaped object.' Guns and torpedoes were fired at it, whereupon it sounded. It avoided their weapons, even evaded depth charges. After two more weeks of hunting it, the Navy tried using a blockade to trap it in the fjord. They failed. Fifteen days later, it disappeared."

Stacy sat her tablet down. "So, you see, the odds are he's been spotted many times. Tracking and stopping him, however, are two entirely different matters."

Callahan contemplated her words. Then he craned his thick neck back and guffawed. "I love it. From the sound of it, he should have my job!"

Dirk rested his chin on one palm heel and grinned. His grin evaporated when he saw the looks on Garm's and Dragunova's faces as they absorbed this information. Still in his seat, he interjected, "There is something else we should point out, admiral. Something that may be useful to our valiant sub commanders, who face the daunting task of capturing this creature."

"What is it?" Garm asked.

"We've recorded *Typhon*'s sonar signature, as well as an audio-profile of his echolocation clicks. His ultra-low frequency emissions match one of the so-called 'bloop' underwater noise phenomena recorded by NOAA, starting back in 1997."

"Which one?"

"The one designated 'train.'" Dirk said. "It's in the file."

"Thanks."

Stacy chimed in. "We've also included updated coordinates and pertinent info from the most recent sightings. That includes the schooner that was sunk and the strange text message from that foreign yacht, which, by the way, you're going to be investigating."

Dragunova frowned. "And what ees our plan of attack?"

Stacy looked at Dirk, who gave her a nod.

"We're looking to launch tomorrow during high tide. *Antrodemus*'s repairs should be completed by then. Our recommendation is you separate with the goal of triangulating *Typhon*'s position. Once one of you gets a lock on him, do not engage. Not individually. Instead, use a *Loki* to hit him with a locator." She folded her toned arms across her chest. "Once you've got him tagged, it will be easier to join forces and corner him."

"Piece of cake," Garm snorted. "I'm sure he'll come willingly."

"And what ees prize for breenging back alive?" Dragunova asked, her stony gaze now falling on Grayson. "Thees animal ees dangerous."

Grayson contemplated her through hooded eyes before nodding his acquiescence. "Normally, I would say this falls under the terms of your contract, captain. But that's arguable." He closed his eyes for a moment, his brow tightening. "Let's make things interesting. Let's do it by the pound."

Dragunova looked confused. "What does that mean?"

"Actually, by the ton," Grayson revised, his fingers tapping on the table edge like it was an old-fashioned cash register. "If you bring him back alive and relatively unscathed, I'll pay each captain ten grand per ton of pliosaur. That means a minimum of two million dollars each."

As Garm and Dragunova exchanged stunned looks, Grayson added, "Oh, and I'll throw in matched amounts, to be divided up among each sub's crew . . . just to keep everyone happy."

Dragunova nodded at him. "You got yourself a deal, doctor."

"Spasiba." Without another word, Grayson leaned forward and pressed his hands against the end of the table. Grimacing, he struggled to his feet. Behind him, Oleg Smirnov realized his employer needed assistance and rushed forward, only to arrive too late and stand there impotently.

"This has been an excellent meeting," Grayson announced, waving off the guard and leaning on the table.

Dirk stood up. "You're leaving, sir?"

"Yes."

"But we haven't touched on current projections, status of negotiations for the caldera, or the serum distributions for--"

Callahan shook his head. "I'm sorry, son. But, as it turns out, that last incident with the guards had dire consequences for my 'Last Chancers' program."

"What do you mean?"

"I've been summoned to Washington to appear before a DOC review board. They're reevaluating the program," Grayson said. He glanced at Smirnov and sighed.

"How soon are you leaving?"

"Right now. And I'll be gone for a few days."

Out of the corner of his eye, Dirk saw Garm's face and wondered if this was how his twin felt when he ran into an unexpected punch. "Uh, okay. Sure thing, sir."

Grayson walked over and rested a confidence-inspiring hand on Dirk's shoulder. "You're in charge until my return." He indicated the nearby guard. "Acting Security Chief Smirnov will be answering directly to you, and all the guards to him. If there are any problems whatsoever, I want you to call my satellite phone, immediately."

"You got it, sir."

Grayson leaned close and spoke in low tones. "I'm counting on you to bring me *Typhon*. He is the <u>future</u>. Do you understand?"

Dirk stood upright and nodded. "I won't let you down, sir."

"I know you won't." Grayson walked over to Admiral Callahan. "Ward, shall we go?"

Callahan got up, gave Dirk a grin and a thumbs-up, then glanced at Garm and winked. "Time to write a few checks, fellas. Keep up the great work," he said, before turning and following Grayson and Smirnov outside.

Dirk felt a twinge of guilt as he watched his mentor leave. His fingers sought and found the portable drive in his lab coat pocket and he hesitated, wondering if he was doing the right thing. Around him, the ORION sub captains and their first officers conversed quietly among themselves. He glanced down at Stacy. She seemed distracted as she sipped her water and stared up at the still-rotating hologram.

Suddenly, a tiny ping interrupted Dirk's brooding and drew his attention down to his personal tablet. He had an incoming email on his secure server, marked urgent. As he sat down and read it, the page's reflection grew in his eyes.

"Holy shit!" Dirk looked around at everyone. "Uh, sorry about that . . ."

"What's wrong?" Stacy asked.

From across the table, Dirk noticed Dragunova eyeing him and smirking.

He stood back up and cleared his throat loudly. "The meeting is adjourned. If you're on shift, please resume your regular duty schedules. Thank you for coming."

As the sub commanders and officers rose to their feet, Dirk added, "Captains Braddock and Dragunova, please stay. I need to speak with you."

Gonzalez and Morgan exchanged glances, but then shrugged and said their goodbyes. Stacy got up and moved quietly to Dirk's side.

"Is everything okay?" she asked. "Do you need me to stick around?"

Dirk ground his teeth. It was better for Stacy if she wasn't a part of this. He put on his most relaxed face, trying to appear nonchalant. "No, it's just a minor personal matter. I'll be fine."

A second later, he cringed as Stacy's amber eyes zeroed Dragunova and a "why-am-I-leaving-and-that-bitch-is-staying?" look came over her.

Definitely the wrong choice of words.

"I'll explain later," he said quietly.

As he watched Stacy cast daggers at an amused Dragunova, before stalking out of the room, Dirk had a feeling he'd be better off sleeping with Gretchen tonight.

"Kat, put your clothes back on. Do it, fast!"

As he listened to his voice bounce around the confines of *Insolent Endeavor*'s tech-crammed bridge, a still-shirtless Judas Cambridge realized those were the last words he expected to hear coming from his mouth. He shook his head, less at the irony than the feeling of regret he experienced as he watched Katerina Feaster bend to retrieve the thong and sweatpants she'd slithered out of, moments earlier. With her eyes locked on their viewing screens, the feisty scientist inserted her toes and pulled upward, wriggling her hips from side to side as she navigated her way back into her shape-hugging bottom-wear.

"What's happening?" Kat pressed as she bent down and snatched up her discarded tank-top. "Do you have a visual?"

Jude blew out some stress, trying to ignore his partner's still-hard nipples. Unfortunately, it was because of pending danger, versus the passionate moment the two just shared.

"Sharky," Kat snapped as she glanced his way and realized he was zoned out. "Can you ID it or not?"

"Sorry." Jude shook his head once more, this time to clear the rosy cobwebs. "Not yet. It's still too far out for our fathometer to latch onto and, with all the zooplankton, the water's too clouded for our hull cameras to be of any use."

Kat frowned and eyed their primary sonar screen. "Autopilot's got us holding position on Ursula's six, three hundred yards back," she announced. "You're right. The signal is big. Whatever it is, it's a half-mile out and heading due east."

Jude sat upright and indicated an array of sonar blips moving erratically to and fro. "The gray whale pod is making a break for it. They've realized their predicament and are running full speed now, trying to get away from Ursula and whatever the hell else is out there."

"Boy, that's a big fucking signal. Do you think it's another *Megalodon*?"

Jude's head swiveled toward her, his surprised expression punctuating her uncharacteristic use of foul language. "I don't know. Hormonal readings from Ursula's gum tissue indicated she birthed her pups a few days before we tagged her, right?"

"Yes, what are you--" Kat's lips pursed then parted. "Wait, are you thinking she's in estrus and a big male has come a-courting?"

"Could be," Jude said. "But it would take one hell of a stud to . . ."

His words trailed off as a warning ping emanated from their ANCILE system's acoustic intercept. The unidentified signal they were tracking had turned. Ignoring the fleeing whales, it was arcing toward the southeast. Its speed matched the *Megalodon*'s as it came about. Seconds later, the giant shark altered course, turning northwest and rising in the water column, but maintaining the distance between them.

She knows something's out there.

Jude felt a lump form in his throat. Based on its trajectory, the intruder wasn't circling Ursula. It was stalking her.

"She's a lot closer to it than we are," Jude announced. Their inability to identify whatever was prowling out of range of their equipment was beginning to irk him. "I'm going to push the locator's zoom and see if we get lucky."

"Sounds good," Kat said. She bent at the waist, one forearm on the top of his chair. With her free hand, she reached forward and gently massaged the back of his neck.

Jude swallowed. Her warm touch was a welcome distraction.

"Pushing zoom to 50X." His hazel eyes intense, he worked the keys. "She's veering to the right . . . definitely knows she's got company. It's just a question of whether we can catch a glimpse while her head's turned in that dir--"

"There it is!" Kat shouted so loudly Jude jumped.

"Jesus, you fucking scared me!" he snapped. His annoyed eyes flung back toward the overhead screen. A full one-third of the infrared viewer was occupied by the starboard side of Ursula's broad head. On the other two-thirds, there was nothing but oncoming sea – clouds of plankton and an occasional fish or jelly. Every so often, the screen would go black as the locator's strobe went off. "What? I don't see anything."

"Rewind the auto-recorder," Kat instructed. "And go back a few seconds. Believe me; you'll know it when you see it."

Jude transferred the feed to one of their console screens and fiddled with the controls. A moment later, he saw. "Holy fucking shit."

"Watch the language," Kat said with a wink. "I've got my mother-in-law's picture in my wallet!"

"Is that . . ."

She nodded. "A *Kronosaurus imperator.* Biggest one I've ever seen."

Jude froze the brief seconds of footage before the scaly behemoth vanished off camera. He could see it outlined by the infrared lens, its four thick flippers undulating, pushing it lazily along. Its head was huge and knobby and its body massive and gnarled. What stood out most to him, however, was that, as far away as it was, its beady eyes remained focused on Ursula.

"It's a full-grown Gen-1 cow," Kat advised. "Has to be. Look at the girth."

"Lord, she's hideous," Jude breathed, leaning forward. He squinted as he examined the black and white image up close. "Look at this enormous dorsal mound," he said, tapping the screen. "Some sort of deformity, perhaps? And look at her skin. Kat, what do you make of that?"

She studied the image. "Humph. The epidermis is very wrinkled and uneven-looking, like something you'd see on a burn victim."

"The military's not using flamethrowers on them, are they?"

"Not that I'm aware of. She probably attacked a boat and the fuel tanks exploded. Do you have stats yet?"

Jude checked the fathometer readouts. "Coming into range now. Confirmed biologic, designate: pliosaur, duh. Overall length is . . . holy fuck!"

Kat threw him a sideways glance and chuckled. "Wow, those are some stats! I'm sorry; I'm a little rusty with your new metric system. Exactly how many 'holy fucks' are there in a kilometer, again?"

"This . . . this can't be right."

"What can't be right?" Kat's minx grin dipped. "Hey, what's wrong?"

Jude tried to master his shudder. "The *Imperator*, according to bio-mass projections, h-he's as big as Ursula!"

"Bullshit," Kat scoffed. "Wait, did you say <u>he</u>?"

Jude nodded. "System confirms an adult male. Length is nearly twenty-nine meters and mass calculated at over . . . two hundred tons?"

"Impossible. That's more than double the world record."

"Look!" Jude demanded, swiveling the monitor and practically shoving it in her face. "This is bad. What are we going to do?"

"What do you mean?"

He pointed at the sonar screen. The gray whales had vanished off the board, the frightened pod making tracks for Tijuana, if they knew what was good for them. All that remained were the pulsing signature readings coming from the *Megalodon* and the approaching *Kronosaurus*. Now at three hundred feet, they began to move on opposite sides of a huge circle. *Make that a spiral*, Jude noted. Like two buses sucked up into an F5 tornado's vortex, they drew steadily closer to one another. The distance between them was down to six hundred yards and shrinking fast.

Kat's eyes protruded like ping pong balls. "They're circling one another!"

Jude nodded. "Sizing each other up."

"They're going to fight?"

"Looks that way."

"So, that's a good thing, right?"

Jude looked at her as if she had two heads. "A good thing?" he echoed. "What are you talking about?"

Kat shrugged defensively. "You wanted footage of Ursula taking on a big pliosaur. So now you'll get it. Hell, we won't even have to go to Rock Key."

Jude's jaw nearly hit his chest. "Are you kidding me? I wanted our shark to fight a pliosaur she could out-mass and outmuscle, not one as big as her! What if she loses?"

Kat's blue eyes narrowed and she pegged him with a look. "So, what do you want to do, tuck tail and run?"

Jude licked his lips, then reached forward and practically attacked his keyboard. His tapping fingers moved so fast it was a miracle the keys didn't melt. "That would be suicide," he muttered. "Air breather or no, that thing is much faster than Ursula. If she turns her back on it, she's as good as dead."

"What are you doing?"

"I'm accessing her program," he stated, his jaw muscles jutting out from him clenching so hard.

Kat moved beside him, concern etched across her angular features. "Sharky, what are you going to do?"

Jude hit the enter key hard and spun around in his chair. "She's already acting on pure instinct. I did the only thing I could to give her a fighting chance. I pumped her full of adrenaline and 'encouraged' her to engage and destroy her enemy."

"And do you think she can?"

He stared at the giant marine reptile's image with hard eyes. "We're about to find out."

TWENTY-EIGHT

With the imperiousness of a 210-ton destroyer, the 84-foot *Carcharodon megalodon* female ascended to the three-hundred-foot mark before leveling off. Despite the steely layers of sinew that coated her massive frame, she moved with deathly silence, powering herself along with slow and steady strokes from her two-story high caudal fin. Her scar-streaked snout bulled its way through the murky waters like a sandpaper-coated battering ram, while her myriad senses extended out as she closed on her target.

The gray whales she had been stalking were gone.

All that remained was the intruder.

Although the female had not yet discerned the identity of the mysterious creature that caused an entire whale pod to flee in squealing terror, she sensed it was a threat, and that she would soon be embroiled in a battle to the death. If so, she preferred to make her stand here, in the twilight conditions near the bottom of the ocean's sunlit tropic zone. Sandwiched between sun and abyss, in a shadowy world of grays and reds, her vision was at its most effective. It gave her a distinct advantage over other creatures.

She had sensed the advancing carnivore from a thousand yards off as it closed on the migrating gray whales. It had remained eerily silent as it approached – a monstrous phantom, slicing through the murk. But, despite its efforts, her sensitive lateral line detected its presence by the compression waves its huge body gave off.

By size alone, she knew she had a rival.

As she curved steadily closer, her soulless black eyes contracted as she strove to target her opponent. All of a sudden, she found herself down-current and its pungent aroma enveloped her like a blanket. Her nares flared wide, drawing in hundreds of gallons of seawater in a single snort as her olfactory system worked feverishly to analyze the scent.

Its odor was reptilian and potent, reeking of testosterone and the smell of rotting flesh. It gave off the impression of being impossibly ancient, yet somehow still alive, like some undead crocodile. One thing about it was abundantly clear: it was big and it was hungry.

The *Megalodon*'s bowling ball-sized eyes narrowed as she continued to dissect the other predator's scent. Just then, a powerful barrage of broadband echolocation clicks slammed into her. The cone of sound was reminiscent of that used by the sperm whales she hunted, only far more boisterous. In fact, the clicks were so loud they were painful. She could feel them penetrating her like X-rays, analyzing her muscles and bones, even the pulsing of her buffalo-sized heart.

With a violent snap of her gigantic jaws, the female accelerated, her huge tail beating powerfully as she propelled herself forward, trying to lessen the maddening racket. Her temper flared and she veered aggressively toward the intruder.

Less than two hundred yards away, she plowed through a hapless school of bell-shaped jellyfish, her serrated skin shredding them like gelatin as she continued on. On the other side of the decimated shoal, her enemy finally came into focus.

It was one of the great shark destroyers.

Brief flashes of recollection sparked within the *Megalodon* female's primordial brain. Among them was an image of her sixty-foot mother, in the midst of birthing a sibling, when the *Kronosaurus imperator* appeared in the distance. The female shuddered at the memory and her protective nictitating membrane snapped tightly closed and opened – the shark's version of a blink. For a moment, she was a helpless newborn once more. Trapped within the recesses of her mind, she took in the ultimate brutality as her already weakened progenitor was torn apart by a fang-toothed terror far larger than herself.

By the same behemoth *she* now faced.

She could see the pliosaur clearly as they circled one another from 150 yards out. It was huge, several times the size of the pugnacious youngster she'd recently faced and, judging by its glittering eyes and craggy skin, very old. As she studied it, she realized it was the alpha of its kind: an insatiable, unstoppable foe that viewed all other species, including hers, as prey.

But unlike her ill-fated mother, the giant female had not been caught birthing pups. Nor was she outclassed in size or strength. She and the great saurian were equally matched. As a cold rage took hold of her, she knew there would be no retreating back to the frigid waters she had fled to as a youngling.

She would fight back. She would destroy her ancestral enemy.

Accelerating to attack speed, the *Megalodon* charged. Back arched and pectoral fins spread, she hurtled forward, her wrinkled lips peeling back in anticipation of delivering a devastating bite. The pliosaur appeared unimpressed and continued toward her, its speed matching her own, its scarlet eyes unblinking. She could feel its sonic pulses increasing in strength as the distance between them melted to nothing.

At the last moment, the female torqued her gigantic body into an underwater roll and threw herself at her target. Her bear trap-like jaws yawned wide enough to inhale a Cadillac and came down with enough force to flatten one.

To her astonishment, her teeth closed on nothing.

Despite its age and mass, the pliosaur was surprisingly agile and sidestepped her with a powerful thrust from its paddle-shaped fins. With viperish speed, it retaliated, its crocodile-like mandibles slashing out as they passed one another, raking her right flank and just missing the blinking red parasite affixed atop her towering gill plates.

The *Megalodon*'s rage-ruled mind registered the impact and injury, but she ignored it. Her opponent's ridged teeth had barely penetrated her thick skin, leaving behind only a series of five-yard white gouges, running down her side.

Aroused now, the *Kronosaurus* uttered a rumbling bellow and went on the offensive. Looping around in the water like some colossal sea lion, it prepared to attack. As it circled her, the female realized the marine reptile was attempting to get behind her. It intended to use its shearing jaws to amputate her tail where it connected to the peduncle. Maimed and deprived of her caudal fin, she would sink into the depths like any finned shark, drowning as she was ripped apart.

Swimming frantically, the female moved in tighter and tighter circles, trying hard to keep the speedy saurian from accomplishing its goal. It was right on her tail and weaving from side to side. Again and again it came on, grunting loudly and snapping its jaws, then drifting back, only to pull rapidly ahead again as it relentlessly searched for a weak point in her defenses.

Suddenly, as her enemy drew parallel and prepared to pass her once more, the female sensed an opening and took it. Banking hard to the right, she threw herself at the pliosaur with the intentions of sinking her teeth into its gigantic rib cage.

The wily marine reptile saw the attack coming and incorporated a powerful reverse stroke from all four flippers. The tactic was sufficient to slow its forward motion, but insufficient to avoid the shark's assault altogether. Jaws spread, the two titans crashed into another with bone-jarring force.

The *Megalodon* struck first, her giant jaws, lined with their rib-chiseling teeth, slamming home. The pliosaur sensed the blow coming and managed to swivel its enormous body a split-second before she hit, absorbing most of the impact with its mound-like back.

The female bit down hard, her eleven-inch teeth carving their way through iron-hard scales and skin, before burying themselves in a yard of fibrous scar-tissue. As she felt her teeth grind along the behemoth's broad shoulder blade, she began to shake her head, trying to excise a multi-ton hunk of flesh and bone.

The *Kronosaurus* fought back ferociously, its wedge-shaped jaws opening wide enough to ingest an Orca. Swinging left and closing with devastating force, its ridged teeth ripped into the left side of the female's neck, directly in front of one of her twenty-foot pectoral fins.

Despite her adrenalized state, the *Megalodon* experienced an explosion of pain. Her enemy's jaws had bitten a ten-foot gash in her gill plates, exposing the frilly red organs below and partially severing two of them. In an instant, a pool-sized cloud of blood spewed into the surrounding sea, turning the dark water a dull reddish-brown.

Berserk with pain and rage, the female twisted her head and, with an astonishing display of strength, wrenched the pliosaur free from her neck and flung it away. Before it could right itself, she surged forward and powered through the growing cloud of blood, barely avoiding the infuriated saurian's follow-up strike as it tried to sink its teeth into her flesh once more.

As she increased the distance between them, the *Megalodon* took in the situation. The pliosaur was on the move, but it was not attacking. Trailing blood from its gaping dorsal wound, it rose to the surface to spout and replenish its air supply.

The female's lips peeled back in a hideous grimace, exposing her triangular teeth. A moment later, she altered course and began to accelerate toward her adversary. Her mighty caudal fin beat faster and faster, increasing her velocity. Out of the corner of one eye, she could see the blood spurting from her ruptured gills. It painted her wake crimson, but she didn't care. Her wounds were of no concern. She had survived worse over the decades.

Up ahead, the *Kronosaurus* descended to the four-hundred-foot mark, its vast bulk hidden in the near-darkness as it crept toward her. It was a wasted ploy; with her night vision, she could see it as plain as day. A snort of bubbles spiraled up from its blowhole and its lips curled back in a snarl-like grimace.

A second later, the pliosaur uttered a roar that shook the sea like thunder and it hurled itself forward. With its fins hacking at the water like giant axes, the beast flew at her. She could sense its fury matched her own. There would be no more feinting, no fancy maneuvering. It planned to dispatch her with raw power – an onrushing mountain of muscle, spearheaded by a maw lined with ivory machetes.

The *Megalodon* accepted the challenge. Matching the marine reptile's depth, she launched herself at it, her giant jaws split-apart and beckoning. The seas before her were a blur as she closed on her mark. The distance between them was 200 yards, then 100 . . .

WHUMP!

The two colossi smashed face-first into one another with a sound NOAA would interpret as icebergs colliding. The impact left both predators stunned and disoriented, with neither of them moving. The seconds ticked by, and like a pair of giant clay figures whose ends were mashed together, they hung suspended in the water column. Their jaws were interlocked, their forequarters obscured by a billowing cloud of scarlet, intermixed with cascading particles of flesh and broken teeth.

As they spiraled slowly in the current, the two finally separated and fell away from one another. The damage they had absorbed was considerable. Both were missing teeth and their gums looked like raw hamburger. In addition, the *Megalodon* had suffered a huge cut in her jaw, so deep that the hard cartilage that made up her mandible was practically severed. The pliosaur was hardly better off. It had sustained horrific facial damage; a six-foot section of its lip hung in tatters and its white tongue lolled from one side of its jaw, half-amputated and gushing blood.

Still comatose, the two began to drift apart. The less buoyant shark started to sink, her massive body turning sideways with the tide as she descended. The *Kronosaurus* drifted gradually upward, its eyes closed and jaw agape.

It was the *Megalodon* that recovered first. Surging to life with a tremendous shiver, she looked around to get her bearings before righting herself and starting forward. With painful slowness, she moved through the darkness, her black eyes staring out from her mangled face, gazing toward the light, six hundred feet above.

Her gaze fell on the drifting body of her unmoving foe and she opened and closed her jaws. A sharp pain shot through her torn mouthparts and an unpleasant clicking told her to stop. In addition to the deep slash in her mandible, two of her gills were terribly damaged. She was hurt and she knew it. Still, she had survived. And if her opponent did not recover, she had won.

A sudden sense of pending danger motivated her to leave the field and she prepared to do so. Blood continued to seep from her wounds and dozens of smaller scavengers appeared. Already, three large Mako sharks circled in the distance, shadowed by a pod of a half-dozen *Xiphactinus*. All had heard the dinner bell and, despite the presence of vastly superior predators, were drawn to a potential meal. The female ignored them and turned northwest. Her stiffness began to fade and she moved steadily, desirous of putting as much distance between her and the battlefield as possible.

Suddenly, her body's floodgates opened and an avalanche of energy surged through her. Despite her wounds, she felt alive and euphoric. Then something else kicked in. She looked back at the immobile pliosaur and realized the battle was not yet over. She could not leave until her rival was finished. There was no choice. She had to deliver a killing blow. She had to gouge out its black heart and eat it.

Tingling in anticipation, the *Megalodon* dismissed her injuries and turned around. The bleeding from her gills had slowed and she absorbed as much oxygen as she could. Then, she angled her torn snout steeply upward and accelerated once more, rapidly increasing her speed to maximum. Any scavengers caught in her path were bowled over by the sheer force of her passing as she shot toward the surface.

She was a vengeful demon, and her target was the immobile *Kronosaurus*.

The battle was nearly over.

As he eyed the view from Ursula's locator camera, Judas Cambridge could already taste the sweetness of his impending victory. If it wasn't already dead, the aged *Kronosaurus imperator* bull was adrift like some whale-sized rag doll, two hundred feet below *Insolent Endeavor*'s slow-rolling hull. Three hundred feet deeper and two football fields away, his monster *Carcharodon megalodon* had just started her attack run.

Jude smiled. In seconds, a pliosaur second only to *Tiamat* herself would be destroyed and he would have it all on video, to ram down Eric Grayson's throat. He was going to ride his shark into Rock Key a conquering hero.

"Are you out of your fucking mind?" Kat Feaster's shoulder-length red locks flared like an angry lion's mane as she wheeled on him. "What the hell were you thinking, boosting her again?"

"She needed the epinephrine," Jude replied defensively.

"She 'needed' it? She's *hurt*, you idiot! She was *leaving*!"

Jude pushed his glasses into place and folded his arms defensively across his chest. He wasn't used to Kat lashing out at him and her icy stare would have chilled him even if he wasn't shirtless. "Look, I need this. *We* need this. We need the win."

"Bullshit. You should have let her go."

He shook his head emphatically. "She's too damaged to fight another day. This is our best chance. We need to record her kill." He eyed Ursula's monitor. "And we're about to."

Kat snorted in disgust. Her blue eyes ascended to the articulated monitor as the wounded *Megalodon* angled sharply upward, heading toward the drifting pliosaur at high speed. The marine reptile was directly under them now, only 90 feet down, and still showed no signs of life.

Jude eyed their fathometer and sonar screens. "She's coming in from the northeast. Speed is sixteen knots, distance seven hundred feet. Make that six hundred . . . five . . . what the *hell*?"

Kat's head swiveled toward him. "See? She broke off her attack."

On the fathometer, Ursula's pixilated image inexplicably veered off. Angling away from her target, she began to descend.

Jude's frustrated fingers turned to talons, frantically clawing at the air in front of him. "No, no, no!" He reached for the keyboard and started typing fast.

"What are you doing?"

"I-I'm juicing her; there's no other option!"

Kat stared at him in utter disbelief. Her eyes swiveled back to the monitors then peeled wide. "Shit! Wait, don't do it!"

"I'm sorry, I have to," Jude said, his fingers tapping away. "Don't worry, she can take it."

"You don't understand. The . . . *no!*"

Jude grunted in surprise as Kat pounced on him, her lithe hands grasping, desperately trying to pull his keyboard away. She was surprisingly strong but he turned his shoulder to her and hit the enter key before she could get a decent grip.

"It's done," he announced. "Relax, she can--"

Buh-thump!

Jude's mouth went slack as *Insolent Endeavor* shuddered and the deck inexplicably slanted. He looked around, befuddled. When he glanced at Kat for an explanation, her look of contempt spoke tomes.

"What happened?"

"You dumbass, I tried to *tell* you!" She speared an accusatory finger toward their hull camera monitors. "It's right under us!"

Jude felt like vomiting. The unconscious *Kronosaurus imperator* had floated up and impacted on their hull, practically lifting them out of the water. It was so huge, he could see parts of it on different screens; its thick-scaled hide on one viewer, a flipper's edge on another, and on the last, a close-up of the side of its huge head. Its crinkled, football-sized eye dominated the lens.

Thankfully, it was closed.

"Shit," he breathed. "Okay. It's okay, it's not moving."

Kat shook her head vehemently. "No, genius. But *Ursula* is!"

Oh, God.

Jude turned the color of mayonnaise as the full weight of his folly hit home. Right under them, the adrenaline-charged *Megalodon* was preparing to breach at flank speed, her giant jaws yawning. She was a 210-ton locomotive and they were dead on her tracks.

"We've got to get out of here!" he yelled, grabbing the yoke and throwing the inboards in gear. "Hold on to something!"

Kat's fear-filled eyes welled with tears as she reached up and gripped the handle of one of their suspended big-game rods.

Jude put the hammer down and held on. The 50-foot Monte Carlo MC5 lurched forward, its engines roaring loudly, but then stopped. He gaped at the monitors in dismay.

"Jesus, we're stuck on him!" he yelled. His heart sank into his feet as *Insolent Endeavor*'s deck boards started to vibrate and then wobble. He'd dealt with enough giant predators to know a displacement wave when he felt one.

"Throw her in reverse!" Kat screamed. "Hurry, she's rising fast!"

The whole ship was shaking violently as Jude changed gears and reached for the throttle. Just as he was about to gun it, he clocked the monitors showing the pliosaur's eye and Ursula's POV. When he saw hers, he cursed aloud.

It was too late.

Then two things happened simultaneously. The strobe light on Ursula's locator went off, blacking out the screen. And the pliosaur's ruby-red eye opened.

There was a tremendous rushing sound and *Insolent Endeavor* torqued savagely to port. A second later, Ursula struck, her steely body a gigantic torpedo, slamming into the awakening pliosaur and them.

Jude had no time to react. All his panic-stricken mind could do was register Kat's terrified shriek and what sounded like a bomb going off.

Then there was black.

Dirk Braddock remained standing as Stacy Daniels, Acting Security Chief Oleg Smirnov, and the first mates of *Gryphon* and *Antrodemus* departed Tartarus's oval-shaped conference room. Stacy was obviously agitated about not being asked to remain behind, but it was Smirnov who was the last to depart. The barrel-chested Ukrainian gave Dirk, Garm Braddock, and Natalya Dragunova an appraising look before nodding and exiting.

"Garm, seal the room, please," Dirk said. "We want privacy for this."

His fraternal twin walked over and pressed one palm against the pneumatic door's biometric control pad, then keyed in a privacy code that, outside of those present, could be overridden by only three other people.

"What ees going on, Doctor Derek?" Dragunova asked with her inimitable Baltic-Russian accent.

Dirk gestured for her and Garm, and the three seated themselves at the far end of the conference room table. At the opposite end, Grayson's empty CEO's chair loomed like some dark-hued sentinel, brooding and silent.

Dirk grabbed his glass and gulped down a quick swallow of water. Between Stacy and his mentor, his chest felt like he was wearing a weighted vest, laden with guilt. There was no helping it; he was committed to his course. "I have some additional information to disclose," he began. "It's for you two, alone."

The two captains exchanged speculative glances.

"What've you got?" Garm asked. The big submariner knew his brother's moods and behavior patterns better than his own and his pale blue eyes shone with curiosity.

Dirk cleared his throat. "I was digging around in mom's quarters and I came across a concealed file on her desktop."

"Sure, she had secret stuff," his brother acknowledged. "That doesn't surprise me. But your take on it does. Concealed how?"

"It was basically hiding in plain sight," Dirk replied. "Under a title that only you or I would notice." He held up the tiny portable drive.

"What ees that?" Dragunova asked.

"Our mother's last lab report." Dirk slipped the drive into a port directly in front of him and waved one hand to activate it.

The room's lights dimmed and a slim LCD monitor emerged from the center of the table. It swiveled until it faced the three of them and then lit up. There was a flash of static and, seconds later, Amara Braddock's face appeared.

Dirk glanced at Garm, gauging his reaction. He'd seen the video several times. His brother hadn't. As the sight of their mother's face, the big man's expression softened. His rugged jaw drooped and his eyes began to widen, like a child taking in some natural wonder.

"Doctor Amara Braddock . . . formal log entry twenty-two-six, January 6th, 2045," she began, glancing briefly down at some notes she carried. Dirk smiled sadly as he took in her visage. Even at fifty-nine, his mother still looked amazing. She had almost no grays or wrinkles and kept herself fit and trim. Only her eyes gave her away, peering over the tops of her vintage horn-rim glasses. They were like Garm's eyes – gleaming, almond-shaped opals. Except hers were tired and sorrowful, worn down by the tragic losses she'd sustained, starting with her husband.

As Amara held up a tiny remote, the recorder pulled back, showing her from the waist up. Dirk could see the footage had been shot in her quarters. She was dressed in her omnipresent lab coat and, over her shoulder, one of her ivy gardenias could be seen, bursting with lush pink flowers as it draped down from its hanging pot.

On the desk beside her, Amara had set up a portable holographic projector. As she pointed, it sprang to life. A swirling globe of colored particles four feet across took shape, flashing and coalescing until they formed a white, movie screen-like shape.

"The subject of today's presentation is captive pliosaur X, designate: *Tiamat*." Amara announced.

As she spoke, black and white security footage of the giant *Kronosaurus* queen appeared, cruising soundlessly within the confines of her paddock pool.

"A considerable amount of time and resources have been devoted toward establishing a breeding program for this animal, with the ultimate goal of its offspring becoming additions to GDT's already formidable collection of bio-weapons."

The camera panned sideways, causing Amara to vanish and the hologram's images to dominate the screen.

"Until recently, we were unable to perform a proper bio-scan on *Tiamat*," she continued. "Her sheer mass prevented her from being transported onto our existing CT scanner, even using our stoutest industrial hoist. Two days ago, however, I was able to import a powerful portable resonance projector and jury rig it to a lift. Using her new neural implant to immobilize her, I suspended it directly above her and got an effective readout."

Amara's off-screen voice took on a morose tone. "The results were disturbing."

On the viewer, a recreated overhead view of two pliosaurs appeared, spread-eagled like mounted butterflies and lined up side by side, with a silhouetted human form inserted in the upper left corner for size comparison. The one on the right was obviously the queen; it dwarfed the other animal.

"*Tiamat*'s size and appearance have always been indicative of her mutative status, but now we can establish just how much of a jump she's made up the evolutionary ladder," Amara narrated. Footage from a moonlit beach, via an infrared lens, began to run. On it, a cow pliosaur dragged itself ponderously from the surf. "Plesiosaurs have been around since the Triassic, with Jurassic and Cretaceous pliosauridae emerging as the greatest macropredators of all time."

The footage did a jump cut. The cow was now up on the beach and using its huge head to scoop out a thirty-foot nursery in the dry sand. "Thalassophoneans are lethal predators and the only real chink in their armor is that they are oviparous and must come ashore to lay eggs. This makes sexually mature females vulnerable to attack during the spawning process."

All of a sudden, bright searchlights illuminated the gravid cow. A swarm of heavily armed troops rushed forward and surrounded it. The absence of sound did little to reduce the intensity of the scene as the giant reptile was mercilessly gunned down, its jaws snapping impotently as it was cut to pieces.

Amara could be heard clearing her throat before she continued. "As a family, pliosaurs were decimated by the Cenomanian-Turonian extinction event after their primary forage base, the ichthyosaurs, was wiped out by sub-oceanic volcanism."

The screen changed to show an assortment of large mosasaurs, compared to a similar number of pliosaur silhouettes.

"Following the C-T event," Amara continued. "Surviving pliosaurs began to be supplanted by encroaching mosasaurs. Although smaller, these marine monitors were highly adaptive. They also had one significant advantage over their more massive competitors – they gave birth to live young. This resulted in higher infant survival rates and the elimination of adult mortality during clutch-laying. Pliosaurs soon found themselves outnumbered. Eventually, only the species we know as *Kronosaurus imperator* remained."

The pliosaur silhouettes evaporated, leaving behind only a single individual, surrounded by mosasaurs. Then the camera pulled back, showing Amara once more.

"Although at first glance, and barring size considerations, *Tiamat* appears as any other pliosaur, our scan revealed significant physiological differences," she said. "Non-mutated pliosaurs have body temperatures that rely on increased activity levels and gigantism to maintain their variance over the surrounding water. Whereas, and regardless of energy expenditure, *Tiamat*'s core maintains a consistent ninety-four degrees – near cetacean levels."

As Amara continued, she pointed at the projector, causing a clip of the *Kronosaurus* queen spouting to run. "In addition to being able to thermoregulate without altering her metabolism, her adipose tissue is denser and more insulating than that of her smaller relatives. It's more like whale blubber."

The camera zoomed back in on the projector as an overhead schematic of *Tiamat* appeared. Cutaways began to pop up, showing her musculoskeletal system and internal organs.

"The scan of *Tiamat*'s reproductive system confirmed my suspicions," Amara announced. "She's not oviparous, she's viviparous."

Garm's jaw dropped. "Holy shit."

"More specifically," Amara's voice continued, "She is ovoviviparous. Although she does not lay eggs, there is no placenta to nourish the young. Her eggs hatch internally and develop inside the womb, with the young feeding on any unhatched eggs . . . and each other."

A grinning Dragunova leaned toward Garm and whispered, "I'm glad she said that part. I was seeting here theenking; can you imagine the size of the afterbirth?"

"Shh!" Garm shushed.

The phantom of Amara Braddock reappeared center stage and continued talking, ignorant of any impoliteness from her audience. "We see this type of inter-uterine behavior in predatory sharks like Makos, tigers, and great whites – evolution's way of ensuring only the biggest and strongest survive." She glanced down at her notes and licked her lips. "Out of an initial clutch size of ten or twenty, I estimate only four or five hatchlings end up going full term," she said. "However, they would be considerably larger than oviparous newborns, with each measuring anywhere from one-fourth to one-third the mother's length. In other words, as much as forty feet."

The screen froze for a moment, followed by a quick jump-cut back to Amara. She was seated with her back to her desk now. Her expression was clinical and she had her hands crossed on her lap.

"I implore GDT's Board of Directors to consider this caveat," she said. "Should *Tiamat* be allowed to reproduce and her offspring escape and proliferate, she and her progeny could cause irreparable harm. Given the size of individual offspring, there is every indication that parental care would be administered. Each hatchling would be a formidable predator to begin with, but with the protection of one or more parents, their survival rates would be astronomically high. Most likely exceeding the near-eighty percent rate *Kronosaurus imperators* enjoyed during the early days of their expansion."

Amara's chest rose and fell as she breathed. "In addition, it is distinctly possible these animals would function in family units, like modern day whales, or worse, like killer whales. Should that happen, the results could be catastrophic."

The camera pulled back as she pointed her remote at the projector, bringing up a flattened image of the globe with its ocean currents highlighted.

"While 'normal' pliosaurs can, via increased activity, endure the freezing temperatures of the abyss temporarily, they prefer temperate waters. *Tiamat* and her descendants would have no such limitations. They could travel all the way to the Arctic or Antarctic, devastating surviving whale populations and upsetting whatever precarious balance we've managed to achieve. They could, conceivably, further alter the ecology of the oceans to the point we may find ourselves facing another extinction-level event."

Amara folded her slim arms across her chest. "If that's not enough, or for those among you whose sole focus is on selling hardware to the military with no regard for keeping nature in balance, consider this: At well over four hundred tons displaced mass and a swimming speed of nearly fifty miles an hour, *Tiamat* has the strength and power to stave in the hull of a nuclear submarine or destroyer."

She paused and her opalescent eyes lowered. "Some people think we deserve this. They say our annihilating sharks for placebo ED treatments allowed pliosaur numbers to explode." When she looked up her jaw was set. "I'm not here to address that. We can't change the past, but we can prevent a worse future. No matter what, *Tiamat* cannot be allowed to breed. Nor can she be set free. And if she ever manages to escape, she must be hunted down and destroyed. This concludes my presentation. Thank you very much for your time."

Just like that, Amara's image froze. Then the screen went black. There was an uncomfortable silence, until Dirk cleared his throat.

"Typhon has to be killed," he stated, indicating the darkened viewer. "Dr. Grayson doesn't realize it and, even if he watched this, he probably wouldn't accept it. But it has to be done."

His brother nodded solemnly. "Is that why you sent Stacy away?"

Dirk nodded. "If there's any fallout it should be on my head, alone."

Garm grinned hugely. "Fuck it, you know I'm in. When do we leave?"

"Tonight."

Dragunova's jaw dipped. "Tonight? But *Antrodemus* ees not yet at one hundred percent! Even eef we complete repairs while underway, she won't be ready un--"

"You're not going," Dirk advised. "This is Garm's fight." He turned back to his brother. "I suggest you investigate the bizarre text from that foreign yacht, first. It's iffy, but it's our most recent lead."

Dragunova's expression turned confrontational. "Excuse me? There ees no way you are leaving me here while your--"

"You have a more important mission," Dirk announced. He was enjoying the feeling of empowerment that came with reining in the powerfully built object of his affection. "One that will allow you to complete repairs to your submarine's sail en route."

Antrodemus's tawny-haired commander rose angrily to her feet. "Meeshun? What 'meeshun'? What ees thees bullsheet??"

Dirk looked up at her and sighed. "I'm sending you to Diablo Caldera."

"*Diablo Caldera*?" both captains echoed.

Now Garm looked stunned. "Say, what? Wait, what's happened?"

As Dragunova cooled her jets and retook her seat, Dirk swiveled his tablet toward the two of them. On it was the email he'd been praying for.

"I've been secretly negotiating with the Cuban resistance," he said, then gave an involuntary shrug. "Ostensibly, with Dr. Grayson's approval.

Garm leaned forward, his wolfish eyes sweeping the page. "It claims their troops have seized a portion of the Cuban surface fleet . . . blockaded that section of their sovereign waters."

Dirk nodded. "We've got just under forty-eight hours to make landfall and survey whatever we can."

"Thees is remarkable," Dragunova breathed as she finished reading. Her expression was guarded, but he could see she was intrigued. "How deed you manage thees?"

"Let's just say I lubricated the wheels of progress."

Garm chuckled. "And how much did that 'lube' cost you?"

Dirk grinned sheepishly. "Actually, *us*. And quite a bit."

"W-what? Did you say *us*?"

"Of course. I knew you'd want to kick in."

For the first time he could remember, Dirk saw his brother flabbergasted. It was all he could do to stop from guffawing.

Garm cleared his throat as he fought to recover his composure. "Well, of course. What's the point of having all that stock if you can't spend a hundred thousand shares of it?"

"Closer to a million shares, actually."

"Even better!"

Dragunova took in Garm's shell-shocked look and smiled. "Derek, why send *Antrodemus*? Why not just take a helicopter to the island?"

He shook his head. "The agreement specifies a clandestine operation. The military situation there is tenuous at best. We don't want to end up getting shot down and cause an international incident."

"So, how do we get inside? As I recall, the caldera cleefs are impossible to climb."

"Underwater."

As Dragunova exchanged confused looks with Garm, Dirk spun his tablet back and pulled up the satellite geo-thermal diagrams he had prepped. "This is Diablo Caldera, pre-eruption," he said, pointing. He touched a key, causing a second scan to overlay the first.

"This is post. The volcano's initial fracturing opened its lake to the sea, which is how the Paradise Cove pliosaur – and Lord knows what else – got out."

"Hell hath no fury," Garm quipped. "Because it all escaped!"

"I doubt that," Dirk stated. He pointed at a huge pile of rubble where the break in the volcanic wall occurred. "A few hours after the initial disturbance, debris from aftershocks sealed the collapsed section." He turned to Dragunova. "There's a lot of magnetic interference from the volcano, but what satellite scans we've managed show a large, crescent-shaped area of what appears to be rain forest, bordering the lake. We have no idea what's in there, so be careful."

She blinked in annoyance. "Be careful of *what*? You steel haven't told me how the hell we are getting een!"

"I'm sorry," Dirk said. He swept his diagrams, removing thick layers of strata with quick finger swipes. "There's a network of lava tubes connecting the lake to the sea. That's how the water has maintained its salinity. They're not completely stable, of course, and the water is superheated, but we don't anticipate any geothermal activity." He touched a section of the screen and enlarged it. "These two shafts are your best bet."

Dragunova's eyes compressed into storm-gray slits as she leaned in close. "Those tunnels wind all over the place and are at most seexty feet wide. *Antrodemus* can never feet in there."

Dirk nodded. "But your *Remora* can. You'll take a three-man crew, detach outside--"

"Da, da, da . . . I got eet," she said, waving him off as she took the tablet and examined it in detail.

As she did, Garm leaned in close. "Let's talk seriously. Is this worth splitting up the team? And what's going to happen with your boss if we succeed?"

"This is the chance of a lifetime," Dirk replied. "Mom would've killed for the chance to go to Diablo. It was her dream. Think of the potential wealth of data we can uncover. Not just discovering how pliosaurs and so many other marine creatures survived KT, but what else might be in there. There may be other animals, plants, trees, pharmaceutical opportunities . . . Hell, we might discover the cure for Cretaceous Cancer!"

"Or bring something worse back."

Dirk's lips pursed as he considered that possibility. "We'll take all precautions. Captain Dragunova knows what to do."

"Da," she said, locking gazes with him. "But what about your brother? You may be sending heem to hees death, facing *Typhon* alone. Aren't you concerned?"

"Whoa, I can take care of myself," Garm protested. He caught Dirk's concerned look and snickered. "Relax, little brother. You know I can throw down. Besides, I've got a score to settle with that overgrown lizard."

Dirk ruminated a tick, then exhaled heavily. "We've got two days at most," he said. "Both from the 'travel visa' they gave us and Grayson's return. Diablo is the primary target. If he comes back to discover we've unlocked the secrets of the island, he'll be dancing on air."

"And *Typhon*?" Dragunova pressed.

"It may take days or even weeks to find him," Dirk said. "*Antrodemus* will commence repairs on the fly, while *Gryphon* begins her hunt. If you sight him--"

"I know," Garm interjected. "Hit him with a locator."

Dirk nodded. "Yes. Once Dragunova's surveyed the island, you two can join forces and finish him off."

Garm scoffed. "Playing tag? I'd rather shove a *Naegling* up his ass."

Dirk laughed. "You're starting to sound like Cunningham."

His brother's face brightened. "Yeah . . . say, where *is* that gabby son of a bitch? I haven't seen him, and he was due in this morning."

"Ever the dutiful husband, right?"

Dragunova cocked her head to one side. "Speaking of dutiful, Derek. Dr. Grayson knows nothing about thees?"

He shook his head. "No, but you saw. I tried to tell him at the meeting."

"You did," Garm confirmed. "I was there."

"And you theenk he won't be mad?" Dragunova asked. Her curious eyes bored into Dirk's.

"I think he will jump for joy when he discovers I got us on the ground inside Diablo," he responded, flushing under her scrutiny.

"What about us keeling the beast he wants to 'wed' to *Tiamat*? He has, how you say, a 'major chubby' for breenging *Typhon* back alive?"

Garm saw the tension in Dirk's face and placed a reassuring hand on his shoulder. "Relax. I've got a feeling it's going to look like an accident."

Dragunova watched their interaction with telltale amusement, but she wasn't finished. "Tell me the truth, Derek," she said. "You are knowingly betraying your mentor, da?"

"I'm respecting our mom's final wish," he said, indicating him and Garm. "And I'm doing what I think is right for all of us, for the world, in fact. And to answer your question . . . yes, I suppose I am."

She looked at him with approving eyes. "Good. I like eet."

Dirk felt his face get hot and he knew he was blushing.

"Alright, enough of this mushy shit," Garm said, hoisting his 245 pounds to his feet. He winked at Dragunova. "You've got a 'Lost World' to explore and I've got a sea monster to kill. So, let's do it!"

Dirk's eyes and jaw muscles tightened. "Yes. Let's do it, people."

———

He was drowning.

When Judas Cambridge's eyelids snapped apart, it was in response to his body convulsing against the seawater invading his lungs. His arms flailed wildly at the enveloping gloom and his head thrust upward, breaking the surface as he desperately sucked in a lungful of oxygen.

A second later, he started puking his guts up.

Brine mixed with blood spewed from his mouth, along with the collective contents of his stomach. When the painful regurgitating finally ceased, his vomitus floated all around him, a vile and viscous broth.

Jude's next inhalation was an agonized wheeze; both from the saltwater that scorched his lungs and a half-dozen cracked or broken ribs. Tossing his shattered reading glasses, he gazed through tearful eyes at *Insolent Endeavor*'s immersed bridge, before taking stock of the damage that surrounded him.

The 50-foot Monte Carlo MC5 was doomed. Ursula's breaching strike had broken her at the keel and, despite the brand's flotation capabilities, she was completely flooded. The sea had rushed in through her broken hull, inundating all below-deck compartments and filling the remainder of the dying vessel to her gunnels. Only her Bimini top and the top three feet of the roof of her spacious cockpit still remained above water, and as he felt his way about the dimly-lit space, Jude could see there was only eighteen inches between him and the bridge's reinforced ceiling.

Things were bad. His high-tech helm was a backwater bay, with debris littering the surface of the water. All their instruments were dead. There was no way to call for help and, judging by the grayish light seeping in from a partially submerged porthole, it was already twilight outside.

It would be dark soon. And in these waters, darkness brought death.

As Jude reached up to grasp one of the few big-game rods that hadn't been dislocated by the impact, a spear of agony shot through his lower back and side. The pain was so intense he shrieked. A wall of blackness smashed into him, threatening to render him unconscious, and the wounded scientist tried his best to stand up on the slippery deck.

A ping of panic pealed through Jude as his legs refused to respond. His fear intensified when he realized he couldn't feel his feet. He tried kicking and stomping, but got nothing. Confused, he grabbed hold of an overhead rod and bore down with everything he had. It was to no avail.

As he reached underwater and felt along his hip and thighs, Jude froze. His face paled and he felt like vomiting again. His pelvis was twisted forward at an unnatural angle and his legs were completely numb to the touch. Terror showed up with its companion, hyperventilation, and he tried doing some of Kat's meditational breathing exercises to keep them both at bay.

Kat!

Realizing he wasn't alone in this and that his partner could come to his aid, Jude envisioned a sudden glimmer of hope.

"Kat!" he called out.

There was no reply – not a sound in fact, except that of waves slapping against the salt-stained porthole and the omnipresent groaning of the ship's ruptured hull.

"Kat!" he cried.

When she didn't respond, Jude felt fear take the helm. *Where the hell is she? Has she gotten out? Is she perched up on the roof, hopefully on the satellite phone and calling for help? Why would she just leave me like this? I could have drowned!*

A sudden shifting of the boat disrupted Jude's disjointed thoughts. *Insolent Endeavor* was beginning to wobble from side to side, her creaky movements causing the water inside the helm to shift back and forth, at times sloshing all the way to the ceiling and nearly drowning him once more.

Despite the direness of his situation, Jude felt a warped sense of pride. He knew what was causing their hull to bounce up and down. Beneath the dying boat, Ursula was feeding on the giant pliosaur he'd sent her to destroy. He could tell from the water, as a frothy area over a hundred feet across appeared all around them. It was his *Megalodon*, tearing off giant mouthfuls of reptilian flesh as she gulped down the valuable protein she needed to recover from her wounds.

Unless . . . unless he was wrong.

What if it was the *Kronosaurus*? What if *it* was eating *Ursula*?

Where the hell is Kat? Annoyance inundated Jude as his useless legs buckled and he went under. He surfaced, sputtering and gasping. *Shit, we need to figure out what happened and how we're going to call for help! Where the hell is she?*

Jude jumped and cried out in alarm as something rubbed against him. He spun around as best he could, his pruned fingers grasping at slippery rod butts and sharp-edged overhead racks as he tried to see what touched him.

"Oh, no . . ."

As Katerina Feaster's dislodged form surfaced from the seesawing of the boat, Jude slapped a hand over his mouth. He reached out, grabbing her by her tank top and pulling her toward him. She was face up in the water, but unmoving.

"Kat! Jesus, Kat!"

When he saw her pale skin and stark, blue eyes, fixed and staring, he knew it was bad. But it wasn't until he cupped one hand under her head and tried to revive her that he realized how bad.

Jude pulled away as if he'd touched a live scorpion and stared bug-eyed down at his hand. Even with the seawater diluting it, he could see the blood caked around his trembling fingers. He howled in dismay. There was no mistaking the mushiness of the occipital bone at the back of Kat's skull. It felt like a rotting pumpkin, two months after Halloween.

As he espied the blood-spattered big game reel suspended directly overhead, a wave of nausea shot up from Jude's stomach like a live moray eel, trying to escape through his mouth. There was nothing left to vomit, but that didn't make the dry heaves that followed any less painful.

An eternity later, Jude found the courage to retake Kat's broken body and pull her close. He gripped her around the waist, holding her against him as best he could, while maintaining the overhead grip that kept him from joining her. As her lifeless head flopped like a rag doll's atop his naked shoulder, the tears started.

"Oh, Kat . . . this is all my fault!" he wailed. "I ruined everything with my stupid f-fucking revenge schemes! I did this! I . . . I killed you!"

Jude hugged her like a life preserver, his plaintive sobs filling the nearly submerged cabin as his hot tears streamed down Kat's cold cheeks. A sudden dizziness permeated him and time seemed to slow. He wasn't sure if it was endorphins or he was bleeding out internally. Either way, it didn't matter. He had gambled and lost, and his best friend – worse, the woman he loved – had paid the ultimate price for his arrogance.

As the boat's intermittent convulsions slowed, then stopped, Jude sniffled and looked up. Whichever giant predator had emerged victorious had stopped feeding. As a low swooshing sound vibrated *Insolent Endeavor* and the floundering vessel spun lazily at the surface, he lifted his face from Kat's, avoiding her lifeless stare as best he could.

Suddenly, he spotted a hint of movement through the waterlogged porthole and what looked like a distant cloud of scarlet. Something was moving out there. Something big.

With an anguished moan, Jude released Kat's body and started toward the porthole. It was almost completely submerged – a dire indication of how much air was left in the cockpit and how much time remained before *Insolent Endeavor* sank beneath the waves, carrying them both into the abyss.

Grabbing onto rod butts and overhangs as he struggled closer, Jude had a brief flashback of playing on the monkey bars as a child. Ignoring the exquisite agony that continued to pulse through his broken ribs and back, he reached the porthole and peered into the greenish-gray murk beyond.

There was a hint of movement nearby: a huge, shadowy form and he recoiled in fear. Was it the pliosaur?

A sudden burst of crimson caused Jude to blink confusedly. He stared dumbly at it as the flash of color repeated itself. It had changed position, moving laterally toward his left. Now, it began to move off, growing steadily smaller. He exhaled and smiled wanly as he realized what he was looking at.

It was the strobe from Ursula's locator. She had emerged victorious, after all.

Even better, he deduced as he wiped away the condensation on the porthole and watched the red blips fade away altogether, she was on the move. A quick glance at the sky above caused Jude's weary smile to upgrade into a satisfied grin.

The *Megalodon*'s implanted programming had reasserted itself. And judging from the sun's position on the horizon, she was headed for Rock Key.

She was going to Tartarus.

Jude held his side as he shook with laughter. The irony was sickeningly sweet. Kat was dead and he was dying, yet their ghosts would emerge victorious. Ursula would home in on Eric Grayson's stronghold and when she got there would establish a huge hunting territory. Then she would do what she was designed to do – kill. She would wreak havoc on everything in the region: boats, pliosaurs, maybe even take out one of their fancy submarines.

In the end, they would have no choice but to put her down. And when they did, they would find the cybernetic implant he and Kat had affixed to Ursula's cranium. They would bring it to their labs, where Grayson and his flunkies, including that punk Braddock kid, would identify the architect of their misery. They would recognize his handiwork and know that it was he who sent the *Megalodon* to terrorize them. They would know he had been right. And in the end, that they had been wrong.

A powerful sensation of lightheadedness suddenly came over Jude and he felt incredibly tired. It was no matter. Ursula was on her way and there was nothing more to be done.

Struggling to stay awake, he monkey-barred his way back to Kat, then lowered himself onto the submerged steering console so he could sit back and wrap his arms around her. He held her close, feeling her cool body against his bare chest. Thankfully, his shivering had subsided. In fact, he wasn't cold at all now.

As Jude glanced outside at the setting sun, he realized it was finally time to go to sleep. Everything was going to be okay. He and Kat were together at last. Oh, sure. It was far from the romantic evening he had envisioned for them, but it was alright. All he needed was a little rest. A quick nap would do the trick.

He would close his eyes for a little bit.

Only for a minute . . .

Twenty-Nine

G arm Braddock's lips bunched up as he and Sam Mot approached the
end of the service corridor leading to Tartarus's sprawling docks.
It was the smell of the place that invariably nailed him like a stiff jab
to the nose; a pungent bouquet of diesel fumes, seawater, *Kronosaurus*
pheromones and excrement, and the omnipresent odor of the assorted
fish and livestock they fed them.

"Whew, this place kicks!" Sam spouted, grimacing. "Or was that
you?" he added with a sardonic grin. There was a low whirring sound
as one of his expensive wheelchair's bionic arms swung up, its silicone-
tipped fingers deftly pinching his nose.

"Probably that poor nurse you took advantage of last night," Garm
shot back. Despite the initial awkwardness whenever he and Sam were
together, he was glad they slipped back into the prerequisite ball-bust-
ing that came with being lifelong friends so easily.

"Dude, she was fucking amazing," Sam said in low tones. His angular face took on a conspiratorial look. "She might be a bit on the 'well-
nourished' side, but let me tell you, she can crack a walnut between
those cheeks!"

"Tell me later," Garm advised. They were approaching one of the
facility's guard posts and he could do without some ex-con eavesdropping on stories of Sam's latest conquest.

Garm felt the dock's warm breeze flow through his chestnut hair
as he looked around. To his left, the black-clad guard – he couldn't remember his name – gave a polite nod and resumed leaning against the
nearby wall, his beefy arms folded across his chest. When he gave the
guard a second glance, the guy avoided eye contact. It was amusing; all

of them were like that ever since his little throw-down in the gym. He wasn't sure if it was the beating he gave Dwyer and his thug underling or the suspensions that followed.

Either way, it was all good. Fear was a great motivator.

"Hey, Big G; what's that thing he's guarding?" Sam asked as they passed into the main docking area.

Garm glanced sideways, scoping the yard-wide wall valve affixed to a riveted steel panel, some five feet across. The entire assembly was vividly marked with red warning labels and covered with a padlocked Lexan cover, three inches thick. It looked like a mixture of a captain's wheel and one of those old-fashioned fire alarms, albeit on a titanic scale.

"That's the release valve for all the paddocks," Garm said, shrugging.

"The paddocks?"

"Yeah, *those*." He pointed up and back.

"Whoa!" Sam's green eyes practically popped from of his head as his chair spun, turning him completely around. Soaring 100 feet straight up, the nearest pliosaur tank loomed over them, a gigantic saltwater aquarium incarcerating some of the world's deadliest "fish."

It was *Romulus* and *Remus*'s enclosure, Garm noted. But the two shell-brothers were too busy having a tug-of-war over the fifteen-foot, genetically-engineered tuna a humming hoist had just dropped to notice them.

"That's nasty," Sam said as billows of blood and entrails spewed from the eviscerated bluefin. "Release valve?"

"Yes. All the pliosaur paddocks and the dockside holding tanks for the fish we use as fodder have water-exchange conduits connecting them to the outside. In the event of an emergency, they can all be opened simultaneously, allowing the animals to escape into the sea."

"You can let them go just by turning that big dial?"

"Or remotely, via the control panel in Grayson's office."

Sam was shocked. "So, you're telling me someone could just turn that and release all those monsters back into the ocean?"

Garm inclined his head. "No, Sam. The valve is guarded 24/7. It's authorized personnel only, and we're talking only in the event of something disastrous, like a reactor meltdown. Besides, they all have control implants. They wouldn't be going anywhere, so relax."

Sam's lips tightened but he nodded and spun back around.

They continued in silence for a few hundred feet, passing the occasional janitor pushing a broom or technician hauling a cart loaded with parts. Garm could see his old friend had gone melancholy and knew better than to press him.

Ahead, Tartarus's docks continued into the distance. The two-hundred-foot-high dome covered a half-mile square, all carved from the gray-hued granite comprising Rock Key. Above them, the steel-girder network that formed the relay system for the facility's assorted cable lifts branched out like an immense orb weaver's web. Despite the late hour, the silence was disrupted by the sounds of men, machines, and the occasional grunts and grumbles from the more cantankerous of their captive saurians.

Of course, Garm noted, the prisoners never got overly boisterous. *Goliath* had made that mistake during her initial incarceration, but just once. A single, earth-shattering bellow from behind the towering black curtain to his right quickly cured her of any repeat performances. The big Gen-1 now sat docilely inside her 400-foot holding tank on the far side of the docks.

Garm snickered to himself. *Tiamat* was not to be challenged.

Fear . . . the great motivator.

As a MarshCat containing two security personnel zipped past, Garm clocked Sam with his peripherals, then looked ahead once more. Still a football field away, *Gryphon* lay poised in her berth, her hydraulic boarding ramps extended like the legs of some colossal insect, locking her in position. Around her, several members of his crew were standing around or hobnobbing with the submarine's technicians as they completed their loadings. Behind his boat, and floating in the center of the three docking berths, *Antrodemus* was similarly positioned, her nose pointing at the Vault's enormous, armored doors. Both subs had already made use of the base's powerful 150-foot turntable to spin around before launch preparations began.

Garm shielded his eyes against the dock's bright overhead lights as he studied *Antrodemus*. A lone loader pulled noisily away from the tail section of the crimson-hulled ORION-class AB sub, and her captain and crew were nowhere to be seen. He exhaled. Apparently, the damaged vessel was already prepped for departure. At least, as well as she could be.

"It's a long walk, huh?" Sam mentioned, gauging the distance. "You know, you could've just hopped in one of those zippy ATVs. It would've been a helluva lot faster."

Garm grinned. "And miss out on us holding hands in front of my crew?"

Sam chuckled as he pointed a mechanical finger. "Is that your bridge crew, all standing around doing a circle jerk?"

"Yep. A regular 'McHale's Navy,' let me tell you."

"Humph. I was thinking more like 'Gilligan's Island.'"

"Whoa, you calling me the fat-ass skipper?"

"Well, you'd make a pretty scary Mary Ann," Sam quipped, arching one eyebrow. "Although with those dreamy moonstone eyes and that thick hair . . ."

"Keep it up, butt-boy, and I'll have everybody calling you 'Lovey' for the entire tour."

"Would that be a *three-hour tour*?"

"Go fuck yourself."

They were both chuckling as they approached Lieutenant Kyle Cunningham and Ensigns Rush, Ramirez, and Ho. Garm felt a tinge of apprehension as he got ready to do the introductions. Cunningham and Sam were old friends, but to the rest of his primaries, Sam was a complete stranger. And a cripple trapped in a wheelchair, to boot.

"Good to see you, Samwise," Cunningham said, leading the pack. He bore a sympathetic look, poorly disguised by a strained smile as he bent at the waist and offered his hand.

"You too, you old horndog," Sam replied. His LJ-3000 chair's actuators whirred as its bionic right arm swung smoothly up and gave Cunningham "the grip." "Now lose that hound dog expression." He used both robotic arms to pat the sides of his chair and winked. "I may be half the man I used to be, but I'm still more than most."

"So, you and Kyle know one another?" Ensign Heather Rush asked as she edged closer and stood next to Cunningham.

"We do, indeed," Sam admitted. "But out of respect for you and any other ladies present, I won't elaborate on just *how* well."

Garm laughed. "Oh, you don't have to worry about Rush. She's 'one of the guys,' as they say."

"That's for sure," the willowy blonde concurred. She brushed her cheeks with lithe fingertips. "See all these freckles? I got one for every curse I've heard onboard. And let me tell you, my freckles have freckles."

Sam's eyes lit up. "So, then I can tell you about the time Kyle, Garm, and I were staying in Miami and he decided he wanted to--"

"Wow, it is getting *late*. No time for reverie!" Cunningham interjected. Garm watched with amusement as he wheeled around and gestured for Ho and Ramirez, who were still lurking in the background. "Hey, guys. Come on over and meet our new AWES operator!"

Garm smiled easily as his sonar tech and helmswoman approached. "Good to see you, Ramirez. How was shore leave?"

"Like my cock," came the disgruntled reply. "Not long enough!"

"That's for sure," Ho lamented.

Garm's head jerked back on his shoulders, less in response to his sonar tech's uncharacteristically surly tone than the sudden realization the two of them were sleeping together. Based on the non-stop bickering, he'd suspected that was the case, but his suspicions were now confirmed.

"Everything okay with you two?" he asked, his aquamarine eyes bouncing back and forth.

"Yeah, we're just hung over," Ramirez grumbled. "Sorry, boss."

"It's his fault," Ho ratted. "Once I wouldn't let him gamble, all I heard was 'tequila, tequila, tequila!'"

Garm intently studied their faces. "Are you fit for duty?"

"Yes, captain," Ho stated. She stepped sharply forward, directly in front of Sam's chair, and extended her hand. "Ensign Connie Ho, *Gryphon*'s primary helmswoman. Any friend of Captain Braddock is a friend of mine."

"Sam Mot, sadly sober civilian," he replied. He smiled and his eyes took on an impish look. "Forgive me for not getting up in the presence of such an attractive young lady."

To Garm's surprise, Ho actually smiled and blushed. Totally out of character for her, he mused. Probably the combination of Sam's disarming good looks and the fact that he was, well . . . "disarmed."

Ho turned and gestured for her partner in crime. "Oh, and this is--"

"Ensign Adolfo Ramirez," the mustached sonar technician said. He pressed the heel of his left hand against his temple as he offered Sam his free hand. "Sorry about being out-of-sorts. It's a pleasure."

Sam nodded, then swiveled his chair so he could take in the bridge crew as a whole. "Boys and girls, your distinguished captain has told me all about you. It's an honor to be working with such an elite band of warriors. I'm fired up."

Ho asked, "So, you're going to be operating the new TALOS Mark VII?"

"That is correct."

"I read your file," she said. "Besides your obvious . . . qualifications, you don't have any military background. Also, no documented combat experience. Not to be rude, but it's no hot tub soak out there; are you sure you can handle it?"

Garm's eyes flashed and he cleared his throat noisily.

"Sorry, captain," she said quickly. "I just want to know--"

"Before my 'accident' I was a master free diver," Sam said. "I also had over ten years of martial arts training and a shitload of street fights." He smirked and glanced down at his missing limbs. "Some you win, some you lose. But we're talking about handling a piece of underwater tech. It's not exactly a *cage fight*, ensign. Know what I mean?"

Ho nodded. "Fair enough."

"Speaking of our AWES, where the hell is it?" Garm asked, looking irritably around. It was almost high tide and they had to launch soon.

Cunningham held up a digital clipboard. "Captain Dragunova was here about it just before you showed up. The crate's on a flatbed by the receiving dock. She and Lieutenant McEwan headed over to get it."

Garm felt a dig of panic as he recalled Lara McEwan propositioning him the other day. He did a quick rewind and relaxed, remembering how he'd shot the CDF officer down. She didn't strike him as the kind to blab, but if she did bring up their conversation, including his "rain-check," he could justify it as him letting her down easy.

Besides, technically, that was true. There wasn't a snowball's chance in hell Nat would buy it, but nonetheless . . .

As he looked back and caught Ramirez and Ho cradling their aching heads, Garm became annoyed. "Okay, you two. Onboard *now*, and take something for those headaches – something non-narcotic. I need you guys at 100%. We're going life or death. There's no room for mistakes."

"Yes, sir," came the synchronized reply as the two picked up their bags and trudged toward the nearest gangplank.

"Same goes for you guys," Garm told Cunningham and Rush. "I want your gear stowed and the boat launch-ready in fifteen minutes. Understand?"

"Of course, sir," Rush affirmed. Without another word, she and *Gryphon*'s Fire Control Officer high-tailed it to their belongings and prepared to board.

Behind Garm, Sam advised, "Here comes the package."

Garm's head swiveled toward the approaching flatbed heading purposefully toward them. Through the windshield, he could see Dragunova driving and McEwan in the passenger seat. Visible above the cab, and sturdily anchored to the bed behind it, was a hardwood crate some nine feet in height.

"Hello, *gorgeous*," Sam breathed as the truck pulled noisily alongside, its brakes squeaking.

"Wow, you're really excited about this AWES suit, aren't you?"

"Screw the suit! Have you seen the two babes driving that rig?"

Oh, hell no . . .

"Oh, yeah. Check out the saucy redhead with the nice rack," Sam said as Lara hopped nimbly down from the truck and headed toward them. As Dragunova climbed out from the driver's side of the flatbed and rose to her full height, however, the former LifeGiver's eyes became the size of ostrich eggs.

"Ouch!" Garm winced as one of his friend's bionic hands involuntarily dug deep into his biceps.

"Holy . . . fucking . . . *shit!*" Sam breathed as he ogled the voluptuous sub commander. "Look at that pulchritudinous mountain of womanhood heading our way!"

"Sam--"

"Fuck off! I saw her first!"

"But, *Sam* . . ."

"Can it! I got dibs on Babezilla. You get the tasty-looking ginger pie."

Garm sighed and resigned himself to the horror-comedy about to unfold. He could tell from their body language there was no animosity between Nat and the petite lieutenant. Both women were focused entirely on Sam, sitting in his chair. Their expressions were sympathetic with a hint of apprehension, as most were when they first laid eyes on the quadruple amputee.

They had no idea what they were in for.

"Hello, tall, blonde, and oh-my-god-you're hot!" Sam opened. He gave Lara a wink and a friendly nod and then ignored her entirely. Surging forward to meet Dragunova, he willed his seat to rise on its suspension system until he matched her six-foot-two stature. Then he extended one hand. "I'm--"

"Meester Sam Mot," Dragunova finished with forced pleasantry, taking and shaking his mechanical hand. As he pulled hers gently toward him and leaned down to kiss the back of it, she wore an amused expression.

"*Love* the accent," Sam said, his warm lips still pressed against her flesh.

"Spasiba," she replied, retrieving her hand and fighting down what looked like an urge to count her fingers. She glanced down at a tablet she carried. "I am Captain Natalya Dragunova, commander of the ORION-class AB-Submarine *Antrodemus*. You are Garm's friend, da?"

"That's right," Sam replied. He puffed up his chest, then reached over with a bionic arm and patted the ex-heavyweight's broad shoulder. "In fact, I saved his life once, back in the day." He gave her a knowing look. "I'll be happy to regale you with the tale if you've got time for a drink in your quarters. You know, before we . . . shove off."

Dragunova grinned as she continued reading. "You are obviously not married."

"Nah, I'm divorced."

Divorced . . . what? As the bullshit started to fly, Garm contemplated *Gryphon*'s nearest boarding ramp. It would be far safer onboard. And judging by her paleness, Lieutenant McEwan looked like she was thinking the same thing.

"Nyet, what woman could possibly geev you up?"

"I used to be a gynecologist, but my wife couldn't deal with me bringing my work home with me."

"I can't imagine why," Dragunova countered. "Weeth a man like you, a woman would want all the help she can get."

Unfazed, Sam continued his assault. "Now, don't sell me 'short,' girl. You know, once you've had a man with no legs, everything else just begs."

As Nat spread a predatory smile and moved closer to Sam, Garm started looking for a hole to crawl into. His foul-tempered Russian fuck-buddy was rising to his friend's challenge and he had a feeling the awkwardness factor was about to go through Tartarus's thick granite roof.

"Tell me, Meester Sam. If I were to, how you say, 'geev you a shot?' How do you plan on making up for your . . . shortcomings?"

Sam pretended to flinch from the deprecating barb, but then grinned amusedly. "Ain't nothing short over here, baby. But I'm more an orator."

"How so?"

"I've got some serious oral skills."

Dragunova's eyebrows pricked up as if he had piqued her curiosity. "Oh, really? Such as?"

Sam smirked. "Are you kidding? You remember the rock group KISS?"

"I have heard of them."

"I've got a tongue like Gene Simmons."

Her brows lowered and she smirked back as she studied his lips and mouth. "Looks like more like Reechard Seemons, if you ask me."

As Sam's jaw dropped and he fought to regain his composure, Garm decided to put a stop to their banter. "Okay, guys--"

"Stay out of this, pal-o-mine," Sam advised. His willed his chair forward, pursuing Dragunova as she turned back to the nearby flatbed. "C'mon, Amazon-dot-com, how about it? One drink, before I leave your lovely port."

To Garm's confusion, Dragunova started to shake with laughter. She knew his history with Sam, so she was obviously cutting him some slack. But what came next was anyone's guess.

"Perhaps you're right," she said, turning back and looking him up and down with those sharkskin eyes of hers. "Perhaps, after I have satiated myself upon you, I put you eenside one of my dresser drawers and leave you there, unteel the next time I am een the mood."

Sam's eyes lit up. "Just remember to feed me and change me, baby, and we're good to go!"

"Jesus, Sam!" Garm shouted in exasperation. Then he wheeled on Dragunova. "You know, Nat, from him I expect this. But from *you*?"

As Sam's eyes ping-ponged back and forth between the two of them, and an "a-ha" followed by an "uh-oh" look came over him, the big submariner realized he'd dropped his guard.

"Shit, Big G," Sam started. "I had no idea--"

"Stow it. Can we get to work, please? We're going to lose the tide."

"Da," Dragunova replied. She gave Sam a look, then gestured for a doe-eyed Lieutenant McEwan to take over. "Commence with debriefing."

"Okay . . ." the CDF officer began, stepping tentatively forward. "I'm glad all the introductions are over."

Garm exhaled as Dragunova hauled out the heavy steel loading ramp from the back of the flatbed, then walked up it and moved around the big crate. As she systematically unhooked the thick nylon belts locking it to the truck bed, she pulled a radio from her waist. There was a brief exchange, then a hydraulic lift suspended overhead lowered with a hum, stopping right above the crate. With impressive agility, she sprang up and gripped the crate's wooden edge, then hoisted herself atop it. She had its ratcheting belts wrapped around the lift and was back down to signal an "all clear" in record time.

McEwan cleared her throat. "If you'll be so kind as to follow me, Mr. Mot," she said, walking alongside the truck's thirty-foot pneumatic-reinforced bed. "I'll introduce you to your hardware."

"Right behind you," Sam said. The blue LEDs on the back of his chair lit up as he powered after her.

Garm followed, trying to pretend he wasn't noticing Sam checking out Lara's backside.

Poor bastard must be making up for lost opportunities . . .

McEwan stopped next to the truck's tailgate ramp, waiting on Dragunova. A moment later, the hydraulic lift rose toward the sky, the thick webbing belts attached to the crate slithering upward and hoisting the huge wooden box up and away, to reveal what lay within.

Without looking up, McEwan started reading from her screen. "Lady and gentlemen, I present JAW Robotics Division's latest underwater AWES combat suit, the TALOS Mark VII."

"Holy fucking shit!" Sam spouted.

"Is that the only curse you know?" Garm asked.

Standing before them like some steel colossus was a massively built, vaguely humanoid-shaped robot. It was a battleship gray in color, with black and chrome highlights at the joints, and had enormous arms. It was bent forward from the hip and, with its metal knuckles resting on the truck bed, looked like a giant gorilla. As it was, it stood nearly seven feet in height. Fully upright, Garm figured it must have been eight feet tall and five feet across. Its torso was thickly armored, with a mirrored oval panel at the top, where the driver's head would be. The arms were weaponized, with the right ending in thick, titanium-steel talons and the left in some sort of cannon-like weapon. The legs were columnar and incredibly powerful-looking, with oversize "feet" that looked vaguely like the base of an old-fashioned Saturn lunar rocket.

"Wow . . . *this* is what I get to pilot?" Sam breathed.

Garm's head swiveled in his direction. "Wait, you're not familiar with--"

"Oh, I am. Relax. I worked on it on the simulator hundreds of times. I just didn't realize it would be so . . . *big.*"

Dragunova smirked and called down from the truck bed. "I bet you don't hear *that* very often. Lieutenant, please continue."

Sam stared in a daze as McEwan resumed.

"Mr. Mot, any questions?"

"Uh, yeah," Sam finally managed. "I, uh . . . I know AWES is an acronym for Armored Weaponized Exoskeleton System, but what does the 'JAWS' in JAWS Robotics stand for? Some sort of shark metaphor or something?"

McEwan smiled. "No. It stands for Jake, Amara, and Willie. Named in honor of the three founding partners, one posthumously," she said, giving Garm a polite nod.

"Gotcha. Thanks, Red," Sam said. He licked his lips and shifted in his chair. "Go on and give me the initial run-down."

"Will do. The TALOS Mark VII is a heavily armored and fully articulated underwater combat chassis," McEwan began. "The unit stands exactly 100 inches in height and, sans operator, weighs just over six tons."

"What can I say? Size matters!" Sam chuckled. He started to shoot Dragunova a look, but then chastised himself and averted his eyes.

"This suit and its variants represent the future of both underwater and terrestrial warfare," McEwan continued. "Over the last six months, JAW has produced both the TALOS Mark VII, for underwater excursions, and its cousin, the larger and more heavily armed Mark VIII, as a bunker-buster and anti-tank/anti-materiel platform. The suits will save many lives. I'm sure the founding partners would be proud."

Garm frowned. He doubted very much that his mother would approve of the company she built around the precepts of using robotics for underwater exploration, construction, and limb replacements, being converted into weapons of war to kill or maim other human beings.

As Dragunova padded her way to ground level, McEwan walked up the flatbed's heavy steel loading ramp until she stood beside the towering metal exoskeleton. She thumped its hard chest as she read from her tablet.

"The unit is powered by an AMS-2409 High Yield Mini-Nuclear Reactor," she said. "Power reserves enable it to operate at peak efficiency for six months nonstop, with occasional prerequisite system checks and updates. Should the reactor need to be brought offline, the suit is equipped with emergency power, rated for twelve hours at fifty percent output."

As Dragunova walked over and stood next to him, Garm studied Sam's face. He was curious how he would handle the notion he'd be walking around with a nuclear bomb strapped on his back – literally. To his credit, although his tan did assume a sudden pallor, he didn't flinch.

"Oxygen is filtrated directly from the surrounding seawater, eliminating the need for bulky rebreathers," McEwan announced. "Barring the need for rest or nourishment, you can operate this thing underwater, indefinitely."

Sam raised a bionic hand. "Uh . . . bathroom breaks?"

"Like an astronaut. You go in the suit."

"I'm sorry I asked."

Garm and Dragunova both grinned as McEwan rattled along.

"Mobility is, predictably, greater on land than in the water," she read, "With traveling along the seabed rated at plus or minus eight miles an hour, depending upon terrain."

Garm scoffed. "He's supposed to help us kill pliosaurs while waddling around on the bottom? That's ridiculous."

"Let her finish," Sam said.

McEwan pushed some stray hairs back from her face. "However, the Mark VII is equipped with a Mako M65 Pump Jet Propulsor in each foot, as well as stabilizing thruster valves at key points in the outer armor. Total horsepower is 700, with a top submerged speed of 45 knots."

Garm nodded. "Now *that's* more like it."

Sam turned to him and grinned. "Jealous yet?"

"No, but I'm getting there," Garm replied. "Lieutenant McEwan, what are the suit's offensive and defensive capabilities?"

She licked her lips as she scrolled to the tablet's next page. "Defensive capabilities . . . With reduced threats from shaped-charge munitions and kinetic energy penetrators, the Mark VII utilizes 'smart-technology' enhanced, non-explosive reactive armor on the outside to redirect impacts, backed by a secondary layer of titanium-steel/ceramic composite armor six inches thick. The reserve armor is designed to flex inward under heavy impact, as opposed to shattering, and, combined with the suit's integrated 'crumple zones,' increases the pilot's capacity to weather prolonged assaults."

Sam waved his bionic arms to draw attention to himself before he commenced driving his wheelchair up the steep steel gangplank. "Okay, enough foreplay. I want to try this thing out."

McEwan looked confused. "Don't you want to know about the weapons systems first?"

"I've read the manuals and done every virtual scenario you can think of," Sam remarked. He reached the truck's bed and gazed wide-eyed up at the technological monstrosity that peered down at him like some metallic ogre. "But keep on reading, Red. I know the captains are interested."

"Uh, okay," McEwan appeared flustered as Sam reached up with his robotic arms and started flipping the external releases that allowed access to the top section of the TALOS's plastron. "Taking advantage of the operator being . . . limbless, the Mark VII incorporates indus-trial-caliber actuators in both arms and legs, making it more robot than exoskeleton in terms of power. Under ideal conditions, and at nominal load, the unit is capable of hoisting five times its overall mass, i.e. thirty-plus tons."

There was a loud whooshing sound of escaping air as the suit's top section, including its mirrored titanium visor, popped open on heavy hydraulic hinges.

"You hear that, Garm?" Sam yelled down. "I'm gonna be like 'Ironman!'"

Garm shook his head and chuckled, then turned to Dragunova. "Thank God Admiral Callahan isn't here. Can you imagine how aroused he'd be by this thing? He'd be pitching a tent for sure!"

The tall Russian wore a disgusted look. "That man ees a complete peeg. I cannot stand heem."

"I can tell," he said. "By the way, I'm sorry about Sam's remarks, earlier. He's a bit of a clown."

She snorted in amusement. "Forget about eet. He ees what he ees – a horny guy who needs to get laid. He's just lucky he's your friend and that we're leaving."

"Why?"

"Because otherwise, I would be tempted to do what I said, just to teach heem a lesson!"

"He might like it . . ."

"Ugh."

They stopped talking as Sam, his cybernetic headband still in place, turned his chair around and backed it up until he was right in front of the TALOS suit. He unlocked his torso's restraining belts using his bionic arms, then had the LJ-3000 grip him under his arm stumps and lift him straight up, lowering him into the Mark VII's high-tech cockpit.

A look of annoyance came over him as he looked around the interior.

"Uh, Garm? A little help over here, buddy?"

"Coming."

With Dragunova following, Garm loped up the ramp. After rolling Sam's wheelchair out of the way, he peered inside the suit's compact interior from the right side, with Natalya leaning in from the left. It was heavily reinforced, with huge internal shock absorbers, and had a padded restraining harness to hold the driver in place. There was also what looked like a slimmed down version of Dirk's cybernetic helmet, complete with a chin strap, waiting to be put on.

Garm reached inside. "Okay. I'll get you strapped in . . ." He looked at Dragunova. "Nat, you wanna give me a hand?"

As the well-built sub commander leaned forward and took hold of him, Sam looked her in the eye and smirked. "I knew you couldn't keep your hands off me."

Ignoring the vulgar Russian expletive that came out of Dragunova's mouth, Garm focused on getting Sam secured. Once his harness and helmet were in place and nothing else stood out, he leaned back. "Okay, now what?"

"I don't know."

Garm looked at him like he had two heads. "What do you mean 'you don't know?' I thought you knew this thing inside-out?"

"On the *simulator*," Sam emphasized. "But the initial connectivity outside the virtual mock-up is supposed to be different."

Garm turned to McEwan. "Lieutenant?"

"Uh, it says he's supposed to power up the suit by willing it to life. If he focuses hard it should just happen."

"Sounds good to--"

"Oh, and it also says, when it powers up, the cybernetic connection through the neural-cranial transmitter is more intense than that of the simulator."

Sam looked at her. "Meaning what?"

"Meaning it's going to feel like hungry ants crawling all over your body. Inside it too, but the sensation goes away after a bit."

"Sounds wonderful," Sam said. He closed his green eyes and concentrated. "Okay, here goes . . ."

In an instant, a low hum and the smell of burning ozone permeated the air and, as the truck bed beneath their feet started to vibrate, Garm and Dragunova stepped quickly back. Moving down the metal loading ramp, they took up position next to McEwan.

A series of bright red LEDs lit up along the Mark VII's periphery and the hum increased in volume until you could feel it in your teeth. Then the exoskeleton's huge arms lifted off the floor and, like a giant waking up from a long slumber, it raised itself stiffly erect.

"Okay, I think I feel that sub-dermal sensation you mentioned," Sam said, leaning back in his harness. His eyes hardened and his jaw muscles bunched. "Yeah, there it is. It's . . . ow! Oh, shit! Motherfucker, that goddamn hurts! Argh!"

As Sam's eyes slammed tightly shut and he let out a God-awful scream, Garm and Dragunova exchanged panicked looks. The TALOS suit came alive and began to stagger about the flatbed, its huge feet clomping down from one spot to another and causing the big truck's heavy shocks to complain noisily from the shifting load.

"Aieee!" Sam cried out, thrashing inside the still-open cockpit. He caught sight of the panicked captains rushing toward him and his struggles started to slow. "I-I've . . ."

As Sam's pained expression morphed into an unexpected grin and he started belting out Sinatra's *"I've Got You Under My Skin,"* Garm and Dragunova both came to a shrieking halt and stood there with their jaws hanging down.

"You fucking dick!" Garm snarled as his friend kept on singing. "I thought you were dying!"

Sam stopped his serenading and chuckled. "Oh, trust me, it hurts like a mother. But I'm not gonna let a little thing like pain get me down."

A moment later, he quit shifting and calmed. He looked around the dock from his perch on the flatbed and then smiled.

"There, that's better," he said. A moment later, the thick cockpit door for the Mark VII swung up and closed with a thump, followed by a loud whoosh and hiss as the pressurized seal took hold. Sam took a lingering look around to get his bearings, then his voice rang out from the suit's external speaker system.

"Stand clear, everybody," he said. "I'm going to bring this bad girl down to the ground and I'm not sure how strong that ramp is."

As everyone backed away, Sam started to guide the six-ton TALOS suit forward. It moved smoothly but ponderously, its huge feet shaking the ground. Although it bowed a bit under the load, the heavy gauge steel ramp held and he made it to the reinforced concrete below without incident.

Lieutenant McEwan stepped forward and stared at her reflection in Sam's visor. "How do you feel?"

"Powerful: like I can lift a house."

"Technically, you can."

"No, it's more than that." He raised his robotic arms in front of him, causing the chisel-tipped fingers on the right side to ratchet open and close. "It's like I can *feel* the added parts, like there are nerve endings in them. And my senses are soaring!"

McEwan nodded. "An accurate description. The Talos cybernetic design includes integrated neural-interactive pathways between your nervous system and the suit's electro-sensors. You can actually 'feel' what it feels, to a point."

"But, my hearing, my sight?"

"All enhanced, especially your vision." She scanned the page quickly. "According to the stats, the visual acuity system was based on that of a mantis shrimp. You've got high speed cameras that can record at up to 200,000 FPS and you can see the entire spectrum. For you, even smells are perceived as colors."

Sam swiveled his robotic head around in wonder, then turned and eyed her with interest. "You're right. And let me say, the colors you're giving off are exquisite, my dear."

"Great . . ." Dragunova shook her head in mock disgust. "You put a horny pervert een a super-suit!"

"Hey, you had your chance, Shorty," Sam said, striking a bodybuilder's double biceps pose.

"Can I shoot heem, please?" Dragunova asked.

Garm laughed and turned to McEwan. "Speaking of shooting . . . what kind of weaponry does this thing have?"

"I can answer that," Sam said, moving a thunderous step closer. "The Mark VII is mainly designed to crush and rend, but it does have one main 'gun' of sorts." He raised his cannon-like left arm and pointed it toward the ceiling. "This!"

"Shit, whatever that is, do *not* fire it," Garm admonished.

"I can't," Sam said. "And even if I could, it wouldn't do anything. Not unless I was right on top of the target."

Catching Garm's confusion, McEwan moved between him and Dragunova and showed them the schematics on her tablet. "See here? It's a Mark-V ADCAP plasma weapon."

"Like in 'Star Trek?'" Garm asked.

She chuckled. "No, more like an overgrown plasma torch. It's a direct-current, hybrid plasma weapon with a range of about ten feet."

"Ten feet?" Dragunova scoffed. "Useless."

"With all due respect, captain, I read up on it and I disagree," McEwan replied. "That sucker's got a blade temperature of over 10,000 degrees Kelvin. That's twice the surface temperature of the *sun*. It can slice through a battleship's belt armor in one pass."

"And against organics?" Garm asked.

"Anything that comes within five feet of the plasma jet will be exposed to a blast of super-heated seawater, effectively parboiling it."

"And a direct impact?"

McEwan's white incisors pressed against her lower lip as she visualized her response. "It will cut through the skull of a *Kronosaurus* like a light saber . . . sir."

"Impressive," Garm said. "And out of the water?"

"I can't use it in the air," Sam interjected. He lowered the barrel of his plasma gun and pointed it toward the floor. "The jet is composed of seawater-stabilized plasma. No seawater, no plasma."

"Good. That means you can't get drunk and punch a hole in the hull."

Dragunova snorted irritably. "Speaking of hulls, eet ees almost time to cast off. My people are already ready, Captain Braddock. I suggest you get yours under control."

Without even a "bon voyage" she spun on her heel and headed toward *Antrodemus*.

"Charming, isn't she?" Garm said to McEwan.

"Actually, she scares me."

"That's because you're a smart girl. I assume you'll make sure the truck finds its way back to the depot?"

"Absolutely." The petite redhead eyed Dragunova's muscular back as she continued to move off, then lowered her voice. "Garm, I didn't want to say anything in front of her because, frankly, I think she's got the hots for you. But I hope you have a safe tour." She locked gazes with him. "And if you're free when you get back, I've got a great recipe for grilled pork chops I'm dying to try on you."

Garm cleared his throat, hoping Sam's enhanced hearing wasn't picking up their conversation. "That's quite an inducement, Lara. Assuming I make it back in one piece, we'll have to talk about that."

Making sure his back was to Sam, he gave her one of his trademark winks, then grinned as she walked back to the flatbed and climbed behind the wheel.

"Okay, Sam," he said, turning around. "It's time to get you and this walking tank onboard."

"Hold on a minute, pal," Sam willed his suit's hatch open as the big truck rumbled to life and pulled away. "It's obvious you're banging the Siberian tigress, over there, but--"

"What makes you--?"

"Oh, please. This is *me* you're talking to. Don't insult my intelligence. It's all I've got left these days, okay?"

He sighed. "Okay, fine. Yes, Natalya and I are . . . involved."

"And the little redhead, too? How the fuck are you managing that?"

Garm sniggered. "Now, *there* you're wrong. I never touched her."

"You swear?"

"Word of honor. She's interested, but I haven't pursued it."

"Oh, thank God. I was worried."

Garm gave him a look. "What, you think I'm a selfish bastard? Geez, Sam. Look, if you want, I'll put in a good word for you."

"Oh, no. I can speak for myself. I just don't want any more of your sloppy seconds."

"What?"

"You heard me. Remember when we traded off those fitness girls in Honolulu – you had the short, Vietnamese one with the great legs? My God, after you were done with her, she was like the Holland tunnel!"

"Get the fuck outta here."

"I'm serious!" Sam said, giving him a playful nudge with one of his giant mechanical arms. "I don't know what you're packing, buddy, but I felt like 'Thelma and Louise' falling into the Grand Canyon! I had to tie a plank across my ass!"

Garm groaned and pointed at the canal where *Gryphon* was berthed. "In the water, forty feet from the bow. Turn on your lights and look for the opened airlock. You'll be storing your AWES alongside our LOKI AUVs."

Sam swiveled in that direction. "What about my quarters? I can't sleep in this thing, you know."

"It's cramped onboard, but we'll do our best," Garm said. "Once they've drained the seawater, my crew will help you out and get you into your chair."

"You can bring it?"

Garm nodded. "Yes, but the only place you'll have room to move around is the galley, so I'll have a cot set up for you in there. Best I can do. Sorry."

Sam's head hung in his harness and he stared at the ground. "Okay."

"What's with the puss?"

"Nothing. I understand I'm a burden, and I know you need your space. It wasn't like I was asking for--"

"Why you devious little cocksucker," Garm swore. "You actually thought I was going to give up my quarters for you?"

"W-what? No way, I just thought . . ."

"Let me tell you something, Samuel Mot," Garm said with a grin. "It's gonna take a lot more than you complimenting my *dick* to con me out of my bunk!"

"Uh, well, how about a hand job?" Sam offered. He held up his suit's huge titanium-steel mitt. "C'mon. This thing's big enough to handle even *your* cock, and with the pistons and actuators it's got, I bet it will do one helluva job. Plus, it's not like I'd actually be *touching* you, so technically . . ."

"Sam?"

"Yes?"

"Get in the fucking water."

"Yes, captain . . ."

THIRTY

"*Afterbirth . . . afterbirth . . . afterbirth . . .*"

Dirk was almost through the concrete corridor leading to the docks when his obsessing over Natalya Dragunova betrayed him. He'd been mentally reviewing the meeting he had with her and Garm when he found himself envisioning each word that came out of her mouth.

'*Can you imagine the size of the afterbirth?*' were the ones that got him.

Out of nowhere, a wave of disorientation swept over Dirk and he was forced to stop and lean against a nearby wall. The cold concrete permeated his skin and he shuddered at the realization. He could literally *hear* the dusty drawer in which he'd compartmentalized unpleasant childhood memories creaking as it was forced open.

Suddenly, he was six years old again and climbing down from the school bus. He was crying and in no hurry to get home, for fear he'd suffer further shame. Thankfully, his dad's SUV wasn't there. Worst case scenario, only his mother would see him in his current state.

"*Afterbirth . . . afterbirth . . .*"

His tormentors' chant was still echoing in his ears as he approached the kitchen door. The razzing had started in the playground. The class bullies, frustrated that he'd refused to allow them to copy his homework, had come up with a new way to torment him.

"*You're so tiny, Braddock – after your brother was born you probably just fell outta your mom's smelly cooch!*"

"*Yeah, she was so stretched out she probably didn't even notice you!*"

"*She probably thought you were the afterbirth!*"

"*Yeah, he's just her afterbirth! Afterbirth . . . afterbirth . . .*"

Outraged by their attempts to denigrate his mother, he'd stood up to them, only to end up getting jumped by all three. If the resultant beating wasn't humiliating enough, he had to listen to their disgusting litany the rest of the day, and all the way home, too.

Garm hadn't been around for the "fight" or the hellish bus ride. He liked to jog the fourteen blocks. But he'd seen the teasing earlier that day and done nothing.

Not that Dirk expected any help. Although the two of them were close, historically speaking, when it came to sticking up for his little brother, Garm was a neutral party. He seemed befuddled by Dirk's inability to stand up for himself and stayed out of it.

And so, it was to Dirk's surprise that, as he crept in the house on little mouse feet with the intention of sneaking up to his room, he overheard Garm and his mother discussing his troubles in the living room. Dreading what was being said, he crept closer, his ears pricking up like an owl's.

"I just don't get it, mom," Garm said. "They were picking on Derek again at school today and he wasn't fighting back."

"What were they doing?" his mother asked.

"They were calling him names, saying bad things, and pushing him around because he's smaller than me."

"And did you stick up for your brother?"

"No."

"Why not?"

Dirk could hear the concern lacing his mom's voice.

"Because Dad said it's a man's duty to be able to take care of himself," Garm stated. "I heard him tell someone that when they asked him why he still trains so hard, even though he's not a policeman anymore."

"You didn't hear the whole thing, sweetie. Daddy works out because he feels a man needs to be able to take care of himself *and* the people he loves."

"*Oh . . .*"

From his vantage point, Dirk could see his mother put an arm around his brother's shoulders. "Did you ever consider, Garm, that the reason you're so much bigger and stronger than your brother is because you're supposed to take care of him?"

"Do you really think so?"

"Doesn't daddy take care of us?"

There was a brief silence. Then Garm said, "You're right, mom. I'm sorry, I'll fix things."

"Fix things? Karma takes care of bullies like that."

Garm nodded. "Yeah, but sometimes karma needs an assistant."

As Dirk brushed against a ceramic bowl on the kitchen counter, nearly toppling it, he gasped in alarm. Fear shot through him and he stumbled backwards, his heart pounding at the possibility of getting caught.

He found himself back in Tartarus.

"There you are, handsome," Stacy said, walking over to him. She wore an unabashedly maternal expression. "Hey, you okay? You're sweating."

Dirk pulled away from the gritty wall and straightened up, his lips bowing as he rhythmically inhaled and exhaled to cool himself. He twitched as a boatload of insight landed smack on his shoulders. He couldn't believe he'd somehow forgotten that relic conversation between his brother and their mom. That was the day before Garm commenced what would be an ongoing mission to beat down every bully that looked sideways at him.

Dirk swallowed the sudden realization he'd solved one of life's little mysteries. "Yeah, I'm good, Stace," he replied. He wiped at his brow. "Sorry. I guess the bourbon isn't out of my system yet."

She chuckled. "I always knew you were a lightweight. C'mon."

"Did I miss anything?" Dirk asked, clearing his throat as he followed her outside. They moved past the guard post, toward a red and black MarshCat she had parked nearby.

"I checked the log and they've already got *Gryphon*'s new AWES suit uncrated and stowed," Stacy said as they both climbed in. She turned the ignition key, causing the rugged six-wheeler to rumble to life. "Both ORIONs are locked and loaded and launch-ready. So, if you're going to wish either of their respective captains a 'bon voyage,' we'd better haul ass."

"Then get us there," Dirk said. He sat back, relishing the feeling of the onrushing dock air flowing over his damp face and hair. Behind them, the immense pliosaur tanks shrank as they sped toward the distant submarine slips.

Stacy was right. Both gray-hulled *Gryphon* and her red-hued sister-ship, *Antrodemus*, were definitely ready to kick butt. Both their bows were pointed at the nearby Vault doors and they had steam wafting from their exhaust ports. They reminded Dirk of hungry dragons, eager to hunt.

He focused hard. Both sub crews had already boarded and he could see Garm and Dragunova conferring like tag team wrestling partners as the ATV moved steadily closer.

Dirk sighed. He would've felt like a real shit if he didn't say goodbye to his brother. Not just because of the compiled guilt over having always been so jealous, which he realized now was considerable, but because of the danger factor. Everyone seemed to think his twin was indestructible – Garm included – but the powerful pugilist was about to go on safari after the most dangerous *Kronosaurus* of all time.

Tiamat might be bigger, but *Typhon* was crafty and experienced. And deadly.

"Well, well," Garm said, turning around as Stacy pulled the ATV up and slapped it in park. "Looks like we're getting a sendoff from the big brass, after all, Captain Dragunova."

"Ees about time," she snickered.

"Glad you made it, little brother," Garm said with a grin. As Dirk tried offering him his hand, he tousled his hair, then grabbed the young scientist in a huge bear hug and hoisted him clean off the floor. "Stay out of trouble until I get back, okay?"

"Oof! Will do," Dirk replied as his feet touched back down. He sucked in a deep breath, trying to get his rib cage to re-expand.

"Doctor Derek," Dragunova said, extending her hand. "Eet ees good to see you again, and *dressed*, I might add!"

Dirk pretended not to notice Stacy's eyebrows scaling her forehead. He shook palms with the towering Russian, then yelped as she unexpectedly yanked him forward and mock arm-wrestled him. She stopped and gave him a playful nudge.

"Doctor Daniels," Dragunova acknowledged, giving Stacy a polite nod.

"Good luck," Stacy replied. "And good hunting."

Garm chuckled. "Oh, don't worry. It's going to be the hunt to end all hunts." He gave Dragunova a knowing smirk then clicked his tongue at Dirk and Stacy before turning on his heel and making for *Gryphon*.

"Hey, Garm?" Dirk said, rushing after him.

"Yeah?"

"I should've said this decades ago, but . . . thanks for always being there."

Garm smiled and clapped a big hand on his shoulder. "No worries, little brother. I always will be."

As the captains split up and started toward their respective vessels, Stacy moved next to Dirk. "Now, tell me honestly; do you wish you were going, too?"

Dirk forced his eyes away from Dragunova's considerable rump and gave Stacy a look.

"With Garm?"

"No, with *her*."

His mouth opened and closed. He'd nearly forgotten he'd kept her in the dark about *Gryphon*'s true destination. "Uh . . . hunting *Typhon*? Are you nuts? Do you know how dangerous it's going to be?"

"Yeah, but just think. The two of you, going down on a submarine, on a harrowing sea voyage . . ."

"*Going down*? Tell me something, Stace. Do you sit around all day, dreaming up these jealous fantasies of yours?"

"Pretty much."

Dirk grinned and shook his head, his eyes flitting back to *Gryphon* as his brother yanked the armored sail door shut behind him with a tremendous thud. Dragunova was almost to her boat when a deep rumble shimmied through the reinforced concrete under their feet. In the distance, the Vault's giant doors began to grind apart.

"So, you really don't wish you were going?" Stacy pressed.

Dirk watched Dragunova scale *Antrodemus*'s gangplank with pantherish strides. He contained his sigh. As unbelievably drawn as he was to the red sub's striking commander, the notion of setting foot on Diablo Caldera and partaking of its prehistoric wonders was equally enticing.

"Not at all," he lied.

"I'm surprised, with all the trouble you two could get into."

He chuckled. "I get plenty of action and adventure right here in Tartarus, thank you very much. Danger too, come to think of it."

"Oh, you think you've experienced danger?" Stacy threw him a coquettish look. "You haven't seen my new garter belt yet."

As a foghorn-like claxon split the air, Dirk mulled things over. His thoughts were punctuated by an earth-shuddering *THUMP* as the Vault's doors locked open. "Is that an invitation?" he asked.

"Duh! Do I have to sit on your face to get through to you?"

"Uh, well, that would work."

"I bet," Stacy said, smirking. She looked around then lowered her voice. "So, my place? In an hour?"

Dirk saw the nearby canal waters churn as *Gryphon*'s maneuvering thrusters kicked in. A moment later, the big pliosaur killer began to creep forward. "There's no place I'd rather be."

He watched Dragunova close *Antrodemus*'s sail door and heard the crimson sub's powerful propulsors roar to life.

Well, maybe one . . .

For the first time in his century-long lifespan, the male *Octopus giganteus* was experiencing creeping terror.

She was extricating herself from their nearby midden, her craggy skin snapping off the remaining reddish-brown rusticles ringing the gash in the sunken submarine's hull like pieces of eggshell. As she forced herself free, a cloud of particles the color of dried blood plumed around her. She waited for the water to clear, then lowered her colossal bulk onto the exposed sand and stayed there.

Other than the rhythmic pumping of her gills, the female was motionless. Her eyes were open but she seemed almost catatonic. Then, without warning, she sprang to life. Her skin had a strange, sparkly look to it and, as she violently shook herself, she sent the coating of glittering black specks that clung to her fluttering away like an obsidian rain shower. Her gleaming yellow orbs widened and she emitted a gurgling grumble as she looked around the surrounding seabed. She took in the barren coral reefs, the drop-off, and finally, her very nervous mate.

As the female's gaze fell upon him, the male shrank down, his body changing color and texture in an attempt to blend into the bottom. For some time now he had kept his distance, and wisely so. She had been increasingly belligerent of late, and there was more to it than just hunger. Her appetite was certainly there; what meager findings he brought back were devoured with a rapaciousness that defied description. But there was anger about her. A rage that came and went that was unlike anything he had experienced in their many years together.

As the female rose, extending her 100-foot tentacles, the male felt a sudden quake of fear. His body tensed and he sucked a room-sized quantity of water into his mantle, preparing to jet away at the first sign of aggression.

To his relief, she moved quietly away from him, her monstrous body flowing up the nearby continental shelf. Her eight arms were a bristling mass of suckers, cascading over one another like a lethal waterfall as they carried her effortlessly forward. Without a backwards glance, she headed toward a nearby submarine rise, crested it and vanished.

The male remained still, his black pupils the only part of his body not able to merge with the concealing substrate. It was unlike his mate to leave the nest for a prolonged period, and he waited patiently for her return. After the better part of an hour, however, he decided she had left to hunt on her own and started to move.

Extracting himself from the bottom, his huge body shed copious volumes of sand as he headed toward the adjacent wreck. It was a moonless night, but the pitch blackness surrounding him mattered not; his eyes were fully adapted to the lightless depths. Peeking inside the entrance of their lair, he studied the thick strings of eggs that hung down from the century-old sub's interior like milky grapes on gelatinous vines.

And a lethal harvest they would be.

High above the mysterious black granules that peppered the midden floor, he could see his offspring squirming within their melon-sized wombs. Their blackish eyes peered hungrily about. There were tens of thousands of them and they were growing fast. By the time they hatched, each would be the size of an adult common octopus and fully capable of surviving on its own.

Temporarily pushing his mate's disappearance from his deliberations, the male pondered a nearby reef. His keen eyes swept its length, pinpointing scores of potential hiding places for his soon-to-be progeny. It was good. Far from the squid-infested hollows, where most octopus eggs were devoured before they could hatch, his brood's chances of survival were vastly improved. Whereas, in the deep, only one or two might survive to adulthood, here in the shallows scores of them would.

They would grow quickly, as cephalopods were wont to do, reaching breeding size in but a year. Then those scores would become hundreds, and those hundreds, legions. Before his time was done, he would see his species do more than simply bounce back from the brink of extinction. He would see them proliferate.

Their spread would go unchecked, and if the great whales they relied on could no longer sustain them they would find new sources of flesh to feast upon. Whether it was the giant marine reptiles they were encountering or the tiny bipeds he and his mate now recognized as a readily available food source, to the great mollusks it mattered not.

In the end, all were meat.

The Adventure Continues In
KRONOS RISING: KRAKEN (Volume 2)
Coming Soon!

Also by Max Hawthorne
KRONOS RISING
KRONOS RISING: DIABLO
KRONOS RISING: PLAGUE
MEMOIRS OF A GYM RAT

ABOUT THE AUTHOR

Heralded as the *"Prince of Paleo-fiction"* by *Fangoria Magazine*, Max Hawthorne grew up in Philadelphia, where he graduated with a BA from Central High School and a BFA from the University of the Arts. He is the author of MEMOIRS OF A GYM RAT, an outrageous exposé of the health club industry, as well as the award-winning KRONOS RISING marine terror novel series. In addition to working as a full-time writer, he is a voting member of the Author's Guild, an IGFA world record-holding angler, and an avid sportsman and conservationist. His hobbies include fishing, boating, archery, boxing, and the collection of fossils and antiquities. He lives with his wife, daughter, and an impossibly large rabbit in the Greater Northeast.

GLOSSARY OF SCIENTIFIC/ NAUTICAL/MARINE TERMS

Abyssal Plains: The vast underwater plains at the bottom of the ocean, with water depths averaging between 10,000–20,000 feet. Largely unexplored, they represent more than 50% of the Earth's surface.

Acoustics: The science and study of mechanical *waves* in liquids, solids, and gases. This includes vibrations, as well as sound, ultrasound, and infrasound waves.

ADCAP: Military Acronym for *Advanced Capability*.

Aft: Naval terminology indicating the stern or rear of a ship. *"Aft section"* indicates the rear portion of a ship.

Amidships: The center/middle portion of a vessel.

ANCILE: Advanced Obstacle Avoidance sonar system with acoustic intercept. ANCILE's active sonar pings target incoming signals and can be fed directly into a vessel's fire control (weapons) systems.

Anti-Biologic: Designed to kill biologics, i.e. living organisms.

Archelon: The largest known sea turtle. Archelon went extinct at the end of the Cretaceous.

Argentinosaurus: An enormous titanosaur sauropod dinosaur, and possibly the largest living land animal of all time. Argentinosaurus is estimated at around 100 feet in length with a weight in excess of 90 tons.

ATV: All Terrain Vehicles.

Autonomous: Independent and self-governing, i.e. freethinking surveillance drones.

Autotomic Response: Self amputation, a defensive response in certain animals wherein a portion of the body (tail, tentacle) is shed to distract a predator. The shed portion continues to writhe on its own in order to keep the attacker interested while the host animal escapes.

Autotomous: Separate parts of an organism that are free thinking and independent of the originating organism's control or influence, i.e. the tentacles of an octopus performing complex tasks while the host animal's attention is focused elsewhere.

AWES Suits: Acronym for *Armored Weaponized Exoskeleton System.* Manufactured by GDT through its subsidiary, JAW Robotics, the AWES Talos Mark VII and VIII are heavily armored, nuclear-powered combat chassis.' Both suits are designed to be worn by quadruple amputees. The six-ton Mark VII is designed for undersea exploration/combat, whereas the larger, more heavily armed Mark VIII is a land-based anti-materiel/anti-personnel weapons platform.

Ballast: In submarine terms, a compartment (ballast tank) that holds water of varied quantities to balance the vessel underway and help control its depth. Pumping water out of the ballast tank ("blow ballast") increases a submarine's buoyancy and can be used for an emergency rise.

Barotrauma: Physical trauma to body tissues due to a sudden and dramatic change in ambient pressure, AKA *"The Bends."*

Barrett XM500: A .50 caliber sniper rifle, circa 2006, developed by the *Barrett Firearms Company.* The XM500 fires the powerful .50 caliber BMG round and is equipped with a detachable 10-round magazine.

Bathymetric Gigantism: A tendency for certain deep-dwelling marine animals, particularly invertebrates, to grow to colossal size in a dark, cold, high-pressure environment. Comparable to *Abyssal gigantism.*

Beam: A ship's width at its widest point.

Bearcat: Also known as the GDT (Grayson Defense Technologies) Bearcat: an ultra-quiet, heavily armed and armored anti-materiel helicopter, known for its stealthy approach.

Bearing: Navigation term as relates to course changes.

Berth: A designated location where a boat or ship is *moored* (attached), usually for purposes of loading and unloading passengers or cargo.

Beta-Endorphin: A neuropeptide found in the neurons of the central nervous system that functions as a natural analgesic. Endorphins dull or numb the pain from trauma-based injuries.

Bioluminescence: The manufacturing and emission of light by an organism.

Blake Plateau: A submarine plateau off the southeastern coast of the United States. The plateau borders North and South Carolina, Georgia and Florida, and stretches between the Continental Shelf and the Deep Ocean basin. It measures approximately 90 by 106 miles and ranges in depth from approximately 500 to 1,000 yards.

BMG 50: The powerful .50 caliber Browning machine gun round.

Bow: The foremost point of the hull of a boat or ship.

Bozhe Moy: Russian for *"Oh my God."*

Bridge: The room or point on a boat or ship from which it is commanded.

Broadband Clicks: High frequency sonar clicks used in *echolocation*.

Brumation: The reptilian equivalent of hibernation. During the winter, brumating marine reptiles sleep on the seabed for extended period of time, breathing entirely through their skins and waking only to drink water.

Bulkhead: A wall within the hull of a boat or ship.

Cachalot: Archaic term for the Sperm whale, from the French word *cachalot*, meaning "tooth."

Caldera: A bowl-like geological formation, usually formed by the partial collapse of a volcano, following an eruption.

Carcharodon megalodon: Binomial nomenclature for a species of giant shark that lived during the Cenozoic Era and fed on sea turtles and marine mammals, including cetaceans. Megalodon had teeth over seven inches in slant height and exceeded 50 feet in length.

Caudal Fin: The tail fin of a fish.

Celazole: (see polybenzimidazole/PBI)

Cenomanian-Turonian Extinction Event: An extinction event during the early Cretaceous Period (approx 91.5mya) that resulted in the extinction of the pliosaurs and ichthyosaurs.

Center Console: A single-decked, open hull boat with all the controls (console) located in the center of the vessel.

Cephalopod: Marine animals such as the octopus, squid, and cuttlefish, wherein limbs or tentacles extend from a prominent head. Cephalopods are also *mollusks*.

Cetacean: Marine mammals, including whales, dolphins and porpoises.

Cetaceanist: A marine biologist who specializes in cetaceans – whales, dolphins, and porpoises.

Charybdis: A mythological sea monster from Greek mythology. Charybdis lived under a rock in a narrow strait and, when ships approached, would suck in huge quantities of water, creating a giant whirlpool that dragged hapless sailors to their deaths.

Chelonian: Turtles and tortoises.

Chemoreceptors: A sensory receptor that detects chemical stimuli in an environment, i.e. taste.

Chromatophores: Cells or groups of cells containing various types of pigmentation or with light reflective qualities. Typically found in animals.

Chronospecies: A species that evolves in sequences over time from an extinct ancestral form.

Circle Hook: A fishing hook with a point that curves sharply inward. Circle hooks are designed to catch a fish in the corner of the jaw and are rarely swallowed.

Claxon: A low-frequency horn used by ships to signal one another.

Cleat: A nautical term for a narrow, anvil-shaped device used to secure a rope or line. Cleats are often used to tie boats to docks.

Clew: On a sailboat, the lower aft corner of a sail.

Cloaca: A posterior orifice found in reptiles, birds, amphibians and a few mammals that serves as a combined opening for both the reproductive, digestive, and urinary tracts.

Coastal Defense Force (CDF): A sub-branch of the military (formally part of the US Coast Guard, now overseen by GDT). The CDF has bases off the coast of Maine, Florida, Washington, and Hawaii, and utilizes Anti-Biologic submarines, such as the ORION Class, to seek out and destroy rogue pliosaurs that threaten America's waterways.

Conning Tower: An elevated platform on a ship or submarine, from which an officer can command ("*con*") the vessel.

Continental Shelf: The extended (and submerged border) of any given continent and its associated *coastal plain.*

Counter-shading: Evolution-induced color patterns in marine organisms designed to make the organism difficult to spot by bother predator and prey. Typical counter-shading patterns are dark above and light below.

Convergent Evolution: The evolution of analogous structures with similar design in different species, i.e. the body design share by both dolphins and ichthyosaurs.

Cretaceous: A period of geologic time from 145 to 65 million years ago. The end of the Cretaceous Period was marked by the sudden extinction of all non-avian dinosaurs.

Crevalle Jack: A species of large saltwater fish, common throughout the Atlantic Ocean.

Cronavrol: A powerful and fast-acting sedative designed to be used against pliosaurs. When injected directly into the spine, Cronavrol instantly forces the recipient into deep *brumation.*

Crustacean: Crustaceans are members of a large group of *arthropods* and include such creatures as lobsters, crabs, and shrimp.

Cryogenics: The study of freezing materials at extremely low temperatures (-238 F or lower)

Cybernetics: Using advanced technology to control a given system.

Dakuwaqa: A shark god from Fijian mythology.

Deinosuchus: An extinct, Cretaceous Era crocodile that once hunted dinosaurs. Deinosuchus reached 40 feet in length and weighed 10 tons.

Detritus: Referred to as *marine snow,* detritus is non-living particles of organic material suspended in water.

Diablo Caldera: A dormant volcano whose upper portion was blown off during a violent eruption during the early *Cretaceous Period.* When the KT asteroid struck, Diablo was flooded by a mega-tsunami and became an eight-mile-wide saltwater lake that imprisoned an assortment of prehistoric marine life. Diablo has a network of superheated lava tubes running underneath it, some of which connect its lake to the sea. In recent years, a portion of the caldera collapsed, allowing some of its inhabitants to escape.

Dinghy: A small boat, often towed behind a larger vessel for use as a ship-to-ship or ship-to-shore boat.

Djöfullinn: Icelandic for demon or devil.

Dopamine: A neurotransmitter in the brain whose neural pathways govern both reward-based behavior and motor control.

Dorsal: The upper side of an animal that swims in a horizontal position. The dorsal *region* refers to that general area on the animal. Dorsal *fin* refers to one or more fins that protrude from that region, i.e. a shark's distinctive, curved fin.

Draft (or Draught): The measurement from a vessel's waterline to the bottom of its hull. Draft determines the minimum water depth a ship or boat requires in order to navigate safely.

Dromaeosaurs: An extinct group of small to medium-sized carnivorous dinosaurs, popularly known as raptors.

Echolocation: In marine animals, the emission of sonar sound waves and the absorption of their echoes to "see" underwater.

Economic Exclusive Zone: An *EEZ* is a sea zone over which a country has specific rights relating to the exploration and exploitation of its natural resources. It stretches from the end of said country's territorial waters (the *12 mile limit*) an additional 200 nautical miles.

Electronic Iridophore: An artificial type of chromatophore with reflective/iridescent properties.

Electroreceptor: One of a group of organs on mainly marine organisms that allow them to perceive and detect electrical stimuli.

Enchodus petrosus: Binomial nomenclature for a Cretaceous-era, predatory salmonid that escaped Diablo Caldera. *Enchodus* are known as the "Sabertooth salmon" of "Sabertooth herring" and have large eyes and long fangs. Maximum length: six feet.

Ensign: Naval rank, equivalent to a second lieutenant in the U.S. Army.

Epidemiology: The study of infectious diseases in defined populations.

ESA: The Endangered Species Act.

Eschrichtius robustus: Binomial nomenclature for the Gray whale. Gray whales can reach 50 feet in length and weigh in excess of 40 tons.

Fafnir: A powerful dragon from Norse mythology, eventually slain by Sigurd.

Fathometer: Passive sonar system that substitutes ambient sounds generated by surface waves and biologics to create a 3-D map of the seabed and surrounding water. Instead of using an active sonar projector, the fathometer utilizes beam-forming and a vertical array of hydrophones to cross-correlate noise from the surface with its echoes from the seabed, thereby reducing interference from horizontally propagating noise.

Fenris: A monstrous wolf from Norse mythology that bit of the hand of Tyr, god of war. During the battle of Ragnarok Fenris kills Odin, the ruler of the gods.

Flagorneur: French for a groveling toady or sycophant.

Flats Boat: A small draft boat designed to safely run and operate in extremely shallow bodies of water, such as the Florida Keys.

Flying Gaff: A specialized gaff designed to land very large fish. The hook portion of the gaff detaches when embedded in a fish and remains secured to the boat by a strong cable or rope.

Fore: The front or *bow* of a ship or boat.

Foredeck: The bow portion of a ship's deck.

Forecastle: The foremost portion of a ship's upper deck. In medieval ships it served as a defensive stronghold where archers could rain fire down upon opposing vessels.

Galley: The kitchen on a ship or boat.

Gangplank: A moveable construct, often formed of strong planks, which bridges the distance between a ship and its mooring station. It enables the loading and offloading of goods and personnel.

GDT: Acronym for Grayson Defense Technologies, one of the largest manufactures of military weapons, pharmaceuticals, and robotics on the planet. GDT both bankrolls and directs the newly formed Coastal Defense Force (CDF).

Gen-1: A member of a first or initial generation.

Gimbal: The receiving point (socket) of a big-game fishing fighting belt or chair. The butt of the fishing rod inserts into this point and can swivel up and down to exert pressure on fish.

Gin Pole: A strong, vertical pole or tower, equipped with an extending arm and pulley system. Gin poles are used on fishing vessels to hoist very large fish onboard.

Gladius: Also called cuttlebone. A hard internal shell found in cuttlefish and squid that gives the body rigidity.

Glycoproteins: Integral cellular membrane proteins that play a role in cell-to-cell interactions.

Gunnels/Gunwales: The uppermost/top edges of a ship or boat's hull.

Gryphon: A powerful mythical creature in Greek mythology, said to have the head and wings (and sometimes forelimbs) of an eagle and the body of a lion. Alternative spelling: *Griffin*.

Harbormaster: The official that enforces the regulations of a particular port or harbor.

Hazmat: Short for hazardous materials.

Helm: A ship's wheel or other steering mechanism (tiller, steering wheel, etc.).

Helmsman: The individual that steers a ship or boat.

Hvalur: Icelandic for *whale*.

Hydrophone: An underwater microphone.

Hydrostatic Pressure: The pressure exerted by water due to the effects of gravity.

Hyperion: one of the monstrous Titans from Greek mythology.

Idling: When a boat sits *idle* with its engine running (in neutral). Idle boats tend to drift as a result of wind and tide.

Intermittent Transients: Hard to track and sporadic radar or sonar readings, usually indicative of a shielded (military) craft.

Isopod: A group of oval-shaped, segmented crustaceans that inhabit land, fresh and saltwater environments. Scavenging abyssal isopods can exceed 20 inches in length.

Kaiju: Japanese for *strange beast.*

Kauhuhu: The ancient Hawaiian's shark god of Molokai.

Knot: A nautical unit of speed equivalent to one *nautical* mile per hour, or about 1.151 mph.

Koshka: Russian word for a female *cat.*

Kraken: A mythological marine monster said to feed on whales and drag ships to their destruction. The Kraken is believed to be based on early sailors' encounters with the *giant squid.*

Kronosaurus imperator: Binomial nomenclature ("Ruler of God of Time Reptiles") for a giant species of pliosaur imprisoned in Diablo Caldera during the KT/Yucatan impact. Males can exceed 60 feet in length, females 80. The species is based on fragmentary fossil remains, including tooth marks on the Mexican pliosaur known as the "Monster of Aramberri," that indicate a creature with a potential tooth crown length of twelve inches.

Kronosaurus queenslandicus: Binomial nomenclature for a mid-sized species of pliosaur from the Cretaceous Period. K. Queenslandicus had rounded fangs, as opposed to the ridged teeth of Pliosaurus, and fed upon plesiosaurs, sea turtles, fish and squid. Size estimate is 33 feet with a weight of 12 tons.

Landing: A designated docking location for vessels at a marina.

Lanyard: A length or cord used to carry something and worn around the neck or wrist. Safety lanyards on boats and Jet Skis function as kill switches and shut down the vessel's engine in the event the pilot falls overboard.

Lazarus Taxon: A species that vanishes from the fossil record, only to reappear later.

Lexan: A clear thermoplastic/polycarbonate, known for its strength and durability.

Livyatan: An extinct raptorial sperm whale that lived during the Miocene Epoch.

LRIT: Long Range Intelligence and Tracking. An international system of tracking ships using shipborne satellite communication equipment.

Macropliosaur: One of the giant species of pliosaur.

Macropredator: A large predator.

Malacologist: One who studies mollusks.

Mandible: One of a pair (mandibles) of bones in the mouth that comprise the lower jaw.

Mandibular Symphysis: Where the two lower jaw bones (mandibles) fuse together.

Manifest: A document listing the passengers, crew, and cargo of a vessel for official purposes.

Marguerite Formation: A defensive formation utilized by sperm whales and other cetaceans to defend their young. The adults encircle the vulnerable calves, typically with either their flukes or jaws pointed outward, in an attempt to ward off attackers.

MarshCat: A six-wheeled, amphibious ATV developed by GDT and used in the CDF's top-secret Tartarus research facility. MarshCats have sturdy roll bars, front row bucket seats, a rear bench seat that accommodates three, and are powered by a 90 hp diesel engine.

Maxilla: One of a pair (maxillae) of bones in the mouth that comprise the upper jaw and palate.

MHD Propulsors: Magnetohydrodynamic Drive Propulsors are marine-based thrust generators typically used in submarines that utilize electrified water as a propellant to drive a vessel in the opposite direction. MHD Drives are powerful and silent and have few moving parts.

Midgard Serpent: Also known as *Jörmungandr* and the *World Serpent*, a gigantic sea serpent from Norse mythology, said to be so huge it could encircle the earth and could bite its own tail. It was Thor's nemesis and during the final battle of Ragnarok was killed by the Thunder God. Thor then perished in the resultant flood of venom that spewed from the dying beast's mouth.

Minke Whale: A lesser Rorqual and the second smallest baleen whale, averaging 23–26 feet in length and weighing 4–5 tons.

Mollusk: A large phylum of invertebrate animals, including gastropods (snails and slugs) and cephalopods (octopus and squid).

Mizzen: A mast on a sailing ship; the Mizzen-mast is the mast immediately aft (behind) the main mast. It is typically shorter.

Mooring: A permanent structure where a boat or ship may be *moored* (attached) such as a dock or jetty.

Mooring Line: Line of rope used to tie off or affix a boat or ship.

Mooring Station: An assigned location where a boat or ship is to be attached or tied off.

Mosasaur: A group of extinct marine lizards that died out at the end of the Cretaceous. The largest mosasaurs reached 60 feet in length and weighed 30 tons.

Nares: Nostrils.

Nematodes: Roundworms.

Neveroyatno: Russian word for *unbelievable.*

NOAA: The National Oceanic and Atmospheric Administration.

Norepinephrine: A chemical in the brain that functions as a hormone and neurotransmitter.

Notothenioid Fish: A group of Antarctic icefish, known for antifreeze proteins in their blood. They have no red blood cells; hence their blood appears as a clear, viscous liquid.

Oceanus: A fictional Florida marine park, named after *Oceanus*, the Greek god of the sea.

***Octopus giganteus*:** A species of gigantic cephalopod, believed to inhabit the ocean's extreme depths. The remains of one reported specimen were calculated to have had a tentacular span of 200 feet.

OMNI ADCAP Sonar: A hull/bow mounted (spherical) ADCAP (Advanced Capabilities) active sonar system using medium frequency broadband clicks to provide all-around coverage. Almost impossible to detect and includes active search and attack capabilities.

Ophion's Deep: A Cretaceous-era submarine canyon named after the Greek God *Ophion*. It starts in the *Straits of Florida* and carves its way 125 miles along Florida's *Continental Rise*.

Outboard: A non-integral and removable propulsion system for boats. Outboard motors attach directly to the transom. Multiple motors can be used for larger boats, with horsepower typically ranging from single digits all the way to three hundred or more.

Papillae (singular Papilla): A nipple or cuticle-like structure.

Pectoral Fin(s): Paired fins in fish that provide dynamic lifting force, enabling some fish to maintain depth.

Peduncle: In fish and cetaceans, the narrow portion of the body where the tail (caudal fin or flukes) attaches to the body.

Pelagic: The portion of the ocean that is neither near the bottom nor close to shore.

Phalanx Anti-Missile Battery: A shipboard anti-aircraft/anti-missile Gatling gun system.

Pheromones: An excreted or secreted chemical that triggers a response in members of the same species.

Phototropic Zone: Also known as the *Photic Zone,* the upper portion of a body of water where sunlight is the primary stimulus for growth and nourishment – typically from the surface down to around 600 feet. 90% of all marine life lives in the Phototropic Zone.

Physeter macrocephalus: Binomial nomenclature (Latin) for the sperm whale.

Pinnipeds: Seals and sea lions.

Pixilated: An image breaking up into visible pixels, typically a distortion when enlarged.

Plankton: Tiny organisms that live in the water column. Plankton are incapable of swimming against either tide or current. They are an important food source for many marine organisms.

Plastron: The almost flat underbelly/ventral portion of a turtle's shell.

Pliosaur: A group of plesiosaurs characterized by short necks and large skulls, armed with sharp teeth. Pliosaurs were fast and maneuverable swimmers and the apex predators of their day.

Pod: A group of whales. Unlike a school of fish, pod members are often related individuals.

Polybenzimidazole (PBI): Also known as *"Celazole,"* it is a space-age polymer/polycarbonate thermoplastic, reported to have the highest compressive strength of any unfilled plastic material.

Polycarbonate: A group of thermoplastic polymers known for their toughness and durability. Some polycarbonates are engineered to be optically transparent.

Port: Direction-wise, turning a boat or ship to the left. *Portside* = the left side of a boat or ship.

Portcullis: A sturdy steel or iron gate with a row of sharpened spikes at the bottom that is lowered to protect or reinforce a castle's gates or drawbridge.

Porthole: A round window on a boat or ship.

POSEIDON M45: Advanced passive fathometer sonar system (see *Fathometer*) using wide aperture arrays and hydrophone complexes set on submarine hulls. Arrays are set both port and starboard. The Poseidon relays readings into a detailed 3D image on the bridge. The system has no sonar projector or active emissions and is impossible to detect. Its only weakness is its limitations in shallow water (waves bounce too repeatedly, reducing range) and under silty conditions (i.e. excessive detritus) which can "blind" it.

Poulpe Colossal: French for Colossal Octopus.

Proboscideans: Modern day elephants and their extinct relatives.

Prop: A boat or ship's propeller.

Proteus: A shape-shifting sea beast from Greek mythology. Proteus could foretell the future, but the creature answered only to someone capable of overpowering it.

Prow: The foremost portion of a ship's bow. The prow cuts through the water and is the portion of the bow above the waterline.

Ragnarok: Translated as the "Twilight of the Gods," Ragnarok represents an apocalyptic battle between the Norse gods and the forces of evil, including the Frost giants and an assortment of inhuman monsters. All major figures perish in the battle, with mankind rising from the ashes.

REAPER: Acronym for: Rail Energized Armor Piercing Electromagnetic Repulsion gun: a close-range submarine-based weapon that fires kinetic energy projectiles using electricity instead of chemical propellants. Powerful electrical currents generated by the sub's reactor create magnetic fields that accelerate a sliding metal conductor between rails lining the barrel. When fired, the conductor launches a projectile at over 5,000 mph. To power the weapon, electricity is allowed to build over several seconds in the pulsed power system. It is then sent through the rail gun as a powerful surge of energy, creating an electromagnetic force accelerating a 2,000 lb. tungsten projectile to nearly Mach 8. The kinetic energy generated exceeds 600 megajoules: equivalent to a 100 ton locomotive striking a target at 250 mph. In order to protect both the weapon and its host vessel during sustained firing, a thermal management system is required for both the launcher and the pulsed power system.

Remora Mini-Sub: A sleek, 4-person submersible designed and manufactured by Grayson Defense Technologies. The Remora is a fast and highly maneuverable vessel powered by pump-jet propulsors. Based on original designs by JAW Robotics, it attaches directly to the outside of an ORION-class submarine via its airlock and remains flush to the hull until detached.

Roman Gladius: The standard-issue sword of Roman foot soldiers. Length: 24–33 inches.

Romulus and Remus: Twin brothers and the mythological founders of Rome, they were purportedly suckled by a she-wolf.

Rorqual: The largest group of baleen whales, including the blue and fin whales.

Rostrum: The crocodile-like muzzle of a pliosaur.

Runabout: A small boat, often used in the service of a larger vessel.

Rusticle: Icicle-like formations of rust that form on the edges of shipwrecks as saltwater acts upon the wrought iron in their hulls.

Saepia inferni: Literal translation: "Cuttlefish from Hell." Binomial nomenclature for a Cretaceous species of heavy-bodied squid that inhabited Diablo Caldera. Inferni are very aggressive. They can grow to thirty feet in length and weigh several tons.

Salmonid: One of a family of ray-fined fish, collectively known as *Salmonidae*. The family includes salmon, trout, char, whitefish and graylings.

Saurian War: Formally entitled a "suppression exercise" – an ongoing attempt by the nations of the world's militaries to exterminate aggressive pliosaurs (*Kronosaurus imperators*).

Sauropterygians: An extinct group of marine reptiles including plesiosaurs and pliosaurs.

Schooner: A sailing vessel characterized by fore and aft sails on two or more masts.

Sclerotic Ring: A ring of small bones encircling the eye that support it. Tiny muscles connect to the sclerotic ring and aid in focusing by helping the eye to compress inward. Found in many prehistoric marine reptiles, including mosasaurs and ichthyosaurs.

Sea Crusade: A fictional animal rights/conservation group, specializing in protecting the oceans and marine life.

Shastasaurus sikanniensis: An extinct species of Triassic Ichthyosaur similar to *Shonisaurus* and one of the largest marine reptiles of all time. Adults were estimated to reach 70 feet in length.

Shoal: A group of fish that stay together for social reasons.

Singulare Monstrum: Individual (unique) monster.

Slip: A reserved docking space for a boat, similar to a rented parking spot.

Sloop: A sailboat with a fore and aft rig and a single mast.

SODOME: Sonar Dome (military designate).

SOP: Acronym for Standard Operating Procedure.

Sound: Also known as a seaway, a sound is a large inlet between two bodies of land.

Spasiba: Russian for *thank you.*

Starboard: Direction-wise, turning a boat or ship to the right. Also, a term for the right side of a boat or ship.

Stern: The rear portion of a boat or ship.

Sub-Aqueous: Beneath the surface of the water.

Supercavitating: A moving submarine object that generates a bubble of gas in its wake to eliminate water friction/resistance and increase speed. Supercavitating ammunition and torpedoes travel many times faster than their non-cavitating counterparts.

Surtur: A fire giant from Norse mythology. During the battle of Ragnarok his flaming sword sets the Earth ablaze.

SVALINN: A submarine-based, active sonar suppression system that targets incoming sonar with out-of-phase emissions. SVALINN can effectively cancel enemy pinging if the sonar is not too powerful or sophisticated. A ship cloaked with SVALINN becomes all but invisible as long as it remains motionless. Moving toward or away from active pinging would still register in an enemy's sonar's signal processors, giving away the sub's position.

Swells: Ocean surface waves moving in long-wave formation.

Temporal Openings/Temporal Fenestrae: Bilaterally symmetrical holes in the temporal bone of the skull through which the mandibular (jaw) muscles travel and attach to the mandible (jaw bone). The connection point at the mandible is called the *Mandibular Fenestrae*. Some animals (including most reptiles) have two pairs of *Temporal Fenestrae*, the upper (*Supratemporal Fenestrae*) and lower (*Infratemporal Fenestrae*)

Thalassophonean: Literally translated as "Sea Slayer," a group of macropredatory pliosaurs including *Liopleurodon, Pliosaurus* and *Kronosaurus.*

Thanatos: In Greek mythology, the demonic personification of *death*.

Thermocline: A distinctive layer in a body of water where temperature changes more rapidly than in the layers above and below it. Thermoclines can be either permanent or transitory, depending on prevailing climate conditions. They separate surface water from the calmer, often colder, deep water below.

Thermoplastic: A polymer that becomes moldable when heated to a certain temperature and solidifies upon being cooled.

Tiamat: A sea goddess from Babylonian, Assyrian, and Sumerian mythology, known as "The Glistening One." Although feminine and a creator goddess, Tiamat appears as a monstrous dragon or sea serpent and is considered the embodiment of primordial chaos.

Titanoboa: An enormous constrictor snake that lived during the Paleocene, 60–58mya. The snake was estimated to reach around 50 feet in length.

Transom: The flat, back panel that comprises the stern of a boat or ship. Outboard motors are affixed directly to the transom.

Triassic: A geological time period ranging from approximately 250 to 200 million years ago.

Typhon: In Greek mythology, the titanic son of *Tartarus* and Earth and the most fearsome of all monsters. Typhon was a deadly enemy of the gods of Olympus and fathered many horrifying creatures, including *Cerberus*, the *Chimera*, and the multi-headed *Hydra*.

Vermitus gigas: Binomial nomenclature for the giant parasitic worms found in the digestive tracts of extant pliosauridae. In appearance, Vermitus look like a mixture between a sandworm and a lamprey. The worms typically grow to 20 feet, but if able to penetrate the host's abdominal wall can continue to grow, reaching colossal size and eventually killing the host animal.

Watch Commander: Nautical term for a shift supervisor on a marine vessel.

Water Column: A theoretical column of water that ranges from the ocean's surface, all the way to the seafloor. The water column consists of thermal or chemically stratified layers, the mixing of which is brought on by wind and current.

Waterfront: A group of manmade structures designed to handle boats and ships.

Whale Killer: Also known as a *Whale Catcher*, a high-speed surface ship designed to hunt and kill whales, then hand the carcasses over to a larger *Factory Ship* for processing. Whale killers typically use grenade-tipped harpoon cannons to disable and kill their prey.

Wharf: A structure built along the shore of a harbor where boats and ships may dock while loading or unloading passengers or cargo.

Windward Passage: A strait in the Caribbean Sea between Cuba and Hispaniola. The passage is 50 miles wide and averages 5,600 feet in depth.

Zodiac: A rubber inflatable boat, equipped with an outboard motor. Used as a dinghy or runabout.

Zooplankton: Drifting clouds of marine and freshwater organisms that range in size. Some are microscopic. Some, such as copepods and jellyfish, are visible to the naked eye.

Zoosexual: A human being who engages in *Bestiality*, i.e. sex with non-human animals.

Made in the USA
Middletown, DE
09 November 2023

42302189R00308